WHISPER OF THE RAVENS
FEHU

MALENE SØLVSTEN

WHISPER OF THE RAVENS
FEHU

Translated from the Danish
by Adrienne Alair

Arctis

This translation has been published with the
financial support of the Danish Arts Foundation.

Danish Arts
Foundation

W1-Media, Inc.
Arctis Books USA
Stamford, CT, USA

Visit our website at www.arctis-books.com

1 3 5 7 9 8 6 4 2

The Library of Congress Control Number: 2024931203

ISBN 978-1-64690-027-5
eBook ISBN 978-1-64690-624-6

English translation copyright © Adrienne Alair, 2024

Printed in Germany,
European Union

For my sister,
who, when I finally admitted I was writing a book about witches,
demigods, and clairvoyants, didn't so much as raise an eyebrow
but simply asked: How can I help?

TRANSLATOR'S NOTE: The quoted passages from Völuspá, Hávamál, and The First Lay of Helgi Hundingsbane are based on the translation of the Poetic *Edda* by Henry Adams Bellows, which is in the public domain. The passages from Hrafnsmál are from the translation of Heimskringla by Alison Finlay and Anthony Faulkes.

HRAFNHEIM

GARDARIKE

NORVÍK

HARALDSBORG

VÁN

DANHEIM

SÉNT

RIPA

ÍVING

SOUTHERN MINES

BARRE

FRÓN

DARK FOREST

IRON FOREST

ISAFOLD

PART I

MAGIC WISDOM

Necklaces had she
and rings from Heerfather
Wise was her speech
and her magic wisdom
Widely she saw
over all the worlds

Völuspá
10th century

PROLOGUE

The New Year's Eve party at The Boatman was spectacular, but my stomach was in knots. All I could see was everyone who was missing. My remaining friends had ominous shadows hanging over them.

It was a good thing I could only see the past.

I looked out over the dance floor one last time before sneaking away.

Od's office with its many doors looked the same, except there was now a cage inside. Bars and all.

In the cage sat Frank, his hands folded. He raised his head when I came in. I ran a few steps toward him, instinctively happy to see him again, before my brain reminded me that he had tried to kill me on my birthday, just over a week ago.

"Have you come to take revenge?" His voice was placid.

"I had no idea you were here. I'm here for another reason, and I would appreciate it if you didn't tell anyone you saw me."

"I owe you that much." Frank looked closely at me. "I meant it when I said I wished it weren't you I had to kill."

I tried to make my face hard. "I'd just like to know why."

Frank stared at his hands again. "I can't tell you that," he whispered.

I did it without thinking. It was dangerous, and it was stupid. But I reached between the bars and took Frank's hands. Then I pushed my clairvoyance into him and pulled the past out. My eyes overflowed with tears of empathy. "The boy," I said. "Ragnara has your . . . is it your grandson? My life for his?"

Frank was still.

"Do you know where he is?"

Frank looked away. No.

I pulled my hands back, and Frank didn't try to hold on.

"What will happen to you?"

Again, his face was serene. "I expect I'll be executed."

Panic shot through my body in a violent surge of adrenaline. All I could think was: No, no more deaths!

"Neither Od nor Niels is executing anyone." It took all the willpower I had to keep my voice from shaking.

"No, but they'll deliver me to Ragnara."

I gathered my courage. "Will you kill me if I let you out?"

"Yes," Frank said without hesitation, and I immediately took a step back.

Evidently, the deal still stood. The child's life for mine.

"As far as I can tell, there's no magic keeping this door locked." I pointed to the door of the cage. "And if I were to give you, let's say, a letter opener, you could get the lock open. After a little while. I get a head start."

Frank sat up a bit straighter. "One hour, max."

"Until early tomorrow morning," I negotiated.

He didn't have to think about it for long.

"Deal."

I pulled a pair of jeans, my biker boots, a black hoodie, and my mom's coat out of my bag. My high heels I kicked off and tossed in a corner, but after giving it some thought, I laid the green dress I'd been wearing in the bag with the rest of the items I'd packed, including the last bit of klinte, Mads's giant crystal, Rebecca's notebook about Hrafnheim, and Freyja's tears—which, if nothing else, I could sell. I was dressed in a matter of seconds.

Outside the door, people started counting down.

"Seven—six—five . . ."

I took a letter opener from Od's desk. "Which door leads to Hrafnheim?"

"It's too dangerous. They'll kill you."

I raised an eyebrow.

"Four—three—two . . ."

"Do you want the opener?"

Frank bared his teeth, then pointed at a blue door.

"One—Haaappy New Year!"

I tossed the letter opener to Frank before I flung the door open and threw myself into the dark.

CHAPTER 1

Two days earlier—Ravensted

The sun reflected off the sand in sharp beams, bright white apart from the wet spots that darkened it here and there.

Dark red spots.

Where was I?

A tattooed hand lay in front of my eyes.

I was lying with one cheek placed directly on the sand. The sun beat down on the exposed side of my face. The bottom part of a pillar stood in the middle of my field of vision. A pillar? This made no sense. Where in the world was I? Confused, I let my gaze glide farther away and saw row after row of spectators stretching up, up, up toward the sky. The wall of people was arranged in a semicircle around me. The crowds filled the stands, but no one made a sound. They just stared breathlessly at something to my right.

A creaking noise from several ropes dangling with something heavy at their ends combined with the stench of blood, sweat, and sheep.

A weak *baaaah* rang out, but it didn't sound like any animal I knew.

Footsteps crunched through the sand, and a pair of feet passed my line of sight. Female feet. Small and delicate in gold-ornamented sandals. The gold was shaped into a tangle of snakes, and the ankles were bare. A strange material of interlocking black stones clinked around the woman's legs like some kind of stone chain mail.

The feet continued moving away from me. Now someone was heaving anguished sobs. For a second, I thought it was me.

No. The sobs weren't coming from me. Just above me, a girl's voice begged: "Please, please."

The enormous crowd drew in a collective breath.

"That's her," they whispered. "That's Thora Baneblood's daughter."

I tried with everything in my power to turn my head, but I couldn't budge.

"Thorasdatter has engaged in conspiracy, and she supports the resistance against us." The voice was high-pitched and almost childlike.

A few faint *booos* sounded from the stands.

"It is our gift to the people that we rid you of her scheming, and of her," a brief pause, "her lifestyle." This last bit was added with chilling acidity.

A sharp *creeeak* indicated that someone or something was being hoisted up. The sound of strangulation made the hairs on my arms stand up.

The spectators roared with excitement.

"Watch her hang," someone shouted. "Out with her tongue. Out with her tongue . . ."

I turned my head to see where I was, but the sun shone in my eyes and blinded me.

Before I could see again, I heard the squeal of metal being pulled from a sheath. This was followed by a sound like a shovel being plunged into sand.

Again, the spectators gasped.

Blood sloshed down over me, and I gagged, nearly choking on the warm liquid. Then I regained enough control over myself to realize I didn't even need to breathe.

A lock of fiery-red hair fell quietly and came to rest in a little curl on the sand in front of me.

I woke with a gasp and raised my hands to protect my mouth from the warm blood, but I ended up flailing aimlessly in the air.

Luna put an arm around me. "Is something wrong?"

We were lying close together on the mattress in the small green room in Luna's parents' house. The room that my best friend had declared mine. The colorful blankets and pillows certainly hadn't been my idea, but Luna insisted that their color energy protected me.

"I'm okay," I lied.

"You do know that whatever you dream at Christmas will come true, right?"

"What?" I turned my face to her in horror at the thought of the blood-spattered sand and the stench of animals.

"I think it's just a superstition." She yawned and rolled onto her back. "Can't we sleep a little longer? I'm still stuffed from yesterday." She patted her stomach. "I don't know if I'll even fit into my dress for the New Year's Eve party in two days."

I sat up and tossed aside a neon-yellow cushion. My movement caused the comforter to slide down.

"Aah, it's cold," she whined.

"It's my blanket," I said and yanked it off her completely. "What are you even doing in here?"

She rubbed her eyes, which were slightly puffy from sleep. "You were shouting in your sleep. First you called out for Arthur. Then Monster."

"Neither of them is coming, no matter how much I shout."

My father was still resting by his body, and Monster was back in Hrafnheim, so he was no help. Luna brushed away a few tangled curls that had strayed across her eyes. Her hair was ash gray at the moment.

17

"We came in when you called for me."

I looked down and picked at an orange thread. "Thanks," I mumbled, but with a jerk of my head, I looked up again. "Wait. What do you mean by *we*?"

The pillows and blankets on Luna's other side moved, and Mathias stuck his gorgeous face up between a pair of blue Indian bolster pillows.

"You guys do know this is a single mattress?" I said.

Mathias reached across the comforter and took my hand, so his strength seeped into me. His divine power—or whatever it was he had—was growing day by day.

I pulled back my hand in mock anger. "What part of 'I struggle with intimacy' don't you understand?"

"It's just the effect of my dad's spells." Luna pulled the comforter back. "You're actually highly receptive to human contact—and color magic." She patted the saffron-yellow sheet.

I imitated my social worker's tight facial expression and smacked the garish comforter. "Would you at least respect my intimacy issues?"

Mathias scoffed. "You don't have intimacy issues. Maybe people have issues being intimate with you, but not the other way around."

I flung myself backward. "You guys are impossible."

Luna pulled down the neck of my T-shirt and traced the thick scar on my chest, where Ragnara had stabbed me as a baby. Inexplicably, I had been healed in Ragnara's hands.

"You look tough," she said, using her other hand to lift a lock of my bright red hair.

Mathias nodded behind her. "But we know you're a total softie."

I pulled up my camisole and pounded on my sculpted abs. "Hey. I'm not soft."

"Wanna bet?" Luna lay on top of me and jabbed her fingers in my sides.

I groaned, smiling but slightly panicked, and tried to get away, but Mathias, laughing, followed Luna's lead and tickled me until I could barely breathe.

Downstairs, Ben and Rebecca were up. I went to join them so my smitten friends could finish kissing.

The Christmas celebrations were still going strong, even though I was ready to puke at the thought of more duck fat and alcohol.

Rebecca was humming in the open kitchen, and Ben was busy arranging some feathers and a cat skull on the shelf next to a figurine that bore an uncanny resemblance to him. With great concentration, he used a yellow, grainy substance to draw a rune on the skull's forehead. "Jólnir, Thor, Heimdall," he chanted, quietly at first, then louder and louder with each word. "Færa," he concluded, and the word was drawn out until it faded into breath.

"Doesn't *færa* mean 'to prevent' in Old Norse?" I asked.

Ben didn't answer. The grainy substance dried and flaked off the skull. He exposed his white teeth and tried again. "Jólnir, Thor, Heimdall, Færaaaaaahhh." This time he hissed the final word in an elongated, insistent manner, but the substance once again sprinkled down onto the shelf like yellow dust. "*Gnit*," he exclaimed, and although I didn't understand a whole lot of Old Norse, it was clear he was cursing. "*Louse*," he translated, followed by a couple of French words that required no explanation.

"They won't take the offering," he said to Rebecca.

Next to the decorated Christmas tree, Ben and his setup looked bizarre. I tried to ignore his outfit consisting of fuzzy pants and a he-goat mask pushed up on his forehead.

Rebecca set a steaming bowl on the table that smelled sweetly of apples. "Dearest Anna Stella. Come and eat."

"Oh goody, even more food." I looked out the window at Odinmont, which sat on the other side of the field, half-hidden in a bank of fog. I had on several occasions tried to fight my way up to the house, which I still regarded as my home, but the hill was magically sealed off, and no one could penetrate the spells. We had no idea why.

Luna came dancing in with Mathias at her heels. She gave her mom a kiss on the cheek.

Rebecca patted her daughter's head absent-mindedly.

"After we eat, we'll place sheaves of grain in the field," she called after Luna, who had already made her way over to the table.

"Didn't you also put sheaves out yesterday?" Mathias asked.

"Odin rides with his ghostly entourage during the nights around jól. His savage, undead oskorei can be appeased if we leave out food for their horses."

My eyes grew wide. "Odin? You mean Svidur? He comes here?"

"He goes everywhere," Ben growled and nudged me onto a chair. When his large hands touched my arm, I felt his humming magic.

At the table, Rebecca said a blessing in which she gave thanks for nature's gifts. The rest of the Sekibo family joined in with hands folded, eyes closed, and heads bowed. Mathias and I looked down awkwardly at our plates, until we could finally turn our attention to the meal. I stared out into space as we ate and chatted—admittedly, the others ate and chatted, while I silently poked at my food.

". . . in turns. That way she can't get close. Right, Anna?" Luna waved a hand in front of my face.

I focused on her. "Yeah, yeah, of course."

Four pairs of eyes looked in my direction, and I looked down at my breakfast, which consisted of chicken thigh, apple compote, and hot mead. When the silence began to hang heavy over the table, I gave in and looked up again.

"I wasn't listening. I'm not used to people talking about me. Not to my face, anyway."

"We were saying we need to take turns being with you. Ragnara will certainly come after you again," Mathias said.

Panic spread through me as I looked at Ben's sparkling gold

teeth in the middle of his dark face and Rebecca's nearly phosphorescent, cornflower-blue eyes. Luna sang a couple of verses in Old Norse, and Mathias looked at her with pride. I didn't dare think about what could happen to them if they came between Ragnara and me.

After the meal, we went to place sheaves in the fields surrounding Ben and Rebecca's house. Luna's bongo drums were strung on a strap she wore slung across her shoulder. Behind the steady *thump-thump*, her parents chimed in with vocals. They stopped when they saw the previous day's sheaf still sitting there, slumped over. Not so much as a single grain had been eaten. Even the birds kept their distance.

Rebecca looked desperately at her husband. "Maybe they didn't come this way."

"Oskorei always pass through." Ben squatted down and picked up a limp ear of wheat. "They rejected our offering."

Rebecca looked toward the misty sky. Her eternally bare feet tapped nervously on the frozen ground. Large flakes fell down to meet us. "We'll put this here, too," she said and lifted a bundle. "Maybe when they see the extra . . ."

But Ben had already stormed off to the barn.

Inside, I sat by the living room window and looked out into the snowy weather.

Once again, my gaze had come to rest on Odinmont without my even noticing. It was so recently that I had lived up there with Monster. My throat constricted. It was just a few weeks ago that Varnar had been there with me.

"What are you thinking about?" I hadn't even heard Rebecca approach me. She laid a cool hand on my cheek. "You're miles away."

Actually just a couple of hundred yards.

I didn't respond.

"He left to protect you," Rebecca said gently. She continued boldly, even though my face must have been more than enough warning. "Varnar knew that you would risk your life for his if he stayed. That's why he went back to Hrafnheim."

My eyes stung, so I clung to my anger. "He left. I don't care about the reason. He left. Monster left. My parents left. That's all anyone's done my whole life."

She looked at me with one of her unreadable smiles. "We're happy that you're here now," she said and walked back to the kitchen.

At the dinner table that evening, Rebecca passed around a small pouch.

"The runes tell us about the year to come," she said.

Everyone pulled out a piece of bone. A symbol had been carved onto each one. Mathias held his up, and Rebecca examined it.

"Sol," she said contentedly. She gave the *l* an elongated, flat pronunciation. "The symbol of heaven. Divine." She stretched her neck to see Luna's. "Reid." She smiled once again. "You will go on a journey both internally and externally. Ben?"

He opened his hand. His palm was lighter than the rest of his skin, and the tattooed symbols stood out beneath the piece of bone. "Tyr," he said.

"Ahh . . . the god Tyr. Protector, just and victorious." I caught a glimpse of a love so strong, it was as if they had just met.

He returned her gaze, and suddenly I found myself liking him a little better.

Rebecca looked down into her own hand. "Bjarka." She inhaled through her nose. "Birch. The mother of all runes. Nature, creation, and equilibrium." Her eyes moved to me. "Anna?"

I fingered my piece of bone and turned it over a couple of times. "It's blank."

"What?" Rebecca took the piece from me. "How did that get in there? It's an extra, in case one gets lost. Pull a new one."

I obeyed.

Blank.

"Again." Rebecca's blue eyes shone.

Same result. I held a blank piece of bone in my hand.

She overturned the bag, and rune after rune tumbled down into her hand. "Take one of these," she told me.

"But then it won't count," I protested. "And I don't believe in it anyway."

"It seems more like the future doesn't believe in you," Ben grumbled.

The words hung over the table, and I impulsively pushed back my chair, stood, and ran.

Outside, it was unusually still. The frost that had lain like a silvery shroud over the landscape on my birthday had been driven away by pouring rain, and an endless *drip-drip-drip* could be heard everywhere. In the spot where the moon was hidden behind a tufted layer of cloud, it was a bit brighter. Everything else was packed in surreal, filtered light, and I was staring out into a wall of dark gray. A short distance up the field sat the sheaves—both old and new—still untouched. It smelled like damp soil. My breath hung around me like a cloud, and I leaned my head back as I got control of my emotions.

A flash of light shot across the sky in the one little peephole through the clouds to the heavens above, and I smiled. Ben would surely say it was Thor, riding across the sky in his goat-pulled chariot, but I held that it was just a shooting star.

I allowed myself one wish. "I hope we meet, Serén," I said silently to my sister, somewhere out there. Maybe she could hear it. Maybe she had already heard it a long time ago. I breathed in deeply and let the chilly night air calm me.

I stiffened when I heard a sound.

It was a raspy breath coming from Ostergaard's field, which was right in front of Ben and Rebecca's house. Right now, I could barely see more than a couple of yards into the field, let alone the imposing mansion down there. I backed toward the door and was about to flee inside when a rough voice called out.

"Anna, are you there?"

I stopped with my hand on the ice-cold doorknob.

"Monster?" I shouted. "Monster . . ."

 # CHAPTER 2

I leapt out into the field, and even though it was pitch dark, I ran as fast as I could in the direction of Monster's voice. My ankle twisted several times in the soft dirt, but I quickly got to my feet and pushed on. It was now raining hard, and large drops struck me like icy pinpricks.

"Where are you?" I called and fumbled around. My hands glided over the cold, wet earth.

"Anna." The voice was closer, but it was strangely faint. It sounded nothing like Monster's powerful voice.

"I'm coming." Crawling on all fours, I patted the mucky ground, unable to see my hands in front of me. Finally I detected an enormous outline, and my fingers found fur.

"Monster," I panted. "Why are you lying down?"

His fur was crusty and covered in warm, wet blotches that I could tell hadn't come from the rain.

I slid all the way down onto my stomach, and the chill from the earth sent a shock through my body, but I didn't care. I snaked my arms under Monster and tried to lift his large wolflike body.

"Anna," he moaned again. "Stop."

"What happened?" I tried again to lift him and felt wounds and more warm liquid on his fur. So much . . .

"Listen, Anna," he thundered, sounding almost like his old self. The illusion was shattered when he let out a very doglike yelp. "We were overrun in the Iron Forest, and your sister was taken by Ragnara's people. I tried . . ." he made a gurgling, disturbing hacking noise, and I didn't grasp exactly what he had tried to do, but judging from his injuries, it hadn't ended well.

"Serén?" I breathed. "Is she dead?"

But twins could sense if the other died. Couldn't they?

"No," Monster said flatly. "She's not dead. Yet."

"Yet?"

"Serén said . . ." He yelped again. "She saw that Ragnara's coming for you. Ragnara wants you two together. She no longer wants to simply kill you; she wants to capture you." His raspy voice ended in a dull bark, but he forced the words out.

"Monster," I cried. "What happened to you?"

"We were captured," he said. "Serén told me what she had seen. She helped me break free, but I didn't have the strength to bring her with me." He moaned again. "I had to warn you."

"What did they do to you?"

He didn't answer my question. "You need to get away from here, Anna. Ragnara is coming, but you can change fate. You have to find Serén before . . ." He stopped to gasp for air. "You have to find Serén."

"What did they do to you?" I asked again.

"I'm irrelevant."

My hands hovered over his body in the dark. "Irrelevant!" I inhaled tremulously. "You're anything but irrelevant."

"You and Serén are all that matter." His voice was paper-thin.

I couldn't bear the thought that he had run through Hrafnheim in this condition. I forced myself to focus.

"Where is Serén now?"

"She's . . ." his voice trailed off.

"Monster," I begged, crying. "Where is she?"

There was no response.

"Monster?" I pulled at his limp body, and I managed to drag him a good distance toward Ben and Rebecca's house through the muddy field. I shouted over my shoulder. "Help me! Luna! Mathias! Help!"

At that moment, the clouds moved away from the moon, and what I saw was so terrifying, I screamed.

"Monster," I sobbed. "You can't. No! No!"

He was my best friend. He was one of my first friends. He couldn't . . .

"Monster!" I was now shouting so loudly, it resounded across the fields. So loudly, it was like I was trying to wake the gods themselves. But there was no help to be had. "No." I shook him. "Come back."

A green flash told me Mathias was at my side, and that he had gone into demigod mode. Luna chanted spells, and, unbothered by Monster's colossal weight, Mathias took him in his giant green arms and picked him up. Ben and Rebecca were there now, too, and they chanted around us, but I was aware of nothing but Monster's glassy eyes, the tongue hanging out of his mouth, and the dark, wet trail we left behind on the pale gravel of the driveway, up the stairs, and on the floor. It smelled salty, sweet, and iron-rich. We entered the living room, and there the light revealed more.

I should have turned my face away, but I stared at him, frozen. I saw every one of his wounds.

"Save him!" I commanded. "Do something."

The witches exchanged a look without speaking.

Mathias tried to press his godliness into Monster, shouting in frustration.

"He's a giant," Rebecca said quietly to Mathias. "You can't use your powers on him."

"Do something." I stroked Monster's snout and ears. "Do something," I repeated, louder.

Ben's buzzing magic shot into me, and a moment passed before I realized that he had grabbed my arm.

"Anna, there's nothing we can do. Witches and gods have no effect on giant wolves."

I shrugged his hand away. "I don't care about your stupid rules."
I looked around with teary eyes. "Elias. I'll call Elias for help."

"His medicines don't work on giant wolves, either," Rebecca
said.

Even though I was gasping for air, I felt like I couldn't catch my
breath. "What the hell are all your powers good for if you can't
save the most important things?"

Mathias, who was on his knees, had let go of Monster, and his
arms hung at his sides. His hands lay on Ben and Rebecca's tile
floor. He had returned to human size, and his neon-green glow was
gone. He didn't speak, but his expression said it all.

On the floor, Monster lay completely still. His sharp teeth were
bloody, and the huge paw I discovered I was holding had started
to grow cold.

I stroked my hand across his forehead, which had always made
him lift his head up to me. Then I shook his paw, but his leg
flopped heavily.

"He's gone, Anna." Someone grabbed me by the shoulders.

I raised my hand from Monster's paw, ready to attack, but when
I realized it was Luna, I lowered my arm, and she wrapped herself
around me and held me tight.

At first, I could do nothing but breathe shakily. I slid down over
Monster's motionless body. Even though I can't see giant wolves'
auras, I had no doubt that he was no longer here. I hugged him
close.

No one tried to pull me back.

Mathias and Luna sat at my side and rubbed my back while I
cried and screamed, not that it made any difference. I barely noticed when someone, probably Mathias, carried me up to bed.
Suddenly, my surroundings were just moving past me, and I landed
on the mattress. I lay there between my two friends and clung to
Luna while Mathias held me, and the few times I was somewhat
conscious, I whimpered helplessly.

I allowed myself this one night of despair. This one night, I could grieve.

But in a corner of my consciousness I knew, when morning came, I had to do something.

Monster's body was gone when I came downstairs on trembling legs. A dark spot on the tile floor marked where he had lain.

Rebecca looked at me with concern from where she stood among dried herbs and decoctions in the kitchen. Ben took a half step toward me but stopped when his dark gaze met mine.

"He was an excellent leader to his people, a valuable ally to us, and the most loyal friend you could have wished for," Ben said ceremoniously. "He was able to see beyond conflicts between men and giant wolves." He was silent as he drew some symbols in the air. A couple of weak sparks around his tattooed hands told me he had cast a spell, but I didn't care.

"Where is he?" I rasped. I had cried so much my voice wasn't working properly.

"In the barn," Rebecca said.

"He's in the barn?" This came out like a squawk.

"He must be returned to his people so they can lay him to rest, but right now there is no passage to Hrafnheim."

I tried to think clearly. "So how do you get to Hrafnheim?"

Her voice was thin. "You can't go there right now."

"At all?"

Ben rumbled. "There's a portal in The Boatman, but only Elias is allowed to travel through it. Not even Od can go to Hrafnheim. There's also a passage down at Ostergaard, but Paul doesn't let a lot of people pass. I don't know how Etunaz got through, but we can't go the other way unless the mission is pressing."

"Pressing?" The word came out like a shout. "But this is pretty damn pressing. He can't just sit out in the barn and . . ." I couldn't finish the sentence.

"We put a stasis spell on him, so he won't decay." Rebecca said quickly. Then she hesitated. "Do you want to see him?"

My hand flew to my mouth.

"He's laid out like a king with grave goods and offerings to the goddess of death. Hel must be appeased, since she can't have him right away."

"Hel?" I asked, disoriented.

"She's the sister of Etunaz's ancestor Fenrir, so she has the right to him."

Something turned in me. "I don't want to see him." Slowly and deeply, I filled my lungs with air. "Where is his . . ." I searched for the word, ". . . soul?" Maybe I could talk to him, like I did with my dead dad.

Now Ben stood right next to me. "Giants have no soul."

I wanted to protest, but Rebecca interjected. "Not like humans, anyway." She gave her husband a long look, and for once, Benedict obeyed and kept his mouth shut.

I tried to stay calm. "Monster was able to tell me something, before he . . ."

Ben rolled his hand for me to continue.

"Ragnara has my sister," I whispered.

Ben let out a violent exclamation I was glad not to understand, and Rebecca gasped.

"Ragnara is coming here to get me, because she wants to have us both."

Rebecca clutched the edge of the table. "We'll send a message to Thora and Varnar. Everyone from the resistance movement is gathered at Haraldsborg in Hrafnheim. Maybe they can come here and protect you."

I jutted my chin out. "It's not enough. Monster said I need to find Serén. I have to go to Hrafnheim myself."

"You'd be heading straight into Ragnara's arms. It must be a trap," growled Ben.

Even though I was hoarse from crying all night, I was shouting now. "Would Monster give his life for a trap? I trust him more than anyone else."

Ben's shoulders grew wider as he stood up even straighter. He wasn't even listening. "You have to stay here where it's safe."

I threw up my arms. "I'm anything but safe here."

Ben was still talking to himself. "I'll have to put more spells on her."

"*Her?* You mean *me?*" I backed up as he aimed his palms at me. They began to crackle and glow as the tattooed symbols stood out starkly.

"Dad!" Suddenly, Luna stood between us. I hadn't even heard her enter the room. She went up to Ben, and he bared his white teeth but held his magic back. Luna took another step forward, so her nose nearly touched his electric hands.

"Do not put any more magic on Anna."

Now Mathias was there, too. He stepped in front of me, so my two friends functioned as a shield.

"Thanks," I mumbled to them. "Thank you."

Ben grumbled but lowered his hands.

I quickly turned and ran up to my small, green room, where I locked the door and, for good measure, placed a chair in front of the handle—not that it would help if Ben changed his mind. Exhausted, I sank onto the bed. I closed my eyes and slipped immediately into a gray whirlwind of snowflakes and branches.

I looked around and needed only a couple of seconds to figure out where I was.

Kraghede Forest?

I turned around in a circle and determined I was in the forest, and that it resembled the many visions I had had since last summer. The visions that had always ended with Frank strangling me and running off across the field to Odinmont.

"Anna," came a voice. "Anna, are you there?"

31

Again, I spun around and gave a little shout when I was looking into my sister's face. "Serén?" I exhaled slowly. "Why are we here?" I pointed at the dreamlike surroundings of the deep-frozen Kraghede Forest.

She looked around as well. "This place is important."

The forest was still, with only the sporadic sound of leaves rustling.

I looked intensely at Serén. "Are you okay?"

Her fiery-red hair was messy. "I am for now."

"Where are you?"

"I don't know. There are stone walls and tapestries, but no windows. And something is blocking my power. It only works once in a while."

"Monster didn't manage to say where you are." The words felt like sharp knives.

She lit up. "He got to Midgard. He made it. The future was so uncertain, and . . ." She stopped when she saw my expression. Then she laid her hand on her heart. "He didn't make it."

Suddenly my vision blurred, but I blinked the tears away.

Serén looked down. "I sent him to you because I hoped—believed—that it was his only chance."

I inhaled shakily and took control of my voice. "He was able to tell me that I need to find you before Ragnara comes after me."

She looked up and nodded. "She will. I'm sure of it. I saw her in Ravensted. She'll come after you in the new year."

An ice-cold sensation snaked down my back. "What about the witches? If I leave, won't it put them at risk?"

"She squeezed her eyes shut and tilted her head to listen to something I couldn't hear. "If you leave before the end of the year, everyone's safe, I think."

"You think?" I repeated, but I quickly realized that Serén's guess was probably the closest I could get to a sure thing. "Did you send me a vision in some kind of arena last night?"

She squinted. "An arena? No. What happened in the vision?"

Serén had enough to worry about, and I wasn't even certain it was a warning. Maybe it was just my overactive subconscious at work. "Nothing," I replied and changed the subject. "How do I get to Hrafnheim?"

She bit her lip. "I don't know. You'll need help."

I scoffed. "Either people can't help, or they don't want to." I thought bitterly of the witches and Od.

"I've seen you in Hrafnheim, so there must be a way." Her eyes grew distant. "And the prophecy does say that Thora's blood can lead to Ragnara's death. You must have the power to kill her. It's somewhere in the future, and she knows it."

"It could also be you who kills her. You're just as much Thora's blood as I am."

Serén laughed, and I saw how pretty she was. Incredible to think she was identical to me. "I don't think it's me. You're the past. You're the destructive one."

I wanted to protest, but ended up just shrugging. She was right, after all.

"But how do I get out of here? None of the people I trust are willing to help me."

She grasped my hand, and it felt so real, I could almost forget we were in a dream. "Then get help from someone you don't trust. I know you can do it. You just have to make the right choices."

"Because I'm known for always making the right choices."

"Just get help." Serén's voice was tense. "From anyone."

The words were still reverberating when I woke up in my colorful bed. I stared up at the ceiling, where Luna had painted a rainbow connecting two worlds together. Tiny people walked along it.

"Get help from someone I don't trust," I repeated.

I knew exactly who that was.

CHAPTER 3

"Pick up, pick up," I begged silently as I pressed the phone against my ear. Elias didn't normally take this long to answer.

"I'm already looking forward to hearing your voice." Elias sounded frazzled despite the smooth words. "You are the only . . ."

"Shut up," I snapped. "I don't have long."

With just one day until New Year's Eve, I was more than a little pressed for time.

"Is something wrong?" His voice was strangely brittle.

"Yes." I did not elaborate.

Elias sounded frustrated. "Are you already in danger again?"

"I need to see you," I said in lieu of answering his question.

A deep sigh was all I heard.

"Elias!"

"Sorry. I just closed my eyes and enjoyed the fact that you said that." Though the words were his normal flirty style, he was short of breath.

"Monster is dead." This was the first time I had said it outright.

"Etunaz . . . but . . . how?"

I clenched my teeth so hard it hurt. "Where can we meet?"

I heard Luna's footsteps on the stairs.

"I'm currently studying at the monastery in Jagd."

"You just up and joined a monastery?"

He stifled a sound with a cough, and I couldn't make out if it was a laugh or an offended sniff. "Meet me in the church."

I didn't answer, but hung up and threw the phone on the bed as the door handle turned.

We sat at the back of the bus. Me in the middle, with Une and Aella on either side. We swayed every time the large vehicle took a turn into the small towns, where no one was waiting at the stops. When the door slid aside with a metallic groan and a hissing noise, we were struck by a cold wind. Une's graying hair was gathered at the nape of his neck, and he looked uncomfortable in the blue nylon jacket Ben had loaned him. Under the jacket, he was armed to the teeth.

"How far is it?" Aella spoke in a monotone. Monster's fate and my sister's capture had shocked her.

"Shouldn't we go together?" I tried.

"My orders are to look after you here in Midgard. We have to stay here!"

"But Serén said I should go to Hrafnheim," I pressed.

She turned away from me and looked out over the slushy, gray Jutland landscape. "My orders," she repeated.

"What happened to you deciding whether you obeyed orders or not?"

Aella whipped her head back toward me. "I refuse orders if I think they're stupid, but I promised your sister I would look after you. I swore," her voice faltered, and Aella quickly composed herself before continuing. "I promised Serén," she said slowly, "that I would stay here, no matter how much trouble she's in. Don't you think I'm fighting every second not to rush back there and help her?" Aella ran a hand over her short hair. "But a promise is a promise, and there's always a deeper meaning behind what Serén requests."

I narrowed my eyes. "What exactly did you swear? That you would stay here, or that you would stay here with me?"

"Same difference."

35

I suddenly grew very focused on looking down at the bus's worn linoleum floor. "I agree with Serén," I said. "You should stay here in Midgard."

My biker boots crunched through the gravel of the parking lot as my protectors turned in circles. The wind tore at us, tasting of salt and sandblasting my cheeks. With my eyes upturned, it struck me that this was another of the region's few buildings above sea level. This hill, however, was significantly larger than Odinmont. I studied the monastery, which had no ornamentation or frills. Just high, smooth, chalk-white walls with elegantly shaped windows. Although my power could clearly sense the activity here, the place instilled a deep calm in me.

"I'm going into the church," I said and walked determinedly across the courtyard. Latin song reached me from inside the building, and I was unsure of whether it was the past I was hearing or the present.

A young monk in a pale robe stepped in front of me. "Welcome," he said with a wry smile. "You must pay to enter the church."

My eyes widened. *A ghost?*

"When the church your money reaps, your soul from purgatory leaps." He clasped his hands and shook them toward the snow-heavy sky.

I squinted at him. "Are you haunting me right now?"

"Uh . . ." he said.

I stepped closer. *Poltergeist?* "What will you do if I go in without paying?"

"I'll call the people in the kiosk." He pointed to the gift shop. "The concert is part of the Christmas market." He straightened his glasses.

Glasses, Anna. He's wearing glasses!

"One, please." Cringing, I paid and was on my way through the low wooden door.

Une grabbed my arm, stopping me with a jerk. "You're not going anywhere alone."

I laid a flat hand on his chest. "Yes, I am."

Une didn't move, but I pushed harder against his torso while looking him right in the eyes. "Look. I can't go anywhere, and I'll shout if I run into any problems." When Une still didn't back off, I added, "You can't do anything violent in a church. That's a rule here in Midgard."

Even though I knew perfectly well that that rule was frequently broken, Une grudgingly relented and took a step back. He walked up to the robed monk.

"Is there another exit?"

The young man touched his glasses again, confused. "On the other side, there's a small blue door."

Une walked off with a serious look as the monk watched him. Aella positioned herself in front of the entrance with a wide stance and a vigilant gaze as I went in.

I crept through the church without seeing Elias. At the altar stood a choir dressed in robes, and the harmonious voices rang out through the interior of the old church, which smelled of wood and candle wax. No one in the mostly elderly audience noticed me.

I looked down at the gravestones in the floor, following the years backward in time until I reached the early 1600s. I had ended up in the little baptistery in the lower corner of the church, and an army of half-naked baby statues stared at me from all sides. I felt a warm hand stroke the back of my neck, and I jumped. Elias removed his hand and prepared to say something, but the words remained on his soft lips.

"I'm sorry," he whispered. Despite his smooth skin, he suddenly appeared ancient.

I knew I'd start sobbing if I said anything, so I kept my mouth shut. For a second, we held each other's gaze, and Elias clenched his fists as if to keep them at his sides.

37

I finally found my voice. "I have to . . ."

"Shhh." Elias looked around at the little statues. "Not here."

"They're made of wood." I furrowed my brows.

Elias didn't respond but pushed on the baptismal font, which slid aside to reveal a staircase. He began the descent, and I reluctantly followed, knowing Une and Aella would be furious if they knew I was willingly allowing myself to be shut in an enclosed space with a four-hundred-year-old mad scientist. Above us, I heard the baptismal font slide back into place as we stepped into a small room outfitted as a study.

"Aah!" I stifled a scream and took a step back. I was alone with a four-hundred-year-old mad scientist *and a brain.*

The beige lump sat in a bowl on the table.

"What the hell are you up to down here?" I panted.

Elias knelt and looked intently into the bowl. "Like I said, I'm studying here. You know of my wish to make divinity, magic, and science work together to reanimate the dead."

I forced the Christmas food back down into my stomach. "Why are you studying *that?*"

Elias was still staring at the brain. "It's gone now."

I took a large gulp of air. "What do you mean?"

"The demiblood that was in Naut Kafnar's veins is gone now." He pointed to the lump. "That confirms my theory that gods' blood is ephemeral. The effect diminishes over time."

I shivered. "Is that the Savage's brain?"

"Of course." Elias didn't even turn to face me.

"That's grotesque."

He shrugged and stood up. "It's a fact."

"Can we talk about what I came here for?" With exaggerated patience I looked at the wall, which was covered in drawings, photos, and formulas. I got the feeling of being in a serial killer's basement. I was also highly aware that Elias had positioned himself in front of the staircase, which was my only way out.

"Shoot." He stood with his legs apart and arms crossed.

I inhaled again. "I need your help."

"Do you have something specific in mind?" His gray-blue eyes traced over me. "Or do I get to choose the manner in which I contribute?"

"I need to get to Hrafnheim."

His arms slid from their pose. He took a step toward me and ran a hand through his unruly curls. I resisted the urge to take a step back. Elias grabbed me by the shoulders. His spicy scent reached my nostrils, and the heat of his hands shot into my arms. "Are you insane?"

"Yeah, probably."

Almost reflexively, Elias cracked a smile, but he quickly grew serious again. "Where did you get the idea that you should go to Hrafnheim?"

"Monster told me so, right before he . . ." I looked down to avoid Elias's eyes, which widened briefly. "I'm certain it's the only choice."

Elias released his grip, but his palms remained resting on my arms. "If there's anything my long life has taught me, it's that nothing is certain."

"Ragnara has my sister, and she's coming after me." I paused briefly. "She wants to have us together."

"She's not the only one." Elias's voice was so brazen that I started to laugh, even though the pain was tearing me up. I'd thought I would never smile again. I looked up at him with glassy eyes.

Elias looked mortified. He let go of me and took a step back.

I regained control of my mouth. "Could you please be serious."

"Sorry. It's automatic." He clenched his fists again. "What's my role?"

"You're gonna help me get there."

I thought Elias would protest, but he was entirely calm. "What's in it for me?"

39

With a groan, I threw my hands in the air. "How about avoiding the end of the world?"

"According to the myth, the world begins anew after Ragnarök. Maybe I'll be the ruler of this new world."

"Serén has seen that we'll both die if I stay in Midgard." The words came out sounding desperate, and I grasped his warm hand. "She can't die. I can't let anyone else die because of me."

Elias stood completely still and looked at me. The hand that lay in mine was also motionless. "Of all the girls in the world, I meet the one with a death sentence." He said *meet* as if it really meant something else.

"What do you want in exchange for helping me?" I asked.

"You think I'm for sale?" I couldn't tell if he was angry or flattered at the thought.

"I *know* you're for sale. What do you want?" I repeated, unblinking.

He cocked his head and his eyes narrowed. "Let me see," he thought aloud. "What do I want?" Finally, he decided. "I think that if you and your sister are able to find each other, you'll have power over time. I want part of that power."

My brows furrowed. "What are you talking about?"

His rough fingertips stroked my knuckles, and I pulled my hand back.

"Past and future meet in the present. I think that if you're together, you can influence events. You have access to the past, and ideally, you'll be able to change it. Promise me you'll change one past event of my choosing, if it's in your power." His soft lips pulled back into a calculating smile. "Then I'll help you get to Hrafnheim. At the New Year's Eve party tomorrow. I can help you through the portal."

I swallowed. "Deal," I said.

"We were about to tear the monastery apart to find you," Aella hissed when Elias and I stepped out of the church. "You were gone."

"I wasn't gone. I was just . . ." Elias sent me a sharp look. "I was hidden."

"Hidden?" Aella scoffed. "Could you give us a heads-up next time you plan to hide?"

"You're utterly impossible to look after," Une growled. "It's like you don't *want* to be protected."

I wanted to object, but my phone rang. I fished it out of my pocket and fumbled with the cold glass screen. "It's not a number I recognize."

Elias looked over my shoulder. He was so close, his curls tickled my cheek. "It's Od."

I stepped away from Elias and glared at the ringing phone without picking up. "Can't he just teleport up here?" It was hard to imagine the ancient demigod making use of something so banal as a cell phone. With a sigh, I swiped my finger across the screen and placed the cold surface against my ear. "Hello."

A dry, warm voice came from the other end. "Took you a while."

"Why are you calling?" Okay, not particularly elegant.

He laughed dryly. It was strange to hear his voice distorted through the phone.

"Meet me at the museum by the fjord. Elias knows where it is."

"Why do you think I'm with Elias? And what are we going to do?" My questions fell over each other, and I wasn't rewarded with an answer before the call was disconnected.

I lowered the phone. "Elias, did you blab?"

"No, but Od tends to know where people are and who they're with."

"Comforting." I stuffed the phone into the pocket of my mother's coat. "Do I have a choice?"

"As to whether you meet with Od?" Elias laughed. "You always

41

have a choice—or that's what he would say, anyway—but funnily enough, he always gets his way."

I looked to the sky, which was already shifting to dark blue.

"Come." Elias pointed to the parking lot. "I'll drive you."

Une and Aella looked uneasy as they crawled into the back seat of Elias's car. Une's broad shoulders brushed against Aella's, even though he rounded his back and looked out the window.

As we drove, all we could see in the dusk was lyme grass, wind-blown fields, and the silhouette of an old, black windmill. My bodyguards jerked back in their seats when Elias gunned the car down the now-dark country road. None of us said anything on the drive, and when I stole a glance at Elias, he looked stiffly ahead and sped up more than necessary.

In no time, we reached the destination, which overlooked the Limfjord.

Next to the museum was a circle of standing stones, but it was now completely dark, so there was nothing to see but the black outlines of the gigantic boulders. The lights from the town formed the backdrop. My power tingled from the activity that had once been here, and I saw people walking past, heard voices, and breathed in a strong fragrance of burnt wood and meat. Trees lined the small gravel path that led from the parking lot to the museum.

"Do you want some klinte?" Elias asked. "Many things have happened here."

I looked at the entrance of the modern building with its posters, copies of Viking jewelry, and a single brightly colored wooden shield. At the same time, I heard an echo of Old Norse and blasts from a hornlike instrument. A parade of slightly transparent torches wound its way down from the burial site, which was on a hill at least as high as Odinmont. The procession was accompanied by a humming song and the sound of weeping.

Elias looked at me with a creased forehead when I nodded.

42

When he unbuttoned his shirt, I caught a glimpse of his smooth chest. He rooted around in the leather pouch that always hung around his neck, which appeared to contain a broad selection of substances, and I shivered in the stiff breeze. Elias held out a finger with a drop of liquid balanced on its tip, and I avoided his gaze when I accepted it. I had to hold on to his warm hand so I could suck it up. When I did look up, I expected a flirty wink, but he just looked at me with concern. I let the klinte work with a deep breath. The voices disappeared, the flames died out, and the smell faded.

A flash of silver flickered at my side when I lifted my head again. Od's warm presence surrounded me, making me dizzy.

Od leaned toward Une and Aella. "Elias will drive you home. Anna will stay here."

Both smiled placidly and got into the car.

I rolled my eyes as I recalled the demagogues of history. Could there have been supernatural factors at play?

Od straightened.

"Elias." He said nothing more, but Elias understood and did an old-fashioned little half bow that betrayed his true age. He got back in with a single glance in my direction before steering the car and my two bodyguards away from us.

I stood alone in the empty parking lot with the demigod. The only source of light, aside from a couple of streetlights down the road, was the silver glow of Od's body.

"What now?" I tried not to look at his face, but I was captivated by his beauty. The high cheekbones, the curved lips, and the dark, shiny hair.

Od pulled on the door, which opened with a little sigh. "Let's go in where it's warm."

"Isn't it wrong to break in?"

"Yeah." Od laughed over his shoulder and suddenly looked very human.

43

The shadows dissolved the walls, obscured the tiles, and darkened the glass of the art cases, while the carved stones stood out clearly along with the axes, coins, and rusty iron swords.

"Why here?" I asked as Od led me down the stairs to the lower level, where the marsh had been reconstructed with reeds, water, and narrow paths. Down here, Od was the only source of light, and his silver glow rendered the space even more surreal. Where most people cast a shadow in sunlight, he cast a light in the darkness.

Od looked at a thick, light-brown braid that appeared to be submerged in sparkling water, though in reality it sat in a plexiglass case. "I lived here."

I looked around. "You lived in the museum?"

His deep-set eyes met mine. "Back when these hills were a town and a burial site. I was a young man of ninety when this was my home." He squatted down, opened the case, and carefully lifted the braid.

"I don't think you're allowed to touch that. You know, historical artifact and all that."

Od's thumb stroked the strands of hair before he laid it back in its glass case. Then he walked to the other end of the basement level. Tentatively, I followed him, mostly because it gave me goose bumps to stand alone in a dark museum basement surrounded by severed braids and broken weapons.

We stopped in front of some glass coffins, and Od's light fell inside. It was a series of skeletons. The skulls' empty eye sockets faced us as though they were looking at us, just as we were looking at them.

I looked at the dead, and the distant past stared right back.

Od's eyes were a little shiny amid all that metallic glow, and I understood that these were people just like me, even though they had passed away many years ago. They once had hopes, dreams, and secrets.

Od stared at the smallest skeleton. A girl, it seemed, judging from the beads and the woolen dress.

"She was six years old when she died. Back then, I didn't know my blood could have saved her." Od's elegant hand rested on the glass. From his hand, a beam of light hit the skull and made the teeth look like a smile. He shifted his gaze to the girl's reconstructed wax head, which was displayed on a pedestal above the coffins. The glass eyes looked straight past him.

"It's a good likeness, but she had fair hair." He let his palm rest on the head's wax cheek. "Time's arrow carries us all in one direction. Even me."

"Okey dokey." I cleared my throat. "I'm sorry. I feel bad that your friends are dead."

Od finally looked at me, as if he only now realized I was there. "There's nothing wrong with death. That's why I brought you here. To show you where we all end up."

"Well, it is cool to be led down into a basement full of dead people. I'm hard-core. I usually live on top of a crypt that holds my father's corpse, so you don't have to worry about that." I waved a hand. "But you could have just as easily told me this at Ben and Rebecca's over a cup of tea."

Od smiled the smile that always made my willpower falter.

I did everything in my power to stare back angrily. "Why am I here?"

"You need to understand where, under all circumstances, you are headed—where we're all headed—regardless of your choice."

"What do you know about my choice?"

He came up close to me, and his breath was intoxicating. His green eyes pulled me in like a dangerous undercurrent in the ocean, and an invisible wind threatened to pick me up and carry me away. I blinked my eyes, bewildered.

"My father believes you and your sister are essential for us. We need you."

"Who's *we?*" I had trouble speaking clearly.

"The gods."

"All the gods?"

"You're essential. For some, you're salvation. For others, doom."

Hmmm—I couldn't put together a lucid thought.

"Odin asked me to tell you," Od whispered in my ear, "that all you have to do is say *All-Father* if you wish to summon him." The words swirled around me like a plume of smoke.

"Summon." Feeling slightly drunk from Od's presence, I giggled when I repeated the ceremonious-sounding word. "Summon," I said again, but it was swallowed up by the darkness. With his back turned to me and the skeletons, Od walked toward the exit.

Instantly sober, I jogged after him with the hairs on the back of my neck standing up and my heart pounding.

Suddenly, Od turned around, and his silvery face was right in front of mine. I didn't have my guard up, so I was overtaken by his divine hypnosis. A trapdoor opened beneath me, and I slid down on a beautiful, golden cloud.

The next morning, I woke up in bed in my colorful little room with no memory of how I had gotten home.

 # CHAPTER 4

The New Year's Eve party at The Boatman was, of course, spectacular, but I had a hard time concentrating on it.

When I stared out over the packed bar, I noticed Hakim's eyes graze over me several times. I hadn't even spoken to him in the days between Christmas and New Year's Eve. He waved cautiously, and when I smiled back, he stood up just a tiny bit straighter. Without thinking about it, my fingers found the little silver hand pendant he had given me for my birthday, right before he saved my life.

In a far corner, Elias stood, keeping an eye on me. When people picked up full champagne glasses and Od took the stage to count down to the new year, Elias nodded his head in my direction.

As discreetly as possible, I backed into the shadows and snuck away.

In front of the door to Od's office, I stopped and looked into one of the large mirrors.

The forest-green dress, which Luna had sewn me for the occasion, was the exact same color as the stones in the ring that adorned my finger. The ring that she and Mathias had made for me together. I pushed the door, and, as Elias had promised, it was open.

Frank looked at me from the cage in the corner of Od's office.
Outside the door, people started counting down.
"Seven—six—five."

I took a letter opener from Od's desk. "Which door leads to Hrafnheim?"

"It's too dangerous. They'll kill you."

I raised an eyebrow. Ironic.

"Four—three—two."

"Do you want the opener?"

Frank exhaled a hiss through bared teeth. Then he raised a finger and pointed to a blue door.

"One—Haaappy New Year!"

I tossed the letter opener to Frank and I just managed to see him grab it before I flung the door open and threw myself into the dark.

My legs moved as if I were running, but they didn't make contact with any surface as I was sucked through the tunnel, surrounded by strips of light. A force stretched, pushed, and pulled me from all sides, although it felt, in a way, like it was coming from deep within me. I crossed my arms tightly across my chest to keep from being pulled apart.

I had no experience with teleportation, but I had imagined it would go a little faster. The passageway stretched out behind and in front of me, and I whizzed through what felt like an eternity.

Elias had said that the portal in Od's office led to northern Hrafnheim, but aside from that, I had no idea if I would plop down into a crowd of people or in the middle of nowhere. If it was a crowd, I also had no idea if they would be friends or foes.

Finally, I felt cold air on my face. My feet continued their aimless cycling, but suddenly there was solid ground beneath them, and I quite literally hit the ground running. At a sprint, I continued into the pitch blackness and was momentarily blinded by the transition from light to dark. Then I crashed into a massive form.

"Ow, shit," I hissed and grabbed my shoulder, which had taken the majority of the impact. My fingers ran over the colossus, and the rough surface told me it was a large tree. High above me, I heard wind hitting leaves.

While I stood panting and waiting for my eyes to adjust to the dark surroundings, a glimmer of light flashed in the expanse of sky. I tried to orient myself, but before I could do so, an explosion brought me to my knees behind the tree.

I was shaking, and nausea caused my mouth to water. After a couple of violent dry heaves, I got my stomach somewhat under control, even though every fiber of my being protested. Had the journey split me into atoms and put me back together again?

Something shook the ground. A sharp, blue flash lit up the sky again, and I saw that I was in a forest.

Fireworks? Or . . . I looked at the strange glimmers. Some kind of light show.

The ground vibrated beneath me once again, and it took a while for me to realize it was a bass beat.

Dum—dum—dum.

From reading Rebecca's notebook, I knew that time had been synchronized between our world and Hrafnheim, except that here, they counted our year 1054 as year zero, because that was when the great migration from our world started. Aside from that, I actually knew shockingly little about Hrafnheim. But I had brought along Rebecca's notebook, which had a map—granted, an eighteen-year-old map—in the middle.

In the pauses between flashes, the forest sank into deep darkness, and I had to feel my way forward.

"Happy New Year," I whispered between thumps in the ground. I hadn't had the chance to say it to my friends, who had all, in one way or another, helped me make it to the new year alive. So quietly, I was practically just mouthing the words without sound, I said: "Happy New Year, Monster. I trust you."

Well then.

Another flash tore through the sky, and I tried to decide which direction to head in, but my surroundings were quickly plunged back into darkness, and I fumbled onward. I tried to find the way with my power, but in a panicked moment, I realized it was numb. I never thought I would miss my clairvoyance, but right now I was terrified at the thought that my only advantage was gone.

Away from the music, I decided, and I crawled away.

Ever so slowly, my clairvoyance began to return, and I saw brief glimpses of the forest in the summer, in daylight, and of people passing by. I exhaled slowly. I still couldn't feel any auras, but I couldn't be sure if that was because my power was impaired or if there was simply no one around.

I stood and took a few steps back. Something splashed.

"Ow," said a deep voice in the darkness; at the same time, my boot hit something.

I spun around, and just then a rocket exploded in the sky, allowing me to see. The man in front of me stared, just as bewildered as I was.

"Serén," he exclaimed. "Thora Baneblood's daughter. What on earth are you doing here?" He quickly buttoned his pants.

I backed away.

Friend or foe?

He took a couple of steps in my direction, until the light burned out, and we were once again plunged into darkness. I couldn't see anything, but my other sense was working in high gear. Finally, his aura emerged, but I had trouble deciphering it. It fluttered with excitement and . . . I examined it as I continued backing away. Beneath the bass rhythm, I heard his hoarse breathing. I cast my clairvoyance at him and forced it, painfully, into overdrive, until I was finally able to pull a memory from his past.

"Oh shit," I exhaled and threw myself backward.

CHAPTER 5

In the man's past, I saw my sister being captured. I saw his calloused hands holding her wrists as she screamed.

"Over here! Hurry!" he shouted and reached for me.

I had the advantage of using my power to get a hint of where he was, since neither he nor I could see very much between the brief flashes of light. We stumbled around, and several times, we tripped over branches lying on the forest floor as I tried to get away.

The man was still bellowing at his companions, and several more people appeared around us. Just when I thought I had escaped, a rough hand landed on my shoulder, where it stuck to my coat as though it were magnetic.

I struggled but couldn't break loose from the suction-like grip, so I kicked him hard in the shin while simultaneously twisting around and wrenching myself free. Before running away, I slammed my fists into his jaw and cheekbone.

He lunged, swearing, but I was quick, and he missed. He smelled of alcohol, and I suspected his slow movements had something to do with that. I ran farther into the forest and tried to triangulate the location of the others.

"Stop in the name of the queen," barked the man who had found me. "I command you."

Shit!

I had run straight into the arms of Ragnara's soldiers. My footsteps pounded loudly on the dry forest floor, even over the bass rhythm, so I slowed down and did a shoulder roll under the trunk of a fallen tree. I tried to muffle my heavy breathing with a hand over my mouth. A bone-chilling cold seeped into me from the ground, and a sharp twig scratched my cheek, but I forced myself to lie still. I got as close to the tree as I could and pulled up my hood to hide my red hair. The men walked around my hiding place. Once in a while, one of them shouted, but finally they came to a stop and began talking.

"Are you sure?" someone asked.

"It was Serén," the first man said. "Without a doubt."

"She's in custody," came a third voice. "I myself was part of the raid. I helped torture the leader of the giant wolves."

My stomach clenched, and I had to cling to the dry tree stump to keep from throwing myself at the man.

The others groaned. "We don't wanna hear about it again, Knut."

Knut. I committed the name to memory.

"Where we put her, she might as well have been in the realm of the dead." Knut growled, irritated. "How could you let her get away?" he said, presumably to the first soldier.

"I'm telling you. She was quick as a mouse, and she fought like a guard. I didn't know Serén could fight."

A new voice joined the mix. "She must still be around here somewhere."

They started walking in the opposite direction.

I lifted myself halfway up on my elbow to make sure they had left. Just then, an impressive flash illuminated the entire sky and most of the trees, and I looked up right into a face. The man who stood over me had no aura, so I had been completely unaware that someone was near me. He quickly grabbed both my wrists in one hand and put his other hand around my throat. None of Varnar's training sessions had prepared me for this, and although I writhed in the man's grasp, I wasn't going anywhere. I had to make an effort not to scream in desperation. Varnar had taught me not to show fear.

"I've got her," he yelled. His hands, too, stuck to my clothes and my neck, and no matter how much I writhed, I only became more entrenched. A familiar electric current ran from his fingers into my skin. It reminded me of Ben's.

The soldiers came back, and before I could twist myself free, eight men were gathered around me in a circle. A crystal shone. It looked like nothing I had seen before, but it radiated light, so I could finally see the soldiers properly. They could also see me.

"It's her. By Ragnara's anfarwol, it's Serén. Gustaf, I knew we could count on you." The voice sounded like Knut, and I stared at his broad shoulders, rough hands, and messy hair. He had a birthmark near his eye, which fortunately made him recognizable.

Some say revenge is wrong. I didn't believe in right or wrong, but I knew what would feel good.

Knut took a small step back. Then he bared his teeth and walked toward me again. "What in all the worlds are you doing here?" he asked. "I myself helped put you under lock and key."

I pressed my clairvoyance into his past to twist out where Serén was imprisoned, but he was unreadable.

He placed his face right in front of mine and stared at me. "It's you, Serén," he said. He exhaled, and the stench of alcohol made my nose wrinkle. "You screamed so prettily when I stabbed Etunaz in the chest. You cried when his blood stained my axe."

I kept my face neutral, which brought him even closer. I could feel the pulse in my wrists and mouth, but I stood stock still. His stubble grazed my cheek, and the tip of his tongue ran over my skin.

At exactly the right time, I flung my face forward and hit Knut squarely in the nose, which made a cracking noise and began to bleed. His teeth bit down on his tongue, which was still in the act of licking my cheek. He grabbed his nose and mouth with a howl, but then he turned and gave me such a slap, I saw stars.

"You better hold her tight. She's a little fighter," the man with no aura said. "Shall we do it here?"

53

"It's too cold. Let's take her back to the camp," the first soldier said.

And so they dragged me away.

The camp was a collection of tents. The reverberating bass was coming from the camp, and now I also heard singing in a Scandinavian language I didn't recognize. The unusual fireworks shot up from large cylinders placed in the ground, and each blast was accompanied by a hollow *thump*.

Whether it was magic or a special kind of gunpowder, I had no idea.

I was pushed into one of the tents, which had massive poles carved with snakes and birds. A strange, branching rune was painted in red on the fabric of the tent. It had one vertical line and two smaller ones reaching up at an angle. At first, I thought it was the rune ansuz, which had been found on the murdered girls in Ravensted, but it wasn't the same. I didn't have the chance to see more before the aura-less man, who was apparently called Gustaf, yanked me under a flapping tent cloth. He pulled me off-balance, so I stumbled forward and had to catch myself with my hands. Then he tied me to a post and forced me to sit down. His palms were tattooed in the same way as Ben's, and on his forehead and cheekbones he had adornments resembling green-and-blue snake scales.

He crouched down, grabbed my chin, and tilted it upward. He was weather-beaten, and his eyes were a cloudy yellowish-green with tiny, almost oval pupils.

"The men will question you," he said. "As long as you answer them, they won't give you any trouble." His words came out with sharp S sounds. "Don't resist. If you do, it'll be a long night."

My blood ran cold, and without answering, I hurled my clairvoyance at him with all the strength I possessed. Like with Ben and Rebecca, I could see nothing of either his aura or his past.

He leaned back on his heels as if I had pushed him. He put his fingertips on the ground to keep his balance. Then he got to his feet and took a few steps toward the tent's opening, where he stopped and turned. "Don't let them know you're a seer. It makes the men uneasy." He vanished.

I tugged on the rope that held me to the post and bound my hands together. It was made of something highly durable, and the knot wouldn't budge. Nevertheless, my fingers grabbed hold of the silver hand that Hakim had given me as a birthday present, which hung on a chain around my neck. Its edge was sharp, and I was able to make a small cut in the rope.

Outside, the strange music thundered on, there was loud clinking, and the Old Norse song was being chanted. Through the tent's fabric, I saw light from both the sky and a fire. The soldiers took their sweet time, and I waited for what felt like several hours. Maybe time actually worked differently in this world. Fortunately, it gave me time to work on the rope, which I alternately cut and pulled at. It was extremely tough. Hooray for my destructive abilities, which eventually got the rope unraveled a tiny bit.

A man entered the tent and interrupted me. It was the first soldier I had met. He, like the others, wore simple blue clothing that, at first glance, resembled coveralls. It was of a rough fabric, however, and had leather reinforcements on the elbows and knees as well as at the waist. The strange rune I had seen painted on the tent was also embroidered with red thread on his chest.

I got to my feet.

He looked more confident here than in the forest. Maybe it had something to do with the fact that I was tied up. Or so he thought. Although my wrists were lashed together, I clenched my fists and, as discreetly as I could, spread my hands to put pressure on the half-cut rope. He tried to look at me, but his eyes kept roaming, as if they slid off me. After spending years carrying Ben's spells around, I knew this look. I estimated the soldier to be a little older than Varnar, a bit skinnier, and maybe just a hair taller. He moved with the clumsy motions of the drunk.

"We're gonna find out how you got away, Serén," he said, but it ended in a burp.

I stood completely still as he approached me. He fumbled with his clothing, which had buttons down the front.

"What are you doing?" It was the first time I spoke. He looked up in surprise but wrinkled his nose when he looked directly at me.

"What do you think I'm doing?"

A combination of rage and sheer terror tore through me. Did he really think . . . ? I inhaled angrily.

He came close to me. "Turn around," he said, but at that moment, I swung at him with both fists, since I still hadn't managed to get my hands apart. I hit him on the cheekbone.

He sank to his knees with a groan.

"Already, Bardu?" someone shouted from outside the tent. I thought I recognized the voice as Knut's. "Guess it'll be our turn sooner."

The ropes would not give, so I had to work with what I had. I wrapped the loose line around Bardu's neck and pulled while kicking him in the ribs. He gurgled, and his hands circled in the air without hitting me.

"She sounds good," shouted another man outside.

A fist struck my knee, and I stopped briefly to change position so he couldn't hit me again. Unfortunately, I had to slacken the rope, and this gave Bardu the opportunity to gurgle once more.

"There's something wrong," Knut said. It sounded like he was getting up.

"Leave them be," another said. "You wouldn't want to be disturbed, either."

Knut pulled the tent flap to the side.

I threw the half-conscious Bardu at him and pulled my hands apart with all the strength I had. There was a boom from the ring

Luna and Mathias had made together, and heat shot across my knuckles at the same time as the rope snapped.

"Get her!" Knut yelled from the tent opening, after which another two soldiers burst in.

On the plus side, my hands were free, but there were also four men surrounding me, even though Bardu didn't seem capable of doing much. Even with Varnar's training, three and a half professional soldiers would be a tall order.

They came closer. One of them reached out, but I had learned to keep my distance from their sticky grasp. Another attacked. He didn't have the elegant movements of the Varangian Guard, but his technique was good, and he landed several blows to my arms.

I kicked him between the legs in a dirty move I had learned from Aella.

He crumpled as I kicked and punched in all directions. I allowed my instincts to take over and Varnar's voice to guide me, but I ended up with raw knuckles and blood spattered up my arms.

The soldiers pulled back as if to decide what they should do. They stood in front of the tent opening and blocked me from getting out.

Knut glared at me. His fingers ran across the axe that hung from his belt. The motion resembled a caress. "Etunaz howled like a wounded puppy when I stabbed him again and again."

Fired up, I took a step forward and swung one leg along the ground, and he landed on his back. In the same motion, I pulled the axe out of his belt and leapt to the other side of his head, so my back was halfway out of the opening, and I faced the remaining soldiers. With a firm grip on the axe head, I placed the sharp edge against Knut's throat and felt how the artery pounded under the iron blade. Knut's nose had taken on a bluish-purple hue from the headbutt I had given him earlier in the evening.

"One step closer and I'll slit his throat," I warned.

They stayed back. Though I suspected Knut's life was worth

more to me than it was to them. I pushed away the thought of what he had done to Monster, fearing it would lead me to murder.

"Where am I?" I spat at him.

"Norvík," he said with some effort. "Near the Hibernian border."

"That's not what I mean. Where did you put me when you captured me in the Iron Forest?"

"What?" Knut struggled to breathe.

"Where did you put me?" I asked slowly, pressing the axe against his throat.

The axe's edge was razor-sharp, and something warm and wet ran over my fingers, but I didn't look down. Instead, I directed my wide eyes at the other soldiers.

I clenched my fist around Knut's collar and shook. "Tell me," I commanded.

"You were placed in . . ." Knut didn't get to finish before something hard hit me in the back of the head.

My head throbbed and dangled forward. For a moment, I had no idea where I was, and when I remembered, I wished I could slip back into unconsciousness. I was half standing, half hanging on a pole. My hands were gathered above my head, and my knees buckled beneath me a couple of times before I got my feet on the floor.

There were people in the room. Both male and female soldiers, all dressed in the blue uniform with the red rune. Behind them, right up against the pale cloth of the tent, stood the aura-less Gustaf, looking at me with his reptilian eyes. In his hand he held a blunt, leather-bound stick.

If my hands were free, I would have rubbed the back of my head, where I could feel a bump growing.

Some people were talking, but they went silent when I blinked my eyes.

"Shhh."

A rough hand grabbed my face and squeezed, so my mouth was pressed together. It hurt my jaw, and I tried as hard as I could to twist free. I was unsuccessful and ended up staring into the shoulder of one of the strange uniforms. The branching rune was just outside my field of vision.

"What's going on, Serén?" Knut asked. He was the only one standing in front of me. "You show up here, even though you're supposed to be in prison." He came closer and I could smell flax, leather, and beneath that, a note of alcohol. He shook my head so my teeth clattered.

Knut forced my face up, so he was looking right at me. His nose had taken on a white tone, and on his neck was an angry, red wound. He narrowed his eyes and turned my face from side to side. "You look ugly. You don't usually. Why is that?"

A light was aimed at my eyes, and it blinded me. I could no longer see Knut's face, but the hand on my jaw was still squeezing.

If I hadn't been so terrified and angry with myself for having ended up in this situation, I would have laughed at the cliché. When it came down to it, the worlds were apparently not so different.

Knut pressed my face to the side, and I looked at the dirty bottom edge of the tent. The blue lights were still flashing through the fabric, but there were longer pauses between them. The music sent vibrations up through the ground and into the soles of my feet.

The hand released me, and I wiggled my jaw. "I want to speak to your leader," I said as calmly as I could.

A laugh came from somewhere in the tent.

"Our leader?" Knut said with mock seriousness.

"You must have a leader. I want to speak with him . . . uh . . . or her."

Behind the other men, I saw Gustaf's head jerk up. Then he took a couple of steps back and disappeared. I tried to follow him with my eyes, and therefore didn't see the slap coming. It struck me so hard, it reverberated inside my skull, and when I sniffed, I felt something warm running from my nose.

"You come with demands?" Another slap landed on my other cheek. "After what you did." Knut hit me again, this time in the stomach, and I would have doubled over if I hadn't been tied up.

I gasped loudly for air.

Knut's knee was on its way up, and since I couldn't protect myself with my arms, I tensed my stomach muscles and tucked my chin down toward my neck in a pathetic defense against the large man.

"Stop," came a voice from the opening.

Knut's knee hovered in the air right in front of my chest, and I noticed a sigh of annoyance from him.

"Stay inside." This was not a voice I had heard before.

Reluctantly, Knut pulled away.

The blood that ran from my nose and down over my mouth began to dry, making my lips feel tight. I looked at the feet moving across the floor toward me.

Heavy boots. Firm steps. Large hands hung at the man's sides. On one hand was a tattoo of a bird.

"Would you also like to question her, Commander?" asked Knut.

The commander said nothing.

He was tall and broad-shouldered, and his hair was so pale, it was almost white. It was gathered in the same type of knot that Varnar sometimes wore. His eyes were dark brown in an unsettling contrast to his light hair. His face was harsh, but I detected youth beneath the hard features. I guessed he was significantly younger than he would like to admit.

Behind him stood Gustaf, still observing neutrally with his small yellow eyes.

Knut continued quickly. "Watch out. She's a feisty one."

I examined the young commander more closely, but he was hard to read, and I got no images from his past.

He raised an eyebrow and looked at Knut and the men with swollen eyes and bruised faces after coming into contact with my fists and boots.

"Just look at the lot of you! How many opponents were there, for you to end up in this state?"

"Just Serén," one answered honestly, running a finger delicately across his cheekbone. Blood ran from his split earlobe.

I wonder when I did that?

"Just Serén?" the commander repeated. He studied me with his lips slightly parted and pulled back. If he had smiled, he would have been attractive, but his face was contorted into a grimace.

I met his gaze defiantly.

Oddly enough, my clairvoyance flared up in a way I had never experienced before. It examined him and recognition tingled throughout my body. As though my very soul remembered his. At the same time, I was sure I had never met him before. He stared at me, and a tiny spark of recognition came back from him. For a split second, we looked at each other with mutual wonder.

"Out. All of you," he commanded without moving.

No one contradicted him, but they scowled at his back as they filed out. Gustaf stayed behind expectantly. The young commander's brown eyes rested on me.

"She has intense witchcraft on her. It was cast by a powerful magician," Gustaf said when the tent was empty apart from us.

"Who put the spells on her?"

"I can't see. But she has strong clairvoyant abilities."

"It's common knowledge that Serén is clairvoyant." The commander's voice had an edge of superiority, and Gustaf's shoulders slumped slightly. "Has she gained other powers? The men looked as if the hrimthurs had gotten them."

"She's just a seer."

The commander looked at me again, and his lip moved in disgust.

The wind made the tent's opening flutter, and I could smell smoke, tar, and grass. Discreetly, I tried to pull the rope apart once again, but this time it held fast.

The commander rolled up his sleeves, revealing that one of his arms was tattooed. The sleeve stopped at his elbow, but the intricate tattoo appeared to continue up under the fabric.

"I want to be alone with her."

Gustaf hesitated.

"Go," barked the commander, and my sense of fear flared.

The moment Gustaf was out, the commander walked right up to me. I tried to lean back, but I was bound so tightly I couldn't move. The commander reached out his large hand, and I saw that the bird tattooed on it was an eagle. A stylized eagle that resembled the drawings on Ben and Rebecca's house or the carvings on a Viking ship. The wings stretched out on his fingers, and its open beak yawned on the back of his hand.

The hand wrapped around my throat. "You're real," he whispered.

"I, uh . . ."

"There are rumors about you, but I didn't know if you actually existed."

The ring on the pole cut into my back. I tried to arrange my face in a mild expression like I had seen Serén do. It felt almost like a violation of myself.

The wind tore into the tent again, and a single flash of light penetrated the fabric.

He took a step closer before sniffing me. His calloused eagle-tattooed hand brushed carefully across my cheek, which burned after Knut's slaps. A strange urge seeped from him and into my beaten face. He kept his own features in a hard mask.

"Thora's daughter?" he said.

"Yes . . ."

Now he furrowed his brows even more. "What are you doing here?"

As I searched for something to say, the commander's other hand reached down. From his belt hung a heavy sword, and he began to slowly pull it.

"I wanted . . ." I racked my brain for a convincing explanation as to why my twin sister would be so stupid as to run right into the clutches of Ragnara's army.

"Help me," I whispered. "The future depends on it."

He didn't reply but continued pulling out the sword.

"I can see your future," I lied. "I can see if you or your loved ones are in danger."

I fumbled for a suitable promise. A suitable lie, but he didn't respond.

"I can see how you'll get rich."

The commander's hand stopped. The sword was halfway out of its sheath. For a split second, he focused on my eyebrow, the one divided by a scar.

"I'm not interested in riches," he said coldly. His hand still rested on the iron hilt.

The weapon was massive and made of matte, dark iron, with runes all the way down. The sword itself had its own aura, and the images that flowed from it told of death and destruction. It had killed hundreds, if not thousands.

"Ragnara will lose." My voice was desperate now. "I swear, I saw it. Wouldn't you rather be on the winning side?"

He breathed heavily. His lips would be nicely shaped if they weren't pressed so tightly together. The eagle-tattooed hand clutched my throat, and the muscles in his forearm were shaking.

"Serén can do the things you promise," he whispered.

"Yes, I—"

"But you're not Serén."

I opened my mouth to protest but didn't get the chance.

He lifted the horrible sword and swung it at me.

CHAPTER 6

Though I tried to get away, the commander's strong hand pinned me to the post, so I didn't budge as the sword sliced through the air.

The sharp blade rushed straight toward me, but instead of getting my head chopped off, I heard a clunk and a moan followed by the sound of a body hitting the ground. I opened one eye and saw Gustaf lying on the ground. He had apparently snuck in behind us, but his lack of aura meant I hadn't noticed him.

The young commander held the sword raised with one hand after having slammed the hilt into Gustaf's temple. The other hand was still around my throat.

"I am Serén," I squeaked. "I am."

His thumb touched my eyebrow. Because he still had the sword in his hand, the blade was just out of my line of sight, and I had to squeeze my eyes shut as the sword's aggressive aura bombarded me.

"Serén doesn't have this."

"It just happened."

"That scar is a decade old." His thumb was still tracing my brow in a repetitive stroking motion. Every time he reached the knotty tissue, the large finger bumped over it.

"You sure know a lot about scars," I mumbled. "Okay. I'm not Serén. I'm her sister."

The commander's breathing sped up. "Where have you been hiding all these years?"

I saw no reason to disclose that I was from an entirely different world. "If Ragnara gets hold of us both, she wins."

"What does she win?"

"I don't know. Power. Time. Everything."

"What are you capable of?"

I looked down but chose to tell the truth. "I think we can influence past events. Or I can, if I'm with her. Maybe I can even change them."

The commander exhaled forcefully. "If you can . . ." I waited as he pondered. "What is your mission?" he asked finally.

"I have to find Serén. If Ragnara kills her, it will spark Ragnarök. The end of the world. I'm pretty sure that would be bad for you, too."

I held my breath and stared straight into his brown eyes while the sword's bloodlust resounded right next to my ear. As if it were whispering: *Kill her, kill her. Blood, blood, blood.*

"Stay out of it," I said aloud and looked at it angrily. "You're just a piece of iron."

The commander appeared to make a decision. "I want you to change something for me, but it has to happen before summer. If you do, I'll find your sister."

I had no qualms about making promises I had no intention of keeping, so I nodded almost imperceptibly.

"Say it." He moved the sinister sword.

"I promise," I said quickly.

Suddenly, his stony expression vanished. He released both my neck and my brow and started pulling at the rope above my head. "Gustaf and his damn knots," he groaned.

Is he helping me?

I held my hands out for him.

I'll be damned, he is helping me.

The commander gave up on loosening the knots manually and raised the sword again. He laid the blade against the rope. "Stand still. Tilarids is very sharp." Carefully, he cut my restraints, and the sword's fury flowed over me, until the rope finally came apart.

The commander knelt to free my feet.

When his fingers brushed my ankles, I once again got the strange feeling of having met him before. He looked up at me, and we looked wonderingly at one another.

I was finally free, and I kicked the rope far away. He stood up to his full height, more than a head taller than me, and I opened my mouth to say something, but he beat me to it.

"Come." He held out his hand and looked toward the tent's opening. "Gustaf will wake up soon."

As if to emphasize the commander's words, Gustaf moaned faintly.

I took the offered hand, which closed around mine so hard, I couldn't have pulled free if I tried. I decided not to try. Not right now, anyway.

"I just need my bag."

Gustaf had tossed it into a corner.

The commander led me out of the tent after I had collected my few belongings.

"It was lucky you showed up tonight," he said over his shoulder. "Most soldiers are celebrating the new year."

We crept through the shadows, the commander with his sword aloft and me dragged behind, unable to figure out if I was his prisoner or under his protection. As a pathetic defense, I clenched my free hand into a fist, not that it would help all that much if we were discovered.

Of course we were discovered.

It was Knut—Monster's killer—who was strolling right toward us.

I had to bite the inside of my cheek hard to keep calm.

The commander pushed me behind him, so I was hidden behind his large form. I sank to my knees.

Knut stood up straight and drew something in the air with his fingers. I wondered for a moment, then realized it was the Hrafnheimish version of a salute.

"Commander," Knut said. He was clearly making an effort not to slur his speech. "I volunteer to escort Serén to Sverresborg."

I ducked in the commander's shadow.

Sverresborg?

He interrupted Knut. "I will do it."

"You?"

"She's mine," the commander said calmly. "You are not to follow us."

It was clear that Knut was swinging between the urge to point out that this order made no sense and the military hierarchy that demanded he follow orders without objection. The hierarchy won out, and he agreed brusquely. "What are our orders, Commander?"

"Take care of Gustaf," the commander said. "He's lying in the tent after she knocked him out."

Hey!

As if my already-tarnished reputation needed any more head traumas under its belt.

Knut cleared his throat. "And then?"

"Stay here and keep a lookout for rebels."

"Shall we send a messenger to Sént?"

"No." The commander's hard voice did not welcome further questions.

"Understood," Knut said and traced the salute in the air again, though it was clear he understood nothing at all. He scrambled toward the tent, and I put my fingertips to the ground and took a couple of deep breaths, forming a cloud around me. The air was freezing, which muted all scents.

"We'd better get out of here." Now I was the one running ahead, with the commander right at my heels.

"Are they after us?" I asked.

We took a short break to catch our breath.

"I ordered them to stay," he said, standing next to me.

"Do the soldiers always do what you order them to?"

The commander lifted his head, irritated. "Of course. But," he mumbled after a pause, "I'm not sure how Gustaf will react when he comes to."

"Is he not one of the soldiers?"

"Magician." He said nothing more.

"What's your name, by the way?" I groaned as I leaned against a tree trunk. The air I gulped down was cold but tasted fresh and clean.

We had been running for over an hour, and I could barely see the commander in the dark forest, but I heard how he inhaled sharply, as if I had asked him a trick question.

"Rorik," he answered finally.

"Rorik," I repeated.

"And you're the sister." This wasn't a question, but a statement. He sounded angry and didn't ask for my name. "We need to find somewhere to hide if Gustaf decides to follow us."

"If he's a magician, won't he find us anyway?"

"I can keep us concealed," Rorik replied.

"It's a good idea to hide while we figure out what to do."

I wondered if I should tell him Frank was also after me. I ran the risk that Rorik wouldn't want to help me if I told him there was also a contract killer from back home out to get me. So, I didn't.

I had caught my breath. "Let's keep going."

I looked at Rorik's broad back in the moonlight that briefly washed over us as we ran through a clearing, where trees didn't block the sky. Though he was tall and muscular, he moved elegantly and quietly, and I wondered whether I could trust him. Not that I had a choice right now.

When the sky began to lighten, he stopped and dug around in his coat pocket. He pulled something out and fumbled with it. When it began to shine, I saw that it was an iron framework in which a crystal was encased. He ran his eagle-tattooed thumb over

68

the glassy surface, after which it glowed brighter. He held it above his head and shone it around him as if looking for something.

"Have you been here before?"

"Never."

"Then what are you looking for?"

"Somewhere we can hide," he said curtly. "Stay here." He took a few steps toward a boulder and took something out of his pocket.

The boulder was covered with moss. A single, scrawny tree and a couple of unruly bushes grew atop it, which looked unnatural. In the delicate morning light, it resembled a large, gray, half-buried bone.

I looked around. The trees had turned into spruces without me noticing the transition, and I inhaled the frosty air. Despite the ice and frost, the smell of spruce came through. It reminded me of Kraghede Forest and my home. The ground was covered in moss, and my footsteps bounced softly as I wandered a bit in the opposite direction. I looked up.

At that moment, the sky was exactly the same color as Mathias's eyes when he went into demi-mode. Mist rose from the ground, enveloped the trees, and broke the light in orange cascades. I held up a hand to block out the sharp sunbeams.

I turned around and inhaled the pure, ice-cold morning air and allowed myself to enjoy the moment as the feeling of longing for my home and friends passed.

There were a few trees between me and Rorik now.

With my face turned toward the sapphire-blue sky, I walked even farther away from the boulder.

Just then, a strange noise made me look down. A claw shot up through the moss-covered soil and closed around my ankle.

I looked straight into a distorted face.

 # CHAPTER 7

"What the . . ." I managed to breathe before the creature used my body to pull itself up. It stood in front of me and stared at me with red eyes. Its head tilted while a claw held on to my coat.

I turned halfway and saw two creatures of the same type rising behind me. They looked like a combination of bird and ape and had somewhat human, yet slightly twisted, faces at the ends of long, buzzard-like necks. Their ears were large and fuzzy, their fingers were webbed, and they were more than two heads taller than me. When one of them spread its long arms, I saw that it had enormous bat wings stretching from its arms to its body. On its forehead, it had small horns like a goat.

Monster had also looked terrifying, but nevertheless my sister had kept her cool and talked to him when she first went to see him in the Iron Forest. Maybe, for once, I should ask first and attack later.

"Can you speak?" I tried, holding on to my mental image of Monster, even though it tore me apart.

The creature in front of me tilted its head even more and listened. It opened its mouth and revealed a row of brown teeth, and a stench of rot hit me.

"What are you?" I asked, backing up.

The creature now bared its full set of teeth and emitted a hissing sound. Its large, funnel-shaped ears lay flat against its head, and its eyes took on an even deeper red color.

"I'm not going to hurt you." I stumbled backward.

This time, the animal screeched and lunged at me, while the other two snapped. When I took another step back, I tripped over a branch and landed on the ground on my back. The red eyes came closer as I crab walked backward.

"Baaaaah," screeched the animal.

A shout came from behind me, and I heard heavy, crunching footsteps. It was Rorik, running toward us with Tilarids unsheathed. Without a word, he buried the blade deep into the chest of one of the creatures. It howled hoarsely and flailed its winged arms before collapsing in a pool of blood. The smell of spoiled meat spread through the air as another of the creatures lunged for Rorik's throat. Now I saw that their teeth were razor-sharp. The animal—or whatever it was—screeched and chomped at him.

The sword appeared to practically steer itself toward the creature's neck, which it chopped through unimpeded. The head tumbled to the ground and landed right in front of me, where it sat gaping like a fish out of water. I pushed it away with my foot, but even though the head was separated from the rest of the creature's body, it still hissed and snapped weakly at me.

Tilarids looked like a magnet searching for metal, and unsettlingly enough, the sword had more of an aura than most people. It bounded gleefully toward the final kill, which was the first creature I had tried to talk to. It quickly sliced through the torso and cleaved the animal in two.

In less than thirty seconds, it was over, and the creatures lay scattered around us.

I lay there with both hands pressed against my mouth amid the inferno of dismembered limbs.

Rorik struggled to get Tilarids under control. Finally, he got it stuffed back into its sheath. Then he turned toward me. "What were you doing?" he yelled.

I stood and took a step toward him. "You don't get to decide if I look around a little. I decide for myself—"

"You tried to talk to a fingalk," he interrupted. "Three of them, actually."

"A fingalk?" *Oh.* I glanced at the shredded bodies. "Are you not supposed to talk to them?"

Rorik looked at me like I was crazy and shook his head. "Everyone knows that."

"What kind of creature are they?" I asked.

"Pests," Rorik said.

With the toe of my boot, I poked at a long, brown, winged arm. "Can they fly?"

"No," Rorik replied indifferently.

I stood looking at the sad remains.

Rorik took a couple of deep breaths. "I told you to stay where you were. Tell me, do you ever do what you're told?"

I looked down. As a rule, no, I didn't. I brushed my hands together to remove the caked-on dirt and tried to change the subject. "Your sword is smeared with blood. And you just stuck it back in its sheath. All wet." I swallowed uncomfortably.

"The blood makes Tilarids kill for me. It's clean by the next time I need it."

"Okey dokey," I mumbled, while Rorik looked at me as if my mere presence made him nauseous. I was used to that, so I barely noticed.

Okay, I'll admit I noticed. I had been starting to grow accustomed to friends and murderers who weren't affected by Ben's spells. And maybe I had a dumb expectation that people in Hrafnheim were exempt from the magic.

"Can we try to get along? There are so many dangers in Hra . . . I mean Freiheim."

Both eyebrows shot up. "Hra . . ."

I waved my hands. I had almost forgotten it was now prohibited to use the old name Hrafnheim. "Did you find somewhere for us to hide?" I asked to divert his attention.

He turned around and started walking. His broad shoulders were stiff, like he wasn't sure he was doing the right thing.

I jogged after him. "I know what I'm doing. I have a map with me and everything."

"Oh, yeah?" He still didn't look at me.

I wasn't planning to share the fact that the map in Rebecca's notebook was more than eighteen years old. I was telling the truth. Technically.

After walking a few minutes through brush and dry branches, Rorik showed me the entrance to a cave. I would have walked right past it if he hadn't pointed it out. Inside, he showed me to a creepy corner, while he placed the shining crystal thing in front of the entrance. It emitted a soft glow and waves of heat, and a hiss of creepy-crawlies fled the light.

And here I had been expecting a campfire.

"Aren't we, like, trapped in here?" I turned around and took a step away from the damp rock wall, where a couple of spiders were crawling. "If someone finds us, I mean."

"We're hidden," he said abruptly, and there was so much certainty in his voice that I accepted it.

I sat down and pulled my legs up under me. "What is Sverresborg?"

"She knows nothing about Freiheim," he mumbled.

"I heard that!"

"Am I wrong?" His dark brown eyes lingered on me.

"Wellll," I conceded. "I'm not super familiar with the place."

A mild understatement.

"What kind of place is Sverresborg?" I asked again. "Knut told one of the other soldiers that Serén might as well be in the realm of the dead."

"I really don't want to go there." A shiver ran through his body.

"The realm of the dead?" I straightened.

"You can't go to the realm of the dead unless you are dead." He turned his eyes to the cave's ceiling. "I meant Sverresborg."

"Where is that?"

Again, Rorik looked at me like I was an idiot.

I sighed.

"Didn't you say you had a map with you?" He spoke slowly.

Yep. He thought I was a moron.

I pulled out the notebook and opened it to the map that Rebecca had artfully drawn. The map depicted an island divided into different kingdoms. Around the whole island she had drawn a fantasy creature. A snake with its own tail in its mouth.

Rorik's brows drew together. "Some of the names are old," he mumbled and looked at the heading, which read *Hrafnheim*.

"This is all I have."

He studied it with a few *hmmms* and *stranges*, while his tattooed hand trailed across the paper. Though his fingers were large and rough, he moved them with precision, as though he were an artist or a doctor. His fingertips traced a little arc in each kingdom.

Hrafnheim, or Freiheim—as I needed to remember—consisted of nine kingdoms, but the map was a little smudged on the right-hand side.

Rorik tore his eyes away and pulled a thin iron rod from his bag. "This is easier," he said. "I can't make heads or tails of that."

The iron rod was only half as thick as his index finger but as long as his forearm. It had a backward rune on one end.

He used the other end to carve into the damp soil, where he drew a square and made two lines in each direction so the square was divided into nine boxes. He pointed to the middle of the top row. "We are here, in Norvík, but the different kingdoms don't actually exist anymore, although most of the areas are still called by the same names." Then he planted the rod in the top left box. "This is Hibernia. Under Hibernia is Svearike, wherein lies Sverresborg. We'll go into Hibernia and from there down to the castle, where Serén is."

"Are you sure she's there?"

74

"Of course she's there," he snapped. "All prisoners are kept in Sverresborg."

"Wouldn't it be easier to curve around this way?" I pointed at the simple map on the ground.

"Can't you just do as I say?" exclaimed Rorik. "You don't know where you are. You have no food. You have no idea of the dangers that exist."

I didn't answer him. Instead, I mentally cursed Ben's spells. They were clearly highly effective on Rorik.

After a small, silent battle in which we stared each other down, he gave up and banged the iron stick into the ground. "We're traveling into Hibernia. There's less risk you'll be recognized there. We need to get you more clothes; it's only getting colder from here." He ran his tattooed hand over the rune on his chest. "I also need to get out of this uniform. Ragnara's soldiers must be after us."

"You *are* one of Ragnara's soldiers. Or you were, until a couple of hours ago. There must be some wild reason for you to betray them. What is it that you want to change in the past?"

He sucked in air between his front teeth while he thought. "Something happened when I was a child. Maybe even before I was born." He paused. "It has to be undone. I'll tell you when the time comes."

I could see that I wouldn't get any more out of him about what he wanted me to change. "What will we do once we've gotten new clothes?" I asked.

"The Bronze Forest goes into Hibernia, and it leads right to Sverresborg."

My stomach did a little flop. The Bronze Forest was where Varnar was born, but there was nothing left of his people after the berserkers leveled their home when he was a kid. Still, it felt mysteriously exciting and forbidden to go there. As if I were stalking him or snooping in his past. I stared at the little scribbles Rorik had drawn to represent the Bronze Forest.

"Get some sleep. You must need it," Rorik said. He sat completely still and stared at the damp rock wall, as though he were in shock over what he had done.

I was exhausted and had no idea when I would get the chance to rest again, so I leaned back.

In spite of it all, I had made it this far without being killed. Points for that. But aside from that, my undertaking seemed impossible. I thought of Frank. Even though I should really be worried about how close he may be, I couldn't help but wonder if he was okay.

I dozed off.

As soon as my eyes closed, I was standing in Kraghede Forest, which was covered in night frost.

"Anna!" came a voice.

My mirror image stood right next to me.

"This place gives me the creeps," I whispered.

Serén nodded thoughtfully. "This place and time should be dissolved, now that your death has been averted." Her reddish brows shot up.

I interrupted her thoughts. "I'm here."

"What do you mean?"

"Here! In Hrafnheim."

"You came."

"Can you see if we make it? Do I find you?"

"I've seen Ragnarök and Ragnara as the victor." Serén raised her hands as I looked at her, horror-stricken. "As one possibility for the future. I've also seen us make it." She shook her head. "It depends on so many factors."

"I'm traveling with someone," I said. "I don't know if I can trust him. Can you see if I should run away and continue on my own?"

Serén scoffed. "I'm clairvoyant, not an oracle."

I flung my arms out to the sides. "Just look."

76

"Okay, okay," Serén said. "What's his name?"

"Rorik. He has light hair and brown eyes."

She squinted, and her gaze became distant, like she was trying to spot something. "Oh . . . there he is. I know a Rorik. He's a soldier in Ragnara's army. High up. A leader."

I froze. "Should I ditch him?"

"Nooo." Serén looked back and forth, as if trying to spot a camouflaged animal. "You can trust Rorik. I see you together." She searched further. "He was loyal to Ragnara, but something makes him switch sides. Right now he's unsure, but he'll become certain. Ha!"

I jumped at her exclamation.

"There he is in the rebels' castle."

"The rebels' castle?" I was struggling to keep up.

"Oh, right. You don't know anything about this world." She spoke slowly. "Our mom's army has a castle—Haraldsborg—just outside Sént. It's got a ton of spells on it, so it's impenetrable."

"And you see Rorik in Haraldsborg?"

Serén nodded. "He's with Varnar. They're friends."

I shivered and exhaled slowly, both from the shock of hearing Varnar's name and from the relief of knowing that I could trust Rorik, however angry he seemed. "Where do you see us?"

Again, Serén searched for something I couldn't see. "It's summer. There are trees." A strange expression flitted suddenly across my sister's face.

"What is it?"

"Uh . . ." she said. "It's possible Rorik dies to protect you."

I tried to form words, but all that came out was a weird moan.

Serén continued hurriedly. "The future can sometimes be changed, but," she had a look of concentration again, "it does look pretty certain."

I tripped over the words. "How do I avoid it?"

Serén didn't answer.

"Tell me! How do I avoid it?"

Flustered, she closed her eyes and considered something inside her head. She tilted her face. "Tell him as little as possible."

"Okay." I was already naturally uncommunicative, so that wouldn't be a problem.

She kept her eyes closed. "There's someone else who's dangerous to you."

"Another one?" I sighed. "Can they just line up, or—"

Serén stopped me with a hand on my arm. "Have you heard about Sverre? Ragnara's son?"

"Yes. Aella mentioned him once. She said he's a little shit."

"He means you harm. Right now, he's more dangerous than Ragnara. I see it very clearly."

"Keep Rorik alive. Stay away from Sverre. Got it?"

I heard a loud snarl.

"Is it just me, or are we being tracked?"

"You don't have long before they find you," Serén said. "By the way, the murderer will cross over soon. If you don't leave, he'll find you and kill you."

Yay. Frank would avoid his execution. My joy dissolved into fear that he would catch us. The growling noise became deafening, and Serén smiled her gentle smile. I looked straight into her blue-green eyes, which must be identical to my own.

"You need to go now," she said, still smiling, "or Ragnara will find you. Wake up!"

"Wait." But I rushed to the surface and landed in the cave, leaning against the rock wall.

Rorik stood bent over the glass thing, which glowed faintly. It was flickering erratically. He had taken off his jacket, and the sleeves of his coveralls were rolled up. I caught a glimpse of muscular arms covered in tattoos before he yanked the sleeves down and rubbed his right forearm through the fabric. "Wait for what?" he asked without looking at me.

"We need to go now," I said, not answering his question.

"Let me just—"

"Not now. They know where we are." I began to gather our things.

Rorik had enough sense to do as I said without asking questions, and we were soon on our way again.

We walked quickly through the forest, and I cast my clairvoyance in all directions to search for anyone following us. I thought I could sense Frank's focused aura, but it may have been my imagination. There were no soldiers nearby—that I could sense, anyway—so for now it seemed that we had gotten away.

It was around midday, and the sun shone bleakly from a nearly white sky. I briefly wondered whether it was the same one we saw back in Ravensted.

"Why do some of you have auras I can't detect?" I asked, a little breathless from our pace.

Rorik stopped. "You're clairvoyant like your sister?"

Don't tell him too much, I reminded myself. "Kind of," was all I said. "I can feel people's energy, but some of you guys barely show up on my radar. That Gustaf guy is totally blank."

"What's a radar?"

"It's a kind of device," I tried.

"A device?" Rorik resumed his pace from before, still without answering my question.

This should be easy.

"I mean . . ." I searched for the words. "Does it have something to do with his tattooed hands?" Gustaf's palms looked like Ben's.

"He's a witch," replied Rorik.

I had figured as much.

"How does he hide his aura?"

Rorik looked to the sky, and I couldn't figure out if he was annoyed by my questions or if he was trying to navigate. "He can

79

hide his soul, or spirit," he said. "Whatever you call it. And he can teach others to conceal theirs. Most higher-ups in the army have gone through training with him."

"Ahhh. So that's why."

"Why what?"

"I can't see you clearly."

Again, Rorik stopped. "That makes you the only one in all of Freiheim," he said.

My teeth were chattering, and I rubbed my hands together through my thin fingerless gloves. Rorik looked at the washing instructions tag sticking out of one of them, but said nothing. Nor had he commented on my jeans or hoodie.

It was late afternoon, and the clouds were already creeping in. Hrafnheim resembled Scandinavia in that it got dark quickly in winter. Rorik offered to stop for the night, but I wanted to go on.

"You'll fall asleep walking," he said.

"Then we'll stop when I fall down," I replied.

Rorik shrugged, and we continued in silence for the following long, dark hours.

"Rorik?" I said to distract myself from the cold and exhaustion.

"Yes." He didn't bother to turn around, so I stared at his broad back.

"How do people feel about Ragnara?"

"I think most people just keep living like they did before she came to power."

"Wasn't there something about her freeing all the slaves? Aren't their lives different now?" I rubbed my arms.

He kept his face forward but shrugged his shoulders. "The former slaves are still workers. The difference is that they get paid now."

"But . . ." I considered. "Have they met Ragnara?"

"She used to travel around a few times a year, but now she mostly stays in Sént."

"What is Sént?"

"The capital." His voice was neutral, but I got a clear sense that he was rolling his eyes, even though I couldn't see them. "Sént is in the middle of Freiheim."

"I know that." *I had no idea.* "If people don't see her, then how does she hold on to power?"

"A couple of times a year, there are celebrations where people have to declare themselves her subjects. The festivals are when the old holidays used to be, so people didn't have to change all that much."

"Okay." I moistened my ice-cold lips but regretted it immediately when the frost made them prickle. "Do people want to do that?"

"They have to. The herders control it."

"Who are the herders?"

Rorik snorted at my ignorance. "They used to be a kind of guard, but now they're more like priests."

"What do you have to do to declare yourself her subject?" I asked.

Rorik sighed and explained like he was talking to a little kid. "In the old days, people just had to say they were loyal and that they renounced the gods. Recently, she's started to require people to make an offering to her. Just a little food, and the people are allowed to eat it afterward."

"Sverresborg . . ." I reached Rorik's side but had a hard time keeping up with his long strides.

"What about it?" Rorik rubbed his cheek with his thumb and index finger, and it looked like the blue tattooed eagle was flapping its wings on his hand in the moonlight.

"What kind of place is it?"

"Sverresborg belongs to Ragnara's son."

"Have you been there?" I walked alongside him and looked at him in the weak moonlight.

81

"Yes." He swallowed.

"What's it like?"

"Ragnara sends people there, but no one comes out alive."

"But you're alive."

"None of the *prisoners* survive," he corrected.

"Does she live there?"

"No," Rorik said. "Sverresborg is Prince Sverre's home, although he's not there all that often. He's pretty much always in Sént."

I had Serén's warning about Sverre in mind. "So the castle is named after the prince?"

Rorik scoffed contemptuously. "More like the prince is named after the castle. It's been called Sverresborg ever since it was built, just after the migration."

He turned his head away from me, clearly signaling the conversation was over. A few long strides took him a good distance ahead of me.

Not my problem if he thought we were done talking. I walked back up alongside him.

"Have you met Prince Sverre?"

Rorik inhaled but didn't look at me. "Yes."

"What's he like?"

Rorik shook his head. "Ragnara's son has the power to do almost anything, but his mother openly treats him like a clown."

"Poor prince." I knew all about what it was like when people had an unshakable bad impression of you.

"You shouldn't say that. He's dangerous because he's unpredictable."

"Okay."

"Maybe he'll settle down when he gets married."

I looked up. "He's getting married?"

"Yes. This summer he will marry Ingeborg something-or-other. She's the daughter of the chieftainess of Gardarike."

"Is there a risk that the prince will be in Sverresborg?" I nearly walked into a large tree as a cloud went in front of the moon, plunging us into darkness.

"Not as far as I know." Rorik's voice came from in front of me.

"Where is he?"

So quickly I almost bumped into him, Rorik turned toward me. "I don't know. How would I know? Stop questioning me."

This close to him, the tip of my nose touched his chest. The cloud moved past the moon, which once again made it possible to see. I leaned my head back and looked up at him.

He was trembling.

"Sorry. I wasn't trying to annoy you."

"Quiet." His strong hand found my forearm and squeezed.

"Ow! I said I was sorry. You don't have to—"

But he only pressed my arm harder. "Shh!"

I stood, unmoving.

Then he threw me to the ground, and I let out a surprised *hpmfff*. He jumped on top of me and held both hands protectively over my face while he tucked his own close against my neck. His fair hair tickled me softly, and he cursed.

His breath was warm against my cold skin.

Ziiiinnnggg—bonk.

A knife protruded from the tree trunk, vibrating, right where my head had just been.

I was struck by Frank's relief and frustration over missing his target. The conflicting feelings tore at me.

Somewhere in the darkness, an owl hooted faintly.

I cursed myself for not having sensed Frank, but his aura was fuzzy, and I was completely exhausted. Now that I was attuned to it, it sliced into me.

Rorik lay on top of me. He was heavy, and his rough hands were still holding my cheeks.

"Roll!" I commanded, and instinctively he barrel-rolled us both away.

83

Again, there was a knife exactly where we had just been. The blade bored deep into the ground, with dead, frost-covered leaves around it.

I peered between the trees, but it was pitch black. "Where is he?"

Rorik jumped to his feet and unsheathed Tilarids. He let the sword swing in a semicircle. Although I couldn't see Frank, I could feel him, and it seemed the sword had the same abilities as I did. It pulled Rorik forward toward the bushes.

Frank gathered his courage. He didn't want to kill Rorik—he didn't want to kill *anyone*—but if it could get him closer to me, he would do it. I noticed it just in time.

"Down!" I managed to shout. Rorik ducked as a blade whizzed through the air. The knife flew over his head and landed inches from my toes.

Tilarids surged forward, and I heard a strangled *arrggh*, though I couldn't see anyone. The sword came back with a bloody tip that glinted in the moonlight, and it pulled Rorik toward the brush, winding his arm back, ready to strike again.

Frank's pain radiated from the bushes, and his aura grew weaker. He ran away, but Tilarids didn't want to let him go, chasing Frank through the trees with Rorik in tow.

I sat on the ground, unable to see them in the darkness.

I stood up and ran after them.

"Stop," I shouted, breathless. "Don't kill him." My voice was desperate.

I finally reached them and saw Frank's back disappear behind a tree. Then his rustling footsteps on the forest floor grew fainter and more distant.

Rorik got Tilarids under control, while Frank's aura diminished. Rorik came back panting as he stuck Tilarids, dripping blood, into its sheath.

"That wasn't one of my men," he said.

I sighed, relieved, when Tilarids was finally put away. "There's someone else after me."

Rorik rested his hands on his thighs and breathed shakily. "Who?"

"A contract killer."

Rorik sounded like something was wrong with his throat.

I tried to calm him. "We made a deal that I would get a head start. But he's caught up to us." I clicked my tongue in annoyance.

"You made a deal with a contract killer? One who wants to kill *you?*"

I shrugged, but Rorik didn't see because his face was still turned toward the forest floor.

"He's my friend," I explained.

Rorik didn't reply. I thought he simply didn't know what to say. He looked at me incredulously. His light hair was disheveled, and he had a couple of red streaks on his cheek.

"He's gone," was all I could get out.

"For now."

I didn't reply.

My voice was still ringing in my head.

Don't kill him.

Actually, I wasn't entirely sure which of them I had been shouting to.

CHAPTER 8

We walked all day in silence, and eventually I was so tired, my surroundings started blurring together. I stumbled on and refused to rest.

Everything was earth-colored. Not even the sky was blue, as it was heavy with snow clouds. Maybe it was my fatigue smudging everything together, but on several occasions, I found I couldn't distinguish the cement-colored sky from the depleted winter soil.

Rorik did not contradict me when I insisted we continue, so we walked on until darkness began to fall in late afternoon. The trees became sparse, and when the road sloped upward, Rorik guided us in the opposite direction. We fought our way through the treacherous dry branches of the undergrowth, which I tripped over repeatedly. I was still shaken after my encounter with Frank and the accompanying near-death experience. Rorik hadn't bothered to wipe the red splatter off his cheek, and I didn't mention it.

Frank's blood on Rorik's cheek was the only color I saw for hours, but gradually, the streak of blood turned brown.

At the top of a hill, I came to a stop.

"Wow!" It was the first thing I had said in hours.

At my side, Rorik looked at me. "That was my reaction, too, the first time I saw Hibernia."

"How can anyone live here?"

"Apparently, people can adapt to anything."

I studied the rock formations, the black sand, and the steaming hummocks. Behind them was a lake, and at the end of the lake was an enormous wall of ice. Large chunks occasionally broke from the ice wall with a sharp crack, landing with a deep splash in the otherwise still water.

Rorik walked down the hillside and sank into the loose, black sand, which was topped with the occasional patch of white snow. I waded after him, my knees quickly frozen stiff. I looked around at the barren landscape. There wasn't so much as a tuft of grass. High above us, a pair of dark birds floated, the only sign of life. The lake drew closer, but the sky had already begun to change color.

"We'll spend the night in Dyflin," Rorik said hoarsely.

The concern I'd felt for Frank's injuries was replaced by fear that he would find us.

"He has to take a break at some point, too," Rorik said, as if he had read my thoughts. Or maybe I had said them aloud. I was so tired, I had no idea. "I'm betting he's doing that now. We need to be rested when he strikes again."

"What's Dyflin?" I asked, trying to move past the fact that Rorik had said *when* and not *if.*

"The town."

I sniffled in the cold. "I don't see any town."

"Wait until we reach the lake."

When we finally got down to the water and rounded a cliff, I saw a small settlement on the other side. It would take at least half a day to walk around the lake, so it was with relief that I spotted a boat—no more than a barge covered with an animal skin—by our side.

Rorik dug through his pack and pulled out a dark gray cloak, which covered most of his uniform. In any case, it covered the rune on his chest.

A tall man leaned against a pole in the boat. He had a long gray beard and beige, shapeless wool clothes. He bowed to us with a toothless grin.

"Come, youngsters," he said with a high-pitched voice. "Hárbard is making his last crossing now."

We went to step aboard, but Hárbard set his pole in front of us. "It costs one piece of silver each."

When I gave Rorik an awkward smile, he rolled his eyes and took out the coins as the old man studied us.

Hárbard waved us aboard and pushed us out into the still water. Rorik didn't seem to notice anything strange about the man but merely looked out over the darkening lake. I stood next to Hárbard, who glared at Tilarids. Far out on the lake I noticed an island. It was nearly concealed by fog.

"What's that island out there?"

Hárbard squinted. "That's Afallon. No one lives there anymore, but delicious apples grow there."

"Huh . . ." I didn't know what to say, so we just looked out over the water while Hárbard pushed us along. Something kept bothering me.

"Have you been sailing people across the lake for a long time?" I asked.

"A long time, yes. But you are late for your journey." Hárbard's voice was an octave deeper now and rather hoarse.

"I only just left," I said. "I couldn't really have gotten any farther."

He looked at me, and instantly I recognized him. The one empty eye socket was a dark hole, and pearly white teeth sparkled behind his shapely lips.

"Svidur," I whispered. "You had two eyes just a minute ago. And no teeth. What's going on?"

He smiled mischievously. "My name is Hárbard."

"I recognize you, Svidur—or Odin—or whoever you say you are."

"I'm not welcome here under my true name."

I realized how much his hoarse voice reminded me of Od's. I glanced quickly at Rorik, who stood frozen like a stone pillar.

Hypnosis.

I turned back to Svidur. "Ben and Rebecca believe you're a god."

Svidur didn't reply right away, instead he looked ahead over the now-dark water. "Do *you* understand that I'm a god?" He stood up straight, becoming markedly taller.

I looked up at him. "I don't know what a god is exactly. So no, I don't understand that. But you exist. I'll give you that." I gestured at him. "I mean, you're standing right there."

Svidur said nothing.

Behind me, Rorik was still motionless, staring across the lake. He didn't even notice my conversation with Svidur . . . Hárbard . . . Odin, who pushed us forward for a while before pulling up the pole, so the boat stopped and bobbed gently in the middle of the lake.

"Why should I believe you're a god?" I asked.

"Look at me. Look how tall I am."

"I know a half giant who's taller," I said. My friend Little Mads would tower at least a head over Svidur.

"I can appear and disappear at the drop of a hat."

"My ghost dad is free from physical limitations, too."

"Well," Svidur said, leaning against the pole, "I can do this."

He raised a large hand and pointed at the ice wall at the end of the lake. A large chunk came away with a tearing sound and hit the water's surface with a deafening crash.

Rorik still didn't react. I wanted to flee, but there wasn't anywhere to flee to, so I gave an unimpressed shrug. "The witches I know can do stuff like that."

"What about this." He came close to me, and I felt him taking over my willpower. His power was hundreds of times stronger than Od's and Mathias's.

"Stop it," I whispered. "That's just hypnosis. That doesn't make you a god."

He leaned even closer to me. "I can kill you on the spot. Right here. Right now." His strong hands reached out toward my neck.

This woke my brain up, and I stared him straight in the . . . eye. "On that point, you're no different from even regular humans. There are plenty who want to kill me."

Svidur's eye glimmered with amusement, and he pulled back his hands. Again, he turned his face toward the water. "Such spirit. So strong-willed. You remind me of your mother."

In profile, he looked like a more terrifying version of Od.

"I'm also a lot like my father. And, above all, I'm myself," I shot back.

Svidur's creepy face tilted to one side. "You're something more than that."

"More?"

"I gave you something. Now you must pay me back."

I wrinkled my forehead. "What did you give me?"

He pursed his lips and reminded me more than ever of an impressive, deadly storm. "Pay me."

"What do you want?"

He inhaled heavily. "Your devotion. A sacrifice."

I stared at him, uncomprehending.

"The more you give, the more I repay you. I will give you whatever you want, if you give me a hangadrott."

"A royal human sacrifice, if I remember correctly." It sounded crazy when I said it out loud, but Svidur merely widened his eye with an intense sigh. "I don't have any royals on me, and even if I did, I probably wouldn't make a human sacrifice," I said sarcastically.

"The god in me desires it."

"The god in you? Is there something other than a god in there?"

He shook his head as if to say I wouldn't be getting an answer.

"At least tell me what separates gods from humans," I said.

"We're a distinct bloodline."

"Then you're no different from humans. Sure, maybe genetically, but that's no more than the difference between a horse and a donkey."

"I am neither a horse nor a donkey." Svidur puffed out his chest, and the boat rocked.

"Relax! It was just a metaphor. I mean, you're just a different species."

He balled up his large fists as if he wanted very badly to hit me in the head. "We're divine."

I raised an eyebrow. "Congratulations."

"We must be worshipped," growled Svidur.

"I don't want to worship anyone."

"You *must*," he boomed.

"You can't force someone to believe."

He had no comeback to that, and he stared at me as he gritted his teeth. "I beg you," he whispered finally. The words were gentle, but his voice was ominous. "Give me your faith, and we can do tremendous things together. You, your sister, and me. All you have to do is worship me."

"Why is it so important that we worship you?" I snarled.

"Because I'm at the top of the hierarchy, and I intend to remain there."

"There is no hierarchy," I yelled.

My shout echoed across the lake. The dark birds that were still flying above us screeched a few times. Svidur glared at me as if I had punched him in the gut.

"I must have your loyalty," he said, and suddenly he appeared old and worn out. The hair at his temples was gray, and deep lines surrounded his mouth.

"And why should we be loyal?" I asked. "Because you're tall, you can move fast, and can do some trick that makes the ice fall down?" I waved my hands.

"Because I can see time." He began to shine metallically.

I cocked my head slightly. "My sister and I can also see time."

"And where do you think your power comes from?"

I searched for an answer, as I had actually never thought about it before.

Svidur whispered. "You must believe that if you worship me, I will serve you." The last bit sounded more like a breath than a statement. His breath hit me and paralyzed me again. If Od's breath was intoxicating, Svidur's was pure narcotic.

I blinked and looked around. We had reached the other side, it was completely dark, and Rorik had already gone ashore.

"Come on," he called.

Svidur gave me a cheeky look and ducked his face into the folds of his long garments. With a firm grip on his shoulder, I shook him, but the toothless face peered over the woolen edge. "Leave me be," piped a thin voice.

Rorik yanked on my arm, pulling me along. "What are you doing? You're supposed to be keeping a low profile."

"But that was—" I began.

Rorik pulled me along as I repeatedly looked back at Hárbard, who was watching us with fear.

We walked up a small hill toward the houses.

When we reached the town, I saw that it was vastly different from small-town Denmark. People were dressed in gray and dark brown wool. Most wore thick sheepskin hats. Again, I noticed the total lack of color.

I gasped when I saw some half-timbered houses with lumber shining like neon. It looked freaky amid all the earth tones.

"Why the hell does their wood glow?"

Rorik looked at the building. "It's not wood. It's bone."

I studied a wall made with boards that looked like something from a rave. "Bone?"

"Lindworm bones are green, and they glow in the dark."

"Are those like garfish?" I asked.

He lowered his voice. "Yes. But lindworms are much larger. The Hibernians don't have access to real wood, so they have to use what's available."

Apparently, glowing lindworm bones were deeply embarrassing in this world. In mine, they would be a marvel.

I tried to compose myself, but some hollow sounds made me look up. It took me a moment to spot the large, dream catcher–like sticks—or bones, as they must have been, because they were glowing as well—which hung from a pole and clanked against one another. They reminded me of the ones that hung in Ben and Rebecca's trees back in Ravensted, except these were much larger.

Rorik walked determinedly along the wide street, which appeared to be Dyflin's main boulevard. The cloak covered his uniform, but he got several looks anyway. When people passed us, their expressions didn't change, but I felt sharp shifts in their auras. They didn't deign to look at me.

"We're getting some attention," I said.

"What do you mean? They're hardly looking at us." He pulled on the door to some kind of inn.

When we walked in, no one reacted to our presence, even though it was as full as Frank's on a semi-busy Saturday. My body reacted immediately to the heat that slammed into us. I had been freezing for so long, it felt like my bones were made of ice.

Like on the street, everything here was brown, gray, or dark green. Even with my affinity for black, I was ready to scream for just a tiny pop of color.

People's pasts assaulted me. I got busy shielding like Elias had taught me, but I managed to see a vision of a boy who came in shortly before we did. He had shouted that one of Ragnara's soldiers was coming. Some had people left, while others started packing up. The contents of most glasses had been swapped out.

Musicians played in the corner. A woman strung a carved board with strings, a man blew a horn with holes in it like a flute, while a third sang, deep and chanting. I had never heard music like that before.

Rorik sat at a table. He kept the gray cloak over his uniform, but I suspected that he hadn't concealed his soldier identity as well as he thought. A young woman came up to us dressed head to toe in dark brown. She smiled invitingly at him. Rorik's face changed noticeably when he looked at her, and suddenly I could see how good-looking he was.

When he looked at me, he scowled, and I sent a silent *thanks for nothing* to Ben's repulsion magic, which clung to me like a nasty fog.

In the girl's past, I saw that just minutes before, she had helped a man leave through the back door.

"Sea buckthorn juice for both of us. Lamb, bread, and preserves to eat," Rorik ordered. "Do you want anything else?" He didn't even look in my direction.

The girl looked around and wrinkled her forehead.

Damned spells!

I sighed and tried to ignore it. "Do you have anything stronger than juice? Maybe some mead or something?" I asked.

The girl and Rorik stared at me in shock.

"My traveling companion is joking," Rorik said quickly. "Just bring us what I ordered."

She left, and he gave me a *you-are-simply-too-much* look.

"What did I do now?" I asked, putting my palms up in resignation.

"Mead?" he said quietly.

"I could use something to build up my strength."

Rorik lowered his voice to a whisper. "Alcohol is dangerous. The punishment for buying, selling, or consuming it is severe."

I now understood why people had been so busy removing glasses and bottles.

"But some of the soldiers were drunk when I met you," I whispered back.

A muscle tightened in Rorik's jaw. "They drank wine we had confiscated."

"Ah . . ." I swallowed the rest of my sentence when I saw his face.

The girl came back with our drinks on a tray.

I raised the clay cup and angled it down so I could see the orange liquid catch the light. It was almost a relief to see the bright hue, and for a moment, I wondered if Luna's passion for colors had affected me.

The girl was now flirting openly with Rorik. In her recent past, I saw the panic in the kitchen where she had just been. Bottles were stuffed into a hole in the ground, and a hatch was closed, locked, and covered with a skin.

She set the tray down in front of us. "I'll be back in just a minute with your food," she purred. "Remember to donate to the wedding fund." Her voice went up in a singsong, and she pointed at a sort of money box that hung on the wall near the entrance.

"What wedding?" I asked.

"Prince Sverre's, of course." She turned to leave.

"Wait." Rorik's voice was muffled, and he stiffened and let out a deep breath.

When she turned toward us, she had a cloyingly sweet smile plastered on her lips again. "Yes?"

"We also need a room. But with two beds. One for each of us." This final bit of information was accompanied by a twinkle in his eye.

"I'll find you one," she said smoothly.

When she was gone, he leaned back in his chair.

"You do know she's afraid of you, right?" I took a sip of juice.

Rorik's self-satisfied expression faltered. "But people can't see that I'm a soldier."

I looked around, and people avoided looking at us to a degree even I had rarely experienced. Everyone bowed their heads and looked away.

"You might as well have it tattooed across your forehead," I said as I swirled the juice around in my cup.

"What do you mean?"

My eyes followed the liquid's journey along the clay walls of the cup.

"When one often does illegal things, one gets good at spotting law enforcement. You don't need to wear a uniform for people to notice you."

"What do you know about that?"

I didn't reply but looked up with a smile that was meant to look conspiratorial, but which apparently ended up looking diabolical, as Rorik jerked back a little.

I tried to explain. "You have a self-confidence. It's the way you carry yourself and look at people. It's unmistakable."

Rorik narrowed his eyes slightly. "But people here aren't doing anything illegal."

Again, the corner of my mouth turned up, while at the same time I raised my eyebrows. This made Rorik study me as if he were seeing me for the first time.

"Maybe I can teach you a thing or two," I said. "Even if I don't know anything about anything or even where I am."

"First of all, you need to stop looking people directly in the eyes," I said. "It's obvious that you're used to getting your way."

We were in our room. I nearly cried with gratitude when I saw the bed, which called to me entrancingly. The cold seeped out of me, but I couldn't quite get warm.

Everything was made of wood, some of it painted. Green, brown, and gray, naturally. The floor, walls, and ceiling were plastered with images of the forest we had just been in and the large lake with the wall of ice.

That was the last thing I wanted to look at right now. A lovely warm summer day would have been better.

Carvings of animals and trees, which I had noticed were very popular here, covered the entirety of one wall. At home, the decorations would probably depict humans in various situations, but here nature clearly was the focus. I pulled a thick blanket from my bed and was hit with the scent of wool.

"I'm not used to getting my way," Rorik protested from his place on the bed. A white shirt hung loosely around his broad torso, and he wore thin, light pants that seemed to be made of flax. It was the first time I'd seen him without the coveralls.

I shook the blanket at him. "Doesn't matter. Just stop doing it."

"I still have these." He pulled his shirt down to reveal his right bicep, which was adorned with the same kind of small scars as Varnar's. All of Rorik's were finely executed, whereas some of Varnar's were clumsily done. Varnar had considerably more of them.

I looked at his arm for a moment before I turned my back to him and fumbled to fold the blanket. "Then you'd better keep your clothes on." I waited a few seconds before turning back toward him. He had fortunately covered his arm back up.

"You seem overly self-confident, too. It's actually really annoying."

He stood and took a couple of steps toward me.

I lamely held the folded blanket in front of my chest.

He sat on the bed again. His fists clenched its frame. "I've never met such an obnoxious girl."

My courage faltered. "I get that a lot."

His lips moved lightly, like he was trying to formulate a question. "Did the girl down there really like me, or was she acting?"

I put my hands on my hips. "Are you interested in her?"

He waved his hand, so the eagle flapped its wings. "No. I just want to know if she liked me." He looked up cautiously. "You can tell, can't you?"

I wanted to say something mocking, but stopped myself. "She

was afraid of you," I said. "But she also thought you looked like a snack."

"A snack? Like food? Is she a witch?" Rorik suddenly looked frightened.

"It's just an expression." I nearly burst out laughing. "It's not about wanting to eat someone." I searched for another word. "She found you attractive."

"Can you sense anything from me?" Rorik asked quietly.

"Not a lot. Just that you think I'm insufferable."

He raked his fingers through his white hair, which he had loosened from its knot. It now hung down over his shoulders. "I wouldn't be able to hide that even with lessons from a magician."

I looked down at the floor.

We took turns keeping watch in case Frank showed up, so I was still groggy when I woke up. I looked out the window at the dark gray cloud that was sailing toward Dyflin.

Ugh. On top of everything else, we would have to go out in crappy weather, and I had only just gotten warm.

I stopped a random person at the inn. "Where can we buy clothes?"

"Gytha. She lives a half day's walk from Dyflin." The man scurried away with a frightened look.

"People find you charming," Rorik observed as he stuffed bread and dried meat into his bag. He had bought it from the girl who, like the day before, flashed him smoldering looks.

"You can also get clothes here." She winked.

"Where does this Gytha live?" I asked her.

"It's much easier for you to buy clothes here. I'll give you a good price."

"Where. Does. She. Live?" The girl was making me more and more irritable with her phony flirting. There was no way I was going to buy clothes from her.

The girl fumbled with her brown sleeve and gave Rorik a look. "You go east on the main road," she said reluctantly.

"That's the way we're heading, anyway," Rorik said.

I smiled sweetly. "Thank you so much."

The smile was not reciprocated.

Rorik opened the carved bone door for me with an air of gallantry.

Out on the street in the weak morning light, the air was dry and ice cold. Small crystals twirled around us as a precursor to snow, and up ahead the dark cloud grew larger and larger. It was coming straight toward us.

We passed two people wearing capes. The branching rune, which was evidently Ragnara's symbol, was embroidered in red on the white fabric of the capes.

I shuddered at the sight of the glaring color.

Rorik hurriedly lowered his head like I had taught him, and they didn't even notice me. One held out a cracked wooden box.

"Those are herders," Rorik whispered. "Ragnara's priests."

"Donate to Prince Sverre and Ingeborg's wedding," the female herder said.

Rorik was still looking down at the ground, but he pulled out a coin. He clutched it for a second before letting it fall into the hole.

"For Ragnara's anfarwol," the man said and traced a salute with his fingers. The shape he drew was identical to the rune on his cape.

"Anfarwol," mumbled Rorik.

It was strange to be in a place where priests were something to be feared. I normally just found them deeply irritating.

"What does anfarwol mean?" I asked when we had passed the priests.

"Immortality," Rorik replied without looking at me.

"But—"

"That's all I know," he said louder, and I knew better than to ask him again.

We continued out of the little settlement. I felt like I was in a weird video game. The surroundings were once again rugged, with black sand dunes and steaming hummocks. The place was wind-blown and inhospitable. The sunlight vanished when the cloud was directly above us, and ill-tempered gusts of wind struck me, pushing me a couple of steps to the side. Just after noon, frozen and hungry, we came to a little house that was largely covered with grass and, at the moment, quite a lot of snow. The facade was made of wood, which was clearly a rarity in these parts, and it was carved with sweeping branches, wild boars, and birds. A chimney stuck up through the turf roof, and the foundation was built from rough-hewn boulders.

"This must be it." I knocked.

Some time passed before the door swung open. A woman with dark gray hair stuck her head out. She was dressed in a long gray dress and had a frayed woolen shawl around her shoulders. Her jawline was very sharp, and she was almost as tall as Rorik. She looked at us with black-rimmed eyes, and when she saw me, she narrowed them slightly. She didn't recognize me—I sensed that clearly—but she recognized something else.

"Are you Gytha?" I asked.

"That goes without saying." Her voice was deeper than I expected. Her fingers trailed over the embroidery on my coat. "Where did you get this coat?"

"Why do you ask?"

"Because I made it, many years ago. For someone other than you." She withdrew her hand, placing it on the doorframe and keeping it there.

"*You* made it?" I had never even considered that my mother's coat could be from Hrafnheim.

She pursed her lips. "Did you steal it, girl?"

I shook my head. "I found it in a barn."

As she was looking at me, I leaned in toward her. "Look at my face."

Her lined, dark eyes studied me. "You look like your mother."

"I do?" My eyes widened.

Gytha nodded. "What do you want?"

"He needs different clothes, and I need something warmer. A hat and some gloves."

Gytha pulled my coat to the side and looked at my jeans, which would otherwise have been hidden. I yelped and pulled the coat back around myself.

"Well, you'll probably need more than that." She looked to both sides before ushering us inside.

Rorik had to duck to walk through the doorframe. "Do you have weapons?"

"You seem to have plenty." Her eyes landed on Tilarids.

"For her." He motioned to me.

Without another word, she went into another room and rummaged around loudly. We looked around the living room, which was so low Rorik's head nearly touched the ceiling. The earthen floor was covered in straw mats. An open hearth was the only source of warmth, and in front of it sat a chair upholstered in black sheepskin. Lumps of meat hung from strings in front of the fire. The room smelled faintly of smoke and meat. Gytha came back carrying an axe with a short, polished handle. I took it and weighed it in my hand. It was light, even though the ax-head was iron. On one side, the metal was decorated with intertwining patterns that resembled the serpent knot around Ben and Rebecca's door. On the other side was an engraved gripping beast. The small teddy bear–like creature grinned, and the handle fit perfectly in my hand. It had some runes carved on it that I didn't understand.

"What does it say?"

"The axe's name."

"Which is?"

"Can't you read it?" Gytha looked at Rorik, who shook his head slightly.

"Auka." She once again disappeared into the other room.

Rorik showed me how to fasten Auka to my belt. I pulled on it a couple of times, which earned me a nod of recognition. Not friendly, but still, not angry.

"What does Auka mean?" I asked.

Rorik's finger traced the gripping beast's arm and ended where it gripped its own neck. "Increase," he said.

"Increase what?" I cocked my head.

"Your chances, I think. It's something you say if your prospects aren't so good." He laid Auka in my hands. "It's just a figure of speech. Don't read too much into it."

"Okay, I won't."

Gytha came back with a stack of clothes and gestured for Rorik to undress. "Let's see if it's the right size."

I turned away. Mostly to avoid seeing the scars again.

There was a sound when his shirt landed on the floor.

I studied the wall intently.

"Let me just check if it fits." There was a pause. "Five. That's not so many."

"Mind your own business," Rorik snapped.

"Don't talk to her like that," I said as I turned around and saw Rorik shoving Gytha's large hand away from his scarred arm. The hand now hovered over his chest. A very broad chest, covered in blue and red tattoos. They depicted entangled animals and people with bows and arrows and raised swords. The tattoos went up his arms and across his chest. The only place that wasn't covered was where the scars were burned into his upper arm. The eagle tattoo started on his forearm and stretched all the way to his fingertips.

I cast my gaze down, but out of the corner of my eye, I saw him pull a gray shirt over his head. He also got a pair of dark brown pants. The black coat Gytha handed him resembled my own, only larger. It also had a red lining and dark embroidery that resembled the figures adorning his skin.

While he got dressed, Gytha handed me a heavy pair of pants and a sweater. In the pile, there were also a leather hat, a scarf, and a thick pair of mittens. Then she looked out through the small window. The weather had gotten even worse.

"It's dangerous to go out in the snowstorm," she said. "You must stay here."

I glanced out and saw the landscape shrouded in mounds of white. The snow had fallen in the short time we'd been in Gytha's house.

I groaned. "Stay here? We don't have time for that."

"Maybe you should have thought of that before you set off on foot in the middle of winter," she said. Rorik suppressed a smile. He looked different in the new clothes.

Gytha's eyes lingered on him as if she were trying to think of something. Then she shook her head and sat in the chair in front of the hearth. "Fimbul is coming," she mumbled.

Rorik sat down next to the little window and looked out into the blizzard.

"Fimbul?" I slid onto the bench next to him, and he let out an uncomfortable *hrmf*.

"That's just talk." The eagle-tattooed hand waved dismissively. "The Fimbulwinter is the prelude to the end of the world." He wiggled his eyebrows.

Gytha looked at him, unsmiling. Then she looked back into the fire.

"How long has this one lasted?" I asked.

"Since fall. It's a totally normal winter." Rorik leaned back.

"Ragnara lets her soldiers wander," Gytha said. "Sometimes they come here to Hibernia." She did not elaborate on what they did there.

"The ones from Norvík?" I was trying, as always, to keep up.

It was Rorik who answered. "And some from Sverresborg. Gustaf comes from there, too."

"Sverresborg," Gytha said and shivered. "That's where they praise the Midgard Serpent."

I had to swallow a couple of times. "The *what?*"

She looked at me. "The serpent. The largest lindworm in all the worlds. Jörmungandr."

Rorik jumped in. "It's so large, it reaches all the way around the world and bites its own tail."

"I know what the Midgard Serpent is." I glared at them. "But are you serious? It exists?"

"Of course." He leaned idly against the wall. "It doesn't hurt anyone, as long as it has a hold of itself." He laughed, and for a moment he looked younger and kinder. "Don't worry."

Don't worry? I had no idea what to say in response to his nonchalant declaration about the mythical beast, so I stayed silent.

Gytha turned her head away from us once more, deep in thought.

A large snowflake had strayed into the window frame, and it was tossed around on the other side of the thick glass. I followed it with my finger.

"Five?"

Rorik had zoned out and was staring at Gytha with a displeasure I couldn't decipher. "What?"

"You have five scars on your arm." I had never dared to ask Varnar about them.

He rubbed his shoulder through the shirt, which I had noticed he often did without thinking about it. "When we kill someone, we mark it with a rune."

I opened my mouth to speak but closed it again. Varnar had at least fifty scars. When I thought about the crooked cuts, and the hardened scab he had had shortly after killing Geiri to save my life, I brought my hand up to cover my mouth.

"I'm a soldier. That can't come as a surprise to you," Rorik said.

"It's not that." I had difficulty getting the words out. "Forget I asked." I desperately needed to change the subject. "How long will we have to stay here?"

"The storm will probably last the rest of the day, so until early tomorrow morning."

"Jesus."

"Who?"

"Nothing."

We sat in silence as the storm raged on. I trembled at the thought of how much ground we had to cover, but I comforted myself knowing Frank surely also had to seek shelter.

"Let's pass the time," Gytha said after we had eaten. It had gotten dark outside, and the wind was howling. She patted the armrests of her chair, stood up, and whimpered when her back made a cracking noise. After digging around in a drawer, she turned back to us with a clinking suede pouch in hand. A small table was dragged in front of the chair.

"Come." She waved her arms. "Let's play hnetafl." She told Rorik to pull the bench over, so we sat on the other side of the table. She dumped out the contents of the pouch, and I saw they were bone pieces with runes identical to Rebecca's.

Rorik studied the pieces critically.

"It's not forbidden to cast runes," she said. "I'm not practicing seid or making prophecies without permission. This is just a game."

Rorik's eyes fell on the hand that held the bag. "No, it's not forbidden."

I slapped his arm to get him to be quiet. "How do you play?"

Gytha's finger tapped the tabletop, and I saw that it had a grid carved into it. Each square had a symbol.

"Here you are." Gytha placed two small pieces in the middle

square. They depicted a man and a woman. She put two more pieces on either side of the grid. Each was twice as large as ours. "These are giants, standing on heaven's rim. They're chasing you, and you have to get away."

I looked at the board. "Two against four. Isn't that unfair?"

Gytha let out a deep laugh. "Who says life is fair?"

"And we're smarter," Rorik added impishly. His lips formed a flattering smile. "Hnetafl is more about strategy than numbers, though strength is obviously an advantage."

Gytha picked up yet another piece and placed it in the lower right corner. "This is the prince. My piece. He's after you, but you're also after him. Pick a square, which only you know, that will lead to your opponents' death. Write it here." She handed Rorik a scrap of paper. "If you lure them there, you can take the piece, and then you can choose a new death square."

"How do you win?" I asked.

"The prince wins if I catch you. You win if you lure the prince into the death square. There's a pattern, but none of us can see it fully until we know the runes."

Hmm.

"When it's your turn, you pull a rune. It dictates how many spaces you can move, and gives you an attribute for the round."

We got started.

I would have to figure out the rules along the way, which seemed to be the theme of my journey. Rorik, who already knew hnetafl, chose a death square, and I pulled a rune.

"Uruz," Gytha said. "The aurochs. It symbolizes determination and strength."

"That's me." I stuck my thumb up.

"But its number is only two."

With a sigh, I moved two spaces.

Rorik pulled a bone piece. "Ken." He moved three spaces after me, so we were still together. "The fire rune. It illuminates the unknown and can change actions." He seemed pleased with being fire-like, and I rolled my eyes.

"I change the prince's position," he declared, and Gytha gave him a look of recognition, while I still didn't grasp the rules. Rorik pushed the prince back a space.

Gytha dug through the pile and pulled a kind of crooked N. "Hagal. It means hail. Destruction, but when the hail melts, the strongest will survive. The number is nine. A magic number." She took three giants and moved them so they surrounded us. There was only one space between one of them and Rorik's piece.

"Hey, are you allowed to do that?"

"It's a magic number, after all." She laughed. "And the magical powers can be shared."

My heart pounded as I saw that our little pieces were surrounded.

"Ha! Death square," Rorik shouted and flicked one of the giant pieces, toppling it.

"Good thing giants can be revived with mead from Heidrun's udders," remarked Gytha.

Rorik chose a new death square.

We pulled runes and got away through the opening left by the dead giant. We could make use of the runes' meanings, but I could never figure out how, so I mostly followed Rorik's example.

We played on, managing to lure three giants into death squares, mainly to Rorik's credit. Eventually, he got close to the prince, while I was a few spaces behind him.

"Shouldn't we stay together?" I asked.

"We'll attack from either side," Rorik said, but his shoulders slumped when Gytha pulled a rune. Evidently, he could figure out what she was going to do.

"Naud. Distress." She took the prince and knocked Rorik's piece away with it. My pathetic little piece now stood alone before the prince, and the final giant was right behind me.

"What do I do now?"

"Pull a rune," Rorik said. "Let fate decide."

I exhaled audibly, not particularly comfortable with fate, and pulled a piece. Gytha looked at it.

"That one's called Eh. Horse. It symbolizes a journey between worlds."

Very subtle, runes.

"But its number is only one."

I moved my piece back a space, away from the prince, who towered over me. I took the paper where Rorik had written the death square, but I was careful not to reveal with my gaze which one it was. If I could just lure the prince one space to the right, I would win.

Gytha pulled a rune, and my blood ran cold when I recognized the symbol. It was the crooked *F* that had been found on the murdered girls back in Ravensted. The rune ansuz. The rune that meant *god.*

Gytha looked sharply at Rorik, who instinctively pulled away from the piece.

"That rune is forbidden," Rorik whispered with an appalled expression.

"I know, I know." Gytha put it away. "It got in there by mistake."

"Why do you have it?" I asked.

"Because the gods were once humans," Gytha snapped. "It has just as much right to be here as all the other runes."

"What do you mean?"

She waved a calloused hand. "All these rules. They're impossible to navigate." She smoothed her dress, and Rorik's gaze landed on it.

"What do you mean, the gods were human?" I repeated.

She glanced at Rorik, who looked at her with furrowed brows.

"According to myth, the gods were once humans who let themselves be worshipped, and so they became gods. How can it be forbidden to worship them when they're . . . *us?*" she concluded.

Rorik stood abruptly, and the pieces clattered on the table.

"Forbidden is forbidden. You should keep that thought hidden. Keep *yourself* hidden." He stomped off.

"Who won?" I asked weakly. "Who . . ."

Gytha packed the game away.

"You'll figure it out," she replied without looking at me. She made beds for us on the living room floor and quickly disappeared into the other room.

Rorik lay down on the blanket, and I lay next to him.

"You were hard on her."

He pulled away from me slightly.

"She lives too dangerously. *He*," Rorik put emphasis on the word, "should suppress his urge to wear women's clothing."

I glanced at him. "You noticed?"

"It's pretty obvious." Rorik wouldn't meet my gaze, and he pulled up his upper lip in disgust. "It's forbidden."

"What does it matter to us? There's so much else we have to deal with." I gave him a scornful look.

Rorik propped himself up on his elbow. A blue-and-red snake peeked out from behind his shirt's loose collar. It twisted across his skin. "I don't like not knowing what's going on."

"Join the club. But unfortunately, I think that's inevitable."

My exhaustion crept up on me. With eyes closed, I began to descend into sleep.

In a glimmer of a dream, I saw Varnar. He smiled and gently placed his lips against my mouth. I enjoyed the dream and reciprocated the kiss. My hands interlaced behind his head, and we continued until it felt entirely wrong.

Suddenly, I could feel the soldiers holding me a few days prior, and Knut's wet tongue on my cheek. Every fiber of my being screamed, and I lashed out violently. My eyes flew open, and I saw Rorik over me. I pushed him away and jumped to my feet in a fluid leap. I wiped my mouth with the back of my hand.

"Ew!"

"Ew?" Rorik clearly wasn't used to girls reacting this way. "Now that we're going to be traveling together, it's only natural."

"Natural?" I sputtered. "You don't even like me."

"I don't like you," he said. "But it would be easier if we were on good terms."

"No *but*. You keep your hands to yourself from now on!"

"Are you like Gytha?" He pointed at the closed door. "Or like your sister?" He folded his arms across his broad chest. "Rumor has it she's with a woman."

My hands flew up. "Oh, right, I must be into girls if I don't want to sleep with you."

Come on!

"It's wrong," he said.

"According to whom?"

"The laws say so."

I couldn't help but laugh contemptuously. "And yet it doesn't seem to bother you that we're breaking all kinds of other laws with this journey."

Rorik was kneeling on the blanket.

"It's unnatural for a man to wear women's clothes, and for two women to be a couple. And it's . . ." he searched for the word, ". . . disgusting. When you have such an abominable desire, you should do everything in your power to suppress it."

I gaped. "What the fuck are you talking about?" I almost accused him of being from the Dark Ages, but even I recognized the absurdity of that statement, considering I was in a parallel world that didn't seem to have changed much since the eleventh century. "Holy shit, how old-fashioned can you be?!" I hissed.

"Everyone feels the same way I do," Rorik snapped.

"Gytha clearly doesn't." I reflected. "The girl at the inn probably doesn't, either, because she tried to keep us from coming here, and now I understand why. She knew you're a soldier, and she knew you would judge Gytha. People don't dare to say they see things differently when the people with the weapons are such lunatics. You're dangerous lunatics."

Rorik looked bewildered, sitting there on the wrinkled blanket.

"But it's illegal," he whispered.

"It should also be illegal to be such an idiot!" I gathered up my blanket and stomped off. I didn't want to sleep next to an idiot. In the other room, I came to a halt.

Gytha had on a thin nightgown, and her dark gray hair was gathered in a long braid. Her rib cage was very flat, her arms were bare, and the parchment-thin skin on her bony right shoulder was marked with a large brand of Ragnara's rune. It was placed in the same spot as the soldiers' kill counts, but where their rune scars were small, this covered the whole of her upper arm.

"Did you kill someone, too?" I asked.

She gave a short, deep laugh. "This?" She stroked a wrinkled hand over the bumpy scar. "The rune is only supposed to be on Ragnara's possessions nowadays, but I can't exactly take it off." She formed her fingers into claws and scratched the nails across the scar. "Fehu. It's an old word that means *livestock* or . . ." She exhaled. "Or *property*. I didn't choose it for myself."

"You were a slave."

Gytha nodded. "Ragnara has an identical one.

"But there are no slaves here anymore?"

"Before Ragnara, there were many thralls. She herself was a slave, but she set us all free. She conquered the whole realm with her slave army."

This sympathetic act clashed with my preexisting notion of Ragnara. I ignored the conflicting feelings.

"How?" I eyed Gytha's flat chest and wasn't quite sure how to word it. "I mean, could you wear women's clothing when you were a slave, when you were someone else's property?"

Gytha's teeth were exposed. I couldn't tell if it was a smile.

"Back then, people like me were called *seidberander*. It was seen as divine that we were . . . different," she said.

"So it wasn't forbidden?"

"Not then."

"But now it is?"

Gytha looked down. "I think Ragnara is using us as a scapegoat. Deep down, she doesn't care, but the people need a clear enemy, and now the gods and the old despots have been removed."

I looked away when she said *the gods*.

"What is your connection to the gods?" she asked cautiously.

"I don't know that I have a connection."

"But you are also . . . different."

"I'm clairvoyant." I didn't know what made me admit it. Maybe the feeling that Gytha and I were, in some way, in the same boat.

"Freiheim is a dangerous place to be different from the majority. It can cost us our lives."

A little more gently, I said: "If it's so dangerous, can't you just stop wearing women's clothes?"

She smiled sadly. "Can you stop being clairvoyant?"

"Good point," I mumbled.

CHAPTER 9

The previous day's snowstorm had not exactly made it warmer, and we walked through what looked like a black, sparkly room when we left Gytha's house in the early morning. The sun hit the ground, which was covered in fine, crunchy powder, and the sparse trees were shrouded in glittering ice crystals. Gytha had sent us off bundled up in warm clothes and with extra food in our packs.

"We'll continue through Vindr Fen tonight." Rorik's voice was muffled by the thick scarf he had wrapped around his head.

I jumped, startled.

It was the first time he'd spoken to me in hours; he was still highly insulted that I had rejected his kiss the night before. "There will be no sleep tonight. Early tomorrow, we'll leave Hibernia and cross into Svearike. There are soldiers. Lots of them. So in Svearike, we'll travel at night and rest during the day."

After pausing to eat on a rock in the middle of the flat plain— snow white on the tops of the hillocks and pitch black in the places where the sand was visible—we trudged on, until the sky began to change color.

We continued in silence for a while, and I was deep in thought about what Gytha had said. Ragnara had freed all the slaves. A good deed. I had difficulty reconciling this with the monster Ben and Rebecca had described. I rubbed my chest through my coat. Even through the many layers of fabric, I could feel the scar where Ragnara had stabbed me as a baby. Not a very nice thing to do.

Rorik jerked me out of my rumination.

"Can I ask you something?" He seemed to regret the words before they had even left his mouth.

"I can't promise I'll answer."

"The gods Gytha mentioned. The ones that were common before Ragnara. Do you know them?"

Surely it couldn't hurt to answer that. "I've heard of Thor and Odin. And Freyja. There are more, but I don't have the full overview."

"Do you believe in them?" Merely asking about the gods seemed to put Rorik on edge, as he kept scratching his cheek nervously.

I tried to act nonchalant. I saw a glimpse of Svidur's empty eye socket and his ability to smash a wall of ice from a mile away. Mathias, who burned the Savage's face with his breath, and Od's glowing, naked body in my dark bedroom.

"There's something," I said. "Some beings are different from normal people. But I don't know if they're gods. Or really what a god even is."

"You're not a believer?"

"No. Unfortunately."

He stopped and turned slowly to face me.

All I could see of his face were his chocolate-colored eyes. Everything else was wrapped in his hat and scarf.

"Why *unfortunately?*" he asked.

I considered this and tried to answer as honestly as possible. "Religious people have it easier, in a way. They can see a greater meaning in things. My friend Hakim is a believer, and he's sure of what's right and wrong. I'm not sure of that at all." I went silent. It was the first time I had called Hakim my friend.

"But believers don't have it easier."

"What?" I asked distractedly.

"Religious people don't have it easy," he said firmly. "No one who breaks the law has it easy."

An image flew from him. Just one.

The people hung from the scaffold. Their ruined bodies rotated slowly.

I opened my mouth, but he turned abruptly and began walking again before I could manage to say anything.

I walked onward in a daze and stumbled repeatedly. I widened my eyes and shook my head to clear it. A couple of lungfuls of frosty air helped.

The black, sandy marsh we were walking across was flat and covered in frozen puddles, which I slipped on multiple times. Here and there, the landscape was interrupted by sandbanks covered in lyme grass and a few lonely windblown trees. The wind had quieted down, and it was ominously silent in the dark of night.

Rorik's broad back in front of me served as my lighthouse.

Mists rose from the earth and shrouded us in a thick soup. Eventually, I could just barely see the back of Rorik's head in front of me.

Suddenly, my senses sharpened.

"Someone's here." I spun around.

"Who?" Rorik peered into the fog and drew Tilarids. "Is it your killer?"

I fumbled for Auka in my belt as I cast my clairvoyance into the fog.

"No." I sighed with relief. "It's not Frank. It's someone in pain," I said. "It's . . ." That was all I could get out before I broke down, struck with a violent roar of fear, uncertainty, and pain. Moaning, I supported my palms on my thighs until I could stand up straight again. "Over here." I walked quickly in the direction of the sensation. Although I couldn't see anything with my eyes, a searing ribbon of agony unfurled in front of me, and I followed it like a bloodhound.

Rorik stumbled after me, and I heard thumps as his feet slipped on the slick ground.

"Come," I called. "Hurry. Come on!" Now I was running. "It's really close."

I nearly tripped on a figure lying on the ground.

The figure let out a terrifying moan, and fear rose toward me. The person tried to crawl away but was too weak.

"We won't hurt you," I said and knelt as Rorik handed me his crystal. With my other hand, I touched what I couldn't see, and the warm, sticky sensation made a lump form in my throat. It reminded me of when I found Monster in Ben and Rebecca's field.

I lowered the crystal and suppressed a gasp.

It was a man. Or, at least, I thought it was. It was hard to tell because he was caked in blood and dirt. Someone had been thorough, but not thorough enough to kill him entirely. Or maybe they had been skilled enough to stop right before he was dead, then left him to succumb to his fate alone on the desolate marsh.

My hands hovered helplessly over his face; finally, I laid my palm carefully on his cheek in one of the few places where skin was still visible.

He flinched and tried again to crawl away.

"I won't hurt you," I repeated. "I'm trying to help." But I had no idea what to do.

I looked up questioningly at Rorik, whose face was a porcelain mask. Agitated. Full of disgust. He backed away.

"Help him," I commanded, but Rorik shook his head.

He looked like he was about to throw up.

"Do something," I tried again, but Rorik retreated even farther into the mist, until he was nearly swallowed up. The last thing I saw was his back, which he turned on me and the dying man.

"Rorik," I hissed, but he had disappeared. I turned my attention back to the man. "Who did this?" I asked, but he didn't answer. His breathing was raspy and shallow.

I ended up just stroking his cheek and whispering comforting words.

The sentence *It's going to be okay* couldn't get past my lips because it was clearly far from the truth, but I told him again and again that I was there, that I would stay with him, that he was safe.

Eventually, the man relaxed. In spite of everything, he understood on some level that I was there with him. I finally felt a sense of safety from him, just before his spirit vanished like an almost burned-out candle going from a glowing ember to a puff of smoke. Slowly, it floated away. The spirit didn't bother to stick around and explain, but I thought he deserved to move on from this place that had caused him so much pain, to go wherever it was he was going.

I sat on the ground for a while with my hand on the dead man's cheek. Rorik still wasn't visible, but I couldn't see more than a couple of feet ahead of me in the mist.

Suddenly, I was unbelievably tired. I fumbled around and discovered that I was sitting at the base of a thick trunk. I leaned against it, exhausted.

"It's over," I said into the night air, assuming Rorik would hear me. "I can't go on right now."

Rorik mumbled from somewhere nearby. "Fine. We'll stay here until dawn. Then we can get him out of the way."

I must have closed my eyes and either dozed off or simply lost consciousness, as I jumped up with a start when a voice rang out. "Kian. Kian?"

I pointed Auka in the direction of the words and saw a man coming out of the mist. He was dressed in simple but well-kept clothes. He was maybe fifty years old, with thin hair that lay in a dark halo around his head. The air was still, so his hair was not mussed by the wind. The fanciest thing about him was his leather boots, which were decorated with intertwining motifs that depicted serpents and dragons.

He knelt with an unhappy exclamation.

"Kian?" he said, not noticing me.

"Do you know him?"

He looked up with a start, and his eyes shone in the light of the crystal. His shoulders relaxed a little when he focused his eyes on me.

"I'm his brother." He hesitated. "Were you with him when . . .?"

I nodded silently.

"Thank you." He exhaled and stroked Kian's hand. "I've been looking for him since sunset, but it's impossible to find your way when the weather's like this."

I lowered Auka but kept my hand on the axe.

"It's very foggy here," I said, because I had no idea what else to say.

The man slumped onto the ground next to Kian. I thought he would start to wail, but he sat completely still. I leaned back against the tree.

"What happened to him?" I asked quietly.

The man's hand still lay on Kian's.

"He didn't live according to the laws," he said, almost imperceptibly.

From the past still clinging to the earth beneath me, I heard the echo of shouts.

For Ragnara's anfarwol. For Ragnara's anfarwol.

"What did he do that was . . ." Oh! I looked forward. Then I focused on the man. "He refused to disavow his faith."

The other man bowed his head. "It's my fault. I didn't hide our religion, and the herders caught him."

"You're a believer, too? The priests did this?" I looked down at Kian. "Are they allowed to do that?" My questions tumbled out on top of one another.

"Ragnara has gradually given them free rein." The man shook his head as if to say he found it despicable.

I couldn't blink. I could only stare straight ahead.

Just when I had allowed myself to think something positive about Ragnara.

"You're lucky you survived," I said timidly and resisted the urge to stroke his back soothingly. "You have to stop living as a religious person."

"I'll stop leading a religious life from now on." He hung his head.

There was nothing I could say to make the situation better.

"What's your name?" I asked instead.

"Hemming," he replied, but his voice cracked on the syllable, ending in a shaky breath.

We sat in silence for a while. Hemming was deep in thought. Then he shook himself briskly.

"Kian is in a better place now," he said.

"Are you sure?" As soon as the words left my mouth, I regretted them.

"I'm sure." Hemming's voice was unshakable.

If imagining the afterlife gave him some form of comfort, that was fine by me.

He focused on me. "What's a nice girl like you doing in Vindr Fen? This place is nothing but death and desolation."

"It's odd you think I'm nice. Most people hate me."

Hemming cocked his head. "How can people hate you?"

"I have these spells on me."

"Hmm," Hemming mused. "Maybe the witch in Jorvik can help."

I straightened. "There's a witch in Jorvik? Is that where you're from?"

"Yes."

The fog was beginning to lift, and the light of dawn was creeping in.

"I can help bury Kian," I offered. "My traveling companion is around here somewhere, although he gets queasy at the sight of blood." I raised my head. "Rorik," I called.

Hemming stood. "I need to get going. I just came to find Kian."

"Now? Can't you help? He was *your* brother."

Rorik's outline came into view.

"What is it?" he asked. "You've been talking to yourself for the past hour. It's giving me the creeps."

"Says the baby who can't handle seeing blood," I snapped back. "And I haven't been talking to myself," I added. "I've been talking to Hemming." I looked around. "Huh. Where did he go?"

The morning sun pushed through the white tufts of cloud, and I saw we were in the middle of a large ring of stones. Rorik stepped through a sunbeam, cutting off the light. It was completely still; even the birds were silent. Fledgling orange beams flowed across the black marsh that gradually came into view. The frozen puddles reflected the light, and I realized this place had probably looked like this for thousands of years.

I stood up.

"He was just here." I turned around as I peered into my glowing surroundings, which became visible as the mist cleared.

The tree next to me glinted with dew, and at the bottom, there were wheel tracks filled with ice. They resembled bloody slashes in the fiery-red reflections of the sun.

In front of me, Rorik had stiffened.

I sighed. "Sorry! You're not a baby. It was just hard to be alone with that, but you can't help—"

He laid his eagle-tattooed hand on my arm and tugged.

"What?"

With his free hand, he pointed up.

I followed the direction but squinted in the sharp morning light. I let out a shout and jumped when I noticed the feet dangling in the branches directly above me.

The hanged man was in equally bad shape as the man on the ground, and in the merciless, revealing light, I saw that both he and Kian had an ansuz painted on their clothes with blood.

The man in the tree swung around slowly, and I saw that his boots were finely ornamented with patterns of twisting serpents and dragons.

We crept into Jorvik late in the afternoon. The town looked like Dyflin, but the houses were much less windblown. Everything was built of wood, but like Dyflin, there was no color beyond earth tones. The simpler buildings were topped with turf roofs.

"I know you want to find the witch, but it's dangerous to be here. We risk getting caught." Rorik looked up and down Jorvik's main street.

"*I* risk getting caught. No one knows who you are now that you're out of uniform." I tucked my red hair under my hood as I followed a house's shadow.

Rorik scowled in the direction of a herder who stood on a corner. The white cape was pulled tightly around her, and Ragnara's rune stood out clearly. She stared probingly at everyone who passed, and pointed at a plaque hanging from a pole, inscribed with gnarled runes.

I wondered if she had helped catch the two men the night before, but I didn't plan on getting close enough to read her past.

Beneath the plaque hung the same money box–type thing I had seen in Dyflin. People hurried to put a couple of coins in the box, after which they practically ran away.

"Can't that stupid prince pay for his own wedding? People here don't exactly seem well-off."

Rorik laughed derisively. "Sverre doesn't have a cent. Ingeborg's parents are providing the dowry."

"Okay." I looked around. "Where might this witch be hiding?"

"I'm sure she keeps a low profile." He pulled his hood close around his face.

Just then, a crash and a jubilant shout rang out, followed by flashing lights. We quickly located an open barn, where the sounds were coming from. A stage was set up inside. From the shadows, we followed the show in progress.

"Clearly, she keeps a super low profile."

A woman of around forty stood on the stage in a dress

reminiscent of Rebecca's seid costume, but dirtier and more ragged. The staff in her hand was not metal like Rebecca's, but it
looked similar, with a carved bird's head on the end. The woman
was in the middle of an intense shaking dance, and at her feet lay
two human skulls. They were arranged so their jaws hung open. A
large mass of people had gathered in front of the stage, and they
bellowed excitedly. A thin man was beating a drum rhythmically.

"*Shhhh*," the witch said as she exhaled audibly.

The crowd quieted down. Some giggled nervously.

"Prophesize," one shouted. "Tell us what the future brings."

I straightened. Aside from Justine in Sømosen, I had never met
another clairvoyant.

The witch began to chant. "For Ragnara's anfarwol. We praise
her."

"Ragnara's anfarwol," someone cheered. "The liberator. She
who protects us from the false gods and greedy lords."

"I see . . ." shouted the witch. "I see . . ." Her eyes rolled back,
and she trembled. She focused and pointed to a woman in the
crowd. "Did someone in your family die recently?"

The people standing near the woman stepped aside. Her eyes
widened and she nodded, her jaw quivering.

"It's your . . ." The witch was shaking even more. "Your . . . sister."

A little movement of the woman's mouth indicated that this
was the wrong track.

Quickly, the witch changed course. "No. She looks like you, but
you're not the same age."

The woman in the crowd was smiling now.

"Your mother . . ." The witch stared intently at the woman. "No,
aunt."

The woman smiled through tears, while my shoulders slumped
in the shadows.

On stage, the witch continued: "You must bury a freshly slaughtered cockerel in the bog under the white tree. Do it tonight.

Then your aunt will be at peace." She stopped herself. "Ragnara's anfarwol."

I narrowed my eyes and followed the spectacle, which I suspected was no more than that. Just a theatrical performance. The witch picked out someone else. An older man standing by himself at the back of the crowd.

"There is also someone you are looking for."

Again, people moved away from the target, until he stood alone. The witch didn't need to fish for information, as he blabbed immediately. "My brothers disappeared yesterday. Are Kian and Hemming dead?"

I flinched when I recognized the names.

The herder had placed herself at the edge of the crowd. She pulled the white cape closer around her and looked at the man.

The witch didn't need the sight to figure out what had happened to Kian and Hemming.

"I see they have crossed over." She glanced nervously at the herder.

"Did they suffer?" asked the man.

"If you place a loaf of bread in the bog along with a silver coin, their passage will be easier. Ragnara's anfarwol." She cast another glance at the herder, who didn't move.

Finally, the scene ended with her slaughtering a goat. Someone led it onto the stage, and the unsuspecting creature had Ragnara's fehu rune painted on its forehead. Ansuz was apparently intended only for shady undertakings.

With a dramatic, unintelligible chant, the witch slit the goat's throat, sending blood splashing onto the stage. I closed my eyes but reminded myself it was nothing more gruesome than what butchers did every single day. The witch cut the animal's stomach open and fished out something squishy that steamed in the cold air. Next to me, Rorik wrinkled his nose but said nothing.

"The liver says," the woman shouted, "that you will all live good, safe lives." She didn't so much as look at the bloody organ.

Pff, I thought.

The woman raised a red finger. "As long as you remember to honor Ragnara and donate money to Prince Sverre's wedding. For Ragnara's anfarwol."

"Anfarwol," the crowd repeated.

Finally, the witch closed the mouths of the two skulls lying on the stage. Because her fingers were smeared with blood, she left fingerprints on the bones. The thin man who had been playing the drum now collected coins and food. He licked his lips when he saw a juicy piece of meat or fresh-baked loaf of bread.

"It's a scam," I whispered. "She's not even a medium. It was just an act."

The false witch sat on a sort of throne of branches and animal skeletons with her eyes closed and appeared to meditate. The staff lay diagonally across her lap. From her past, I caught a short film of her and the thin man roasting a chicken. With a sigh, I turned to leave, but an electric pulse hit me in the back. Slowly, I turned around to look at the woman again.

She hadn't moved, but an energy field gathered around her. She opened one eye slightly, pulled the animal skin costume around herself, slinked off the throne, and left the stage.

I brushed past Rorik.

"Hey, where are you going?" He ran after me.

"I need to find the white tree in the bog."

The bog looked like something out of a horror movie, with fog, gnarled trees, and ditches full of stagnant brackish water. It was completely dark at nightfall, so Rorik had lit the crystal, and its light cast a circle around us. We found the white tree, which resembled a skeleton's hand with its fingers pointing to the sky. Beneath it sat a round loaf of bread along with a coin. There was also a freshly dug spot in which a chicken lay neatly wrapped in a cloth.

Rorik watched as I dug it up. "Isn't it supposed to stay down there?"

"Are you superstitious?"

"No, but there's just something wrong about removing an offering."

"It was never intended to stay here." I stood up from my kneeling position and brushed the dirt from my knees.

When the witch and her sidekick arrived a little later on a rickety cart pulled by a pair of mangy horses, I was sitting on the other side of the road. I let them dig in the ground before I jumped out of the shadows.

"Looking for this?" I shook the bird carcass.

The woman whipped around and pointed her staff at us.

"I can curse you," she warned.

The staff emitted a golden light from the end, but the glow flickered like a defective lamp.

Rorik stood behind me and rested his hand on Tilarids's hilt—mainly to hold the sword in place. It quivered agitatedly in its sheath.

I stepped forward. "You can have your chicken, although we would appreciate it if you shared with us."

She kept her staff aimed at us. "What do you want?" The energy field gathered around her again, but it seemed even less controlled than Luna's.

"Lower your staff. It could go off by accident." I ducked out of the staff's path.

She looked over the staff. "Who are you?"

"It's best if you don't know. For your own protection," I added.

She looked at Rorik with narrowed eyes.

"He looks like a soldier, and he has an Ulfberht sword." She pointed at Tilarids. "I've done nothing wrong," she said to him, head bowed. "I always praise Ragnara when I take the stage." There was real fear in her voice. "And I have a permit to practice seid."

I tried to act as though I knew what she was talking about. "He doesn't care if you keep the offering for yourself."

She raised her staff but still looked at us with suspicion. "What do you want?"

"Could you give us a lift to your camp? I promise we don't wish you ill."

With another look at Tilarids, she pointed reluctantly at their cart. "Hop in."

In silence, we reached a clearing amid the brush and trees. The man unhitched the two scruffy horses. They were docile, but they followed everything we did. Rorik jumped down and helped pull the horses away.

"Start a fire," she ordered.

The thin man immediately started heaping sticks into a pile. From his belt hung a piece of iron, which he pulled loose. With great care, he banged it against a stone, so sparks flew in all directions. With a glance at the now-roaring bonfire, she praised the man. "Looks good. Well done."

He squirmed with pride.

"What are your names?" I asked.

"I'm Védis. And that's Gretter." She pointed at the man, who still hadn't said anything. "The horses are Jørund and Mår."

They looked up when their names were spoken.

Védis looked at me with a determined set to her mouth. "So, what do you want?"

"You're a witch." I spoke so quietly the men couldn't hear us.

"I can speak to the deceased and help them reach the realm of the dead." She straightened.

"No you can't. That requires years of training in seid if you aren't a medium or clairvoyant, and you aren't trained. At least, not very well."

She slumped a little. "How do you know? Are you a witch?"

I shook my head. "If I were, I wouldn't need you."

126

"Then what are you?"

"I'm clairvoyant."

A strong breeze stirred the leaves around us, making a crackling sound. Dust from a dry patch in the middle of the clearing rose in a miniature whirlwind. Védis's mouth rounded as if she were searching for the right words. "What do you want from me?"

"Can you see that I have spells on me?"

She took a step back, closed her eyes halfway, and looked me up and down with the expression of a professional. "There's magic on you. It's complicated. And there are several layers."

"I need you to remove it." Even though I had nagged Luna to try to break the spells, she had outright refused. She claimed it was too dangerous.

Védis raised her hands reflexively. "I don't know how."

I dug around in my bag and found the heart-shaped jewel, Freyja's tears. "Here is your payment."

Védis exhaled heavily. "Where did you get that?" She reached out for it.

Rorik had seen the jewel and stretched his arm between us right as I was about to drop it into Védis's palm. Instead, it landed in Rorik's large, rough hand.

"Hey," both the witch and I exclaimed.

He stepped away and held the red pendant in front of the fire. Filtered through the jewel, beams of burgundy bathed his face. "What is it?"

I walked after him. "It's mine."

Deep in thought, he examined it. "I've never seen anything like it."

"That's because there's only one. Give it." I was ready to lunge at him. The piece of jewelry was my only item of value, aside from the gifts from my friends, and I wasn't planning to part with those unless it was a real emergency.

Rorik turned as if just noticing my presence. He handed the

jewelry back to me, and I exhaled slowly. Carefully, I laid it in Védis's outstretched hand. Rorik walked over to one of the horses and stroked its neck, but his eyes lingered on us.

Védis's voice cracked. "Is this what I think it is?"

"Well, I don't know what you think. I'm not telepathic. But it is very special."

"It's beating. Like a real heart." She held the pendant in both hands like it was a fragile baby.

"Do we have a deal?"

She wavered. "It's at your own risk, and I don't know if I can."

I took the jewel back. "You only get it if you successfully lift the spells. But if something happens to me, you're not responsible."

"Fine," she spat. She grumpily gathered the animal-skin costume around herself and started rummaging around in the cart. She pulled several dried herbs from a bag, and in a box she found a blue powder.

It felt magical to see something that color after all that brown. Védis carried the box as though it were highly valuable.

She handed me a knife. "Cut yourself."

I stood, bewildered, with the knife in my hand. "What?"

"I need your blood."

"What good will that do?"

"Are you the witch, or am I?" She took the knife and dragged the blade across my palm.

"Ow, shit!"

"What are you doing?" Rorik came running when he saw the blood. His lips drained of color, and he breathed through his nose.

I studied him but couldn't interpret his expression. My hand was dripping red.

Védis set a bowl beneath it and collected some of my blood. When she thought she had enough, she took the bowl away and handed me a dirty rag to wrap around my hand.

Rorik snatched it away before I had the chance. "I'll do it." He took a clean piece of fabric from his bag. For a moment, I wondered if he'd faint at the sight of blood, but he didn't waver. As with the first time I met him, an intense feeling of recognition rushed through my body. He stiffened, and for a second our eyes met. Our looks of bewilderment must have mirrored one another, but just then, Védis called to me.

"I'm ready."

Quickly, Rorik bound the fabric around my hand and released me.

Védis, who was crouched on the ground, had put the dried herbs in the fire. They were now smoldering. The blue powder was poured into the bowl with my blood, and she mixed it until it formed a purple paste. She used her fingertips to paint it on her face and beckoned me over.

Slightly uneasy, I sat in front of her.

As she dragged purple fingers across my face, Rorik watched us. "What's going on?"

"Védis is just going to try something." I removed a lump of the paste from my nostril with my little finger.

"You said yourself she was a fake." He looked from me to her.

"She's a fake medium. But she's a real witch."

Védis began to chant, and I saw the unstable force field gather around her.

"You should probably stand back." I closed my eyes and tried not to cough in the thick smoke from the herbs. "In case she explodes."

"Explodes?" Rorik grabbed me by the shoulder and tried to yank me up. "Whatever it is you're doing, I forbid it."

"You can't forbid me from doing anything. Now away with you. I don't want you to get hurt."

At that moment, Védis's magic hit me, and everything went black.

CHAPTER 10

I had never before been on the receiving end of magic, aside from Luna's persuasion and Ben's spells when I was a child. But this time, it felt like someone was trying to break me apart with their bare hands. Rorik's voice pushed weakly through the fog, but I couldn't make out the individual words. Védis's magic pressed deep inside me, and I saw her entire past as clearly as if it were my own. I found out several things about her.

She was not forty. More like two hundred and forty. At one time, she had pursued a real education in witchcraft and was well on her way to becoming a skilled witch. Her mentor appeared in the vision with his back turned, wearing an old-timey white wig.

As I witnessed her past, Védis's magic powers hammered against my spells, which were as solid as bulletproof glass. They didn't budge, even though she tore at them as if she were trying to pull a couple of my ribs out.

Despite the wig and old-fashioned clothes, the man in Védis's past was familiar—even from behind. He stood bent over a table covered with densely written books and vessels and bottles that seethed and bubbled. Just as he turned, Védis's magic recognized the spells.

I gasped for air when I saw her teacher's face.

Védis screamed—or maybe it was her magic that screamed. In any case, it immediately broke the spell.

Although my eyes flew open, I still saw the image of Védis's long-ago mentor. His nearly black skin contrasted sharply with the white wig. A silver ring shone in his nose, his broad lips parted, and his gold teeth glinted in a fierce grin.

"Ben," I said.

"Benedict," Védis said simultaneously.

For a moment, the witch and I looked at each other with equally baffled expressions. Then I jumped to my feet and ran to the nearest bush, where I threw up. Despite the cold air, sweat moistened my hair. I collapsed on the frozen ground.

Rorik came over and crossed his arms, looking down at me.

"Do you still think I'm horrible?" I asked dully.

"Yes! And on top of that, I also think you're incredibly stupid."

"Shit. They're still there."

"What's still there?"

"I have these spells on me. That's why you don't like me." I swallowed some vomit-tinged saliva.

"There are several reasons why I don't like you. Mostly because you're the most reckless person I've ever met." He was shouting by the end.

"That's kind of my thing," I mumbled.

Rorik ignored me. "You almost died. You were convulsing and frothing at the mouth."

I wiped the corners of my mouth on my sleeve and stood up slowly.

Védis sat where I had left her, still with a shocked expression.

I dragged myself over to her.

"You know Ben?" I picked the heart pendant up off the ground, where it had fallen out of my pocket.

She didn't even look; she just stared ahead absently. "I haven't seen him in many years."

"Could you be more specific about how many years?"

"Over two hundred." Her voice was monotone.

I knew it! Ben was much older than he looked.

"Why are you so old? Have you spent a lot of time with demi-gods?"

Finally, she woke up a bit. "Witches get to be very old unless someone kills us. Unfortunately, that happens a bit too frequently."

So there was an even better chance that Luna and Mathias could live together for many hundreds of years. I couldn't wait to tell them. That is, if I ever saw them again.

Védis pulled me out of my thoughts. "Are you Benedict's enemy?"

"What? No, no. He sees himself as a kind of guardian to me, even though he has a pretty strange way of showing it."

Her eyes narrowed. "The spells he put on you are not friendly."

"Like I said, he shows his concern in a strange way." I bit my lower lip. "What can you do to remove them?"

Védis shook her head forcefully. "Only Benedict can remove them. His spells are stronger than any other magician's. If they were cast by a different witch, I definitely could, but not his. If I tried again, we would both die. Besides, I respect him too much to change his magic, even if I could."

"You can take your respect and shove it," I snapped. There was no chance that Ben himself would lift the spells.

"Stop fighting for a second," Rorik cut in. "Is it Benedict Sekibo you're talking about?"

We both stared at him.

"How do *you* know Ben?" I asked.

"I know the sorcerer of Midgard by name only. But I know that he is evil, highly dangerous, and nearly impossible to defeat."

"He's not evil." I remembered Ben in a yellow raincoat and top hat. "He's friends with my parents." My inner eye saw him throwing energy balls at the berserkers. "The other two things may be true." Despair crept in. I would be dragging Ben's stupid magic around with me for the rest of my life. No one would ever like me.

I thought of how Aella, Frank, and Varnar were somehow un-affected by the magic. "If you can't remove the spells, can you at least give Rorik magical immunity?"

"Yes, of course," Védis said.

"Then do that." I once again pulled the heart pendant from my pocket and held it out to her.

"No, no," Rorik said. "I just saw how you were lying there, con-vulsing."

Védis shrugged. "I'm happy to do it, but I can't accept the jewel, no matter how much I would like it." Her eyes lingered on Freyja's tears. "The payment should be equal to the service."

"It's illegal to do magic on someone without their consent," Rorik protested, but we ignored him.

I dug in my pocket and found a Danish coin with a hole in the middle. "This is all I have."

Védis accepted it reverently. "It's so rare and so valuable. It's al-most too much."

"Believe me. It's really not a lot."

"But I don't want to," Rorik tried again.

"Do you need his blood, too?"

Rorik backed away.

"No. I just need to do like this, and like this." Védis waved her staff and bent to toss a few more herbs into the fire. Her aura sput-tered unsteadily, and I heard a bang as a cloud of smoke rose to-ward us. The flames were dampened, and we were thrown into foul-smelling darkness.

We both coughed.

"Oops—I'm pretty sure I also gave you immunity," she said to me. "I can't fully control it." Védis waved the smoke away. The flames regained their strength.

"I don't think you got me. I don't feel any different," I said. The smoke made my eyes water. When I could see again, I couldn't stop my startled cry.

Half of Védis's right lower jaw was missing, and the other side of her face was disfigured by a large burn scar. The creature that had previously been a man was now a dog, and the two horses were actually men.

"What the hell!" I whispered.

Rorik's expression must have resembled my own. He stared at the men, his mouth open. They looked back at him sadly, saying nothing. Both had ropes around their necks and were tied to a tree.

"Should . . . Shouldn't we help them?" He struggled to maintain his composure.

"They did this." Védis pointed to her jaw and the scar. "They actually got off easy. Benedict would have given them three hundred years of suffering. Their only punishment is to pull my cart."

"Did Ben do all this?" My gaze returned to the men and the dog.

Védis followed it. "The horses are Benedict's work. I transfigured Gretter myself." She patted his head and grinned. "He's such a good dog."

Because her teeth were exposed where the jaw was missing, the grin looked sinister.

"Okay." I started to gather my things.

Rorik's eyes landed on me, where they lingered.

"We're leaving now," I said.

"Don't you want any chicken?" Védis pointed at Gretter, who was wagging his whole body and nudging the roasted bird with his snout.

"No, not after all. Thanks, though." My heart was pounding heavily.

We turned and started to go. Without a magical filter, the reality of Védis's camp was too harsh, even for me.

Behind us, Védis called out. "Find me if you need help again."

"We'll remember that," I shouted without looking back.

And before we knew it, we were both hightailing it away from the smiling Védis, the wagging Gretter, and the two sad horse-men.

"Stop looking at me like that."

I tried to concentrate on the porridge, but Rorik's eyes followed my movements.

We sat in a cave, moisture dripping down the stone walls.

"Sorry, but it's really weird."

I sighed. "What's weird?"

"You. There's such a big difference."

I set the bowl aside. "What's different?"

"I don't want to strangle you anymore, and you look like a real person."

"Did I not look like a person before?"

"No. I mean, you looked like Serén, but like a doll, or a drawing. Like I could do anything to you, and you wouldn't feel it." He suddenly looked horrified. "I tried to kiss you when you didn't want me to."

I looked away, my lips pressed together.

"Now I can see that you're an actual human being. That you can feel happy and sad."

"I've been able to do that all along." I plopped my spoon into the porridge a couple of times.

"You must have had a hard few months, living with spells making it so no one could stand you."

Months? Try years.

"I suddenly want to ask you all kinds of questions."

"What do you want to know?"

His lips moved as if several words were trying to come out at once.

"What's your name?" Rorik's voice was timid.

"What?"

"I never asked for your name."

I cleared my throat. "Anna."

"Anna," he said. "That's a strange name. Anna," he repeated. "Anna. Where have you been all this time?"

"Uh . . ." I racked my brain. "In that land . . . um . . . to the south . . . north." I wasn't prepared to suddenly explain my presence in a mythological parallel world that I didn't know particularly well.

Rorik cocked his head. "South-north?"

"It's . . . on the coast of Ván." I grabbed one of the names I remembered from Rebecca's map. I quickly lowered my gaze to the ground.

"Ván doesn't have a coast," Rorik said, his eyes narrowed. Then he stiffened. "Ohhh," he said, standing. "Ohhh." The sound repeated as comprehension flowed across his face. "You're from," he gasped, pointing at me, "from . . . Midgard."

I flashed him an awkward smile. "Yeah, kind of."

For a second, he was at a loss for words and simply stared at me. I squirmed uncomfortably.

"Your strange clothes, your lack of knowledge, and your weird way of talking."

"I talk weird?" I asked, surprised.

He didn't reply. "What's it like in Midgard?"

What was it like in the place I'd spent my whole life? I searched for a fitting description. "It's different from here," is what I ended up with.

He sat distractedly on a large rock closer to me. "Different how?"

"Well, we can travel faster." I rubbed my deep-frozen toes, which I had freed from my boots.

"Do you have faster horses?"

"We don't use horses in day-to-day life anymore. We drive. But not in carts like yours. They're powered by gasoline."

Rorik's upper lip rose. "What's gasoline?"

"It's a kind of liquid."

He stared at me, still uncomprehending.

"We fly if we have to go really far." I pointed at the cave's ceiling.

"Fly." He gaped. "Is everyone a witch there?"

"No. Magic is only mentioned in fairy tales. People don't believe it exists. The witches who do live there keep it secret."

"Then how do you fly?"

"In these big machines. I haven't tried it." I flapped my hands to indicate that I didn't know what I was talking about.

Rorik leaned back. "Tell me more," he demanded.

"I haven't seen a whole lot. Just the town where I lived, and the surrounding area."

"What do people in Midgard believe in?"

"Hardly anyone believes in Odin and Thor anymore. Most believe in a different god, but a lot of people aren't religious at all."

Rorik's forehead crinkled. "Then what do they believe in?"

I considered this. "Science."

"What?" He ran his tattooed hand along the rock he sat on.

"Like research," I said, but when he still looked confused, I added, "In space exploration and technology, for example."

Rorik was struggling to follow. "I don't know what those things are."

"Actually, I'm surprised you guys haven't progressed further. Back home, they've invented all kinds of things, but here, people still drive horse-drawn wagons. It's been a hundred years since we did that."

Rorik looked at me. "In the past, it was forbidden to invent anything that threatened the gods' position."

"Hmm." I scoffed. "That's why I hate religion. Everything ends at *because God said so*, and then you can't go any further. Back home, people actually thought that the earth was flat for thousands of years because no one dared to contradict the Church."

"But the earth *is* flat."

I started to laugh. "No, it is definitely round."

Rorik's eyes narrowed. "But if it were round, the Midgard Serpent would fall off."

I widened my eyes with a smile.

"The Midgard Serpent exists. It does."

"Yes, yes . . . of course it does." I rubbed my toes again. "When religion was abolished here eighteen years ago, there was plenty of opportunity to invent something new, but not much seems to have happened."

Rorik looked away. "I think Ragnara thought it was best to preserve the old traditions."

"Mhmm. Because it's easier to control people when they're ignorant."

He didn't comment on that. "What's it like, then, where you're from? If there's neither gods nor dictators? What do you believe in?"

I exhaled. "Most of all, the people in Midgard care about sex and money."

"Then we're not so different," Rorik remarked dryly.

"I think we're similar in a lot of ways. People in Midgard love their families. They fall in love. They have ambitions. And they hate and care for one another."

"Maybe," Rorik said, "people aren't so different when it comes down to it. Even if their circumstances are."

"What's the weather like in Midgard?"

"Really windy and rainy. Where I live, anyway. In the north it's cold, and in the south it's warmer."

Two days had passed, and Rorik was still grilling me. I was almost starting to miss the spells. We had set off through the Bronze Forest, heading toward Sverresborg. Rorik had told me we would arrive the following day. He wouldn't meet my eyes when he said it, probably because he feared I would rush into the castle without thinking.

I don't know where he would have gotten that idea.

Evening came, and it quickly grew darker among the trees. It was no wonder the forest was called the Bronze Forest, as it had a golden hue, and even though it was just as cold as Hibernia, it was more pleasant here in the soft, reddish light.

I enjoyed the calm for a while until Rorik asked again. "And you travel in huge iron boxes far above the earth? Without magic." He was particularly interested in airplanes. "Why don't they fall down?"

"It doesn't make sense to me, either, but they stay up there."

"And people always fly to get places?"

"Sometimes you drive or take a boat. But not a little barge like in Hibernia. There are huge ships, so you can sail on the ocean."

"Oh," Rorik said with awe. "They sail on the ocean?"

"Don't you do that here? You descend from the Vikings, and they sailed all over the place. This is an island. It's surrounded by a huge ocean."

"But you can't sail out on the open ocean. It's far too dangerous because of the Midgard Serpent. It makes the waters violently choppy, so the ships capsize."

"Have you seen the Midgard Serpent?"

"No."

"Has *anyone* seen the Midgard Serpent?" I asked innocently.

"That's impossible, as long as it stays in place with its tail in its mouth." He rolled his eyes.

"Could it be a superstition?"

Rorik looked at me angrily. "It's there! The myths tell of it and of what happened to those who were dumb enough to try to find out if it was real."

I mumbled something unintelligible to signal that I didn't want to continue the conversation. My hint sailed right over Rorik's head.

"What language do you speak in Midgard?" he asked.

"The same as here."

"What kind of swords do they have?"

"They don't carry swords."

His forehead creased. "Then how do they defend themselves against fingalks and lindworms?"

"Those don't exist in the other world."

"Are there—"

"I really don't feel like answering anymore." I sniffed. A scent in the air was becoming more and more familiar, but I couldn't place it.

"Just one more question."

"Okay. One." I inhaled through my nose again.

"What do you do if you get sick or injured?"

"Then you go to the hospital," I said distractedly. "What is that I'm smelling?"

Rorik didn't answer me. "What's a hospital?"

"It's a big building where all the sick people and doctors are."

"What's a doctor?"

"Someone who heals."

Rorik's head jerked up. "So it's a big building with sick people and women who heal them?"

"Both men and women can be doctors." I walked on like a hunting dog on the move. Where did I know that smell from? Longing spread through my body from somewhere deep inside. From a place where something was thoroughly packed away. I studied a fiery-red shrub and looked up into the golden canopy.

"So both women and men are allowed to heal in Midgard?"

"Of course. Women are allowed to do all kinds of things. It's not as patriarchal as here."

"What's that? Patriarchal?"

"The men control everything."

"No they don't!"

I snorted. "Men assault girls, and it's totally legal."

Rorik's lips pressed into a straight line. "Only the soldiers have that privilege. And they can only take women who are prisoners."

"Privilege?" I accidentally shouted the word. I had felt with my own body what that *privilege* meant.

"I don't like it, either. But aside from that, women have a lot of rights here." He rested his hand on a reddish tree trunk.

"I haven't seen them."

"Our ruler is a woman, and many of our warriors are women. Some of the herders are women."

I sniffed again. "Then it's probably just patriarchal in different ways."

The scent was overwhelming. The longing I felt was both seductive and sad.

Rorik walked after me. "There is actually one aspect where there's more equality between women and men in Midgard."

"How?"

"Men aren't allowed to heal here. Healing is a form of seid. And seid is only for women."

"What is that smell?" I asked again.

Rorik looked around.

"It's the trees' bark. The copper trees always smell like this at sunset."

I spun around. The scent filled everything, and it mixed with the smell of forest and fresh air. I realized where I knew it from, and I thought my heart would burst.

Right there, Varnar jumped out in front of me.

PART II

THE GLADNESS
OF RAVENS

The gladness of ravens
In wolf-wood asked the mighty leader
of the southern maid,
If with the hero home would she
Come that night
The prince will come a few nights hence
The maid to take

The First Lay of Helgi Hundingsbane
12th century

CHAPTER 11

He was just a child. A little boy with dead eyes and an axe in his hand.

I shouted, startled, although I quickly figured out I was seeing the past. At the same time, Rorik drew Tilarids without knowing where he should point it. I stared at child-Varnar and reached out to him.

Varnar ran into the undergrowth. The smell of smoke filled the air, and a growl came from the bushes, followed by a thump. Varnar came out again, and his right arm and the axe were smeared with blood. Someone shouted angrily. A man stumbled after him, and with a chilling shock, I saw it was Naut Kafnar—the Savage. I shouted instinctively, terrified. *No.* I cleared my head and realized it wasn't the Savage—but his matted hair and outfit of animal skins were identical. The berserker grabbed for Varnar, but he scurried up a tree and pulled his small legs up.

Rorik turned around and pointed Tilarids at the invisible enemy. "Where is the danger?"

I gasped loudly when the translucent berserker looked up into the tree for Varnar, and there was a hollow sound, like when you split open a watermelon. The berserker stood still for a moment before he tilted forward. The axe was buried in his forehead. I managed to jump out of the way, but the berserker fell straight into Rorik, who, for obvious reasons, couldn't see him.

"Tell me what's going on!" Tilarids trembled excitedly, and Rorik moved in a circle, unaware that he was ankle-deep in a transparent corpse.

"Something happened here once," I stammered.

The dead body dissolved and was gone.

Panting, Rorik lowered the sword. "Of course. The Forest Folk lived here." He did a double take. "Did you see something from back then?"

I avoided looking at him but nodded, then I leaned my head back to look up into the tree canopy. Maybe I could call the vision of Varnar back.

"That must have been more than twelve years ago." Rorik put Tilarids away. "You gave me a shock."

That's nothing compared to what I got.

My curiosity got the better of me. "What happened here?"

"The berserkers stormed the Forest Folk. All the adults were killed, and the Varangian Guard came to the rescue," Rorik rattled off.

I was about to mutter something when a thin voice piped up from a tree.

"That's not exactly what happened."

Again, we spun around, and once again Rorik drew Tilarids. I had been so busy spying on Varnar's past, I hadn't even detected the aura from within the tree's branches.

"Show yourself," Rorik barked.

"Yeah, yeah." A figure climbed gingerly down the thick trunk. A small old man landed on the path in front of us. His face, arms, and clothes were brown and green. I couldn't tell if it was camouflage, the typical Hrafnheimish color code, or simply dirt.

"I neither can nor wish to do you any harm." The man was several inches shorter than me. "I only want to ask for something to eat."

"Who are you?" I asked.

"Glaus," he said.

I noticed his high cheekbones and slightly tilted eyes.

"You belong to the Forest Folk?"

"No," Rorik interjected with a grim expression on his face. "The oldest survivor was only eleven when the place was abandoned."

Varnar.

Glaus looked away. There were furrows down his face and a shameful look about his mouth.

"You hid," I whispered. "While your people were slaughtered. Even when the children were captured. You coward."

Glaus didn't comment on this. "Could I have some food?"

Rorik rummaged in his bag, but I laid my hand on his arm.

"Don't give him anything. He can rot here. Hungry and alone."

"He's skin and bones." Rorik pried my fingers off. He found a piece of bread and handed it to Glaus. "Come, old man. We'll set up camp here. I want to hear what you have to say."

Half an hour later, I sat with my back to the two men and the fire. Rorik had chosen not to light his glass thing, and I didn't ask why. I shook my head when Rorik offered me a bowl of food. He shrugged and walked away. They spoke quietly, and I listened closely to what they were saying.

"Have you lived alone here in the forest since the attack?" Rorik's voice went down an octave and seemed indifferent as to whether Glaus answered or not. But he was far from indifferent.

Glaus didn't notice. "Not a lot of people come through here. Most know that this place is cursed."

"But, surely, it's not cursed," Rorik said good-naturedly.

There was the sound of spoons clinking in bowls and food being scooped up with large plops.

"No, it's not cursed," Glaus said between two mouthfuls. "But people are well aware of what happened here, so they stay away."

"Tell me about what happened."

My stomach contracted, and even though I sat apart from them with my back turned, I leaned back so I wouldn't miss a word.

"When the berserkers attacked, I was at the edge of the forest," Glaus said.

I also saw his memory clearly. It reflected what I had once seen from Varnar. The adults were massacred, and the children were rounded up.

"I know this part," Rorik said. "Soon after, the Varangian Guard came and liberated the children."

"No," Glaus said. "They came after four days, and by then, seven of the berserkers were already dead."

"Dead?" It sounded like Rorik stopped mid-bite.

"There was one child the berserkers didn't capture."

I turned involuntarily. At the same time Glaus said the name aloud, I thought it.

"Varnar." Glaus didn't notice that we were staring, and he continued between bites. "The berserkers' victory was swift. We are not warriors. But one boy evidently had fighting skills."

Rorik leaned slightly away from Glaus.

"Varnar," he whispered.

"You said that seven berserkers were dead when the Varangian Guard arrived," I said.

Glaus looked up. "Yes. And Varnar freed all the children. So the berserkers sent for reinforcements."

"For more berserkers?" Rorik asked.

"No, for the Varangian Guard."

Rorik opened his mouth, but a few seconds passed before anything came out. "The Guard didn't come to save the children?"

Glaus shook his head slowly.

"But no one wants to help the berserkers." Rorik's voice cracked. "They live in the Dark Forest. I don't think anyone's seen them since before Ragnara came to power, and even then, they plundered anyone they saw."

"Glaus is right," I whispered. "Ragnara is working with the berserkers."

Rorik turned toward me. "How do you know?"

"They attacked me . . . back home." I looked at the ground.

Rorik seemed to be struggling to understand. "Eskild and Ragnara loved Varnar like their own son. More than their own son." He looked down.

Glaus didn't notice Rorik's expression.

"Are Eskild and Ragnara together?" I asked cautiously. I had never gotten clarification as to what the relationship between the two actually was.

"They're not a couple," Rorik said brusquely.

"But is it true that he's the father of the prince?" Aella had once implied this.

Rorik snorted. "No one knows. If he is, their relationship isn't exactly characterized by fatherly pride."

Glaus interrupted us. "Now it's your turn," he said. "I haven't heard news of my people since then. Are the little ones okay?"

"They're not little anymore," I said, since Rorik seemed unable to speak. "Most of them are in the Varangian Guard."

"What about Varnar? He must be a big hero now."

Rorik looked into the flames. "Varnar is dead. He was killed and eaten by the giant wolves."

Even though I knew Varnar was very much alive, hearing this still made my heart lurch. Serén had said she saw Rorik and Varnar together. Were they already friends? Or would they become friends in the future?

Glaus clucked in dismay. "What about little Geiri?" he asked. "He was the apple of my eye."

I closed my eyes when he said Geiri's name. I heard the cracking sound of Monster eating him, and I absent-mindedly brought my hand to my throat, recalling how Geiri's leather cord had nearly strangled me in Ravensted.

"I don't know how Geiri is," Rorik replied. "He was sent on a mission by Eskild."

It was my turn to change the subject.

"What have you been doing out here all these years? Everyone thought there were no adult survivors."

Glaus looked into the fire. "I buried the dead, and now I maintain the settlement so that it's ready."

"Ready for what?"

"For the children to come back." Glaus looked at me with sincerity. "For us to become a people again."

When I opened my eyes the next morning, the fire was already going, and something was bubbling in the pot. I squinted in the light of the rising sun. *Where is Rorik?* I looked around frantically and could feel my pulse pounding in my throat.

"Rorik is fine," Glaus said, seeing my searching look. "The forest says so."

A few months ago, I would have refused the notion that someone could understand the forest's language, but now I knew of Varnar's ability to do the same. Slowly, my heart rate lowered, and I stood up. The many nights spent sleeping on the ground were starting to take a toll on my body. I was stiff and sore all over.

Thunk—thunk—thunk, my pulse hammered in my ears.

I walked over to Glaus. "Do you know Sverresborg?"

His movements stiffened. His eyes were watchful. "It's a place people want to avoid."

"Do you avoid the castle?"

He busied himself with looking into the pot.

"Glaus?"

His voice was barely audible. "There's a trash heap outside. Sometimes I'm lucky and find something edible."

Luck was probably the last word I would associate with Glaus, but I kept that thought to myself.

"Sverresborg is one of the most dangerous places in the realm," he whispered. "I wish I didn't have to go there." His gaze flitted toward the bag that held my remaining food rations.

I closed the top. We needed every last crumb ourselves.

He took a step forward. His bones were visible even through his clothes, and his teeth protruded as if being pushed out of his mouth.

"Give him some food, Anna."

I jumped at the sound of Rorik right behind me. Because I had gotten used to acting unbothered when my ghost father showed up without a sound, I replied with calm in my voice: "We can't spare it."

I turned and saw Rorik standing with reddish branches and larger pieces of wood in his arms.

"We can spare it more than Glaus can."

"Are there creatures at night?" I asked as we fought our way through a thicket early the next morning. "Fingalks?"

"Creatures?" Rorik's voice was tense. "There are no creatures here. They're afraid of the Kyngja Swamp." He pointed diagonally ahead of us.

"The what?"

"It's over there, and it swallows anything that comes near it. Everyone knows to stay away from it."

Before we could see the castle, we found a cave, which we crept into just as the sun's first orange arms reached through the trees. I said nothing, as it was clearly the safest place to be, but I was getting really sick of caves.

We lay down in a little side tunnel, after Rorik had lit the glass thing. I wrapped myself up in my mother's coat and shuddered as I stretched out on the cold ground. I rested my head on my bag, but it was hard and bumpy and didn't really cut it as a pillow. Fortunately, I was so exhausted I fell asleep.

When I opened my eyes, snowflakes were swirling around me. The spruce trees creaked, and Kraghede Forest was clear before me.

"Serén, are you here?" I called, not quite sure whether I meant in the vision or in Sverresborg. "Here in the dream?" I specified.

"Yes." The word sounded fluid and came from the trees. Our connection was poor.

I looked around, but I was still alone in the dark forest.

"We're here," I shouted. It echoed. *Here . . . here . . . here . . .*

"I can't manifest myself," the voice fluttered. Without a body connected to it, it sounded like the trees themselves were speaking. "My clairvoyance is impaired." *. . . paired . . . paired . . . paired.*

I tried to clear my mind. "Can you sense us?"

"Ahhh," Serén's voice sighed from the trees, and as it coincided with wind pushing against the treetops, it sounded like a gust of air.

Through the tree trunks glittering with frost, I glimpsed Odinmont atop snow-covered fields. A car honked. The other times I had had the vision, I hadn't even noticed the honk, but after weeks in Hrafnheim, the blaring sound was both eerie and familiar.

Serén was silent. "I can sense Rorik. But everything's blurry."

I exhaled. Relieved.

"I'm on my way, Serén," I said. "I'm coming for you."

"Hmm," Serén said from up in the trees. "I see something. What? There's . . ." Her voice disappeared so quickly, it sounded like an audio recording put on pause.

I leaned my head back. "Serén?" I called. "Sereeeen." *. . . ren . . . ren . . . ren.*

No response but the echo of my own voice.

A twig snapped behind me. "Serén?" I shouted again, turned around, and cried out in fear.

A version of myself, hypnotized and wearing the dress Luna had sewn for my birthday, was coming straight toward me. Behind this other me, through Kraghede Forest, near Ravensted, a world away, Frank came stomping with his face tilted down and the leather cord dangling from his hand.

CHAPTER 12

My eyes were glassy beads.

I tried to make eye contact with the other me. For an instant, her gaze darted in my direction, but then it looked blankly forward again. The other me staggered by.

"What," I whispered breathlessly. "But this didn't happen. Serén. Are you seeing what I'm seeing?"

Serén was silent in the treetops.

"Is this the past or the future?" I shouted upward.

Still no answer.

Frank placed the cord around my neck. I didn't need to watch because I knew every second. I had seen it over and over again for the past six months. The choking sound still made me turn my head. I was more angry than afraid.

Dying-me gasped for air.

Okay. I was terrified.

"This didn't happen," I screamed. "You didn't kill me, Frank."

Thump.

"I didn't die," I yelled again.

Frank tore open my dress and carved the rune into my back, after which he stood, leaned against the birch tree, and snapped it under his weight. Then he ran across the field toward Odinmont.

I remained in the forest with my arms hanging uselessly at my sides. In front of me lay myself, cast aside, bloody and in an unnatural position.

What the hell just happened?

Hands gripped my face, and I tried to twist myself free. My fist hit skin.

I woke to see Rorik kneeling in front of me with his tattooed hand on my cheek.

"You were screaming," he whispered. "What did you see?"

I pushed his hand away more brusquely than was warranted.

"It was just a dream." I compartmentalized the vision, so the scariest parts were pushed furthest away. "Serén sensed you."

I pointed toward the cave's opening and Sverresborg, which lay somewhere out there. Then my fingertips found my neck, and I gulped down a big mouthful of air.

Rorik's brows furrowed.

"She can sense me?" He raised his hand.

My sharp look made him lower his hand again. "What else did you dream?"

"There was nothing else. That was it."

In the afternoon, we crept toward Sverresborg.

Rorik repeatedly admonished me: "Don't do anything stupid."

"Me? I would never."

This comment earned me a grin, his brown eyes lingering on me.

My thoughts kept turning back to Kraghede Forest and the bloody rune on my back, but I pushed the dream away. Right now I needed to find my sister. Soon, I would meet her. I trembled. Together, we would solve the mystery of what the vision in Kraghede Forest meant. Together, we would prevent Ragnarök. I stopped. It would work only if Rorik and I were successful now.

I looked at the large fortress.

I'm on my way, Serén.

She replied immediately. *You are? Anna, are you here?*

I exhaled a tiny sob at the sound of her voice, and Rorik glanced quickly at me.

"What?" he mimed.

"Hurry. She's right in there," I replied, moving as quickly as possible on all fours, but my stomach fluttered with joy at the thought that we would soon be able to speak to each other outside of a dream state.

Rorik and I crawled onward in front of the giant red sun that was about to slip behind the horizon, far out at sea. Right now, it hovered just over the edge.

I had expected Sverresborg to look like a papier-mâché castle from an old movie, but that was far from the case. The fortress sat on a little promontory jutting out into the sea. A wooden defensive wall surrounded the entire structure in a semicircle. The rest of the castle was thrust out toward the sea. There were two massive entrance gates of wood and iron, each guarded by six soldiers.

From our position, I could see the buildings sticking up within the walls. They were shaped like large, beached fish, with overlapping wooden shingles on their roofs.

In a way, the fort resembled The Boatman. Like Od's bar, Sverresborg sat on top of a cliff with a sheer drop to the beach many yards below.

Rorik pointed to the cliff, but his eyes traced the fort again and again, and he wrinkled his nose like he had the first several times he saw me.

"There's an entrance down there," whispered Rorik. "I think we can get in that way without being noticed."

I shuddered involuntarily at the thought of us toppling over the edge, but it was not the time to be afraid of heights.

When we reached the castle, I was struck with the stench of the trash heap. Dark figures crawled around on it, but they were so filthy and shabby, I couldn't make them out.

We snaked our way around the dump, and I breathed through my mouth as we got close. The only way down to the beach was right up against the corner of Sverresborg, and we ducked down as far as possible in the shadow of the wooden palisade.

Rorik climbed backward over the cliff's edge, and he seemed so confident that I followed suit, even though every fiber of my being protested.

We moved with extreme care as the salty wind tore at us. There wasn't much aside from lyme grass to hold on to, and the sharp blades sliced my palms. I ignored the twinges of pain, and finally we reached the bottom. The waves lapped the beach in a violent surge that did not match the relatively mild wind. At home, there would need to be gale-force winds to create such large waves.

"There." Rorik's finger aimed at a small hatch in the dune. It was well hidden, and at first glance, I didn't notice it because a bigger entrance sat just beside it. A large gate.

I brushed the sand off my pants.

The beach was full of footprints and splinters of wood. Pushed up a canal that led into Sverresborg, there rocked a battered, dark, glistening raft. In the middle, a pole stuck straight up, but it was cracked and splintered. Over the smell of fish there hovered another scent. I sniffed. It was a faint, sickly smell of urine and animals.

I reached out with my power.

At first, there was just a faint sound. I tilted my head and strained to hear.

I heard a falsetto-like song, but I couldn't make out the words. The song was controlled and formal, but it sounded plaintive and shrill. Someone pounded a drum, and the rhythm blended with the voices. Then came deep, prolonged blasts from some kind of wind instrument.

"Someone was just here." My voice was swallowed by the crashing of a large wave.

"What?" Rorik asked.

"Something just happened here," I said, louder, and closed my eyes.

In the past, I saw people in white capes with Ragnara's fehu rune on them. They were the ones who were chanting.

I studied the vision with my eyes squeezed shut. "It looks like a religious ritual."

It reminded me of when I was forced to participate in ceremonies in an evangelical church in North Jutland. But then something happened that reminded me neither of North Jutland nor of churches. In the vision, a raft was pushed out into the sea. The planks were encircled with torches, and in the middle, tied to a pole, was a bull. Its large forehead was carved with the fehu rune. The bull rolled its eyes back and strained against its rope. Two men used poles to push the raft along, but once it was far enough out, they jumped off and waded back to shore. I shivered at the thought of how cold it must be. The bull floated on, alone. The rhythmic song and drums continued.

The contrast between the bull's deep bellow, the plaintive blasts, and the priests' nasal howls sent shivers down my spine.

"Lúgh, Ragnara, Jörmungandr," shouted the priests. "Lúgh, Ragnara, Jörmungandr."

The water's surface rippled in wide bands, and the smell of sulfur and seaweed reached me.

"Anfarwol," a herder sang out over the water.

"Anfarwol," another joined.

"Anfarwol," they all sang.

I opened my eyes. When my gaze landed on the raft in the canal again, I saw it was the same one the bull had stood on, now in somewhat worse condition.

"We'd better hurry and get inside." Rorik nudged me, and we approached the little hatch next to the gate leading into Sverresborg. He opened it with a metallic creak, and we walked in. We had to duck to fit in the low-ceilinged passageway, and the air around us smelled musty.

"Why is neither the gate nor this door guarded?" I breathed through my mouth to avoid the smell. Squeaks and scratching sounds told me there were rats, but I didn't care. I had encountered far worse than rats in my life. It was pitch black in the tunnel, and it took a few seconds for me to orient myself.

"There aren't many who dare to come down to the beach," came Rorik's voice in the darkness.

I didn't have the mental space to ask him to elaborate.

Serén? I called inside my head instead. *Serén. Hello!*

Anna? Serén said.

It sounded hollow.

"Ow!" Just then, I banged my head on a beam in the ceiling. "Could you light the crystal?" I asked Rorik, rubbing my forehead. "I literally can't see my hands in front of me."

Where are you, Serén?

Something blinked. Like a defective TV that was fighting to pick up a signal.

Anna, I'm . . . Silence.

I turned around just as Rorik got the crystal working.

"Where did she go?"

"Who?" Rorik raised the shining glass over his head, and there was a *whoosh* as a bunch of small shadows disappeared.

"My sister. We can talk to each other in our heads, but now she's gone."

"Can you . . ." Rorik's voice trailed off, probably because he had no idea what to ask.

I went a few steps ahead of him, calling out silently.

Serén, Serén.

A short distance away from Rorik, she showed up again.

Anna.

I exhaled with relief. *I can't sense you.*

It was quiet for a moment, long enough for me to think I had lost her again, but I reasoned that it was just because she was thinking. Sverresborg was teeming with auras, but they were all rough. People who were used to struggling. People who always had to fight. With effort, I cast the net further than I ever had before, and I felt like my brain was being stretched out like a rubber band. I let out a muted whine of exertion.

A tiny, harmless aura with the texture of a rabbit skin flickered, until Rorik caught up to me and it disappeared.

"What's wrong?" he asked, agitated.

It suddenly dawned on me. "She disappears when you come close."

"What are you talking about?"

I ran ahead, and her mild aura popped up again.

Warmer. Warmer.

Be ready. I'm coming, I screamed silently and ran to the right. The aura grew a touch stronger.

Warmer. Warmer.

Miraculously, there were no soldiers in the hall before us. The passageway branched off again a few yards ahead. I went to the left.

How will we get out? Serén asked desperately. *The door is locked.*

I'll improvise, I promised. *We're gonna get you out. Rorik is here with me. We're almost there.*

Her aura grew stronger, and I ran as quickly as I could without making noise.

Rorik was behind me, but he stayed a few yards back as we raced in the direction of the silky aura.

Warmer.

Something's coming closer, Serén faltered. *I can hear steps. I can sense something, too. Something violent.*

I was almost there. Soon I would be with my sister for the first time.

I stopped in front of three identical doors, then took a few steps toward one of them.

Colder.

Shit!

I ran back to the middle door.

Warmer. Getting hot.

I grasped the handle.

Is it you?

It's me, Serén. I'm coming for you.

Someone turned the corner.

I looked over my shoulder and suppressed a scream when I recognized the man stomping toward us.

Gustaf! He had no aura, so I couldn't sense him. I should have guessed he'd put a spell on the place so he would know the second anyone snuck in.

Presumably because Védis had made me immune to magic, I saw him as he really appeared. He looked like a snake with a narrow face, high cheekbones, and slanted eyes with vertical pupils.

Gustaf looked at me and seemed totally unsurprised to find me there. But he took a couple of steps back when he saw Rorik. Then he turned to look at me again. His pupils were almost gone now, and he held his hands out in front of him. They were glowing, and the symbols on his palms pulsated.

"Svefn," he shouted, and an energy or electric current shot out.

I just barely managed to kick the door open and throw myself into the room. I slammed it shut before the walls shook with a bang, and a flash of blue was visible between the panels.

Rorik was out there, but I couldn't think of that now.

"Serén? Serén?" I called, this time aloud, as I spun around in circles.

Anna . . . I heard inside my head. *Is it you?*

The room I stood in was quiet apart from the crashes coming from outside. It was also, at first glance, empty. An animal hide lay on the floor, and embroidered tapestries hung on the walls. There was a bed covered in blankets and pillows. Something wavered around it. It looked like haze or a mirage.

"Serén?" I ran to it.

A hand stuck out from the pile, and a body was buried in fabric.

I ripped the blankets off. I stared, but my eyes didn't want to comprehend what I saw.

Another insistent bang rammed the door, and it flung open.

"Don't move," Gustaf said.

I stood completely still as Gustaf approached from behind.

Serén? I asked slowly. *Where in Sverresborg are you?*

It was quiet for a moment.

Sverresborg? I'm in Sént.

"Crap!" I said into the room. "Crap, crap, crap." I looked down at the bed.

A head rested on the pillow. Fair, disheveled hair. The boy appeared to be sleeping, but his lips were blue, his fingernails purple, and his eyes were open and staring ahead, lifeless. For a second, I thought the child was dead, but then I realized the soft aura was coming from him. The shield around him was magic. He was enchanted, like Arthur's body back in Denmark.

The light grew stronger as Gustaf came closer.

"If you move, you die."

My breathing was rapid, but I stood completely still as Gustaf's footsteps approached.

I squinted and focused on the boy. He was familiar.

Gustaf's hand struck me and shot energy into my body like a taser. I sank to my knees, still staring at the boy, and I realized where I had seen him before.

In Frank's past. It was his grandson.

CHAPTER 13

Gustaf dragged me through the corridor. I stumbled along after him, still half stunned. Suddenly, cold air hit me. Evidently, we were outside, but I was too dazed to get my bearings.

Where is Rorik? Did you kill him?

Maybe I asked this aloud. I wasn't sure, and in any case, Gustaf did not respond. His strong hands were impossible to fight back against, his fingers stuck to me, and although I wriggled, I couldn't break free. He pulled me into a building, and I squinted. Along the walls, torches were held in thick iron rings, and the floor, walls, and ceiling were made of large boulders. There was no decoration. Just stone and fire.

We took a sharp swing down a side hallway. We soon reached a narrow staircase. Groggy, I stumbled and slid down a few steps. I hit my shoulder and my back but miraculously slipped out of Gustaf's grasp. I tried to quickly jump to my feet, but a ball of energy landed close to my head. The wooden railing by my ear smoldered.

"The next one will land in your chest." He moved his fingers, and suddenly all I could see was Gustaf's face, coming closer and closer. The tattoos on his cheeks and forehead were now pulsating like real scales. His eyes were yellower than before, and his pupils morphed into thin lines. His tongue flicked like a snake's. Maybe I was seeing things. I shook my head in an attempt to clear it, but Gustaf narrowed his eyes. There was a faint crackling in the air around him.

At first, his magic met resistance. That must have been the

magical immunity Védis had given me. Then he murmured, and it was as if something inside me let go and fluttered away.

My willpower seeped out of me. I had the feeling of having absolutely no control over my own muscles and thoughts, even though I was fully conscious, and I *wanted* to obey. I wanted to do whatever it took to please him. The panic of being nearly blind vanished.

"Come." Gustaf laid an arm over my shoulder, and I leaned into him. He was the safest person in the worlds. We started walking again, and he led me, humming, the rest of the way down the creaking stairs. The sound mixed with Gustaf's chirpy song, which reminded me of something, but my brain wasn't working right.

"Lúgh, Ragnara, Jörmungandr," he chanted as if he were calling to someone.

Finally, we reached a dark room. I stepped willingly onto a surface that, though I couldn't see what it was, rocked beneath my footsteps. Gustaf let go of me and rummaged around for something.

I waited obediently.

Gustaf guided me backward until I hit something hard.

"Arms behind your back," he murmured.

I obeyed willingly. In fact, I giggled, because his rough palms tickled my arms as he bound me to a pole like the first time we met. He was so close, his flicking tongue hit my neck. Was he sniffing me? Then the light in his eyes went out. His pupils contracted and became round again. My head instantly became clear, and with my heart in my throat, I pulled against the ropes, but it didn't do much good. I was bound to the pole. I still couldn't see anything, since it was pitch black, and panic set in with full force.

Something beneath me made a sloshing sound, and whatever I was standing on swayed a little.

Gustaf's voice was harsh, and it resounded as if we were in a large room or a cave. "You won't feel much."

"Much of what?" My voice was shrill, and I tugged frantically at the ropes.

He didn't answer. I tried again to pull myself free, but the ropes didn't budge. I grasped for my last chance. The truth.

"If you kill me, you risk starting Ragnarök. That's what the prophecy says."

"What exactly does it say?" Gustaf asked.

"If Ragnara or her people kill me, the world will end."

There was a click, and I could suddenly see as light bathed the room. We were in a hall that reminded me of a large factory.

Gustaf lifted a torch, and it illuminated his face beneath his hood. He wore a white cape, like those worn by the herders. Ragnara's symbol stood out starkly on his shoulder. He dipped a finger in a bowl that sat on a table.

"I'm not going to be the one to kill you." He was now very close to me. "Not me, nor anyone working for Ragnara."

"Ragnara wants me alive," I said desperately. "She'll be furious with you if I die."

"*Pff*. You're lying." His finger touched my face, and with a wet substance, he drew a rune on my forehead. Then he yanked up my sleeve and placed his finger on my forearm. His nail moved, and I screamed as a searing pain shot into my arm.

The stench of burnt flesh rose. My own burnt flesh.

Gustaf engraved something into my skin, as though his finger were a woodburning tool.

Because my hands were tied, I couldn't see what he'd drawn. A hot, stinging pain spread through my arm.

"What the fuck," I protested.

Gustaf didn't respond. He jumped into the water and moved forward with difficulty. He opened a large gate and pushed the barge—on which I stood bound—down the canal and then onto the open water outside Sverresborg. We passed the raft I had seen when we came in, and I realized it was identical to the one I was standing on.

The setting winter sun colored the water pink, and I felt like I was being pushed straight into it.

Gustaf chanted like the priests did in my vision when the bull was . . . *What actually happened to the bull?*

Now Rorik's voice rang out. "I command you to stop, sorcerer."

He had apparently caught up to us, and I felt a wave of relief that he was alive.

Gustaf looked over his shoulder with a mocking grunt.

"That's an order," Rorik barked from the beach.

"I don't take orders from traitors," Gustaf yelled over his shoulder and continued pushing the raft forward.

Eyes wide, I leaned back against the pole, as if I could somehow brake that way. A short distance ahead, the water's surface began to show small ripples. Something large was moving in the water. A sulfurous smell with a hint of chlorine hit my nostrils.

From somewhere behind me, I heard another shout. It was Rorik, coming after us. I could hear him making his way through the water.

The sea roared again, and the raft made a large, yet smooth, movement as a wave passed us. Behind me, it crashed onto the beach with a splash. Yet another large wave struck, even though the air was still.

"Don't go any farther," Rorik yelled.

Gustaf pushed us stubbornly ahead, even though his feet lost contact with the bottom several times, and he had to cling to the barge.

Duck! I suddenly heard Serén's voice in my head.

What?

Now! Duck, she screamed. *I just saw it.*

I obeyed instinctively and slid down the pole, bowing my head as far as I could. An oversized reptilian tail swished up out of the water and hit the wood above me. It splintered, and I shut my eyes.

What the hell was that?

The tail slid back into the water.

Gustaf shouted, dove below the surface, and came back up coughing. We must have crossed some kind of shelf, as it didn't seem he could reach the bottom anymore. With loud, splashing strokes, he left me, and I floated alone.

The raft was so far out, it was close to reaching the highest waves. A massive shape glided just beneath the surface. The barge bumped a few times and there was a dull, choppy sound as something slid along the logs from below.

There was an exclamation when Rorik and Gustaf bumped into each other, but I couldn't turn my head far enough to see them.

The barge was tossed around, shaking me like a rag doll.

My pathetic vessel jerked backward as I stared at the large waves rising before me. Never before had I felt so small in the face of nature's power.

"What's going on?" I screamed to Rorik.

"The Midgard Serpent is out here." Rorik's voice was tense with effort, and I realized it was him pulling me backward. "The serpent is writhing to free itself from its tail, and you'll be crushed if you end up under its body."

"I just saw a tail that wasn't in a . . . in a . . ." I couldn't say more. Not a word. A head rose from the deep. It was as big as a house. Prehistoric-monster big, and it was heading directly toward me. Its scales shimmered a metallic blue in the final rays of the setting sun. Along its back, hard plates overlapped like a scorpion, giving its body an impenetrable appearance. Its eyes were iron-colored, and its maw looked like that of a whale, with gills under its chin. A row of densely packed, sharp teeth protruded from its mouth.

I knew what had happened to the bull.

Serén, I called desperately in my head.

You won't die at Sverresborg, she assured me.

What the hell are you basing that on? I stared at the gigantic Midgard Serpent, which placed its monstrous head in front of me. Its enormous body trailed behind it.

Rorik made a violent *huugghh* sound and pulled a final time. My barge nearly smashed into the shore.

The Midgard Serpent gnashed its teeth, and when its jaws came together, they produced a crash that shook everything around us. Its tail flicked and appeared to come from the other side of its head. Then it dove down into the waves again in a wild movement that disturbed the water even more.

A cascade of water poured over me, and Rorik was thrown even farther up the beach, where he dragged himself on his stomach in the sand, leaving a deep trail behind him.

Gustaf, who still lay in the water, was sucked farther out when the wave retreated. He shouted when the monster reappeared from the water. It turned its head to the side and looked at him with one gray eye the size of a window.

"I've given you offerings," Gustaf yelled. "You're supposed to protect those who give you gifts."

The serpent looked at him with its narrow lips pulled back.

"I've *fed* you." He looked like a tiny mouse in front of the gigantic snake.

Glowing venom flowed from the Midgard Serpent's sharp teeth, which were each the length of my forearm. When the venom hit the water, there was a long sizzling noise. A drop of venom splashed onto Rorik's pants, and a hole appeared. The liquid floated like bright green oil spots on the water's surface.

"No," Gustaf begged. "No."

A mouth the size of a barn door opened just above Gustaf. The serpent pulled back its lips, revealing another row of sharp teeth behind the first. Gustaf's head turned slightly in Rorik's direction, and he looked like he wanted to say something. Before he had the chance, the Midgard Serpent struck. Gustaf turned to flee, but the serpent's jaws closed around his body, and I closed my eyes. Although I didn't see it, the sound will stay with me for the rest of my life.

With Gustaf in its maw, the snake slinked back into the deep.

CHAPTER 14

The sea was now completely smooth. Only small splashes, patches of neon floating on the surface, and the splintered raft indicated that a violent drama had taken place just moments ago. The sun had fully set, but a stubborn orange light flared from the horizon like flames from the underworld.

The water sparkled like quicksilver and was topped with bright green spots as Rorik cut me free from my restraints.

It was completely silent on the shore as we looked out over the gurgling, glimmering water.

The venom dissolved in the water, and I realized how many people had been watching breathlessly from the palisade wall. They took off, and soon thereafter, the alarm sounded.

The soldiers had to leave the castle to pursue us, which gave us a slight head start. But only slight. We clambered up the steep cliff. I barely noticed how I pulled myself up, but when I looked down, my palms were full of cuts from the sharp lyme grass and thorny bushes. We sprinted toward the forest as quickly as we could, which was frustratingly slow.

"Your sister?"

"She's not there," I shouted back. "She's in Sént."

"Sént?" Rorik groaned. "But Ragnara never keeps prisoners in Sént."

Behind us, dogs barked, and voices moved in our direction.

"That's what Serén said."

We reached the forest and began creeping through the trees, but deep down, I knew we would never make it to the cave. We would not escape the soldiers.

"*Psst.*" A small head poked out from behind a tree.

Rorik raised Tilarids, ready to strike. He had drawn the sword during our frantic run.

My heart was pounding, but I reached my arm across Rorik's chest so he would lower the sword.

"It's just a little girl." I panted from exhaustion, shock, and cold.

The girl stepped out from her hiding place behind the tree. She wore dirty clothes, her hair was a rat's nest, and her eyes were enormous. Her face was so emaciated that all her features stood out sharply.

"Come," she said. "This way."

And then she ran.

Rorik and I exchanged a look and made our decision simultaneously.

"You have to step exactly where I do," the girl said as we ran through an area that grew wetter and wetter.

The water reflected our surroundings in a distorted way, so trees and bushes looked like frightening creatures. In one place, I strayed too far to one side and stepped on something that looked like solid ground, but with a squishing *pop*, my foot went through the moss, and I sank to my knee in swamp water. The water was painfully cold, and it felt like something down there was pulling on me.

Rorik cursed, but it was the girl who reached me first. Despite her unassuming appearance, she yanked me up.

"Step *exactly* where I do," she hissed. "Kyngja is hungry."

She stomped off again, and where she stepped was solid ground.

I prodded tentatively at the place where I had gone through. It had closed up and once again looked like normal forest floor, but the surface quivered, and I pulled my foot back immediately.

It quickly grew completely dark, and we had to make an effort to stay on the girl's path. The dogs were right behind us, but I heard splashes and heartrending barks when they tried to follow us into the swamp. There was a terrified shout when a man screamed for help. More soldiers arrived.

"Grab his hand," someone shouted. "Grab it, grab . . . where is he?"

We were running faster than was safe.

"Did they run in there?" I heard someone ask somewhere behind us. "Then they've been swallowed up by the swamp by now."

We continued in silence, the only sound the branches we broke on our way. Finally, we reached a small arrangement of standing stones covered with branches. The stone walls appeared ancient and were covered in moss and half collapsed in some places, but the makeshift roof was new.

The girl waved us in.

"The soldiers won't dare come here." She led us farther inside. "Even if they make it through the swamp."

After crawling through a labyrinth of low, narrow passageways, we reached the center, which wasn't much more than a circular covered space. A fire crackled in the middle, but it produced more smoke than flame. Around it sat huddled figures. It was impossible to see if they were children, women, or men. They stared at us in fear. I gasped when I saw their missing fingers and noses, the red, oozing wounds.

"They fought the Midgard Serpent," the girl said to the terrified figures, but none reacted. "They were the ones who gave Glaus the food."

She pointed to a corner, where, on a platform that resembled a primitive altar, the remnants of our rations sat.

Dirty hands reached out and grabbed our clothes. One kissed the leg of Rorik's pants, while my perception of Glaus was turned on its head.

"What's wrong with them?" I whispered to Rorik.

"Splittr."

I furrowed my brow. "What is that?"

"Leprosy. They're called untouchables." Rorik spoke more loudly into the room: "Can we stay here until morning? The soldiers are looking for us in the forest."

A space was quickly made for us in a corner near the smoking fire.

Rorik scrutinized my side, which had been hit by a large splatter of venom. Fortunately, it had eaten away only the fabric of my mom's coat and a little of the shirt underneath. Gytha had apparently made the coat from something very sturdy, so I was unharmed, though the skin underneath was red and irritated.

"Your leg!" I exclaimed when I caught sight of his thigh. His pants had dissolved in a large hole, and I could see a yellow, oozing wound beneath.

He looked down at himself with an indifferent snort. He twisted my coat off me and pulled the remains of my sleeve up to look at the wound Gustaf had burned into my arm.

I just managed to see some charred lines before I pulled my arm back. "I think you should take first priority."

"It'll heal."

Pus soaked the wound on his thigh.

I rolled my eyes. "Of course you have to play the macho guy."

"The what?"

"Take off your pants," I ordered. "I need to bandage it."

He raised an eyebrow in surprise and started to smile.

"What's so funny?" I asked bitterly.

"It just isn't like you," he said as he loosened his belt, pulled the pitiful remains of his pants off, and placed them on the ground. They smelled as if they had been on fire.

I knelt and looked at his ravaged leg. My hands brushed aimlessly over the unharmed skin, and he made a little sound above me. His legs, too, were tattooed. It seemed his whole body was, minus the one bicep. The image of a battle scene had been ruined by the wound. A warrior had been where there was now raw flesh. Only an arm with a sword stuck out from the patch of destroyed skin, the warrior himself having been eaten away.

"I have no idea what to do," I admitted. "I'm not particularly good at fixing things. Or people."

"There's some salve and bandages in my bag," Rorik said quietly.

I rummaged around and found clean fabric and a jar.

"Wipe the venom away," he instructed.

I obeyed and dabbed carefully at the wound.

Rorik clenched his fists but said nothing. I breathed through gritted teeth in sympathy.

"You lost some ink," I commented when I had finally removed the last drops of green.

"Ink?"

"Your tattoo got ruined."

He looked down at his leg and pulled lightly at the skin to assess the damage. "I never liked that one. I got it for the wrong reason."

"Do you need a reason to get a tattoo?"

"All the marks on our bodies mean something. Maybe we don't know what it means, but it has a meaning."

"What do I do now?" I asked.

"The salve is medicinal. Spread some of it on."

I held up the jar. "Do you just go around with a portable hospital?"

"We soldiers have to have more skills than just killing people. Fortunately." This last word was mumbled quietly.

I remembered how Varnar had examined me when I was attacked, and how he had wanted to bandage my hand the time I broke my finger.

"And this is?" I asked as I took a dollop and spread it across Rorik's thigh.

He whimpered as the milk-white salve sank into his leg.

"It's called laekna," he said tensely. "We buy it from the Brewmaster, although I've never met him personally. It's great for healing superficial wounds."

"You call this superficial?"

"No broken bones or torn muscles. Yeah, it's superficial."

I read the small label, which was written in Elias's handwriting. Then I glanced at the wound, which had already started to close and now looked more like a bad scrape. I hoped it would heal completely.

It didn't, though it did stop flowing with yellow fluid. Elias hadn't bothered to sell them real laekna.

"Ahhh." Rorik closed his eyes as the salve did its work. Then he looked at me again and took my arm. He ran his fingers carefully over the red skin on my forearm where Gustaf had burned me. It looked more like a tattoo than a burn, as the lines were deep blue underneath the red swelling. The end of the mark cut into my palm.

I studied it more closely and cursed. Ragnara's rune now adorned my arm.

"I've often thought about getting a tattoo, but I really would have liked to pick it out myself," I said in an attempt to sound sarcastic.

"Gustaf must have wanted to mark you as Ragnara's property." He looked at the fehu symbol and let his fingers trace the perimeter of the wound. His touch was gentle. "Does it hurt?"

I looked down, feeling awkward under his searching gaze. "It's nothing compared to your wound."

"Still." Rorik carefully rubbed some of Elias's salve over my arm.

The salve's effect wasn't as intense as real laekna, but a pleasant tingling spread all the way up to my shoulder. I leaned back, my arm still in Rorik's grasp.

Real laekna removed injuries and left no scars, so I hoped the fehu tattoo would disappear. But a blue scar bubbled up under the salve and ended up printed into my skin. It would surely last for the rest of my life, however long that might be.

"What did you find inside Sverresborg?" Rorik asked quietly.

I looked at him drowsily. "A little boy. I know him, sort of, but he's spellbound. Gustaf must have cast a stasis spell on him."

"Gustaf," Rorik repeated.

The name hovered between us as we said nothing. The large, open mouth of the serpent and the sound it made when it crushed Gustaf echoed in my mind.

"FUCK!" I shouted.

"What?" Rorik stood halfway and reached for Tilarids.

The huddled shadows quickly crawled away from us.

"Frank's grandchild is still enchanted. And now Gustaf is dead, so he can't lift the spell." *Shit, shit, shit.* I closed my eyes and pinched the bridge of my nose.

"Anna?" Rorik said.

"Give me a second." I crawled into the damp passageway that led out of the building. With the back of my head up against the frigid, moss-covered wall, I exhaled and tried to organize my thoughts. Then I heard a voice in the darkness.

"Seer."

I let out a frightened shriek as Gustaf's spirit came closer. He did not have the disoriented eyes of typical ghosts.

"You. Are. Dead," I said, trying to keep my voice steady.

He continued toward me.

"You were eaten by the Midgard Serpent," I said with a touch of desperation. My trick of bringing up ghosts' deaths and thereby compelling them to return to their earthly remains didn't seem to be working.

Gustaf's outline didn't so much as flicker, but he looked in the direction of the castle. Then he turned his head back toward me.

I cautiously stepped backward, and it occurred to me that it might be a good idea to keep him there.

Gustaf bared his teeth and studied the collapsed wall. "You're hiding in the ravenous swamp among the half-decomposed living."

"The *decomposed* helped us, actually." I gathered my courage. "Why are you hanging out here? Haven't you like . . . moved on?"

Gustaf looked at his nearly transparent arms. "I was at the gate to the realm of the dead. For an eternity, but at the same time only an instant. Modgud wouldn't let me in. Hel wants me to haunt you."

"Why does Hel want that?"

Gustaf's ghost waved a transparent hand. "I've never understood politics, but Ragnara was behind it."

"Okaayy." I stretched the word out, mostly because I had no idea what to do about the ghost. The idea of dragging a frustrated spirit around with me was not exactly appealing.

"You're supposed to disappear when I mention your death," I said so quietly, it sounded like a breath. "That usually works on ghosts."

Gustaf's yellow eyes were now the most solid thing about him. The rest was like smoke.

"I'm a magician," he said, as if that explained everything. He pointed his fingers at me, and I waited, squinting, for a spell to fly out of them, but nothing happened. He shook his hands as if he were holding a defective TV remote.

"You *were* a magician," I corrected.

He took another step in my direction with a vexed expression, but I stayed where I was and stared right into his slanted eyes. "I need to ask you something."

Gustaf grimaced scornfully. "It's your fault I'm dead."

He raised his hand to hit me, but I didn't budge.

"I may be able to get you in somewhere else," I said.

"In?"

"I can try to pull some strings to get you out of haunting me. It sounds like a really boring way to spend your afterlife." I raised my eyebrows. "Haven't you done enough for Ragnara?" I put all my effort into holding my face in an angry expression. "You busted your ass for her your whole life. Now you're gonna keep working for her in death?"

Gustaf seemed to waver. "What do you want in return?"

"How do I remove the spells from the boy?" I asked.

"You can't lift the spells. You're not a witch."

"Can another witch do it?"

Gustaf waved a half-transparent hand. "Yes, but I'll only tell you how on one condition."

"Let's hear it."

He leaned forward.

What was it Od had said about calling on his father? I walked farther down the hall when Gustaf was done speaking.

"Svidur," I whispered. "Svidur," I hissed a little louder.

Gustaf's spirit hung over my head.

"You're crowding me," I snapped.

"I'm what?"

"Just stay there." I turned a corner and suddenly remembered it. "Hey! All-Father. Come here."

A gust of wind hit me, and Svidur was very close. "Have you realized it, little seer?"

"Realized what?" I looked up at his frightening, beautiful face with the missing eye.

"That I'm a god and must be worshipped."

"Actually, all I've realized is that you have a bunch of kids."

He turned his face, so it was hidden in shadow. It was impossible to tell if he was smiling or scowling. "So why did you call me?"

"I have something—someone—for you."

Svidur's breath sounded like a violent sigh. "Hangadrott? You know I'll do anything for you if you sacrifice a royal to me."

"It's not exactly a hangadrott."

Svidur was about to say something, but I laid a hand on his arm. It was blazing hot without being uncomfortable to touch. "Just hear me out."

He nodded.

"I have a soul for you to take to Valhalla." It dawned on me that Svidur might not even want Gustaf's spirit. In that case, I was really in trouble. "He wants to go."

Now that I've convinced him, but Svidur didn't need to know that.

Svidur's breathing grew heavy. "One who wants to come to me. Are you offering me a willing sacrifice?" His hot hand came to rest on my shoulder.

"He's already dead."

"How did he die?" The words did not match his bedroom voice. I tilted my head.

"He was eaten by a sea serpent." I chuckled when I heard how crazy that sounded, but Svidur didn't so much as raise an eyebrow.

"Was he in battle?"

"Yes! Very much so."

Svidur exhaled heavily and squeezed my shoulder.

Okay, this is weird.

Hurriedly, I called out: "Gustaf."

He appeared immediately.

Svidur released me and looked bitterly at the ex-magician. "I know this one all too well! He rejected me when he was alive."

"But he's ready to come with you now," I said, almost desperately.

Svidur snorted.

"Times have changed, and I can't allow myself to be picky." He studied Gustaf more closely. "A magician."

"I'm sure he's as good as anyone else," I said, still worried that Svidur would refuse to take my potential clingy spirit.

"It's an even greater gift. I am a master of magic. Together we can—"

"Okay." I raised my hands. "Just take him."

Svidur's eye lingered on Gustaf before he turned his attention back to me. He smiled, which blew my willpower completely off course. Then he carefully traced my arm with his hand, from shoulder to wrist. For a moment, his fingers hovered over the fehu tattoo.

"I didn't want it," I rushed to say.

He stroked it.

"You are *my* slave." When I looked up in anger, he continued hoarsely. "And I am *your* slave."

Then he unclenched my fist and kissed my palm.

"You've acted like a true Valkyrie. You've given me a magic soul who died in battle. And you've helped your first spirit cross into the realm of the dead. You. Are. A. Völva," he said slowly, emphasizing each word. "Völvas who served the mead of poetry brought me back to life when I was hanged dead on Yggdrasil."

I pushed his warm mouth away. The breath that hit my wrist felt like scalding-hot steam, but it didn't hurt. In fact, it was alluring. The dilapidated building spun around me.

"What's a völva?"

"Someone who can get help from those who are either no longer here or not here yet. Hejd—the mother of all völvas—saw you long ago. You have always belonged to the past, but now it also belongs to you."

"What can I get help to do?" I asked, but I had trouble controlling my voice.

Svidur shrugged. "I don't know yet, but even I—the king of the gods—need the völvas' help from time to time."

"And völvas can revive gods with the mead of poetry?" I asked, dazed.

"Tsk, tsk," replied Svidur. "Not gods. But I am of giant descent."

We stood at the entrance to the run-down building. Our faces turned toward Sverresborg. There was still a dull sound of bells, and behind them, crashing waves played like background music, just as on the west coast of Denmark. A faint smell of sulfur still hung in the air. Svidur inhaled slowly, as if he were tasting the air.

"People made offerings to me here in the swamp." He exhaled again. "Food, weapons . . ." his long tongue ran across his teeth, ". . . people."

"People tossed things and bodies down to you in the deadly waters?" My lower lip curved down. "Nice!"

"Did you meet it?" Svidur asked.

"The Midgard Serpent? Yep! It was really . . ." I searched for a suitable word.

Terrifying, nightmare-inducing.

"Big," I concluded.

"I moved it here from Midgard and put its tail in its mouth over a thousand years ago."

"Why? I thought the people who immigrated here worshipped you. Wasn't that kind of mean of you to throw the Midgard Serpent over here?"

He chuckled, and the sound swirled in my body.

"The sea is the portal to Udgard," he replied. "The Midgard Serpent encircles Hrafnheim and protects it from chaos."

"I don't think people perceive it as protection," I said. "And in any case, it's not encircling anything anymore."

Svidur lowered his brows. The skin folded around his missing eye. For a second, I saw an endless abyss in the socket.

"What do you mean?" This sounded like a gust of wind.

"Its tail isn't in its mouth anymore, so it's not encircling anything."

Svidur seemed truly frightened by this information. "How . . . when . . . why did it let go?"

"The herders gave it a bull. They wanted to give me to it, too." With a shudder, I rubbed my wrists where they had been lashed to the pole. "Most likely to keep it from eating them."

"Either that, or they're bribing it with offerings," Svidur contemplated. "Bribing it to let go. Why would Ragnara do that?"

"No idea."

"So they can come in," he mumbled and stroked his long white beard.

Had his beard been white just a second ago?

"Who can come in?" I stammered.

"The forces of chaos." He let go of his beard with a sigh.

"But the Midgard Serpent," I started, "isn't it also part of the forces of chaos? Aren't they evil?"

"Evil?" Svidur tilted his head as if he didn't understand the word. "The forces of chaos simply *are*."

"What about you? Are you evil or good?"

Svidur let out a low, hoarse laugh that sounded very much like Od's. "These are new words."

"New? Good and evil are pretty well established."

"Not for me."

"Svidur," I whispered.

"Yes, little seer."

"My sister has a dream where I get killed in Kraghede Forest in Ravensted. Do you know if that happens? I mean, you are clairvoyant, aren't you?"

He put the tip of his thumb just above the bridge of my nose. A current hit me, and I wanted to pull away, but he grabbed the back of my head.

"I see that you see. I see that she sees. You see each other, and if I stand in the middle, if you will let me. You must worship me. None of us is anything without the others."

"Could you be a little more specific?" My voice sounded flat, as if I were speaking directly into his palm.

"Your sister has seen the future," Svidur said.

Well, shit! My death by Frank's hand in Kraghede Forest was on the schedule, even if I escaped him in Hrafnheim.

Svidur traced his thumb over the symbol Gustaf had drawn on my forehead several hours ago. His finger bumped across the dried lines. When he touched the drawing, it flaked off like golden powder.

I raised my hand. "I had totally forgotten about that."

Our fingers intertwined, and his nails followed my knuckles in a rather pleasant way.

"Mine," he whispered. The sound of his voice, the power of his eye, and the intoxicating scent of his breath made me lightheaded.

And then he was gone.

Unsteady on my legs, I wobbled back to the large room. Rorik's leg was nearly healed, though it was covered with a dark scab.

The iron-encased crystal was lit and warm, and clear light streamed out into the room. The emaciated people had gathered around it to take in its heat. Weeping sores on their limbs glittered in the light.

I sat down next to Rorik, who sat on the hard-packed earthen floor. I studied his wound. My finger traced the outline, and he shivered.

"You'll have a scar."

Svidur's touch was still like electricity in my hand, and I felt that I transferred some of this to Rorik. His hands twitched, but he kept them flat on the ground behind him.

"It doesn't matter."

"You saved my life. You nearly died because I was in danger." Suddenly it became very important for me to study my knees. I clasped my hands.

"Hey." Now his tattooed hand found my chin, and he forced me to look at him. "I'm doing this of my own free will."

My eyes burned. "It's all my fault. The girls back home were murdered. My father is dead. Monster is dead. Frank's grandson is being held captive. And . . ." I pushed myself to continue. "And you almost got eaten by the Midgard Serpent. Do you realize how crazy that is?"

Neither of us said anything for a while.

"What now?" He ran a hand through his white hair.

"I have to go to Sént." In my head, I pictured Rebecca's map. "It's right in the middle of Hrafnheim, right?"

Rorik shivered when I said *Hrafnheim*. "I'm worried about going to Sént. It's the most dangerous place in the realm."

"Are you more worried about Sént than about . . ." I gestured with my thumb over my shoulder, ". . . the Midgard Serpent?"

"Yes!" The word came out fast and sharp.

"I have to go there." I stopped and looked at Rorik. "Can I still count on you?"

I held my breath, hoping that whatever he wanted to change in his past was important enough for him to be willing to help me get to Sént.

"Yes. But it needs to be before Sverre's wedding," he said abruptly.

"Why?"

He didn't answer.

"The soldiers will be looking for us all day, so we should stay here for now." His eyes flicked toward the worst-off of the people. "Tomorrow night, we'll leave this place."

Just then, we were approached by the girl who had found us in the woods. Rorik looked from the dirty rags to an angular wound on her cheekbone. Her nose was a little crooked.

She sat down with a determined set to her mouth. "What are your names?"

"Anna and Rorik. And you?" Rorik was still looking at her with a frustrated expression.

"Merit." She carefully scratched her crooked nose. "The two little ones over there are my brothers."

A pair of half-starved boys slept in the clear light from Rorik's crystal. They were six or seven years old. It was hard to tell because they were so thin. One's leg was exposed and had visible sores, and a couple of fingers were missing from the other's hand.

"Is everyone sick?" I asked and looked around.

Rorik looked away, clearly nauseated by the disfigured children.

I suppressed the urge to smack him. He could at least be a little more discreet.

One of the small boys whimpered in his sleep, and Merit quickly stood to go comfort him.

Through the incomplete ceiling, I saw that the sky had begun to lighten.

"We might as well get a little sleep. I'll take first watch," I announced. Rorik looked like he was about to fall asleep, and he agreed.

That gave me about two hours before he would discover I was gone.

Dawn was breaking, but it was completely still. I was lucky I could recall the past and see where we had stepped, otherwise I would have sunk into the bottomless swamp.

I stopped when I reached a pool with two dead dogs, frozen solid, their heads under the icy surface. They must have drowned yesterday. A raven sat on the back of one of the corpses, pecking at it. The spine had broken through the skin and stood out with fresh red blood in the midst of the white frost. With a moan, I forced myself back onto solid ground.

No soldiers were searching the forest, and the alarm bells were silent. I breathed deeply in the cool morning air. The cold oxygen cleared my brain and gave me courage, which I desperately needed.

"You can come out now." I hoped my voice sounded calm.

The raven from before, or an identical bird, flapped through the dense underbrush, but aside from that, there was no reaction.

"Let's get this over with." Now I was annoyed.

From my back, footsteps approached. Someone stood close behind me, and I could hear their breathing. Without meaning to, I turned and flung my arms around Frank.

Whatever he had been expecting, this was not it, and he stiffened. Then he embraced me.

"I've missed you so much," I whispered.

He cried into my ear.

I looked up at him.

"Anna," he said. "What are you doing? I'm going to kill you."

CHAPTER 15

Frank's last word came out like a sob.

"Can you make up your mind? Are you overprotective or dangerous?" I forced myself to stay standing.

He held me at arm's length. In the light of the sunrise, I saw that his hair, which was normally coiffed with pomade, hung loosely past his ears. He fit right into this world with his brown wool clothing and leather armor over his jacket.

"No," he said. "I can't decide."

The hands that gripped my shoulders gave a little squeeze.

I looked at him without reproach. Even when Frank's fingers moved, I didn't budge. His strong hands closed around my throat. Ever so slowly, I felt my airways narrowing as I stared at him. A ringing in my ears told me I was about to lose consciousness, but I let him continue without a fight. The only thing I did was look at him, even as I felt my pulse pound behind my eyes.

A beam of pink light washed over us through the treetops. His grip weakened, and finally Frank let go entirely. His hands fell to his sides, as if they each weighed a ton. With a violent cough, I gulped down air and leaned against a tree trunk for support.

"I can't," Frank whispered.

I gasped for air and held up my index finger to signal I would answer in a moment.

Frank's legs gave out, and he landed on the frozen earth.

"He's going to die," he said. "They're going to kill Halfdan."

I knelt, mostly because I was still on the verge of fainting.

"He's up there," I rasped and sat heavily next to him. The cold seeped into my legs.

Frank lifted his head. "Where?"

I pointed toward Sverresborg.

Frank rose halfway to his feet. "Prince Sverre sent a child here?"

"He's under a spell," I croaked through my sore windpipe. "He's about five years old, and he appears to be sleeping. Gustaf put a stasis spell on him."

"How did you recognize him?"

I had to swallow a couple of times. Painful flames warmed my throat. "From your past."

Frank squinted. "Gustaf trained me to conceal my spirit."

"Maybe some of it gets through, if it's meaningful enough." I spoke quickly, even though every word caused me pain. "I know a way in, and I know where he is."

Frank narrowed his eyes. "Why, in all the worlds, would you want to help me?"

"You're my friend."

"I've tried to kill you. Repeatedly."

I cleared my throat. "I don't have a whole lot of friends."

He tried to say something, but I interjected.

"I knew you wouldn't do it, Frank."

"How? I didn't even know that myself."

I didn't blink, but I turned my eyes away when Frank kept staring at me.

"Or . . ." I said to the ground. "I was almost completely sure."

"You gambled."

I gave a thought to Serén's vision from Kraghede Forest and Svidur's statement that my sister had seen the future. If Frank killed me, it wouldn't happen here.

"Don't I always?"

"Halfdan looked to be okay?" Frank asked for the fourth time.

"Yes," I replied. "When was he kidnapped?"

"Four years ago."

"Four years?" I struggled to keep my voice low. "Have you been after me for four years?"

Frank didn't meet my eyes. "Yes."

This single word made the hairs on my arms stand up.

"Did you set fire to my foster family's house? Was that you?"

"I spent months tracking you down with that family. You kept slipping away from me, so I set the whole house on fire."

"There was a family in there, Frank. Other children." A chill ran down my spine at the thought that I had nearly been the cause of so many deaths.

Frank looked down at the ground. "Afterward, you were gone without a trace."

"I was sent to a group home because they thought I was the one who started the fire."

"That was lucky for you. I realized that you must be under a spell, so Gustaf gave me magic immunity. I wanted to be sure . . ." He was quiet for a moment. "I wanted to be sure it was only you I killed when I found you again."

"You killed others besides me. Tenna and Belinda."

Frank sighed. "I despise myself."

I glanced to the side, where Frank's overgrown, graying hair hid his face.

"Why you?" I asked, deciding not to mention the fire again. I walked sideways toward the cliff with my back pressed to the palisade wall.

"I was part of the resistance movement. I came here for love many years ago, but I was born in Denmark."

"You fought against Ragnara?" I asked instead of digging into Frank's love life.

"I fought alongside your mother. That was no lie. But Ragnara found me, and . . ." He lost his breath. "It cost me my family. Halfdan is all I have left."

Aha.

"She knew that, with my knowledge of both worlds, I was her best chance at finding you."

The words hung in the air, unanswered.

Frank didn't even hesitate as he climbed down the cliffside. He flexed his calloused fingers. I had never noticed that his hands looked like they could be a blacksmith's.

The beach resembled a war zone, with brown spatters, green and black scorch marks, and the two wrecked rafts. Fortunately, the sea was relatively still, so I knew the Midgard Serpent wasn't on its way. Nevertheless, I pressed myself up against the bottom of the cliff. Frank gave me a look.

"What are you doing?" he asked.

"Just stay as far back from the water as you can," I said.

We reached the small door, and with a sigh of relief, I noted that it was left as it had been the day before. No one was expected to come this way, and with the Midgard Serpent in mind, I could understand why.

Inside the low tunnel, I cast my clairvoyance out around me. It was becoming easier and easier for me to control, and even though I couldn't see anything with my eyes, I was able to navigate our way forward. With Frank's broad hand in mine, I pulled him along as I homed in on Halfdan's gentle aura.

Finally, we reached the room where Halfdan lay, and I pointed to the door with my other index finger to my lips. There was still no one in sight, and I cautiously grabbed the doorknob. The door was locked, but before I could consider how I would break it open, Frank's bootheel landed right next to the lock with a quiet but forceful kick. It was clearly not the first time he had broken open a door; shockingly enough, it swung open at once. Within seconds, he was standing over Halfdan's small body, stroking his hair.

I couldn't see the boy properly, as Frank stood between us. He stepped to the side so I could look down at Halfdan, and an exclamation stuck in my throat.

The fehu rune was drawn on his forehead.

"Oh no," I sighed. "They want to offer him to the Midgard Serpent."

The sound of boot-clad footsteps came from the hall outside. Frank turned his head toward the sound. Then he pushed his arm under Halfdan and went to lift him, but something jerked him back. The blanket that lay over the boy slid off, revealing he was chained to the bed.

Frank cursed and pulled an axe from his belt. It was twice the size of Auka. He hit the lock with the blunt edge, and the metal gave a sharp bang.

The footsteps were coming closer, and now we could also hear voices.

Frank swung again, sparks flying in all directions. The lock was almost open but needed one last whack. Frank had a look of pure concentration on his face. The voices stopped just outside the door. We covered Halfdan with the blanket and both hid behind the bed. The door opened, and soldiers walked in, apparently too preoccupied with their task to notice that the door had been tampered with.

"Is he ready?" asked a deep voice.

"He has the symbol." The other voice was a little higher.

A key ring jingled. Next to me, Frank squeezed the axe, and his eyes were closed as if he were trying to triangulate their location within the room. To me it just sounded like a mess of voices, but Frank opened his eyes and held up a hand to me, fingers stretching out to signify five people were in the room.

There was another jingle, and footsteps approached as Frank sat crouching. If he attacked, he had no chance of defeating all of them and getting out alive.

I pulled off both gloves and put my hand into my pocket, pulled out Freyja's tears, and pressed the pendant into Frank's hand.

"Find the witch called Védis. She can lift the spells," I whispered. *I hope.*

"What?" Frank mouthed.

I didn't reply before jumping out from my hiding place.

"Found it," I said, waving one glove. Then I looked innocently at the soldiers, who, like Gustaf, had green-and-blue scales tattooed across their cheeks and foreheads. There were no herders, and I was betting that none of the soldiers would recognize me.

I made a bad bet.

"What are you doing in here?" the one with the longest beard asked. It had a sprinkling of green in it.

"Are you a servant?" asked another. "I haven't seen you before."

"I just came here from Hibernia." Technically, this was not a lie.

"Ugh." I had come too close to the bearded one. "You're hideous."

His gaze slid off me, but he forced it back.

I said a silent thanks to Ben's spells.

"The boy isn't ready yet," I said.

"The herders told us to come get him."

"They told me he . . ." I looked at Halfdan, whose eyes looked lifelessly out into space. "Uh . . . he just needs to be bathed first."

One of the soldiers narrowed his eyes. "What does it matter? He's going into the sea."

I put on a look of outrage. "Do you want to disobey the herders' orders?"

He raised his hands. "No."

The green-bearded man was still looking at me.

"You guys get going," I said with as much confidence as I could muster. "I'll just—"

But I didn't get the chance to say what I was going to do.

The green-bearded man grabbed my wrist. "I have a better idea."

They left Halfdan there but dragged me away. I was worried about what would happen to me, but after all, Serén had seen that I wouldn't get hurt in Sverresborg.

Hey, wait!

Now that I thought about it, the point was that I wouldn't *die* here. That didn't tell me anything about what state I would be in after my visit. It was a little late to reach that conclusion.

"What do you want with her?" another of the soldiers asked.

"Just wait. I have good news," the man with the green beard replied. He had my wrists gathered in his sticky grip.

I tried to dig my feet into the ground, but he just picked me up when I resisted.

"I'm a witch," I tried. "Let me go or I'll cast a spell on you."

"Cast away," the man said. "Curse us, transfigure us."

They didn't believe me for a second.

I dug into the soldiers' pasts.

Afraid of dogs, trauma after nearly drowning . . . hmm . . . claustrophobia.

"I can send wild dogs after you, who will chase you down into the forest. But you'll fall into the swamp and drown like the mongrels I saw down there." I made eye contact with the claustrophobic man. "They were frozen in the ice and couldn't get away from the birds who started eating their flesh before they were even dead."

The men paled but carried me onward.

I moved my hands like I had seen Luna do. "I can make all that happen if you don't let me go."

One of them loosened his grip, and I had a flash of hope that they would let me go. Then we reached a room where another fifteen soldiers were gathered.

Shit!

"See what we found?" the one with the long beard said. They tossed me into the arms of another pair of soldiers, glad to be rid of me.

191

"What are we supposed to do with her?"

"Look at her."

I was held at arm's length. "Oof. She's repulsive."

"What about the ceremony with the boy?" someone asked.

"This is better. Look at her," the soldier repeated.

Someone grabbed my face.

"I know this mug." It was a short, wide man, who looked like he would be easier to jump over than to walk around. "I saw her in Konungsborg in Sént. She doesn't usually have this." He pointed to the scar running through my eyebrow.

Oh . . .

"But it's definitely Serén, daughter of Thora Baneblood."

. . . crap!

The squat man stroked my cheek and lifted a lock of my red hair. Instinctively, I tried to throw myself at him, but too many hands were holding me still.

"Ragnara will reward us if we bring her Thora's daughter. But before that, we can do with her what we will."

There were a few excited gasps.

"But you're right, she is disgusting. We'd better wash her," the one with the green beard said.

And so they got to work on me. Someone dumped ice-cold water over my head, and I gasped. The silver hand Hakim had given me was yanked off.

"This can be melted down," someone said.

Furious, I swore I would get my revenge, which was optimistic, to put it mildly. I was doused with cold water again. I tried to fight them, but they beat me. I kicked out indiscriminately and got a thwack on the nose that resulted in a nosebleed.

"Careful. Ragnara has to be able to recognize her."

I shook my head. I would get through this with my head held high. Held high and gushing blood, apparently.

Hands pawed at me, and one unbuttoned my pants.

Panic surged through me like a force of nature. I squirmed, trying to get free, but this only made the hands hold me tighter. I screamed like an animal.

I looked to a distant corner over the soldiers' heads for something I could hold on to.

A man stood watching the activities I found myself in the center of. His face was tilted, displaying neither disgust nor pleasure. Just neutral interest.

When I recognized him, the shock was more paralyzing than the ice-cold water.

"What are you doing here?" I writhed, but too many hands were holding me down. "You traitor."

CHAPTER 16

Elias crossed the room.

"Do you know her, Brewmaster?" one of the men asked, and they all paused.

I stood there, dripping wet, with blood gushing out of my nose. Elias studied his nails.

"Serén? I've never had the pleasure."

"The pleasure will be short-lived," the wide man said. "We're sending her to Ragnara as soon as we're done with her."

Elias's face was expressionless. He would be a fool to help me. But he *was* rather foolish at times. The look he gave me was so cold, my hope faded. Elias would always look out for Elias, first and foremost. Despite the warm blood running from my nose and down over my mouth, I was cold with fear. Elias stepped back with his hands raised.

"I don't mean to disturb you, if you have work to do." He turned and took a few steps.

I inhaled, preparing to expose him. I was going to shout that I knew him and that he knew me, and that on multiple occasions, I had seen him act directly against Ragnara. My mouth formed the words, but they didn't have a chance to come out before he walked back over to me and placed his hand over my lips.

"Unless you'll let me have the first turn with her."

One of the soldiers laughed. "There are more than a dozen girls here in the castle that you could have totally of their own free will. They fawn over you. Let us take care of Thora's daughter."

Elias looked at the soldier. "I want to have her before you." When no one said anything, he added: "I'll pay for it. Ten ampoules of laekna, twenty of opium from the other world. And wine."

It was still quiet.

". . . and a hundred pills of both Skoll and Hate," he added.

Most of the men agreed, and the rest didn't dare say anything. Elias started to haul me away, but the short, squat man stepped in front of us and put his hands on his nonexistent waist.

"You can do it here. And we want the payment up front."

"Don't you trust me?"

In response, the scarred soldier laughed and pulled his head back, creating a double chin.

Elias shrugged and opened his backpack. He pulled out several ampoules and a couple of bottles. He also fished out blue and pink pills in two transparent bags. While the soldiers drank, we stood in the middle of their circle. The room was large, and long tables ran along the stone walls on either side. A large iron serpent hung on the wall. Aside from that, there were no decorations.

I jutted my jaw out and looked directly at Elias.

"What are you thinking of doing?" Against my will, my voice came out thin.

"You know what I've always wanted."

"You psychopath."

"Brewmaster, were you planning to simply converse with the lady?" The scarred one took a sip from his horn.

"I just needed to prepare myself." Elias gave me a mocking half bow. "I'm ready now."

The hairs on the back of my neck stood up, and I searched for the most effective words that would turn the men against Elias. Maybe it would work if I said he had often helped me. But he saw me open my mouth to speak, and he quickly grabbed my hair, pulled my hair back, and kissed me. His lips forced mine apart, and he pulled my hair so painfully, I whimpered into his mouth. This bore no resemblance to the sincere kisses he had given me before.

I was so shocked, I went stiff. Then I bit his lip, and his blood mixed with my own. Elias's hands slid over my body, but even though his fingers were all over, it felt nothing like his usual touch.

"I hate y—"

Before I could finish the sentence, he once again closed my mouth with his own. He brought me down to the ground, while I wriggled and hit him as hard as I could. He was stronger than I thought, and the weight of his body pressed me against the cold stone floor.

He covered my body with his.

"Lie still," he whispered.

"No, I don't want to, you idiot." I kicked desperately and squirmed around beneath him.

"Just a little longer. Any minute now . . ." The rest of his words were drowned out by hacking coughs. One of the men collapsed. Then another, and another. In just a few seconds, all the men were writhing on the ground. Elias must have given them the same poison he gave the Savage. Bloody foam surrounded their mouths, and a deep-red fluid flowed from their eyes, ears, and noses.

My body stiffened beneath Elias, but my insides were a pit of horror.

Several of the soldiers pounded their limbs rhythmically against the floor. One had evidently abstained from the poisoned wine, and he stood completely still, looking around, eyes wide. With such speed that I almost couldn't follow the movement, Elias pulled out a knife and threw it. It hit the man's neck, and he toppled over, the terrified expression still on his face. Elias lowered his arm with resignation.

"Well, there goes that business opportunity for the next couple of hundred years."

I didn't need to ask if they were dead, because suddenly the room was devoid of auras apart from Elias's. I suppressed every impulse to scream loudly over the lifeless, bloodied men. Elias stood and reached out a hand to me.

I stood up without his help. My feet and fingers were almost completely numb.

"You're welcome! I just killed twenty men for your sake." Elias's voice was dry as he pulled the knife out of the soldier's neck.

"You missed one," I mumbled. My hands were shaking, so I clenched them into fists.

"Who?" Elias spun around.

"That one, in the corner."

The green-bearded man met my gaze. He took a few bewildered steps toward us, but walked through a chair along the way.

"My bad." I narrowed my eyes. "You're dead," I said hatefully and pointed to his body on the ground. The ghost collapsed, shaking, and it warmed me a little to watch his painful double death.

"It won't be long before the other soldiers discover that their comrades were killed." Elias wiped blood from his mouth and tenderly dabbed a finger in the spot where I had bitten him.

I walked over to the short, squat man's body and took Hakim's khamsa, which he had ripped from my neck. I tried to avoid the bloody foam, but it smeared on my hand, so I wiped it off on his shirt.

Elias followed me with his eyes. "What are you doing here?"

"I had to help Frank get his grandson back." I fastened the silver clasp behind my neck.

Elias did me the kindness of not commenting on how much I had risked to save a child I didn't even know. I could tell by looking at him what he would have done in my position. Or, more accurately, what he wouldn't have done.

"Isn't Frank trying to kill you?" he asked instead.

"Not anymore. I hope." I added this last bit quietly, as I recalled Serén's insistent vision from Kraghede Forest. My hand flew involuntarily to my sore neck.

Elias exhaled intensely. "You are the most reckless person I know. I can't believe I thought you were a survivor."

"Well, I am still alive."

"Thanks to whom?"

I turned toward him without answering his question.

"Have you considered how grateful Frank is that I helped him?" I waved my hands in a gesture that signaled I was ready, and that Elias should lead the way.

"Have you considered that you wouldn't have needed to make him happy if you hadn't let him out in the first place?" Elias walked out, and we hurried down the hall.

"Ragnara would have executed Frank."

"That was actually my point." Elias looked straight ahead. He stopped and pushed me against the wall as a group of soldiers came stamping down an intersecting hallway. My body twitched at once again being trapped under Elias.

"Yeah, but I don't want him to be executed," I whispered, mainly as a means of distracting myself. "Actually, I really want him on my side."

"Do you know where he is?"

"Nearby."

Elias didn't probe any further.

"What are you doing here?" I asked.

"At Sverresborg? I just got here a couple of hours ago, and I found the place turned upside down after Gustaf's death. I was surprised, to say the least, when I saw you."

"You didn't answer my question. Why are you here?"

"Business."

We made our way through the forest, and I shivered in the cold. My clothes were still wet from the soldiers dumping water on me. A snowstorm had moved in, which, on the plus side, made it hard for the soldiers to follow us, but on the other hand, it also made it difficult for us to move forward.

"Where are we going?" Elias took off his jacket and draped it over me. I had left my own coat in the collapsed building.

"The ruins." I pointed, but my bare hand trembled, and I quickly stuck my fingers in my armpits.

"The ruins? The old blót site was abandoned when Ragnara came to power. You can't get through the swamp without being swallowed up."

"I can," I said, teeth chattering.

Elias put his arm around me, and I was so cold, I let him do it. He walked with me into the bog, and I let my clairvoyance lead us while he held me upright.

"You lead the way. I have enough energy to get us both there," he whispered. "See, we make a good pair."

I ignored his comment.

Elias glanced sideways at me. "Why are you hiding among the lepers?"

"The soldiers can't get through the swamp." We had reached the dogs' corpses, but they appeared only as small mounds in the snow. "First we slept in a cave." I kept talking, mainly to keep warm. "My traveling companion found it. He loves caves."

A gust of wind blew me to the side, but Elias held me tighter.

"Why am I the one running from soldiers in a snowstorm, and not this traveling companion of yours?"

I tried to orient myself in the gray sea of snow. Even though it wasn't much past noon, it was dark beneath the heavy clouds spewing snow over us.

"He doesn't know I went to Sverresborg. Well, I guess he does now." I coughed discreetly.

"My guess is that he's just as outraged by your bullheadedness as the rest of us. Most likely mixed with sheer fascination." Elias added this last bit quietly.

"I hope Védis can lift the spells from Frank's grandson." I was no longer sure what I said aloud and what I simply thought. "She's no match for Ben, but I think she can remove Gustaf's magic."

"Védis?" Elias stopped in his tracks, and because we were intertwined, I stopped, too.

"I met her in Jorvik. I tried to get her to remove the curses Ben placed on me, but she couldn't."

We walked a bit farther. I concentrated on the past to follow Merit's tracks, and if Elias hadn't had his arms around me, I would have tripped several times. My body was shaking uncontrollably.

"They aren't curses, what you have," Elias said, and I suspected he was keeping the conversation going so I wouldn't collapse.

"They sure feel like it." I trembled.

"You wouldn't be alive without them."

"Are you taking the adults' side?" I furrowed my frozen brows.

"Hey." Elias laughed, taken aback. "I'm older than all of them."

"I don't actually think of you that way," I said.

"Then how do you think of me?" He held me a little closer.

I staggered on. My irritation with him gave me a tiny bit of fuel. When my knees began to buckle under me, Elias took more of my weight.

"So, have you found him?"

"Who?" I groaned.

"Varnar of the Bronze Forest."

Simply hearing his name was like a punch to the gut, but it warmed me up a little. "That's not why I came here."

"You can have multiple reasons."

"You would know all about that," I snapped.

"Do you long for Varnar, or have your thoughts moved to other things?"

Something made me hesitate.

Elias immediately interpreted my pause. "Someone new?"

"No, Elias." I sighed. "There's no one new."

"There's no reason not to mix fighting for your life with romance." Then he contemplated further. "It's not Hakim. You're not ready for him."

"Shut your—" I growled, but Elias kept talking.

"Me." He sighed. "We would be a fantastic pair—in every way—but you can't see how good we are together. Yet."

"—mouth!"

"Frank is too old; Mathias is too sweet; and Od is too . . . divine."

"If I were in love with someone—which I'm not—would you really want to hear about it? I mean . . ."

Surprisingly enough, Elias laughed again. "It would make me happy if you were swooning over someone else. That would mean I also have a chance. There's nothing more nauseating than unbreakable coupledom."

I wanted to snap back, but at that moment, the crumbling stone wall emerged from the chaos of snow. I stopped before we got all the way there.

"Would you have helped me if you didn't have to?"

Snowflakes collected in Elias's hair and turned it nearly white. "What do you think?"

"I don't know. That's why I'm asking."

He didn't answer but asked a question instead. "Would you have given me away if you were sure I wouldn't help you?"

"Yes," I replied without hesitation. "I would have told them that you've had several opportunities to deliver me to Ragnara but didn't."

For a second, Elias's face showed surprise, before returning to his usual cheeky expression. "Sometimes you're like looking in a mirror."

I wanted to say something else, but he turned and took long

strides toward the ruin. I staggered after him. In front of the building, he laid a hand on the wall.

"Ha-have you been here before?" I stammered through my chattering teeth.

He bowed his head, and for once, I could see his age. His back hunched slightly. The laughter of a child echoed in Elias's past.

"It was many years ago. Come." He walked through the collapsed entrance and stepped over a couple of fallen branches.

I walked into the central chamber. Rorik, who was pulling on his jacket, lowered his arms.

"Where have you been?" he yelled.

He had his pants on again, and I saw that a patch had been sewn over the burned hole.

"I was just . . . out."

Elias stepped into the room and looked around. His eyes lingered on the deformed figures.

Rorik stopped mid-motion. "Who are you?"

I fumbled for the wall to have something to support myself against. "The Brewmaster."

Elias held his fingers out toward the crystal thing, which shone and spread blessed waves of heat. He looked first at Rorik, then into the crystal.

Rorik turned back to me.

"What the hell were you doing?" His voice was piercing, but it slid into the background like a faint yapping. I could sense he was yelling, but I didn't hear it. My movements were clumsy as I rummaged in my bag. Rorik took it from me in annoyance, found some dry clothes, and threw it back to me. I tried to catch it, but it fluttered past me. Normally I had fast reflexes, but right now I could barely even lift my hands. I couldn't be bothered to ask the men to turn around, but they hurried to look away when I took my clothes off. I finally got my shirt changed, but when it came time for the pants, I fumbled with them. Elias, who apparently had already been looking anyway, stood behind me and carefully helped me pull them up.

Rorik studied me, too. "Where were you?"

Elias shook his head. "Not now."

My stiff, cold fingers still wouldn't obey. I let out an *ughh*. Only now did Rorik notice me struggling. He took a step toward me, but Elias stopped him by raising a hand.

"The soldiers tried to rape me," I said, still fighting with the buttons on my pants.

Rorik walked toward me again, now with an appalled expression. I jerked my head back as if I'd just been slapped. Right now it was impossible to keep other people's feelings out.

"In their minds, they had every right to do what they . . . almost . . . did," Elias said so quietly I could barely hear it.

"How can Ragnara put up with women being exploited like that?"

"I think," Elias said, "Ragnara accepts that some things have to be the way they are for her to maintain power."

"She'll do anything to stay on the throne," added Rorik.

"Hypocritical woman."

"Says the girl who set a murderer free," Elias said dryly.

"It's different with Frank."

"He killed two girls before he found his way to you."

"And you sold demiblood to Naut Kafnar, who killed three other girls," I snapped. Then I shouted in frustration: "I can't button my pants."

Elias moved in front of me.

"My hands don't work." Suddenly, I couldn't hold back the tears. Only now did I realize how much I was shaking.

"Come here." Elias tried to pull me close to him, but I instinctively jerked away with a violent jolt. My body remembered the multitude of brutal hands, including his.

He looked at me. "Even after all these years, I can still misjudge people's reactions."

"So I'm reacting wrong?"

Images of the Midgard Serpent and Gustaf's dangling legs swirled around in my head, and I saw a soldier's stiffened face smeared with red foam. Kian lay on the ground, and Hemming hung from the tree in Vindr Fen. I pressed my temples with both hands.

With his eyes still directed at me, Elias found the leather pouch that always hung around his neck. Then he looked down and dug through the ampoules, while I stood there sobbing with unbuttoned pants and wet, messy hair.

Outside, the wind whistled, and it sounded like a fierce animal.

Rorik came closer. I sensed that he wanted to help but didn't know how. The hobbled shadows had retreated as far away from us as they could without going out into the snowstorm. Elias found a vial and a syringe.

"Your reaction is completely normal. I was just led to believe that you were supernaturally strong."

"Sorry to disappoint you with my humanity." This was meant to be sarcastic, but my lower lip twisted down again.

"*Shhh.*" Elias reached out for me again, and this time, I didn't manage to pull away, although I tried. He held me close, and finally I relaxed in his arms. I inhaled his sweet, spicy scent.

"It's me who has become inhuman," he whispered. "I forget how a healthy mind functions."

He held me away from him, grabbed my arm, and rolled up my sleeve. In a routine manner, he pulled the liquid up into the syringe with one hand while he squeezed my upper arm with the other.

"What is that?" I sniffed.

"Something that'll help."

After a twinge of pain, calm flowed into my body. I suddenly didn't care about the soldiers' hands, the tortured men in Vindr Fen, or even Halfdan.

Elias pulled the needle out of my arm, and I sat down on the floor in front of him with a thud. The sound of heavy breathing made me even more relaxed. I realized that it was my own. My mother's coat was wrapped around me, but I had no idea who did it. I just stared into the shining crystal.

I got a glimpse of Elias's distant past. It stretched out like a tunnel behind him. He was sorting through piles of paper in an old library, brewing things in large vats, and bringing bottles to his mouth. In strange clothes, he walked across a field toward a hill that I recognized as Odinmont without the house on top. He met someone up there, a blurry figure I couldn't see properly. They shook hands.

My consciousness returned, and I blinked my eyes. My hair had dried in thick tufts, and I turned my head to look around.

Elias met my eyes gravely. He had been keeping an eye on me.

"What did you give me?" When I spoke, I felt how dry my mouth was.

"A break." He looked down and rubbed his own forearm through his shirt.

Rorik handed me a jug, which I drank greedily from. He squatted in front of me. "How are you feeling?" He tentatively took my hand.

I tried to speak, but my voice failed, so I took another sip. Finally, I could say something. "I'm as okay as I can be."

"We'll leave as soon as the snowstorm is over. Merit can help us get through the forest unseen." Rorik cleared his throat. "Isn't it best if we find somewhere you can rest? Hide? I can try to find your sister without you."

I turned my head, and it felt like I was dragging it through mud. "I have to keep going. I have to find Serén myself. Otherwise I can't help you with . . . whatever it is."

Now Rorik's voice was gentle. "I don't want to lose you."

With effort, I focused on him. "If Ragnara gets her way and kills me, Ragnarök will start, and you'll lose me anyway. And you'll lose everything else."

"What do you mean?"

I didn't answer.

He let go of me, cleared his throat, and ran his eagle-tattooed hand over the crumbling wall. "What about you?"

I rubbed my eyes with my knuckles. "By then I'll be long gone. I can't avoid my fate, and it's been foreseen that I'll be killed if I don't find my sister."

"Why doesn't Ragnara just kill Serén? That way you couldn't meet."

I sighed. I had thought quite a lot about that myself.

"Maybe something happened that Ragnara needs to change." The pain of the thought of my sister's death was about to pass, and Rorik looked at me indignantly. I held my hands in the air. "It's just a theory."

He leaned back on his heels. "What do we do?"

"Keep going," I said.

He squinted, like he did when he was thinking. "Why are you so sure this is your responsibility?"

I ran my fingers through my matted hair. "I'm not. But someone has to do something."

Elias interjected. "It *is* Anna's responsibility."

CHAPTER 17

We looked toward Elias.

His blue-gray eyes came to rest on me. "Are you ready for me to show you something?"

"Yes!" I sat up straight and pushed my hair out of my face.

"While you've been running around playing the heroine, I've been putting this time to good use."

"I won't dare guess what you consider to be good use," I replied.

His soft lips pulled back into a smile when he heard me sounding somewhat like my normal self. "The only good use of time there is. Studying." He pulled out a few papers. "The solution may be right here."

"Let's hear what shady formulas you've come up with."

Elias bit his lower lip. "They're poems."

"Poems?" I sat up a bit more and whimpered when a pain in my back let me know how long I'd been sitting hunched over. "Haven't we moved past the point of caring about poetry? You just killed more than twenty men." I stalled but pushed myself to continue. "I was hoping you had invented an explosive or a biological weapon."

Elias made a *tsk* sound. "This could be more powerful ammunition than anything explosive or poisonous."

"Okay." I shivered in my heavy coat. "What did you find out?"

Elias unfolded the papers. "I'm going to read some verses, mainly from 'Völuspá' but also from 'Hávamál.'"

My breathing quickened. "The last time I heard those, I threw up and passed out."

Elias opened his mouth, but a few seconds passed before he spoke. "I know. That's why I need you."

"Need?"

He continued quickly. "If you start to feel really bad, I'll stop."

"Hasn't she been through enough?" Rorik asked, scowling at Elias.

I rushed to interject. "I think I'll go through just a *little* more."

Elias suppressed a smile. Then he grew serious and waved the pages around. "I think only fragments of the poems are the real prophecy. With your power, you can sense the true words."

"What are you basing that on?"

"Hejd recited the prophecy to Od before she died."

"And Hejd is the clairvoyant Od knew over a thousand years ago?" I narrowed my eyes, trying to wrap my brain around this.

Elias nodded. "The mother of all völvas."

I twitched. Svidur had made me a völva, even though I wasn't quite sure what that entailed.

"Wasn't 'Völuspá' only written down hundreds of years after it was first recited?" I asked to coax some information out of Elias. I didn't want to reveal what Svidur had said.

"The poems were first written down after the turn of the millennium." He caught himself and paused. "The first millennium, that is."

I was silent as I considered Od's extreme age.

"Did Od make the poems cryptic to hide the truth?" I asked.

"Hejd recited the prophecy, but she didn't even understand it herself. I think Od was waiting until the right person could make sense of it," Elias said.

"Are you the right person?" I rubbed my lower back.

"No. You are."

"Ow." Another cold zap ran up my spine.

Elias recited.

The sun, the sibling
of the moon, from the south
Its right hand cast
Over heaven's rim;
No knowledge it had
where its home should be,
The moon knew not
What might it had,
The stars knew not
Where their stations were

I felt the weight of the words. My head spun, but it went away when Elias stopped.

Rorik listened to the words. "I've never heard that poem before."

"I'm certain it's about Serén, Anna, and her friends," Elias said.

"Luna and Mathias," I said. My heart felt a twinge, and I wondered at the feeling. I wasn't in the habit of missing anyone.

Elias continued reading, and I breathed in to fortify myself.

I saw for Baldr,
the bleeding god,
The son of Odin
his destiny set:
Famous and fair
in the lofty fields,
Full grown in strength
the mistletoe stood

"The gods' blood," I said when the shock of the words had passed. "It's Baldr's blood that Ragnara has. That's what she uses to stay immortal?"

"I mentioned that to Od," Elias said. "All he'll say is that he's made sure Ragnara can't get any more. So what she has now is her last portion. Once that's gone, and it works its way through her system, she'll be mortal again."

"Mortal," Rorik contemplated. "Then there's free access to the throne."

"There's more in the poem," Elias said.

"What?"

"In the lofty fields," he said.

"Odinmont."

Elias spoke slowly. "You must be the one Hejd saw."

"Not necessarily," I said. "Odinmont is ancient."

"Famous and fair," Elias said.

"She's both, that's clear," Rorik said with a smile. "But that doesn't mean—"

"—mistletoe," Elias interjected.

Rorik looked at him, uncomprehending, but I closed my eyes.

"Ahen Drualus," I whispered.

"*Drualus* is an old Gaelic word for the druids' herb. The same as mistletoe." Elias's voice hung in the air as I looked down. "Does that have something to do with you?"

In my mind's eye, I saw Varnar wrap his arms around me as he whispered that name in my ear. I inhaled shakily.

"There was someone who called me that once. He got it from an old song." A chill spread down the back of my neck when I remembered that Justine had said I would bear a name given in love. I composed myself and took a piece of paper. "What is this?"

"That's from 'Hávamál.' I think there may be verses that are also real prophecies."

I read a random verse.

If high on a tree
I see a hanged man swing;
So do I write and color the runes

That forth he fares,
And to me talks.

I tossed the paper aside, both because I felt the prophecy and because of the words.

"Well, that hasn't happened." Elias's voice trailed off when Rorik and I inhaled at the same time.

"Vindr Fen," Rorik exclaimed. "You spoke with the hanged man. With his spirit."

Elias read aloud from another poem.

When the eagle comes to the ancient lake,
He snaps and hangs his head;
So is a man in the midst of a throng,
Who few to speak for him finds.

The dilapidated room spun around me. I looked at Rorik's hand with its eagle tattoo. I'd met Svidur at the old lake in Hibernia, and he had few to speak for him. I moaned in frustration.

Elias read:

A hall she saw, far from the sun
On Nastrond it stands, and the doors face north;
Venom drops through the smoke-vent down,
For around the walls do serpents wind.

Again, my surroundings rotated. There was also something familiar about this poem.

"Serpents," I groaned. "As in the Midgard Serpent?"

Elias looked down at his papers. "No. This is supposed to be a description of Helheim."

I was breathless and could hardly speak. Hadn't I heard this poem before?

"But," Elias continued, "the Midgard Serpent is key, because it's a sign that Ragnarök is coming if he lets go of his tail. As I understand it, he has let go."

"Are there other signs of Ragnarök?" Rorik asked.

"Tons," Elias said. "But who knows what's mythology and what's true. For example, one legend says that Ragnarök will be heralded by Loki breaking free and leading the forces of chaos."

"Loki?"

"Keep reading," Elias said.

"No thanks." I scoffed. "We can't do anything about it anyway!"

"I think you can change fate," he said. "Prophecies are an educated guess at the future—not written in stone. Maybe when you know what the future could be, you can shape the present so that it affects what will happen." He pointed at the papers. "Read these two verses."

I looked down and reluctantly read them to myself.

She saw there wading through rivers wild
Treacherous men and murderous wolves,
and workers of ill with the wives of men.
There Nithhogg sucked the blood of the slain
And the wolf tore men;
Would you know yet more?

The giantess old in the Iron Forest sat,
In the east, and bore the brood of Fenrir;
Among these one in monster's guise
Was soon to swallow the moon from the sky

"That didn't happen." I gasped.

"Yet," Elias said.

The words spoke clearly to me, even though the events hadn't taken place.

Wolves.

I squeezed my eyes shut. The Iron Forest was where Monster's people lived. Raw grief hit me like a hammer. I had to repress the feeling, otherwise I would sink into misery.

The giant wolves descended from Fenrir.

Swallow the moon from the sky.

The thought knocked all the air out of me. One of them would swallow the moon.

Oh no! Luna!

"I'm not going with you," Elias said as he pulled me aside, away from the others.

The snow stopped late at night, so we couldn't leave until morning. Merit was eager to show us the way. She was talking with Rorik, both of them looking in our direction from time to time. Elias's curls moved slightly in the wind.

"Why aren't you coming with us?" I asked and ran my hand over the spot on my coat that had been eaten away by the Midgard Serpent's venom. Merit had sewn a patch over the hole without me asking her to. Something about the gesture touched me.

Elias pursed his full lips. "Do you want me by your side?"

I looked down at my boots.

"I'd prefer to avoid starting rumors that I'm helping Thora's daughter," he said.

I put my hands on my hips and raised my head. "Don't you think there will be rumors when people find out you killed all those soldiers at Sverresborg?"

"An unfortunate accident. They drank something they shouldn't have." Elias's gray-blue eyes looked up to the treetops.

"What about the one who got a knife to the throat?"

His teeth glinted, and for a second, Elias looked like a predator. "He had an unlucky fall."

"Very unlucky." I scoffed. "So you're bailing on us?"

"I think I've done my part." He took my hand.

I wanted to jerk it away, but he pressed a cold ampoule into my palm. I looked at it. "Is this laekna?"

Gently, he turned my hand over and closed my fingers over the ampoule. Like he did the first time we met, he raised my closed fist to his mouth. This time, though, he didn't have a mocking expression on his face. He was completely serious when he kissed the back of my hand. I let him do it, suppressed the urge to ask him to stay, and shoved the vial in my pocket.

"If you don't have anything pressing to attend to, could you do me a favor?"

"For you, I'll do anything."

I knew what was coming.

"But it'll cost you."

I sighed. "Of course. You never do anything for free."

Elias was about to say something, but my warning look stopped him. He jumped to the next sentence. "What can I do for you?"

"We found two men in the stone circle in Vindr Fen. Dead men. We didn't have time to do anything more than bury them in the sand under the tree. We placed stones on the graves to mark them. Would you go to Jorvik and tell their brother where they are? Their names were Kian and Hemming. They should probably be buried properly or burned or . . ." My voice faded.

Elias cocked his head and studied me without saying anything. I couldn't interpret his expression. Sympathy? Cynicism? Then he came right up to me.

"What do you want in return?" With a flat hand, I held him away.

Elias leaned his head closer toward mine.

"Forget the way I touched you at Sverresborg." He closed his eyes. "I wish you hadn't seen me like that."

"I can't forget that. And I can't figure out if you were playing a role up there, or if that's what you're doing now."

214

An ancient sadness crept over his face. "Then I'll just ask you for one thing."

"What?"

"Say my name." He opened his eyes again and looked at me. There was no ulterior motive in his gaze. Just a strange desperation.

"Nothing else? Just your name?"

He nodded.

"Elias." My voice went up at the end, questioningly.

He leaned in toward me. "Whisper it."

Uncomfortably, I forced myself to stand there. This was a small price to pay for notifying the men's family. I placed my mouth against his ear.

"Elias," I whispered.

His fingers stroked the back of my hand and sent small shivers through me, but before I could pull my hand back, Elias let go.

"Thank you." He bowed. "Almost everyone else calls me Brewmaster." He looked at me one last time. "Farewell, Anna."

Then he turned and disappeared between the trees.

I watched him, then turned toward Merit and Rorik. "Let's go."

Merit started walking into the forest. She had my scarf around her neck and Rorik's mittens on her hands. The terrain sloped downward, and through the tall trees I glimpsed open land. I settled into a quick pace between them.

"How long does it take to get to Sént?"

Rorik glanced sideways at me. "It takes four or five days, but we shouldn't get too close to Frón, since it's right up against the Iron Forest." He stopped.

"Why shouldn't we go near the Iron Forest?"

"The giant wolves are dangerous."

"I'm friends with Etunaz." A pain sliced into my stomach, so sharp I almost fell to my knees. "I was friends with him," I amended. "Even though he's . . . not in the Iron Forest, his wife and children are. They've heard about me."

"If you say so."

"Come on," Merit urged us along.

The snow thinned out the farther we went down the hill; we were nearing the tree line. We reached the edge of the forest. Merit insisted that she had chosen a route the soldiers weren't familiar with, but she kept looking back. Now she stopped and turned toward Rorik. The mitten traced across the thin, cracked skin on her cheek and landed on her crooked nose.

"I have a little more feeling in my face now," she said, surprised.

Rorik's eyes flashed over to me.

Merit's small head tilted slightly.

"Splittr can't be healed with medicine." She squinted in confusion. "Only with seid."

Rorik looked down silently at the snow-covered ground. The forest towered behind us, and before us lay a plain that sloped steeply down and ended at a hill. On the horizon, I glimpsed green leaves, and I was struck by a faintly warmer gust of wind. We were near the border of Særkland.

"On the other side of those hills, you'll reach one of Ragnara's forts. It's abandoned now. There aren't too many of Ragnara's soldiers in Særkland, and she doesn't even have any strongholds in Miklagard, but she has many spies." Merit pulled off the mittens and held them out to Rorik.

He shook his head and pushed her hands back. "You're a good scout."

Merit's mouth pulled into a crooked grin. "No one notices a little girl with splittr."

Rorik focused on her cheek, where previously a red, weeping area had taken on a normal skin color.

She laughed again and dashed into the trees, quick as a mouse.

"What is this place called?" I asked when we crossed the hill on the marsh that Merit had pointed us toward. In the distance, I spotted another hill, which was colored pink by the rising sun, now a couple of breadths above the horizon. We must be in some kind of valley. The air was moist and tasted stagnant. There was no sign of a fort, but standing stones were arranged in ovals. Many of the stones had toppled over, so the ovals were incomplete. The grass was short, as if it had been bitten down, and there were skeletons of horses, cows, and even dogs lying around. The bones cast long shadows in the morning sun.

"We're still in Svearike. Særkland's border is on the other side of the hill."

"Why is it so deserted here?" I asked, skirting around a cadaver. Its white ribs had been picked clean of every shred of flesh, but some skin still clung to the bones. "And why are there dead animals everywhere?"

Rorik contemplated a large skeleton. "I don't know. I've never been here before."

A heavy silence hung over the landscape. Not even birds or insects could be heard, even though reflective areas showed how marshy it was. I would have assumed the place would be a mecca for birds and toads, but everything was mired in frightening silence. We stopped in front of an enormous flat stone that stuck up straight from the ground. It rose at least three yards above us, and I squinted into the sunlight when I looked up toward its top.

"A stone doesn't land like this on its own," Rorik said with a flat hand against the megalith. He looked down at the ground where the bottom of the boulder was buried. "There must be as much under the ground as there is above it. Otherwise it wouldn't be able to hold itself upright."

"How did people get it to stand up like that without a crane?" I balked.

"What's a crane?"

"It's like a huge car with a grabber thing on it." An echo of the past vibrated up into my feet from the earth, and I squatted down and laid my hand on the short grass.

"A grabber?" Rorik studied me curiously.

"It looks like a big claw." I made a grabbing motion with my fingers. "But it's made out of iron."

"And what's a car?"

"A car?" I stopped moving my hand. "Forget it."

Suddenly, the orange morning light turned grayish, and I shivered. A large storm cloud was heading toward us, and winds that hadn't been there just seconds before now blew ominously. A single bolt of lightning flashed in the sky, followed by a thunderclap.

"Come," Rorik said. "We'd better find a cave."

I groaned. "I swear, if I get out of this alive, I'm never going in a cave again."

Rorik smiled crookedly and started walking up the hill at the end of the marsh. We climbed it as the black clouds glided toward us with more threatening flashes followed by rumbling. When we reached the top, we saw a large, round building in the middle of a flat area even swampier than where we'd just come from. There was more water than land here, and the building seemed to have been placed on the only patch of earth. The scrawny trees, some of which protruded directly out of the water, rustled with every gust of wind.

We ducked down in the grass and scouted for foes, but it appeared to be just as abandoned as the stones behind us. The building had a kind of moat, full of sharp stakes and spikes. Around it was a tall rampart. Leading up to the fort itself was a footbridge that ended with a large gate. It was open and banged in the wind.

Rorik studied the place with the look of a professional.

"This is military construction." He stood and walked over the hilltop.

When I didn't move to follow him, he waved me on. "There's no one here. Come on."

I flung my clairvoyance into the place. It was clearly empty, though I sensed human activity in the not-too-distant past.

I got up and tromped after Rorik as more lightning flashed. The air was now humming with electricity, and the mist gathered around us.

"We can seek shelter in there." Rorik walked toward the building.

"Is it safe?" My voice was skeptical. "We'll be trapped if someone comes."

Just then, another bolt of lightning came down, and soon after came the crash of thunder. We didn't even feel the rain fall. The mist just formed into drops.

Rorik looked over his shoulder with a teasing grin. "Of course, we could also look for a cave."

With a decisive motion, I waved my hands toward the footbridge.

"Lead the way." I looked around. "What is this place?"

Rorik was still walking in front.

"I had no idea it was here, but it looks like a totally average fort." He looked at Ragnara's branch-like rune, which was carved into a wooden plaque at the end of the bridge. "Normally these fortifications are placed like beads on a string along a wall. I've never seen one out in the middle of nowhere." Before he stepped onto the bridge, he turned around as if to make sure no one was waiting to ambush us. He mumbled to himself. "But it must protect something?"

Cautiously, we walked across the long wooden bridge toward the open gate, which was now swinging agitatedly. It, too, was adorned with Ragnara's rune, which stood out darkly with charred edges. The wind had picked up, sometimes shrieking in a falsetto when it met resistance. Another flash of light and a crash made us run, the footbridge creaking beneath us. The wood of the guardrail shone with oil, and the railing had been repaired recently.

Rorik studied the bridge. "This is weird. Really weird." He stopped and looked over the railing, down into the trench with its many sharp spikes. Then he focused his attention on the rampart that surrounded both the moat and the fort. "This doesn't look like anything I've seen before."

"It looks like Sverresborg, just in a smaller version," I said, passing him.

Rorik stayed back, still looking ponderously at the exterior rampart, while I hurried inside as large raindrops fell. I passed through the rattling gate and stepped out of the rain.

Pitch black. The violent flashes from outside illuminated the building sporadically. I got the impression of being in one large, round room, and rows of sticks followed the wall all the way around.

"What—" I began but was interrupted by a loud crunch when I stepped on something. I looked down but couldn't see anything.

More footsteps crunched behind me, and my heart flew into my throat before I realized it was only Rorik. He hadn't noticed the strange ground covering.

"If you're going to keep enemies out, the moat should be outside the rampart. But here, the rampart is on the outside, and the moat is inside. It makes no sense."

The back of my neck began to prickle.

A bolt of lightning illuminated the room, and I looked down.

Eggshells? Enormous eggshells.

But the lightning was soon gone. Something rustled near us. Even though my clairvoyance couldn't detect anyone apart from Rorik, there was something moving in the dark. Rorik's large hand found my arm and pushed me behind him.

"I should have seen it," he said as he shoved us back toward the doorway.

Beneath us, the shells were crushed.

"What should you have seen?" I whispered, but it was muffled by the return of the scratching noise, after which a thunderclap drowned out my words completely. A flicker lit up the hall, and I saw an oval shape next to us. It was almost as tall as me, and it was swaying. It resembled the stones in the field on the other side of the hill, but this one sat completely upright, was mottled gray and black, and was rocking uncontrollably.

"Rorik?" I whispered. "What should you have seen?"

His eyes had also landed on the quivering egg.

"That this place wasn't built to keep anything out." He stopped as another crash of thunder sounded, and the egg began to crack. "It was built to keep something in."

CHAPTER 18

We backed up toward the exit, staring at the trembling egg. Long cracks tore down the hard shell. Rorik drew Tilarids and pointed it at the egg. Whereas I was moving away, he moved forward, shifting the sword from one hand to the other to ready himself for whatever was inside the egg.

The rain pounded noisily on the roof, lightning flashes were followed by loud crashes of thunder, and I wasn't sure if it was more dangerous to be inside or out. When a particularly intense bolt of lightning ripped through the sky, the egg's deepest cracks grew longer, and a translucent, sticky fluid bubbled out. It smelled rotten. Another flash revealed that the liquid was a dirty green. With a crack and a swoosh, the egg broke in two. A creature flapped around in the half shell that had rolled onto the ground, resembling a horror-movie version of an Easter egg. Small brown arms with limp, transparent, leathery skin reached out, and something howled like a bizarre-sounding baby.

Tilarids was right against the edge of the eggshell, and Rorik prepared to attack. He held the sword's hilt with both hands and pulled his arms back. Just then, a head peered up. Orange eyes blinked, and the pupils bounced around, as if the creature was having trouble focusing. The animal was slimy and brown, with a grayish-white spot around its left eye. It yawned, and a sour smell escaped from between its gums, reaching me several yards away. It called out again as it twisted its long neck.

Rorik stopped mid-motion.

"A fingalk," I said, breathless. "Is it a baby?" I looked at the many shells on the floor. "This looks like a poultry farm."

"I've never heard of a poultry farm," Rorik said slowly, without taking his eyes off the little creature.

"There must have been hundreds of them here." I stopped in my tracks. "Oh shit! Do you think Ragnara's created a fingalk army? That's why all the grass was eaten down by the standing stones."

The fingalk finally gained control of its orange eyes and focused first on me, then on Rorik, who stood frozen with Tilarids in his hands. The little fingalk emitted a mysterious sound and reached out to Rorik.

"Baaahh."

Rorik relaxed a little and started to lower his hands, but Tilarids took that opportunity to jerk toward the newborn creature's long neck. With effort, Rorik regained control of the weapon. If the sword had a voice, it would have protested loudly.

The fingalk stared at Rorik.

"Hey," I said. "You do understand what this is, don't you?"

Even though Rorik's back was toward me, I could sense he was gathering his courage. Again, he lifted the sword toward the baby fingalk. The small creature jumped up from its shell but slipped in green slime, and it fell right on its face on the ground. The cry that came from its broad mouth, which resembled an open wound, was heartrending. A couple of times, Rorik prepared to swing the sword, but he finally lowered it.

"We should just go," he said and turned away from the out-stretched arms. He took long strides toward the open gate. Outside, the rain was still hammering down, but evidently, Rorik found that more appealing than staying inside with the mini fingalk. It got to its feet and staggered after him.

"We can't just leave it here." I hopped backward when it came closer. Its head came up to my thigh, and the smell that came with it was nauseating.

Rorik lit the crystal and studied the fingalk with a wrinkled nose. "It's disgusting."

"That's what people say about me," I said quietly.

Rorik walked faster, but the animal ran after him.

"No," he told it. "Stay here."

It stopped and moved its lips like a fish out of water. "Baaah?"

I looked around the empty room.

"It can't stay here. It'll die of hunger, and," I looked at the multitude of empty shells and a couple of desiccated fingalk skeletons, "and loneliness." With considerable effort, I found the words. "It would be more humane to kill it now."

With its head cocked, its orange eyes studied me, and I hoped it didn't understand what I had said. The creature once again began to waddle toward Rorik with its long arms spread out. The flaps of skin, which must have once served as wings for its ancestors, were nearly transparent.

"Should I do it?" I asked. I most definitely didn't want to, but I reached back for Auka.

Rorik looked at me gratefully. The fingalk also stood still and stared at Rorik, unblinking. I raised Auka toward it, and now it looked at me instead.

"Grrriiiik," it said, and it jumped, as if frightened by its own voice.

I pulled my arm back but hesitated. Then I raised my arm even higher as I gathered my willpower. Before I could do anything, Rorik stepped between us.

"We have to come up with something." He held a hand between the fingalk and Auka.

I lowered the axe, half-irritated, half-relieved. The fingalk moved its mouth, searching. Finally, its gums latched on to Rorik's jacket, which it munched on with gusto.

"Stop it. Shoo." He tried to brush it away, but it only gnawed harder. "Get it off me."

I found the last piece of bread in my bag and waved it at the animal. "Here."

Its large nostrils flared, and a funnel-shaped ear turned in my direction.

It snatched the bread and swallowed it while Rorik shook out the drool-soaked corner of his jacket. In its excitement, the little creature got the food stuck in its throat and coughed. Instinctively, I thumped it on the back, and the half-dissolved piece of bread came up with a retching sound and plopped onto my boots. I jumped back and shook my feet. The fingalk wagged its scaly tail and slurped down the soggy bread.

"What are you doing? We don't have time to . . ." I didn't finish my sentence because the fingalk had already finished eating and was looking up at me. It wagged its entire ugly body and nestled up against me.

"You mean, what are *we* doing," Rorik corrected.

My hands hovered over the fingalk as its long brown arms wrapped around my legs. Finally, my palms came to rest on its tufted head, and it rubbed its cheek up against my thigh. "What's going on with it?" I asked.

"I think," Rorik said, "it believes we're its parents."

We stayed in the hall until the rain died down. The fingalk curled up and fell asleep with its head on Rorik's leg and its tail curled around my boot. It snored with its wide mouth open. Every time it exhaled, it emitted a horrible smell.

"Should we sneak away? Maybe it won't notice." I felt bad even suggesting it.

Rorik tried to formulate his thoughts as he looked at the sleeping creature. "We can't bring it with us. That's completely idiotic."

Neither of us moved.

"The rain stopped," Rorik said, looking forward. "We should leave now while it's asleep."

Again, we sat in silence and looked at the animal. It rolled over onto its back and kicked its legs in the air.

"Baaah," it laughed.

"I wonder if it's dreaming," I said.

It chuckled again in its sleep.

"Yeah," Rorik said. "It seems like it."

I stood up. With heavy steps, I walked toward the gate, but I looked back. Rorik carefully lifted the fingalk's head from his thigh. It reached out and whimpered in its sleep. Rorik stuck part of a shell in its hand, which it squeezed, and then it calmed down. He opened his bag.

"This is the last of the food I have." He placed some dried meat and bread next to it and looked up at me. "What if it gets stuck in its throat again?"

I rolled my eyes.

"Come on." When he didn't move, I added: "I feel really bad about this, too, but we have no choice."

Together, we walked toward the exit. The wooden bridge creaked beneath us, and my stomach was full of hard knots that kept growing and growing. Rorik's face was nearly as white as his hair.

"It just feels wrong to leave it," Rorik said.

"Don't say that word," I snapped. "I hate that word."

"Wrong?"

"No. Leave."

We trudged on in silence. Even though it had stopped raining, the air hadn't cleared up. Moist air filled my lungs, and I looked across the flat plain below that ended in a deciduous forest.

We reached the bottom of the hill, a good distance from the empty fort. The almost empty fort. There was a meadow, where the wet grass reached my shoulder. Normally, I would have balked at having to walk through the sodden brush, but right now, I welcomed the distraction of ducking between raindrops and sharp blades of grass.

"Baaaaahh," came a sound when we were in the middle of the field.

Rorik turned around and looked toward the castle.

"Griiiik." We heard squelching stomps, and tall grass was shoved to one side. Only the tops of the plants quivered, but something was clearly moving toward us. Something alive. Out of the vegetation, the little fingalk threw itself at us. It howled, and my heart leapt at the sight of it. Without thinking, I spread out my arms, and it jumped into my embrace. A sour smell of spoiled meat permeated the air, but I didn't care.

"Oh, Finn," I said, on the verge of tears. "Finn."

"What are you doing?" Rorik's tone was anything but angry.

"What do you mean?" I concealed a shaky breath with a cough. "I didn't do anything."

Rorik's hand found the back of the fingalk's neck, and he squeezed it gently. "You gave him a name. Now we can't leave him."

Finn stayed behind us, and he ate everything we came upon. Frogs, insects, grass, and leaves. He was insatiable, and he grew at lightning speed. I could practically see him getting bigger from one hour to the next. The first night, we slept in a cave, and he lay between us and the exit. When he looked at us, his eyes were orange, the color of flames, but when he sensed danger, they turned deep red.

At one point, when we were on the move again the next day, he disappeared. We had started to search frantically when a growl reached us from the bushes. We fought our way through and found Finn crouched with a dead deer in his mouth. He had eaten half of it, and he wagged his tail when he saw us. With his snout, he nudged the meat toward Rorik, who shrugged.

"Dinner?" he asked over his shoulder, running his fingers through his white hair with a smile.

Shortly after, when we had found a cave where we could spend the night, the cooking pot hung over Rorik's crystal, full of bubbling venison stew.

"Can we be sure he'll stay away from people?" I muttered.

Rorik looked up from the crystal.

"Finn," he said. "Do you understand what I say?"

Finn cocked his head and slowly moved it up and down.

"You cannot eat people," he said. "You can't even harm people."

The fingalk flapped its arms angrily as if to refute him. Its wings had gotten thicker and had taken on a darker brown hue.

"Unless one of us says so," I added.

Finn pursed his broad lips in an expression I chose to interpret as acceptance.

The next morning, Rorik trained with Finn, who now stood a head taller than him. Rorik threw a bone from a dead wild boar, and the fingalk fetched it and brought it back to him, scaly tail wagging and eyes pale orange. Rorik gave him a friendly swat. Finn reciprocated by turning around and sweeping his tail toward Rorik's feet. He laughed and hopped over the tail. Then Rorik whipped his body around while simultaneously lunging out with clenched fists.

"Let me see that again," I said and walked down the hill toward them.

Rorik looked up.

"This move?" He copied what he had just done. "I came up with it myself. I don't think anyone else can do it just like that."

"Let me try." I reached out with my clairvoyance and captured the movement.

Rorik widened his eyes. "No one's ever been able to do that before. Not even Varnar, back when he was the leader of the Varangian Guard."

I quickly looked down, and even though I hardly caught anything from Rorik, jealousy flowed from him. It didn't surprise me.

It was almost impossible to be a warrior and not feel jealous of Varnar's abilities.

I never thought I would be glad to see the vision in Kraghede Forest again, but that night, I closed my eyes in one of Rorik's many caves and opened them again among tree trunks glistening with frost. I glimpsed black fields topped with silver snow and smelled spruce and moss. The air itself crackled with cold, and right in front of me, the little birch tree stood, upright and resilient.

No Frank. No me with a bloody rune on my back. Just the cold of winter and the feeling you get right around the winter solstice. It's the feeling of being submerged in the deepest part of the ocean, with a long, long way back up to the surface.

I exhaled, and my breath looked like smoke. Maybe I really had averted my murder by freeing Halfdan.

"Serén," I called.

At first there was no reply. Just the tops of the trees grating against one another, and a car speeding along Kraghede Road just beyond the forest.

"Serén," I called again.

"Anna."

I let out a sigh of relief when I spotted my sister. I saw her from behind, and her long red hair reached almost to her waist. She stood bent over, her arms wrapped around herself, like she was trying to give herself a hug.

I ran over to her.

"You're okay, you're . . . What's wrong?" I grabbed her by the shoulder and turned her around. A scream forced its way out of my mouth.

"What happened?"

Serén stared straight ahead. She looked directly at me, but her eyes didn't register me. They were milky white.

"Anna?" She squeezed my hands, and her voice was terrified and miserable. I slung my arms around her. Even though it was a dream, she felt real.

Her long fingers felt their way up my arms, over my hair, and landed on my cheeks.

"What happened?" I whispered.

"Magic," whispered Serén. "Ragnara's people have done something to my eyes so I can't see."

My hand waved in front of her face, but she didn't even move her head back.

"I can't see," she repeated.

"I know."

"No, I can't see what happens. In the future."

"Ragnara took your power? But you're here. This is a kind of clairvoyance, too."

Her red brows furrowed. "I've been trying to reach you for days, but I hit a wall every time I called. Suddenly there's a way through."

"What happened?"

She didn't want to answer.

"Did you do something?" I pressed.

"I was desperate," she whimpered. "I would rather have sawed my arms off than lose my clairvoyance."

"Serén!" Even though she stood as defenseless as a baby bird, I couldn't keep the crabby edge out of my voice.

"I asked the All-Father for help," she whispered. "He promised to make me a völva. He said it would bring the two of us closer together."

"What did he want in return?"

Serén sounded a little confused. "I just have to worship him."

Ahhhh.

"So are you a völva now?"

"Not yet. I have to make an offering."

I leaned my head back.

"Svidur!" Then I corrected myself. "All-Father."

Rustling leaves swayed behind me, and I had no doubt who was coming.

"My soldiers," he said. "My shield maidens, my . . ." He appeared in front of us.

Serén turned her head toward the sound.

Svidur stood in front of her and held her face, which almost disappeared in his large hands.

"Little bird," he whispered. "What have they done to you?" He leaned forward and kissed her on the mouth.

"Cut it out," I exclaimed and tried to pry them apart, but I might as well have been trying to move mountains.

The kiss went on for a long time, as if he were sucking something out of Serén. When he pulled back, the gray haze slid away from her eyes.

"I can see again," she breathed, widening her eyes when she looked directly into Svidur's face. "I can . . ." She squeezed her eyes shut and fumbled around. "The future is there, but it's smudged and chaotic."

"That has more to do with the future than with your powers." Svidur sighed. His one eye blinked knowingly.

"What did you do?" I was still mad that he had kissed my sister.

"It may well be that Ragnara rules over magical powers, but I am the greatest magician." His hand slid behind Serén's neck.

"If Ragnara does it again, call me." He leaned forward as if to kiss her again.

"She has a girlfriend, you know," I said and pushed him away. It sounded ridiculous when I said it.

Svidur laughed. The hoarse laugh sounded like Od's.

"Why did you help her?" I asked tersely.

"I'm helping you both," he said. "You're in grave danger. Time is working against you—and I mean that quite literally—but you're mine."

"Your . . . what?"

He whispered:

Odin rode without joy
on the eight-legged one
where Baldr's pyre was built
Valkyries and ravens accompanied him
Victorious, happy again

His index fingers touched our foreheads.

"Muninn." He pressed his rough finger into my skin, and for a second, it felt like he had reached all the way into my brain. "Memory. The past."

Next to me, Serén moaned, so he must have done the same thing to her.

"Huginn," he whispered. "Thought. The future."

He released us. His arms spread out, and we were encircled in his embrace.

I looked up, and he towered over us.

"You are mine," he said again. "I gave you gifts, and you must give me gifts in return." He paused briefly. "You are my ravens."

The word echoed a few times, and then he was gone.

We were left in the woods, breathing heavily. Serén's hands were still raised in an embrace, while my palms were out as if pushing back against Svidur's chest.

CHAPTER 19

The weather was much milder in Særkland, and the land stretched out farther than in the other kingdoms we had traveled through. Some places were dry and barren, others were lush with large forests, and others were fields, currently black expanses of soil with only a tiny hint of green on top.

With only one or two days to Sént, I urged us along with the feeling that a large clock was ticking far too quickly. Maybe it was just the constant racing of my heart that made me feel that way.

Something kept tickling the back of my neck as we walked down a road in the morning sun. I slapped it, and it went away, only to come back soon after. When this had happened a few times, I heard a laugh and whipped around. Rorik giggled. Even Finn seemed amused. Rorik held a long, thin branch in his hand. He had apparently been using it to tap me on the neck.

"Hey," I shouted, but I couldn't help but smile when both the fingalk and the warrior burst out laughing.

"You are so childish," I scolded. I playfully hit Rorik on the shoulder with my fist. He hid behind Finn, so my next punch hit the fingalk on the chest instead.

I tried again to strike Rorik, but he held on to Finn and used him as a shield. Finn clapped his brown hands with their razor-sharp claws together in delight.

I let out a grunt and rolled my eyes, then strode away from them. "We don't have time for this," I yelled over my shoulder. But out of sight of the others, I smiled to myself.

"We'll arrive in Ván tomorrow, right?" I asked. "Then we'll be in Sént—in what? One and a half, two days?"

"Yes," replied Rorik. "There's plenty of time before the wedding. We should definitely be able to find her."

I walked in front of him and turned around, so I was walking backward. "Why do you want to get there before the wedding? Does it have something to do with the thing you want to change?"

Rorik walked around me. "I'll tell you when the time comes."

I got a strange feeling. "Do you know them? The prince and the woman he's going to marry?"

Rorik wouldn't answer.

"Do you know Ingeborg?" I caught up to him and walked alongside him with long strides.

Rorik rolled his eyes. "No, Anna. I don't know them."

"Does it have to do with the throne being up for grabs if Ragnara dies?"

Rorik stumbled as if I had tripped him.

"What are you talking about?" He turned toward me.

"I'm just asking. I have no clue about how anything works in this world."

"Of course it doesn't have anything to do with that." He started again and walked away from me.

Hmmm.

We walked for a while without saying anything, while Finn looked nervously from Rorik to me.

"It's more fertile here than the other places I've been," I said in an attempt at reconciliation. I knew it calmed Rorik down to talk about Hrafnheim.

"Særkland supplies crops to the rest of the kingdoms," Rorik said. "Ragnara distributes them, so no one goes hungry."

I coughed. "Aren't the lepers at Sverresborg evidence against that?"

Rorik's shoulders shot up. "I didn't know they were there. I thought everyone got what they needed. That's what the traveling skalds say."

I did him the favor of not commenting further on this. "Is every kingdom in Hrafnheim responsible for something different?"

He turned around and hissed, "You don't even notice that you're doing it, do you?"

"What am I doing?" I asked, stunned.

"You keep saying the old name. It's incredibly dangerous. No one is allowed to use it." Rorik's tattooed hand found my arm and squeezed. He was clearly still annoyed that I had asked about the wedding, as he had never corrected me when I'd said *Hrafnheim* before.

"Hey. Let go."

Finn came rushing up to us, clearly uncertain as to which of us he should help.

"Hrafnheim?" I tried to pull my arm back. "Surely I can say it when it's just you?"

Finally, Rorik let go of me. "This isn't the ravens' home any-more. You should never say that name. You can't trust anyone." I was reminded that Varnar had told me the same thing. "If Ragnara's people hear it, they'll kill you on the spot." He walked ahead of me with long strides, while the fingalk nudged me with his forehead.

Late in the afternoon, we encountered a small group of people walking toward us on the road. There was no time to hide.

Rorik stopped and turned his back to them.

"Put your scarf on," he commanded.

I looked down at the piece of green cloth hanging around my neck. "I already have it on."

"Around your head," he said.

"What?"

He grabbed it and raised it up over my head, leaning in close to me.

I stood completely still as he held on to me.

"Sorry about before," he whispered. "I let my feelings get the better of me."

I didn't reply, but my eyes followed his fingers as they carefully tucked red tendrils up under the fabric.

"It doesn't look weird for me to be wearing a scarf?"

"We're in Særkland. It's totally normal here."

I didn't have time to figure out what that had to do with anything before the party reached us. There were two men and three women.

"Stay quiet," Rorik admonished both me and Finn, pointing a tattooed finger at each of us. Then he shoved his hands in his pockets and turned back to face the people.

"Hello," they said and smiled. "Anfarwol."

The wish for Ragnara's immortality was repeated by everyone like a strange echo, and I forced myself to mumble it, too.

"Anfarwol," Rorik replied. The word sounded different coming out of his mouth than how he normally spoke. Or maybe it was actually me he spoke differently to. He pushed Finn behind him, which was pointless, since the fingalk was a head taller than him anyway.

"Where are you heading?" asked a man in a moss-green hat. The hat looked like something I had seen in one of Mathias's fashion magazines back in Ravensted.

"Miklagard," lied Rorik. "And you?"

"Ripa," answered one of the women. She wore a thick wool dress that looked like what I'd seen people wearing in Jorvik. She leaned forward and looked over Rorik's shoulder at Finn, who followed the conversation with a curious expression.

I realized that he had never seen humans besides me and Rorik.

"A fingalk," she said.

"Are you performers?" asked the man with the green hat. He pointed at the other man, who looked different from the rest of his companions. He wore leather pants and had long blond hair, half of which was gathered in the middle of his head, and his neck and hands were covered in tattoos. "We met this skald a couple of days ago. He knows a lot about what's happened in Freiheim."

Rorik and the skald looked at each other. I noticed Rorik kept his eagle-tattooed hand buried in his pocket.

"We're not performers," Rorik said, and paused, surely trying to come up with a plausible explanation. We were dressed in clothes from Hibernia, with patches over the holes caused by the Midgard Serpent's venom. On top of that, we had a fingalk with us. Even I, who was relatively clueless about this world, could see we were an odd bunch. "They've started selling tame fingalks in Miklagard," Rorik said. "This one's going to market."

Finn let out an unhappy squeak.

"How droll." The woman who had spoken before laughed. "It's as if it understands us." She looked at Finn with fascination.

"He's tame," Rorik hastened to add. "He won't hurt anyone."

"A tame fingalk." She put her hands on her hips. "That's just fantastic."

"Yes, yes." Rorik nodded. "Well, have a safe journey to Ripa." The words came out sharply, and he walked past them. Discreetly, he grabbed my sleeve and pulled me along. "Ragnara's anfarwol," he said over his shoulder.

"Let's set up camp together," the skald from behind us said. "It'll be dark soon, and I've heard there are rebels in the woods. They're not just staying in Haraldsborg anymore."

Rorik stopped.

"Good idea." This sounded more like a curse than an agreement.

"I would rather keep going tonight," I whispered, but Rorik shook his head in warning.

A little later, we all sat around a bonfire.

237

Rorik kept the crystal out of sight.

The people had come from an area just west of Sverresborg, but they were heading to Ripa—which was apparently somewhat more prosperous—to work from spring until late summer.

Rorik paid them for a little food, and both Finn and I tore into the bread and dried berries. We had more or less been living off Finn's kills for the past few days.

"Is there anything to report from Hibernia?" the man with the green hat asked.

"Nah." Rorik bit off a piece of bread. "It's the same. Wind, cold, and sheep. Is there news from Svearike?"

The woman, who was still looking curiously at Finn, leaned toward Rorik. "The magician from Sverresborg died."

"Oh." Rorik made an effort to sound surprised. "How?"

The other woman interjected. She had long brown hair gathered in a braid that hung over her shoulder.

"We don't know. Some say he was attacked by rebels, but that can't be right. He could easily overpower them, unless they can also do magic. There's also a rumor," she laughed dismissively, "that Jörmungandr ate him. But that has to be made up."

I kept my eyes trained on my clay cup full of warm juice.

Rorik hurried to change the subject. "What about the rest of the realm?"

The man with the hat pointed at the skald, who hadn't said anything since inviting us to spend the night with them. "He knows a lot more than we do."

Rorik looked at the skald inquiringly. "Any news?"

The skald set down his bowl. He had a half-moon tattooed on his throat.

"It costs four copper coins," he drawled. His accent was different from any I had heard before.

The other woman, who had kept quiet so far, laughed. "He says that every time we ask. We don't have the means to pay."

238

Rorik bit his lip. He still held his eagle-adorned hand hidden in the shadow of his leg. Then he dug in his pocket and pulled out a couple of coins.

They held each other's gaze until Rorik, with his un-tattooed hand, dumped the money into the skald's palm.

The skald looked at the coins, and his lips moved as he counted them.

I resisted the urge to roll my eyes. How hard could it be to count to four?

The skald wiped his mouth on his sleeve and dropped the copper into his breast pocket. Then he stood, and I felt like someone had turned on a TV.

"To honor Ragnara highly as the eternal leader of Freiheim is an expression of noble sentiment and a desire common to all among her people. To Ragnara, there is no difference between general, farmer, hunter, or chieftain. She is fair to all."

I suppressed a derisive snort, but all around the bonfire people nodded.

"Ragnara helped my family when all our animals died," the woman with the long braid said. "She gave us two new horses, a pregnant sheep, and grain to get us through the winter. We only had to give one of the lambs back when spring came."

"The herders give lessons," the man with the green hat said. "My children are learning runes."

"And she freed all the slaves," the last woman said. "Don't forget that."

The skald waited for it to be silent again before prattling on. It seemed to me like a speech he had learned by heart, and I couldn't see where the news part came into it.

"While Ragnara has spent her whole life dedicating all her energy to the realm's success and the happiness of the people, she's never done anything for herself. Freiheim has never seen a leader like this before, and she will always live in the hearts of the people."

Rorik also looked like he had heard this all before, as he raised an impatient eyebrow at the skald.

"Prince Sverre is set to get married this summer," the skald said.

This wasn't news to us, either, but the others pricked up their ears.

"I've heard he's getting married, but who's the unlucky bride?" the woman with the braid asked.

The skald didn't react to hearing this slander against the prince. "Ingeborg. She's the daughter of the chieftainess of Gardarike. A princess."

Rorik raised an eyebrow when the skald said *Ingeborg*.

"Right, so everyone's equal, but of course, the prince has to marry a princess." The words were out of my mouth before I could stop them.

Around the fire, spoons stopped on their way into mouths, cups paused halfway to lips, and all eyes were aimed at me. I saw animosity in their gazes.

"Uh, I mean, he could just as well have married one of us. Someone from the common folk of Hr—" Rorik kicked my foot. "Freiheim," I finished and ducked my head down in my scarf.

"She's right," the woman who seemed taken with Finn said. Then she stood and wiggled her body. "I'd be happy to live in the castle in Sént."

"Even if you had to take the prince with you?" The one with the long braid laughed.

"Oh. I hadn't really considered that."

Everyone giggled except for me, Rorik, and the skald, who actually didn't seem capable of mirth.

"But the prince is gone," he continued.

The smiles grew stiff, and heads turned.

"Why didn't you tell us that earlier? This is unprecedented," the one with the braid said.

"You didn't pay," the skald said flatly.

"Doesn't Ragnara pay you?" Rorik asked. "I would think it's your job to spread the news."

The skald scoffed. "I can't survive on those crumbs."

"What happened to Prince Sverre? Is he dead?" Rorik had to strain to remain seated, and I set my bowl on the ground. I pricked my ears. Serén had warned me about the prince, after all.

"No one knows. He disappeared a couple of weeks ago. Ragnara thinks he's out sowing his wild oats before the wedding." The skald laughed coldly. "She doesn't want him to spread his seed all over the realm, since she doesn't want to fight with even more people who could challenge her seat on the throne. Or maybe he was captured by the rebels."

I gasped. "Wouldn't Ragnara care if her own son was taken captive?"

"Pfft. The biggest blow to her was when Varnar died. She loved him like he was her own. Sverre and Varnar were like night and day, and they hated each other. Ragnara was disappointed that Varnar was the one to die." The skald looked around. It was clear that this story was familiar and part of his set repertoire.

What if everyone knew that Varnar wasn't dead, that he had turned against Ragnara?

"She and Eskild have gone looking for the prince." The skald's words pulled me out of my thoughts.

Rorik lifted his gaze. "Are they riding around the kingdoms? Now?"

"We passed them a couple of days ago," the man with the hat said. "I only noticed the Varangian Guards." He stared at the skald. "You showed up not long after. Were you traveling with them?"

The skald's face returned to its apathetic expression.

"*Were* you traveling with them?" I asked, now unable to keep my mouth shut. I tried to pull something of the past out of him, but it was blocked.

The skald patted his pocket, so the coins clinked inside.

I looked desperately at Rorik, who, thankfully, found a larger coin. He held it out to the skald, but with the hand with the eagle tattoo.

The skald's gaze slid down to the hand, and the two men each held their side of the coin.

"I also think she's looking for something." The skald narrowed his eyes. "Ragnara has been tracking something since Hibernia, where she interrogated the man-woman."

My lips began to prickle.

Gytha.

"In Jorvik, where she was looking for the witch."

Védis.

Shit, had Frank found Védis before Ragnara did? Had she lifted the spells from Halfdan? Was she okay?

"In Sverresborg, where Gustaf was dead, and an important prisoner was gone."

Rorik and the skald were still each holding their end of the coin, while Rorik's free hand fidgeted with Tilarids's handle. The skald noticed this at the same time Rorik let go of his end of the coin.

"Where are they headed?" Rorik asked. His voice was an octave deeper than usual.

"Here," the skald said, his eyes still on Tilarids.

As soon as the camp was quiet, Rorik nudged me. He and the skald had had a mysterious staring contest in the hours after he revealed that Ragnara and Eskild were on their way.

Personally, I was in favor of running away immediately, but Rorik shook his head faintly when I, eyes wide, tried to signal this to him.

The skald's eyes kept landing on Tilarids, and eventually, I could plainly see how Rorik had to strain to keep the bloodthirsty sword in its sheath. It was clear the skald had figured out there was something fishy about us. Right now, he was lying on his mat with his eyes closed, but a quick look with my clairvoyance revealed that he was absolutely not asleep.

Rorik didn't say anything. He didn't need to, either, as I got up fully dressed and pulled gently on Finn's ear.

The fingalk had been snoring peacefully, but he woke up as soon as I touched him. At first, his eyes were pale yellow, but they shifted to burgundy when he saw our faces.

As quietly as we could, we snuck away.

Once we were out of earshot of the little group, Rorik began to run.

I followed him as Finn's large feet slapped against the road.

"The skald was—"

"A spy. Yes." Rorik finished my sentence and started running even faster.

"So he's on his way to Ragnara and Eskild now."

"He just has to kill those people first."

I stopped, my stomach churning. "Is he killing them right now?"

"There's no time for this," Rorik chided. "Anna. Come on!"

He took my hand and pulled me along. I started running again, this time nauseous with fear.

"Why didn't he attack while we were there?"

"Tilarids."

"But the others have nothing to defend themselves with." I exhaled, but I was so out of breath, I had to inhale twice as hard. "They were loyal to Ragnara."

"That means nothing. They're in the way."

I didn't want to dwell on that information. "Shouldn't we help them? Can't Tilarids—"

"They're already dead." Rorik's voice snapped like a whip.

No. Oh no.

"How much time do we have?"

"An hour until he fetches Ragnara and Eskild. Maybe two." He was also breathing heavily. Then he turned into the woods.

Branches hit me in the face and tripped me, and I was grateful when Rorik stopped at a rock face and ran around it, patting it with his hands.

"Here." He pushed me into a little crevice. I had never seen him so panic-stricken before.

It was nothing like the large caves he had been finding for us thus far. This was no more than a narrow split in the rock, but he squeezed all three of us in there. Quickly, he lit the crystal and exhaled slowly.

We stood packed together. I was pressed up against his chest, and his arm rested on the stone behind me. Finn had placed himself in the opening, where he looked out watchfully. Whenever he turned his hairy head, I saw his bright red eyes.

"How long do we need to hide here?"

Rorik's mouth was right up against my ear. I could feel his every word as a warm gust of air. "We should stay here for a while."

"A while?"

"They're close by. I had no idea they were so close. I knew they might take off, but I wasn't expecting them to come this way. Ragnara knows you're here." I got the feeling he was speaking more to himself than to me. "If they find you, they'll kill you."

I didn't say anything. I couldn't find the words, but I kept picturing the people. The long braid. The green hat. Even more people would die because of me.

I closed my eyes, suddenly extraordinarily exhausted. I actually slumped forward, but because it was so cramped, I just fell into Rorik.

His strong arms were around me when my knees buckled.

"Anna," he said. "Anna . . . Anna . . ."

The trees sighed, and I glimpsed Odinmont on the other side of the field, while a dry branch cut into my bare foot.

I looked around, faintly aware that I was still leaning against

Rorik in the cave on some other plane, but the image felt just as real.

It was freezing cold. Colder than it usually was in the vision. I inhaled some snowflakes. They froze my esophagus and ended up in my stomach. My body should have melted them, but instead, the frost spread until my insides were thoroughly frozen. This was different from a normal winter chill. This was . . .

I was as close to death as I could get.

The dream version of me walked past me, and soon after came Frank.

Shit!

Every time I thought I had evaded my murder in Kraghede Forest, it popped up again like an insistent cork. I felt like I couldn't get free of this vision.

The cold spread through my flesh and blood, and eventually I stood frozen solid, covered in ice. The only warmth came from the tears running down my cheeks. But they, too, froze and solidified, until I found myself completely immobile.

"Run," I whispered to the other me through unmoving lips. "Do something. Anything."

Frank strangled me.

But the other me didn't react, and in my head, I heard a rhythmic *thump-thump, thump-thump . . . thump . . .* The spaces between the heartbeats grew longer, until, finally, they stopped completely.

The rune was carved into my back.

I could hear how the knife pierced the skin.

"Do something," I breathed powerlessly. Was I talking to the version of me that now lay lifeless and bleeding on the ground, or the version that was standing frozen solid?

Shit!

I tried to move, but I was encased in ice. I tried again, and a very low, crackling sound scratched at my inner ear.

Thump . . . My heart fluttered, and the cracking sound repeated.

Thump . . . thump . . . thump-thump. I could move a little, and I tensed all my muscles.

Finally, with a crash like shattering glass, I was free from my coating of ice. On wobbly legs, I staggered away from the dead version of me lying on the forest floor. Frank ran across the field, and I ran after him, but my legs gave out and I landed on the ground. Still, I kept moving, crawling despite the frozen clods of earth that tore at my hands and knees.

In the middle of the field, I almost collapsed on the rock-hard, black soil topped with shining silver snow. My willpower kept me going, and I made it halfway to Odinmont, which was now my beacon. Frank's form had long since disappeared, but I continued.

The house was illuminated; I could see people inside, and I felt heat emanating from it.

Arthur's voice was audible, and he laughed. I found myself smiling, even though I was frozen half to death and lying in a field. The silhouette of a curly-haired woman appeared in the window, and she held a bundle in her arms.

Then, just when I'd nearly made it to the house, eyes appeared in my field of vision. "No, Anna!"

I wanted to scream, but I had no voice.

My own features were before me, and they were angry and contorted.

"Serén?" I asked.

"You can't come here."

She was so angry, I crawled backward.

"They're right in there. Our parents." I pointed to Odinmont, and again I could hear Arthur's soothing voice.

Someone came out through the front door. It was our mother. She had a child on her arm, and for a split second, in the light of the moon, she and the baby were identical to the ice sculpture that had adorned the equinox ball at The Boatman.

What kind of place is this?

Serén also looked at the scene with longing. She took a small step toward our mother but then turned back to face me. "This exists only in our dreams."

"Maybe we should just stay here." I reached a frozen hand toward Odinmont.

Pain once again flooded Serén's face when she looked toward the hill. Arthur had appeared with another child in his arms, and our parents stood close together, looking out over the dark fields.

Serén and I stared up at them, and for a second, Arthur's eyes locked on mine. He looked into the distance as if trying to spot something, but then looked down at the bundle in his arms.

"This isn't real," Serén whispered.

"I don't know what reality is anymore," I whispered.

Serén jolted from the reverie. She gave me such a frightening look, I was suddenly forced to consider how scary I must be at times. She shouted: "Get out of here."

"But—"

She stomped in front of me, her eyes locked on mine, while I crawled backward toward Kraghede Forest and my own corpse.

"No," I begged. "No. I don't want to."

She brought her face all the way down to mine. Her expression was so furious, I was momentarily afraid of my own reflection. More afraid of my sister than what awaited me between the trees. I turned my head to avoid looking at her, but in doing so, I saw my own lifeless face, eyes open, on the forest floor.

"You don't have much time." Serén was gone, but her voice rang out in the woods.

"What do you mean?"

"Ragnara will make her move at Prince Sverre's wedding this summer."

"Make her move how?"

"I don't know. I don't know," Serén repeated. "They're always talking about how she must be worshipped, so she . . . something."

"*She* must be worshipped? Ragnara?"

"That's why she wants to find the prince now. She needs him to come home for the wedding so people can worship her. So they can sacrifice something to her. She's going to find you."

"We ran away." I put all my energy into collecting my thoughts. "We ran away from her. I think Rorik has it under control."

"I still see him dying while protecting you," Serén said. "I see that he gives his life for yours."

I looked to the sky, and a car honked on the road below.

"Ragnara's plan," rang Serén's voice. "She's planning something. They're talking about it."

"What do you mean? I don't understand."

"Anna," Serén roared. "They're blinding me again. Ow! Ow! Anna!"

"Anna." Someone was shaking me. "Anna, wake up."

As with every time I fainted, it took me a moment to orient myself. I stood up. The cold of a stone wall seeped into my back, but my front was warm. Hands stroked my forehead, and red eyes peered at me.

"Aah!"

I clung to a muscular arm.

"It's just Finn."

"Rorik?" I suppressed a wave of nausea.

Rorik's arms wrapped around me, and I pulled him close to me. His broad chest was solid and warm. So warm. And so alive.

He planted a kiss on my hair. "Were you dreaming?"

"It wasn't a dream." I hiccupped. "Or, in a way it was real, and it can't stay that way, or else I'll disappear."

My words didn't make sense, but Rorik didn't ask me to explain. He simply held me as my breathing slowed. Through our coats, I could feel his heart beating, steady and calm, and my breathing fell into step with its rhythm. Just when I thought I'd regained control of myself, I was struck by the image of my own chalk-white hand, and I let out a long, tremulous sob.

Rorik squeezed me tighter. "Shhh."

Anyone else would have asked me what I'd seen. Anyone else would have drilled into what my visions revealed. But Rorik simply held me. When my tears subsided, he reluctantly let go, but we still stood so close that I could lean against him.

I went to wipe my face, but Rorik beat me to it and ran his palm over my cheeks. His hand smoothed my chaotic hair. The scarf had slid to my neck during our frantic flight.

"Ragnara is planning something for Prince Sverre's wedding." I hiccupped. "Serén said so. That's why she's here. That's why she's looking for him so intently."

"What is she planning?" The fear was clearly visible in Rorik's features in the weak light of the crystal.

"Serén doesn't know, but she sees people worshipping her." I leaned my head back and looked up into the moist darkness above my head.

"Worship? That's forbidden."

"I don't know." My voice was hysterical. "I don't understand." Then I stopped. "Worship is forbidden?" I repeated.

"Yes. It is strictly prohibited to worship anything at all."

"You aren't allowed to worship the gods. Odin and Thor and all the other gods. But you are allowed to worship Ragnara. In fact, you have to. You have to make offerings to her. And people make offerings to the Midgard Serpent." Something was simmering in my battered brain.

Around me, I heard drips and rustling, but I didn't care what lurked in the depths. I continued slowly.

"When we were with Gytha in Hibernia, she said that the gods were once human. I didn't give it a second thought back then."

"Didn't the gods create humans?" Rorik asked.

I was reminded of Od, who had only said the matter wasn't settled.

"If it's true that the gods came later, then they didn't create everything." I stopped myself and took a deep breath. "They were created, and they stop being gods when no one believes in them anymore. That's why she prohibited all forms of faith. To deplete the gods."

The words hung between us.

"She prohibited all faith," I repeated, while for the second time in just a few minutes, a chill spread across my body. "And she does rituals for herself. The largest will be at the prince's wedding, where she'll most likely kill Serén. Or should I say *sacrifice* Serén?"

I struggled to breathe. "Maybe she'll even sacrifice something bigger."

"What could be bigger than sacrificing your sister? What does she want to achieve?"

I couldn't see much of Rorik, since the crystal was flickering, but I felt his heart beating faster through our clothes.

At first, he couldn't speak, but after a while, he got the words out.

"Ragnara wants to become a goddess herself."

PART III

THE SON OF A RULER

The son of a ruler
Shall be silent and wise
And bold in battle as well
Bravely and gladly
A man shall go
Till the day of his death is come

Hávamál,
9th century

CHAPTER 20

Rorik was pale when we finally left the cave early in the morning.

"Can you feel her?" His voice was hoarse.

"I don't know what she feels like." As I spoke, I cast out my clairvoyance, and I flinched. It was as if a giant, dark hand were trying to strangle me, and I instinctively laid my fingers over the scar on my chest. "She's close," I croaked.

Rorik, who was walking a few paces ahead, ran back to me.

"Where?" He didn't draw Tilarids. He probably figured it was pointless.

My body shook, and I pointed with a trembling hand toward the sun, so I assumed it was directly east.

Rorik cursed. "Let me see your map."

With hands that refused to work properly, I pulled Rebecca's notebook out of my bag.

Rorik flipped to the map and turned it so it was aligned with something, and looked over his shoulder.

"I think," he began, but he paused as he followed the battered map with a finger. "That way is the kingdom of Frón."

I simply could not keep my body still, and I began to walk in the direction opposite Ragnara.

Rorik clapped the book shut and followed me. "We can swing around to the south in Frón. It'll take a couple of days longer, but the risk of meeting them in the other direction is too high."

"What if they come toward us?" The thought alone knocked the wind out of me.

"Then you'll be able to feel it, right?" He looked at me inquisitively.

I pressed my lips together in response.

We kept to the woods, far from the road.

I alternated between freezing and sweating, and on several occasions, I noticed that, without thinking about it, I had folded my arms protectively across my chest, in front of my old scar. I was so focused on my own misery that I didn't speak for several hours.

But someone else did.

"Nana," a voice said.

I turned around with my hand on Auka, but I didn't see anyone among the brush and branches.

"Nana," the strange voice insisted again, but I couldn't feel anyone apart from Rorik.

Iron rubbed against leather as Tilarids was drawn behind me. Rorik had heard it, too.

"Krik?"

It was very close to us now, but I couldn't detect anything.

"What is that?" I whispered, but Rorik shrugged as he peered between the trees.

A long brown arm attached to a deadly hand with sharp claws slid around my shoulder.

"It's okay, Finn," I said and patted the tufted forearm. "We'll protect you."

The fingalk had put its other arm around Rorik.

"Nana and Krik."

Hmm.

I looked up at the tall fingalk, and on his other side, Rorik did the same. Finn laughed his putrid, open-mouthed laugh.

"Finn!" I exclaimed. "You can talk."

His eyes were pale orange, and his scaly tail wagged proudly.

"I didn't know fingalks could talk!"

Rorik was just as perplexed as I was. "I've never heard of one that could. But on the other hand, it's never been investigated."

"Nana." Finn jumped at the sound of his own voice. "Nana . . ."

"Okay, okay." I laughed and scratched his chin. "Very good."

Finn stamped his foot on the ground.

"Nana and Krik." He pressed us against his body, and for a second, I was overwhelmed by how tall and strong he was. His leathery wings folded around my back and felt like thick plastic. Fortunately, he let go quickly and ran ahead.

"Krik?" I looked at Rorik.

"Nana." He smiled back.

I couldn't help but laugh, and it felt wonderful. My shoulders dropped a little, and I exhaled slowly as I watched Finn's back. All three of us were unharmed, we were on our way to save Serén, and there was enough time before the wedding.

"Oh no," I whined. "Not another cave."

It was now evening, and Rorik led us to the mouth of a grotto. Dank, foul-smelling air emanated from it.

He turned halfway around. "This is the safest place to stay. We'll be hidden in there, and we need to rest."

I sighed, and with eyes closed, I recalled cotton sheets, soft pillows, and fresh-smelling blankets. And to think something so banal as a bed could seem like the wildest luxury.

Inside the cave, the stench was worse.

"Have I already suppressed the memory, or does it smell worse in here than usual?" My nose wrinkled.

"It does smell pretty bad in here." Rorik fumbled with the crystal, but he couldn't bring it to life. Finn smacked his lips in the dark, and my foot hit something hard. Finally, light streamed out into the space.

Finn moved forward with a *slurp*, and I gasped and jumped back, while Rorik let out a small cry.

I had stepped on a skeleton. Empty eye sockets pointed up at me. Small, dried bits of skin still covered the forehead, and long, honey-colored hair flowed over one of its bony shoulders. I turned my back, not wanting to see more.

"Finn," I commanded. "You may not—"

"Nana," begged the fingalk. "Food."

"No. That is not food. That's a person. And there's nothing left for you to eat, anyway."

Rorik breathed heavily, and I guessed he was trying to breathe only through his mouth. His steps receded farther into the cave, while I stood with my back to the skeleton.

"Shouldn't we leave?" I couldn't stop myself from inching toward the exit, in the direction of the fresh air.

I heard Rorik fumbling with his pack and then a dragging noise as fabric was unfolded.

"I covered her."

"Her?"

"It's a woman. Or . . . it was." Another pause. "Can you feel her?"

I reached out mentally but shook my head.

"The skeleton feels just like the dirt and rocks. But I can sense something else in here. Hmm . . . uncertainty, fear mixed with a strong craving for . . . power, I think." I tilted my head and concentrated even harder. "Someone's doing something that's necessary, but it's highly dangerous. Someone, no . . . She . . . she's afraid of the forces she's setting loose." The old, nearly evaporated aura in the cave reminded me of the sinister dark hand I'd felt earlier. I saw a glimpse of long black hair, and heard a scream of exertion when she hammered something against stone, crushing it. "I think it's Ragnara. She's been here, but it was many years ago."

I heard the scratching of Rorik's footsteps around the grotto, along with Finn's unsteady, tiptoeing feet. "Anna. You have to see this."

Grudgingly, I opened my eyes and saw the details in the space.

I had been so focused on the dead body, I hadn't noticed anything else.

The cave, which was shakily illuminated by Rorik's crystal, wasn't particularly large. On the ground, next to the now-covered body, lay two broken stones. They had once been round, with holes in the middle, but now they lay in four semicircles in the dust.

They were what I had just seen Ragnara crushing in the past.

Dried-up ropes or shreds of skin had been tossed in a pile on the ground, and even though there were no ghosts in the cave, I felt a violent aggression flowing from the discarded items. I looked closely at a shape, and with a groan, it dawned on me that it was the shriveled remains of a gigantic snake whose head had been chopped off. I spotted a bony hand sticking out from the cloth Rorik had draped over the woman. The hand was clenched around a wooden bowl. It was yellowish-green in some places and corroded black in others.

Rorik scanned the interior of the cave, then narrowed his eyes as he thought aloud.

"That can't be right. It can't be . . ." He trailed off as he paced back and forth between the stones and the dead snake.

"Do you know this place?" I tried to close my nostrils, which made my voice nasally. The smell was sickly and stagnant with a sweet undertone.

"Maybe." Rorik spun around. "Or maybe I've heard about it."

I accidentally sniffed, and my stomach churned. I turned and ran out into the pleasantly cold evening air, gulping down large mouthfuls of it. Rorik and Finn came slinking out after me.

"I'm not doing it." I crossed my arms. "I'm not spending the night in there."

Warmth at my shoulder told me that Rorik's hand was hovering right over it, but he didn't set it down.

"The rocks will shield us," he said. "We'll sleep out here."

"Thanks," I mumbled and sank down along the large stone that formed one wall of the little indentation.

Rorik set the glowing crystal on the ground and removed the cooking pot from his bag. He added water and tossed in some herbs.

Then he looked into his pack again and cursed. "I put my blanket over her."

"Take mine." I wasn't able to get up.

Rorik found the blanket in my bag and rolled it out. Then he sat and patted the other end.

With great effort, I dragged myself next to him, and he handed me a cup of tea. I took it when I smelled mint. For a moment, I held the cup under my nose, letting the fresh, tingly fragrance fill my nostrils.

"Do you know what happened in there?" I asked finally.

"Not what happened. I have no idea why she's dead. It looks like it happened many years ago, judging from her"—he cleared his throat—"condition. But I think I know what kind of place it is."

I blew on the tea and enjoyed the warm minty smell that wafted back. "Tell me." My voice sounded hollow because I was speaking into the cup.

"It's just a story my mother told."

I sat up straight. In the whole time I had known Rorik, he had never mentioned his parents.

He looked at the sky, which was now cobalt blue with small pink whisps of clouds. "The old stories are banned. But this one was allowed to survive because it's about Loki's punishment."

I sipped on the tea, careful not to provoke my nausea.

"Loki?" I asked after taking a sip. "I thought everything to do with the gods was forbidden."

"It is. But Loki's not a god. He's a jötunn. A giant."

"Ahhh." I set the cup on the ground and lay down. My upper body could fit on the blanket, and with my knees bent and my feet on the ground, it was actually pretty comfortable. The stars winked above me. The top of my head nearly touched Rorik's thigh, but

Finn squeezed himself between us. Even though he stank, I laid my head on his leg, and a hairy claw stroked my shoulder.

Rorik continued. "Loki was condemned, bound in a cave under a snake that dripped venom on him. He was held there by two millstones. His wife stayed with him, holding a bowl over his head so the snake's venom didn't hit him." Rorik took a slurp of tea. "It's an old poem. One I heard when I was a child."

> *One did she see in the wet woods bound,*
> *A lover of ill, and to Loki like;*
> *By his side does Sigyn sit, nor is glad*
> *To see her mate: would you know yet more?*

The words rang out, and the prophecy echoed in my head, even after Rorik's voice faded. I squinted. "I've heard that somewhere before."

"It's from Midgard. I interpreted it as a story about true love," he said softly.

"I'm not so sure her love paid off. *She* must be Loki's wife, and the sorrow his fate caused . . . well, we saw the result in there." I pointed in the direction of the cave.

"I don't know."

"Do you really think this is the place?" I turned my head to look at Rorik.

"If you had asked me that a couple of weeks ago, I would have said it was just a legend. The story was already old by the time of the great migration, so I don't know how they would have ended up here in Freiheim. But now . . ."

"What does it mean?" I asked.

A few moments passed before Rorik answered. "It means Loki got away. He's in charge of the forces of chaos, and as I understand it from what the Brewmaster was saying, then that's yet another sign that Ragnarök is near."

That night, we took turns sleeping and keeping watch, but for many hours, no one was near us aside from the woman in the cave.

I woke Rorik after a few hours, and we sat for a while, side by side, silent in the dark. There was something unbearably sad about this place.

"Go to sleep, Anna," Rorik said when I hadn't said a word.

I stretched out on the blanket but had a hard time relaxing. Meanwhile, Rorik stood and stared pensively into the crystal's dull light.

I must have dozed off, as I woke with a start when I heard voices approaching. Someone groaned, another cursed, and feet tramped in our direction.

I jumped to my feet and held Auka in my hand.

Rorik was already standing with Tilarids drawn, and Finn's long arms were spread out, wings stretched in front of us like a shield.

"She's bleeding out," a man's voice said.

Standing as we were in the cleft, we had nowhere to flee. If we went out, we would run straight into the arms of whoever was coming, and if we withdrew, we would end up in the cave with the remains of the snake and the skeleton.

We backed up. In spite of it all, the corpse and the snakeskin were the more attractive option.

Finn smacked his lips, and when he turned his head, I saw that his eyes were rust red and his nostrils were flared.

I reached out with my clairvoyance and detected eight people. As soon as I started to feel around, one of the auras reacted. It poked inquisitively back at me.

"There's someone here," came a quiet female voice.

"You just said there wasn't anyone here, Taliah."

"There wasn't before, but now I can feel something." Her aura pressed against mine.

"There's something hiding them, but they're over there in that opening."

Rorik and I looked simultaneously at the crystal, which was now flickering on the ground. I tightened my grip on Auka, and Rorik raised Tilarids. Finn growled quietly like a cat backed into a corner.

"Edith doesn't have much time left," another man's voice said.

The eight people came into our little cleft. A group that, to my eyes, was at least as mysterious as our own.

Rorik raised Tilarids, Finn hissed, and I prepared to swing Auka.

A tall man with a red beard led the way. He was dressed in a long tunic that looked vaguely Middle Eastern, and over it, a loose jacket. Despite the Arab attire, his skin was just as pale as mine, and he had freckles that were starkly visible in the crystal's light. Close to him were four children: two little girls who were four or five years old, and a teenage boy and girl. They all had bronze-colored hair, blue eyes, and freckles.

The group also included a man and a woman who were carrying a third woman between them. Her pale jacket was stained dark red on one side; a rag was tied around her chest, but it was completely soaked through. What was worse, an unsettling yellow hue spread across her face, and she seemed to be having trouble keeping her eyes open.

The woman carrying her was tattooed from her fingertips to her jawline. She was dressed in black, and her skin had the same dark tone as Hakim's. She was who I had sensed, and now her clairvoyance was crashing into me. Taliah, one of the others had called her. Her free hand clutched a long knife.

The man on the other side had a long dark-brown beard and a mouth that looked even softer than Elias's. He pointed threateningly with a spear, aimed more toward Tilarids than Rorik.

Taliah gave me the sensation of never-ending reflections, but it was different from with Justine in Sømosen. This was like a copy of my own experiences, where the camera was turned at a slightly different angle. A swirling force surrounded us both, like water draining out of a sink, threatening to pull us down.

261

We all stood with weapons raised, even though both Taliah and I were swaying, trying to stay upright.

The new arrivals stared at Finn and Tilarids, but no one took notice of me. No one but Taliah, who held my gaze.

The injured woman whispered something unintelligible.

"Who are you?" The redheaded man's words came out raw.

Kudos to him for speaking before attacking.

We didn't answer. I searched frantically for a sign that they belonged to Ragnara's people but found none. The redheaded man came closer and lifted a hammer-like weapon with a longer handle than Auka, but it was also decorated with a serpent knot. He had finally noticed me, and, breathing heavily, he pointed at me.

"Fimm," he said.

"What?"

The man repeated himself. "Fimm." His finger came closer, until he was almost touching my throat.

I raised my fingers and touched Hakim's gift. *Right—the silver hand.* The neckline of my shirt had slipped down. I grabbed the pendant.

"What about it?"

"Hamsa," the man said.

"You mean khamsa?" That was what Hakim had called it when he gave it to me for my birthday. It felt like just yesterday but also, somehow, years ago.

"Wait, have I been running around with a religious symbol around my neck? Jesus!" My hands flew up, which sent every weapon toward us.

Finn snapped his teeth.

"Hey, hey, hey . . ." The red-haired man held up a freckled hand to us and his own people.

"Not Jesus," I corrected myself quickly and considered my words. "I'm not religious. There are probably people who say they're gods, but they can kiss my—"

"It's not a religious symbol," Rorik interrupted. "People from Miklagard often wear them, but it doesn't mean anything."

"Maybe it means something in Miklagard that you aren't aware of," I whispered.

Everyone stood still for a moment, then the group started pulling shirts and collars aside to display various versions of hands that looked like my own.

"Miriam's hand," the man with the brown beard said.

"Mary's hand," the injured girl whispered.

"Fatima's hand," Taliah said, never taking her eyes off me.

The redhead dangled his pendant. "Fimm," he repeated.

I stared at him. "Why do you call it *Fimm?*"

"*Fimm* means *five*. The hand has five fingers." The redhead's middle finger landed on his collarbone. "We all call it something different, but the common name is Fimm. It's also the name of the cause."

"What is the cause, exactly?" I asked. My eyes were wide, and I tensed all my muscles, ready to run.

Taliah held her own hand up, and I saw that the tattoos adorning it looked nothing like Rorik's eagle and snakes. They were dark, intricate designs with elegant curves and dots. "The freedom to believe what we want."

Ahhh, so they are religious. Just not the religion I expected.

"What happened?" I took a step toward the wounded woman, but all the weapons were raised again.

Rorik stepped away from her slightly. The knuckles clenched around Tilarids were chalk white.

"The Varangian Guard," the redhead said. "They found us while we were worshipping our gods outside of Miklagard." He said nothing more.

In his past, I saw his group had been about fifty people, and that these eight were the only ones left. In the vision, I saw some of the white-clad figures running directly into the raised swords and knives. "We are martyrs," they shouted before being impaled. The people who stood before us had been sensible enough to run away.

The bleeding woman moaned again, and Rorik backed farther away from her.

The man with the brown beard laid his hand on her cheek. "At least she'll die free, with God to comfort her."

I wanted to say that, in my opinion, gods didn't seem to make a difference when it came to dying, but I held my tongue. Then I jumped. "Hey! I can help."

"Are you a healer?" Taliah asked.

"Nope. I'm just clairvoyant. But I have some of the Brewmaster's potion. Laekna." I pulled the tiny vial from my pocket. "Let me see the wound." I tried to sound as convincing as Elias.

The sodden, makeshift bandage was removed with a sticky sound, and Finn inhaled forcefully. With the laekna in hand, my courage faltered. I was in no state to fix anything.

"Rorik. Come here," I called.

But he was now pressed all the way up against the rock opposite us and shook his head.

"Come on," I commanded as the wounded woman was laid on the ground. I could see how her aura was growing thinner and thinner.

"Shhh, Edith." Taliah's voice was surprisingly gentle.

When the man with the long beard had disentangled himself from Edith's arms, he reached for the ampoule.

I gave it to him, relieved. "Drop laekna into the wound."

I stared at the vial as the last drops disappeared into Edith's shoulder, and I looked at the empty vessel that the man set down on the ground. Even though there was nothing left in it, I tucked it back into my pocket.

The bleeding hole in Edith's shoulder closed up. There must have been a splintered bone, as there was a crunching sound inside. It sounded like a creaking glacier.

Edith's cheeks turned red, and she breathed heavily. She looked down at her completely healed shoulder. Her shirt was torn up and covered in blood, but her skin was smooth. Tentatively, she prodded the muscles and bone.

"It's a miracle," Taliah said. "Even with a healer, there would still be a scar."

"No!" I shook my head. "It's not a miracle. It's just medicine."

"Divine intervention," the brown-bearded man said as he reached his hands up toward the dark sky.

"It's just a potion, it's not . . ." I stopped when it occurred to me that the laekna was made using Od's blood. "If you believe in that kind of thing, then in a way, it is divine intervention. Half-divine."

Edith massaged her shoulder. "Right now I feel . . ." she searched for the word as a goofy smile spread across her lips, ". . . blessed" she finished.

"That's just because Elias put drugs in it," I commented dryly.

It was quiet for a while.

"Can we stay here for the night?" the redhead asked. "Edith can't travel right now, and the little ones need to rest."

We nodded, and they sat down.

Finn positioned himself as a lookout at the entrance, and Taliah sat next to me. Her mere presence made my surroundings wavy.

"You're a seer." It wasn't a question.

Taliah pulled her black jacket tightly around herself. "So are you."

She clearly shared my affinity for short sentences and black clothes.

We were quiet until I couldn't stand it any longer. "Can you only see the past?"

She confirmed this with a nod.

"Can you see auras?"

"Aura?"

"I don't know what else to call it. The way people feel."

She thought, and I used the pause to look into her past and saw a foreign place with colorful buildings, Arabic writing, and the scent of spices. Cinnamon, grilled meat, lime, and coriander. This little glimpse contained more colors and smells than all my time in Hrafnheim so far.

"Do you mean life-thread?" Taliah finally asked.

"I don't know what that is, but maybe. Can you also send visions?" The question flew out of my mouth.

"Send?"

"I mean . . ." I searched for the words. "Can you contact other clairvoyants in dreams?"

She narrowed her eyes. "Well, yeah? All clairvoyants can. It's part of our power."

"Not mine. Or maybe I just never learned how."

Taliah sighed. "It's called *lucid dreaming*. In the dream, you find the other clairvoyant's life-thread and follow it, and then you can talk to each other."

"Uh . . . life-thread again? So, their aura?"

"I have no idea what an aura is," Taliah said, irritated. "It's the thread spun by the Norns."

I grinned, but Taliah looked at me with a furrowed brow.

I quickly wiped the smile off my face. "Are you serious? But you clearly follow a different religion." I looked at her arabesque tattoos.

"Of course I'm serious. We clairvoyants are tied to the Norns, regardless of what we believe in." She shook her head at my ignorance.

We sat in silence for a while, and several times, Taliah looked at me with narrowed eyes. Suddenly, she gasped.

She held a hand in front of her mouth. "You're . . . you're from . . ." she whispered between her fingers. She had evidently been snooping around in my past.

"Shh, it's kind of a secret," I said as I shushed her.

She pressed the tattooed hand harder against her lips, squinted her black eyes and studied me.

"It's dangerous for you to know. You risk torture and execution. Just like your . . ."

She slowly lowered her hand.

"Thora Baneblood's daughter is imprisoned in Sént, but there are rumors that Thora has another daughter. And Ragnara is looking for her."

We parted ways with the believers early in the morning.

Rorik, Finn, and I headed directly south, but it was slow going because we were staying away from the road. Ragnara's giant strangling shadow grew fainter.

On one occasion, we saw a group of cloaked herders on their way to who-knows-where. As they passed, the three of us hid behind a bush. I studied the white cloak fabric with the dark red fehu rune. A couple of the priests carried boxes, appearing to be yet more collection for Prince Sverre's wedding.

Finally, they were gone, and we continued on our way.

In front of me on the acid-green field, Finn ran ahead like a hairy scout who once in a while came back to deliver unintelligible reports.

"Rees," he screeched.

Rorik called back. "What is *rees?*"

Finn was panting. He had a stick in his mouth, which he dropped at my feet. He pointed at the hill. "Rees."

"Yes, I know there are trees over there. There's a forest. I can see it from here."

For a moment, the fingalk pursed his broad lips in disappointment and looked at Rorik with his large head cocked.

Rorik quickly reached up and scratched his ears. "But it's still nice that you told us."

Finn broke into a happy grin, and his large tail swung. Then he turned around and ran across the ridge. He came rushing back. He was breathless and extended a long claw toward the forest. "Peep."

"You hear birdies in the trees?" I went to scratch his neck, but he brushed my hand aside.

"Peep." He flailed his long arms. "Sor."

He pointed down at Tilarids, which began to quiver.

Now I detected auras, too, and cursed. The priests had simply been the vanguard, but now I felt auras that were aggressive and authoritative. Definitely soldiers.

Again, Finn squirmed and pointed. "Peep. Sor."

"I got it," I said quietly. "There are people, and they have swords."

Rorik reached for Tilarids, but he didn't draw it. Instead, he concealed the sword with his long coat, although no one would doubt he was armed.

Rorik scanned the small figures that came into view on the hilltop.

"Varangian guards," he said.

Prickles of fear spread across my body. "Are they the ones looking for me?"

Rorik took a small step backward and squinted his eyes.

"No." He pulled his hood down over his forehead, so his light hair was hidden. He held his eagle-tattooed hand behind his back.

The first soldier drove a cart, while the rest of the troop marched behind him.

"They've seen us. We can't hide now," he said quietly.

The green scarf hung around my neck, and I hurried to pull it over my hair. I looked down at the ground to hide my face.

Some of them were among those who massacred the believers. My heart pounded.

Rorik looked at Finn. "Don't talk."

The tall fingalk held a hairy hand in front of his mouth. The sunlight reflected off the thin webbing between his long fingers.

The soldiers came right up to us, and with my heart racing, I pulled my head even farther within the scarf while I laid a hand on Auka.

"Let me do the talking," Rorik said.

There were five soldiers, and they positioned themselves around us. Rorik stood up straight.

"Can I help you, comrades?" Despite the obliging choice of words, his voice was gruff.

I jumped when I heard the brusque tone, so far from his normal way of speaking. The leader didn't bother to descend from the cart. I forced myself to stand still and look at my feet, while Finn fidgeted uneasily.

"Who are you?" He spoke with the same tone that Varnar and Rorik used when they stepped into military character.

Rorik didn't move. "Don't let my clothing fool you. I am in the service of Ragnara, and I'm transporting this girl to Sént."

I opened my mouth when he disclosed our destination, but I didn't say anything.

The Varangian Guard leader, who had a dark, closely trimmed beard and a mythical creature tattooed on his cheek, looked me up and down. "What did she do?"

Rorik bared his teeth. The cold expression was so far from his normal warm smile, the hairs on the back of my neck stood up. "Do? She didn't do anything. She is to be part of the wedding festivities."

I looked angrily at Rorik, but he didn't so much as look in my direction.

"Huh," the bearded man scoffed. He studied me thoroughly. "She's nothing special. She's ugly. Gross."

In the group of soldiers, I saw a couple of women with indifferent expressions.

The smile vanished from Rorik's lips.

"There's someone who likes this type." He wiggled his eyebrows. "We want to take care of all the guests, you know." He grabbed the back of my neck and shook me.

I looked to the female soldiers in appeal, but none of them re-acted. Either they didn't care, or they didn't dare interject. I shot Rorik a death glare, but his uneasy vibe made me stand still.

The leader, who seemed to accept Rorik's explanation and er-rand, climbed down from the cart and walked right up to us. "Why aren't you in uniform?"

"I couldn't just waltz into Miklagard like that. The slave trader I bought her from can't be seen with soldiers."

The leader growled. "I've heard that they still have slaves in Miklagard. It's a disgrace." His gaze shifted to Finn. "And you have a fingalk," he said. "Let me do you a favor."

He pointed his spear toward Finn's neck. He would have stabbed him without further ado, but I protested loudly and laid both hands on the man's arm.

"Know your place, thrall." Rorik slapped me hard across the face, and with eyes wide, I brought my hand to my cheek. "The fingalk stays alive. It's valuable," he said to the leader, who lowered his spear.

Finn whimpered.

"Why do you have that beast with you?" The leader wrinkled his nose.

"It's trained." Rorik shoved Finn, who looked at him in confu-sion. "Say something."

The large lips pumped without making a sound.

Again, Rorik prodded him. "Come on, you brute."

Finn kept looking at him, uncomprehending, until Rorik kicked him in the thigh, causing him to howl. I flinched.

"Speak," commanded Rorik with a shout.

Finn twitched.

"Nana," he tried. "Krik mad at Nana."

The soldiers glared at first, then they roared with laughter. Finn looked at them, flustered, as my heart broke.

The face-tattooed leader wiped his eyes. "He sounds like a moron."

"Oron?" Finn repeated with large red eyes, and another chuckle spread through the group.

Rorik shrugged. "They want spectacular things for the wedding. The prince won't be satisfied with anything less."

The leader threw up his hands. "Prince Sverre." He said nothing more, but it was clear how he felt about the prince.

"Agreed," Rorik said. "I also have better things to do than escort a girl and a monster to this wedding."

"Yes," the leader said after a brief look at Rorik. "We have our hands full with maintaining order in the realm. And now we're wasting time on a party."

Rorik shook his head as if to concur. I held my breath, but the leader didn't seem to care to waste any more time on us. He turned to climb back onto the cart, but then turned around again. His eyes narrowed as he studied Rorik. "There's something familiar about you."

Rorik stood up straighter. "I don't know you."

The leader racked his brain. "I know your face."

The corners of Rorik's mouth turned down. "I go to Sént once in a while. Maybe you've seen me there."

The man tilted his head and raised his upper lip. Then he waved with one hand.

"That must be it." He boarded the cart. "For Ragnara's anfarwol," he said in parting.

Rorik nodded back. "Anfarwol," he repeated.

The soldiers went back the way they had come, and we stood and watched them.

Rorik's shoulders drooped, and he couldn't look at me.

"Sorry," he said finally.

"It's okay. You had to play that role. They would have killed Finn if you hadn't."

Finn gave a frightened howl next to us. I wanted to stroke him comfortingly on the arm, but I found that my hand was shaking.

"I'm sorry I implied you were . . ." Rorik's voice broke. "Sverre's wedding was just the only thing that came to mind as an excuse."

"I hate that prince. He sounds horrible," I mumbled.

"He is," whispered Rorik.

Finn pointed at his hairy thigh.

"I had to." Rorik looked desperately at me. "How do I explain to him that I did it to save him?"

Finn let out his characteristic *baaah* and pointed at my cheek. "Krik hit Nana."

I looked from the uncomprehending fingalk to Rorik, who looked back unhappily. Then I draped my arm around Rorik.

"Friends," I said to Finn, who pursed his floppy lips and shook his head. I moved my hand, so it held Rorik's. "See?" I pointed at our interlaced fingers.

Rorik looked down, too.

I shook our hands. "I'm not mad. He did it to help."

The fuzzy back of Finn's hand stroked my cheek. "Ow, ow," he said.

I nodded. "Yes. Ow, ow. But it's okay now."

Finn sent Rorik an angry, red glare. He hissed at him and put his funnel-shaped ears back. The small horns stood up straight in the air.

I took Rorik's face with the hand that wasn't holding his and kissed him with a big *smack*. "It's all good, Finn."

Rorik's free hand wrapped itself tentatively around my waist, while mine still held his face.

Finn sniffed doubtfully. "No hit."

"No, no, we're friends." I laid my cheek against Rorik's.

Rorik turned his face toward mine, and I let him do it. Finn was still looking at us skeptically.

Cautiously, Rorik's lips brushed against mine, even though I stiffened. My instinct was to jump back, but I stayed where I was. I let Rorik's mouth rest on mine for a moment before I twisted free. "See?"

Finn seemed to accept this. His whole body wagged, and his long tail knocked our feet out from under us, so we ended up in a big smiling pile on the ground. Finn rubbed his head up against both of us, and we hugged him in spite of the smell. Just then, as we lay on the ground, I felt the Varangian Guard coming back, heading straight toward us.

They were determined, and they brought reinforcements.

CHAPTER 21

They surrounded us.

Rorik got to his feet in a fluid leap and, in the same motion, drew Tilarids. But I feared that even the murderous sword would have a hard time keeping up with the . . . I looked around . . . *eight*, *nine*, *ten* warriors beating on their shields and swinging spears and axes.

Finn's claws came out of his long fingers with a series of *plings*, and his eyes took on a deep, dark shade of red. His scaly tail whipped back and forth, and I rolled off the ground in a move Varnar had taught me.

"Thorasdatter," shouted the leader with the mythical creature tattoo. "It took me a while to realize it was you with that rag on your head, but there's no mistaking it."

"This isn't Thora's daughter," Rorik said loudly. His voice was steady, but his aura sputtered with panic. "I'm escorting her . . ."

The man focused on Rorik, who stood slightly hunched with Tilarids pointing out. "Are you sure you haven't ended up on the wrong side?" he asked and slowly walked forward.

Whether he was speaking to Rorik or to Tilarids was unclear. It wouldn't even have surprised me if the sword responded that it actually wasn't sure if it was fighting for the right people. But Tilarids remained silent, as did Rorik.

I spun around so Rorik and I stood back-to-back. I pulled Auka from my belt, but I knew we were laughably outnumbered, and suddenly it hit me that Serén's prediction—that Rorik would die

protecting me—was about to be fulfilled. The thought turned my
breathing to sharp gasps.

"You can't fight them," I whispered.

"I don't have much choice." Rorik's warm back was massive
against my own.

"I'm the one they want. If I give myself over now . . ." I couldn't
complete my sentence.

"What'll they do to me afterward?" His voice should have been
sarcastic, but it was soft.

"Okay, we'll fight."

Finn stood next to us and spread his legs, reaching out with his
razor-sharp claws. His wings flapped impressively, even though I
knew he couldn't fly.

The soldiers came closer, and I picked three to lure away from
the group. Maybe Rorik—or more accurately, Tilarids—would
stand a chance against the remainder.

I lunged, and Rorik shouted behind me. I got three of the soldiers to come to his other side. One was a woman, the only one
bearing a sword. She had a harsh appearance, and I felt her desire
to be the one to catch me. The other two were male Varangian
guards, each swinging a spear. With a jab in my heart, I noticed
that one had Aella's high cheekbones and Varnar's coloring. He
must have been one of the children taken from the Bronze Forest.
Their movements were familiar, since Varnar had clearly been the
one to train them, and it didn't take me long to decode them.

I bent my knees and let them stab at me, not striking back until I was ready.

Tilarids had already felled the leader and the other woman, and
they lay dead on the ground. Three other Varangian guards fought
against Rorik, but their auras surged with fear when they saw the
unruly sword. Tilarids was practically singing with glee over the
fighting and blood. Rorik fought to keep his grip on the handle,
and it looked like the weapon was jerking him around.

In a flash, Finn reached out his long, hairy arm, and even though the soldier standing before him raised his shield, the pointed claws pierced through his defense and sliced a thin line across the man's throat. For a moment, the soldier just looked down in disbelief, but when red liquid started rushing out, he sank to his knees with a gurgle. Upon smelling the blood, Finn smacked his lips loudly before turning toward the next man, who backed away but didn't get very far before Finn split him open from his neck to his groin.

The three soldiers came closer to me, and one of them lunged with his spear. I jumped over it and swung my axe at him. I missed, stumbling forward with the weight of the weapon. I still wasn't used to fighting with Auka, but fortunately, I had Varnar's training sessions in my muscle memory, so I quickly regained my balance. The woman's sword sailed through the air, and she would have hit me if I hadn't instinctively done Varnar's trick of jumping behind her with an elegant dance-like movement.

She widened her eyes and lowered her sword slightly.

"How—" but before she could finish, Finn slit her throat. I hadn't realized he was nearby.

The woman fell, her face frozen in a baffled expression. Finn didn't even turn around as his long tail wrapped around another soldier's ankle and pulled. The man landed on his back, and his spear rolled away. As he reached for it, Finn's large jaws closed around his neck, and the crunch sent chills all over my body.

Finn looked toward Rorik, who had three men around him. Tilarids fought determinedly, but the men were faster, and for a second, it looked like one would hit Rorik with his axe. Finn jumped with his legs together like a kangaroo and, in a single leap, arrived at Rorik's side.

I turned to face my final opponent.

The soldier who resembled Aella looked at his fallen comrades, flung his spear to the ground demonstratively, turned around, and started running.

As he ran past Finn and Rorik, the fingalk let out a terrifying sound somewhere between a tiger's roar and a hissing snake. He jumped onto the fleeing soldier's back and flapped his arms, and the two of them lifted slightly off the ground. They landed, and the man kept running.

"Let him run," I shouted, but Finn took no notice.

The soldier ran on with Finn on his back, and they made it a short distance before teeth and claws stopped him.

The last soldier had knocked Tilarids out of Rorik's hand, while simultaneously lunging at Finn's back with his axe in an attempt to help his comrade. Rorik looked briefly at Tilarids, but chose to help Finn. He threw himself between the large animal and the axe, blocking the weapon. He was able to turn the soldier's arm, so the axe ended up buried in the man's own side. The soldier made a noise I wish I could forget, while a sour smell spread from his stomach region.

Finn's nostrils fluttered as he looked from the half-flayed man to the soldier with an axe sticking out of his side. He jumped on him, pulled the axe out, and sank his teeth into the large wound.

Then the soldier's aura went out like a busted light bulb. An intense flash of guilt emanated from Rorik, while Tilarids lay on the ground and trembled with anger that Rorik had killed without it.

"Did we win?" It was my own voice, but it took me a moment to realize it. I could smell iron, and my fingers were sticking together.

I heard shouts and lifted my gaze. More soldiers were coming toward us.

Crap!

I swung Auka when the first soldier reached me. The axe hit the soldier's temple, and their aura popped like a piece of popcorn. I didn't even register if the soldier was a man or a woman. Almost immediately, three other people stood around me, and through red mist, I lunged and kicked like Varnar had taught me. I don't know how many I killed. But I killed.

People say there's a dividing line, once you have a human life on your conscience, you never feel the same, but I felt nothing beyond a grim determination to survive.

Suddenly I was on the ground, or maybe I had been lying there for a while. Varnar's words rang out in my head. Even in this moment, when I was more animal than person, I heard his voice as if he were standing right next to me.

You're lying down, Anna. You have to get back on your feet.

A soldier sat straddling me. He swung his knife, and it was heading right toward my chest.

No, no, I thought. *I don't die like this. I'm going to die in Kraghede Forest, in winter. This is all wrong.*

I should have been thinking it would be wrong to die at all.

But I didn't die, and the man above me stiffened. He looked down and pricked his fingers on something pointy sticking out from his diaphragm. Something had impaled him from behind. I managed to make eye contact with him before he fell to the side, revealing my savior.

I stared. "Frank?"

"Get up," he hissed, with blood spattered across his face. Gone was the kind small-town bartender, but I no longer resembled a normal high school student, either.

"Fight," he commanded and shoved the bloody Auka back into my hand.

I watched from the corner of my eye as Finn hammered his tail into a soldier's chest until he fell to the ground.

Finally, there was only one soldier left. He fled with his spear in his hand. It wasn't much more than a pointy stick. Just when I thought he would get away, he turned and sent the spear flying toward us. Immediately, Frank threw a knife, and it bored into the soldier's heart.

I looked down at the red grass, not quite grasping that we had survived. The salty-sweet smell was overwhelming, and I wished I could sense the many people we had collectively killed. Feel guilt or sadness. But I was completely numb.

Just then, Frank gave a shout, and I looked over my shoulder as if in a daze.

"Halfdan." Frank took long strides toward the small figure. "You were supposed to stay in the woods."

"I wanted to help you, Grandpa. You were shouting." The child was blond and blue-eyed, like I had seen him so many times in Frank's past. Védis must have succeeded in lifting the spell. But then the boy went to speak again and was stopped by a strange sputter. I squinted, uncomprehending, while Frank ran to him in what appeared to be slow motion.

The spear had gone through Halfdan's little body. A red spot quickly spread across his chest. Blood stained his lips when he tried again to speak.

Then he collapsed.

CHAPTER 22

"No!" Frank shouted. "No," he pleaded again as he reached for Halfdan, who fell backward in the grass. When the boy hit the ground, the spear was pushed out of his little body, landing next to him with a muffled sound.

My hands fluttered helplessly, my brain refusing to understand what I was seeing. I couldn't think clearly, but suddenly everything came into focus.

Laekna.

I dug in my pocket and pulled out the little ampoule. Breathing heavily, I held it up to the light. Only a few oily drops clung to the glass. I had used it all on Edith's shoulder. I wanted to say I was sorry, but my words stayed where they were when I looked at Frank. Even if I screamed into his ear, he wouldn't have registered me.

He had pulled Halfdan's shirt to one side, exposing the circular wound. He stared into the boy's eyes, and he forced himself to smile at him, even as his rough, bloody hand clenched the boy's tiny jacket.

Halfdan's aura was fading quickly, and I watched as Frank used his free hand to stroke the boy's cheek as he mumbled softly. He held back his desperate screams, but I knew they would come soon. When it was over.

Rorik knelt close to them, shaking with sobs.

No, he wasn't crying. He was just shaking. As if some force within him were spinning out of control. I grabbed his shoulder but quickly let go. It was scorching hot, even through the layers of clothes.

"A child," Rorik whispered. He focused on the grotesque wound where the spear had been.

Halfdan's life force was now almost gone. His eyes were closed, but he whimpered softly. Just one more breath, then the pain would be over.

Frank held back his tears so they wouldn't be the last thing Halfdan heard. He kept whispering loving words to him.

Next to him, Rorik's clenched fists were turning white, and he swayed from side to side. Then he let go and aimed his hands toward Halfdan's chest.

First, beams of light poured out of Rorik's palms. Then the current changed direction, and Rorik pulled something back toward himself. At the same time, the wound closed up and left a knotty scar. Rorik sank back to his heels with a deep sigh.

When Frank finally understood what had happened, he stared incredulously at Rorik, then back at Halfdan. The wound was now completely closed, and Rorik fell sideways with an exhausted groan. His forehead glistened with sweat, and he gasped for air as if he had just sprinted.

The scar on Halfdan's chest shone intensely, but he didn't seem to notice anything. He blinked. "Why am I lying here?"

Frank couldn't hold back any longer, and he sobbed as he pulled the boy close. He disappeared in Frank's embrace.

The living, pain-free, uncomprehending Halfdan spoke in his high voice. "Why are you sad, Grandpa?"

"I'm not sad." Frank clutched him tighter. With the little body in his arms, he met Rorik's gaze. "I owe you everything, whoever you are. And I promise, I'll keep your secret."

Rorik looked at his hands, appalled, as if he wanted to cut them off. He rose unsteadily to his feet and slowly, head low, staggered away from us.

I walked after him. "That was incredible. That was . . ." I went silent when he turned and I saw his face. "What?"

"I couldn't hold it back this time," he whispered. "Not with a child."

"You're a healer. I had no idea. That's amazing." I took a step back when Rorik looked at me angrily.

Just then, Finn came ambling back from the soldier Frank had killed with his throwing knife. His long arms swung cheerfully, and he had blood around his mouth. His eyes were such a pale orange, they were almost yellow. He passed me, and with a big smile on his broad lips, the fingalk held out the knife toward Frank, who accepted it, baffled, as he looked up at the large creature.

"I think you need to explain some things, Anna," he said, still cradling the disoriented boy.

Rorik, Finn, and I carried the bodies into the woods. I forced myself to look at each face.

"They'll be found," Rorik said. "But hopefully not until the next unit realizes they never came back."

I didn't know what to say, so I stayed silent and looked around for ghosts that may need help crossing over to the realm of the dead. But there were none.

Later, we set up camp in the forest, far from the battleground. For some reason, Rorik hadn't brought out the crystal. He instead lit a fire, which glowed faintly. Frank and Rorik insisted that we had crossed into Frón, and that we should now be relatively safe from Ragnara's soldiers, who didn't have regular patrols here.

Finn sat with his back straight and gazed into the forest. His pride in having protected the group was unmistakable. Whenever he turned his head toward us, I saw that his eyes were nearly phosphorescent. It seemed he could see just as well at night as during the day.

Rorik stared into the embers with an empty look in his eyes.

Frank sat leaning against a tree trunk with Halfdan in his arms. The boy was asleep, and when Frank kissed him on the head for the tenth time, I understood that Rorik had saved not only Halfdan's life, but Frank's, too.

I squatted beside them and stroked Halfdan's fair hair. He turned his head toward me in his sleep. His cheek was pink; far from the yellowish white it had been in Sverresborg.

I spoke softly to not wake Halfdan. "What are you doing here?"

Once again, Frank's lips brushed against Halfdan's forehead. "After we found Védis, and she lifted Halfdan's spells, I wanted to make sure you were okay."

"Thank you," I said. "You saved our lives. But if it hadn't been for Rorik . . ."

Rorik raised his head and gave me a reproachful look from across the fire.

I turned back toward Frank. "Go back to Ravensted. Halfdan will be safe there. I'll write a message to Ben and Niels telling them to give you immunity."

Frank wrinkled his forehead. "You don't have that authority."

"But I will." I don't know what made me so certain. "They'll give you asylum, at least until I get home."

Frank started and stopped several times before finally speaking. "I don't understand why you're helping us."

My hand brushed Halfdan's forehead again. "He's never done anything to hurt me. And you . . ." I stopped.

"You have every reason to hate me." Frank's voice cracked.

"Yes," I conceded. "I do. But I also have every reason to care for you."

"Anna . . ."

"You're caught up in this mess just like I am."

Frank looked to the stars, and—not for the first time—I wondered whether they were the same as the ones back home in Ravensted.

"I hate myself. If it weren't for Halfdan, I would have ended my life."

"I get that," I replied honestly. "Ragnara put you in an inhuman situation, but she's not in control of you anymore, and you're much more helpful to us alive than dead." I searched for the words. "Halfdan needs you."

Though Frank wasn't smiling, the smile lines appeared around his eyes. He looked at me with so much tenderness, I wanted to throw my arms around him.

I resisted the urge, but added quietly, "I need you, too."

"As an ally?"

"As my friend."

He said nothing, but his eyes lingered on me. Then he got to his feet, the sleeping Halfdan still in his arms. He stood next to me for a second, still silent, and I felt the heat from his body.

I found a blank page in Rebecca's book and tore it out. With a ballpoint pen that Rorik regarded with curiosity, I wrote a short message, which I handed to Frank. We looked at each other for a moment before he disappeared into the forest carrying his sleeping grandson.

I sat next to Rorik.

He looked at me, then back into the embers. "I'm guessing Frank is your killer," he said.

"I was hoping you'd figure that out."

"It's hard to get a read on you." Rorik exhaled. "Some things you brush off like they mean nothing. Others, you hold a grudge over."

I didn't respond. He was right. I thought of the time Varnar told me he could have just as easily been my killer. I had dismissed that as well.

"Where is he headed? To Ragnara, to tell her where to find us?"

I didn't even hesitate. "He's going home to Midgard."

Rorik looked intently at me, as if to figure out whether or not I was right. With his head bowed, he seemed to accept my answer.

"Why are you so sad?" The question got out before I could stop it.

He spread his hands and stared at them. For a long time, he said nothing.

"What you saw today—" he started, but then interrupted himself. "It's forbidden for men to practice seid," he started again. "It's dishonorable, and it's shameful for us to heal others."

Ahhh. His aversion to wounded people. And here I was thinking he was squeamish.

"Isn't that better than fighting and destroying all the time?" I asked.

Rorik's eyes flashed. "That's what men do. What we're meant to do. I was raised to kill." He bowed his head again. "But I always have the urge to fix everything."

I exhaled. "I was actually talking about myself. My impulse is always to fight and tear things apart. For as long as I can remember, people have been telling me how wrong that is."

Slowly, Rorik lowered his hands and hid them behind his back. "I've also been told I'm wrong. We're quite the pair."

Pair?

I ignored his last word and changed the subject. "It's a gift, being able to heal. I don't understand how you can think it's so awful."

"How many times have people tried to convince you of the same thing regarding your clairvoyance?"

I didn't answer and tossed a stick into the fire.

"Do you remember," Rorik asked, "when we talked about how men heal in your world?"

I nodded. "But soldiers also have to be able to treat wounds, and many soldiers are men." I thought of Varnar, who wanted to splint my broken finger.

"Soldiers need to be able to patch people up. That's not the same as healing."

I looked into the flames. One of the burning pieces of wood crackled.

"That really made an impression on me. In this world, I've always envied women," whispered Rorik.

I raised an eyebrow in surprise, but he continued quickly with a crooked smile. "Although, there are things about being a man that I wouldn't want to give up." He reached out and tucked a lock of red hair behind my ear.

I sat completely still, my heart pounding. He quickly removed his fingers.

"I've always hidden behind Tilarids and let it do the killing for me. These," he rubbed his scars through his shirt, "have never really belonged to me." He closed his eyes. "But today, I killed. I don't know which feels worse: that I killed, or that I healed."

"You killed someone, and you saved someone."

"The two don't cancel each other out. I will always have the taking of a life on my conscience."

"I still think what you did for Halfdan was good," I whispered.

The crooked smile again. "But you don't believe in good and evil."

"Nah," I admitted.

Rorik took a deep breath. "Would you help me with something?"

"What?"

He dug around in his bag and pulled out a thin iron rod tipped with a mirror image of a rune. I had seen it before, but I never found out what it was. Rorik laid it in the embers and took off his shirt. The tattoos on his torso moved when he moved, and the illustration of a man appeared to breathe at the same pace as he did. The thin scars on Rorik's right bicep appeared as small ridges, and I felt the urge to trace them with my fingers.

Rorik's hand ran down over them until he found an empty space at the bottom. "Here," he said to me. "I want you to do it."

My voice failed, so I just nodded. Quickly, before I lost my nerve, I stood and yanked off my own shirt to expose my smooth right bicep. "You should do some on me, too. But I don't even know how many people I killed today."

Rorik gasped for air as his dark brown eyes took in my bare torso. They lingered on my scar—or at least I thought that's what he was looking at. He reached his hand toward it but lowered it again. Then he composed himself and nodded.

It hurt like hell, and the pain ignited a feeling I hadn't had before. The recognition that I had killed. Tears sprang to my eyes as I remembered the unfamiliar faces that, from now on, would be imprinted in my memory.

Suddenly, the pain was gone, and I looked down.

"Hey, you healed me." The scars were pink and delicate.

Rorik clenched his fists. "I couldn't help it. It's getting harder to control."

Without thinking, I took his hands. "You don't have to control it."

He moved backward slightly.

I pulled him back toward me. "It's valuable. And . . ." I gathered my courage.

Tell him the truth, Anna.

"You shouldn't hide it. Not from me, anyway." My free arm dangled at my side.

He formed his lips into a smile. "I like your gift, too. You can see me like no one else can."

We stood that way for a while, facing each other without saying anything, our fingers interlaced.

"Why did you let Frank go?" Rorik asked in a low voice. "It wasn't just for strategic reasons."

I didn't know if it was the shock of having killed, discovering Rorik's healing power, or seeing Frank again, but my breathing became unsteady, and the corners of my mouth turned down.

"Anna." Rorik's free hand caressed my cheek. "What is it?"

A flood of images bombarded my mind. The ones I always saw, of myself in an institution, with a strange foster family, or at a new school. In all of the images, I was alone. Maybe I would be alone for the rest of my life. If I even had a life to speak of.

"Anna," he tried again, but I shook my head.

"If you don't tell me, I can't help."

"It's too dangerous," I mumbled. "You can't know anything."

I let go of his hand and held my hands in front of my mouth.

Gently, he took my hands and pushed them down carefully, but firmly, so he could see my face. "Stop trying to protect me all the time."

I struggled not to let out a sob. "There's nothing wrong."

He was still holding my hands, but leaned back slightly. "Tell me."

My gaze reached the ground. "Sometimes I can sense my sister, and it feels so right, but sometimes the connection drops, and then it's lonely," I whispered. "I don't know why she's hidden from me sometimes."

"Maybe she's near a giant crystal."

I made a face. "A what?"

Rorik pulled out the glass object he had been dragging around since I met him. "One of these. When it's lit, you can't be traced."

"So that's why you were so sure we wouldn't be found?"

Rorik nodded.

"Of course! That's why Serén got cut off when I was talking to her at Sverresborg. Every time you came close, I couldn't hear her." I had a realization. "Did you have it lit while it was in your bag, too?"

Rorik looked sheepish. "I thought it was safest. But when we got too far apart, I was the only one hidden."

I sat down abruptly on a rock. "Shit!"

Rorik's head tilted. "I've come to understand that this word is never followed by something good."

"That was why Serén couldn't see that I risked dying at Sverresborg. I trusted her prediction, so I called on Frank." I studied the crystal as Rorik ran his finger across the slightly frosted surface, which began to glow faintly, this time a pale pink. The whole

288

object was the size of his outstretched hand, but the crystal alone, without its iron holder, was the size of a fist.

"Giants make them," Rorik said. "That's how they keep themselves hidden from their enemies, and they allow your loved ones to stay connected to you. The closer a connection, the more easily that person can find you. It glows red when those you care about are nearby."

I thought a while longer.

"Shit!" I shouted again.

Rorik smiled. "There's that word again. What now?"

I ignored him and rummaged around in my bag. Then I fished out the crystal that Mads had given me for my birthday. It was rougher, and it wasn't encased in a holder. "Is this the same kind?"

The smile froze on Rorik's lips. "Where did you get that?"

"One of my friends made it for me."

Rorik cautiously lifted the stone. "You know a giant?"

"He's only half giant. I went to school with him in Midgard."

"I don't know what *school* is," Rorik said, turning the crystal in his hand. He suddenly dropped it as if it had shocked him. "It's extremely powerful." He looked at Mads's gift with reverence. "Your friend must be a giant with very strong powers."

I jutted my jaw out and shook my head. "Mads? Nope, he's just a normal guy."

". . . with hidden powers," Rorik continued. "Who else do we know who fits that description?"

"It's also because of the crystal that Frank found us. Even though he wanted to kill me, we have a close relationship." I took the crystal and ran my hand lightly over the cool surface like I had seen Rorik do with his. "How do I make it glow?"

Rorik cleared his throat. "You have to think of someone or something you care about."

"What do you think of?"

Rorik coughed. "That's private. But it's subject to change." He aimed his finger at my giant crystal. "Try again."

Someone or something I cared about.

Hmm.

I tried thinking of training. Nothing happened. Then I thought of Odinmont, and the stone flickered a little, then went out. Then I closed my eyes and saw Luna in my mind's eye. She grinned, and I felt a jab in my chest. In my head, Mathias stood next to her, and he placed his arm around Luna and smiled his familiar godly smile. Frank stood there, Mads laughed, and Rebecca hummed as she stirred something in a pot. And on it went. Arthur, Aella, Hakim, even Ben tumbled forth from my memories, where I had carefully packed them away. It was like a punch to the gut, and I opened my eyes to see my crystal glowing.

The sharp sensation spread, and I pressed a flat hand to my stomach. The pain grew stronger as my crystal shone brighter. I couldn't stop it, and before I could stem the flow of memories, Monster came trotting up. I tried to hold back the sniffles as I sat down on my blanket, but tears ran down my cheeks. Overwhelmed, I lay down and rolled over so my face was turned away from Rorik.

He sat down behind me.

"May I?" he asked softly.

I couldn't answer, but he took my silence as consent. He lay down and draped his arm around me. His breathing was slow. He held me gently, and I let my own ragged breathing fall into step with his.

"You miss them," he noted.

"Yes." Much more than I had realized. "But it's not that."

"Then what is it? You're fortunate to have so many people in your life."

Again, I gasped for air, and I felt Monster's fur between my fingers and his warm breath on my palm. Now that the floodgates were open, I couldn't hold the feelings back.

"Until pretty recently, I had no one. I was completely alone. Now there are so many people I love," I whispered.

"You're lucky."

"But I could lose them again. I've already lost my best friend." This came out almost as a shout.

Rorik pulled me closer. "It's those who have tried having nothing who most fear losing what they have." His fingers found mine and wove our hands together. "Loving comes with a price."

"I've always been jealous of those who weren't alone, but making friends has made me vulnerable as hell."

"It's also made you strong." When I didn't respond, he whispered, "Tell me about them."

I took in a gulp of air and trembled violently. I could feel his warm breath and his soft hair against the back of my neck. It took a while before I could answer him.

"On one condition."

"What?"

"Heal me."

"You aren't hurt."

"Yes, I am. There's been something wrong with me since I was a kid. On the inside." I pounded my chest for emphasis.

For some time, Rorik said nothing. His grip on me tightened, and as with every time we touched each other, I thrummed with recognition. He made a decision, and without moving, he released his power and let it flow into me.

I closed my eyes and accepted it.

His healing patched the gaping holes and filled in the longing I had always carried with me. The scars would always be there, but I no longer had open wounds. In the end, we just lay there, our bodies pressed together.

Finally, I started to tell him about how much I missed Monster, how Luna and Mathias had insisted on becoming my friends, even though I'd done everything I could to push them away. About my father, Arthur, whose love had kept me from becoming completely hardened, and Frank, who had supported me when no one else would stand by me. About Aella, who loved my sister, and my mother, who was gone. I told Rorik about them all.

But for some reason, I didn't mention Varnar.

CHAPTER 23

The next day, we didn't say very much.

My thoughts were clearer and happier than they had been in a long time. The storm that usually raged inside me had subsided. Rorik had healed my deepest, most inflamed wounds, and I saw everything in a new light.

We crested the top of a hill and looked out over Frón. It was a broad, flat plain that reminded me of North Jutland. The heath was a timid pale green, and a mild breeze reached us along with the smell of grass.

I spotted a few buildings across the plain. "What is that?"

"The town of Ísafold." Rorik pointed. "It's a small settlement. Not too many people live here in Frón. Down there, at the end of the plain, is a grove known as Barre. On the other side, there's a river called Iving. The river marks the end of Frón." His mouth pulled back in a crooked grin. "It's a very small kingdom."

I looked to the blue sky, where just a few white tufts of cloud were scattered. A few birds circled high above us, but they were too far away for me to discern which type.

"What's on the other side of the river Iving?"

Rorik started taking long strides down the hill. "The Iron Forest is behind it. The giant wolves live down there."

Finn ran ahead of us through the trees.

Monster's family lives in the Iron Forest. Despite Rorik's healing, missing my best friend was still unbearable.

In my eagerness to drive away the sadness, I picked up my pace, but my foot got stuck on a root that was hidden in the grass. When I stumbled, Rorik instinctively reached out for me, and for a moment I held tight to his strong arm. We looked at each other, and through his shirt, I felt a muscle tighten in his shoulder. Then I let go and hurried past him.

"Shit!" I cursed quietly. This was NOT supposed to happen.

Rorik made every effort to appear unfazed. He walked alongside me. "Legend has it that ice never forms on the river Iving. Even during Fimbulwinter."

"Mhmm." I wasn't fully listening.

"And they also say there are elves here." He wiggled his brows.

I giggled, playing along with his attempt to keep things light-hearted, but my stomach was doing somersaults.

Rorik steered us to the right, toward a low stand of trees. "If we go through the forest, the Ísafolders won't notice us. We need to find a place to hide out for a day or two to avoid Ragnara."

We ducked between the trees. Rorik tried his best to stand up straight and look around.

I forced myself not to look at him.

There were tiny, verdigris-green buds on the thinnest branches, and there was a soft squishing sound with every step we took. Finn sniffed loudly. Despite the stillness among the nearly bare trunks, I could hear insects buzzing, birds chirping, and . . . suddenly, I stiffened.

I stopped abruptly and turned to face Rorik.

His mouth hung open, and he looked as though he'd been punched in the gut when I looked directly at him. "Anna . . ."

I laid my hand on his, and it felt warm and rough.

He stood completely still. "Finally," he breathed.

"Shh."

"I don't know what's happening between us, either," Rorik said. "But we have to—"

"There's someone here," I interrupted with a low voice, casting my power in all directions. Nothing about the calm forest indicated that four people were currently watching us.

Rorik raised his brown eyes and let them glide around, seeing no one.

"Are they hostile?" he whispered.

"They seem mostly curious." I tried to relax, but the thought of having to fight again—and maybe take another life—made it hard to breathe.

Rorik laid his hand on Tilarids. The sword immediately hummed with anticipation.

"Shouldn't we just go?" I had an almost uncontrollable urge to remove his hand from the murderous sword's hilt before the weapon did something stupid. "They might not wish us any harm."

Rorik rubbed his cheek. The eagle on his hand flapped its wings with the motion.

We walked slowly in the opposite direction, but a woman's voice shouted. "Stop, strangers."

Before I could see what had happened, Tilarids was in Rorik's hand. It's possible that the sword had jumped into his palm of its own accord. Rorik looked at it as though he himself were surprised.

"Come out so we can see you," I called. "There's no reason to hide."

There was a short laugh. "Sure there is. You have a fingalk, and your companion is armed with an Ulfberht sword."

"Put that away," I hissed to Rorik, who, with great difficulty, forced the quaking sword back into its sheath.

"Finn, try to look harmless," I told the fingalk, who immediately exposed his pointed, brown teeth in what was meant to be a smile, while his eyes took on an orange glow. The grayish-white spot around his eye was stark.

I sighed. "Just look down at the ground."

"Neither of them will hurt you. You have my word," I called.

"I don't know what your word is worth, stranger." The woman's voice was hard.

"Either you come forward or you let us continue on our way," I said brusquely.

Rorik cleared his throat. "Or they'll send arrows into our hearts from a safe distance."

I covered my mouth. "Oh."

"We need shelter," Rorik said. "We'll give you gold in return."

"We can take your gold ourselves, from your cold, dead bodies," someone retorted darkly.

"Nice," I mumbled. "Now they're even more interested in stopping us."

"I was trying—" he said.

Now the woman laughed. "Stop. Just stop. We have no interest in killing travelers."

We heard footsteps treading on the dry branches on the forest floor, and a girl with hair a shade lighter than mine appeared from behind a bush. She held a bow in front of her, with an arrow ready to be fired. Behind her were another girl and two men with spears. They all wore pieces of fur on their clothes that looked remarkably like Monster's pelt. I tried not to dwell on this fact.

Rorik raised his hands to show he wasn't looking for trouble. Finn glanced at him and mimicked the gesture. It looked absurd with his long arms and useless wing flaps.

The girl, whose bow I noticed was carved with intricate patterns of twists and curlicues, came up to us. She was a little taller than me. I anticipated the usual. Being either overlooked or insulted. My repulsion spells had shown themselves to be particularly effective in Hrafnheim.

But none of that happened.

She reached her hand out to me and smiled.

"My name is Faida." She gestured over her shoulder to an older girl wearing armor. "That's Birna."

They shook our hands as we looked at them in wonder.

Rorik's eyes flickered between me and them.

"I'm Rorik, and this is Anna," he said, seeing that I was at a loss for words.

The men introduced themselves as Tíw and Styrr. Something—I don't know what—made me suspect that Tíw was the leader but let Faida run the show.

"Come with us," Faida said. "We have food and drink in Ísafold."

Rorik and I exchanged a glance. He shrugged his shoulders.

"Well, we do need a place to stop." He might as well have said *hide out.*

"And we could use the gold," Birna said as Faida shushed her.

"We Ísafolders are known for our hospitality," she said. "That's why we're inviting you."

She gave Birna a long look, while Tíw concealed a grin behind his fist.

So we followed them to the town.

Birna chatted and joked with Rorik, while Faida looked shyly at him. Tíw fell into step alongside me.

"It's not every day you see a trained fingalk."

"He's not trained."

"Then what is he?" Tíw looked more closely at the large creature. Finn swung his arms and scratched his forehead.

For a moment, I watched Finn, and my chest grew strangely warm. "He would probably tell you he's part of our flock, if that's what we are."

"Flock." Tíw laughed. "You could also call the Ísafolders that."

"You're the leader," I observed.

He ran a hand over his full dark-brown beard. I noticed a silver ring on his middle finger.

"What makes you say that?" he asked.

I shrugged. "You're older than the others, and you seem more mellow."

He was about to say something, but I cut him off. "And you're always looking at them with concern."

He smiled to himself as he used his own carved bow as a walking stick. His hair was long and hung loose, with thin braids here and there, fastened at the ends with small gold rings. When we walked up a slope, he held out his hand.

I shook my head, which made him chuckle. "You're also the leader of your little trio."

"Why do you think that?"

He nodded in the direction of Rorik's tall figure, which was flanked by the girls. "Because you let him go first, but you always keep an eye on him."

I didn't mention I was starting to suspect there was another reason I couldn't keep my eyes off Rorik's broad back. I focused my efforts on walking up the hill.

"Then we're a lot alike." I quickened my pace and joined Rorik, Birna, and Faida.

"Is this your first time in Ísafold?" Birna asked, and once again, I looked at her, astonished. I had learned to be on guard when people acted friendly toward me, but when I nodded silently, she just kept talking.

"Okay, I'll show you everything. We so rarely get visitors." Her arm wrapped around mine, and she pointed out the buildings, but I wasn't really listening. I just looked down at our interlocking arms.

". . . the women's house," she finished a sentence I hadn't really heard. She studied me critically. "You're staying the night, right? No offence, but you really need a bath." She leaned toward me. "Your husband does, too, if you don't mind me saying it. He's attractive, but you can't see it through all the dirt."

"He's not my husband," I squeaked.

Faida turned her head toward us.

People came up to us as we walked between the houses, and Faida pointed proudly at us, as if to say she deserved credit for bringing us—which, in a way, she did. Curious eyes followed us from doorways and windows.

The men I saw had long hair and full beards. Their locks were interspersed with thin braids finished with the same small metal rings as Tíw's, though I noted that his rings had more of a golden shine. Some women wore dresses and some wore pants, both in the familiar earth tones, and their long hair, too, hung loose down their backs. Most had red or blond hair, with pale skin and freckles. Tíw's brown hair was an anomaly.

A child ran up and grabbed Tíw's hand. "Guess what!"

"What?" Tíw said.

"The black mare's mane was braided again this morning, but no one had been there all night."

Tíw looked seriously at the boy. "Then the elves must have been here again. We'd better make sure to stay on their good side."

"Should I leave a loaf of bread in the grove?"

He furrowed his brows. "Of course not. We don't make offerings. You know it's forbidden to make offerings to anyone but Ragnara."

A questioning look spread across the boy's face, and a woman came running up and pulled him away.

I snuck over to Rorik. "Are we prisoners?"

He looked around and stumbled to the side when Finn pressed himself up against him. "It's okay, Finn. They won't hurt us."

"Okay," the fingalk repeated.

I raised an eyebrow. "Have you started using words from Midgard?"

Rorik changed the subject. "Ísafolders are known for their hospitality."

"Why do they like me?"

Rorik shrugged.

Birna grabbed me by the sleeve. "You're going to the women's house. Come on."

We were separated.

"What about Rorik?"

Birna gave me a confused look.

"The men's house," she said cautiously.

"And Finn? Our fingalk, I mean."

"Oh." Birna bit her lip. "He can stay in the stables with the other animals."

"Just a second," I said and grabbed Finn's hairy arm. "You're going to stay with the animals. Do *not* eat them." I paused. "Or kill them, or even hurt them. You'll get food later."

Finn's orange eyes grew round. "Not with Krik and Nana?"

I tried to find the words to explain. "The Ísafolders aren't used to fingalks."

He cocked his head. "What is fingalk?"

"Um . . . uh . . ." I scratched him behind the ears and resisted the urge to fling my arms around his smelly body. "I'm just going to take a bath, and then I'll come find you. Will you go over there?"

He watched as I was pulled toward a long building on a corner of the street. I looked over my shoulder a couple of times but eventually forced myself to go through the door. Inside, I saw sauna benches lining the walls. It smelled like smoke and people but also a hint of lavender and thyme. The other women were reserved at first, but when they saw that Birna and Faida were talking to me, it didn't take long for them to throw themselves at me. I was washed and combed before pulling on clean clothes. Birna took my dirty clothes away, holding them out between her thumb and index finger with a grim expression.

In the end, I smelled of their spruce-scented soap and was as clean as I could get. I refused to have my hair braided, but gathered it in an elastic, which Faida studied curiously.

"What is that?"

I acted like I hadn't heard her.

"Is it from Miklagard?"

I nodded quickly. "Yep."

"Is that where you're from?"

I rummaged aimlessly in my bag to hide my face. "Not really."

Birna came back from her expedition to the laundry room. "They need to soak. I've never seen such dirty clothes before."

Faida continued speaking as she placed a clean piece of cloth on a bench.

"Where are you from? Your clothes are a strange mix. The axe is from Hibernia. You talk like someone from Danheim, but Rorik sounds like he's from Sént. Most fingalks live in Norvík or Svearike, and I've never seen a bag like yours." She pointed at my backpack, which was made of durable fabric with leather straps. To my knowledge, it was made in a factory in Sweden.

Again, I mumbled something vague in response.

"And this is to designate Ragnara's property." She pointed at the fehu brand on my forearm.

"I didn't choose it," I said quietly.

"Maybe Anna doesn't want to talk about that," Birna interjected with an admonishing look.

Faida's hands stroked the bench. She didn't comment on the correction, but her jaw tightened. Then she smiled again. "Everyone's entitled to their secrets. It's none of my concern."

Come to find out, it would become very much her concern.

We hid out in Ísafold for one day, while the intense feeling of Ragnara's presence weakened. Rorik wouldn't dare continue toward Sént if I could still sense her, even though I felt like I was sitting on a ticking time bomb. At first, Finn was unhappy to be relegated to the stables, but he quickly made friends with the horses and cows, and later in the day, I found him sleeping arm in arm with a pregnant pig.

I stood for a while, watching him, and I swore a silent oath that I would always do whatever it took to keep him out of harm's way.

Rorik and Tíw went for a long walk, during which, Tíw showed him the sparse crops and hunting grounds. Tíw had been put in charge of Ísafold after his father died last winter. He had been chosen, even though the Ísafolders had never had such a young leader before.

I hadn't even noticed how exhausted I was until I laid my head on a clean pillow in the women's house. I woke twelve hours later, ravenously hungry, my whole body stiff from lying still. I met Rorik in the common house, and he looked just as groggy as I felt. His hair was clean, and he smelled good.

We ate bread and dried berries silently, with a view over the flat plain at the other end of the town.

"We went down to Barre yesterday," Rorik said after a long silence. "Tíw showed me the grove."

"What's it like?"

Rorik looked out over the flat, heather-covered landscape with its small, spiky thorn bushes. The place made me homesick for North Jutland. I never thought I would miss its windblown expanses and clean air. The grove wasn't visible, as there was a steep drop at the end of the plain.

"It's peaceful," he said, taking a sip of milk. "Tíw said that it was once a holy grove, though obviously not anymore. Now it's just sitting there. It's beautiful. The Iving runs down there and marks the end of Frón."

We sat a while longer in silence and let the calm descend over us. A few older people came in. Two women and one man each sat down with a bowl of porridge at the same long table as us. One woman had a beige scarf draped loosely over her gray hair.

"There were footprints in the hoar frost this morning. They were this big." The woman without a scarf used her hand to demonstrate how small the prints had been.

The older man looked at her gesture. "Did the children go out in the field before we got up?"

"It wasn't the children. A whole row of blackberry bushes was missing," said the woman.

The other woman—the one with the scarf—made an expression that indicated she knew exactly where the prints came from.

Rorik moved closer. "What tracks are you taking about?"

He used his questioning voice. The somewhat casual tone he used when he was pumping people for information. I had him figured out. The people didn't notice and spoke willingly.

"The little footprints appear all the way up here sometimes," the old man said. "A couple of days ago, there were prints in the dust on the main street."

"Is it animals?" Rorik asked, taking a nonchalant sip of milk.

The woman with the scarf laughed. "Oh, no; it's elves."

I snorted. "Elves?"

The other woman gave me a sharp look, and it was clear she thought this was no laughing matter. "You don't know the stories?"

"No."

Rorik took his mug and swirled the milk around, as though elf stories were trivial. "I've heard a little, but I don't know what's myth and what's truth."

"They're all myths. There are no elves here," the man said with a pointed look at me and Rorik.

"Yes, there are too elves!" the woman with the scarf interjected. "They come here sometimes from their world, Alfheim."

The man laughed nervously. "Then tell the story again, Granny. Now that there's finally outsiders here who don't know it. But remember," he said to us, "it's only a fairy tale. Granny here just has a very active imagination."

The woman rubbed her hands together and raised her shoulders. "They say, over a thousand years ago in Midgard, a herd of seals arrived at the coast. This was at a fjord in the northern part of the Danes' land, where row after row of linden trees grew."

"Seals?" I asked the woman.

"Yes! Seals. But these were no normal animals. They were elves who went ashore. They placed their skins in a cave and emerged in all their beauty and danced and feasted among the burial mounds. A farmer—he was our forefather—walked past the cave. He saw the many sealskins and thought they were beautiful. He didn't know they belonged to magical beings."

Rorik tilted his head to the side. "Did he take the skins?"

The woman, who now sensed that she had an audience—me, Rorik, and the other two old people—leaned toward us. "He took one skin." She extended a wrinkled finger. "Just one. The shiniest one, with the loveliest golden color. Then he went back home. The elves returned to the cave, dressed themselves in the pelts, and jumped back into the fjord. But one elf had to stay on land, as she was missing her skin."

I inhaled. The thought of the abandoned elf struck something in me, even though it was just a story.

The woman continued. "The elf woman, who was as beautiful as the sun itself, went to the farmer's homestead. He found the naked elf woman in his bed. He . . ." The woman wiggled her fingers, and we started to laugh. She waited patiently until we were quiet again. "He married her!" she summarized with a grin.

There was a chuckle from behind me, and I turned around. More people had joined us, and they were nudging each other excitedly.

"Together they had many children. The farmer's hair turned gray." With an apologetic expression, she tugged on her friend's gray braid. "But the elf woman remained as young as that first night. One day, her granddaughter found a golden seal skin hidden in the attic. The girl showed it to her grandmother, and the elf woman took it in her hands, saying nothing."

It was now completely silent in the common house as everyone listened. Some people came in talking, but they were quickly hushed.

The storyteller looked around, building up the suspense before she spoke again. "The elf woman didn't say a word. Not to her husband, nor to her children, nor her grandchildren. She simply walked to the fjord, where she pulled on the skin and disappeared beneath the waves without so much as a backward glance."

You could have heard a pin drop in the room. A child shifted in his father's lap.

"The farmer's descendants later came to Freiheim during the great migration." The woman whispered, "We Ísafolders have a tiny bit of elf blood in us, because the elf is our foremother. Legend has it, the elves still keep an eye on us, because we are their kin. They wander through the fields at night, and sometimes they come all the way up here to beautify our lives with flower petals, or," she looked directly at the child, ". . . perhaps braid our horses' manes."

The boy gasped and clutched his father's shirt.

"Elves can become angry if we don't give them food and drink. They bring sickness and misfortune to people. That's why we leave bread and ale for them, so they know we're their friends."

"But that's forbidden," came the clear voice of a child.

The woman looked gravely at the child. "You're right, it is forbidden. But what's worse? Ragnara's wrath, or that of the elves?"

For a moment, silence hung over the common house, but then applause broke out.

The woman bowed elegantly—it seemed she had entertained people many times before.

I clapped, too, and by my side, I heard Rorik whoop, but when I looked at him, he bore a ponderous expression. The crowd dispersed, and soon, we were once again alone in the common house.

Faida stuck her head in the door. "Remember, there's a party tonight. You *must* come."

The girls were ecstatic. They giggled and flitted around the building reserved for the women. I sat at a small table and studied Rebecca's notebook as I tried to ignore the squeals around me.

"What are you going to wear?" Birna was suddenly standing in front of me. Her golden hair had been slicked back and arranged in a sophisticated, braided updo. Gone was the dusty leather armor she's been wearing. Her dress was ochre, with small green leaves embroidered on it.

I looked up. "What do you mean?"

"Tonight? For the festivities."

"What festivities?"

Now Faida came over. She lifted my red ponytail. "I can put your hair up."

I pulled my hair out of her hand.

"No, thanks." With a protective grip on my elastic band, I studied the girls' hectic, flushed appearances. "What is happening tonight?"

Faida sat on the table in front of me. Without noticing, she placed her butt right on my open book. Her hair hung to her waist and was a shade lighter than mine. A couple of twists embellished her tresses.

"Anna, if I didn't know any better, I would think you weren't even from Freiheim." She laughed, and I quickly looked down.

Birna squatted and looked up at me with a teasing smile on her pursed lips.

"Today is hálfa." When I looked at her uncomprehendingly, she elaborated. "We're celebrating that winter is halfway over."

"Okay." I tried discreetly to grab the book from under Faida's butt.

"All the girls and women aim to look as beautiful as possible. It's a special evening for us."

"Because it's a chance to get all dolled up?" I pulled on the book, causing Faida to shift. Finally, it was safely back in my hands, and I clapped it shut.

"You could have just asked me to move." Faida scowled, but her excitement made her smile again. "It only happens once a year."

"What only happens once a year?" I tucked the book into the pocket of my coat.

Birna rolled her eyes. "The women get to pick out the man they want."

My hand stopped halfway into the pocket. "You need a special day to do that?"

Now Faida clapped her hands.

"Girls aren't . . ." she searched for the right word, "the pursuers, when it comes to that kind of thing."

"Wow, that's so old-fashioned. In my opinion, gender roles are made to be broken." I scoffed, and Faida ignored me.

"The men aren't allowed to say no tonight, during hálfa. Because life is slowly returning to the earth, and women are the fertile ones, it's our celebration." She let out an excited *eeeeee* and twirled around. "I've never taken part before."

"I have." Birna wiggled her eyebrows deviously. "I mean, I didn't go all the way, but I—"

"La, la, la . . ." I covered my ears.

When the girls looked at me questioningly, I lowered my hands. "I'm sort of embarrassed by that kind of thing."

"But it's completely natural for women and men to—"

"La, la, la," I repeated, grimacing.

Birna flashed an understanding grin.

"Do you follow all the seasons so slavishly?" I asked.

Faida jumped in. "Equinoxes and solstices are magical. Nature reaches out to us on those days. During the summer solstice, we're as close as we can get to the perfect world. The fall equinox prepares us for the winter and protects us from the deepest sleep, and during the winter solstice, we're so close to death, we can nearly see into the realm of the dead."

Yep—you're right about that one.

"Hálfa, on the other hand . . ." Birna closed her eyes and enjoyed a delicate sunbeam peeking in the window. "Now is when everything begins, and bonds are formed. Now is when the magic of creation starts to crackle. I already know who I want."

"I've decided, too," Faida said.

"Good luck with assaulting a couple of innocent men," I said, widening my eyes.

Faida shoved my shoulder with one hand.

"You're not getting out of it." When she saw my warning look, she hurried to continue. "You're not getting out of dressing up, anyway."

I gave in only when Birna threatened me with a heavy gown embroidered with flowers. I might have even caught sight of a butterfly or two on it. When I realized I wouldn't be allowed to leave the house in pants—it was either a skirt or nothing, Faida teased—I pulled the green dress Luna had sewn me for New Year's Eve from the bottom of my bag. I hadn't thought I would ever wear it again.

A murmur traveled through the group of girls.

"It's just a dress." I sighed.

Birna cautiously stroked a hand over the green fabric. "What's it made of?"

I shrugged. "Silk, I think."

There was a collective moan.

"What?"

Faida was the first to compose herself. "Silk is unfathomably expensive. You can only get it in Miklagard, and even there it's unaffordable." She stared again at the fabric. "For us, anyway."

I turned the dress around in the weak sunbeams trickling in through the open window. To me, what made it spectacular were Luna's creative abilities, but apparently the girls were more impressed by the material.

"Where did you get it?" Faida narrowed her eyes.

"I was a gift." Before she could ask anything else, I added: "From a friend who's really good at sewing."

Faida said nothing more.

"Put it on, put it on." Birna jumped up and down.

"I was gonna wait until right before the party."

But the other girls joined in, whooping.

"Put it on, put it on." They stomped their feet rhythmically and clapped.

Defeated, I looked out the window, where some men, including Rorik, were peeking in our direction. There must have been an awful racket coming from the women's house. I imagined it sounded like a henhouse.

I walked away from the opening and pulled on the dress. In bare feet and with my hair still in a messy ponytail, I flung out my arms. "There—are you satisfied?"

It was completely silent.

Faida crept forward and carefully undid my ponytail. My hair fell down over the deep back neckline.

There was a deafening screech as the women threw themselves on me and—talking and laughing all the while—began to comb and braid my hair, paint my eyes, and smooth my dress.

All my objections were drowned out by clucking and shouting.

I was pulled along in a maelstrom of excited girls. Wedged between Faida and Birna, I ended up at the long table, which was overflowing with food. They plunked me down between Tíw and Styrr.

For the occasion, both men had combed their beards and hair, which was, as always, adorned with small metal rings. Their clothes were freshly washed and smelled like spruce.

The beard made Styrr look grown up, though I estimated him to be at most two or three years older than me. Tíw must have been a little older, but not by much. Again, I noticed the ring on his right hand.

Tíw poured juice in my glass, and Styrr placed meat and cheese on my plate.

A bit farther down the table sat Rorik. His long, pale hair hung loose, and here and there it was braided and fastened with silver rings, as was customary among the Ísafolders. He wore a clean dark-brown shirt that matched the color of his eyes.

Faida sat at his side, and she spoke with a smile and repeatedly touched her hair and lips. She had placed the woman with the beige scarf, who was apparently her grandmother, on his other flank. At one point, she had him sniff her wrist, after which she whispered something in his ear. Her finger followed the blue eagle tattoo from the back of his hand and down across his fingers.

I felt a twinge in my stomach, but I kept my face neutral. With a raised eyebrow, I lifted my glass in his direction, and he returned the gesture with an awkward grin.

I concentrated on the food and tuned out Tíw and Styrr's conversation. Fortunately, Birna sat on Styrr's other side, and he quickly turned his attention toward her when he gathered that I was—to put it mildly—not interested.

Tíw was more persistent. He pointed downward. "Guess what I have under the table."

I wrinkled my nose and scratched my forehead. "No idea."

He leaned in toward me and ran a hand over his beard. The silver ring on his finger caught the sun's rays. He pointed down. "Take a look."

"Are you serious?"

"Go on," he said again and leaned closer to shield us from prying eyes.

I looked down cautiously. Fortunately, it was only a bottle.

"What is that?" The corners of my mouth crept up slightly.

"It's moonshine. And it's as strong as they come." He scratched his cheek. "Gimme your cup."

As discreetly as I could, I chugged the elderberry juice. Then I lowered my cup under the table, and Tíw poured an oily, clear liquid into my clay cup and then his own.

I sniffed and nearly sneezed from the sharp alcoholic fumes.

"Isn't it illegal?" I whispered.

Tíw bit his lower lip. "Very."

From where he sat, Rorik was following my conspiratorial conversation with Tíw, but Faida tugged on his sleeve.

I took a tentative sip of the moonshine and had to breathe in and out quickly to keep from spluttering. Tíw followed suit, but drained his cup without so much as a shudder. I gave up and coughed. To conceal it, I hid my head in Tíw's shoulder.

He put his arm around me and patted my back. He kept his arm there, but no one seemed to notice.

No one except Rorik.

The party wore on, and even though no one advertised the fact that they were drinking moonshine—or other alcoholic beverages—the atmosphere became more relaxed. Unfathomable amounts of food were placed on the table, all exotic and foreign to me. There were small, crispy cookies with salted fish, salads of green sprouts, long rows of eggs, and butter mixed with smoked ham that could be spread directly onto freshly baked bread.

A couple of shriveled apples made the rounds, and everyone took a bite. When the brown, half-chewed core came to me, I stared at it uncertainly.

"Take a bite," Tíw said.

I glanced at the well-stocked table.

"There's quite a lot of food already," I leaned in toward him and whispered, "food that's, you know . . . fresh."

He leaned his head back slightly. "Don't you know the superstition?"

I shook my head.

He looked suspiciously at me, but then understanding flowed across his face. "It's because you're not from Ísafold."

"Yes, that must be why," I said, then cleared my throat.

"There's a belief that, on hálfa, you should eat an apple from last year's harvest."

I looked at the wrinkled, half-eaten fruit. "This is definitely from last year."

Tíw interrupted me with a smile. "Then you'll be protected from misfortune in the year to come."

Maybe not such a bad idea.

My teeth sank into the mealy, spongy apple, then I passed it to Styrr.

The juice ran from my mouth, but Tíw caught a drop on his finger. I jerked my head back and held a hand in front of my lips as I chewed. Without saying anything, he stuck his finger in his mouth and sucked the apple juice off while maintaining eye contact.

I felt an intense urge to leave the table, so I tumbled backward over the bench and got to my feet. Even though I had held back on the moonshine, I could feel the alcohol surging through my blood when I stood up. I felt dizzy, and I jogged behind one of the low buildings. I leaned against a clay-plastered wall and took big gulps of cold air. My hands reached behind me, and I found a straw sticking out of the clay wall. I pulled it out and squeezed it.

In front of me lay the flat expanse that made up the Ísafolders' front lawn. It was as if it suddenly stopped. Simply disappeared into nothing. I knew it was because Barre, the deep-set grove, and the river Iving dove down, but as I stood there, I felt like I was standing on the edge of nothingness.

"I'm sorry."

The voice made me shudder. Tíw was standing a few paces away.

"You don't need to apologize."

"Yes, I do."

He walked closer.

"I was hoping . . ." He turned his head and looked out across the plain. "You know what I was hoping."

"Why do you even like me? Why do all of you like me?" My voice came out sounding more desperate than I wanted, and I squeezed the dry straw even harder. It cut into my palm.

Cautiously, Tíw came closer.

"Why wouldn't we like you?" He scratched his beard. "You're tough, but you're a good person. That much is clear."

I looked at him. "No, it's not."

He looked at me, uncomprehending.

"I have these spells on me," I explained. "They're permanent. I've tried to have them lifted." My voice cracked. "Most people think I'm repulsive. But here . . ." I waved my hand, the words getting caught in my throat. "You're friendly."

To my surprise, Tíw's laughter rang out over the nothingness. "We aren't affected by that kind of thing here in Ísafold. Maybe it's that one drop of elf blood that allows our people to see through spells."

"So no one here hates me?"

"Of course not." He stood close to me now. "You should stay here. With us."

Suddenly, I felt compelled to study my feet in their soft, brown slippers.

Tíw's hand stroked my hair.

"The girls like you. The elders like you." His mouth was right up against my ear. "I like you."

Moisture sprang to the corners of my eyes.

We stood like that for a while. Me with my eyes directed at my feet, and Tíw with a hand on my hair and his mouth to my ear.

"I have something to show you," he whispered.

"Oh, I don't want . . ." I began.

"No, no. Nothing like that." He smiled. "It's the women's day. I was overeager. But I still want to show you something."

"All right, then."

With long strides, he walked toward his house. We ducked through the doorway and into the dark living area. He disappeared into an interior room.

"Come in here," he called.

I followed him and found myself in his bedroom.

313

He gestured to the bed. "Can you help me out?"

"Hey . . ." I said.

"Help me move it."

"Ohh."

With our combined efforts, we were able to move the heavy bed. Beneath it, there was a trapdoor in the floor.

"I'm sure you've never seen anything like this before," Tíw said with a sly look on his face.

"Uh, nope. Never."

He pulled up the hatch to reveal a short staircase leading down to a cellar beneath the house.

It wasn't as deep and gloomy as the crypt beneath Odinmont, but nevertheless, the hairs on my arms stood up as we descended underground.

Finally, we reached a bookshelf on which there sat a box. The cold light of day struck the shelf from above. Tíw inserted his ring into an indentation on the front of the box and turned his hand until there was a little *click*.

"Nice camouflage," I remarked.

He laughed as he looked at the ring, which was apparently also a key.

"Even something small and beautiful can serve an important function." He winked at me when he said this.

Inside the box, there were several small objects packed in a moldering piece of fabric. His large hands carefully unwrapped little figurines and placed them in a row on the shelf.

I studied them.

One depicted a small, chubby man with a golden hat, sitting in lotus pose. The next was a person with an elephant's head and four arms. The third was a nude woman with her arms upstretched, and the last one showed a figure standing tall with a bird on each shoulder, two wolves lying at his feet, and—unmistakably—he was missing one eye.

Tíw unwrapped a final object from the fabric and handed it to me. A silver cross with a person nailed to it. It wasn't the typical suffering Jesus, but a proud, strong-willed man with a calculating expression on his mouth. He looked like he could jump down off the cross at any time.

Carefully, I laid the crucifix at the end of the little row.

Tíw put his hands on his hips. "They're very old. My ancestors brought them here from Midgard."

"Do you know what they are?" I probed.

Tíw nodded.

"Even though it's forbidden now, my father told me about Odin when I was a kid." He pulled the one-eyed man forward slightly. "And Freyja." He pushed the nude woman toward me.

"But the others, those are totally different religions," I said, tracing the cross with my finger.

"Before Ragnara, they were all accepted. The residents of Miklagard believed in many different gods. It was allowed, even though most of the people here followed the Norse faith."

I turned the Buddha around. "But isn't it super dangerous for you to have them?"

Tíw looked at me, dust motes dancing in the beam of light from above. "It's our heritage."

"That won't help you if someone finds out. You shouldn't even be showing them to me."

Tíw pointed at the little silver hand that hung from a chain around my neck.

I placed my hand over it. "This? It was a gift."

"It's a symbol."

"It's just for decoration."

He narrowed his eyes.

"You don't seem that big on decoration." He shrugged. "But of course, you can always just say you bought it in Miklagard. Then it doesn't mean anything."

"Why are you pointing at it? And showing me dangerous things?" My voice grew a bit shrill.

Tíw's forehead wrinkled.

"Because *you* aren't from Miklagard." I wanted to protest, but he cut me off. "I don't think you're even from Freiheim at all. I think you're here to free us from Ragnara, and if that's the case, I want to let you know that the Ísafolders stand behind you."

My mouth opened, but I couldn't say anything. I squeezed Hakim's gift.

We heard voices from the house above us, and Tíw hurriedly packed all the figurines back into the box. He locked it and returned it to the shelf. Then he led me back up the stairs.

In the room, he shoved the bed back into place with a routine motion, while loud laughter resounded from the living area. We stuck our heads out of the bedroom to find Birna and Styrr in a tight embrace. Birna giggled, and Styrr kissed her neck. Both swayed slightly.

Tíw's deep voice rang out. "Did the lady lay claim to you, Styrr?"

Styrr caught sight of us. "Very much so." He exhaled.

Birna laughed again.

Authority flowed from Tíw, and I got a glimpse of the leader he was to his people. "You could end up with a baby if you keep going."

Feeling awkward, I wanted to sneak out. In my opinion, this was a very private matter that neither I nor Tíw should have anything to do with, but Tíw held me back.

A touch of sobriety reached Birna's face.

Styrr stood up a little straighter.

"We'll hold back. We just want to be alone." He glanced toward the bedroom. "Are you done?"

I held my hands over my eyes and made a mortified noise.

Tíw swung open the door to the bedroom.

When I stepped out, embarrassed both on their behalf and my own, the couple hopped onto the bed behind me.

Tíw returned to the feast, while I ran across the flat plain toward Barre.

Finally, I found peace down in the little grove. It was warmer there than on the plain and in the town, and a few yards away from me flowed the river that bordered the Iron Forest. A loaf of bread sat on the ground not far from the water.

I let my back slide down the trunk of a birch tree, and the soft moss gave way beneath me when I landed on it. I leaned my head back and enjoyed the quiet. High above me, the clouds floated lazily across the pink afternoon sky, and somewhere in the forest a bird chattered, while the river Iving babbled steadily.

Branches and twigs cracked, and footsteps came running in my direction. I fumbled for Auka, until I realized it wasn't part of my formal wear.

Stupid dress.

I got up, standing as tense as a coiled spring as the sound came closer.

It was Rorik who appeared in the grove.

"What's wrong?" I shouted and bent my knees, ready for an attack.

"She's after me." He panted. His hair was matted, and he looked over his shoulder.

"Who's after you?" I looked around.

"Faida."

I lowered my hands. "Faida?"

Again, Rorik looked around. "She said the words *I choose* . . . and then I ran."

The river sloshed a bit more wildly, and a breeze caused the treetops to creak.

"You ran away?" I suppressed a smile and eyed his broad shoulders.

He answered seriously. "Yes. But I think she's right behind me."

"Say no if she catches you." I squinted. "I mean, unless you want to."

"I don't," Rorik said quickly. His brown eyes lingered a second too long on my face. Then he peered between the trees again. "But you're not allowed to say no. Not today."

We heard Faida's voice through the trees.

"Of course you can say no." My arms folded across my chest. "You can always say no."

The treetops whistled again, and more birds joined in.

Rorik looked desperately at me. "Say you choose me."

"Absolutely not!"

"She can't claim me if someone else already has."

I backed away, bumping into the tree trunk. "It should be possible to politely say, *no, thank you.*"

Faida's voice came closer. "Rooooriiik?"

"Not now. There's magic in the air today." He looked at me pleadingly.

It must have been my imagination, but it felt as though the ground trembled beneath me when Rorik said *magic.*

"All this talk about witchcraft."

Faida emerged from between the trees. She ran toward us, breathless. "Rorik, I wanted to choose you."

Rorik tugged on my sleeve. When I didn't react, he shoved his elbow into my side.

"Ow!" I rubbed my rib. "Dibs." I gestured at Rorik with my thumb.

The corners of her mouth turned down in disbelief.

"I didn't think there was anything between you." She came closer, suspicious. "Do you *want* to choose him, or have you chosen him? Do I still have a chance to say it first?"

Now Rorik stepped on my foot.

"Hey!" I looked up angrily, but his desperate expression made me mumble: "I've chosen him."

"Say it," he hissed through gritted teeth.

"I choose Rorik."

The birds chattered again, and the soft moss bulged beneath my feet.

Faida's lips pulled back regretfully.

"Well, congratulations, then," she said with a dignified air, and she took a couple of backward steps before turning around and running off.

We stood alone. Rorik was still holding on to my sleeve, and the ground spun beneath my feet. The waters of the Iving flowed more powerfully than before.

"I feel something," he whispered. The hand clutching my sleeve loosened its grip.

A force shot up between my legs.

"I only said that to help you," I said, short of breath. "I didn't mean it."

The earth pulsated, and Rorik's fingers found the back of my hand and stroked it softly.

Unthinking, I interlaced my fingers with his.

Something about this felt familiar.

I didn't hear the wind or the water anymore, but their energy became one with my body.

Rorik pushed me against the birch tree. Not a hard shove, but a gentle nudge. His tattooed hand found my cheek. "You meant it."

The tree's power ran through me and into Rorik. A pleasant, warm wind flowed from the eagle on his hand.

If I hadn't known what was happening, I would have resisted. I would have said the magic was acting on us against our will, and I would have tried to push it away. But I knew love magic. I had encountered it before, and I knew it worked only when people were already in love.

Rorik's grip on my face grew stronger, and now he cupped both hands around it. My arms found their way around his body, and through the fabric of his shirt, I felt him trying as hard as he could to hold back.

"What's going on?" he asked. "Are we under a spell?"

Tilarids quivered furiously in its sheath. Something told me the sword didn't care for love.

"Yes," I whispered and held him closer. "This is magic."

His face was now close to mine.

"How do we dispel the witchcraft?" He pulled me close, trying to push me away at the same time.

"We can't cast off the magic because it comes from us," I whispered, leaning forward.

At the same time, he gave up on holding back, and our lips met in a passionate kiss. My entire body felt like it was exploding, and colored lights flashed before my eyes. Rorik's fingers traced my neck, and the touch sent even more pleasant electric shocks into me. His hands moved to my shoulders, and then farther down.

His kisses became deeper as he pressed himself harder against me. His shirt dropped slowly to the moss-covered ground, and his bare skin felt like silk beneath my fingers. His tattoos formed small ridges on his skin, and I found myself thinking of his body as one big topographical map.

I don't know if we fell, but suddenly we were lying down. The force from the earth flowed into our bodies, and the large heart pounded all around us.

"Creation," Rorik mumbled. "This is the power of creation."

Neither of us said anything coherent after that.

Rorik slept naked on the soft moss, but I was wide awake. Above us, the sky was deep blue and full of tiny, twinkling stars.

It should have been colder, but the combination of magic and the power of creation allowed our little patch of earth to stay warm and green. Frost glittered on the trees just yards away from us, and the sound of the Iving was once again calm, small splashes.

I studied Rorik intently, because I wanted to remember every inch of him.

Most of his body was decorated with ink, and with each of his steady breaths, the figures on his skin moved as though they were running, fighting, or . . . I tilted my head and looked at a couple . . . dancing. I felt the urge to run my hand over the small scars on his shoulder, but I clenched my fist and pulled my arm against my body. With a sigh, I stood and took a few steps around our little area. I found my dress, which lay a few feet away, covered in a layer of frost. With a shiver, I pulled it on. The cold helped clear my head.

I took another look at the sleeping Rorik, and a feeling I had felt before threatened to break my chest open. My fingers touched his cheek one more time before I turned and ran toward the settlement.

It was still and clear in the little town. Even the animals were sleeping at their posts.

I snuck into the women's house and saw that, in most beds, there were two people. Men and women slept in each other's arms. Faida lay alone, her fiery hair forming a wave above her head. Guilt gnawed at me when I saw the skin under her eyes was red and swollen.

After locating my bag and changing into my normal clothes, I crept over to her bunk. I carefully placed my green dress next to her with a note on top. Though I still wasn't great with the runic alphabet, I had scratched something I was pretty sure resembled her name.

Then I left.

As quietly as I could, I ran toward the river Iving, and with great effort, I managed not to look in Rorik's direction as I passed our place in the forest.

It would be best and safest for Rorik if I got as far away from him as possible. I would do whatever it took to make sure Serén's prediction that he would die protecting me didn't come true.

I thought of Finn, and my heart threatened to explode. It would also be safest for him not to be near me. I hoped the two of them could take care of each other.

As I hopped barefoot, my slippers held above my head, into the Iving—which, like the story said, had no hint of ice on its surface—I inhaled sharply.

On the other side of the river, I jumped up and down to warm myself. I sat on a rock and put my socks and shoes back on. Things didn't look much different on this side of the river.

A wealth of ice crystals sparkled below, and clear stars shone above. But I was now in Jötunnland.

I stood and began walking into the forest. Everything around me looked like it came from a fairy tale, cloaked in shimmering crystals with silvery moonlight streaming down. I walked for a while, and I felt resoundingly alone.

"Where did you come from?" came a sweet voice from the bushes.

I looked around and reached for Auka.

CHAPTER 24

A curly head stuck out of the crystalline thicket. He had dark ringlets and large, amber-colored eyes. His lips curved upward when he smiled at me, and I totally melted under his gaze.

"Are you a demigod?" I breathed.

He let out an effervescent laugh. "No."

I laughed, too. I don't know why, but he was so warm and inviting, I couldn't help it. The smell of caramel intoxicated my senses. In a far corner of my consciousness, something was screaming that witchcraft was at play, but maybe it was the love magic still flowing through my veins. Or maybe this magic was even stronger. My hand abandoned its place on Auka's handle.

The boy stepped out of the brush and stood up straight, not much taller than me. His torso was bare beneath a silver vest, and a transparent, iridescent material hung from his shoulders like a cape. His skin was smooth and golden, and despite the cold that turned my breath into fog around me, heat emanated from his body in thin, flickering waves.

Without thinking, I stroked his forearm, which was just as soft as I expected.

He let me do it as if it were the most natural thing in the world.

"Who are you?" I couldn't get the smile off my lips.

He bowed toward me, and I inhaled his scent again as his curls brushed my face.

"I'm Nore. Who are you?"

"Anna," I said.

Nore drank in my scent with a deep breath.

"What a lovely Christian name. Very unusual here." He took my hand, and—as though it were totally normal—I let him do it.

"Are you from Ísafold? I didn't see you in the town," I asked. I definitely would have noticed him.

Nore shook his head.

"Things have been tough for us since Ragnara came to power, and we've had to get closer to humans than we should to get what we need."

I didn't have the wherewithal to ask what he meant by *us*.

"I was drawn by all the love," he explained, though I still didn't quite understand what he meant. "Where's your handsome friend?"

Heat pulsed from our interwoven hands, up my arm, and into my chest.

"Over there." I pointed. "He's on the other side of the Iving."

"If only I could take both of you." Nore shook his head regretfully, so the brown curls caressed his face. "But that's human land over there, where only the bravest or most foolhardy of my people dare to go."

"I can go get him," I offered, ready to jump across the river to please Nore.

"No," he whispered in my ear and pulled gently on our hands. "I don't want to risk losing you."

I went with him without asking where we were heading. As it turned out, we weren't going very far. Or, in any case, it didn't feel like we went very far.

We reached a mound, and Nore pulled me into it through a long passageway covered in hexagonal decorations. Some were filled with a golden liquid that splashed softly. Others contained small, twirling, white half-moons. The room at the end was hemisphere-shaped and covered in the same gold and white hexagons. Light filtered through them, giving the entire room a surreal glow.

There were rings of dancing women and men, all with the same translucent capes as Nore. They moved in circles, spinning around one another so quickly, I could barely follow them. The capes fluttered behind them.

"What is this?" I asked with wonder.

Nore looked at the dancers. "It's the Halling dance."

I stared, enchanted.

On the floor sat a glass bowl full of ripe fruit. Garlands of flowers tumbled over the sides, giving off a smell as sweet as honey. We reached the bar, behind which a black-haired woman stood. She was just as beautiful as Nore, and something about her seemed faintly familiar.

"What would you like? The Bog Wife's beer or saltpeter wine?" Nore asked as his hand slipped around the back of my neck, under my hair.

"Uh . . . beer." The other option sounded a little dangerous. I needed to look out for myself.

The bartender's lips parted, and I stared, enthralled. She placed an elegantly shaped glass in front of me, filled with a dark liquid. It was exactly like the ones used at The Boatman's equinox ball.

Nore, his hand still on my nape, bent down and kissed me. Drowsily, I let him do it, not even considering I had only recently kissed Rorik.

Was it that recently?

Beside us, beautiful people kept coming up and taking fruit from the glass bowl. They curtsied or bowed and laid their hands on me each time they passed. Perhaps it was my imagination, but it seemed like more and more people were around us.

When Nore released me from the kiss, I took the glass to drink. A large hand closed around mine.

I looked to my other side, and it felt as though my head were moving in slow motion. An exclamation of surprise left my lips when I recognized the man behind me.

"Od."

He wasn't smiling his usual serene smile. In fact, he looked extremely serious.

"What are you doing here?" I asked slowly. Even my voice stretched out like a long thread I couldn't stop.

I didn't get any farther, as Od raised his hand, and, to my shock, slapped me in the face.

I shook my head. "What the hell are you doing?"

He slapped me again, this time on the other cheek. He didn't hold back at all, so his divine power nearly ripped my head off.

"Wake up, Anna," he shouted metallically. He had a silvery glow and was significantly taller than he normally was.

The bartender nodded to him from her place behind the bar.

"Cut it out! Stop hitting me," I protested and looked around for help. Nore was closest and was, after all, the person I'd come here with, but he merely growled at Od. His cape had blown up behind him. It whirled quickly, and he moved jerkily around us.

That was when I noticed the long stinger protruding from his back.

What?

The colors of the hexagons began to fade, and the white half-moon shapes popped out of their cells. They landed on the ground, where they writhed and squirmed. Golden, oily liquid flowed from the other small compartments and sent an overwhelmingly sweet, sickly smell toward us.

A loud buzzing sound made my body vibrate, and the other guests stopped their dance and came closer.

"She's ours," one whispered. The words came out more like a hum than a voice.

Some of the girls hovered over us, and only then did I see their backs were hollow like rotted-out trees.

Od had a firm grip on my arm, and a wave of divinity surged into me as silver beams of light shot from his eyes.

Nore pursed his dark lips. "She came here willingly. It's our right."

"I'm familiar with the elves' views on free will."

I had never seen the otherwise gentle Od like this before, not even that night he showed up at Odinmont unstable and hyped up on divinity.

"She's ours," the elves repeated.

"You can't have her." Od backed away, dragging me with him. He pushed me behind his back, and with a glance at the whirring figures, I didn't resist.

The elves came toward us, now on all fours and with their heads tucked into their bodies as if they had no necks at all. Their capes lay like wings; occasionally they spread out, causing the elves to rise into the air. They surrounded us, and I couldn't see how we would get out.

Od turned and shook me.

"Wake up," he hissed.

"What do you mean? I am awake," I shouted, turning around as the elves drew closer, buzzing from all sides. Several of them now had extra legs, and their stingers stuck straight out behind them.

Nore still had a hold of my other hand in a brown, bony claw, its surface sticky and cold.

"Use my strength." Od's voice was close to my ear, and without understanding what he was talking about, I clung to his arm and mentally embraced his divinity. Whereas previously he had sent it flowing into me, this time I pulled it out of him. Finally, I freed my hand from Nore's grasp and held tight to Od's body.

The ground vanished beneath my feet, and we rushed upward as the cave beneath us collapsed in a deafening buzz.

The last thing I heard was a communal roar of rage.

CHAPTER 25

I heard the sound of buzzing insects and started to panic, until I realized they were only harmless bees. Sunbeams caressed my face and penetrated my closed eyelids, so I was submerged in gentle, red light. I was lying down, and the ground beneath me was warm and soft.

Something tickled my nose, but whatever it was quickly fluttered away.

I opened my eyes and saw Od lying next to me in the grass. He was on his side, studying me, with one hand on my cheek. Water trickled, birds sang, and I had a strong suspicion that the demigod had teleported us into an animated film aimed at seven-year-olds.

Od smiled his disarming smile, which dissolved my willpower, but not in the same nightmarish way as Nore had. This was sweet, intoxicating.

"Finn. Rorik." They were the first things I thought of.

Od squinted, and it was clear he had no clue who I was talking about. "Did you sleep well?" he asked instead. His voice was, as always, a little hoarse.

I propped myself up on my elbow.

"You hit me," I complained.

"I had to. You were captivated."

"Captivated?" I shook my head to remove his hand.

"You were literally taken captive. Taken into the mound."

"What kind of place was that?"

"An elf mound."

I sat up fully, though an intense dizziness nearly toppled me over. "An elf mound."

My words hung in the air.

Od didn't respond.

I looked around at the summery landscape. It was lush and green, and I recognized the river Iving and the place in the forest where, mere minutes before, I had met Nore. We had been surrounded by ice crystals and bathed in moonlight.

"Shit!"

Od lifted himself onto an elbow, as I had just done.

"Anna. Language," he said gently.

I didn't bother snapping at him. My voice was desperate. "How much time has passed?"

"About six months." He sat up the rest of the way.

"Half a year! I was only at the party for a few minutes."

"You were in an elf mound. The elves drain human life force in there. A clan can live for forty or fifty years from a single human. You don't realize how much time is passing."

"But . . ." When I realized how lucky I had been to lose only six months, I nearly fainted. "Is Serén okay?"

Od looked me straight in the eyes. His divinity pulled at me like a forceful undercurrent. "Serén is alive."

I rapidly counted on my fingers. If I had been gone for six months . . . "The wedding must be happening soon," I stammered. "Where Ragnara will almost definitely sacrifice Serén."

No, no, no!

"In four days." Od's hand stroked my cheek again, but he said nothing more. I let the revelation sink in, and my pulse rose at the thought of how much time I had wasted.

"What do you mean by *sacrifice?*" Though Od was still speaking calmly and softly, his voice had a dangerous undertone.

I looked down into the grass. "I think Ragnara wants to become a goddess herself. If enough people worship her, it'll happen. If she gets Serén and then me out of the way, she'll start Ragnarök, and it's been prophesied that the old gods will be vanquished. Then she'll have free reign. At the same time, she'll remove the possibility that someone . . ." I swallowed, ". . . that I could go back in time and prevent her from coming to power in the first place."

After over a thousand years of life, I would have thought Od was incapable of being surprised, but right now he seemed pretty close to it.

"So that's why my father was so insistent that I help you."

"You didn't come of your own free will?"

"I always have free will." He tilted his head. "My will was just nudged in a particular direction by my father and my wife."

"Your wife? You mean Freyja?"

"She and Odin work together. Neither of them wants to fade into obscurity."

"If Ragnarök comes, they'll die."

He rubbed his forehead. "Ragnarök." Od's voice was no more than a puff of air. "I've always known, since Hejd told me, that doomsday would come. Nevertheless, I'm trembling now that it might actually be here."

"Right now, all signs indicate that it's happening."

"What signs?"

"The Midgard Serpent let go of its tail, there was no ice on the Iving, even in the frost, and Ragnara set Loki free."

"Loki's on Ragnara's side?" Od asked. I wasn't quite sure whether he was surprised or if he had known this all along.

"It would appear so," I said.

"The giant wolves are loyal to Loki."

I inhaled sharply. "What? But Monster wasn't loyal to him."

"The giant wolves trace their lineage to Fenrir, who was the son of Loki. The wolves are most likely to follow him. With them fighting against us, our chances don't look particularly good."

"But Monster's family . . ." My voice died out.

"They think humans are to blame for his death."

"I wish I could talk to him again." I sniffed. I hadn't even noticed the tears starting to fall.

"You can." Od's face was serious.

I heard the words. I registered the words. I simply didn't understand them. I couldn't even formulate a question.

Od moved closer to me, and for a moment, I wondered if he wanted to kiss me, but he merely spoke: "My father appointed you as a völva."

"Okaaayyy."

His intoxicating breath reached me as he continued. "The mead of poetry, when served to a giant by a völva, will bring him back."

At first, I was unable to speak, so I just stared at him with eyes wide. I brought my hands to my temples. "Your father told me that. I should have figured it out ages ago."

Od simply looked at me.

"You have the mead of poetry," I finally managed to say. "I remember you said you had mead from Heidrun's udders."

Od nodded slowly. Then he held out one of Elias's small bottles, but this one was filled with a brownish liquid, with a little foam on top.

I took it and inhaled, but coughed.

"And there's a stasis spell on him. He's back home in Ben and Rebecca's barn." My words tripped over one another. "I can get him back." I was still staring at the bottle. Then I raised my head to him.

A sincere smile made Od's smile shine, and I quickly looked down to not be paralyzed by demi-hypnosis.

"If the giant wolves are about to turn against us, they need to know that I can and will get Monster back." I had already stood up and was heading into the Iron Forest. "Monster's family needs to know he'll be okay."

Od's lovely fingers interlaced themselves with mine.

"There's something I have to tell you first." I got the sense he was back to the bad news.

"What?" I whispered. I could tell from looking at him that it was bad, and I didn't want to hear it, but Od continued mercilessly.

"Ísafold was attacked by Ragnara soon after you disappeared. Some were wounded, others killed. And she took some of the Ísafolders captive."

"Why?" I interrupted myself, "Oh. They were looking for me." I lay down on my side again. I turned my head and lay there for a while looking up into the blue summer sky, at the birds flying around without a care.

"Yes. They were looking for you, but they found evidence of god-worship in the cellar under their leader's house."

I buried my face in my hands. "Is Tíw dead?"

"He's awaiting trial in Sént. Ragnara also captured some religious fugitives from Miklagard."

I moaned into my hands, recalling Taliah's arabesque tattoos.

Everyone was in Sént. My sister, the Ísafolders, and the believers from Miklagard.

"I'm getting them out," I swore. "I'm gonna get help, and we'll get them out."

Od's face was unreadable. I didn't know if he thought I was crazy or heroic. Probably a combination of the two.

"How did you know where I was?" I asked.

Od looked into the Iron Forest. The trees and leaves sparkled like silver. "I have elves working for me. Word gets around when they catch a human. They come from miles away to feed."

I bit my lower lip.

"Was Veronika planning to go there?" I remembered the small black-haired woman who worked at the bar at The Boatman.

Od met my gaze again. "She had already left."

I let out a timid *huh* sound. "That's why the bartender in the mound was so familiar." I touched my hair and found that it had grown quite a bit longer.

"She was honest or loyal enough to tell Elias what was going on. I found out a month ago. I was in the mound for several weeks myself." Od got to his feet and held out a hand. "Your giant crystal led me to you."

Mads, what a gift you gave me.

I was starting to pant from the heat. "Let me just change before I get heatstroke."

Crouching, I rummaged in my bag for a camisole and the loose pants Aella had given me. Unconcerned with propriety, I changed in front of Od. When I pulled off my wool sweater, he reached out a hand toward my chest.

"What are you doing?"

His hand touched the gnarled scar.

"Oh, that." Something dawned on me. "Were you there when I got it?"

"Yes."

"Do you know why I healed in Ragnara's hands?" My own hand landed on top of Od's, and I felt the uneven scar tissue through his fingers.

He made a face. "I have a guess, but . . ."

I let go of him and stepped back, so his arm fell. "I know that expression."

"We don't talk about other people's powers."

Normally, I would have snapped at him, but I was actually starting to understand the rule. I looked around. Heat and humidity wafted toward me, and butterflies swarmed around us. Where we stood were bushes, grass, and trees in every shade of green, but just a few yards into the forest, the trees took on an iron-like glow. Plaintive creaking noises reached my ears.

"What now?"

Od smiled mildly. "I can only accompany you to the nearest

333

portal so you can return home to Midgard. I can protect you along the way and fill you with divine strength so that, when you get home, you're strong and full of energy."

"I'm going into the Iron Forest." My heart skipped a beat as I stared into the trees. "I have to win the wolves over before it's too late."

Od, too, looked into the bare, twisted branches. "I can't go in there with you. If you go that way, you'll have to go alone."

Hmm . . . Travel with a supernatural, handsome demigod, or continue alone into a dark forest full of man-eating wolves.

"I'm going into the forest," I maintained.

Od held my gaze, and for a second, I feared he would force me to change my mind, but instead he cautiously came closer to me and pressed his lips to my forehead.

With eyes closed, I accepted the wave of pure love. I don't know how long we stood like that, but when I opened my eyes, Od was gone and dusk was falling. Before I could lose my nerve, I took decisive strides in between the metallic trees.

It was like going from color to black-and-white. The earth was various shades of gray, and even the sky above me had a strange colorless tone. The leaves on the bushes and trees were dark. A small stream resembled quicksilver. There was no smell, and the sound of my footsteps was muffled. My clairvoyance captured nothing from my surroundings.

I cast my power around, but it was resoundingly empty, as I found myself in a vacuum.

Shit! I had lost half a year. My stomach twisted. If I had been at the party a minute longer, I would have lost the chance to avert my sister's death. I shuddered and pushed the horror away. There was simply no time—especially not now—to think about it. But I imagined Finn's gentle *baaah* and Rorik smiling in the afternoon sun. I nearly sent a prayer to the gods I didn't believe in for them to be okay.

There was a low noise.

Quietly, but with so much force the ground trembled beneath my feet, I heard something. It was a continuous, threatening growl.

"Don't you need to breathe?" I called out into the trees, where it was now completely dark.

Something glimmered between the trunks. It was a pair of shiny eyes, with so much space between them I didn't even dare imagine the size of the creature they belonged to.

A soft noise followed by the crack of breaking branches warned that a heavy animal's paws were moving toward me. When the giant wolf stepped out of the thicket, I gasped for air.

It was the same height as Monster, but somewhat thinner. Its fur was completely black, and its ears more pointed. Its hackles were raised, its teeth were bared, and, despite its size, I sensed that it was more frightened than angry.

It snapped its teeth with a slobbery sound.

Okay, it was mostly angry.

Despite every impulse, I didn't back away. "Who are you?"

The wolf didn't answer, but the menacing rumble in its large chest continued.

"I'm Anna. I have news of Etunaz." I inhaled shakily. "And my sister has been here. She looks just like me."

Slowly, the wolf came closer, and it took all my willpower to stand still. When it reached me, it pressed its snout against my neck and sniffed. I broke out in a cold sweat, and in my mind, I heard the crunch that had resounded when Monster ate Geiri. But I let the wolf smell me without moving an inch, even when its sharp canine tooth scraped across my jugular.

Finally, the giant wolf spoke.

"There is no news of Etunaz," it said in a guttural voice. "He's dead."

"I can change that," I said, breathless. "I want to change it. He's my friend."

335

"Who says I'm on the same side as Etunaz?" As if to emphasize its point, the wolf snapped its jaws right next to my throat.

I hadn't even considered that. Monster had never told me if there were different factions of giant wolves. For the umpteenth time, I kicked myself mentally for not knowing much about Hrafnheim. "If you want to eat me, eat me. If not, let's talk."

The wolf sniffled, then composed itself. "We are kin, but I saw Etunaz being tortured with my own eyes. He can't have survived."

"He didn't. He died in my arms," I said bluntly.

The wolf whimpered.

I held up a finger. "But I just found out I can bring him back if I give him the mead of poetry. His body is with some witches I know, and they've placed a stasis spell on him. So if you help me, I can go back to Midgard and bring him back to life."

The wolf squinted as if struggling to follow.

I slowed down. "It's true. I wouldn't risk my life by coming into the Iron Forest if it weren't."

The wolf considered this. "It's a fair trade."

I exhaled.

"You reek of elves." It sniffed again. "And of demigod." It scoffed with a very doglike hacking sound. "Why?"

The scoff sounded just like Monster, and my heart spilled over.

"I wandered into an elf mound." I tried to make my voice brusque.

The animal's mouth hung open, and I saw a row of sharp, pointy teeth inside. A large, bright red tongue lay in the middle.

"Elves are useful to have around. They catch unwanted guests." It laughed hoarsely. "How did you escape?"

"That's why I smell like demi."

"Hnnhh," the wolf snorted. "The demis are our enemies. Giants and gods have been fighting each other for a thousand years."

I didn't respond. It had nothing to do with me, but I suddenly understood Monster's reluctance the night Od showed up at Odinmont.

"Are you gonna eat me or not?"

Wrinkling its nose, it grumbled. "You stink too much."

"Then stop trying to psych me out." I laid a hand on its snout without thinking. That was what I always did with Monster when I wanted to stop him, but a glance at this wolf's menacing, sparkling eyes made me stiffen mid-motion.

"Unhand me." The wolf was quivering with agitation, its voice even more nasal than before with my hand closed around its nose.

I slowly lifted my hand. "Sorry."

"Sorry?" It shook its head. "Come," it rumbled, but somewhere deep in its gray eyes, I saw amusement. An amusement I recognized.

We walked through the gray forest.

Evidently, giant wolves weren't much for small talk, and I had a lot to think about myself, so we were silent. The wolf came up to my armpit, and once in a while, it turned its head toward me, its eyes sparkling. When I stepped on fallen leaves, I noticed they were as sharp as razor blades.

Deep in the forest, I saw flames between the trees. Shadows danced, resembling monsters with long ears, sharp teeth, and large claws. I wondered how the wolves had managed to start a fire with their paws when some entirely different shadows fell to the ground. They were long and skinny and looked like aliens.

"What . . .?" I breathed, before I was struck by the auras of the creatures creating the shadows. One was clear—friendly and a little sad—and the other was like a crackling freight train of creative energy.

Panicked, I gasped for air.

The poem. "Völuspá."

The brood of Fenrir
Among these one in monster's guise
Was soon to swallow the moon from the sky

One of the giant wolves was going to eat the moon.
  "Luna!" I screamed.

CHAPTER 26

Before I knew it, I was standing amid seven enormous wolves.

"If you've eaten Luna, I . . ." I shouted, but I couldn't really threaten them—I realized I was the one in danger as the wolves studied me with their ears back.

Before I could say anything more, I was pressed up against the trunk of a tree. A shower of corkscrew curls flowed around me. There was orange and purple fabric and a long red chain. Even though Luna was dressed in Hrafnheimish gear, her style still shone through.

I would have preferred to act cool about our reunion, but the sight of my best friend knocked the wind out of me. Great sobs forced their way up my throat, and I squeezed her tightly. We ended up in a pile on the ground amid a group of baffled giant wolves.

I wiped my eyes with both index fingers. "What are you doing in Hrafnheim?"

Luna replied with a question of her own. "Where have you been?"

"I've kind of been right here."

Luna, who seemed not to believe her own eyes, held my face. "We've been looking for you. Mads's crystal told us you were here, but you weren't. It's been a month since we left home."

"We?"

I noticed a tall figure standing on the other side of the bonfire. "Mads!"

He timidly walked closer.

I looked from one friend to the other. "I'm so happy to see you, but you guys are crazy. It's way too dangerous for you to be here."

Luna's large eyes didn't blink. "We had to flee."

I opened my mouth. "Flee? Why?"

Luna took my hand. "Ragnara's people attacked."

"Who?"

"Berserkers on demiblood."

"Shit!"

"My parents fought, but they couldn't protect us, so they sent me and Mads here. We ran down to Ostergaard."

"Are Ben and Rebecca okay?"

"Mathias fought alongside them, and with his power, they should have been able to handle the berserkers." Tears filled her large eyes. "But I don't know."

Mads squatted down. I wasn't on hugging terms with him, but we grasped each other's hands. "It's so good to see you," he said.

"You seem so," I searched for the word, "comfortable?"

"I'm among my kin. They accepted me immediately."

The wolves around us had sat down, and one of them was checking itself for fleas.

I pulled Mads's hands closer. "You also belong with us. Never doubt that."

He smiled again. "I know, Anna. But here . . ." He flung out his long arms. "Here among other giants, I can be myself."

He looked taller, no longer bowing his head and hunching his shoulders.

Luna blew a stray curl from her face. "My dad was about to kill Frank."

"Frank?" I had to close my eyes for a second. "Oh right, it's been months since he left. What happened?"

Luna held a slim hand in the air. "I intervened. I mean, I'm still really pissed he tried to strangle you, but if you can forgive him, then I respect that."

"He couldn't have done anything differently."

Luna pursed her lips. "Frank killed two girls."

I fingered a sharp leaf that resembled polished iron. "In a way, it was Ragnara who did that. And Frank is responsible for Halfdan. It wouldn't do Halfdan any good for the only adult he has left to be sent to prison or executed. And punishing him wouldn't bring Tenna and Belinda back."

Luna didn't answer.

"How is Halfdan?"

She shrugged. "He's going to kindergarten in Ravensted."

"It's probably best if he never finds out about all that—" I stopped myself when I realized this was the exact same reasoning my own parents and their friends had arrived at when I was a child. I inhaled and vowed: "I promise, if I survive this, I'll tell him everything when he's old enough. Everyone has the right to know their history."

"What's happened since you left?" Luna opened her eyes wide.

"I came here to find Serén. Now I'm almost certain Ragnara is planning to sacrifice her at Prince Sverre's wedding. We have to figure out a way to free her." I continued reluctantly. "But I've discovered that Ragnara has a bigger plan." I told them what I had figured out along the way. About worship, the religion ban, and Ragnara's plan to become a goddess.

Both of my friends stared at me in silence.

"I need to get to Sént as quickly as possible," I concluded.

"We're going to cook you for dinner." The wolf that had found me was suddenly standing before us.

"What?!" I sputtered.

"I mean, we're going to cook dinner for you." Its giant mouth pulled back, and because I knew Monster, I knew it was grinning.

Later that night, when the wolves were sleeping and Mads had gone to bed on the other side of the fire, I sat and stared into the flames. I was struggling to adjust to the humid summer heat that wrapped itself around me. My body was still tuned to the chill of winter, and I had to force it to understand the change. It was as if my soul didn't want to join me. It was still with Rorik in the forest, six months ago.

Luna, who apparently couldn't sleep either, sat down next to me. "What's wrong?" She scratched at her curls.

"Everything. But haven't we already summed it up?"

She looked at me. "Anna. There's something wrong with you. Something besides Ragnarök. Something more serious."

"What's more serious than the end of the world?"

"I know you." She spoke quietly. "You don't want to admit it, but there's something bothering you."

I sighed. "Varnar."

She waited for me to say something more, but I stayed silent. Then she furrowed her brows. "Varnar broke your heart. But I knew that already. Something else happened."

I looked at the sky, which was a sea of flickering dots. "I met someone else."

A grin spread across her lips. "But that's a good thing."

I shook my head. "No, it's not. Serén saw that being around me will cost him his life. So I had to leave him."

"And now you miss him."

I shrugged. "Yeah," I admitted.

"Who else do we know who left someone to protect them?" Luna wondered with a finger beneath her chin.

I shuddered. "Varnar."

Her eyebrows shot up. "I tried to explain that to you a hundred times, but you could only see it as a rejection."

I rested my forehead against my knees for a while as Luna stroked my back.

342

"What about Varnar? Are you over him?"

I turned my face but kept my cheek on my knees. It was easier to stay curled up in a ball. "I'm in love with both of them."

"Tell me about the other one."

"His name is Rorik, and he's a—" I stopped myself before I could say *healer*. "Oh. We don't talk about people's powers. I always forget that. I told him about you guys."

"That's okay. If you trust him, I trust you." Her electric aura flowed from her warm hand down my back. "What's he like?"

"Rorik tries to fix everything, even though that's not the masculine ideal here. He always feels wrong, because men are supposed to fight, and he doesn't want that. He put some parts of me back together. Things that had been broken since I was a kid."

"So he's good for you."

I looked down. "But Varnar is, too. I understand him because we're a lot alike. And I understand him even better now that I know his background."

"You love them both," Luna noted.

"You could say I love Rorik *because* of something. I love Varnar *in spite of* something."

"Hmm." Luna turned her face up to the sky. "It's hard to say which of the two ways of loving carries more weight."

I straightened myself out from my curled-up position. "It doesn't matter. I'm not with either of them."

Luna pulled me into a recumbent position and lay behind me with an arm around my waist. "Try to sleep. You need to rest."

She was right. I needed to sleep. To dream. I knew exactly what to use my dream for.

Sømosen looked just like it had the last time I saw it, except it was now nighttime, and a swarm of spirits were creeping and crawling around the trails and hills.

I had no idea if I was doing it right, but I tried to do as Taliah had said. Fumbling for Justine's aura or life-thread, or whatever I should call it, I stumbled around. Suddenly, I sensed an elongated aura that I recognized. I grasped it mentally and pulled.

"Justine," I called. "Justine." I followed the line.

Sømosen in North Jutland responded with splashes and rustling leaves as the spirits mumbled. Towering spruce trees swayed, and the smell of swamp and dirt hit my nostrils.

I forced my way ahead through the throng of ghosts. When I turned my head and looked at a slope, chalk-white fingers were digging their way toward me. A body broke through the wall of earth and crawled out.

I started to run.

"Justine," I shouted again, desperate as I tried to follow the mental thread.

The ghosts had noticed me. Their phosphorescent eyes were directed at me, and they placed themselves in a semicircle, blocking my way.

"Living," said one.

"Warm," said another.

I had my back to the lake as they took small steps in my direction.

"Breathing." A gray hand reached out toward me.

Maybe I should abort the mission. Maybe I should wake up now.

I spotted brown curls in the crowd. The little boy looked at me curiously. He was covered in grime, his feet were bare, and his clothes tattered.

"Hey, I know you. You're the myling." I had seen him when I visited Justine with Elias.

The boy put a dirty finger to his lips and shushed the other ghosts. They stopped their unsettling talk and steps in my direction, but they continued looking at me.

"I need to talk to Justine," I told the boy as calmly as I possibly could.

344

He tiptoed to me. The top of his curly head only reached my hip. He hadn't said anything the last time I was in Sømosen, but now he opened his mouth.

"Help me go to the realm of the dead," he said in a voice as light as a flute.

"Uh."

"I wasn't sent off properly," he continued. "They just tossed me in the bog. You can do it. You're a völva now."

I fumbled for words. "Get Justine. Then I'll do what I can when I come home to North Jutland."

If I come home.

The boy nodded, his soft curls bouncing around his face. He took my hand in his. His fingers were ice cold, but I held on tight. Then he pulled me through the sea of ghosts, who watched mutely as we passed.

He quickly found the cave, which was once again completely covered. I had to compose myself before I went underground so soon after being in the elf mound. With a snort, I reminded myself that no elves were there, and that, besides, it was just a dream. Nevertheless, I trembled as the myling pulled me through the passageway, and—somewhat embarrassingly—I clung to the dead boy.

"Little seer," came Justine's cracked voice. "You're visiting me in a dream. Your powers are getting stronger."

"Yes," I said, breathless and relieved that my dream communication had actually worked. "I need to know something."

Justine emerged from the shadows and pulled her ragged shawl tight around her shoulders. The space we were in—Pondbottom, she had called it—was greenish and smoky. Firelight flickered across the walls, but I couldn't see the flames themselves. Justine looked gray and transparent.

"Do you know if my friends Mathias, Ben, and Rebecca survived the attack of the berserkers?" I asked.

Justine squinted and chewed the inside of her cheek. "The witches are alive, and the demigod is as quick as ever."

I could hardly wait to tell Luna.

Justine held up a wrinkled hand, skin as thin as parchment. Her head tilted to one side. "But the berserkers *stole* something from the witches."

I took a step forward. "What did they steal?"

Head still cocked, she listened in the darkness. Did she have contact with Ben and Rebecca in some way?

"No, they didn't steal something. They stole some*one*. Someone Ragnara is afraid will end up in your hands."

"My hands." Dumbly, I looked at my own palms and pursed my lips. "Who? Ohhhh . . ." Terror immediately crept across my skin. "No."

Justine started to flicker. The fear had affected my concentration. "Tell me," I said. "Is it . . .?"

But my line to Justine was severed, and I rushed up to the surface, where I woke, still spooning with Luna.

"Monster," I whispered. "Monster's body."

CHAPTER 27

The black giant wolf walked us back to the Iving the next morning. Once again, I studied the metallic leaves, the shining gray bark, and the pure white flakes of ash dancing in the sunbeams, but this time, it was to avoid looking the wolf in the eyes. The news that Ragnara had stolen Monster's body was almost too much to bear, and I had decided not to share it. I had to maintain the lie that I could bring him back to life. If I could just find his magically preserved body, I could revive him.

"Are you all together?" I asked.

The wolf grumbled. "What do you mean?"

"Do the giant wolves all fight together?"

It scoffed. "We are two clans. Etunaz's father is the king of ours. We don't see the others very often, apart from the gathering attended by the mother of all."

I squinted. "Who is the mother of all?"

The wolf wiggled its snout.

"The old one." It exhaled. "I've never met her. I'm too young."

I studied the wolf. "You don't look particularly young."

It laughed in the same hoarse way Monster always did. "Ask my dad once you've brought him back. He sees me as a pup."

I stopped, nearly causing Luna to stumble into my back. "Wait. Are you . . . ?"

The wolf stretched out one of its front legs and curtsied elegantly. "Rokkin. Daughter of Etunaz and Boda."

Shit!

347

I closed my eyes. "I have to tell you something." Reluctantly, I shared the information of the berserkers' theft with Rokkin. She had the right to know her father's fate. But when I saw her expression, I wished I had kept my mouth shut.

Rokkin lowered her head, the fur on the back of her neck stood up, and her white teeth were bared. "You said yesterday that you could bring him back."

"I didn't find out he was gone until last night. I thought I could bring him back, too. I'm so sorry, but we have to work together, otherwise Ragnarök will start." I tried to lay my hand on Rokkin's head, but she snapped at me. It was a warning. I was certain that next time, she would bite my arm off. I held my fingers close to my body. "Can I talk to your mother?" I asked quietly. Monster had spoken of his wife, and I had a feeling she would listen to me.

"My mother?" Rokkin snarled.

"Yes, your mother."

"We can't talk to her."

"Why not?" I backed up discreetly.

"Eskild captured her when she tried to protect your sister. My father died, and my mother might as well be dead."

So Boda was with all the others in Sént.

"I am so sorry," I whispered.

"They're gone because of you. Because of humans and gods." These last words were delivered with a sneer. She ambled menacingly toward me, reminding me of a large, ill-tempered lioness.

Luna, Mads, and I backed farther away, while Rokkin stared at us, her head lowered. She growled threateningly.

There was nothing I could say. I understood her anger.

She seemed to regain a bit of composure.

"The only reason I'm letting you live is the giant." She gestured at Mads. "If I see you here again, I'll eat you, no questions asked. That goes for your sister, too."

"Listen . . ." I began, but I was interrupted when Rokkin leapt toward me, planted her paws on my chest, knocked me backward, and pinned me to the ground.

Her snout was right in front of my nose, and her sharp teeth nipped at my upper lip.

"So fragile," she said. "So delicate."

"Monster said he didn't even like human meat," I whispered.

"My father," Rokkin growled, "had strange tastes. I love human meat. Remember that."

Rokkin licked my cheek before hopping off my chest and running into the woods.

I lay there, my heart pounding.

Luna and Mads were immediately at my side and helped me up.

"Shit! Just when I thought they were on our side."

I was almost more upset that I'd gotten my hopes up about bringing Monster back, only to have those hopes dashed.

We continued walking and reached the edge of the Iron Forest. The valley where I had lain with Od was covered in a carpet of green grass, and behind it the Iving sparkled blue. From this angle, the wide arc of the river looked more like a large lake.

When we passed Ísafold, I saw that many buildings were burnt and smashed, but reconstruction was underway. I sensed fear and aggression even from a distance, and I caught a flash of soldiers running toward the town. There were screams and shouts.

I shook the vision away and suppressed the urge to run down there. Anyone who came near me was apparently in mortal danger. It would be best to get away from Ísafold and the Iron Forest.

It took no more than half a day for us to reach Ván, where Sént was located.

Along the way, we discussed how we would free Serén. My idea was to sneak into the city and then assess how my sister should be freed. If I got close enough to her, maybe we could change the past so none of this mess ever happened.

The kingdom of Ván was directly north of Frón, and it was clear that we were close to Ragnara's capital. Luna and I let Mads walk ahead, as though he were the leader of our little group, and whenever we passed someone, we bowed our heads. Fortunately, no one bothered us.

Luna gathered her now completely black curls in an elastic. Her hair had grown to the length it had been before a berserker set fire to her in my front yard. After all, it had been almost—I counted on my fingers—*five, six, seven months* since I had seen her. It just didn't feel like it to me.

"What's up with your hair color?" I stroked the unruly ringlets with my hand. "I thought you hated black."

Her eyes grew somber. "I do. But I knew I would have to draw from the ultimate color energy, the situation being what it is."

My brows furrowed. "The ultimate color energy?"

She didn't detect the amusement in my voice. "Yes. Just think of how many years black kept you alive before we found you."

Mads looked over his massive shoulder at me. "She's right."

"Yeah," I whispered. "She is."

Our surroundings changed the farther into Ván we went. The roads were wider and better maintained, the towns had stronger defensive walls, and the carts shone, freshly painted with Ragnara's distinctive rune. The clothing was colorful, the houses whitewashed.

All the bright colors nearly hurt my eyes after spending months in the colorless, impoverished regions of Hrafnheim.

The people didn't seem to feel the need to use every last bit of everything, like they did in the other regions. I suspected that Ván, despite Ragnara's reputation for fair distribution of goods, snatched up more for itself.

We trudged onward in silence but stopped when we reached a wide wall with a large iron door. I studied the tall palisade, which was made of oiled wood. Each pole ended in a deadly point.

"Is there a way around it?" Luna stretched her neck, but the wall extended for miles in either direction.

I pulled out the notebook and flipped to the map.

"Yes, but it's a substantial detour. There's a big city over there. Ripa." I pointed. "The wall goes all the way around it. It would definitely be faster to go through."

Mads leaned his head back and looked up at the spikes. My gaze landed on the door, which opened at that moment. A cart emerged, bouncing on the bumpy road. It was empty, and a man sat on the seat.

"Clearly, supplies come in and out here," I said when yet another cart passed the first, heading in the opposite direction. It was filled with crates. I looked at Luna. "How good have you gotten at hypnosis?"

The poor woman sat leaning against a tree, mouth open and drooling. She stared into space, smiling blissfully. A few yards away stood her cart, which was painted in bright colors and smelled like fresh wood.

Luna studied her critically. "I may have given her a little too much."

We had stopped her a half mile from the gate, where Luna doused her with persuasion magic.

"Will she be okay?" Mads carefully closed her mouth.

"Yes, yes." Luna rummaged around in the cart and found a blanket, which she draped over the woman. "She'll wake up tomorrow. I put another spell on her so no one will see her."

"But when she wakes up, her cart will be gone!" I flung out my arms. "I didn't come here to hurt anyone."

Without thinking, I rubbed my forearm where the brands were.

Mads grumbled: "Do you want to get in or what?"

I turned halfway around.

Mads climbed up onto the driver's seat, and the cart creaked threateningly. Luna and I hopped into the back between crates of eggs and plums and bags of grain. Mads grabbed the reins, and we lurched forward a bit, wobbling before he gained control of the vehicle. Luna and I clung to the sides, and I held on to a stack of crates to keep them from toppling over.

"You're pretty good at driving," I said when Mads got the cart to move forward in a straight line.

He laughed. "There are some benefits to growing up way out in the country in darkest Jutland."

At the entrance, we were stopped by a pair of guards who seemed more apathetic than usual. The female soldier, wearing a simple uniform with the fehu rune embroidered on the back, looked uninterestedly at the goods. Her gaze lingered briefly on Luna and not at all on me.

For once, I silently gave thanks to my spells.

The guard waved us in.

I exhaled tentatively as the male soldier rifled through his papers. "Take the goods down to the chieftain. He's having a party tonight to raise money for Prince Sverre's wedding."

Just hearing about the wedding made my stomach clench.

Mads flicked the reins.

"Thanks." He continued down the road, which split after a few yards. "Which one should I take?"

"No idea." I frantically flipped through the notebook, but there were no details of Ripa.

"Just pick one and hope you're right. They'll realize we don't know where we are if we stop here." Luna sighed.

"They'll also realize that if we go the wrong way," I said tensely.

Resolutely, Mads turned to the right.

Nothing happened, and we continued for quite a bit.

"Hey!" came the voice of the female soldier. "You're going the wrong way."

CHAPTER 28

We stopped, and Luna cursed under her breath.

"You don't know this area?" the voice from the gate asked.

Mads turned toward the soldier and gave her one of his most innocent expressions. He often made the same face back home in Ravensted.

"No. We've never been here before," he said.

I stared stiffly down at the bottom of the cart bed as the soldier's footsteps approached. Slowly, I reached for Auka. At my side, energy crackled in Luna's palms.

The guard had now reached the cart, and from the corner of my eye, I saw her rest her hand on its edge.

My fingertips brushed against Auka, but fortunately, the soldier spoiled my plans.

"My shift is almost over, and I'm heading that way, too. Let me ride with you, and I'll show you the way." The cart rocked as she climbed aboard.

I resisted the urge to look behind me.

"I'm excited for tonight," she began, as Mads turned the cart around.

"What's tonight?" Mads asked.

"You don't know?" Her voice was surprised. "We've received instructions from Sént. We'll be the first to try the new ritual."

"Oh," Mads mumbled. "We don't get a lot of news."

"We don't know what it's all about, either, but it's something we must do for Ragnara."

Mads mumbled good-humoredly.

The soldier sat on the driver's seat next to him, and the large rune on her back swayed right over my head.

"Did you hear what they're doing with the prisoners?"

"What are they doing?" Mads continued in the same jovial tone, but I could hear that he had grown tense.

"Prince Sverre has requested that they be punished at his wedding."

"What kind of person would want that?" I whispered to Luna. "If I ever meet him, I'm gonna strangle him."

"What are you saying down there?" the soldier asked.

"Nothing," Luna replied as she interlaced her fingers with mine. "What's the punishment?"

"The arena," the soldier answered.

I pressed my hand over my mouth to keep from crying out.

"Are you going to the wedding?" Mads asked, probably to distract her.

The soldier exhaled loudly.

"I bought tickets. Front row. First, we'll see the wedding, and then comes the fight." She inhaled. "The last time I saw a gladiator battle, I got blood spatters on my clothes, that's how close I was."

"Gladiator battle?" Mads's voice was somewhat thinner than before.

Fortunately, we had arrived at the chieftain's homestead, which was situated on the outskirts of Ripa.

The soldier hopped down, and Mads said goodbye as politely as he could muster. She stuffed a couple of plums into her pockets and ducked in through a door.

"For Ragnara's anfarwol," she said over her shoulder.

"Anfarwol," Mads echoed faintly.

We sat in our colorful stolen cart in the middle of the yard.

"How do we get out of here?" Luna didn't dare turn her head.

"Maybe no one will notice if sneak away really quietly," I said.

Just then, someone shouted.

"Finally! We've been waiting for this delivery." He stopped. "Where's Gunnbritt?"

"Um . . ." Mads drew out his words. "She had to stay behind."

"In Laxdaela?"

"Yes. Right. In Laxdaela."

The man, whose clothes were coarse but clean and well-kept, brushed his hands together.

"Okay, well, go ahead and start unloading." He clapped at us. "The festivities are starting soon."

Mads guided the horse to what was clearly the kitchen entrance, and Luna and I started carrying crates and sacks inside.

"Is this a good idea?" I said as I passed her, her head buried under a grain sack.

"We don't really have a choice," she whispered. "When the cart is empty, we'll slip out of here."

Mads, who could carry a stack of five crates, quickly reduced the amount of food in the cart, and I figured we would be leaving soon.

Hidden under two bags of grain, I bumped into someone and mumbled an apology, before hurrying on my way.

"Easy there." Someone laughed. It was a man's voice, whose owner I couldn't see behind the canvas sack. "What incredible hair you have. It blazes like fire," he said.

I looked up, and when he saw my face, he involuntarily wrinkled his nose.

Leather pants wrapped tightly around his legs, looking like something I'd seen in Hibernia. His mid-length, brown hair was braided and fastened with small rings like in Frón, though his shirt was clearly made in Miklagard with arabesque embroidery. There was a smattering of tattooed scales on his cheekbone, but another tattoo on his neck was nearly identical to the serpent knot on Ben and Rebecca's house—except one of the snakes was larger and in the process of eating a human. Set deep between the snakes was a yellow half-moon. The man's eyes were slightly slanted, like Aella's, and his cheekbones were high, like Varnar's. His dark mustache was twisted upward, and when he took a step back, he moved like a self-assured rock star. I recognized the half-moon on his neck from the skald I had met with Rorik.

The man's upper lip was pulled up in a sneer as he looked at me, but his face changed when Luna came up behind me.

"Last crate," she said and wiped her hands.

The man licked his lips. He took a step back and bowed, like Elias did from time to time. When Elias did it, it looked almost derisive, but this seemed sincere.

Mads came over to us, and when he saw the man, he puffed out his large chest and clenched his fists.

"What kind of a group are you?" His voice was curious.

None of us answered.

"Let's start over. I'm Tryggvi."

"Huh," I said and turned. "Let's get out of here," I whispered to the others from the corner of my mouth.

They turned, too, and we began walking, but Tryggvi overtook us.

"You aren't from around here." He trotted backward.

"Neither are you," I said.

Tryggvi, who was still staring openly at Luna, turned back to me with a sharp look. Then his expression transformed into a smile. "I'm a guest here, a guest *of honor*."

"Good for you," I growled and started walking faster.

"You can't go," Tryggvi whined. "I can't bear it." He looked at Luna, and it was clear who he meant when he said *you*.

"We just came to deliver some food," she deflected. "We have to go back to Loxdale."

"Laxdaela," Mads corrected quickly.

Tryggvi looked suspiciously at Mads but turned back toward Luna. "You lovely dark maiden. Are you a princess from Miklagard?"

356

"Huh?" Luna tilted her head.

"You—that is, all three of you—should stay for the party. I insist." With a theatrical gesture, Tryggvi fell to his knees at Luna's feet. He fondled her green-and-orange dress and finished by kissing her purple slippers.

She hopped backward and shook her feet.

We were starting to attract attention, and people stretched their necks in our direction. Someone laughed, and I heard someone say: "Check out what Tryggvi's up to."

"Stop it," Luna hissed. "Get up."

He looked up through his long eyelashes. "Will you stay?"

She yanked on his arm. His hand, which was heavy with rings, closed around hers and pulled her down, so instead of bringing him to his feet, she landed in front of him on her knees and he clung to her.

"Hey." Mads grabbed their hands. "This isn't funny anymore."

"Funny!" The back of Tryggvi's hand went dramatically to his forehead, and he leaned his head back with eyes closed. "This isn't funny. This is tragic. I'll throw myself from the cliffs of Sverresborg and let myself be eaten by Jörmungandr if I can't have more time with the dark princess." He opened one eye a crack. "Fortunately, it's a bit of a trek to Svearike, and maybe the beautiful women of Frón will make me reconsider along the way." He winked at one woman who had come closer, and she snickered.

More people flocked around us and followed the show with laughs and jeers.

Tryggvi looked back toward Luna. "If you don't stay, I'll die of sorrow." He turned to the crowd in appeal. "I'll DIE."

Someone cried out "No!" and another shouted to Luna: "Can't you see what you're doing to him?"

His ring-bedecked fingers grabbed the collar of his shirt, and for a second, I thought he would rip it open.

357

"I don't know what you have in mind, but I'm in a relationship," Luna said in a flat Jutland accent.

People in the crowd gasped. So much for not attracting attention.

Tryggvi stopped mid-movement and slowly looked Mads up and down. "Is it him?"

Luna shook her head.

Tryggvi looked at me in horror. "Is it *her*?" He bared his teeth in a grimace. "That's strictly forbidden."

"She's just a friend," Luna said.

Tryggvi's eyes lingered on me, and it was clear he didn't understand how anyone could be friends with me.

"Is this person . . . dangerous?" he asked Luna.

I recalled Mathias's bone-crushing fingers and scalding-hot breath.

Luna pursed her broad lips. "No, he's really sweet."

"Then I'll defeat him in a duel!" Tryggvi shouted wildly. He stood up and turned around with his arms raised toward his audience. He was clearly speaking more to them than to Luna.

I nudged her.

"But," she hurried to add, "my boyfriend can get terribly angry, and then he has a bunch of powers." She stood back up.

"Is he a giant?" Tryggvi rolled his eyes.

"Noooo." Luna glanced toward Mads, who looked down.

"Is he an elf?" Tryggvi bit his nails—exaggeratedly, so it could be seen from the back of the crowd.

Luna shook her head and laughed, and again there was a "No!" from the audience.

I personally didn't think there was anything funny about elves.

"Is he . . ." Tryggvi wiggled his eyebrows. "A witch?"

"*Oohh*," someone jeered.

Luna clenched her fists. "No, but I know people who are. Actually, my boyfriend is a . . ." The rest of her words were muffled when both Mads and I put our hands over her mouth.

It was completely quiet. Tryggvi's grin had grown stiff, and he was staring at us. Gone was the theatrical banter.

"We'll stay." Mads panted and laughed awkwardly toward the crowd. "We'll stay for the party."

Tryggvi composed himself and addressed the spectators. "I think it's clear to us all that this woman belongs to a . . ." He paused for effect. "Troll."

A man in the crowd nodded understandingly. "Of course. So she can't kiss anyone else. They'll turn to stone."

An older woman took a step back, as if Luna were planning to plant a big juicy kiss on her lips.

Tryggvi stepped in front of us and stretched a hand back to signal that we should keep our mouths shut. He cleared his throat and started working up to the grand finale.

"Thus concludes my pursuit of the dark maiden. I'll have the chance—if only for a single evening—to sit by her side at the honorable chieftain's table. Her guardians," he pointed at me, "are an ugly hag . . ."

I rolled my eyes as people shouted "Eeeww" and "She's hideous!"

". . . and a . . . uh . . . a very tall man." He glanced at Mads and made a show of how frightened he was by his size. "I can't touch the princess, not so much as brush her lips with mine." He ran a finger across his lower lip. "And I definitely can't . . ." He coughed while doing a suggestive twist with his hips, which made people shriek with laughter. "But I can enjoy her company until night falls, and she must once again return to the troll's clutches."

Tryggvi bowed and his audience clapped. He waved to the people in the back and bowed again.

After a while, the crowd dispersed. We remained standing there, and Luna's eyes were shooting daggers.

Tryggvi bowed his head. "I have to do at least one performance a day."

"That's fine for you, but maybe we don't want to be part of your show." She scowled.

There was no trace of a smile beneath Tryggvi's pointed mustache. "Life is one long show. In fact, so is death."

I put my hands on my hips. "Okay. Sure. But now we're leaving."

Tryggvi looked at me and shuddered. "You really are ugly."

"Hey!" Mads said.

Tryggvi laughed, but this time it wasn't an act. "You promised to stay. Everyone heard it, and believe me, if there's anything these idiots keep an eye on, it's unfamiliar faces."

"That's not really our problem," I said.

Tryggvi shrugged. "It will be once they start looking for you. It's really weird to get an invitation to party with the chieftain and then not show up. And you're," he looked at us one by one, "pretty easy to recognize."

I tipped my head back with a moan.

"Come on." Tryggvi gestured for us to follow him. "You don't have anything to hide. Do you?"

"Are you a skald?" Luna asked Tryggvi as we sat on a bench overlooking a neatly mown lawn next to the chieftain's yard. The summer evening had taken on an orange tinge, and a fine layer of dew settled on the glasses and plates we had filled from the large buffet that stood at the end of the banquet tables. It was piled with meat, bread, and fruit, and I couldn't stop thinking of the skeletal, leprous children outside Sverresborg. Actually, when I thought about it, it was the same way in my own world. Some gorged themselves on far more than they could handle, while others—the vast majority—had nothing.

On the adjacent field stood a tall, covered form. It was hard to see it clearly in the twilight. Pale canvas flapped around it, and the orange sunbeams penetrated the fabric here and there, revealing what looked like black, gnarled arms. There were laughter and conversation all around us. I was shielding like mad as the many guests' feelings assaulted my mind.

The chieftain, who was getting on in years but still seemed lucid, stood at the end of the banquet table and gave a speech. His young wife stood next to him with a watchful eye on his notes. The chieftain pointed out the small baskets the soldiers were bringing around the tables.

"We've gathered here this evening," he said, "to honor Prince Sverre's marriage to Ingeborg. I expect everyone to willingly donate a silver coin or more."

The basket was thrust in between us, and the soldier who had ridden in with us looked around admonishingly.

Luna scrambled to find some coins. Fortunately, she was better prepared for the trip than I, who by now didn't even have any Danish coins left.

The chieftain shuffled his notes, and his wife pointed down at them so he could see where he was.

"Also, we have received new instructions from Sént. We are lucky to be the first to benefit from Ragnara's grace and justice." He pointed to the covered form behind him. "Let us all rise."

People got up from their seats. Cautiously, we made our way toward the covered object. The chieftain's wife gestured for us to stand around it. When we had formed a circle, the chieftain went to the middle, along with his wife.

He studied the fabric around the form and found a ribbon embroidered with a snake design. He stood up straighter, and everything grew still.

People stood breathlessly as a strange mood spread through the crowd.

Then the chieftain pulled on the embroidered ribbon.

The fabric fell away, and gasps could be heard around the circle. The fiery sunset contributed to the supernatural scene.

A tree was revealed when the fabric slid down, but it wasn't

361

brown and green and alive. No, it was hard and smooth, as though it had been buried in a bog for years.

It took me a moment to figure out why it looked so strange, but finally I realized it had been turned upside down, so the crown was buried in the ground and the roots spread above our heads. The middle of the tree's trunk was carved with Ragnara's crooked fehu rune.

"From now on, this will be here. This fehu."

Goose bumps spread up my arms and the back of my neck.

"The fehus will be close to everyone in Freiheim. As we speak, they are being erected in every city in the realm. They will be finished for Prince Sverre's wedding. You should come to our fehu for guidance and comfort. At midsummer and midwinter, we must make an offering."

A chill ran up my spine when he said *offering*. Ragnara was putting her plan in motion.

A man and woman wearing long white gowns with a rune on them stepped into the circle. They looked like herders, but their robes had become more uniform-like in the six months I had been in the elf mound. Around their necks lay twisted bands of gold, like thick plate armor, and their faces were frozen in ceremonious expressions. The cloaked man pulled a piglet behind him. The creature oinked and looked around in confusion. It had a rune painted on its forehead.

"The herders will help with the rituals." The chieftain stepped back with arms raised.

"Ragnara started her life as a slave." The female herder pointed to the rune on the tree. "Ragnara sacrificed herself so we could all be free. With this symbol and this tree, we commemorate her sacrifice." Her hand stroked the symbol. "For Ragnara's anfarwol," she said clearly.

Several people repeated the words to themselves. "For Ragnara's anfarwol. For Ragnara's anfarwol."

The hairs on the back of my neck stood up. This way of chanting the words was familiar to me from my time with the evangelical foster family. The people continued whispering excitedly. The many years when all faith and worship were banned had left a void that was screaming to be filled.

"Now it is time for us to give back. A humble expression of thanks to Ragnara." The herder's voice cut through the noise of the crowd. "We will show her our allegiance." She spread out her arms, palms facing up. "You step up to this fehu." She walked up to the tree and bowed her head, her arms still outstretched. The other herder came up behind her, still dragging the piglet. In a rapid motion, he tied a rope around its hind legs, and it squealed in terror.

I spotted the knife in his hand.

Ohh . . .

He skillfully tossed the rope up over a root and pulled, so the animal hung with its head pointing down. It writhed and continued to squeal, and I had to force myself not to cover my ears.

In front of him, on a small altar, sat a bowl with a bundle of twigs inside, and with a firm grip on the pig's snout, he pulled, so its neck was exposed. Its front legs twitched in the air, but the herder seemed very experienced.

The piglet managed to let out one more terrified squeal before its throat was slit. Its screams were drowned in an unsettling gurgle. The herder's white cloak was stained red across the shoulder by a large spray of blood. There were shudders and gasps from the crowd. A single whimper rang out, but then it was completely still. The herder held out the bowl and collected the splashing blood. The female herder, who had stood motionless with her back to the drama, reached out and took the bundle of twigs, which was submerged in the red liquid. She lifted it, and the blood ran down her arm until her cloak was stained as well.

This theatrical performance worked exactly as it was intended.

Titillated, fearful, and enthusiastic auras hit me from all sides, and the only things keeping me from passing out were my viselike grip on Luna's hand and Elias's lessons in shielding.

The herder dragged the dripping twigs across the fehu symbol on the tree trunk.

"With this blood, we honor Ragnara," she shouted. The liquid appeared black as it glistened down the ebony tree.

A murmur went through the crowd as the fehu rune glowed faintly, as if the tree itself were alive.

The herder looked at a man in the circle and gestured for him to come closer.

He slowly walked forward with eyes wide and took the bundle of twigs. Then he dipped it and dragged it down the trunk and the carving. When the blood hit it, the rune flared even brighter.

"With this blood, I honor Ragnara," he whispered.

The herder handed him a drinking horn, which he brought to his lips.

"For Ragnara's anfarwol," she chanted.

The man took a large sip, but he quickly pulled the horn away and looked inside. He licked his lips tentatively.

A new person came forth and repeated the ritual and the words, then took a sip from the horn, followed by the words "For Ragnara's anfarwol." Then came the next, then another, all the way around the circle. Then it was our turn, and there was no getting out of it.

It wasn't the first time I had been forced to utter religious words and perform ritual acts, so I knew it was just a matter of singing *crap, crap, crap* in my head the whole time. That was what worked for me, anyway.

I copied the others.

The rune didn't glow, but no one seemed to notice.

I brought the horn to my mouth, and I was surprised to discover that the beverage was sweet and alcoholic. I looked more closely at the horn, and I gave a little start when I saw the symbol carved

364

on its side. It was the crooked *F* that had been on all the murdered girls in Midgard. Ansuz. The one that meant *god* in Old Norse. I quickly handed it back.

Then Mads splashed the blood, mumbled the words, and drank from the horn, but Luna's large eyes went blank when it was her turn. She was the last in the circle.

"I can't," she whispered and shook her head. "I believe in something different."

Everyone waited, watching her.

"Come on," I urged through gritted teeth as I pushed her forward.

"No." She shook her head again.

People were starting to whisper, and the herder took a step toward us. The knife was still glinting in his hand. The bloodless pig hung in the tree behind him.

"Just do it," I hissed. "It doesn't mean anything if you don't mean it."

She looked at me. "It does mean something, Anna. Can't you feel it?"

Desperately, I looked at the blood-spattered herder.

"She's overwhelmed," I told him. "Just give her a moment."

The herder stopped and looked at us, unblinking.

"Come on, Luna," I pleaded. "Do it for my sake."

Large tears ran down her cheeks. "For you?"

I nodded eagerly.

"If you say *crap* in your head, then it doesn't mean anything." My voice was barely audible. "It works for me."

She looked me in the eyes with so much trust, my heart overflowed. Then she took a step forward and grabbed the wet twig bundle.

I exhaled, and I saw Mads do the same at my side. Luna went through the motions perfectly, and I sighed with relief when she was finished.

"For Ragnara's anfarwol," she said clearly.

That's it. Good job.

"Crap," she bellowed in conclusion.

Oops.

It was completely silent.

Luna looked around, smiling. She hadn't even realized she'd said it out loud. Mads and I exchanged a horrified look as the herder raised the knife to her back.

"It's an expression of praise!" I shouted. "In Særkland, this word is an honor. It's a sign of subservience."

"Crap," someone in the circle mumbled.

"Crap," I joined in.

A man nodded. "Crap, crap, crap." He clapped rhythmically and seemed totally high.

"Craaaap," Tryggvi screeched and did a little dance.

Mads raised his arms, and soon everyone was screaming the word, whose real definition was fortunately unknown in this world. It was as if they were releasing their ecstasy over the ritual, the killing, the sacrifice, and the blood. The herders made eye contact for a second, then shrugged and joined in.

Luna ran back to the circle, and I caught her in a big hug.

The voices faded out, and people stood panting, red-cheeked and fired up. The chieftain made some final remarks that no one really registered. Then he waved us back to the table.

With my pulse pounding in my throat, I walked back as well. Luna and Mads were right behind me, both with alarmed expressions. We all just wanted to get out of there. We inched ourselves away from the table, but Tryggvi beckoned us to our seats.

"You were asking me something before." He fluttered his long eyelashes in Luna's direction.

"What?" She was distracted and looked down at her palms, which were sticky with pig's blood.

"You were asking . . ." He rolled his hand.

"Oh, right. Are you a skald?" Her voice shook.

"Am I a skald?" Tryggvi was clearly a fan of this subject. He twirled his mustache, making the ends even pointier. When he was done, he pointed at the moon tattoo under the serpent knot on his neck. "Surely you know that this moon is the symbol of skalds."

"Mhmm," Luna hastened to confirm.

Tryggvi studied her, then shrugged. "I get paid to travel all over Freiheim and bring news to even the farthest reaches. There is not one corner of the realm I haven't visited."

"I've always wanted to meet a skald," Luna said. "What an adventurous life."

"And I've always wanted to meet a gorgeous, dark temptress." Tryggvi wiggled his brows.

Luna ignored him. "What exactly can you do?"

A smile revealed that Tryggvi was only playing the lover boy role, and that his pride in his profession was sincere. "I can recite sagas and poems for days on end. And I can recite all the laws, but that's boring."

Mads moved closer. "Do you write anything yourself?"

Tryggvi threw his arms to the sides in an elegant motion. "Of course. It's very difficult."

"Isn't it just a bit of rhyming?" I asked. "Desire/fire, and so on?"

Tryggvi scoffed, but I didn't know if it was because of my repulsion spells or my comment. "It takes years to learn."

"Okay, okay . . . I didn't mean to disparage your livelihood." I glanced at Luna, who clearly wanted to hear more. And maybe I could get a little help with the prophecies, which I was starting to realize contained a lot of answers. "Would you be so kind as to explain how you write a poem?"

Tryggvi still had an insulted look on his face. But his love for the skaldic arts overtook him. "If I'm asked to write a poem, I start with a sitting."

"A what?"

"I sit under a hanged man—if I'm lucky and there's one nearby."

"Ewww! You mean a dead body?" Luna's shoulders shot up.

Tryggvi's brows furrowed. "Yes, of course. But I'm usually not that fortunate. Normally I just sit on a grave or at a crossroads." He pointed down the now-dark road leading to the gate. "There's a crossroads just down there. I sat there to write this evening's poem."

Mads took a sip of juice. "What do you do while you're sitting there?"

"I let the poetry come to me."

"How so?" asked Luna.

Tryggvi's slanted eyes narrowed even more. "Don't you know anything about the skaldic arts?"

I shook my head.

"We're pretty isolated," Mads rushed to explain.

"Yeah, you must be." Tryggvi paused and looked at each of us. Then he turned the corners of his mouth down in a what-do-I-know expression. "It's an art form that stretches back centuries. All the way back to the other world. Poetry is a riddle to be solved. Nothing can be taken literally. Everything is told in metaphors."

"Metaphors?"

Tryggvi stretched his long, ring-clad fingers toward a platter of cakes. "Here's an example. Say I'm supposed to write something about a boat—I would never write the word *boat*. I would write *the Midgard Serpent's prey* or, if it was a warship, *conqueror of foreign shores*. Whatever hints at the ship's fate."

I widened my eyes. "Are you a seer?"

Involuntarily, I raised my mental barricades, until I realized I could normally sense if people were clairvoyant.

Tryggvi laughed. "No. But maybe there's an old prophecy about it, or a rumor. Or maybe I just make something up. You can influence fate by stating with confidence that something will happen."

Hmm.

368

Tryggvi, who had just taken a large bite of cake, finished chewing and swallowed. "Listen to this:"

She saw there wading through rivers wild
Treacherous men and murderous wolves,
and workers of ill with the wives of men.
There Nithhogg sucked the blood of the slain
And the wolf tore men;
Would you know yet more?

The giantess old in the Iron Forest sat,
In the east, and bore the brood of Fenrir;
Among these one in monster's guise
Was soon to swallow the moon from the sky

There was a loud bang in my head when the prophetic words reached me, and I nearly fell backward off the bench.

Luna discreetly placed a hand on my back to hold me up.

"Where's that from?" she asked, though she knew very well that it was from "Völuspá."

Tryggvi shrugged. "Dunno. It's from the old world. But the point is, you can't understand it. Which men are treacherous? Whose wives are we talking about? The poem also mentions wolves and monsters. But those could be metaphors for something else, and we'll never know what, because the author is long gone."

I involuntarily made a loud wheezing sound.

Mads drowned me out with his deep voice. "What about your own poetry?"

Again, Tryggvi twisted the ends of his mustache. "In addition to following the rules for a poem's structure and rhyme, the skald's foremost duty is to always walk the line of the offensive. A skald risks losing his head every day. We can get away with saying more than most—you saw that for yourselves over in the yard," he gestured with his thumb, "but with regular people that's fine. It's when I'm talking to—and about—the people in power that things can go wrong. I've known several skalds who have crossed the line." He mimed a noose around his neck and stuck his tongue out the side of his mouth. Then he waved his hand. "But that risk is part of the job."

"It sure sounds exciting," Luna said.

"Watch this," Tryggvi dabbed his mouth with a napkin. He stood and clapped his hands. There were noise and laughter, but it grew quiet when Tryggvi climbed up on the table. Those who hadn't seen him were shushed by their neighbors at the banquet table.

"We'll just listen to this," whispered Luna, "then we'll sneak away."

"Greetings, stalwart men and," he bowed and winked, "lovely ladies."

There was a loud hoot and a few giggles.

"I have prepared for you a few stanzas from the Saga of Harald Fairhair. Harald was the greatest warrior of the other world. When Harald was young, he was eager to fight. When it came time for battle, he was made sovereign. But he ended his days in bed, powerless."

Tryggvi recited a poem about Harald, who was already the most handsome man in Norway by the time he was ten years old. I sat spellbound, hanging on his every word, and Luna and Mads leaned forward.

He will drink Yule at sea if he decides the matter,
the prince forward-looking, Freyr's game he will play;
bored from youth, by fireside basking, indoors sitting,
with ladies' warm bower and wadded downy mittens.

"The war comes," Tryggvi whispered, but the crowd was so quiet, everyone could hear him. "And Harald and his men go to battle. They must fight for their lives and their honor."

The story was so engrossing, I lost all sense of time and place.

Tryggvi strutted up and down the table, jumping over the occasional pitcher or flower arrangement, as he recited the verses. At one point, he snatched a cup from a man's hand and poured its contents down his throat. He started to speak, but he stopped with an exaggerated cough and sniffed the cup with a horrified look while everyone laughed.

The man held up his hands in an expression of innocence.

"Tsk, tsk." Tryggvi pointed at the man, and the guests laughed again. He tossed the empty cup, which the man caught. Then Tryggvi returned to the poem, which had come to a gory description of warfare.

> *With a roar of raised axes and ringing of spears, men were*
> *bitten by black-polished blades of the great king's forces,*
> *when the enemy of Gautar got victory; loud over*
> *the necks of spirited soldiers sang spears flight-bidden.*

There were cheers when Harald finally won the throne. Even Mads pounded on his plate, and Luna clapped.

"But," Tryggvi said, sighing. "Nothing lasts forever. Harald died an old man in his bed, surrounded by his children, without strength, beauty, or power. Was he lucky?" Tryggvi shrugged. "Or was he without honor? You decide."

He finished by bowing in all directions to rapturous applause.

This went on for a while, but Tryggvi hushed them again.

"Now for a poem I composed myself." He leapt jauntily down the planks of the banquet table, and people moved their cups to safety, chuckling. "It's an ode to our very own Prince Sverre, soon to be bound in wedlock." When he said *bound*, he crossed his hands at the wrists and stretched his arms over his head.

People laughed again, but this time with contempt.

"What! This is our honorable prince we're talking about." Sarcasm dripped from Tryggvi's voice.

I shared this sentiment. With a little luck, I would never meet the prince. The luck would be all his.

I wasn't alone in thinking so, as I could sense animosity toward the man rushing through the crowd, but no one said anything out loud, and the guards standing along the perimeter shifted uneasily.

Tryggvi cleared his throat.

We've gathered tonight to honor a man
With gold overflowing his purse
Who's leaving one lap to take up with another
He loves his mother, but no longer shall nurse

There was a low "Ooohh," and Tryggvi opened his mouth to say something but stopped with a cheeky grin. He threw up his hands as if to say he had nothing to do with Prince Sverre's situation.

The throne will never be his
Unless, of course, his mother dies
Oh, what a shame it is
But he does get a consolation prize
That's where Ingeborg comes in

Tryggvi tiptoed daintily, pursed his lips, and swung his head.

She's beautiful, a work of art

He tapped his temple.

Though, apparently, not so smart

"No, she must not be," called a woman. "Since she wants to marry the prince."

"Who said that?" The guards stretched their necks trying to spot the offending guest, but they couldn't find her.

Tryggvi's mouth was open, and a seedy smile played at the corners of his mouth. He waited for the crowd to settle down. Then he whispered:

On his wedding night, Sverre aims to be
Upstanding
And wield his sword shall he

When Tryggvi said *sword*, he wiggled his eyebrows, and people tittered. He made his eyes wide and pursed his lips. Then he bent over and squinted his eyes as if to make out something very small.

Now everyone was gasping with laughter, and even Luna wiped her eyes.

The sword his foster father wrongfully stole
Perhaps Eskild already took it for a spin?
Is innocent Ingeborg really free of sin?
Prince Sverre does not draw his weapon
It's his weapon that draws him

Tryggvi made a highly inappropriate gesture that indicated what metaphor he was going for. Then he ran down the table, as if someone were pulling on an invisible line attached to his pelvis.

I laughed, too, and hid my face in my hands.

It stands erect of its own accord

Tryggvi swung his arm around with his elbow placed in his crotch, and I let out a groan.

Then it was time for the big finish. He stuck his nose in the air,

373

and his black hair fanned out from the back of his head, making him look like a crowing rooster.

He bellowed:

Tilarids, the mighty sword!

CHAPTER 29

Everyone screamed with laughter as I sat there, stunned. Next to me, Mads laughed, too, after Luna elbowed him in the side.

My lips were numb.

Tilarids?

I looked around to see if anyone shared my horror, but the unbridled atmosphere only made people laugh harder.

Tryggvi jumped down from the table in an elegant motion and bowed exaggeratedly to the audience, prompting them to clap even louder. He walked up to the table of food and drink to signal that his work was done.

I scrambled backward over the bench as the guests raised their glasses.

"Let's go now, Anna," Luna whispered, but I didn't answer her.

On unsteady legs, I followed Tryggvi and grabbed his arm.

"Look at them." He grabbed an overripe plum. "I had them in the palm of my hand."

With a squelch, he squeezed the fruit, and juice ran down his arm.

"Are there a lot of swords named Tilarids?" I was somewhat out of breath. "Is that a common sword name?"

Tryggvi licked some of the plum's juice off his wrist. "What?"

"Just tell me! Is it?" I may have raised my voice, but no one apart from Tryggvi noticed.

He looked at me in surprise. "No. It's completely unique. No one else would dare use that name."

He bit into an apple with his chalk-white front teeth, and the skin made a popping noise when it burst.

"And Tilarids is Prince Sverre's sword?"

Tryggvi shrugged his shoulders. "Eskild stole it from someone. He gave it to the prince as a betrothal gift."

"Who did Eskild steal it from?" Desperation turned my stomach into a hard knot. "Was it someone named Rorik?"

Tryggvi shook the remaining juice off his arm. "No idea. All I know is the sword's original owner suffered a grim fate. Something to do with torture and intestines everywhere."

My face felt frostbitten as pictures of what might have happened to Rorik swam around in my head. My imagination didn't pull any punches, and each possibility was more horrific than the last. I forced myself to stay calm.

"Tell me about Prince Sverre."

Tryggvi scratched his upper lip through his mustache. The yellow half-moon on his neck contrasted boldly with the serpent knot.

"I make fun of the prince. Ragnara encourages it because she doesn't want anyone to think Sverre is a real threat to her."

With my hand pressed to my solar plexus, I turned around and walked toward the grain field on the other side of the lawn. The previously golden grain was now submerged in solemn darkness. If Rorik was still alive—the mere thought that he could be dead sent ice-cold chills down my spine—I would slay the prince, if necessary, to help him. Maybe, I thought in a panic, he had already died to protect me, just as Serén had foreseen.

My legs could no longer carry me, and I had to sit on the ground.

The field was cool and dark, and insects were humming. The ground was damp, and the moisture soaked through my pants, but I didn't care. The crisp scent of straw enveloped me, but an emptiness formed, dulling my senses.

"Rorik might be dead," I mumbled, sucking down oxygen in a

large gulp, but I still couldn't catch my breath. Images bombarded me, scenes of him smiling in the sunset in Ísafold, joking around with Finn, healing Halfdan. I placed my hands over my eyes as I felt, once again, how he had healed my psychological wounds.

Someone was approaching.

Tryggvi had followed me. He sat next to me in the short grass and looked into the wall of grain.

"Have you encountered that sword before?" he asked quietly.

I didn't answer. It was impossible to squeeze out even a single word.

"Maybe Tilarids killed someone you cared about." Tryggvi's voice was soft. "It has felled many, if the rumors are to be believed."

"I know . . ." Again, the words caught in my throat, and I began to feel nauseous.

"Is it true that there are runes all the way down the blade?"

I looked at him, unable to decode the words. My brain refused to understand anything at all.

Tryggvi looked down. "There are very few who have gotten close enough to see the runes and lived to tell the tale." He paused. "In the brief time Tilarids belonged to Eskild, many people got a good look at those runes."

My stomach clenched at the thought of the fearsome sword in the wrong hands.

"That was a metaphor, in case you weren't sure," Tryggvi said. He turned his head, and the little moon on his neck caught the sun's final rays in the twilight.

I stood, then slumped forward with a stomach cramp. Shaking, I hunched over and looked down at the ground. Tryggvi got up and laid a hand on my back. His hard rings pressed on my spine through my shirt.

"Where is she?" came Luna's voice from the lawn.

"She was just here," Mads said. "Annaaaa . . ."

Tryggvi whispered something.

377

I tried to tell him I couldn't hear what he said, but then I realized he hadn't even been talking to me. Too late, I heard someone sneaking closer.

Tryggvi's hand covered my mouth, muffling my protests.

"I have her," he called, and a soldier threw herself on me. It was the guard who had ridden with us to Ripa.

I kicked and punched, but I was unprepared and still numb from shock. They quickly got my hands lashed together.

"I've seen your face many times, Serén," Tryggvi whispered in my ear. His hand still covered my mouth, and a particularly sharp ring on his little finger dug into my chin. "I can't comprehend why you didn't run away as soon as you saw me."

I managed to headbutt him right in the mouth, and he cried out. He spit out blood and part of a tooth. Furious, he clutched his jaw with one hand and looked at the tooth in the other. Then he threw it far into the field.

"Fuck it. I'll be rewarded with riches and honors when I deliver you to Ragnara."

I was tossed onto the bed of a cart, which screeched into motion with a violent jerk. My hands and feet were bound so tightly, I couldn't stop myself from rolling around, and I banged my head on the side. Behind us, Ripa became smaller and smaller.

"Anna?" Luna's voice quickly grew fainter.

Heavy footfalls told me Mads had run after us. Now I could see his large outline tailing the cart. Something rattled, and I recognized the sound of a bow being drawn. Tryggvi steered the cart at breakneck speed, and my head banged against the bottom.

Mads came up alongside me, but because I was lying on my side, I could see only his stomach.

"Anna." His voice was tense, and he made a choking noise as he dodged an arrow fired by the soldier. It swished just past him.

There was a bang as one of Luna's energy balls hit a wheel. The cart lurched. Tryggvi jumped down in front of me. Now the soldier was steering the cart.

Energy crackled in Tryggvi's palms. He narrowed his eyes and aimed at a spot behind Mads.

Mads lunged toward Tryggvi's legs, causing him to fall to his knees and miss when he cast his magic toward Luna.

Mads was now hanging off the back of the cart as it clattered along.

On the side of the road, Tryggvi's energy ball hit the middle of a tree, splintering it into a thousand pieces with a flaming crash. As the cart sped along, we traveled deeper into the forest that lay on the other side of Ripa.

Tryggvi gathered more energy by rubbing his palms together. This time, he directed his hands toward Mads, who was clinging to the back of the cart.

"Get rid of that hrimthurs!" the guard howled.

I rolled over, so Tryggvi, still on his knees, tumbled down and landed on top of me. I wrapped myself around him, pushing him so that his arms were turned away from my friends, which unfortunately meant his glowing hands were aimed right at my face. They hovered right in front of my forehead, and Tryggvi stared at me with such rage, I was certain he would blow my head off. I squeezed my eyes shut and waited for the bang. It came, but it didn't hit me. Instead, I heard a shout and a splat as Mads hit the ground.

I opened my eyes and saw that Tryggvi had simply blown up the back of the cart. It glowed and smoked, and the smell of the burning wood made me cough. Tryggvi gnashed his teeth. His hair stuck out in all directions, and his previously smooth mustache bristled.

"You're a sorcerer?" I whispered.

"Of course, all skalds are," he spat. "In Sént, you knew all our secrets. Sometimes you even knew what we were going to do before we knew it ourselves. But now you don't know anything."

379

He was right about that.

"It's obvious," Tryggvi hissed, "that the big guy is a giant, and your little witch friend's powers are so poorly hidden, she might as well have a sign around her neck."

The cart sped off, and the back of my head smacked against the bottom.

"What's going to happen?" Tryggvi screeched, shaking me. "You must have something up your sleeve if you can show up here, of all places, acting this nonchalant."

Somewhere far behind us, Mads and Luna shouted.

"What's going to happen?" Tryggvi repeated, then he punched me in the face. The clang in my head was deafening, and spots flashed before my eyes. "What's happening?" he yelled and hit me again, then again.

"I don't know," I yelled back and tried to raise my bound hands to my head.

Tryggvi looked at me as understanding reached his face. His hand hovered, ready to hit me again, and the rings on his knuckles shone.

I pressed my lips tightly together to signal that I wouldn't answer, and he hammered his ringed fist into my temple.

My consciousness flickered, and Tryggvi moved his hands to my stomach, where he began punching wildly.

"*This* is for stopping me from taking down your friends," I heard through the ringing in my ears. "And *this* is for my tooth." He hit me again.

The last thing I saw was his raised, clenched fist, heading straight toward my nose. His rings glinted, and with my hands tied, I could do nothing but turn my head.

I heard large, soft feet hitting the ground alongside us.

The fist soared toward me, but just before it struck, I heard a deep growl as claws landed with a *rittshh* on what remained of the cart.

An enormous set of teeth closed around Tryggvi's forearm, and I looked away when I heard a crunch.

Tryggvi wailed as his hand fell onto my chest, followed by spurts of warm liquid.

I looked up just as Rokkin's mouth closed around Tryggvi's neck, and I caught a glimpse of the moon tattoo surrounded by the serpent knot with the man-eating snake, before the large maw covered it entirely.

Tryggvi did not scream again.

PART IV

THE FATE
OF THE GODS

Now Garm howls loud
Before Gnipahellir.
The fetters will burst
And the wolf run free
Much does she know
And more can see
Of the fate of the gods,
The mighty in fight.

Völuspá,
10th century

CHAPTER 30

The cart swerved to the side, where it listed into the ditch due to the broken wheel. In the driver's seat, a second wolf was attacking the soldier, and I heard a scream followed by a crunch. Fortunately, I couldn't see what was happening. Rokkin barked some orders, and the weight of Tryggvi's body was lifted from my chest. A dragging sound grew distant through the trees.

The black wolf sat by my side in the tilted cart and studied me with shining eyes.

Mads and Luna caught up to us, out of breath.

The collapsed cart, the back of which still smoldered, was smeared with blood, but they composed themselves quickly. While Luna loosened my restraints, Mads and Rokkin looked at each other.

When I was finally free, I buried my head in Rokkin's fur and wrapped my arms around her neck, totally disregarding the fact that she wasn't used to physical contact.

"There, there," she said awkwardly, resting her chin, which was soaking wet—a detail I chose to ignore—on my shoulder.

A voice growled from the trees: "They're gone now."

Nausea rose in my stomach, but I forced it down.

"We have to get out of here." The sound of Rokkin's rusty voice, which reminded me of Monster's, caused a pang in my heart. I recovered, got to my feet, and hopped down from the sorry remains of the vehicle.

Luna supported me. "You have scratches all over your face."

"It's nothing." I flinched as a sharp pain radiated from my stomach where Tryggvi had punched me.

Luna's finger ran along my temple. "Nothing? You have a gash here."

I waved her away. My legs were shaking, but I tried my best to hide it as we jogged into the woods and away from the broken-down cart. We hurried along for quite a while, and I noticed I was the most normal one in the group, which was saying a lot.

Finally, we were a sufficient distance from the scene of the crime, and I turned to Rokkin.

"What are you doing here?" I asked. "It's super dangerous if you get caught. Your dad . . ."

"You're welcome." She laughed.

I had to force myself not to embrace her again. She reminded me so much of Monster, it was almost unbearable.

"Thank you so much for saving my life," I said. "I'm really glad you did. But you're here in Ván. Close to Ragnara. Close to Sént."

"Close to my mother and to my father's body. Maybe we can get them out," Rokkin said bluntly.

"We?" I couldn't help but ask.

She looked at me stoically.

"I thought about it after you left." She paused briefly. "You see beyond race. You're friends with a witch and a demigod." She looked toward Mads. "And a giant." Her gray eyes found mine again. "Your worst enemy is a human."

"But—"

"Do you want our help or not? Is that not why you came to see me in the Iron Forest?"

"No," I protested. "I went to you to prevent you from siding with the enemy. I never asked you to risk your own life by coming so close to Sént."

Rokkin sniffed. "That's our choice. It has nothing to do with you and your sister."

"But it's our fault," I whispered. "If we didn't . . ." My voice cracked. "Your parents."

"It's Ragnara's fault!" Rokkin rasped.

I sighed, breathing shakily.

Rokkin looked back at her pack, which numbered six giant wolves in addition to herself. Some were black, others gray, and one particularly large wolf was pure white. All had sat down to wait while we talked.

"What's your plan?" Rokkin asked.

"Uhh . . ."

"You *do* have a plan?" She didn't blink as she looked at me.

I squirmed.

"I got delayed a little." About six months. "So the plan isn't fully nailed down."

"There are three days until the wedding," Rokkin said as she lowered the bushy eyebrows she had most definitely inherited from Monster.

I picked up a leaf from the forest floor and studied it to avoid meeting her critical gaze.

"In broad strokes, the plan is that I go to Sént and get my sister, free my friends and allies, and find your father's body so I can bring him back to life."

"So, you and your two friends are going to attack the headquarters of the regime?" Rokkin asked dryly.

"Actually, I thought I would ditch Luna and Mads soon." I looked away. "I don't want them to get hurt."

Rokkin exhaled, her tongue hanging out of her mouth. Then she smacked her lips with thinly disguised sarcasm. "Oh, okay then. You'll storm the seat of power alone?"

"I was thinking more along the lines of an ambush."

"It's a good thing we came," Rokkin remarked.

"Yeah." Understatement of the century.

"Now that we're here, anyway," Rokkin said, a clear attempt to elegantly jump over my plan—or lack thereof, "how should we go about it?"

"The resistance movement has a base not too far from Sént. Haraldsborg. They should be notified that I'm on my way to Sént, but with only three days left, I don't have time for both."

"What do you know about Varnar's army?"

My stomach jumped at the mere mention of his name. *Oh!* I cocked my head to the side. "Varnar is dead."

She laughed hoarsely. "I know perfectly well that my brethren didn't eat him back then. Word travels about that kind of thing."

I laughed at the thought of the deadly wolves exchanging gossip. Then I grew serious.

"All I know is that the resistance fighters are in Haraldsborg, near Sént. Their castle has all kinds of spells on it, so Ragnara's soldiers can't get in. The fighters need to be summoned so they're ready for the wedding. Ragnara plans to elevate herself to a goddess there, and I'm planning to stop it, but it would be nice to have some backup from the resistance."

"We stand behind you, too," Rokkin declared bombastically. "My pack does, anyway," she added, somewhat less confidently, looking at her six companions.

"I don't want you to get hurt, either," I wailed. "Jeez, it's so hard when you care about people."

I tossed the leaf into the air, but it circled slowly to the ground.

"My parents believed in you and your sister," Rokkin said. "So I believe in you, too."

After Rokkin and I talked, we all found an undisturbed spot in the forest. Mads gathered stones, which he squeezed to form crystals. Then he placed them around our campsite. They glowed red, because Mads was near us. I looked around at the wolves and Luna.

"It's so cool that you can do that," I said to him.

He shrugged dismissively.

"You're so tough." Luna hugged him, and he nearly lost his balance.

"Okay, okay," he grumbled and patted her on the back, then hurried off in the opposite direction and placed the crystals on the ground.

"What's up with him?" Luna ran her fingers through her black curls.

I didn't answer.

"I can cast spells now," she said proudly. "My mom taught me to do protection magic."

She flailed her arms in the air and chanted something in Old Norse. Blue light crackled around us and formed a dome around our camp.

I took a step back as the energy field around her flickered unsteadily, and I remembered clearly how Védis had nearly killed me with her untamed magic.

When Luna had finished without any serious mishaps, she washed my cut.

"If only we had a healer." She dabbed at my temple with a damp rag.

My stomach contracted. "Yeah, if only."

"Or Elias were here," she added.

"I don't know about that," I said, wincing.

She inhaled sympathetically. "My dad can hypnotize people to not feel pain. I'm almost certain I could figure it out."

Almost?

"Uh . . . I think I'm okay." I removed her hand. "I'm sure it'll heal on its own."

"We'd better get some sleep," she said. "I'm guessing we'll take off for Sént early tomorrow morning."

I stared intently at a tree trunk so she couldn't catch my eye.

"Yeah, it's a good idea to get some sleep," I said.

My friends and the wolves were asleep. Or, more precisely: my friends and *most of* the wolves were asleep. Rokkin and the white wolf, whose name was Vale, were awake.

We walked a short distance away from the camp.

"You'll explain to Luna and Mads tomorrow?" I asked Rokkin and cringed. "They'll be so mad!"

Rokkin scoffed. "I would prefer to go with you."

"I just need to find out where in Sént my sister is. I think I'll be able to sense Serén's aura if I get close enough."

"My father would not have left you. I—"

"Nope!" My hand rested on her snout, and the white wolf made a surprised noise to see me touching her so nonchalantly.

"You need to find the resistance fighters and explain everything to them. You're the one who knows the most. And take good care of Luna and Mads. I don't want them to get hurt." What I didn't say aloud was that I couldn't bear losing anyone else.

"What if the resistance fighters don't believe us?" asked Rokkin.

I shivered at the thought of the fighters mistakenly killing the wolves—or vice versa.

"If there's any problem, tell Varnar . . ." I bit my lip, hard. "Tell him Ahen Drualus sent you." I removed my hand from Rokkin's snout, and she wrinkled her nose.

"Ahen Drualus?"

"Just say it."

She sniffed as if taking a deep breath and directed her large eyes at Vale. "I can trust you."

It was unclear whether this was a question, a statement, or a threat. Vale seemed to understand it as all three.

"I'll guard her with my life," he said in a voice deeper than even Monster was capable of.

The black and white wolves looked at one another for a moment.

Rokkin nodded.

We looked into each other's eyes. Then I hugged her and breathed in the scent of her fur.

"Take care of yourself!" I whispered.

It was unusual for me to be the emotional one, but Rokkin was apparently growing accustomed to human contact and let me do it. She even exhaled into my hair the same way Monster used to, and it made tears spring to my eyes. We stayed in that position for a while, until I let go and turned my back. I carefully picked up my bag, which Luna had fortunately had the presence of mind to bring from Ripa. Vale lumbered after me, and soon we were far from the camp.

Now that I was walking alongside him, I realized he was even bigger than Monster.

"Hop up," he rumbled.

"What?"

He stopped. "Do you want to reach Sént exhausted tomorrow afternoon, or do you want to get there in a few hours at dawn?"

"Well, when you put it that way." I looked at his broad, white back. His shoulders reached my chest.

Damn, he's big!

"How do I do it?" I tentatively placed my hand on him.

He crouched down so I could clamber up. Neither of us said what we were both thinking. A giant wolf kneeling before a human.

"Thanks," I whispered. I hoped he understood how much the word meant.

"Hey," came a voice behind us, and Vale assumed an attack position, so I had to cling to his fur.

Luna and Mads emerged from the underbrush.

Crap!

"Did you really think you could sneak off?"

"Uh . . . Yeah, I did." I stared at her. "You have to go to Haraldsborg."

She crossed her arms. "We're coming with you."

"It's too dangerous," I tried.

"Yes, it's incredibly dangerous," Mads said. His deep voice rumbled. "That's why you shouldn't go alone."

"Absolutely not."

Luna ran to my side. She had to stretch to reach me where I sat on Vale's back. She wrapped her arms around my waist and hit me with her largest portion of persuasion magic yet.

"Hey, come on. That's not fair."

"And sneaking off is?" Luna said into my stomach.

Totally incapable of resisting her magic, I leaned down and embraced her.

"You're not getting rid of us," she whispered. "You're my best friend, Anna."

She let go and walked over to Mads. The top of her head only went up to his chest.

"May I . . .?"

He looked down and nodded with one of his wide grins. He turned around, and she climbed onto his back.

"Are you ready?" She slung her arms around Mads's neck.

In response, Vale bowed, and I once again had to hold tight to his fur.

"We're ready," he bellowed.

And so, we took off. I closed my eyes, partly because the howling wind was making them water and partly to avoid throwing up from fear of slamming into trees or falling into the creeks, which Vale crossed with long, elegant leaps.

Behind us, I heard Mads snapping twigs and breathing heavily, and a single *whee* from Luna. When I finally dared to turn my head and look at them, I saw Mads running with ease and grace. There was no trace of the giant awkward boy from Ravensted in him. In fact, he reminded me more of Vale than a human.

I held tight to the wolf and hid my face in his long fur. I pretended it was Monster, though Vale's fur was much softer, and it felt like I was sitting on a sheepskin rug.

The forest flickered past, and eventually, all I took in were the smells of leaves and fertile soil.

We reached Sént first thing in the morning. We stood at the edge of a forest and looked at the city, which rose from the other side of a red plain. The sun was already warming our surroundings, and I was sweating in my lightweight clothes. I climbed down from Vale and saw that his back was wet where I had been sitting. His silky fur was in disarray, and he shook so it fell back into place. When he straightened his neck, I was struck by how beautiful he was.

Luna slid down from Mads's back and brushed off her colorful clothes, while Mads massaged his neck and looked around at the green forest.

I had changed my shirt back at the camp, but Tryggvi's blood had also saturated my pants in some places. Now it had dried, and the stiff spots scratched my legs. There were brown blotches on Vale's back, but he licked himself clean.

"Wouldn't want to let perfectly good blood go to waste," he said. The first thing he had uttered in several hours.

I gulped.

Beautiful, yes, but also a deadly, man-eating giant wolf.

What did it say about me that he was on my side?

We crouched behind some bushes and observed the city.

Sént was the closest thing I had seen to a big city in Hrafnheim. In the center stood a castle with four towers. This was most likely Konungsborg. It was built of a greenish stone, and each tower was a different color: gray, black, rust red, and white. It looked like the air was shimmering around one of the towers. The white one. I squinted.

There was a vibration coming from there. Both a push and a pull, as though I were one of two magnets both attracting and re-pelling. Like the pulsation of an intense aura.

An intense aura. Or just one that I feel intensely.

"She's in there," I said. "She's alive."

The relief was nearly palpable, and I had to lean against a tree to keep from toppling sideways to the ground.

Luna's warm hand stroked my back.

"We'll find her," she whispered. "We'll find your sister. She'll be just as much my friend as you are."

The aura responded by blinking, but apparently my sister was still unable to really communicate with me.

Imagine cold water running through your veins. Keep your head clear, Anna, I admonished myself.

There was a narrow path of red clay between the city and trees where we hid, so it would be difficult to sneak up to the city. My gaze swept over the walls in search of weak points, unguarded areas, or anything else that could be of use to us.

Whereas the other towns I had seen in Hrafnheim resembled Norwegian or Icelandic villages (though I was just guessing; aside from my journey to this parallel universe, I had never gone farther from Ravensted than Hjørring and Aalborg), Sént looked like my idea of a medieval town, with a moat surrounding a high wall. The buildings inside were rectangular, and in the middle, elevated above everything else, was the castle. In a notch in the city wall, I noticed a smashed building that had once stood taller than even the castle. In a flash from the past, I saw a gleaming lighthouse. The vision fluttered away, and I was once again looking at the ruin.

The gate nearest to us was closed, but I tried to figure out whether we could get into the city that way. Maybe I could cover myself with a scarf again? I dug around in my bag for the piece of green fabric that Rorik had given me. For a moment, I held it in my hand and stroked it with my index finger. I fidgeted with the scarf and felt a jab of longing. I was about to wrap it around my head when one of the city gates opened. A cart lurched out. I pressed myself farther down behind the bush.

"What's going on?" Luna whispered.

"Shhh."

A small group of soldiers was on the cart, and they were heading straight toward our hiding place. Ragnara's rune was painted on the cart's side in bright red.

When they came closer, I recognized the man in the driver's seat. It was one of the soldiers who had detained me my first night in Hrafnheim. I was pleased to note that his nose was unnaturally flat, and he was missing the bottom part of his earlobe. I recognized the man behind him as Knut. He was the one who had tortured Monster. There were a couple of other soldiers I didn't recognize. In the cart bed, I spotted a bound figure who sat hunched over with a hood on their head—the same kind Luna had had when the berserkers captured her in the yard in front of Odinmont.

She gasped next to me.

One man wasn't wearing a uniform.

"The magic is crackling off him," Luna whispered. "That's a sorcerer."

A familiar yet foggy aura reached me from the cart, and my first thought was Serén, but the broad shoulders suggested there were only men on the cart.

The cart stopped, and Knut looked directly at the clump of bushes we hid behind. With a groan, I pressed myself completely flat against the ground.

Then he shouted: "Surrender and come with us willingly."

No one else was around, but there was no way he knew we were lying there. As quietly as possible, I loosened Auka from my belt.

Next to me, Vale bared his teeth, and Mads's eyes glittered ominously.

"Thorasdatter," Knut called. "I know you're in there."

My pulse pounded, and a cold sweat broke out across my forehead.

395

How the hell does he know where I am?

"Thorasdatter," he barked again. "Surrender now!"

There was a pause in which the only sound was a creak from the cart.

The man with the half earlobe drew his sword and pointed it toward the bound figure in the back of the cart.

Who is that?

Knut hopped down from the cart. His boots crunched in the dry red soil. He nodded at the man with the sword, who poked the hooded figure in the neck. A small red stripe spread across the hood where it covered the man's throat.

One of the soldiers roughly jerked the man's hands up, and my whole body went cold. A tattooed eagle flapped its wings on his thumb and index finger. I inhaled sharply and nearly stood up but forced myself down.

Cold water in your veins. Keep your head clear.

Knut shouted again.

"Thorasdatter." He yanked the hood off. "The decision is yours."

I whimpered and gripped Auka as Rorik squinted against the weak sunlight. He scanned the trees with a look of desperation on his face.

"They saw my giant crystal," he shouted. "They could see you were nearby. Stay away."

"Choose," Knut yelled. "We'll let him live if you surrender."

Cold water in your veins . . . I moved a fraction of an inch closer.

"No," Rorik begged and peered into the trees again. "Don't. They'll come after you regardless. It's just easier for them if you surrender yourself. Run away while there's still time."

Cold water . . .

"Is that Rorik?" Luna whispered.

I nodded in anguish and wiped my eyes on my sleeve. "Is there anything you can do? Cast a spell or something?"

Her forehead wrinkled as she concentrated, then she shook her head.

"There's magic around them." She raised her fingers in the air, but she pulled her hand back as though she felt an electric shock. "Ow, shit," she snapped. "I'm not good enough to break through it."

On the cart, the sorcerer's yellow eyes glowed even brighter than before.

I looked at Rorik again.

His white hair shone in the sun, and his dark brown eyes searched for me. I tried to discern whether he was frightened or banged up, but he simply looked miserable. They had given him one of the robes with Ragnara's rune on it, so people could see he was in her custody. He was relatively unharmed, and he was alive, but this small relief dissolved into a shudder when I realized Serén's prophecy was about to be fulfilled. She had seen Rorik and me together by a forest in the summer, and he would die because he was protecting me.

Cold . . . I bit my lip, hard. *Hell no!* I couldn't let any more people die because of me.

Knut pressed the sword closer to Rorik's throat. The edge rested on his skin.

"Go to Haraldsborg," I ordered Luna, Mads, and Vale.

"Anna!" Mads protested. "You can't go to them."

I gave him a look that he probably considered typically me. Then I turned my face away from my friends.

"Go on. I'll be fine." With a loud, clear voice, I shouted: "Wait!"

The bloodied sword remained where it was. Now the whole front of Rorik's pale shirt was shining.

I lifted the leaves so I could duck under a branch.

"Anna." Luna reached out, but I skillfully evaded her grasp so she couldn't hit me with persuasion magic.

"No!" Rorik shouted. "Don't."

But I stepped down to the plain.

When he saw me, he gasped for air, and I realized he hadn't seen me for six months. I smiled with tears in my eyes and held his gaze.

I reached the soldiers on the red plain.

"Anna," Rorik whispered. "You don't have to do this for me."

"I'm so tired of everything being immovable, predetermined," I told him. "I have to try to change fate."

Rorik's brown eyes glinted in the sun, which was now just above the horizon. Longing and tenderness flowed from them.

"I can't let anyone else die for my sake." I could feel my eyes going soft. "Especially not you."

I raised Auka as a sign of surrender and took a few steps toward Rorik, who looked like he wanted to say something.

Slowly, Knut pulled the sword away from Rorik's neck, while the other soldier came toward me. He stood behind me and fastened my hands together.

I thanked the gods I didn't even believe in that the others had stayed in the brush. The men didn't know my friends were in there.

The soldier tied me up as my heart pounded. *To hell with the consequences.* I didn't care that I was in Ragnara's clutches. As long as I could save Rorik. Not one more person could be allowed to die for me to live.

"Let him go. He has no value to you anymore."

Knut studied me for a moment, unmoving. Then he shifted his gaze to Rorik.

"No value." The corner of his mouth crept up. "Ragnara doesn't think he's valuable anymore, either. He betrayed her. She said he must be punished."

"You promised to let him go."

"Promises made to enemies don't count," Knut said.

What?

Knut fingered his sword.

Every muscle in my body was trembling.

Knut raised the sword and pulled his arm back.

I threw myself forward when I realized what he was doing, but the ropes held me back.

Knut thrust the sword, and I saw it in slow motion as he plunged it straight into Rorik's chest.

CHAPTER 31

I threw myself forward again, but the soldier jerked me back. I screamed, letting out all the pain of being unable to change fate. Knut pulled the sword out, and blood spurted from Rorik's chest.

He collapsed in front of me.

Vale left the thicket with a *grrooaaw* and jumped on Knut.

No!

In Ripa, I had been lying with my back turned, so I hadn't seen what efficient killing machines the giant wolves can be. This time, I got the full picture.

Luna and Mads followed, throwing themselves at the soldiers.

"Run away!" I shouted as I pulled against my restraints. "I told you to run away."

"As if," Luna replied. Balls of energy shot from her hands, but they bounced off an invisible wall, as though there were a transparent shield around the soldiers.

The sorcerer raised his hands toward Luna and Mads, emitting a blue beam. They leapt to either side, and the beam shot between them.

Rorik lay on the ground as a red puddle grew larger and larger around him. He opened his eyes wide when he saw the gigantic white wolf. The blood was absorbed into the ground, and the hard clay surface became an even darker red. Suddenly, the whole plain appeared damp and red in my mind's eye.

The sorcerer sent out another beam, freezing Mads, who stood as still as a stone pillar. Only his eyes remained mobile, opened wide and desperate.

Luna tried to cast another energy ball, but it rebounded right in her face, and she went down, knocked out by her own magic.

Vale's white fur had turned red, and it stuck out from his body in thick, wet clumps.

What was left of Knut lay on the ground in disarray, but to my horror, I discovered he wasn't dead. He reached for his sword, which had fallen out of his hand, but Vale's paw, which was the size of a dinner plate, stepped on the blade. When Knut pulled weakly on the hilt, dragging his ruined body slightly forward in the process, Vale lowered his head and placed it right in front of Knut's.

"You killed my prince, Etunaz," he said in his deep voice and opened his bloody maw, his sharp teeth glinting in the morning sun. "Vengeance."

I turned my head.

Another soldier hit me hard in the back of the head, while the remaining men brandished their spears at Vale.

I fell to my knees, and for a split second, I made eye contact with Rorik.

"I'll find you," he whispered, clutching his chest. Sticky liquid trickled out between his tattooed fingers, and the eagle looked like it was spewing blood. Reality undulated around me, and only in the very center of my field of vision was I able to focus on Rorik.

Vale aimed his gray eyes at me as all the blood flowed around us. His nostrils flared.

"It's—" Vale said, before a spear slid into his side.

"No!" I screamed.

Luna lay on the ground, and Mads stood, immobile.

Vale growled ferociously and turned toward the soldier, the spear protruding from his flank. Very little of his fur remained white.

"Anna, they're deceiving you," he snarled. "They . . ."

401

"What?" I shook my head, trying to cling to consciousness, but the soldier hit me again.

Everything went black.

One moment, I was on the plain, and the next, I was in a cool hallway, the sound of feet echoing. Something whined and snarled, but I couldn't figure out where it was coming from.

Vale? Is he alive? Are Luna and Mads?

The sound disappeared down another hall, and now there were only the footsteps.

I had the sensation of being carried as people talked around me. Their voices sounded like distorted loudspeakers. The sound of iron clanged, and a metallic whine suggested hinges swinging open.

Something rustled, the hinges creaked again, and I was bound with something cold. Magic electricity crackled, and a chain tightened around my wrists.

I didn't know if I was lying down or sitting up. The only things I could discern were a scratchy surface, cold tiles, and metal digging into my hands. The door creaked again, and I was blessedly alone.

Then I let myself be swallowed up by hopelessness and darkness.

Eventually, I couldn't cling to unconsciousness any longer, even though I would have preferred to remain huddled in my little corner. With my hands fastened behind my back and attached to the wall with a thick chain, my sore muscles cried out, and this pushed me the rest of the way into a wakeful state.

I blinked and looked around.

Bars. Yellow-green tiles and mats on the ground.

There was scattered conversation, but in my little cell were only three of us. The other two were not tied up. Only a fragment of daylight crept in through a tiny window high up by the ceiling, and I heard faint whimpers in the dark.

The intense aura, Serén's, rushed all around, like when you're about to pass out.

Wooosh . . . Woooosh . . .

I reached out mentally for Luna and Mads and sensed them down here somewhere. They were, at least, alive.

I leaned against the cold tile wall.

My two cellmates and I were separated from the rest of the dungeon only by iron bars. A man lay on the floor in our cell, and he looked to be nearly dead. I couldn't go to him, because of the chains, and even if I could have, I had no idea how to help him.

My other cellmate was a broad-shouldered woman with a dark shadow over most of her face. She was crouched next to the man. Something about her was familiar, and I tried to focus, but my vision kept going blurry. My eyes widened when I finally realized who it was.

"Gytha! What are you doing here?"

She looked at me, and despite the bruises and dirt, there was warmth in her face.

"I'm sorry we're meeting again under these circumstances, Thorasdatter. Things have clearly gone downhill since I last saw you." It wasn't a shadow covering the bottom half of her face. It must have been months since she'd had access to water, soap, and a razor. Maybe not since she was in Hibernia.

"They captured you because of me." I gasped with dismay. "I'm sorry. Oh . . . I'm so sorry."

There were purple bruises on her cheekbone and neck. Through the holes in her shirt, I glimpsed scratches and scars.

"They *questioned* me because of you." She pulled her tattered, stained skirt tight around her legs. "They arrested me because I don't live according to their rules."

"I wonder if it's a coincidence that we ended up in the same cell."

She squinted. Without makeup on, her eyes looked stark. "Nothing is a coincidence."

The sleeping man moaned, and Gytha laid a grimy hand on his forehead.

"He's burning up with fever," she mumbled.

I looked at her, huddled and beaten on the floor of the filthy cell.

"Where's Rorik?" she asked. "I liked him. So handsome and feisty."

"He . . ." I inhaled forcefully to keep from crying. My conviction that I had no more sadness left in me after losing Monster was quickly disproven. I didn't know what had happened to Luna and Mads, just that they were somewhere in the dungeon.

Everything had gone wrong, and it was all my fault.

Gytha sensed my misery and crawled over to me. Since she wasn't in chains, she was free to move around all one hundred square feet of the cell. Her strong hands, which were covered in bruises, touched my cheeks. "Has your companion gone to the realm of the dead?"

Her concern nearly pushed me over the edge.

With gritted teeth, I nodded. "Rorik is dead." I might as well get used to saying it aloud, but my lower lip quivered.

I could see into the other cells through the iron bars. In the one next to ours sat a pair of men. The rest of the cages were lost in shadow, but I could hear chatter and coughs, and beneath Serén's intense aura, less powerful ones began to show up. With my mind frayed as it was, I had a hard time shielding myself from them, but I tried as hard as I could to remember Elias's instructions. I took a deep breath and wrinkled my nose at the sharp stink of humans. This actually helped, so even though I felt like throwing up, I concentrated on sweat, urine, and unwashed skin.

One of the neighboring men came up to the bars and peered in at us. "Who are you?"

"Shut your mouth," Gytha said. "Can't you see she's upset?"

"We're all miserable here." He leaned as close to me as the bars would permit. "What did you do?"

I looked up slowly through thick, red tangles. "I planned to kill Ragnara and Eskild."

Our neighbor gasped. "The worst death must await you. The very worst."

"Shh!" Gytha tried to hit him through the bars, but he hopped back, out of reach of her long arms.

"Death is death," I said. "The outcome is the same."

I didn't feel nearly as brave as I sounded.

The man continued as though he didn't hear me. "There's garroting, burning, being skinned alive, the rack . . ."

The fear, anger, and frustration all around me, combined with my own grief over far too many losses, bombarded my brain, and everything swirled around. I looked down at the dirty floor and took a few deep breaths.

In the other cells were people from Ísafold, and I saw a film reel of all the horrors that had occurred. I let out a terrified sob when I saw the dead and dying people, with burning houses in the background.

It's all my fault.

On top of the misery, the desperate people around me, and my own hopelessness, it was too much. Everything began to disintegrate.

It was impossible to flee. The only thing my brain could do to stop it was check out again.

When I opened my eyes, it was brighter in the small cell. I guessed it was around noon, but it was hard to tell. I stretched, surprised to notice I wasn't freezing and that my head rested on something soft. I sat up, and the chain clinked faintly behind me.

A large, soft blanket was draped over me, and there was a pillow where my head had been.

What?

I looked around. Next to my mat was a goblet of water and a plate of food.

Gytha crawled over to me. "You're awake. Smelling that bread has been torture. Eat it quick so the rest of the prisoners aren't tormented by it."

"Who brought it?" I was still groggy.

Gytha shrugged. "A guard."

There was a noise from the cell next to ours. Our neighbor leaned against the bars and licked his lips. "Give me some food."

I stood, and even though Gytha didn't reach for my plate or my blanket, she looked at them longingly.

"Why didn't you just take it? You know I would rather let you have it."

"Give it to me," the man in the other cell called again, but I ignored him.

Gytha shook her head with a stubborn set to her mouth.

"Give him some water and put the blanket over him." I pointed my foot toward the still-unconscious man.

This spurred Gytha into action. She grabbed my bedding, crawled over to the man, and gently placed the pillow under his head and the blanket over him.

I squinted. "Do you know him?"

Gytha carefully poured a few drops of water between the man's lips.

"No," she said. "But he's suffering."

I waited for her to say something more, but she was silent.

The man instinctively accepted the water. Gytha poured some more, and once again he swallowed. I could almost see his life force glowing a little stronger. Gytha laid his head back on the pillow.

"Eat," I said. I tried to convince Gytha to eat all the food, but she broke off only a piece of the bread and handed the rest to the man in our neighboring cell.

"Thanks," he mumbled, as they each held one end of the bread.

Gytha tilted her head elegantly.

"You're welcome, my good man," she replied with a dignified air before letting go. "Take a piece and distribute the rest to the sickest and youngest."

She kept the water and got the man to swallow some every few minutes.

His breathing grew a little stronger, but he did not regain consciousness.

I passed the time by walking back and forth, as far as the chain would allow. I really should have been doing something more meaningful, now that I was awaiting my death sentence, but I spent the time thinking about the food I wanted to eat. Rebecca's chicken with cinnamon, Frank's burgers, Milas's french fries, and ice cream with whipped cream and chocolate sauce. My mouth watered, and my stomach rumbled.

Oddly enough, I thought about North Jutland. This was the first time I was forced to stay in one place, and my thoughts flew homeward.

Home.

I had never thought about my surroundings when I lived there, but now, in this strange place with its unfamiliar sounds and smells, I was constantly thinking about Ravensted and the surrounding areas. I longed for the harsh western wind, the flat expanses, and the endlessly roaring sea, unconcerned with our small human lives. I missed Odinmont's placement, its view over the stark landscape. The thought of walking into the warmth of Frank's on a cold winter day made me homesick.

After a few hours, when the gray darkness began to gather in the cell, the suffering man moaned, blinking with the one eye that wasn't scabbed shut.

I narrowed my eyes as I studied him.

Something about him was . . . not familiar. I'd never met him before, but . . .

He looked around, and his gaze landed on me. He squeezed his eye shut and moved his cracked lips soundlessly in shock.

"Serén," he whispered. "Serén. You're alive. I've tried to find you in my dreams, but you've been hidden from me."

I stood, and the chain clattered behind me.

"I'm broken," he whispered. "But it's me. Bork."

Oh, right. Bork was Serén's foster father. He had been Ragnara's clairvoyant adviser, revealed to be a traitor. This was apparently the punishment Ragnara had given him.

He didn't understand that I was just as much a prisoner as he was, if in somewhat better shape. Though his clairvoyant abilities fluttered around him, he was too delirious to see that I was not my sister.

"I never thought I would see you again, Serén," he cried. Tears streamed from his intact eye. "I tried to keep the secret. I tried. Even when they took my eye." He raised a mangled hand to his eye socket. "They cut people's eyes out as a way of mocking Odin." He inhaled shakily. "I came up with it myself." His voice faded into a hollow cough. "I revealed nothing, but then they gave me a potion." He coughed again. "They'd gotten it from the Brewmaster. Then I told them everything."

Stjórna!

"What did they want to know?" A combination of willpower and a slightly too-short chain held me back.

"They wanted confirmation that Thora is your mother. They asked where you were." He squirmed. "I knew you were in the Iron Forest with the giant wolves, and I told Eskild that." He whimpered softly. "Forgive me."

I opened my mouth to respond, but he moaned again. Something flashed deep inside him, and I saw his vision. It was like when I was with Justine from Sømosen. I felt as though I stood between two mirrors and saw an endless series of reflections. Time was a large plane that was at once fixed and in constant flux.

My mother handed Bork a baby. She was haggard, and she looked intensely at him, as if to ensure he kept his word. The baby in his arms had a little crown of thin red hair. It squeezed his rough finger and smacked its lips in its sleep, and Bork's heart swelled. The vision of my sister smiling as a baby rushed toward me. She looked exactly like me, although the smile was unfamiliar.

Maybe I smiled, too, when I was younger, but I couldn't remember it.

Bork ran after Serén in a playful game of tag. I saw her sitting with her eyes closed, concentrating on sending him a vision, which he received. They both raised their arms in victory when it succeeded. Then the vision shifted to war, blood, pain, and death. Like when I read passages of "Völuspá", I heard terrified screams and had the sensation of being in an elevator plummeting down. Then I saw his vision of himself lying here on the floor. He knew very well what was coming. He might have known—or at least been aware of the possibility—for years. I gasped as I felt ice form around my arms and hands. It crackled and creaked in my ears, and I had to shake myself to get rid of the chill.

He mumbled weakly. "Fimbulwinter. It will come if Ragnara kills you."

"And if Fimbulwinter comes?"

"After Fimbulwinter comes Ragnarök. The end of the world."

I took a couple of steps toward him, but the chain held me back. "Where? Which world?"

Bork shifted on his mat. "This one. The other one. Both. Maybe. It keeps changing. I can't see it."

He groaned as the image of my own dead face fluttered from him. It lay on the forest floor, and behind it I glimpsed Odinmont. Despite everything, it seemed the future didn't plan for me to die here and now.

"I see too much," he said weakly.

"He doesn't have much longer," Gytha said.

"Forgive me," Bork wailed. "Forgive me, Serén."

"I don't know if I can."

Bork opened his one eye and looked at me, and I bit my lip until I tasted blood. His aura flickered and became nearly transparent.

I exhaled.

"I forgive you." With these words, a giant boulder rolled off my heart.

Bork closed his eye and let out a long breath. He didn't inhale again, and for a second, I thought he was dead, but he was simply unconscious.

"I forgive you," I whispered again.

Me. *Forgive*.

I crawled back to my mat and sat there, staring blankly into space. First my hands, then my arms, and finally my shoulders had lost feeling from being forced behind my back. With a little luck, I would be completely numb when they came to get me for my execution or torture. Probably both. Though I tried to push the thought away, our neighbor's words continued to reverberate in my head.

Garroting, burning, being skinned alive, the rack.

The last three were things I had heard of. I didn't know what the first one was, but it didn't sound particularly pleasant. I slid down the wall and closed my eyes against the strengthening daylight.

Gytha didn't move from Bork's side. She spoke to him, even though I wasn't sure he could hear her. His color shifted to a waxy yellow, but Gytha continued to feed him water and breadcrumbs.

I woke with a start when someone stroked my cheek. I had apparently fallen asleep again, leaning up against the cold tile wall. I turned my body and leaned into the warm hand. It was so familiar and comforting.

Through the little crack of a window, I saw pale morning light.

"Anna."

My name sounded like a caress, and I raised my head toward the voice.

"I came to get you."

"You can't save me. You couldn't even save yourself."

"I can try." There was a smile in the voice that was so heartrendingly familiar.

"But you're gone." Even half asleep, I felt the tears fall.

"Shh." The sound was gentle. "I'll get you out of here. You're coming with me."

Death had been breathing down my neck for a year now, but to get the message directly from a ghost was a bit much. Reason took over my brain and chased away all traces of sleepy dreaminess. My eyes flew open, and I was looking right into Rorik's warm gaze.

"Did you upgrade to poltergeist? Why haven't you crossed over?" The words came out on top of each other.

He was crouched in front of my mat.

"Rorik," I said again. Tentatively. "You're gone."

"You're right. Rorik is gone now."

"Cross over. You don't belong here." I racked my brain to remember how to send spirits to the realm of the dead. "Your fight is over," I tried. "I'll be there soon. This winter, at the latest."

"I'm not going anywhere," Rorik said softly.

It would be best if he wasn't here when . . . I still couldn't get myself to think it. I had to send him away in the only way I knew how. I took a deep breath.

"You're dead," I said, tears running freely. I pressed my face against his hand. I wanted to touch him. Just one last time. "You're dead, you're dead, you're dead." Now I was crying loudly. "I saw it myself. You were stabbed in the heart."

But he didn't falter. He simply stared at me with his brown eyes, and the hand holding my face was warm and solid.

I blinked a couple of times and focused on him. With difficulty, I sat up, and he let go of my cheek. Gytha was sitting pressed up against the wall on the other side of the cell, eyes wide. She held a hand over her mouth.

I stared again at Rorik. Familiar . . . and yet.

He was clean. And he was dressed in military clothes again, Ragnara's symbol emblazoned on his shirt. His pale, almost white hair lay in shining waves over his shoulders. Tilarids hung at his side, and the sword radiated with joy and victory.

"Rorik?" I said cautiously.

He shook his head. "I'm not Rorik. That has never been my name. My name is Sverre."

CHAPTER 32

For a moment, I stared at him. My brain refused to accept what he'd said. "I saw you die."

He patted his heart with his free hand.

"You saw me bleed." When I still looked at him, uncomprehending, he continued. "I'm a healer, so I healed myself. Knut knows about my flaw, and he uses it to torment and humiliate me. Ragnara gave him orders to punish me. I never know when it's coming. It was the greatest torture for me, that you saw me die without me being able to explain."

I was mute as it sank in.

"The whole time," I finally whispered. "You lied to me the whole time."

I got to my feet.

He stood, too, slowly.

Then I hissed: "Traitor!"

He flinched but quickly regained his composure, towering over me. "How am I a traitor?"

"You lied to me. And to everyone else. You lied about who you are." The anger cleared my head. Out of pure frustration, I slammed my head back into the wall behind me.

Rorik—*no, Sverre*—took a step forward and raised his hands but stopped himself.

"Our whole journey. In Ísafold . . ."

Hatred must have been shooting from my eyes, because he took a step back, placing a hand on Tilarids's hilt. Then he recovered himself. "You left me. What do you think it was like for me to wake up and discover you were gone? I looked for you. Finn was upset. He cried and searched for you, but it was like you'd vanished into thin air."

"Finn," I whispered. "Where is he?"

"In the stables with the other fingalks."

"But he doesn't even know what a fingalk is."

"It was either that or death," Rorik snapped back. "Was I supposed to kill him? Our . . ."

"Our what?"

Rorik gave me a long look. "I could tell from my giant crystal that you weren't dead, so my only conclusion was that you had left me. And that you had always planned to leave me. *You* lied, and *you* left me."

"I thought," I began but stopped when something dawned on me. "Were you there when Ragnara attacked Ísafold?"

I caught a glimpse of pain on the prince's face before he gained control over his emotions. "They were looking for you, but they found me. I was at least able to convince my mother to give them a fair trial. The ones who survived."

"Ragnara is your mother." The words hung in the air.

"She's furious with me for running away in Norvík. I'm under nearly constant supervision by the soldiers."

"But—"

"The soldiers found you through my giant crystal. That was how they caught you. I tried to get rid of it, but they caught me."

I shook my head.

"But they couldn't have seen that it was me. I don't believe you."

"They could see that someone I cared about was nearby, and they grew suspicious."

I looked at him, uncomprehending.

"I've never cared about anyone before," he said quietly. His expression was sincere, but I couldn't tell if he was lying.

"You acted like you were my protector," I whispered.

"And I'm a terrible protector."

"What did you want out of it? Out of traveling with me?"

"I can lead Freiheim much better than my mother can." The way he said the word *mother* sounded like a curse. "I know the people. I want the best for them. But this damned healing power is in the way. No one wants to follow a seid-man."

Comprehension came to me. "*That's* what you wanted me to change in your past. You were going to ask me to take away your healing ability."

He nodded.

I furrowed my brows.

"You must have had it since before you were born." I wanted to say more but stopped and looked down at the scar that peeked out above my shirt. Suddenly it made sense why, from the moment I met him, I felt like I knew him. *I had met him before. I had met him before we were even born.*

Standing before me, Sverre wore the same facial expression I did.

"I recognized you," he mumbled. "I thought it was because you looked so much like Serén, but I've always known you." He stepped toward me, and I pressed myself against the wall. He leaned over me and reached out his hand. Absent-mindedly, he ran a finger down the scar.

"It was you," I said. "That was why I healed. Why my mom healed, when Ragnara touched us. She was pregnant with you."

"You were the first," he whispered. "Your life was the first one I saved. It may have even been you who awakened my horrible powers."

"If I take away your ability, I would die back then," I said. "Do you want that?"

"No, Anna. No, I don't want that."

Neither of us said anything as we followed the thought to its conclusion.

415

"It's strange that we happened to meet when I came to Hrafnheim. Of all the people in the whole realm, I met you."

Rorik's mouth hung open.

"Your sister," he said. "Your sister said it, many years ago."

"What did Serén say?"

"That my fate could be changed if I went to Norvík right before my wedding." He bowed his head. "I wanted so badly to change my fate, but it turned out to be fate that changed me."

I wanted to move away from him, but I was attached to the wall.

"Leave," I said quietly. "Get out of here."

He ignored me. "I want to be with you."

"Why should I believe that?"

A wounded shadow flitted across his face before he composed himself. "Can't you feel it?"

"I don't trust my ability to feel anything right now, Rorik." I bit my lip, hard. "Sverre! Where did you even get the name Rorik?"

He closed his eyes. "I pulled it out of nowhere. There was a Rorik in the army. He's working for your mother now. I took his name."

"Why didn't you say who you are?"

He looked down. "I knew our time together would be over as soon as you knew the truth."

"You're right about that."

Rorik—*Sverre, damn it!*—sighed.

"I can help," he hissed through clenched teeth. "We're on the same side."

For a moment, I stared at him, not understanding. "No, we aren't."

Again, he brought his mouth close to my cheek. "Ragnara isn't at the castle. If she were, you would be dead by now. She's on her way, so I need to get you out of here as soon as possible. I would have come for you earlier, but I couldn't get away. All I could do was send down food and blankets.

My pulse rose. "Does Ragnara know I'm here?"

He nodded gravely, his light hair swaying around him, and the scent of lavender reached my nostrils.

I didn't want to think about what I probably smelled like.

"I need to get you out now," Rorik insisted. "It won't be long before she arrives."

Damn it, Anna, his name is Sverre!

"I don't trust you," I snapped.

"Do you have a choice?"

"Um, yes. I can choose to stay as far away from you as possible, and if you drag me away with you, I can fight you every step of the way and expose what you're trying to do." I clanked the chain behind my back demonstratively. "But you've kind of IMPRISONED me."

He inhaled a long, controlled breath. "I'll smuggle you into my quarters. You can stay there without my mother and Eskild finding out. Ingeborg means nothing to me. You and I can . . ."

I stared at him. "We can what?"

The words remained on his tongue.

"You think you've figured it all out yourself, don't you?"

He didn't say anything.

I glared at him. "What about the others? The Ísafolders, Monster's wife, the people from Miklagard?"

"My mother wanted to kill them on the spot, but I insisted on the arena as a way of buying time. As a wedding present. I was hoping . . ." He laughed bitterly. "I don't know what I was hoping. Maybe divine intervention. It backfired."

"What do you mean?"

"There are going to be gladiator fights. It's a demonstration of how a battle between Ragnara and the resistance movement would go. Everyone's excited because now there are two giant wolves. A black and a white one. If the prisoners win, they'll be set free." He waved a hand. "In reality, it's just entertainment for the masses."

I was breathless for a moment. "You captured Vale? He survived?"

"Vale?" The prince balked.

"The white wolf?"

"Didn't it want to eat you? I thought it was your enemy."

"He was protecting me, you idiot!" I shrieked. One more would die because of me. I resisted the urge to bang my head against the tile wall again.

Sverre stared, realizing his mistake, but pulled himself together.

"Anna, let me help you," he urged.

I clenched my fists behind my back and wished I had knocked him out the very first time I met him. Now the iron chain held me to the wall.

"You can help me if you free all the other prisoners," I said, clearly enunciating each word. "Including my friends Luna and Mads."

"They . . ." he stopped. "I can't save them."

I tilted my head to one side as I looked at the man I knew so well, but was, at the same time, a complete stranger.

"I can't," he said desperately. "I'm not sure if I can even save you."

I widened my eyes and shook my head. I felt a pinching sensation, and I realized that the gash from Tryggvi's blow to my temple was still there. Meanwhile, a dull ache at the back of my head indicated where the soldier had hit me. I tried my best to keep from wincing. "You're useless."

He pressed his lips together. "I'll do whatever it takes to save you, even though I can't help the others."

"There's just a little hole in your plan," I said slowly.

"What?"

"All the prisoners—our friends—my best friends—will be ripped to shreds!" I didn't bother to keep my voice down. In fact, I screamed in his face and threw myself toward him with a clatter of the chain.

"This is my only chance to save you and your sister," he yelled back. "My mother is going to sacrifice her at my wedding."

Invisible ants crawled all over my body.

He lowered his voice. "You and Serén. You're who I'm focused on. I can't save everyone, and isn't Serén the most important to you?"

I looked at him coldly. "And you still need us together. If you want to be king, you need to have both the past and the future on your side."

Suddenly, there was calculation in his eyes. It was only a glimmer, but I saw it.

"So you have to help me."

"But I'm useless. You left me when I wasn't useful to you anymore."

I interjected. "I left you to protect you. You and Finn." My voice broke. *Shit.* I couldn't hold the tears back. I looked down and gulped down a couple of tremulous breaths. I forced myself to focus. "How are you going to get ahold of my sister?"

Sverre squinted. "I've searched the entire castle for her, and most of the city. I simply can't find her."

"I can feel her. I know where she is."

"If you can feel her, then I can find her."

I took a step forward but was halted by the chain. "So let's find her now."

"I can't move about the castle freely. We have to do it when everyone's busy with something else."

"Like what?"

He cleared his throat. "The preparations for my wedding."

"What do you want in return? For helping Serén and me?"

He looked at me in surprise. "For you to live."

"What. Do. You. Want?" The words came out sharp as the crack of a whip.

He looked down. "Let me think about it."

That's when I realized what I would have to do to save everyone. Almost everyone.

CHAPTER 33

The prince handed me the green cloth.

"Cover yourself," he said quietly.

I wrapped it around my head until only my eyes were visible.

Gytha stroked Bork's forehead. We couldn't stand to leave her in the dungeon, so she came with us.

Bork opened his good eye, and for once, he appeared to be lucid. Feebly, he reached up and clasped Gytha's hand. Then his arm fell back down, and he closed his eye.

Gytha's long hair, shredded dress, and beard garnered jeers from the other prisoners, and I gritted my teeth to keep from shouting back. Gytha could have ducked her head and lowered her eyes, but she held her head high and looked every single heckler in the eyes. I hid my head in my shawl and looked down at the tile floor of the hallway.

Sverre led the way and appeared confident, but I sensed panic in his aura. Finally, after what felt like a nerve-racking eternity, we reached an isolated wing, and he showed us into an apartment that was larger than all of Odinmont.

"I'll come back tonight," he said. "Until then, take the time to eat and rest." He turned around and disappeared through the door.

I looked around.

There were high ceilings, soft carpets on the floors, and a huge bed in each of the two rooms. All the furniture was upholstered in colorful silks from Miklagard, printed and embroidered with intricate patterns and animal motifs. The beds, tables, and cupboards were carved from wood and looked like ones I had seen in other parts of Hrafnheim. A peek into the room in the middle of the apartment revealed a gigantic tub filled with hot water, a powder-blue tile floor, and jars full of perfumed soaps and oils. I longed to sink into the water and cleanse myself.

A bowl of fresh fruit on the large table in the middle of the room made my mouth water. I was struck by the contrast between Gytha in her filthy rags and our opulent surroundings. She looked around at the wealth on display.

"A mere fraction of this could support everyone in Dyflin for a year," she muttered.

"It's unjust." I wrapped my arms around myself. "But it's like this where I come from, too. The rich are parasites."

Gytha patted me on the shoulder. "It's even more unjust if it goes to waste. You won't win any battles if you're starving and be-draggled."

I couldn't help but smile. It had been so long since I had smiled, it made the corners of my mouth hurt.

Gytha nudged me into the extravagant bathroom.

When I looked at the blue tile wall, I stiffened. There was a switch that looked very familiar, even though it was made of metal and carved with delicate arches that looked like seashells.

Gytha studied it. "What in the worlds is that?"

I tentatively flipped the switch, and we were suddenly bathed in light from above.

Gytha hightailed it out of the room.

"It's just electricity," I said, amazed, looking up at the lamp hanging from the ceiling. It glittered with crystals and gold. In the middle sat a light bulb.

Gytha came back and looked up as well. "Is it magic?"

"No. It's from my world. Electricity is normal there, but I haven't seen it at all in Hrafnheim."

Gytha jumped when I used the forbidden name, but then she waved her hand.

"Everything we're doing is illegal anyway. Hrafnheim!" she shouted toward the light bulb. This seemed to exhilarate her. "Hrafnheim!" she shouted again, then stood panting a bit. She turned a knob on the bathtub, and hot water poured out. "Is this from your world, too?"

"Yes. But running water was invented hundreds of years ago, although," I stopped to think, "for a long time it wasn't something everyone had."

"Those in power have always had their comforts, but they've kept them from the people. Ragnara is exactly like the old kings."

I nodded in agreement.

Gytha helped me out of my ruined, dirty clothes and then into the water. She washed herself as well, and hesitated slightly when she caught sight of a razor sitting on the edge of the sink. Her fingers stroked it, and I cursed at the thought that Sverre had been the one to put it there. I really didn't want to like him right now.

I rinsed my hair, and Gytha rubbed hers with a fragrant oil. She stood for a moment with a towel wrapped around her and studied the tiles, which were stamped with Ragnara's symbol. She turned her own arm and looked at the brand on it, which was identical.

I looked down at my forearm, where Gustaf had marked me with the same symbol.

"It's awful how she flaunts that rune," I said as I floated in the warm water, turning my arm so I didn't have to see my tattoo. "I would totally understand if you can't stand seeing it on everything."

"She set us free," Gytha whispered. "Regardless of what happened afterward, Ragnara did free the slaves."

I turned my head. "But you weren't free down in the dungeon. Are you free now?"

"I live my life the wrong way." When I was about to protest, she cut me off. "Or *she* thinks I live my life the wrong way."

Neither of us spoke before we returned to the bedroom. Our clothes were gone. Instead, there were clean clothes on the beds. For me, there were loose blue pants, a soft white shirt, and finely ornamented slippers. Again, I had to squint my eyes against all the overwhelming colors here in Sént.

For Gytha, there were a red dress and a shawl, and she put them on immediately. I glared suspiciously at my bright clothes.

At that moment, a small figure entered the room. She was hidden behind a tray of steaming food. Large pieces of meat, boiled vegetables, and a fragrant green sauce.

When she lowered it to the table, I exclaimed.

"Merit!"

The girl's color was much improved, and her cheekbones no longer protruded, though her nose was still crooked from where the leprosy had damaged it. Gone were the tattered clothes, and instead she wore a pastel dress.

"Oh!" she exclaimed. "You're here, too."

I shook my head in disbelief. "What are you doing here?"

Merit scratched her cheek, where a scar indicated that it had nearly been consumed by the disease. "The prince saved us." Merit hopped enthusiastically on the soft carpet. One shoe was significantly smaller than the other. "My brothers are here, too. We're going to school." She nodded proudly. "The others were sent to Ripa."

I struggled to figure out where this fit into Sverre's plans.

"You did a great job of hiding the fact that he was a prince." She smiled at me, and even though one side of her mouth was pulled back stiffly, I could see the admiration in her eyes.

"I only just found out he's a prince."

"Ohhhh . . ." Merit's non-scarred cheek turned pink. "So your feelings for him have nothing to do with his origins?"

"What feelings?" My brows furrowed.

Merit patted my shoulder. "It's obvious that you're in love. Oooh—it's so romantic."

"It's not romantic," I said, my voice hard.

But Merit interjected. "The prince is so good and noble. And handsome, too." She whispered this last part. "I would do anything for him."

Ahhh—that's how she fits in his plan.

I didn't mention this, but instead I asked, "Where are our clothes?"

She looked at me in surprise. "They were thrown away. They were barely hanging together by a thread."

My mother's coat was the only piece of clothing I'd wanted to keep, and it had gotten lost in the fight along with my bag, but I felt vulnerable with the towel wrapped around me and my hair dripping onto the expensive carpet. I noticed then that Gytha had thrown herself at the food.

Merit's little head tilted, and she laughed as she backed toward the door.

"I'm so glad he found you. The prince has been looking for you for months." Then she grew serious again. "I know he's marrying Ingeborg tomorrow, but maybe Ingeborg would be okay with . . ." She stopped herself. "Goodbye," she said with a little bow before running off.

I watched her go, then pulled on the clothes with a sigh.

I also took some food. I realized how ravenously hungry I was, and before I knew it, I was eating and drinking in large mouthfuls. When my stomach was full, my eyes began to close.

With a firm grip on my shoulders, Gytha led me to the large, soft bed.

"You remind me so much of your mother," I heard Gytha say through the mist. "Let go of your anger for once. Then you'll have the strength to keep fighting."

She nudged me under the blanket, and I was asleep before my head hit the pillow.

As soon as I closed my eyes, I was struck by a sour stench of animals, blood, and fear. I tried to look around, but I couldn't.

This was familiar.

"Serén?" I called. The name came out in a sputter through my clenched teeth.

I saw the vision sideways. I tried to move, tensing every muscle in my body, but I couldn't even make my eyes budge.

This wasn't coming from Serén. I couldn't feel her at all. I finally knew her aura, and it wasn't here.

The sun reflected off the sand in sharp beams, and though it was bright white, there were wet spots here and there.

Dark red spots.

A tattooed hand lay in front of my eyes, but I couldn't see if it belonged to the body I was in, as my vision blurred at the edges. There was something familiar about the dark lines on the hand.

Heat flowed toward me, and the side of my body that faced upward was baked by the sun.

This was the dream I had had just after my birthday back in Ravensted.

The bottom part of a pillar stood in the middle of my field of vision. I focused farther away and saw row after row of spectators stretching up, up, up toward the sky. The wall of people was arranged in a semicircle around me. The crowds filled the stands, but no one made a sound. They just stared breathlessly at something to my right.

An *arena*.

A crunching sound grew louder, and a woman's delicate feet walked past, a strange stone skirt rustling around her ankles.

The feet continued moving away from me. I couldn't follow them, but I heard them stop. Now someone was heaving anguished sobs.

No.

A voice above my head repeated my silent plea.

"No," she begged. "No."

I knew that voice.

The enormous crowd drew in a collective breath.

"That's her," they whispered. "That's Thora Baneblood's daughter."

Serén or me?

"Thorasdatter has engaged in conspiracy, and she supports the resistance against us." The voice was high-pitched and almost childlike. "It is our gift to the people that we rid you of her scheming."

Someone or something was hoisted up. The sound of strangulation made the hairs on my arms stand up.

The spectators roared with excitement.

"Watch her hang," someone shouted. "Out with her tongue. Out with her tongue . . ."

I heard the squeal of metal being pulled from a sheath, followed by the sound of something hard plunging into flesh.

Again, the spectators gasped.

Blood sloshed down over me.

A lock of fiery-red hair fell quietly and came to rest in a little curl on the sand in front of me.

I blinked and realized I was wrapped in a blanket and that I had wormed my way under the pillow. With a desperate gasp for air, I yanked it off and sat up in the dark room. My fingers wiped at my mouth, which was, of course, free of blood. The question was, for how long would it stay that way?

Sverre sat at the foot of the bed, staring at me. He jumped, frightened, when I looked directly at him.

My first instinct was to fling myself into his arms and seek comfort from the terrifying vision—which likely would become reality tomorrow—but I gained control over my erratic breathing.

"What are you doing in here?" I held the pillow up threateningly.

He let out a laugh. "Are you going to attack me with that?"

"With my bare hands, if necessary."

He wiped the smile off his face, which was for the best, as I couldn't bear to see it. He looked too much like Rorik. He looked like *himself*.

I rubbed my eyes.

"My sister," I said, closing my eyes, and saw the lock of red hair falling in front of me.

"Tell me where she is."

I was silent for a moment.

"You never named your price," I said.

He hesitated.

"I've been thinking about that. I don't want you to remove my healing powers, because then you would die before you were born. You could get rid of Ingeborg, but she's done nothing wrong." He wouldn't meet my gaze. "Then I considered asking for us to have never met, or at the very least, to erase what happened in Ísafold."

My voice grew thin. "Then I'd be erasing it from my past, too."

He looked intently at me. "Is that what you want? If that's what you want, we can do that."

"Do you wish we hadn't?"

He shook his head.

"Me neither." Despite everything that had happened, I didn't want to lose that memory. "Then what do you want?"

"I just want to see you walk free. And even if I can't have you for myself, at least I'll know you're alive in another world."

I should have thanked him, or told him I also just wanted him to live, even if it was without me in a bizarre parallel universe, but the words wouldn't leave my mouth, because I knew it wasn't going to happen.

"Let's find my sister," I said instead. Without thinking, I jumped out of bed. "Now!"

The prince stayed seated on the edge of the bed.

"What?"

"It's the middle of the night. We'll get her tomorrow morning when the guards change shifts."

Waiting. Not my strongest skill.

"I'm getting married tomorrow," Sverre whispered.

"Yeah," was the only word I could get past my lips. "But it's not binding if you're forced into it, is it? I don't believe in marriage. People don't own each other just because they're married, and they don't love each other less if they aren't."

He considered this. "You're right. My heart isn't in it. My heart is . . ."

I couldn't handle this. Not now.

"I slept all day," I said abruptly.

Sverre sat up straight. "You must have needed it."

"The people in the dungeon need it more," I snapped. "They're your friends down there, too."

He looked down at the carpet.

I leaned my head back. "I saw Merit."

Sverre lit up with a smile that looked completely genuine.

"Merit is fantastic." The smile faded when he saw my critical expression.

"She worships you."

"So what?"

"You're brainwashing the kids."

"Isn't that better than them dying of hunger and disease?"

"Didn't Eskild and Ragnara do the same thing when they took in the children from the Bronze Forest?"

Sverre searched for the right words. "Ragnara used the children from the Bronze Forest as soldiers. They were the first to worship her unconditionally. That may be where she got the idea that worship could change her."

I tilted my head and let him complete his line of thought.

"But she loved them. She still does. Especially Varnar." Fortunately, he was looking down, because hearing that name come out of his mouth made me flinch. "Varnar was everything I wasn't," Sverre said. "He was a warrior, good at fighting, and at peace with the act of killing."

My lips remained pressed together, and I was more and more relieved that I had never revealed that I knew Varnar—or how intimately. I imagined how the two boys must have competed. So different, and both with incredible qualities. I glanced up cautiously. Varnar's abilities as a fighter were unrivaled in Hrafnheim, but to be able to save lives . . . to be able to heal my inner wounds.

I shrugged, then flinched as a searing pain shot through my back. Being chained to a wall had left my body stiff and sore.

Sverre's hands flew out toward me, but he lowered them.

I pretended I hadn't seen.

Sverre smoothed the blanket with his palm.

"I have something for you." He picked something up off the floor.

"My bag!"

"It was in the forest at the end of Vigrid."

"Vigrid?"

"The red plain around Sént." Then he took out Rebecca's notebook.

"You went through my stuff!"

"This is fascinating." He flipped through the handwritten pages of notes and drawings. "There are things about Freiheim in here that I had no idea about. The religion, the creatures, the migration. It's lucky that the witch used runes in some places. The other symbols," he tapped on a page of regular words, "mean nothing to me."

"I mainly have it for the map."

"How can you not have read it? It has all the essential information about our realm."

429

"I didn't have time to study. But," I exhaled slowly, "you're right. I should have read it more closely." My forehead hurt, and I raised my hand and rubbed it until I realized the pain was due to my severely furrowed brows. I forced myself to relax. "Keep it. It's your realm. You should have it."

"Thank you, Anna." Sverre's brown eyes lingered on my face.

"I'm going to get the prisoners out. All of them."

A small smile warmed his face. "If anyone else said that, I wouldn't believe them, but you . . . you can do the unfathomable."

Sympathy and love made me say what I felt in my bones. "I miss Rorik. I just miss him so much."

Sverre's hand found mine in the semidarkness. The eagle flapped its wings, and he felt familiar and warm.

"I miss being Rorik, too," he said softly.

For a while, we just sat like that, holding hands without saying anything.

Sverre's voice was barely audible. "Anna . . ."

I lay down and pulled him with me. The feeling of his body against mine relaxed me. His healing powers bored into me and patched up my sorrow and fear. It was like lying against a pleasantly warm surface that smoothed out my cramped muscles.

He kissed me tentatively, and I accepted. In spite of the deceit, in spite of the lies, in spite of everything. He gently cupped his hands around my face and held it.

I let him do it, leaned forward, and slid my hands around his familiar body. I took my lips away for a moment.

"Goodbye, Rorik," I whispered, a chill running down my spine. Then I pressed my mouth against his and kissed him again.

Later, as Sverre slept, half covered by the blanket and with my hand in his, I followed the scars on his bare arm with the fingers of my free hand. On his chest there was a pink line where Knut had stabbed him. My fingertips traced it slowly.

Then I pulled my hand away and slipped silently out of the bed. "All-Father," I called in a low voice, as Od had taught me. "All-Father, I have something for you."

CHAPTER 34

When I opened my eyes, it was morning, and Sverre lay next to me, staring at me. His tattooed hand rested on my cheek, and the bare torso that peeked over the edge of the blanket was decorated with an intricate pattern of animals, people, and curlicues.

The wedding is today.

I gently removed his hand, got out of bed, and looked out the window.

If I tilted my head slightly, I could see the towering Konungsborg. Intense pulsations came from the white tower in the farthest corner. I felt like a tiny ant in relation to the high walls.

The prince stood behind me and wrapped his arms around me. The skin of his chest was warm against my back, and he kissed my hair.

I clung to the moment before he let go.

He laid something over my hair.

It was the green cloth he had given me on our journey. He wrapped it carefully around my head. "If you wrap yourself in the scarf, we can walk through the castle unnoticed."

"Okay."

Rorik—*ugh! Sverre*—got dressed.

He went to take my hand, but I dug my heels into the soft carpet and jerked my arm away. "What are you doing?"

"We have to . . ." He cleared his throat.

"Hmm," I said. "They're used to seeing you running around early in the morning with different women." He looked sheepish, and

I rolled my eyes. "How you've used your position up until now is none of my business," I said. "If it can help us, great."

With a sigh, I grabbed his hand, and it closed around mine quite pleasantly.

"Where are we headed?" he whispered.

"The white tower."

He stopped in his tracks. "Eskild's quarters." He looked at the ceiling of the hallway, which was whitewashed and covered in delicate designs. "I haven't looked there. Eskild never has prisoners."

We walked through the beautifully decorated halls. There were fine carvings, golden adornments, and detailed tapestries on the walls.

"I need to ask you for a favor. I have nothing else to give you in return." I had to push the words out.

Sverre looked at me. "Anna, I'll do anything in my power for you."

"I think your mom has my best friend's body."

He wrinkled his nose. "A body?"

"Etunaz," I clarified.

"Ahhh." Sverre still didn't appear to understand what I was talking about.

"There's a stasis spell on him. Or at least there was, last I checked." I clutched the little bottle in my pocket, which contained the mead of poetry that Od had given me. "Do you know where his body might be?"

I kept my eyes down while we walked as quickly as possible.

"He's probably in my mother's bedchamber," he whispered out of the corner of his mouth. "That's where she keeps her trophies. You can check while everyone's busy."

"Busy with what?" I stopped. With a jerk, he stopped, too, as our fingers were laced together.

"The wedding. Everyone will be there." His eyes fell on our interwoven hands.

I forced my voice to remain steady. "You kind of have to be there, too."

"But *you* don't."

Quietly, I asked, "What's going to happen at the wedding?"

He squinted his eyes as though I had pinched him.

"Ingeborg and I will be married in the arena, followed by entertainment." He said *entertainment* with a grimace. "Afterward, the people have to worship my mother. Herders in every corner of Freiheim will ensure that everyone makes an offering at their nearest fehu tree."

My whole body went cold, but I started walking again when I saw a couple of servants giving us curious looks.

"My mother has a big fehu tree in the arena. It's connected to all the other ones in Freiheim," Sverre explained as we hurried along.

She would sacrifice my sister as the pièce de résistance, if my vague dream vision held true, thereby clearing the last obstacle. The last obstacle apart from me, that is. She would become a goddess, all-powerful, and have the ability to annihilate us all.

I walked faster while focusing on Serén's pulsating aura.

People rushed past; I ducked my head into the folds of the scarf. Sverre looked conceited and insufferable, and though the passersby didn't show it, their auras hummed with animosity. But I had to admit, it was convenient to accompany the reviled prince. No one looked twice at me because their eyes were on him.

The closer we got to the white tower, the more Serén's energy surged toward me. Eventually, I had to push my way forward.

Sverre looked at me curiously. "Why are you panting?"

"I can feel her," I said through gritted teeth. "A lot."

"Maybe it's hard for the past and the future to meet," he wondered.

We entered the tower and ascended a spiral staircase.

"Where is she?"

"Higher up," I groaned and struggled onward.

At one point, the energy simply knocked me over, and I fell a couple of steps down, but Sverre pulled me back to my feet.

Suddenly, we heard footsteps on the narrow stairs above us. Sverre shoved me onto a landing and pressed me up against the wall.

"What are you doing here, Prince?" The voice alone sounded like an accusation.

"Staying away from prying eyes." There was a pause. "Eskild."

Eskild.

My heart did a terrified backflip. At the same time, Serén's intense aura shoved me sideways, so I had to dig my fingernails into the stone wall to keep myself upright. I pressed my head down into my shawl, but fortunately, Eskild didn't deign to look at me.

I would have to thank Ben for the repulsion spells; I was lucky that Védis had failed to remove them.

I kept my gaze lowered, but out of the corner of my eye, I saw steel-gray hair and a very tall, broad man. He looked strong and tough, and he was dressed in simple leather armor that creaked every time he moved.

One of my nails cracked against the rough stone wall as I was pressed to the side.

"You're marrying someone in less than an hour," Eskild said coldly.

"All the more reason to spend my time wisely," Sverre said, laughing as I clenched my teeth. His strong hand resisted as he sensed I was slowly sliding away from him.

I forced myself not to cry out when another nail was torn off, sending a jolt of pain all the way down to the quick.

"Your girl is moaning like a bitch in heat," Eskild said, and though I hadn't thought I could hate him any more than I already did, here I was.

I stared intently at the floor.

"Don't let anyone see you," he concluded and continued down

435

the stairs. "Your mother is arriving soon. We'll see you in the arena."

His boots and voice echoed through the tower.

"What a . . ."

"Yeah, yeah," Sverre said. "Let's keep moving."

Knowing that Ragnara was on her way made me gasp for air.

We reached the top of the stairs, but now I could barely fight my way forward. A stiff headwind blew me back, and Sverre pulled on my arm. Finally, he picked me up, but he nearly fell to his knees.

"You weigh more than lead." He panted as he walked forward with effort.

"I think it's this door." I pointed to a carved wooden door with a large bolt across it, but even the simple act of lifting my hand was nearly impossible.

The prince set me down and approached the door, suddenly unimpeded.

I, on the other hand, ended up flat on my stomach and was pushed several yards down the hall, until I grabbed an iron bar that protruded from the wall.

"Go get her," I said. "Get her to safety. I can't come any closer. Hide her with my scarf. We're identical. No one will notice."

Sverre walked back to me with ease, while I clung to the iron bar with my legs straight out on the floor behind me.

The hallway extended past the stairs.

He took the scarf from my head and hesitated for a second. Then he laid his tattooed hand on my cheek.

"I'll send Merit. The two of you can look for Etunaz." Then he ran toward the door as I tightened my grip.

Just when I thought there was no way he could get through, he drew Tilarids, and the sword cut through the iron bolt as though it were made of butter. When he opened the door, I was hit with such intense pressure, I could no longer hold on. My fingers slipped from the bar, and I flew down the hall, still lying flat, until I reached the end, where I lay smushed up against the wall.

Sverre came out the door with a girl wearing my green scarf. He struggled to pull her along, and I knew it was the pressure between us that caused it.

I rolled up into a ball, and somehow, they reached the stairs.

The girl looked down the hall, and I sensed that I should duck my head, but I stared at her back when she'd taken a few steps.

It was the very first time I saw her.

"Anna," she exclaimed, but her voice was nearly swallowed by the wind produced by our energies.

"Serén," I shouted, but Sverre pulled her away.

As she got farther away, the pressure lessened, and I could relax.

I chanted to myself. "My sister is alive, my sister is alive, my sister is alive . . ."

A dark aura flowed over me, and it felt like a giant invisible hand was trying to strangle me. Ragnara must have arrived at the castle. My chest burned in the spot where she had stabbed me as a baby.

I closed my eyes. "My sister is alive, my sister is alive . . ."

"Anna!"

The face in front of me swam into focus, and a small hand was shaking me.

Confused, I shook my head. I must have fainted when Ragnara's violent aura came closer. It was everywhere, and I coughed, gasping for air.

Merit crouched in front of me.

"The wedding has started."

My stomach did a somersault. "It has?"

She nodded, and outside I heard a rhythmic hum.

"Is my sister safe?" My voice sounded strangely hoarse, and only then did I realize how dry my mouth was.

"Yes. She's in your room." Merit laughed her bubbly little laugh. "I thought it was you at first." She grabbed my hand and pulled it. "I'm supposed to accompany you to . . ." she lowered her high-pitched voice, ". . . to Ragnara's chambers."

Resolutely, I got to my feet, and she handed me a hat to hide my hair.

Merit led the way down the stairs and farther into the castle. She shoved all her body weight against a door, which opened with a creak. Something told me we were close to Ragnara's chambers, as the shadows grew deeper, and a heavy, distrustful vibe seeped from the walls themselves. Everything was arranged in straight lines, and there was a total absence of ornamentation. My stomach sank as I realized this was how I would have decorated the place—if I were a maniacal dictator with a large castle, that is.

There were open windows facing the center of the castle. I sensed that the middle was a large square. Or an arena. Ragnara's aura rushed in through the windows.

I stopped by a wall on which there hung a necklace, framed by carved pieces of wood. A small plaque with runes was underneath, but I couldn't read it. I cautiously ran my fingertips over the cool metal.

I saw a vision of a small dark-haired woman, whose eyes resembled Rorik's. She wore the necklace around her throat, her face was covered with blood and soot, and she stood at the end of the plain called Vigrid in front of Sént, not far from where I had hidden with Vale. Columns of smoke rose from Sént, and smashed statues lay on the ground. One, carved from wood, lay splintered with its face turned toward the sky. The statue was, unmistakably, missing one eye.

Eskild stood behind the woman and pried the chain apart with pliers. She held the necklace straight up over her head. Her neck bore a deep wound where the chain had been.

"I swore," she shouted, "not to remove my slave chain until we defeated the tyrants."

On the plain stood thousands of people, all filthy, some with identical chains. A collective war cry rose from their throats.

"Freedom!" shouted the woman, who must have been Ragnara, and despite everything, I couldn't help but feel a rush of victory. The people cheered and praised her. "Freedom from oppression, freedom from the gods, freedom from slavery. I set you free."

A wave of worshipful energy hit her as the people shouted her name again and again.

"Ragnara, Ragnara, Ragnara."

She inhaled. Her eyelids closed halfway, and suddenly her face flared with hunger for even more power.

"Ragnara, Ragnara, Ragnara." The wave of energy flowed over her.

"Anna, come on." Merit's small hand tugged me, and my fingers slid from the framed chain, the vision of Ragnara's past fluttering away.

"Ragnara, Ragnara, Ragnara," I heard from an open window. The people were praising the queen outside.

I looked around in confusion as Merit dragged me along.

The halls were deserted. Everyone must have been gathered in the large arena. We passed no more than a couple of servants, who didn't even look in our direction.

We came closer to the center of the castle, and through an open window, I heard the crowd outside even more clearly.

"For Ragnara's anfarwol."

I couldn't stop myself from looking out, and I muffled a whimper when I saw the enormous crowd. Walls stretching toward the sky. Stands with seating for thousands of people encircled the round arena. In the middle stood the same kind of black bog oak tree that I had seen in Ripa, but this one was five times as big. A circle of herders stood around it, and the trunk flowed with a dark liquid.

Dead animals hung from the branches. Pigs, dogs, goats, and sheep. I could smell wool, feces, and hay from where I stood. It was the same stench as in the dream I'd had, and the arena was the same as in the vision. I was pretty sure I had changed what otherwise had been destined to happen.

Soldiers milled around among the spectators.

"They're looking for you," Merit said. "Ragnara knows you're here somewhere, and that your sister was set free."

My stomach churned with fear as a soldier grabbed a red-haired female spectator by the collar and studied her. He shook his head and let her go.

At one end of the arena was a platform, where I immediately spotted Rorik—*no, Sverre*. At his side stood a small figure I couldn't see clearly, nor did I want to. She wore a blue dress, and glittering gold thread and gemstones were visible even from where I stood. They were far away, but I thought I detected that both his and her shoulders were slumped.

Diagonally behind Sverre stood Eskild with his hand on his sword. Where everyone else's eyes were fixed on the black tree in the middle of the arena with its roots in the air and its crown buried in the sand, Eskild's eyes swept across the rows of spectators, where the soldiers were looking for me.

I ducked when I felt his gaze fall on me. Cautiously, I looked up again, and he was looking in a different direction.

A black-haired woman sat in front of the others. She was so small, I didn't see her at first. But when the herders began to chant: "Ragnara's anfarwol, Ragnara's anfarwol," whisps of their auras fluttered toward the tiny figure.

She grew a little with each shred she absorbed. Her physical body didn't change, but her aura increased in size.

The fehu rune on the tree's trunk glowed like I had seen in Ripa.

My heart pounded faster. The time had come. She would now try to elevate herself to the status of goddess.

Her aura was already pulsating like Svidur's, and I didn't dare think about how much energy it would have when people across the entire realm made offerings to her. If things went according to plan, at least she couldn't sacrifice Serén now that we'd gotten her out of the way.

I had seen enough, so I forced myself away from the window.

"Hurry," Merit squeaked. Her crooked mouth twitched, but she shook it off and pointed to a door where five Varangian guards stood watch. "The prince said you could handle them easily."

I rolled up my sleeves.

I'm not proud of what I did, as the three men and two women probably hadn't asked to guard Ragnara's bedchamber. And I tried not to kill anyone. I succeeded, but two of them would likely have raging headaches the next day. I stepped over the limp bodies and pried the door open.

I trembled. Monster could be right in there. I pulled out the bottle of the mead of poetry before I had even entered the room.

"Unbelievable," Merit gasped. "That can't have taken more than twenty seconds."

I silently thanked Varnar's training sessions, which had made me a pure fighting machine. I took a few steps into the room and stopped with a little gasp.

Monster lay on the ground diagonally behind the bed.

Yes!

He was there. I would save him. Bring him back to life. I started to pull the cork from the bottle. I was going to get my best friend back. He was . . . I looked closer.

What?

Monster looked oddly deflated, and to my horror, I realized it was only his skin lying on the floor, paws spread out and bushy tail behind him. His ears were floppy, and his eyes had been replaced with glass beads that stared blankly ahead.

My heart pounded, and if it weren't for the intense surge of adrenaline rushing through me, I would have fainted on the spot.

I inhaled raggedly and leaned on Merit, who stroked my back comfortingly as my knees threatened to buckle beneath me.

"Is it him?" Merit asked delicately.

I couldn't speak. How could this skin be all that was left of Monster?

"Yes," I finally said, sniffling. "It's him."

I was hyperventilating, and though I tried to speak, my voice wouldn't obey. I knelt and ran a hand across Monster's soft forehead.

Hands shaking, I focused on Monster's mouth. His sharp teeth were exposed as though frozen mid-growl. The large wounds were gone, and he was actually in better shape than the last time I saw him—aside from the fact that he was now a rug, of course.

"Anna?" came a voice behind me. Sverre entered the room, breathless.

I whipped around. Wordlessly, I threw myself at him and hit him with clenched fists. I sobbed angrily as I hammered my hands into him.

He looked over his shoulder. "My mother's troops are on their way. They've already caught your sister."

I shouted in frustration.

"The fighting will start soon," he continued quickly. "Your friends from Midgard will be in the arena, too."

Oh no. Luna and Mads.

Merit turned on her heel.

I looked at Sverre. The prince. His nearly white hair was unruly, but the gold band across his forehead held it in place. The dark brown eyes I knew so well shone frantically.

There was no way out of this.

My eyes landed on a ring of braided straw that sat on his finger, encircling one of the eagle's wings.

I opened my mouth.

"All-Father," I called. "Come and get your hangadrott."

Everything froze. Even time itself. Sverre stopped in the middle of a word, lips apart; Merit's hair fanned out behind her mid-turn. Even the dust motes hung in the air. Sverre had one foot raised, stiffened in an unnatural position.

I turned around, and when I had made a full circle, I almost bumped into Svidur, who stood right in front of me.

"Little seer," he said hoarsely. His breathing was heavy. "Do you have what you promised me?"

I took a step back. "You have to free all the prisoners, like you promised me."

Svidur stretched his neck and grew a couple of inches taller. He looked me up and down. "I can save them," he said, almost nonchalantly. "And you and your sister. My ravens," he teased coyly and caressed my cheek.

I smacked his hand away, which made him growl. If I hadn't been so desperate, I would have been terrified.

"The prisoners, Luna, Mads, Gytha, Finn, and my sister," I said. "We had an agreement."

Now Svidur looked directly at me. His eye smoldered, and the empty socket on the other side was unfathomably deep.

"So demanding." The understated amusement made me want to hit him again, but I restrained myself.

My voice quavering, I pointed to the frozen Sverre. "He's a royal."

"And you're offering him to me?" Svidur whispered and licked his lips. "You're giving me a hangadrott?"

"If you pay for it."

Svidur let his red tongue glide over his shapely lips. "Can I have his blood?"

I ignored his inappropriate tone. "You can do whatever you want with him."

Svidur inhaled with an excited sound.

"That's the deal I'm offering." My fists clenched.

He looked at me a moment. Not angrily, but curiously, as though I were an exotic animal, and he wasn't sure how I would react.

"We made an agreement," he confirmed. "I stand by my word."

"Spoken like a true Viking," I said after a powerful exhalation. "Take him, then." I pointed at Sverre but turned my face away. "And do what you promised."

"I won't do anything until you give me the sacrifice."

"I mean, he's standing right there." I waved my hands in Sverre's direction but avoided looking at him.

A dry laughter encircled me, and when I looked down, I had a sword in my hand. Not just any sword. Tilarids. How had it gotten from the sheath on Sverre's belt and into my hand?

"No," I whispered. "I can't."

"That's the deal *I'm* offering."

I closed my eyes. In my hand, Tilarids trembled expectantly. Still averting my eyes, I walked over to . . . I took a breath.

Sverre stared straight ahead, unaware that I stood in front of him with the sharp sword. My breathing quavered again when I laid the blade against his neck. Against Rorik's neck. I bit my lip.

Not Rorik. Sverre. This is Prince Sverre.

I tensed the muscles of my biceps and pulled my hand back, ready to slit his throat.

Red drops ran across Tilarids's runes and down my fingers.

CHAPTER 35

"Stop, Anna!"

I looked around. No one else had entered the chamber.

"Stop!" the voice repeated, and this time I knew it had come from inside my head.

Serén.

My hand froze in the already-frozen vacuum. Although the cut wasn't deep yet, blood trickled to the floor.

Drip, drip, drip . . .

Serén spoke so quickly, she nearly tripped over her words. "Don't kill him."

I lowered Tilarids slightly.

"You're interrupting something," I said through gritted teeth.

Svidur stepped closer, a desperate look on his face.

"Kill him." His eye searched the hall and the arena on the other side. "Kill him. Then I'll be just as strong as before."

I raised Tilarids again, but a violent, invisible force swiped the sword out of my hand. It clanged to the floor, where it lay and hummed furiously.

"Hey!"

Svidur took an angry step forward.

"You can't do it." Serén spoke intensely. "This action will lead to the end of the world. I can see it."

"That's starting to seem inevitable under all circumstances," I snapped and knelt to pick Tilarids back up. "You are all on your way to the arena, and I know how that ends."

Svidur's head turned.

"I can hear you, raven," he said. He was speaking to Serén.

I was impressed by my sister's calm voice.

"You can't have your hangadrott, Odin."

I flinched when she said his real name.

"It's my right," he snarled. "In the past, the sacrifices came pouring in. The little people were more than eager to shower me with blood."

"Times change." Serén's clear voice rang through my head. "Believe me, my sister. I know."

Again, Svidur growled. "I should never have given you clairvoyance."

"I wish you hadn't," I spat back.

He didn't respond but made a movement with his fingers, and Tilarids was back in my hand. Almost involuntarily, I once again pointed the blade toward Sverre's neck.

Serén turned her focus to me. "Anna. Don't become a murderer."

"I already am," I whispered. Suddenly, my shoulder burned. "You said before that Sverre was dangerous to me."

"He is very dangerous to you . . . dangerous to all of us. If you kill him. I only just realized that is how my vision should be interpreted. I had misunderstood it."

"Interpreted?" Hysteria colored my voice. "Am I in the middle of a human sacrifice with a Norse god right now because you misinterpreted a vision?"

Tilarids quaked in my hands, and it took all the strength I had to hold it back.

"Things have changed."

"Since half an hour ago?" I shouted shrilly.

"We're on our way into the arena," Serén said.

"Ragnara aims to steal one of my ravens," Svidur bellowed, growing larger. "She wants to take my power." The sound was more supernatural than the times Mathias had produced his deep, metallic shouts, and he raised his hands, which were now the size of bike tires. His face swayed high above me. "Kill her son! Kill him and save yourself."

"Anna," Serén urged.

I focused on a drop of blood that fell from Sverre's throat. Because time was warped, it took several seconds for it to hit the floor with a splat.

"Just one cut," I whispered. "Just a little flick of my wrist. Svidur will save us all. He'll send you and our mother home, and with Elias's help, we'll get our father back." My words were now barely audible. "We can be a family."

"Not like this." Serén's voice crept into my head.

I tuned her out and squeezed a little harder. "It's just steel going through air and blood. Nothing more."

Tilarids's metal hilt was cool in my hand. Tempting. It was all right there. I could almost see my parents waving from Odinmont, together with Serén and me.

"Trust me," Serén said. I heard tears in her voice.

I stopped.

"You can't kill Sverre."

"He deceived me. He lied to me."

"If you sacrifice him, you're just like Ragnara."

I breathed deeply. "You're right. You're always right." I nearly cried at the thought of what I had been about to do. I looked at Svidur. "It's not happening." I let go of Tilarids. It fell with a clatter, and this time the sword remained lying on the ground.

Wrath smoldered in Svidur's face. Divine fury, and the heat radiating from him singed me.

"Little seer," Svidur said. "This is going to cost you another life. You will pay dearly for this."

Then he backed into the shadows and was gone.

CHAPTER 36

Around us, time started up again.

Merit's hair settled on her shoulders, and she ran off. Sverre completed his step forward and looked, puzzled, at Tilarids lying on the floor. He brought his hand to his neck, where fresh blood seeped from the thin cut.

"What?"

I moaned. His blood was on my hands. But he was alive.

Sverre looked from my fingers to Tilarids, shaking his head.

"Now," he said as he stuck Tilarids back in its sheath. "We need to get out of here."

We took off running down the hallway.

"In here." Sverre's voice was strained, and he reached back to grab my hand so he could pull me down a side hall.

I dug in my heels.

"What can we do to help?" I tore my eyes away from the narrow, red line on his neck. If I had cut deeper, we would all be safe now.

"We can't do anything. I have to get you out of here."

"My sister is down there. My best friend. I have to help them."

Sverre thought for a moment, then changed direction and led us to a staircase. He guided us down, and we ended up in front of a door. When he pulled it open, we were met by the roar of the crowd outside.

We were in the passageway that encircled the round space in the lowest part of the arena, the middle of which still decorated with the grotesque tree and its bloody fruit. The stench of animal, blood, and fear invaded my nostrils. Just like in the dream.

The audience, which must have numbered in the thousands, screamed and cheered wildly. There was only an iron grate between us and the sandy ring, and above us loomed the walls with rows of seats. I leaned my head back.

Up, up, up.

Soldiers were still running around up there, searching—probably for me. I pulled my hat farther down on my head.

My eyes glided over the spectators and tried to find humanity, but all I could see were faces warped with bloodthirst. I had never been around so many people before, and their effect nearly brought me to my knees. I saw their memories, felt their emotions, and most of all, the collective enthusiasm for the coming fight, which came crashing toward me. On top of it all flowed Ragnara's violent aura. I shielded more than ever and wished I had the little bottle of klinte that was in my bag. My bag, which was in the bedroom in Sverre's quarters. The only thing I had on me was Auka.

I looked at the little platform, where Sverre's place was glaringly empty. Ingeborg sat next to it in her fine blue dress, looking lost. I felt bad for the girl, sitting there with her hands clutched together. Ragnara—I shivered when I finally saw her clearly—sat on a carved throne at the very front of the platform. I trembled, not because she was scary, but because she seemed so small and fragile. I just couldn't understand that this person—this soon-to-be goddess—had done such horrible things.

Her wild aura engulfed me like thick black smoke. I stifled a cough.

Ragnara's long, dark hair was curled and half-up on her head, and her dress was made of black stones that glimmered in the sunlight. Like a hot, hard husk that couldn't possibly be easy to move around in. But she sat calmly, and the stone dress didn't seem to weigh any more than a feather. Her face was pretty but nothing more. Not supernaturally beautiful or eerily captivating. Just a regular face with an indifferent expression. Her eyes—my own gaze flitted to Sverre—her eyes were familiar. Dark and alert. They were much better suited to her golden skin tone and black hair than to Sverre's almost white locks.

Ragnara sat like a statue but made a small movement with a delicate hand that caused the thousands of people to quiet down. It grew completely silent; the only sound was the slight creaking of the ropes from which the animal carcasses hung, turning in the breeze.

She didn't raise her voice when she spoke. Even with her fledgling powers, her high voice carried all the way up to the top row.

"Someone," the thin voice rang out, "has committed a crime against us."

I don't know if she meant that as a royal *us*—speaking of herself in the plural—or *us* as in the people.

"Someone wants to destroy the freedom we have fought for."

Again, *we*. Was she talking about herself or the people of Hrafnheim?

"We will do whatever it takes to live in peace. We must therefore punish those responsible." A little movement of her dark eyebrow indicated that this pained her. Maybe. Or maybe it delighted her. Without looking back, she raised her hand, and Eskild, with his steel-gray hair, stood. One eye was pale blue. The other was black.

Eskild Black-Eye.

Unlike Ragnara, he was truly scary in his understated leather outfit covered in metal buckles. Buckles that held knives, swords, and spears. The only adornment he wore was Ragnara's rune stamped into the leather on his shoulder. He took a step forward, and in that step lay all his authority. All his power and determination. Even if the world came crashing down, he would not leave Ragnara's side.

"Open the gates." His voice was sharp, like the crack of a whip.

Eskild sat back down, and a deep, metallic sound swirled along the curved walls of the arena. At one end, a gate opened, and a small group of people were shooed out.

I clutched the grate involuntarily when I recognized them.

There was Taliah. She was easy to recognize with the arabesque tattoos running from her neck to her fingertips. With a pang, I felt her clairvoyance, and at that moment, she raised her head, as though she sensed me. She held a crooked spear.

Luna came out, and I had to restrain myself from pounding on the grate. She had a bow, which was loaded with an arrow. A quiver at her hip held two extras.

Only three arrows!

My heart sank when I saw her move her hands to gather magical energy. Nothing happened. Someone must have restrained her powers. Her colorful clothes were dirty and torn, but she appeared to be in one piece. Unharmed, for now.

Taliah's red-haired friend appeared, tied up together with Tíw. The redhead raised a war hammer against an unseen foe. I looked at Tíw. Someone had gone to the trouble of combing Tíw's brown hair and decorating it with golden rings, like when I saw him in Ísafold. He was dressed in clean clothes, and he resembled an ancient Celtic folk hero. Tíw straightened his back, despite his disadvantageous position lashed together with the redhead. He had a sword. Rusty and crooked with a blunt blade, but at least he had something to defend himself with.

The crowd in the stands got to look at the prisoners for a good while. They shouted curses and spat down into the pit in the middle of the round structure.

Luna looked around questioningly.

There was a rumble, like distant thunder. In the impenetrable darkness deep in the opening, two pairs of gray eyes shone. A gigantic wolf stepped out, teeth bared and ears pressed back. It was coal black, like Rokkin, and just as tall but quite a bit broader.

451

The people gasped at the sight of the wolf, which must have been Monster's mate, Boda.

Behind her, Mads walked out. Next to the wolf, it was easy to see that he belonged to the race of giants just as much as that of humans. He looked angrily at the spectators, and for the first time, I could see just how terrifying my classmate was.

"The beasts will turn against the other prisoners," someone shouted. "Giants will eat any human in their path. Slay the monsters at once."

Boda turned her gaze up and stared directly at the person who had spoken. Her expression promised the man a grim fate, but he merely laughed.

Behind Boda and Mads, Vale paced. He had a slight limp, and his whole side was stained brown with old, caked blood from when Sverre's people wounded him.

"Is that it?" I asked breathlessly as my eyes swept over the prisoners.

But one more person walked out, and with my heart pounding, I saw it was Gytha.

A roar of gleeful laughter rose from the stands, and unthinkingly, I looked up at Ragnara, whose expression remained neutral. She had gathered pretty much everyone I knew in this world, plus a couple from Midgard, and I felt like the whole spectacle was being put on purely to hurt me.

"Lady man," someone shouted at Gytha.

"You get what you deserve," another voice said. "Shameful. Disgusting."

Sverre grasped the iron grate as Gytha walked in, standing tall with as much dignity as possible. In her hand was a small knife that didn't seem good for much beyond chopping herbs.

Sverre frantically searched the grate for an opening, but it was smooth and solid. His hands froze and remained raised in horror as the final figures entered the arena.

It was Merit, her brothers, and the four children from Miklagard. Merit's arms were around the two trembling boys, and she looked around pleadingly. Her crooked little nose was clearly visible, and the scarred skin on her cheek caught the light. The children, Merit, and her brothers were shoved into the middle between the other prisoners. The adults formed a circle around the children.

The audience roared with excitement. There were scattered shouts of *boo*, but there were also some who remained silent. Certainly not all of them enjoyed seeing children in the arena.

"Leave the little ones out of it," the redhead pleaded to Ragnara. His voice quavered with fear. Not for himself, but for his children.

She didn't even look in his direction.

"I'm begging you." He fell to his knees and stretched out his non-chained hand. The hammer landed in the sand with a thump.

After a couple of glances among themselves, the adults bowed to Ragnara. Even Boda and Vale prostrated themselves, but their teeth were still bared. All weapons were laid in the sand as a sign of submission.

"Let the children go," the redhead repeated.

Now Sverre ran toward the platform where Ragnara, Eskild, and Ingeborg sat, but there was a grate between them. He looked at his mother.

"Not the little ones," he shouted. "I'll do anything."

Behind Ragnara, I saw Ingeborg looking at her new husband with an unreadable expression.

Slowly, Ragnara turned her head. Her dark curls swished over the stone dress. Her face was emotionless when she looked at her son. Again, her eyes sought out the large fehu tree with its bloody ornaments, as though it beckoned her. Then she looked down the passageway.

I ducked behind a column, but I don't know if she spotted me. Maybe the repulsion spells worked on her, too.

"Ragnara, Ragnara, Ragnara," chanted the crowd.

Now Ingeborg stood on wavering legs. She leaned toward Ragnara and said something in her ear.

Ragnara's brow lowered by a fraction of an inch, but she didn't reply.

Ingeborg tried again, but Eskild laid a large hand on her shoulder and guided her back to her seat.

Ragnara leaned back slightly and said something to Eskild, after which he made a signal to a couple of soldiers and pointed down into the passageway where we stood.

I looked out into the arena again as soldiers pushed their way through the crowd toward us. Fortunately, they had trouble getting through the many excited people.

The gate at the other end opened slowly, and the chained prisoners reached for their weapons in the sand. They stood and positioned themselves in a circle with the children in the middle. Boda and Vale stood in front of them, snarling through long, white, bared teeth.

There were strange sounds from the open gate. It sounded like leather against bone. A flapping, groaning sound together with a swarm of red, glowing dots. They walked toward the sunlight.

"Baaahh . . ."

I gasped. They were fingalks. They must have been part of Ragnara's fingalk army. Ten gigantic, red-eyed fingalks flapped their useless wings and looked at the huddled prisoners at the other end of the arena. The apelike faces with red eyes and tufted ears turned as they studied their prey.

Soldiers prodded them forward with short, sharp sticks. Several of them left bleeding wounds on the fingalks' backs and long arms, and some got stuck under their skin, protruding at odd angles. The fingalks snarled every time they got poked. The guards let them stop at the big, black tree, where they sniffed toward its top, and one of them opened its mouth and lapped up the blood dripping from a sacrificed lamb.

One of the fingalks was lagging. It looked around, confused.

I felt my heart break right then and there, and Sverre looked miserably at me.

Out in the arena, among the other fingalks, with a round white spot around one of his red eyes, Finn dragged his big feet.

He looked around, and his nostrils fluttered.

"Nana," he called, taking a couple of steps in my direction. His red eyes flickered as he sniffed. "Krik?"

A soldier prodded him in the back with a sharp stick.

Instinctively, Finn spun around and hissed at the soldier, his eyes taking on a deep-red tone.

A murmur spread through the crowd at the sight of the angry fingalk, which was a head taller than the others.

Whether he was there purely by coincidence or was chosen to torment Sverre, I didn't know, but just then, I didn't care if Ragnara caught me, if Eskild killed me, or if the other nine fingalks skinned me alive. I wanted to go in. I wanted to go to the children, the wolves, my friends, and Finn. I cried furiously and ran the other way to find a way in.

Eskild noticed my movement and raised his head like a dog sensing danger. He shouted an order to the last soldiers on the platform, and they, too, moved toward the ring.

Sverre ran toward me. "I had no idea," he shouted. "Not about the children."

Meanwhile, the fingalks crept closer to the prisoners, who raised their pathetic weapons and positioned themselves to fight. Boda's hackles rose, and she snarled at the frightening creatures.

Each time Finn tried to get away from his fellow fingalks, a guard prodded him back to the group. Eventually, foul-smelling blood ran from Finn's back. A sharp stick was embedded in his thigh.

Sverre and I continued around the arena, our hands and eyes searching for even a small hole in the iron grate.

In the arena, two fingalks made the first attack. One snapped at Taliah, but she swung at it with the axe. At the same time, the second fingalk lunged at one of Merit's brothers, but Tíw whacked it in the side with his sword. The sound of splintering bone and the stench of wounded fingalk flowed over us.

The mob whooped.

As Sverre and I searched the fence, I sensed something coming closer. It was a pulsating, intense aura that nearly pushed me backward.

"Serén?" I called out, but she didn't answer.

In the arena, another fingalk had thrown itself on Boda, but only a few seconds passed before her sharp teeth tore it apart. It now lay in several pieces, like a dog's chew toy, as she moved on to the next one.

The spectators roared with bloodlust.

Mads smashed a fingalk's head with a clenched fist. His hair stuck to his forehead as he swung his strong hands.

The crowd shuddered and hooted.

I was starting to think they could actually win. The children in the middle spun around, the youngest ones crying. Merit spread her arms protectively over them, while Vale and Boda alone killed four fingalks.

There were now only two fingalks remaining—three if you counted Finn, but he looked so hesitant and disoriented, I mostly feared for his life.

I saw the fury in Tíw's face, and stubbornness in Taliah's. Luna looked focused, shooting an arrow that bored into a fingalk's chest. The giant wolves snapped and snarled, and the children remained standing in the middle.

Eskild had leapt back onto the platform and shouted something again. The hint of optimism I felt was dashed when another ten fingalks ran in on large, slapping feet. They threw themselves into the fight, and for a few minutes, it was nearly impossible to follow.

Meanwhile, the soldiers had made it halfway through the crowd.

Luna's final arrow plunged into a shoulder, but another fingalk was about to slash her chest with its long claws. At the last second, Gytha threw herself between them and shoved her little knife into the fingalk's neck. It gurgled and turned, dragging its razor-sharp fingers over Gytha's cheeks. She fell to the ground with her face in her hands.

There were blood and gore everywhere, and the audience cheered. Taliah had a wide gash across her cheek. Tíw's ability to fight off attacks was hindered by his being chained to another person.

A fingalk jumped onto Taliah's back and closed its claws around her throat. She flailed with her spear but couldn't hit it.

I couldn't stop the shout that blurted out of my mouth. It didn't matter now, anyway. Eskild and the soldiers had already spotted me. I pulled the hat off my head, so my red hair flowed down over my shoulders.

Taliah fell in front of the large tree on her side, her arm stretched out. She moved weakly as the fingalk leapt forward.

"You have to get out of here, Anna," Sverre begged. "It's now or never."

"I don't give a shit!" I shouted. "Finn, Luna, Mads. If they all die, none of it matters. I have to go in."

He nodded, and we sprinted around the arena, separated from the fighting only by the sturdy fence. I started pounding on it to find a way in. I saw a tiny hole but again was struck by a wave of Serén's energy.

I started hacking at the grate with Auka. Next to me, Sverre realized what I was doing, and he used Tilarids to break the iron grate apart. He alternately hacked and pulled at the opening, which slowly—all too slowly—grew larger.

Three fingalks set their sights on the children in the middle of the circle, and they snapped and chomped to get to them. Mads and Luna did all they could to resist, but the gate opened, and four large figures entered the ring. Another murmur traveled through the crowd when they saw berserkers with long, matted hair, dressed skimpily in leather.

There was a shout from the stands. "Are the berserkers on our side now?"

"Ragnara has strong allies."

"This is the best gladiator battle I've ever seen!"

I pounded on the grate and kept my eyes on a woman with unruly hair, brown teeth, and a knife that was even larger than the Savage's. Fortunately, these berserkers didn't seem to be under the influence of demiblood, but they nevertheless threw themselves fearlessly into the fight, and though the prisoners fought back, I eventually realized it was impossible. Luna had picked up Taliah's spear and was using it to defend both herself and the children.

A fingalk launched a violent attack against Tíw. If it took him down, there would be free access to the little ones. Just then, it was like something kick-started Finn's brain. He bleated and crept closer, though he had been staying on the fringes.

No, Finn, I thought. *You can't kill our friends.*

But he was heading toward the fingalk that was attacking Tíw. I saw that, but I wasn't sure if Tíw did.

Finn flapped his wings, and everyone shouted when he lifted off the ground. No one believed fingalks could fly, but Finn rose above the bloody scene and hovered over them all.

Tíw looked up. He had one second to decide whether to stab Finn or the fingalk in front of him. Just then, another fingalk ran toward his side where he was chained to the redhead.

Tíw squinted, and I sensed that he was looking at Finn and focusing on the white circle around his eye. Then he turned around and plunged his sword into the side of the standing fingalk. He placed his other arm, which was still chained, between the final fingalk and his friend, protecting him. A howl of pain reached me when the fingalk's claws tore through bone and flesh, ripping Tíw's arm in half. But this gave Finn room to turn around and whip his tail, knocking several of the fingalks and two of the berserkers to the ground.

Ragnara had stood up. A small motion of her wrist caused silence to fall again. Eskild barked something, and the fingalks and berserkers froze.

The prisoners stood, panting, and the giant wolves growled. Vale was no longer putting weight on one of his legs, and the wound in his side had reopened and started bleeding. Mads clenched his large fists, and Luna's curls stuck out in all directions.

Ragnara's thin voice rang out.

"There's been a change. Or rather . . ." The corners of her mouth turned up. This was the first smile I had seen on her mouth, and she was suddenly terrifying. Blood-chillingly, overwhelmingly terrifying. She continued in her childlike voice. "It's more of an addition. We have captured both of Thora Baneblood's daughters."

An intense gasp ran through the stands, and I looked around in confusion.

Both?

The soldiers had almost reached us, but I hadn't been captured—yet. Maybe she was so sure she would catch me, she was willing to proclaim it in front of everyone.

Again, the ground buckled beneath me. Serén was close by.

A gate opened, this time at the opposite end from where we were, and a small figure with flaming red hair in a green dress staggered into the arena, led by a soldier.

"Serén?"

But I felt no aura from her. None of the energy that bowled me over.

459

My heart sank nevertheless when I recognized Faida, who had tried to seduce Rorik at the hálfa festivities in Ísafold.

She looked lost, with a thick rope around her neck. I almost couldn't bear it when I saw that she was wearing my green dress, which I had given her with the best of intentions.

"No," I whispered.

Sverre also looked aghast at Faida, and Tíw shouted.

Faida blinked in the sharp sunlight, as though she were struggling to orient herself. When she noticed the spectators, she furrowed her brows. Then she looked at the fingalks, who stood between her and the other prisoners, and her eyes grew wide.

There were a few faint *boos* from the stands, and Faida's head turned in their direction, perplexed.

Ragnara knew full well what my sister and I looked like. She knew this wasn't either of us. Faida was playing the role of one of us without even knowing it herself.

"Why is she wearing your dress?" Sverre whispered.

"I gave it to her. After that night in Ísafold, when we . . ." I couldn't say it. "I felt bad."

Rorik looked at Faida again.

Without thinking, I yelled out: "I'm here. Take me. You have the wrong girl," but it was drowned out by all the noise from the stands.

Ragnara's eyes flitted from me to Eskild, and his grating voice shouted an order.

The fingalks stood between Faida and the prisoners, and although they tried to reach her, they couldn't.

Ragnara stood slowly and stepped down into the arena. She walked with long strides past our friends.

The spectators whispered. "So brave."

Ragnara's sandals crunched through the sand, and her stone dress rustled around her. She passed Taliah's motionless body and stopped just on the other side of her head.

I moaned when I saw the angle. My dream. It had been seen through Taliah's eyes, and the tattooed hand was hers. At that moment, as her final act, she must have been trying to send the vision to me in the past.

I cursed myself for not having understood it. If I had known Ragnara would use Faida in her game, I would have stayed far away from Ísafold, the party, and the innocent red-haired girl.

Faida sobbed in fear.

"No!" I screamed.

"No," she begged. "No."

The enormous crowd drew in a collective breath.

"That's her," they whispered. "That's Thora Baneblood's daughter."

"Thorasdatter has engaged in conspiracy," Ragnara said, "and she supports the resistance against us. It is our gift to the people that we rid you of her scheming."

The soldier threw the other end of the rope up over a branch—which was actually a root—of the large, black tree. He hoisted her up.

Faida twitched and gurgled, and her feet were right over Taliah's motionless head.

I pounded on the fence, and at my side, Sverre pulled as hard as he could. There must have been a spell on the grate, otherwise we would have already gotten in.

The spectators roared with excitement.

"Watch her hang," someone shouted. "Out with her tongue. Out with her tongue . . ."

Ragnara quickly pulled the sword from the soldier's belt and stabbed it into Faida's back.

The spectators gasped again as blood sloshed down over Taliah's body.

Faida now hung still, and Ragnara pulled the sword out. In doing so, she severed a small lock of Faida's red hair.

It was dead silent in the arena as it floated down past Faida's bloody body and landed in a little curl on the sand.

People stared at Ragnara. Some with admiration, others with horror. But from all of them fluttered small golden whisps. Worship, whether it came from love or fear.

Ragnara's aura grew with each whisp that reached her.

If I had hated Ragnara before, it was vague. Abstract. I couldn't picture her, and she had been more like a concept than a person of flesh and blood. Now I hated her with my whole heart.

Eskild barked again, and with Faida's blood on her hands, Ragnara walked calmly back toward the platform.

Just then, we broke through the grate, but the soldiers had finally worked their way down to us, and they attacked with swords raised. Sverre turned toward them and swung Tilarids. Fortunately, the sword was effective enough to give me the chance to pry the fence aside.

The prisoners were still hopelessly outnumbered, but the redhead was fighting better now that he was no longer lashed to Tíw. He used the dripping chain as a metal whip. Blood poured from Tíw's half arm, but he still swung the sword around.

"Bring in the other sister," Ragnara shouted, and Serén was pushed into the arena.

I was struck by an intense pressure, and she looked instinctively in my direction.

When our eyes met, time sloshed around me, and I heard an explosion.

Okay, time really is fucking huge.

Serén and I flew in opposite directions as the wall in front of me collapsed.

Anna, I heard inside my head.

Serén! Can we change the past? I thought desperately. *Can we undo all of this?*

Try.

I don't know how.

We looked at each other again, and there was another crash. A good chunk of the wall behind me simply vanished in a cloud of dust, and Sverre shielded his face as bits of stone and mortar rained down on him. One of the soldiers was struck by a flying brick and fell to the ground.

This didn't happen, I commanded time and looked at my sister.

There was a bang as a crater spread before my feet. A large hole appeared in front of me, and I nearly stumbled into it.

It's not working. We're just blowing everything up. Even inside my head, I could hear that Serén was desperate.

Maybe we have to touch each other for it to work, I thought, trying again to push myself forward as I looked at her, but I was quickly shoved back.

The grate surrounding the arena bent backward with a whining, metallic sound.

I dropped to my knees, the twisted iron forming an arch over me. Instinctively, I looked at Ragnara.

Surprise flitted across her face. This was the first time I had seen any emotion. Whatever she had been expecting, it wasn't this.

Again, I thought frantically to Serén. *We have to blast our way out.*

We both stood, wobbling, and looked at each other. When our eyes met, I felt a violent shock, and I didn't think it was because of our clairvoyance. It was more like being reunited with a missing half.

Kapow!

The wall behind me collapsed, creating a clear path out. All the way out. Behind houses and buildings, I saw Vigrid—the red plain—and even better, I also saw wolves and humans streaming in through the hole.

Rokkin and her pack galloped in and sank their teeth into the fingalks and soldiers who had the misfortune of trying to fight them off. The humans, who must have been resistance fighters, also ran in, shouting and swinging weapons wildly.

With a sigh of relief, I saw that Finn flapped his wings and kept himself aloft above the fighting.

Each time Serén and I looked at each other, we blasted new holes in the wall and were slammed to the ground. But every time, we got to our feet and looked at each other again.

It didn't take long to defeat the fingalks. Eskild jumped into the fight, while the Varangian Guard circled Ragnara protectively. In no time, the prisoners and the children were gathered up and led out through the hole in the wall.

Someone pulled Luna and Mads along.

Vale limped away, bleeding, and Tíw was carried, collapsed and gushing blood. He wouldn't last long, but he would at least die in peace.

Sverre jumped out in front of them.

"Rorik," Tíw whispered.

"That's Prince Sverre," a female rebel said with disgust. She raised her spear toward him, but the redhead stopped her.

"What do you want?" he asked Sverre.

"I don't care," the prince said. He seemed to be speaking mainly to himself. He grasped the stump of Tíw's arm, and an intense current flowed from his hands. "Nothing matters now."

The rebel could do nothing but stare at him, mouth agape.

"Let him," I managed to say.

Sverre looked focused as calm spread across his face. He let go of Tíw's arm and leaned against the wall, exhausted. The end of Tíw's stump had healed with new, pink skin.

They carried him away, and someone pulled on my shoulder, but I twisted free.

Serén was gone; I sensed the pressure fade away in the direction of the forest. I exhaled. She had escaped. She survived. I was about to follow her, but I stopped.

The tree.

In the center of the arena stood the gigantic black oak tree. Faida hung there, along with the dead animals, from the upright roots. The trunk shone wetly, the fehu rune glowed, and I focused on it.

"Is the tree connected to all the holy trees in Hrafnheim?" I asked Sverre.

His eyes were still closed, but he nodded.

"We have to destroy it." It had just sunk in.

"What?" Now Sverre opened his eyes. His forehead glistened with sweat.

"If we destroy it, it can't connect to the others. It's like the server for a large computer network."

"A what?" He straightened.

I ran all the way into the ring, which was full of dismembered fingalk parts and people no longer living.

Gytha came over to us, the gashes forming four lines down her face.

The three of us moved against the rebels. In the stands, there was chaos. Some tried to flee, while others stared breathlessly.

I was heading straight for the tree. The stench of the animals invaded my nostrils. I fumbled with Auka, which was pathetically small in comparison to the massive trunk.

Two people stepped in front of us just before we reached it.

Ragnara's dress made hollow clanking noises as the black stones rubbed against one another. She was so small, she only reached my shoulder. Eskild was tall. He and Sverre looked each other right in the eyes.

For a chilling moment, Ragnara's dark eyes locked on mine. The sinister darkness felt like a hand closing around my throat.

I saw her childhood as a slave, her struggle against those in power, the birth of Sverre, and her eighteen years as ruler. Just as I was feeling sympathy for her, I saw a knife in her past. Its carved verdigris handle lay in her palm. The handle was shaped like a snake. In the vision, the knife plunged into my mother's stomach, then into my baby chest.

I instinctively flinched and clutched my chest. She walked directly toward me, and my stomach dropped with fear.

Gytha stepped between us.

I shook my head to clear it, but Ragnara's eyes had already moved to Gytha, whose torn dress revealed the rune on her upper arm. The rune that showed she, too, had once been a slave.

I realized that some of the spectators were still watching. There was total silence in the stands.

Gytha smiled, breathless.

"Freer of slaves," she whispered. "You . . ."

But Ragnara had already swung the knife. She pulled back her hand, and at first, Gytha simply looked surprised. She continued looking at Ragnara in wonder, but then fell to her knees. Her neck gaped with a gigantic wound.

The spectators shouted.

Sverre looked from the bleeding Gytha to his mother. He threw himself to his knees and laid his hands on Gytha's neck to heal it. In the nick of time, he managed to close the wound, and Gytha knelt, coughing.

Sverre raised his face toward his mother. He was trembling with anger. "This is my friend."

Ragnara pointed the knife at her son. "Not one more word."

She stared at me.

"Finally, Thorasdatter. Finally." She raised the blade again, but Sverre stood and grabbed his mother's wrist.

"You can't . . ."

"I can't kill the seer? Do I need your permission?" Ragnara cocked her head.

"She's done nothing wrong."

"Her parents are to blame for this," she said so quietly, only those of us standing close to her could hear it. "Her parents and their friends. Gentle Od." She raised her upper lip in disgust. "Even he who was once in chains. They drove me to this."

She pointed at herself, but I wasn't sure if she was referring to the divine powers, the fine dress, or the green knife.

"What?" I gaped. "What happened back then? What did my mother and father do?"

"Ask them."

"She hasn't done anything," Sverre pleaded.

Ragnara's brown eyes shifted to me. "I'm killing her for what she *will* do."

But Sverre squeezed her wrist harder. "No."

"You are a prince," Ragnara hissed. "Not the son I should have had, but maybe you can still be of use." She raised the knife. "Hangadrott!" she bellowed.

The spectators inhaled simultaneously in a giant gasp as Ragnara thrust the blade forward.

"Baaaaahh . . ."

Finn was suddenly there. He threw himself on Ragnara and buried his claws in her chest. His eyes were such a deep red, they were almost black.

His jaws opened and he bit her neck.

CHAPTER 37

The thousands of spectators seemed to hold their breath as Finn's sharp teeth closed around Ragnara's neck, and his claws bored deeper into her rib cage.

When I observed her aura, I saw that small whisps of energy had been pulled out, returned to the people in the stands, but it didn't flicker, despite the fact that a fingalk's claws nearly skewered her tiny body.

Eskild let go of me, pulled his sword, and, without a second thought, stabbed Finn in the back.

"Noooo," I screamed. "Finn, Fiiiiinn."

Finn's large body went limp and dropped to the ground. His claws slipped out of Ragnara's body, and Eskild pressed both hands to her chest. His sword fell in the sand.

"Nana," Finn moaned.

I squeezed his brown, fuzzy hand, but its force weakened in my grasp.

He looked up at Sverre. "Krik."

Then he closed his eyes, which had shifted to an amber yellow as he looked at us.

The stench of fingalk blood spread, but he lay completely still.

"Finn," I whispered.

"I can't heal fingalks," Sverre said, his voice quavering.

Ever since Monster died, I had been painfully aware of the fact that some creatures were not receptive to healing.

In front of us, Ragnara stood up. She brushed off her shoulders and neck with an irritated grunt.

"What the hell?" I said.

She took a step toward me, and this time her brown eyes blazed triumphantly.

Immortal. Ragnara was immortal.

Amid everything else, I had completely forgotten.

Sverre was still staring down at Finn in horror. Then he raised Tilarids toward Eskild.

Ragnara pointed the knife at me.

"You!" Her voice was high, like a little girl's. Her dark eyes held mine, and that single word crept into my bones and took over all my willpower.

Auka fell to the ground, I lost the ability to move, and I just looked at her. The hand with the verdigris knife handle moved toward me, but I didn't even have the wherewithal to be afraid. An influence, very similar to Svidur's, took over my body. All I saw were her eyes and the small golden whisps around her.

Eskild and Sverre fought each other, but it was clear that Eskild was a stronger fighter. In fact, he fought very similarly to Varnar.

I fell to my knees and reached weakly for Auka, but Ragnara placed her foot on my hand, and I heard Varnar in my head.

You can't let them take you down. You can't lose your weapon.

I had failed on both counts.

Sverre saw me on the ground, trapped under Ragnara's foot and with Auka just beyond my reach. Despite Ragnara's diminutive size, she was exceptionally strong, and I couldn't move from beneath her. Besides, I wasn't aware of much beyond the brown eyes commanding me to lie still.

"Anna!" Sverre called.

I couldn't even turn my head in his direction.

"Anna!"

I finally managed to force my head sideways, and my gaze locked

469

on the prince's. So much like Ragnara's eyes, but with love shining deep within them.

This helped clear my head, but I still couldn't get free.

Sverre seemed to make a decision, and he threw Tilarids to me, making him vulnerable to Eskild's blows. He got ahold of Auka and managed to block Eskild's attack.

I gripped the sword, and its fury shot into me. The feeling gave me the force to pull myself halfway up, though my arm was still trapped under Ragnara's foot. I raised Tilarids toward Ragnara, and the sword—more so than me—parried the jabs of her knife. Eventually, all I saw were streaks of neon green from the handle as she thrust it.

Finn couldn't kill her, but maybe I could. The prophecy said I could.

I swung Tilarids with the intention of killing, and miraculously, the sword struck her chest.

It cut through stone and string, and black lumps rained to the ground. Vibrations went up my arms as it sliced through her flesh and bones.

I *could* kill her. I could . . .

But she straightened, and the wound on her bare chest closed.

Oh shit!

I tried to think clearly as she once again swung the knife like a half-naked Fury. I couldn't defeat her, even if I got another stab in.

The tree! I thought again. *Worship. Sacrifice.* I looked to the pulsating rune on the large trunk. Then I raised Tilarids one last time and threw the sword.

With a splintering sound, the blade bored into the glowing fehu rune.

Ragnara clutched her stomach as though I had hit her.

Flames burst around Tilarids, and soon the fire was climbing up the tree. The dry oak ignited like paper.

Eskild backed up with his arm around his queen, but everyone

saw her, exposed and horrified at the sight of the great tree burning.

Sverre's dark eyes filled with tears. He took Finn's hairy hand as
the large tree blazed behind us.

Ragnara and Eskild ran toward the gate the prisoners had entered through, and Sverre and I remained in the middle of the
arena by the burning tree, next to the lifeless Finn.

A crash made me flinch. It was the tree, cracking in the middle.
At first, the top half hung on by a few fibers, but finally, it tore
away completely and fell to the ground in a cloud of embers. It felt
as though an electrical current pulsed through the ground beneath
it, and I suspected that had to do with the tree's connection to the
other fehu trees in Hrafnheim.

"Anna," Sverre said.

I looked at his broad shoulders, the bold tattoos, and the scars
on his bare arms. His pale hair nearly outshone his gold headband
in the sunlight, but the braided ring on his finger was long gone.

I looked down at Finn, who lay with his eyes closed and his head
on Sverre's leg. His brown hand with its sharp claws was slack.

I breathed shakily. "Is he dead? I can't see fingalk auras."

"Almost." Sverre laid his hand on Finn's chest.

"Come with me," I begged.

He tried to lift Finn, but the fingalk let out a heartrending
whine.

"I can't move him, and he shouldn't die alone."

I studied them both, sitting there.

"Run," Sverre commanded. "They'll come back for you if you
don't hurry up and leave."

I brought my head down to the fingalk's face. "I love you, Finn."

He replied with a little snort.

Sverre looked behind me and nodded at someone.

Whoever it was grabbed my shoulder, and a woman's voice said
in my ear: "Go, Anna."

I didn't have a chance to wonder how she knew my name. "You're not safe here."

Sverre looked up at the many spectators, then back at me.

"You have to go." He pushed me, and the person behind me pulled.

I took a couple of steps backward and looked at him one last time before I turned and hurried away. The woman led me out of the arena, through streets and alleys and out through the corner of the city wall, where the lighthouse had once stood. Everything flashed past, and I didn't register much as images of Faida, Taliah, and Finn continued to bombard me.

Finally, we ducked into the forest outside of Sént, and the woman pulled me behind a bush.

I woke from my trance and instinctively swung my fist, but it hit someone's palm. I was staring straight into a pair of wide eyes in a slender face surrounded by dark curls. There were a few white hairs among the black ringlets. The woman looked at me inquisitively.

I recognized her from various visions.

"You're . . ." I couldn't finish my sentence. "You're—"

SMACK!

The woman threw a knife right past my ear, and it sank into someone's chest right behind me. The soldier fell forward, gurgling.

I hadn't even noticed there was someone following us. Again, I stared at the woman, whose stubborn expression resembled my own.

She gripped my arm, and before I knew it, we were once again running at full speed through the trees. I tried to catch even a single glimpse of Thora as arrows flew and shouts rang out behind us. She pulled me behind a boulder, where we sat with our backs pressed up against the cool surface. She whistled quietly and signaled to the bushes.

I couldn't see anyone, but I assumed her people were in there. If not, my mother had really lost the plot.

She looked intently at me.

I could *feel* that I knew her. Feel that we had shared a body for many months. That I came from her. I reached out.

If I was expecting a loving embrace and gentle words, I was disappointed, because when she opened her mouth, her voice sounded like a harsher version of my own.

"I'm going to avenge your father, destroy Ragnara and Eskild, and then I'll come back to you and Serén."

I didn't know how to respond, so I just stared at her.

She waved her hand decisively. "Stay here. One of my men is coming for you." She pressed Auka into my hands. She had apparently brought the axe from the arena. "Fight, Anna," she exhorted me. "You have lived long despite all odds. Keep it up."

Then she took off in a burst of dark curls and threw herself into the battle that was taking place some distance behind us.

I sat there, my mouth hanging open.

"Bye . . ." I whispered, ". . . Mom."

Someone sat down next to me.

"The others will take care of your pursuers. I'm here to escort you to Haraldsborg." The young man waved a hand in front of my eyes. "You're totally out of it." He snapped his fingers. "Wake up."

I shook my head. "I'm ready."

His blond hair was gathered at his nape, and he walked ahead of me with steady strides.

"It's not too far," he said over his shoulder. "The headquarters are right over here."

He was around eighteen years old, and despite his self-assured tone, he quivered with pride that Thora had entrusted me to him.

We walked for a while in silence as my brain churned.

"What's your name?" I asked.

His boots made crackling sounds against the plump green branches beneath our feet. The forest was lush, above us the sky was blue, and dark birds were circling. The summer heat radiated around us.

He turned his head.

"My name is Rorik."

CHAPTER 38

"Your name is WHAT?"

He looked at me, uncomprehending. "Rorik," he repeated.

I grabbed his arm. "How long have you been called that?"

He tucked a strand of hair behind his ear. My forceful movement had caused it to escape from its leather cord.

"Since I was born." He contemplated. "Longer, actually. It's a family name."

I spun around and peered through the trees.

Shit, shit, shit.

"Get away from me," I said frantically.

"No. Varnar and Thora made me promise to protect you with my life."

I was on the verge of tears. "Can you please go away?"

Rorik—that is, the real Rorik, whose name Sverre had stolen—looked around as well. "There's no one around. What's wrong with you?"

It all fit. Serén had seen me in a forest with Rorik. She had seen it as an almost unchangeable part of the future. But she had seen the real Rorik, and I had erroneously believed it was Sverre. Serén had seen him die protecting me. I could barely breathe, and my eyes flitted to the boy at my side.

"You can't protect me," I shouted and started sprinting away from him. "Run the other way."

Rorik followed me, pushing sticks and branches out of the way to reach me.

"Stop!" he yelled.

I tried to get away and even flicked a springy branch toward him to get him out of the way.

"Cut it out," he shouted. "What in the worlds are you doing? Varnar will be furious if I let you get away. Ow."

"Varnar is always mad at me," I shouted back. "I'll survive."

But right now, there's a good chance you won't.

"Stop," he called from far behind me, but he wasn't prepared for my magical Teflon.

I crouched behind a fallen tree and scanned the area. Why hadn't I discovered the people watching us?

Maybe the real Rorik had a chance, as long as he wasn't protecting me.

"Anna . . ." I heard his voice call out again.

Shut your mouth! I closed my eyes and wished I could warn him, but if I called back, it would lead the soldiers directly to me.

My eyes flew open.

If I called, it would lead the soldiers directly to me.

I stood up.

"Helloooo," I called. "I'm over here."

A man emerged from the underbrush, but he crumpled when I karate-chopped him in the neck.

I had learned from the psychopath Christian Mikkelsen back in Ravensted that you should strike before your opponent can even see that you're getting ready to. I smashed my fist into his cheekbone and saw him go cross-eyed.

The soldier fell to his knees, swinging his sword in the wrong direction. I jumped over the blade and kicked him in the temple, and he was out like a light. Then I put two fingers in my mouth. A high-pitched whistle shot out across the forest.

"Over here!"

Several more soldiers came running. It didn't take me long to knock them out, leaving them unconscious on the ground.

My pride in having taken down—I counted six, seven—eight trained warriors was replaced by fear as even more came pouring through the trees.

My journey had trained and hardened me, and I wasn't scared to fight up to eight people at a time. But the number of soldiers around me in the clearing surpassed what even I could handle.

A female warrior stuck her head out of the brush and fixed her eyes on me. She let out a war cry, but it ended in a choking sound, her face frozen in a grimace. An arrow protruded from her neck. The other soldiers whipped around, and another arrow landed in a man's eye.

Rorik's footsteps came closer. He stepped out from behind a bush with his bow raised.

"I have to protect you." He looked around, his eyes wild.

"I can protect myself just fine."

"I can't say I completely agree," he shouted and drew his sword.

"Can you please go away," I bellowed as one of the soldiers swung his weapon toward me.

Rorik turned around and blocked the knife from hitting me. The way he got down on his knees resembled Varnar.

Someone hit me in the back of the head.

I looked over my shoulder and found a soldier with a slingshot.

He fired again, this time hitting me in the ear with a metal ball. Black spots danced in my vision.

"Get away from here, Rorik," I whistled. "You'll die if you don't."

"I'm not budging." He swung, taking a woman down.

Someone slammed a sword's shaft into my forehead, and I blacked out.

When, lethargically, I looked up, Rorik was circling the final three soldiers. Again, I could see who had taught him to fight, and I shouted when he took down another man. The ground in front of us was full of dead and unconscious bodies. The two remaining warriors went after Rorik, and he moved so quickly and elegantly,

I thought he had a chance. I watched through the blood that ran into my eyes from a gash on my hairline.

One of the soldiers turned toward me and threw his spear. Rorik saw this and seemed to make a split-second decision. He launched himself sideways and smacked the hand just as the spear left it. This changed the spear's trajectory just enough that it whistled past me, but the movement left Rorik's flank open, and the last soldier buried his sword in his side.

Rorik sank to his knees.

I crawled forward as my surroundings blurred. The only thing in focus was Rorik, who collapsed with the weapon protruding from his body.

"No!" I screamed.

We made eye contact.

Then the soldier grabbed Rorik's hair, yanked his head back, and in one clean slice, slit his throat.

I was sobbing violently and fell forward, landing on my side, as the soldiers slowly walked toward me.

I saw their feet sideways as I lay in the grass, unable to move.

I hate you, fate! I cursed quietly. *I hate you so much.*

Everything I had fought to prevent had happened. What about my murder in Kraghede Forest? Was fate impossible to outsmart?

Boots came closer and stopped beyond my field of vision. I heard an enthusiastic voice.

"Is that her? Serén?"

A foot prodded my leg. "I think so."

The other one was about to say something, but then an exclamation rang out instead. Again, there was noise above me, but I couldn't see what was going on. My consciousness wavered, and I closed my eyes, glad to escape the bloody scene. With eyes closed, I waited, and it wasn't long before it was once again completely silent.

A scent grew stronger as it approached. A scent I knew well.

Warm hands stroked my bloody face, and without opening my eyes, I laced my fingers with theirs.

"I never thought," the voice said softly, "that I would see you again."

I suspected I was in a fantastic dream—or that I was simply dead, and that the afterlife was unexpectedly delightful. I was being carried, and the wonderful fragrance enveloped me. I flung my arms around the man's neck and inhaled hungrily as everything swam around me.

A gate opened, and an echo of footsteps and voices surrounded us. Someone laid me down carefully, and a moist, warm cloth washed my face. There was chatter, but it, too, faded away. Then it was quiet.

The image of Rorik, the real Rorik, getting his throat slit flickered in my head, and I was suddenly freezing, even though it was a warm summer day. I saw Faida being strangled and heard again and again Finn's faint voice. My teeth chattered, and with a weak motion, I tried to rub my arms. Or maybe it was someone else rubbing me.

Wood was stacked, and flint struck against stone, after which a crackling sound was followed by a wave of warmth. I didn't dare open my eyes. Instead, I reached out my hand and ran it over the surface I had been placed on.

It was smooth and soft, and heat billowed toward me.

Tentatively, I cracked one eye open and discovered that I lay in a large bed with the softest sheets I had ever touched. The walls of the room were draped with tapestries, and the floor was made of stone. Flames roared in an open fireplace. A man stood in front of it with his back to me. His dark hair went past his shoulders.

There was something familiar about this.

The man turned around. It was Varnar. I held my breath. His hair was longer than the last time I had seen him, and his clothes were different, but otherwise he looked like himself. He smiled, and his smile warmed me more than the blazing fire. With two long strides, he was next to the bed and leaned toward me.

"I've been waiting for this. For so long." He spoke slowly.

Very familiar.

I said nothing, just stared at him and tried to figure out why I had such a strong feeling of déjà vu.

The bed creaked as Varnar lay down next to me. I was once again enveloped in his scent, and instinctively, I wrapped my fingers around his neck.

He leaned in closer toward me, and when his lips nearly touched mine, I made a strangled noise.

Without thinking, I stroked a hand over his dark, silky hair. The fragrance was overwhelmingly comforting.

"I've missed you so much," I breathed.

The sound of my own voice made me focus. Why did I feel like I had experienced this moment before? Then it dawned on me. I *had* experienced this before. In dreams. I sat up abruptly, and a nasty headache nearly knocked me over.

"Anna." Varnar's hand lay on my cheek, and it sounded like the mere act of saying my name gave him pleasure. "Ahen," he said and closed his eyes. "Ahen Drualus."

"You can't call me that," I whispered. "It's a name of fate."

He looked at me, uncomprehending.

I looked around the room. It was very familiar, as most of my fantasies about Varnar had taken place here. Serén had sent me the dream a long time ago because she knew I would fall in love with Varnar. Or had I fallen in love because of the dream? Or maybe it would have happened under any circumstances?

Damned fate!

I held my head and squeezed, but I winced when I accidently pressed directly on the gash at my hairline. It intersected the one that was already on my temple.

Varnar removed my fingers and carefully touched my face, but I wriggled free and got to my feet in a daze.

My knees threatened to give out beneath me.

"Am I in a time warp?" I asked, looking at the ceiling. "Serén?" I called. "Serén! This isn't funny."

"What's wrong?" Varnar asked. He had stood up and was trying to turn me toward him, now with a firm grip on my shoulders.

I stared at him as though I were afraid he would evaporate.

"Is this the past or the future?" I asked, confused. I didn't know if I was asking Varnar, Serén, or myself.

"It's now," he replied with his signature furrowed brow. "Right now."

"Now." I said the word as though I didn't understand its meaning.

Slowly, Varnar lowered his hands. "It's my fault. I never should have left you."

Anger bubbled inside me. "No. You shouldn't have left."

Then he scowled, and I was almost relieved to see him irritated. It was much more like him. He searched for words. "I thought it was the right thing to do."

Now I stood up straight and struggled to keep my voice somewhat calm, but even I could hear how shrill it was. "*Right?!* There's no such thing as right. There are actions, and they have consequences. But right and wrong—those don't exist."

"It was to protect you." He stood, and his warm hand touched my cheek.

I wanted to yell at him. A thousand times, I had gone through what I wanted to say to him if I ever saw him again, but my arms just hung limply at my sides. "I know."

"You do?"

I nodded weakly.

"I still love you," he whispered. "That hasn't changed."

All I could do was answer honestly.

"I love you, too. But . . ." I delayed, because I knew as soon as the words left my mouth, I couldn't take them back. The thing I knew I had to tell him. Then Varnar would be lost forever. I swayed precariously.

"But . . . ?" He gently pulled me back to the edge of the bed.

We sat, and I stared down at the floor. My head ached, and the room was spinning around me.

"That you love me is all I need to know," he whispered and kissed my hair.

I leaned into him heavily.

Tell him, Anna! Tell him who you slept with last night.

I turned my head.

Dark brown hair framed Varnar's face as always. His eyes, with their small flecks of green, stared into mine, and his lips were soft, the way they only were when he looked at me.

Say it.

He put his mouth against mine. A million comets exploded inside me, and I kissed him, unable to stop. My thoughts were chased away, and I was aware only of his lips and his hands that repeatedly stroked my hair, and the smell I had missed so much.

He leaned his head back slightly and twisted a lock of hair between his fingers.

"Red." He smiled.

"Oh, right. You haven't seen it," I said. "It happened . . ."

He closed my mouth with another kiss.

"Shhh . . ." he whispered. "Tell me later."

Yes, I sighed to myself as I kissed him again.

Later, or maybe never.

I woke to Varnar carefully pressing on my forehead.

Outside, it was almost dark, but I could make him out in the twilight. He was propped up on his elbow and moving his fingers around on my head.

"What are you doing?" I mumbled.

"I'm examining you." There was a smile in his voice, and under the blanket, I felt his naked body against mine. "I was worried you might have a concussion, since you were talking in your sleep." His mouth landed on my forehead, just below the gash. "You don't usually talk in your sleep." The back of his hand brushed my collarbone. "But you aren't badly hurt."

I was flooded with joy by the fact that someone knew me so well, he knew whether I normally talked in my sleep.

"What did I say?"

Varnar's face grew serious. "You kept saying 'Rorik.'"

I stiffened instinctively, retreating slightly from Varnar's embrace.

"I'm sorry about that," he said quietly.

"You are?" My breathing quickened.

"Of course. That shouldn't have happened."

"I didn't think you knew."

He narrowed his eyes. "I saw it happen."

I flinched in shock. "You saw it?"

"He was aware of the risk."

"The risk?" The words made no sense. Then I sank back onto the pillow. "Ohhh," I exhaled when I finally got it.

"He was a good soldier," Varnar continued, lying back next to me.

"Yeah." I stared up at the ceiling, my heart pounding.

"But now he's gone."

"You're right about that."

We were silent again as Varnar's hand held mine on top of the covers.

"There was something you wanted to tell me," he whispered.

"Yes." I searched for the words. "Well, it's been a while since we saw each other." My voice faded out. "I've missed you so much, but I thought it was over between us."

Varnar's eyes glinted in the semidarkness.

"You've found someone else," he said.

The shock that went through my body paralyzed me.

"It was . . ." I gasped for air. "It's over now. In a way, it never even happened." My words dropped to a whisper. "He doesn't exist anymore."

Varnar was grave. "Was he a good man?"

I reflected.

"Yes," I said. "The side of him I knew was good. I have to tell you who it was."

Varnar's eyes closed. "I knew this could happen. I accepted it, but I don't want to know any more."

I exhaled, extremely relieved that I didn't have to admit to anything.

"I've always wanted you to be happy, but I don't want to hear his name." There was pain in his words.

"But I'm not happy without you," I blurted.

His brows furrowed. It was barely visible in the semidarkness, but I was so familiar with his features, I just knew it.

"I'm not happy without you, either," he whispered. "But your safety comes first."

"Safety?" I exclaimed.

"Ragnara will come after you again."

"Is Ragnara the only reason you want to keep me alive?"

At once, his strong arms were around me again, and I lay flat on my back, with him on top of me.

"No," he whispered. His lips found mine, and he kissed me tentatively. Then the kiss grew deeper. He pulled away slightly. "Actually, I'm pretty self-serving when it comes to your survival."

In the morning, I was sitting at the table in the chamber and nibbling on some bread when there was a knock at the door.

Varnar had left early, because he had to attend to his duties, but not before he had walked back and forth between the bed and the door several times. He always had to have just one last kiss. Happiness and infatuation swirled around in my body, and despite the horrifying events of the last few days, it was hard to wipe the smile off my face.

I was having a hard time controlling my thoughts, so it was a welcome distraction when Aella stuck her head in.

I shouted with joy.

"You're okay! Is Une here, too? Wow, your hair's gotten long. Where's my sister?" My words tripped over each other. "What about Luna and Mads? And the giant wolves?"

Aella gave me a big hug. "What happened to you?"

I pulled away. "What do you mean?"

"You've just spoken more words in a row than in all the time I spent in Midgard."

"Oh." I laughed. "I'm just happy to see you."

Aella plopped down at the table.

"To answer your questions one at a time: Une is here, and we're both okay. Your sister is at the other end of the castle, because clearly you can't be near each other without blowing things up."

My stomach sank at the thought that I might never get to meet my sister properly.

"The giant wolves are fine, though Vale needs a bit of care. Luna and Mads are still resting. They're okay," she rushed to add as I rose halfway from my seat. "But they're in shock and pretty banged up. You can see them in a few hours."

"Thora?" I asked.

Aella looked down. "She had to leave. She went to Miklagard with Jorfur and his kids."

"Jorfur?"

"The guy with red hair."

"What is she going to do there?" I asked, disappointed.

485

"She's organizing contact with the town. We are becoming more and more unified—thanks in part to you. The Ísafolders are also involved."

"I hope some protection comes with that," I mumbled, thinking of the children and elderly people in the town. "They don't stand a chance if they're invaded by Ragnara's soldiers again."

Aella exhaled. "We're sending troops down there, and sorcerers on our side are casting spells on their bases."

"Did my mom really just leave? I didn't even get to talk with her." My throat felt oddly scratchy, and I shivered in the loose clothes Varnar had loaned me. Once again, my clothes had been beyond saving.

"Your mother isn't a big talker," Aella explained. "She reminds me a lot of you in that way. Actually, she's a lot worse than you."

I quickly changed the subject. "What now?"

"Do you want to see our bastion?"

"Bastion?"

"Haraldsborg is our headquarters." She stood.

In the hallway, I studied the decorations, which were typical of Hrafnheimish. Viking art mixed with Arab-style ornaments, and—in contrast to the rest of the realm—images of the gods.

A life-sized statue of Odin with his two ravens on his shoulders stood proudly against the stone wall, flanked by a voluptuous woman and a man in a long white cloak, his eyes blazing blue. Something about the eyes brought me to a halt.

"Who is he?" I asked. I thought I had a pretty good command of the Norse gods.

Aella stopped. "That's the white god. Heimdall."

"He's not as well-known as the others, is he?"

"He was very important once. And he plays a role in doomsday." She said this with a shrug, as if she didn't really believe that it was right around the corner.

"Is that why he's included?"

486

She shook her head. "Serén insisted that he be here so that he could be worshipped in line with the other gods. She says he will be important, so he needs all the power we can give him. Or he has a son who's important. I don't know. She's seen something or other, but she's always seeing things."

And she's always right, I thought, studying the statue's sapphire-blue eyes, which now seemed to stare at me. "A son?"

"Yeah." Aella laughed. "They've been busy, he and Odin. Come on."

She kept walking, and I followed, though I looked over my shoulder at the cloaked god, whose eyes followed me down the hall.

In the courtyard, combat practice was underway.

Varnar stood in the middle of a small enclosure, while five soldiers moved around him. Three women and a man. I realized how privileged I had been to have him to myself for all those months.

At first glance, it looked like Varnar had an impossible task before him, but I knew better. When the soldiers finally attacked, he flew around them in his usual dance-like way. Though he was careful not to wound anyone mortally, he inflicted bloody noses, black eyes, and bruises.

I narrowed my eyes, looked critically at the soldiers, and caught sloppy footwork, too-low parries, and a skull that smacked into a forehead.

They limped off to the side.

"Again," Varnar barked, and I recognized his brusque demeanor.

The soldiers scowled, and one of them leaned against the railing.

I couldn't help myself, and I walked over to them.

"He's a little slower on his left side," I whispered to them.

They looked at me.

"Serén?" one of them said. "But you don't know anything about fighting."

487

"Just listen to her." Aella laughed.

"You can see your opponent's direction in their eyes. A split-second before they change direction, their gaze darts over. Varnar is no exception." I lowered my head and gave them a few more tips. A couple of times, I looked at Varnar, who was watching me. If I hadn't known him, I would have thought he was planning the best way to strangle me. I knew him, though, so I knew his thoughts were of a different sort.

"Come on, soldiers," Varnar shouted sharply. "You have a lot to learn."

"Try again," I told them, and they trudged back to the enclosure.

It went better this time. In fact, the last one—a tall woman—stayed upright for almost a minute before Varnar took her down. A crowd had formed, and there was a scattering of applause when the fight was over.

Varnar didn't help the soldiers to their feet, but he didn't chew them out, either. I knew that was as close to praise as they could ever dream of getting from him. He took off his shirt in the beating sun, and I felt an urge to touch him when I saw the fine network of muscles on his abdomen and back. A shiver ran through my body as I looked at the many scars on his upper arm. I now knew what they meant.

He gave me a look of mock reproach, and I threw up my arms.

"I just pointed out a few of your weak points," I said loudly.

"Weak points," he said with a menacing glimmer in his eyes. "I don't have any of those."

Only I saw the smile that grazed the corner of his mouth.

The spectators followed our exchange as though it were a tennis match. Varnar's words sent shock waves through the crowd.

"Pff," I said. "Of course you have weak points. Have you dazzled them into believing you're invincible? Don't think they can't beat you."

The soldiers turned their heads toward Varnar, eager to see what he would do.

He wagged his finger. "Can you do it better?"

"I would think so."

"Come on, then. Let's fight—until one of us goes down."

A murmur ran through the crowd, and someone shouted: "Come over here! Varnar is fighting one-to-one against Thora Baneblood's daughter."

Someone else whispered, "How long do you think she'll last? I give her ten seconds."

"Twenty," wagered another.

Money changed hands as I crawled between the boards into the enclosure. My hair caught on the dark, splintered wood, and I gathered it into a ponytail.

Varnar studied me as I slowly approached. The way he looked at me made my blood pump faster. I concentrated on the fight. The other thing could wait.

"Are you sure?" he asked, smiling.

"Are *you?*"

"I'm not holding back."

I pursed my lips and sucked in air. "I wouldn't expect you to."

We stood facing each other for a moment, until his hand whizzed toward me.

I ducked and spun around with my leg straight out, aimed directly at Varnar's knee.

He quickly hopped over it while kicking at my head, which was at the same height as his foot.

I leaned back but shot my hands forward, grabbed his ankle, and pulled.

The rebels let out a collective gasp as he was jerked backward, about to land on his back. At the last moment, he planted his palms on the ground, did a backflip, and landed on his feet again.

"Ten seconds, and she's still standing," someone shouted.

Varnar's intense eyes locked on mine, and the pleasure of fighting with him nearly surpassed spending the night in his arms. I bit my lip to force the corners of my mouth back down.

"Stop holding back," I said.

He leapt toward me.

My palms landed right in his solar plexus, stopping him, but he got a punch in and hit me in the lip, causing hot blood to spill down my chin. I let the pain flow through me because I knew it was coming. That was the price of getting close enough to karate-chop him across the cheekbone.

There was another roar from the crowd, which was growing quickly around us. "She's up to forty."

Varnar wasn't looking after me, and I wasn't looking after him. We moved around each other and kicked and punched, and the soldiers around us screamed and shouted.

"She's winning. Holy shit, I think she's winning."

Varnar's teeth were red when he smiled, and I spat blood. He ran right toward me, and I knew he was about to do his elegant little move where he would land behind me, delivering the blow that would send me to the ground. Involuntarily, I turned and spun around the way Sverre had taught me.

Varnar widened his eyes, and in that moment, comprehension reached his face.

I didn't notice that he was standing there, paralyzed, so I hammered my fist directly into his stomach, and he crumpled and fell into the dust.

Around us, the soldiers hooted and clapped, and the one who had placed all his money on me shouted triumphantly.

At that moment, I realized why Varnar was frozen.

He looked up at me, coughing, from his position on the ground. His expression was one of pure horror and disbelief.

"Prince Sverre," was all he could force out.

CHAPTER 39

Aella handed me a white rag, which I pressed to my lip. It quickly turned red. She looked at me with arms crossed.

"Varnar said he didn't want to know anything." My voice was warped by the damp cloth in front of my mouth.

"I feel like there might be an exception for your intimate relationship with his archnemesis."

I flinched as though Aella had slapped me. "I thought Ragnara was his archnemesis."

"Sverre and Varnar have been rivals for as long as I can remember." Aella sighed. "And Sverre lies every chance he gets."

"That's not true. I know him. He said he wants . . ."

Aella's arms wrapped tighter across her chest. "Did you not hear what I just said? He lies all the time!"

I bowed my head. "Sverre did actually lie about his identity during our entire trip."

"So tell Varnar that." Aella threw up her hands. "I'm sure he'll accept that explanation."

I looked up again, eyes blazing. "Accept! Varnar won't accept anything. He walked out on me—which is only about the worst thing someone could do to me. I don't owe him an explanation."

"Glad that's cleared up," came a voice from the doorway.

I closed my eyes. And the day had started so well.

Aella hurried off.

With a sigh, I turned toward Varnar and armed myself with a deep breath. "The prince is a potential ally."

"The only reason for him to remove his mother from power is to usurp power himself. And he's just as bad as Ragnara, if not worse." Varnar's eyes were hard. "You're forgetting that I've known him for years."

It reminded me of the way he'd looked at me nearly a year ago back in Ravensted, before we got together. The feeling that a door had closed forever made me press my lips tightly together.

"He was putting on an act to protect himself. He's nothing like that in reality. He's a . . ." I laid a hand across my chest, and I could feel my long scar through my shirt. I had nearly said *healer*, but I stopped myself at the last second.

"He saved my life. Several times."

"I'm grateful that he could fulfil my role in my absence." Varnar didn't sound even the slightest bit grateful, and I wasn't sure which of his roles he was referring to.

I decided quickly that I didn't need to know. "We have to focus on the political strategy. I'm starting to understand that."

"Everyone thinks strategically," Varnar continued mercilessly. "I thought you were different."

That was the last straw, so I stood up.

"I had to take care of myself in your *absence*." I hissed the final word. "Was I supposed to just sit on my ass at home in Ravensted, unchanging, so you could run back here and play the hero?"

He took a step back. "And what have you achieved with your journey? You were fooled by the prince. You were caught by the elves. You got Rorik killed."

My mouth hung open until I found my voice again. "My sister is free, and the fehu trees have been destroyed. I may not have won, but I delayed Ragnara's plan. She would have been a goddess by now if I hadn't taken action."

"You did all that?" For an instant, Varnar's brows drew closer together, and he forgot what he was doing, which was apparently trying to wound me as much as possible.

"We did it together."

"You and Sverre?" A muscle tightened in Varnar's neck.

I nodded without meeting his eye.

He alternated between opening and clenching his hands. His mouth formed a circle, as if he were going to say something, but then he turned around and disappeared.

His footsteps grew quieter and quieter down the hall.

When he had left, I sat heavily on the stool and buried my head in my hands. I longed for solace, but there was only emptiness. I longed for someone who would understand my relationship to Varnar.

"Monster," I said out loud, my voice full of self-pity. "I wish you were here, but I don't have any friends left among the giant wolves."

"That's not true."

I jumped at the sound of the hoarse voice, and I turned in my seat. "Rokkin."

The giant wolf ambled closer.

"Monster . . ." My eyes stung. "Your father . . . I found him, but he can't be saved."

Rokkin squeaked but regained her composure. "You were the best friend he could have hoped for."

My eyes squinted as I blinked the tears away.

Warm arms embraced me.

"Luna." I turned on the stool and held her as she stroked my hair.

Behind her stood Mads.

"Are you guys okay?"

"I'll never forget it," Luna whispered. "All that hatred and bloodlust."

"You should not have even been there," I cried. "It's my fault."

"Shut up about your guilt! I don't want to hear it anymore."

I looked up in surprise. Luna was rarely so blunt.

She pursed her soft lips. "It's time for us to go home."

"How?"

"Your sister will help."

Suddenly, the ground buckled beneath me, and I was struck with a force that felt as though I were in a room with thousands of people. I nearly collapsed when the current came closer. The force drew nearer, and the walls began to flicker, as if the outlines were simply dissolving.

"She's figured out a way," Luna said. "You have to unite your powers."

I gasped for air as the enormous, all-consuming aura pressed down, and the ground rolled beneath me. Beneath us.

"Is now when we change the past?"

No, I heard inside my head. *We're not ready. Or time isn't ready. It's in too much turmoil. But we can travel between the worlds with our combined power.*

Rokkin stumbled, too. The intense current made everything tremble.

"What's happening?" I shouted, but the violent blast drowned out my voice.

I repeated the question inside my head.

You have to go home, Serén said.

If you come in here, it's all gonna explode.

Inside my head, Serén laughed. *Then I'll keep my distance.*

Yet another wave rushed toward me, and, as always, I had the feeling of standing between two mirrors with endless reflections.

Luna, Mads, and I were lifted off the ground, and I saw that time around us was just a big imprint, where we were plopped down in a random place. I could see myself in the past and vaguely make out something in the future, while at the same time, it all flowed around me like a muddy expanse. The worlds also ran together, so time and space were one big soup.

The earth ripped, and an opening came into view. Beneath me, I clearly saw the outline of Denmark. We quickly zoomed in on North Jutland, though we were still very high up.

"It's a long way down," I shouted.

Goodbye, Anna. I'll see you in dreams, Serén said in my head.

She let go of us, and we plummeted.

"Serén," I yelled. "Serén, for fuck's sake."

But there was no response.

We hit the cloud cover, which was thick and wet.

Luna and Mads vanished between the clouds, but I could hear them both screaming.

I tumbled downward, and suddenly trees, fields, and the sea were fast approaching. There was a flicker of colors, smells, and sounds, and I closed my eyes.

Then there was a crash.

It was me, landing heavily on the ground.

PART V
NASTROND

A hall she saw, far from the sun
On Nastrond it stands, and the doors face north;
Venom drops through the smoke-vent down,
For around the walls do serpents wind.

Völuspá,
10th century

CHAPTER 40

I blinked a couple of times and stared up at the blue sky without moving. High above me circled a bird—I couldn't tell if it was a raven or a seagull—and it was impossible to determine whether I was in Hrafnheim or back home in Ravensted.

My body thrummed. The feeling of Serén's clairvoyance was still vibrating in me, as though someone had punched me in the head.

Tall, golden straw reached toward the heavens, and an ant crawled across my cheek. A car horn honked in the distance, and a machine rumbled.

Okay. Home.

I exhaled slowly.

Well, I'm not dead.

My eyes widened.

Or am I?

I dug my fingernails into my palms.

Ow!

Alive.

I lay there for a while, trying to gain control of my thoughts as the rumbling sound drew nearer. I was back in boring, regular old Ravensted.

The straw in front of me moved.

Maybe I had finally escaped rulers, gods, and giants. I inhaled sharply. And impossible men in a crazy parallel world. Maybe I was safe.

Safe! Whoa!

The combine harvester was very close. I hadn't registered that the large machine had almost reached my toes, or that we were even in the same field.

I leapt up and started running, the sharp blades right behind me. I was surrounded by grain as tall as I was, and I struggled to move forward.

"Stop!" I screamed to the person high above me. "You'll run me over."

Having grown up in a place consisting primarily of fields and pig farms, I knew very well that hearing protectors are a farmer's best friend, and that it would be impossible to spot someone on the ground in front of an industrial harvester, especially when up to their ears in wheat.

The harvester's teeth snapped right behind me, and I was hit with a dust cloud of broken seed heads and dry soil that blew across my arms and legs in the places where my clothes were ripped.

I fought to get away from the rotating metal blades, my arms moving in front of me as if I were swimming, but the wheat held me back. I ran diagonally from the harvester, like when you swim away from a rip current.

After a few nerve-racking seconds, I reached the other side of the metal beast and tumbled out of the tall straw, landing on all fours on the closely trimmed field. Behind me, the vehicle's driver finally spotted me and braked with a whine.

"What are you doing, girl? You know you should never be in the fields during the harvest."

I looked back, though I still didn't have the breath to do anything but gasp for air.

The man stopped.

"Thora and Arthur's daughter." He approached me cautiously. "Anna?"

I nodded as I took in large gulps of air.

He squatted in front of me. "What in the world are you doing here?"

When I still didn't answer, he stood and held out a rough hand to help me up. "Come with me. I'm sure Mina has some clothes you can borrow."

I had never been to Ostergaard before, even though the estate had been my view to the north the whole time I lived in Odinmont. The Earl led me across the manicured driveway, and the gravel crunched under my embroidered slippers. I looked toward the hill on the other side of the driveway and fields, where the small white house sat.

"Anna?" My classmate, Mina, stood at the top of the stairs by the large oak front door. "What are you doing here?"

Paul Ostergaard answered for me. "Do you have some clothes she can borrow?"

Mina took in my slightly oversized, torn, handwoven clothes with a raised eyebrow. "Aren't you coming to school?"

"School?" Not that I expected much concern over the fact that I'd been missing for more than half a year, but I thought my fellow citizens might show at least a little bit of surprise at my sudden return.

Mina cocked her head. "We're supposed to be there in an hour."

I pursed my lips. "I haven't been thrown out?"

She flashed her father a confused look, then looked back at me. "Why would you be?"

"Well, I mean, I've been away," I said tentatively.

Mina was clearly wondering if I was on drugs. "You've been in school every single day since the break. Or . . . I'm sure you have."

"Are Luna and Mads okay?"

"Luna?" Again, she looked at her father. "I think they're just as okay now as they were when you were sitting in Frank's yesterday evening." Her eyes darted again. "I'm sure I saw you guys down there."

I exhaled hard. "Is Frank back?"

"Where would he have been?"

I kept my mouth shut, ran my fingers through my hair, and picked a piece of grain from the red mess.

"Go get some clothes for Anna. She's evidently ruined her running clothes." The Earl looked sideways at my chaotic ensemble and ushered us into the old mansion.

Mina walked off toward her room, looking back over her shoulder a couple of times.

Paul Ostergaard folded his arms. "I think Benedict had something to do with this."

The Earl's hair was a graying medium-blond, and his build was like every other fifty-something-year-old man, but his light blue shirt was from an expensive brand, and though he spoke with a Jutland drawl, he sounded different from the rest of us.

"Ben?" I brought a hand to my mouth, and only now did I see how dirty it was. Wide, dark lines indicated where my wrists had been locked together, and my nails were broken and black. Two of them had been ripped off, and dried blood caked the cuticles.

The Earl studied me.

"No one knows that you've been," he searched for a suitable word, "away."

Mina came back with a pair of jeans—the most expensive designer brand, of course—and a nice-smelling blue sweater. She silently handed me the clothes and pointed in the direction of the bathroom.

Inside, with a sense of foreboding, I looked at myself in the mirror. With recent events in mind, I didn't have high expectations, but I nevertheless gasped at the sight.

My hair was a big red bird's nest, and I was smeared with dirt and had bruises, cuts, and scratches all over—some of them from my fight with Varnar. The runes branding my arm were visible through my torn shirt. An old gash on my temple intersected a fresh one along my hairline. But what was worse, my eyes were wide and manic.

Cautiously, I leaned in toward the mirror to study myself. With a dirty finger, I tapped on the glass.

"Serén," I whispered, and my stomach twisted with disappointment at the thought of how close we had been to each other.

"What are you doing?"

I jumped at the sound of Mina's voice right behind me. I quickly removed my hand from the mirror's cool glass.

"I . . . uh . . ."

"Were you attacked?" She looked at my bruises. "Because if you were, you should report it to the police."

I rubbed my wrists. "It's nothing, really."

"Whoever did that needs to be held accountable." She pointed at the gash on my forehead. "Otherwise, they'll just keep doing it."

"You're right about that, actually." When she continued studying me, I added: "I'll talk to Hakim."

I washed my filthy fingers.

Behind me, Mina grabbed a brush and pulled it through my hair.

I forced myself to stand there, hunched over the running water, and splashed a large handful over my cheeks and nose. Mina pulled a long, dark splinter—which clearly didn't come from either the field or the driveway—out of my hair. It came from the enclosure where Varnar and I had trained just an hour earlier.

She turned it between her fingers, but finally just placed it on the edge of the sink. "You're really good friends, huh?"

"Who?" I looked at her in the mirror. Drops of water stuck to my eyelashes and made me blink frantically.

"You, Luna, Mathias, and Mads."

I shrugged.

The movement caused my loose shirt to slide farther down, exposing the brand marks on my upper arm.

"You didn't have those yesterday." Mina traced the scars with her finger, and her eyes fell on my forearm, where the blue fehu tattoo shone. "Or that."

I turned abruptly, making her hand slide away. With a brisk motion, I pulled off the ragged shirt and pulled the sweater over my head. I looked down, mainly to avoid Mina's probing gaze, as I changed into her jeans.

"I like them, too," she said quietly. "I really like all of you."

I looked up with a start. "Even me?"

She nodded.

"Aren't you friends with Peter?" The question flew out of my mouth.

She lifted the brush again to detangle my hair. "I can be friends with both of you."

"No, you can't."

The hand that held the brush sank, and she took a step back.

"Peter and I are enemies. It goes way back. Much further than you and him."

"Are you sure?"

"Yes! I'm sure." When I turned back toward the mirror, without the dirt and with smoother hair, I looked a little more like myself. There wasn't much I could do about the gashes, but I pulled my sleeves all the way down past my wrists to hide the bruises. "There."

Mina took a step back and looked me up and down. "You look good now."

Paul's voice rang out: "Are you decent?"

"Yes, Dad," Mina shouted back.

He stuck his head into the bathroom.

"Anna just needs to go over to Ben and Rebecca's to get her bike. That's where you said it was, right?" He raised an eyebrow.

"It is? I mean, yes, it is." I collected myself. "I'll see you later, Mina."

She stopped me. "Where's your school bag?"

I looked around, half expecting it to be leaning against the wall. Of course, it wasn't.

"Oh, it's . . ." I had no idea what Ben had enchanted people into thinking.

"You must have left it at your apartment."

"My what?"

"Your apartment. Above Frank's."

I muffled an exclamation of surprise with a cough. "Yes, I must have."

Ben and Rebecca welcomed me at the door as if I had been gone only for an afternoon. As always, they leaned against each other's force fields. Their house had gotten a little more charred since I last saw it, presumably from the attack when the berserkers stole Monster's body.

My bag leaned against the painted exterior wall. Luna must have brought it from Hrafnheim.

Rebecca stroked my hair in a motherly way. As always, her bare toes stuck out beneath her long dress. "It's wonderful to see you, Anna Stella."

I looked into Ben's brown eyes surrounded by chalk white.

"Niels Villadsen from the DSMA wants to speak with you." His voice was a deep rumble.

I formed my mouth into an *oh* followed by an awkward laugh.

The Department of Supernatural and Magical Affairs was probably pretty annoyed with me.

"I'm sure he does." I cleared my throat. "I have a greeting for you."

Ben's full lips retracted, the silver ring in his nostril tilting.

I inhaled sharply when he exposed his gold teeth.

"From whom?" he boomed.

"Védis."

His smile—because that's what it was, even though he looked more like a hungry predator—stiffened. "How is Védis these days?"

I shrugged my shoulders. "She keeps company with a couple of horses and a dog."

The laughter that flowed from Ben was so gleeful, I shivered. "She is far too forgiving."

"She's one jewel richer." I kept my face neutral, but Rebecca gasped.

"Freyja's tears are priceless."

"What Védis did in exchange was also priceless," I said calmly. "At least Frank thinks so."

The witches stared at me, and Ben's eyes narrowed.

"Ben." I struggled to continue. "Your spells saved my life several times."

He put a hand on his hip. "Anna Stella Sakarias. Are you thanking me?"

I raised my head. "*Thank you* would be taking it too far." I suppressed a smile. "I'm just saying I'm not quite as mad at you as I usually am."

He laughed loudly. "You remind me so much of your mother."

I didn't know what to say, and we were fortunately interrupted by a yelp.

"Anna," came Luna's voice, and my heart stopped. "I have the craziest news. The craaaaayziest news."

"What?" I looked at her, confused.

She was about to speak again, but someone else shouted.

"Anna!" Mathias was right behind her, and before I knew it, I was in the middle of a tangle of honey-colored hair and black ringlets. My friends hugged me and talked over each other.

Tears formed in my eyes, and I flung an arm around each of them as we danced around.

"I've missed you so much," Mathias whispered. "I wanted to go to Hrafnheim, but Luna convinced me to stay and protect her parents."

"I managed it," I said. A version of the truth.

"It was also about the journey," Luna said sensibly, as though she had heard my thoughts. "Not so much about the destination itself."

Taliah's dead body flashed across my retinas, along with Finn's amber-colored eyes and Faida in my green dress. "I'm not sure I agree."

Behind us, Rebecca climbed a ladder to hang a piece of bacon and a loaf of bread from a branch of a large tree. There was more food up there than usual.

"Come," Luna said. "We have the best surprise for you."

"What is it?" I asked, not really a fan of unknown elements.

"Just come."

Mathias positioned himself behind me and covered my eyes with his large hands. When his palms touched my skin, it tingled, and energy coursed into me. His divinity had grown markedly stronger.

Reluctantly, I went with them. Luna held my hand so I wouldn't fall.

Something creaked, and then I felt the warm sunlight vanish. We were enveloped in shadow.

Mathias took his hands away, and I squinted until my eyes adjusted to the dark.

We were in Ben and Rebecca's barn. I had never been inside before, but it seemed to be set up as a kind of workshop. A magic workshop, that is.

Dried flowers and herbs hung from the ceiling, and everything from African masks to drums and carved staffs leaned against the walls, and in the middle of it all, there was a platform. It was covered with a white sheet. Around it were lit candles, fresh flowers, and various kinds of food. Bread, berries, and sheaves of grain. Skulls and bones were arranged around the strange form at the center.

Luna pulled the sheet away and shouted: "*Tadaaaa . . .*"

I gasped for air and clapped my hand over my mouth to keep from crying out.

I never thought I would be so happy to see my best friend's corpse.

On the platform, stiff and cold, lay Monster. He had been cleaned up, but his side and chest bore deep wounds and gashes.

I fell to my knees and wrapped my arms around him. He was motionless, very much dead, but his fur was soft, and there was a body under it. It wasn't just a pelt.

"How?" I whispered. "I saw him. He was in Ragnara's bedroom."

"You saw his brother," Luna said. "That was Liutpold lying there."

Monster's brother. I groaned. *Of course!*

"But Justine said Ragnara had stolen him." I thought back to our conversation. On closer inspection of my memory, I realized that she had only said the berserkers stole *someone.*

"They stole that little figurine that looks like Ben. Odion," Luna said. "My parents say this is a catastrophe, but I think it's still better than if they'd stolen Monster."

I stroked Monster's forehead.

"He's here. He's . . ." I gasped for air. "I need the . . ."

Luna handed me the bottle containing the mead of poetry.

Hands shaking, I took it. "What do I do?"

"Serve him the mead of poetry. Like the völvas did for Odin when he died on Yggdrasil." Luna giggled, though this was not at all appropriate for the serious topic at hand.

I pulled the cork from the bottle, even though my fingers refused to work properly. I finally succeeded, and a tingly, alluring smell rose from the neck of the bottle.

"Should I say something?"

"Just give it to him," Luna said. "That must be how it works."

I tipped the bottle and poured a bit of the golden, fragrant liquid onto Monster's snout and mouth. Then I set the bottle down and leaned over the large body.

"Monster," I whispered. "Monster. Come on now. Come back to me."

Some time passed. I have no idea how long.

From beneath me, I heard first a groan, then a sneeze. Warmth was spreading through flesh and tissue, and his heart began to beat.

"Anna," came a rusty voice that I had missed so unbearably much. "Anna," Monster repeated.

 # CHAPTER 41

I refused to leave Monster's side.

"Anna. You'll get marked absent now," Luna said. "My dad's hypnosis isn't active anymore."

I ignored her.

"Surely she can take one day off," I heard Mathias say, but I was too busy burying my face in Monster's fur to lift my head. "No one knows she's been gone for the past six months."

The mead of poetry—whatever it was made of—healed Monster's wounds enough that he wasn't bleeding anymore, but he would still need time to recover, and the long scars down his sides would be with him forever. I wasn't ready to let him out of my sight. We sat on the lawn in front of Ben and Rebecca's house.

He asked again and again if his family had survived.

"They're doing fine," I said. "I saw both your wife and your daughter escape from Sént."

Monster's dark eyes sparkled. "I should have been fighting alongside them."

My gaze fell on his back, which was still marked by a large wound. "But you did fight alongside them. In the Iron Forest. And if you hadn't come here and warned me, Serén and I would be dead now. So would your wife, for that matter. And I know you don't want to listen to me, but your kin managed themselves quite well in your absence."

"You met my kin," he boomed and laid his large head on my leg.

"Some of them," I corrected. "Vale."

His ears perked up.

"I didn't know giant wolves could get so big."

Monster gave a rusty laugh.

"Our forefather, Fenrir, is many times larger." He reflected. "But you're right. Vale surpasses most of my kind."

"I only met the ones led by Rokkin."

He raised his head, but winced, presumably still sore all over. "What do you think of my daughter?"

I sniffled. "She has the same dark sense of humor as you."

Monster opened his mouth, and I could see his white teeth glisten.

"She's amazing," I added and scratched his ear. "I even gave her a hug."

You wouldn't think a wolf's jaw could drop, but that was what Monster did. I could see that he didn't believe me.

"She didn't run away?" He paused. "Or bite you?"

"Nope!"

The hoarse laughter flowed around me, and I carefully leaned against him, afraid of touching his wounds.

Monster placed his chin on my shoulder in the way he always did.

"That was one of the reasons why I liked you from the start," he whispered. "You remind me of my daughter."

My fingers burrowed in his fur. "It's an honor to be compared to Rokkin."

"Did Ragnara try to kill you?" Monster's rough voice was unusually soft.

"Yes," I whispered. "She is very determined. However it's meant to unfold, she's very interested in preventing the prophecy that I can lead to her death. Which I can totally understand, to be fair."

"Can you? I mean, what the prophecy says. Can you kill her?"

I couldn't meet his gaze. "I got close to Ragnara, and it's true, she's immortal."

The sound of Finn's claws piercing Ragnara's chest echoed sharply in my head, followed by the hollow noise when Eskild stabbed him in the back.

Monster sighed. "I know. Liutpold tried to bite her head off before Varnar killed him."

I trembled and spared Monster the knowledge that his brother was now serving as a rug.

"The prophecy says that Thora's blood can lead to Ragnara's death, but that doesn't necessarily mean I can literally kill her, and Ragnara isn't stopping. She will strive for power for as long as she is able."

"Well, she is immortal."

"Yeah. And if she gets what she wants, she'll become a god." I lay down in the grass and looked up at the bright blue sky. Inexplicably, I imagined for a moment that it was the same sky they saw in Hrafnheim. "She's immortal as long as she consumes gods' blood. Od has made sure she can't get any more, but she has some stashed away somewhere."

Monster rested his bushy head on his paws. "Then we need to cut her off from it before we can kill her."

"Yes . . . I guess that is what we need to do."

"Anna . . . Anna . . ." Serén's voice splashed, as though carried through water.

I must have fallen asleep on the lawn with my head resting on Monster's stomach. In a corner of my consciousness, I knew I was sleeping in the sun.

In another part of my head, I was in Kraghede Forest on a cold winter night.

"I'm here," I said into the cold air, not quite knowing what I meant by *here*. "I came home to Ravensted, and Monster is alive again. Serén. He's alive! You have to tell his family."

My sister stepped out from behind a large tree.

"Did you hear what I said?" I asked.

"Yeah . . . I saw that he's alive."

"Then maybe a little *yay* is in order." I jokingly raised my arms in victory, but I lowered them when Serén appeared neither happy nor relieved.

"I see something else," she said. "Ragnara is on her way to your world, and it will lead to death."

"Whose death?"

Suddenly, Serén slammed her fist into her temple and closed her eyes. "I don't know. It keeps changing. But she'll be there. Soon! It's the same as what I saw on New Year's Eve."

My shoulders sank. "So me going there didn't even make a difference. Everyone who died . . ."

Serén's blue-green eyes, which must have been identical to my own, locked on to me. "You did exactly what you should have done."

"Says who?" I asked. "It's starting to feel like I have absolutely no influence on fate, regardless of how much I fight against it."

"Fight against it?" It sounded like Serén had to suppress a bitter laugh. "Fate always wins. And it says Ragnara is coming. The question is simply whether or not you're ready."

I woke with a start on Ben and Rebecca's warm lawn. A fly landed on my cheek but flew away when I swatted at it.

"What is it, Anna?" Monster mumbled drowsily.

"Nothing."

But my heart was beating hard in my chest.

I had a lot of updating to do with Ben and Rebecca, as they were hopelessly unaware of what had happened in Hrafnheim over the past several years. Arthur appeared out of thin air, and my father's ghost embraced me and wouldn't let go. The chill of death slipped from him into me, and I held tight, terrified of losing him. It must have looked strange to the three other people, who could see only my half of the embrace.

I considered confronting them with what Ragnara had said about how they bore some of the responsibility for this whole mess, but for some reason, the question remained on my tongue.

Ben beamed with pride that Védis had lifted the spells from Halfdan, and Rebecca shivered when she heard how Gytha had nearly died in the arena. They evidently knew each other. Monster sat at the end of the table as I talked, and Rebecca poured me cup after cup of different herbal brews, each one more pungent than the last. One for healing, one for strength, one for sorrow, and even one for a broken heart, though she did me the favor of not saying that aloud in front of my father. The smell invaded my nose, and Arthur made a farting noise with his mouth.

"There's something I don't miss about being alive." He nodded in the direction of the steaming mug, which reeked of juniper, ginger, and garlic. "It smells frightful."

"It tastes okay," I replied, and Ben, Rebecca, and Monster looked at me questioningly, since they couldn't hear Arthur.

"Nothing," I said to them. I took a sip of the foul-smelling, hot substance, and flinched when the taste hit my tongue.

"What about . . ." Arthur had difficulty finishing his question. "Your mother. Did you meet Thora?"

"Yes. She says hi."

He narrowed his eyes and tilted his head.

I corrected myself. "Or rather, she said she would avenge you, destroy Ragnara and Eskild, and return to Ravensted."

Arthur laughed, but it sounded more like a sob.

"That sounds more like her." He laid his hand on my cheek. "You remind me so much of each other."

"I know it was reckless to go there," I said. "But if I hadn't, Ragnara would be a goddess now, and it would all be over."

Arthur looked at me with equal parts pride and anger. "Can you promise me you'll take care of yourself from now on?"

"Okay." I winked innocently at him.

"Anna, I'm a ghost. I can see that you have your fingers crossed behind your back."

"Hmm," I said and uncrossed my fingers. "I'll do what I can."

He sniffled. "I guess that's the closest I'll get."

When I didn't have the strength to talk anymore, I just lay in the garden on a blanket next to Monster and looked up at the North Jutland sky. The smell of dirt and land was completely different than in Hrafnheim, the sounds of car horns, tractors, and barking dogs took up residence in me, and white clouds floated high above us. I had never noticed these things before, but now I was grateful for each and every one of them.

Finally, I closed my eyes and let myself drift off to sleep with one hand on Monster's warm paw. His breathing, too, grew deep and slow.

Walking into school the next day was like a surreal dream. I had never thought I would see the place again, and the sight of the colorful acrylic carpets, red bricks, and funky seventies artwork was more exotic than Ragnara's castle in Sént.

Mathias and Luna flanked me, and they felt more like bodyguards than regular classmates.

Luna lit up with a wide smile. "Hey, Mads."

Mads! I spun around, his long arms enveloped me, and we continued walking, arm in arm.

When we reached Yellow Hall, I couldn't stop looking around as though I were in a bizarre fantasy. Inside the classroom, I studied the tables covered in plastic film, the chairs with their red legs. I walked up to the window and ran my hand over the metal grate.

Mr. Nielsen came in and immediately began handing something out. "Here are your graded papers."

A white, paper-clipped stack of papers landed in front of me, but Mr. Nielsen didn't so much as look in my direction.

I looked at the pile.

"I really wrote a long paper on . . ." I studied the front page, ". . . tenth-century literature."

I flipped to the last page, where Mr. Nielsen's assessment was written in red pen.

"Hey," I whispered to Luna. "Couldn't your dad have conjured me a better grade?"

She giggled. "Apparently, your magical mirage wasn't a diligent student."

During the break, I swung into Yellow Hall and saw a broad-shouldered person leaning against the wall.

"Hakim!" I ran up to him, and only willpower and the awareness that people were watching us kept me from embracing him. I clenched my fists but smiled.

He returned my smile. His green eyes lingered on my face, then glided down to my neck. "You're wearing my present."

I fingered the cool silver pendant. "I almost never take it off."

"I would have gone after you, but I didn't know how to get through. The DSMA wouldn't tell me."

Without thinking, I grabbed his arm.

He stood completely still and held my gaze.

"It's good that you weren't there." I focused on the tattoo of the Arab-style snake that wrapped around his upper arm. It peeked out from under his T-shirt sleeve and suddenly reminded me of something. The snake was biting its own tail, and I got an ice-cold lump in my throat when I remembered the Midgard Serpent, which certainly did not have its tail in its mouth any longer. "It was far too dangerous."

"Yeah, it was dangerous—for *you?*" Hakim raised his voice on the last word, and a couple of students looked over at us.

"But I managed it."

He opened his mouth to say something but stopped himself.

Instead, he traced the crusty wound on my forehead with his finger. "But what did it cost you?"

I brushed his hand away. "How's it going working for the DSMA?"

Hakim regained his composure and held his head up. "Let's ask them."

My forehead creased. "What do you mean?"

Hakim cleared his throat. "Niels Villadsen wants to talk to you, so I asked Janitor Preben if we could borrow one of the rooms here."

"Something tells me Niels is pissed."

"That's why I asked for the meeting to be held here."

"There are a lot of witnesses here."

"Just to be on the safe side," Hakim said.

"The music room?" I looked around when Hakim led me into the room. A piano stood against one wall, and the rest was filled with percussion instruments, amplifiers, and a drum set.

"If we need help, we can always bang on the drums." He pointed. "And there's a back door."

We remained standing close to the door as footsteps approached.

Niels Villadsen, director of the Department of Supernatural and Magical Affairs, stuck his head in. To my shock, he gave me a friendly look.

"Anna. It's so good to see you. I'm glad you made it home unharmed." He looked at me through his inconspicuous, gray wire-rimmed glasses. His eyes landed on my cuts and scrapes. "Relatively speaking."

Maybe this wouldn't be so bad.

Niels pulled a piece of paper out of his briefcase. The top bore a logo from the Danish government, and beneath it was a bulleted list. Even though I was reading upside down, I could see my name.

Niels cleared his throat.

"Anna," he began, smiling again. He peered over his glasses at me. "You traveled to Freiheim through Od Dinesen's passage, which is reserved for Elias Eriksen. That is forbidden."

I didn't respond.

"You broke into Sverresborg and freed a prisoner of war."

"A little kid—" I protested.

"That is forbidden." Niels's voice was flat. "You stole a fingalk."

"Finn was abandoned. He would have died. He's dead now . . ." My voice faded, and Hakim looked down at me with a furrowed brow.

"That is forbidden." Niels took a breath before continuing. "You fraternized with the giant wolves. Forbidden." His finger moved down the list's many bullet points. "Forbidden, forbidden, forbidden." He didn't even bother to read out the rest of the allegations.

"I can explain everything. I did it to save my sister. It's bec—"

"You killed some of Ragnara's soldiers!"

I stopped mid-word. I involuntarily ran my hand over my arm.

Niels continued. "You destroyed Ragnara's large fehu tree, and you blew several holes in the Sént arena, after which you spent time in Haraldsborg with the rebels, including Varnar and Aella of the Bronze Forest and Serén, daughter of Thora Baneblood."

"Have you heard anything? Are they okay?"

"Ragnara and Eskild are furious, so I assume they're all okay." Niels busied himself by looking down at his papers.

"What about Prince Sverre?" I held my breath. My thoughts were haunted by Ragnara's threat that he was only useful as a hangadrott.

Niels still didn't look at me. "The prince has gone to Sverresborg with his young bride. A honeymoon of sorts, I suppose."

My stomach dropped. At least Sverre was alive.

Niels waved his papers again.

"You face severe punishment, Anna Stella Sakarias."

"I should absolutely not be punished. I saved all your asses! Ragnarök would have started if I hadn't freed my sister."

Niels looked patiently at me. "Would you rather be handed over to Ragnara so she can deliver your punishment? Our diplomatic agreements oblige me to cooperate with her."

"I prefer not to be punished at all."

Niels rubbed the bridge of his nose. "I'm trying to avoid a war, Anna. I'm doing everything I can to use my diplomatic channels to maintain the peace and keep you alive, even though you're really not making it easy for me."

"There is no peace anymore," I shouted, my voice echoing off the percussion instruments around us. "You should have seen Ragnara. She'll do whatever it takes to get what she wants."

The others were quiet.

"And you know what she wants?" Niels finally asked, tentatively.

Very quietly and slowly, I replied: "She's trying to become a goddess by forcing people to worship her."

The corners of Niels's mouth turned down as though he were suddenly nauseous.

I continued coldly.

"Ragnara is still immortal because she consumes gods' blood. She must have some left. We tried to destroy her." I didn't say who *we* were, and I quickly continued. "But it didn't work. We need to figure out how to make her mortal, so we can . . ." I couldn't say it out loud.

Niels's eyes closed halfway. "I'm trying—"

"No," I said. "The only thing to do is get rid of Ragnara."

"Peace." He was short of breath.

I slowly shook my head. "Peace is an illusion."

I took the indictment from his hand and tore it to pieces. Then I slammed the bits of paper down onto a laminate table.

"You remind me more and more of your mother."

I didn't answer before I dramatically strode out of the room full

519

of electric basses and tambourines. I couldn't waste one more second arguing with this bureaucrat. Ragnara was on her way, and I had to figure out what to do.

Back in the classroom, the next lesson had started, and people looked at me curiously when I walked back in.

"That cop came to talk to her," someone said quietly.

"Again," another said.

"Wonder what she's done now?"

On the far side of the room, Peter laughed maliciously.

I sighed. Despite it all, some things hadn't changed.

"I'd totally get it if you don't want to live with Frank," Luna said as she locked her beat-up cargo bike. She shook her pink curls. One of the first things she'd done after we got home was change her hair color. "The room at my house is still yours, if you want it."

I trembled slightly at the thought of Ben and Rebecca following my every move.

"I mean, Frank did try to kill you. And he could try again," she said.

"No, he won't. He wanted to kill me because of Halfdan, and we saved him."

"Okay," Luna said. "But maybe Frank would try again if someone threatened Halfdan."

"If Frank does anything to hurt me, it won't be until winter," I blurted.

"What do you mean?"

I didn't have the energy to explain to her how Serén kept seeing my murder in Kraghede Forest.

"I'm going to his place," I decided at that moment.

"We're coming, too," Mathias said. He had just joined us.

"Suit yourselves," I said.

Just like when I'd stepped into my high school, it was surreal to see Frank's Bar and Diner again. For a second, I wondered whether

I had even been gone. Maybe the past half year had been a figment of my imagination. But when I spotted Frank—who looked like himself with pomaded hair, a white T-shirt with the sleeves rolled up to expose his sailor tattoos, and black jeans—my heart did a backflip in my chest.

He looked up, and when he saw me, he jumped out from behind the bar and came over to us in three long strides. He hesitated for a moment in front of me, as if to see whether it was okay, but when I stepped toward him, he folded his strong arms around me and lifted me up with a long hug.

"You're alive," he mumbled into my hair. "You're here. You're back."

"Grandpa," said a high voice behind him, and Frank let me go.

I peered behind his back.

Mina stood there holding Halfdan's hand. The boy wore green sweatpants and a yellow sweater with a dinosaur on the front. He had a colorful tote bag slung from his shoulder.

Frank took Halfdan into his arms. "Did you have a good day at preschool?"

Halfdan started talking, and I didn't understand even half of what the excited child said.

"Are you his babysitter?" I asked Mina.

She nodded, her brown ponytail bouncing behind her.

"I pick Halfdan up every day and watch him in the evenings when Frank has to work late. You've seen me a bunch of times in the apartment . . ." She narrowed her eyes.

"Oh, right . . ."

"Thanks, Mina." Frank patted her on the back, in the same place where I'd seen him carve a rune into my own. "Halfdan can just hang out here in the bar."

"Okay." She stroked a finger over Halfdan's soft cheek and mussed his hair.

I looked around my little apartment.

It was clearly meant to look like I had been living with Frank for half a year, and whoever had arranged my things had done a great job. It looked like I had done it myself. Everything was there, but there was no decor or knickknacks. It occurred to me that movers could have unloaded everything indiscriminately, and it still would have looked like I'd arranged it myself.

A knock at the door caused me to stiffen. It was Frank's aura on the other side of the thin wood, but he was waiting until I gave him permission to come closer.

I opened the door, but he remained on the other side of the threshold.

"Do you want to come in?" My eyes darted to the room behind me, then back to Frank.

"Actually, I was wondering if you wanted to come over to mine. So you can say goodnight to Halfdan."

"Goodnight?" I repeated, doubtfully.

"He's heard so much about you, he feels like he knows you."

"You've told him about me?"

"He knows you're the lady who saved Grandpa's life." Frank smiled crookedly. "But he doesn't know how, of course."

In Frank and Halfdan's apartment, I froze at the sight of Frank's axe, which hung on the wall like a brutal decoration. Before I could back out, Halfdan came running and clung to my leg.

"Will you tuck me in, Anna? Please?" he begged. The cartoon bear on the front of his pajama top bounced as he jumped excitedly.

In the bedroom, I stared at the book Halfdan handed me. Uncertainly, I began to read as the boy snuggled up to me.

When Halfdan fell asleep with his little hand clutching mine, a lump formed in my throat. I eased a stuffed animal into his grasp and looked down at the red-cheeked boy.

Back in the living room, Frank was sitting on the sofa. He looked at me expectantly.

"Can I still live here?"

He cocked his head and scratched a sideburn. "Do you want to?"

"Yes," I said without hesitation. "I might move in the winter, but for now I'd like to stay."

"Why would you move in the winter?"

I declined to answer.

"If you're staying for now, I'm happy," Frank whispered quietly. "That way I can look after you."

CHAPTER 42

"Can you remember anything?" I asked as Monster and I took a rest in Kraghede Forest on one of our long runs. "From when you were dead?"

Monster had lain down on the forest floor, and I was leaning up against a tree. The smells of the forest reminded me of the ones in Barre, the grove outside of Ísafold. I sighed as my hand ran across the nubby trunk. It was clearly my lot in life to belong to everywhere, yet at the same time not really belong to any place at all.

Monster made a doglike hacking sound.

"It was like only a single second passed, but also an eon. I stood on the edge of eternity, about to fall in." His large nostrils flared. "There was someone who spoke to me. Held on to me. A forefather or foremother."

"Hmm." I dug my sneaker into the moss and disturbed a colony of ants marching in a straight line, carrying a leaf many times their size. "What are you going to do now?" I asked cautiously, even though I didn't want to hear the answer.

"I have to go back to my kin as soon as I'm fit to travel," Monster said. "There are plenty of people to protect you here."

I looked at his side, where a large scar branched out. He would always be marked by what had happened.

"It's not just about my protection. You have to be safe, too," I said, and I forced my eyes away from the scar.

"My family," he said. "Rokkin. And Boda."

We set off again and ran back toward Ben and Rebecca's house. He was right. Of course he was right.

When he left again, I had to exert every ounce of strength in my body to even say goodbye.

"Until we meet again, Anna," Monster whispered as I cried silently into his neck.

I clutched him and buried my face deeper into his fur.

"Stay," I whispered desperately. "It's so dangerous for you to be in Hrafnheim."

"It's dangerous for my family, too. I have to be there for them."

I pulled my head back and gave him a wounded look.

"You're my family, too," he assured me. "That's how I see you. But there are many people here who also see themselves as your kin."

I realized that I had gotten the family I'd never had. An incredibly mysterious and strange family, but there were people who loved me.

So I let him go.

He lumbered down toward Ostergaard as I stood on the field and watched him with my arms folded around myself.

After a couple of weeks, I had read up on all the schoolwork I'd missed, as I refused to let Ben update me magically, even though he insisted it would only take a minute. I didn't want any more of his magic in my system.

Every time I thought about the fact that Ragnara was on her way, I got short of breath. She might arrive at any moment, but I couldn't figure out how I was supposed to kill her when she was still immortal.

I would have to resort to drastic measures.

The country road was deserted, and the fields dark brown after having been plowed. It was the middle of September, and the darkness and cold had begun to creep in. A single car passed me, but aside from that, I didn't see a single person as I biked down the road against a stiff headwind. Elias's house appeared in the middle of a little grove of trees in Store Vildmose, halfway between Ravensted and Jagd.

He met me out front, his unruly curls matted by the wind. I hadn't seen him since Sverresborg. For a second, he seemed to want to reach out, but then he clenched his fists and kept his arms at his sides. His blue-gray eyes swept over me.

"I had heard you survived, but it's still a relief to see it for myself."

I made a *brrr* noise from the cold. "Fate evidently has other plans for me."

"What are you doing here?" he asked after some time had passed with neither of us speaking.

"I don't have anywhere else to go." I looked toward the sky, which had taken on a dark blue tone.

"You're always welcome with Od." Elias straightened his posture. "You know that."

"I'd prefer to be around someone who's a hundred percent human." I kicked at the gravel.

"Are you sure you've come to the right place?" Elias peered at something far away in the twilight.

"Can I stay here or not?" I threw up my arms.

"Why do you want to be around me?" There wasn't so much as a hint of flirtation in Elias's voice. No teasing undertone. Just the question.

"With you I at least *know* you're not to be trusted." This came out sounding more desperate than I'd wanted.

He looked at me for a moment without blinking. Then he smiled softly and did one of his old-fashioned little bows. "I won't disappoint you." He pointed toward the round building in the yard. "Let's go in there."

We went in as dusk fell. The wind rustled through the trees in a way that probably would have made some people uneasy. For me, it instilled a deep sense of calm and the assurance that the weather is completely unconcerned with us little people.

"What was it you called this place?" I followed him up the spiral staircase.

"My observatory? Stjerneborg." Elias's flat hand followed the wood-paneled, snail-shell-shaped wall.

The upper floor was one big room, and one entire side consisted of a large window with a telescope aimed at the sky, which was now almost black.

"What do you do up here?" I looked around the sparsely furnished room. There were only a mattress on the floor and a little stool next to the telescope.

"I look away from this world." Elias stood with his back to me in front of the gigantic glass surface. He stuck his hands in his pockets and raised his face toward the starry sky.

To me, it just looked like a piece of black fabric with tiny holes in it.

"There isn't really anything out there, is there?" I asked cautiously. When he turned, I added: "I mean, I know there's something out there. Planets and stuff. But why do you look at them?"

"I study the celestial bodies."

"Why?"

"Their age makes me feel young."

"I guess you probably don't get that feeling often."

For a moment, silence hung between us. The wind made a branch knock against the outer wall, and the scent of oiled wood perfumed the air.

"No." His soft mouth turned up. "It doesn't happen very often. Come. Can I show you something?" He held his hand out.

I hesitated but took it. His hand was warm, and the fingertips and palm were rough. Elias pulled me up to the telescope and adjusted the apparatus.

"Look." He pointed to the telescope.

I leaned over and looked into its end. "What am I looking for?"

Elias leaned over me and twisted the lens. The heat of his body hit me, and I inhaled his sweet, slightly spicy scent. I concentrated on looking.

"Holy crap. What is that?" I exclaimed and took a step back, nearly bumping into him. Then I went forward again and stared intently into the telescope.

"A supernova."

"Which is what?" I sat down on the stool and studied the view in the little lens again.

"A dying star."

"Why are you showing it to me?"

"It's both an ending and a beginning. What is created in its death becomes other stars and planets. The building blocks of everything and everyone in the universe originate there." He carefully lifted a lock of my red hair. "We come from star stuff, you and I."

I moved my eye from the telescope, but I kept my face pointed toward the universe. I didn't push his hand away, but after a while, he dropped it.

"We're eternal. Or rather, what we're made of is eternal."

"What do you mean?"

"In time, everything gets remade into something different," he said. "The saying 'From earth hast thou come, to earth shalt thou return, and from earth shalt thou rise again,' isn't exclusively religious. And it covers much more than just the human body."

"Where are you going with this?"

Again, he moved a little bit closer.

"Two people's energy can also create something bigger. Something better than when they're alone or with other people." He stood completely still. Expectant.

"You do know you were my first kiss, right?" I had no idea what made me say that.

For a split second, Elias's eyes widened, but he quickly composed himself.

"I'm honored to have been the first person to kiss your lovely mouth." He brushed his fingertips across his lips, then laid his hand across his heart. "But right now, Anna, I'm more interested in finding out if I'll be the next."

I leaned back slightly. "If we're going to be friends, you've got to drop that bullshit."

He looked innocently at me. "I'm extremely serious."

"No, you're not. I can *feel* it when you're putting on an act. I'm not falling for it."

His lips gathered in a typical Elias smile. "You're so demanding."

"You're the one who invited me in." I reached out and stroked his temple. His curls tickled my hand.

The smile disappeared and was replaced by a deep sadness. "I barely know who I am anymore."

"Then it's a good thing I know who you are." My hand cupped his cheek.

He brought his own hand up to mine and squeezed it.

"I'd like to sleep over. Up here, if you don't mind," I said.

He let go of my hand and took a step back. "In that case, I'll leave you alone."

"Stay here with me."

We lay on the mattress. Elias was behind me with a hand around my waist, while I looked out the window at the starry sky. It felt both chaste and highly intimate to lie fully clothed with him, without doing anything but being close to one another.

"We tried to kill Ragnara," I whispered as though admitting a major failure. "But we couldn't."

"What held you back? Humanity? Sympathy?"

"Oh." I shook my head. "My fingalk pierced her with his claws, and I stabbed her in the chest with an Ulfberht sword."

Elias gasped. "You did what now? Where did you get the sword?"

"I actually don't know what an Ulfberht sword is," I mused.

"They're from Midgard. The blacksmith puts part of their soul into the sword, so they're extremely precious," Elias said.

"Rorik—who, by the way, is Ragnara's son—has one, and it's bloodthirsty as hell."

"I did learn Rorik's true identity later on," Elias said quietly. "I would have told you if I'd known. For free."

I shrugged and returned to the subject of Ragnara. "But there wasn't a scratch on her. She's immortal. So we *couldn't*."

My voice must have given something away, as Elias stroked my back. "What happened with your fingalk?"

"Finn?" I cleared my throat. "Eskild killed him."

Everyone else had seen Finn as a pest. Everyone but me and Rorik. But Elias squeezed my arm. "I'm sorry to hear that."

For a moment, I couldn't say anything, but I shook it off.

"Immortal," I repeated. The word echoed in the room.

Elias's voice was soft. "It must be because of the blood."

"The gods' blood? Baldr's blood?"

"It *must* be," Elias mumbled behind me, but I wasn't sure he was talking to me. "Even though Od cut her off from the blood, she must still have some somewhere."

"I saw for myself how close she is to becoming a goddess, and how badly she thirsts for it." I debated with myself over how much I should tell him. "Ragnara is coming here," I said quickly. "Serén has seen it, and it will bring death."

Elias inhaled sharply but didn't comment.

"Serén said I had to be ready to meet Ragnara."

"Ready?"

"She'll become mortal if we find the rest of the gods' blood."

"I've searched exhaustively," Elias said.

"*You* have?"

"If I'm to have any hope of being able to reverse death, I'll also need to use gods' blood, but it's not in Hrafnheim, nor is it here in Midgard."

"Ragnara is enemies with the gods and the giants, so it can't be in their worlds," I said.

"She has no connection to the elves. Otherwise, they would have turned you in when you were in that elf mound," Elias continued.

I shivered when he said *elf mound*.

Again, we said nothing for a while. I changed the subject.

"I don't understand why you're so fascinated by outer space. It's not like you can really use it for anything. I mean, with regard to your other projects." My finger traced a line in the weave of the blanket.

"The stars remind me of how small both we and the gods are. How insignificant we all are when it comes down to it."

I turned and snuggled up a little closer to him.

He tightened his grip around my body. "Both science and religion have creation stories. Of how everything started," he whispered.

I exhaled slowly.

"I know the Norse creation myth. Odin and his brothers created the world from a giant. His brain became clouds, his blood the seas and rivers, and his bones mountains." I made a *tsk* noise. "It's totally unrealistic that the whole world could come from just one giant."

Elias laughed. "Is it more realistic for the whole universe to originate from something the size of a pinhead?"

"No, I guess not," I mused.

I turned onto my back, and he propped himself up on one elbow above me.

"You're talking about the cosmos, right?" I asked.

"I suppose I am."

"How paradoxical."

His free fingers ran along the top of the scar on my chest. The part that peeked over the edge of my shirt.

"Why is it paradoxical?" he asked absently. His fingertip drew circles on my skin.

"Everyone else says chaos is coming." I moved his hand, as I couldn't bear him touching me on the scar that Rorik—no, Sverre, damn it—had made.

"Everyone else?" Elias's fingers stopped briefly but then continued along my collarbone.

"Svidur talks about chaos. Serén also says it's on its way. Bork talked about it, and Gytha mentioned Fimbulwinter."

Elias stopped. "You met Gytha? She's fantastic."

"Yeah. Ragnara almost killed her."

"All things pass away."

"Yes. Even the gods. Maybe it's impossible to fight against impermanence. Even Lough, the Celtic god, disappeared when no one believed in him anymore. And he used to have thousands of worshippers. Od said so himself."

Elias spoke as though he had forgotten I was there.

"Lough." He laughed. "Have you heard the theory that Loki was originally the god Lough, who saved himself from oblivion by becoming a giant in a completely different religion? So maybe Lough didn't disappear after all. Maybe he just let himself be transformed into something else."

"We found a cave during our travels. The one where Loki was bound." I yawned.

Elias was suddenly alert. "What was inside?"

I shivered with my eyes closed.

"He was gone. But his wife's body was there. Rorik . . ." I stopped and let the sharp twinge of pain pass.

If Elias noticed my strange expression, he pretended not to and waited silently until I was ready to carry on.

"Rorik," I continued, "said that during Ragnarök, Loki will lead the forces of chaos."

Elias contemplated this. "Loki is the father of Fenrir, the

Midgard Serpent, and Hel. Ægir, who brews the mead of life from Baldr's blood, is his brother."

I breathed in slowly and yawned again.

"Well, he's got the right connections." Exhaustion was coming on fast, but there was something that bothered me. "Od said Ragnara can't get more of the blood from Ægir," I mumbled and closed my eyes. "So there really aren't many worlds left where her remaining stash of blood could be."

The mattress shifted, but I kept my eyes squeezed shut.

"That's enough about gods and worlds for now," Elias whispered. His face was right above mine.

I reached up and caressed the nape of his neck.

"Is there someone else?" he asked hoarsely.

I saw a glimpse of Varnar, who had chosen a greater cause over me, and who had rejected me because of Sverre. And Rorik, who healed my inner wounds, but in reality, Rorik didn't exist.

"There's no one." I tried to sound resolute. "And I'm tired of love magic controlling what I do."

Elias brought his lips to my neck and kissed it. It was completely different from the way he had touched me in Sverresborg. This was cautious, and he moved so slowly I nearly begged him to go faster. My breathing grew heavy.

First, I let him kiss my neck without doing anything myself, but then I ran my fingers over his shoulder blades under his shirt. His weight on top of me was not unpleasant, and his scent enveloped me. Elias's hands found my shoulders and caressed them.

I relaxed completely and allowed myself to be in the present. For once, I had control over the situation, and Elias let me decide exactly how far we would go and at what pace. I wasn't thinking about the past or the future or what I had to do. Everything I hadn't achieved, all the impossible tasks that awaited me, all the horrible things that had happened.

And just then, it clicked into place in my head.

533

CHAPTER 43

I pushed Elias away and gasped as though I were drowning. Then I sat up and pressed my hands to my face as if to hold on to my thoughts.

"I thought that was what you wanted," Elias said from behind me.

"Shh." I squeezed my temples harder.

No, that couldn't be right.

Elias laid a warm hand on my back. "Anna. It's different with you. It's not like with the other girls. You are—"

"Just shut up," I hissed.

"Is it because of what I did in Sverresborg? I told you, I didn't have a choice. It was awful."

I pushed his hands away. "Help me figure this out."

Finally, he moved to sit in front of me and focused on me. "Figure what out?"

"Lough—Loki. They're the same."

Elias let go with a resigned expression. "It's just a theory."

"Loki has escaped, which signals Ragnarök." I held up a finger. "I'm pretty sure it was Ragnara who set him free. I saw it when I was in the cave where he'd been bound." I scratched my forehead. "Ragnara wants to be a goddess . . ."

Elias inhaled sharply, about to say something, but I cut him off.

"If Ragnara is now in control of Loki, and his brother Ægir has Baldr's blood, then that's where she's getting it from. Loki is the leader of the forces of chaos. They're his children. The Midgard Serpent." I trembled. "I've seen it. It let go of its tail. The line of Fenrir," I nearly choked, "Monster's kin. They're also becoming more powerful. That was what Serén meant when she told Monster that an alliance between us and the giant wolves was the only way to avoid chaos." I contemplated further. "So then all that's left is Loki's daughter."

Elias concluded my train of thought: "You've figured out where Ragnara's remaining gods' blood is."

"It must be with Loki's daughter in Helheim, but why would she go along with it?"

"Maybe Loki promised her a better position on the other side of Ragnarök." Elias clawed at his curls, which became even more unruly. "But—"

I jumped up from the mattress. "How do you get to Helheim?"

Elias laid his hand on my arm. "If you're not a god, there's only one way to get there."

"How?" I asked eagerly and reached for my mom's coat, which I had tossed on the floor. "I have to go right away."

Elias placed both hands on my shoulders and tilted his head so he could look me directly in the eyes. "You can only get there by dying, Anna."

"Oh." I furrowed my brows. "But then how will we get down there?"

Elias kept his hands on my shoulders.

"We can't go down there. It's impossible." A sly look glimmered across his blue-gray eyes. "But we may know someone who can."

"Arthur," I called. "Arthuuur."

My father appeared out of thin air. Suddenly he was just there in Elias's yard.

He grabbed on to me and shook me. Even though he wasn't as

535

strong as a living person, the combination of his anger and his poltergeist abilities caused me to sway back and forth.

"What in the worlds are you doing here?" he shouted. Arthur looked around at Elias's yard, furious.

"What's he saying?" Elias asked.

Arthur shifted his gaze. "What are you doing with him?" He took a step toward the unaware Elias.

I objected before my ghost dad could attack him.

"Elias is helping me figure something out." I skipped over the fact that, five minutes earlier, I had let him kiss my neck.

"Elias is not to be trusted!" Arthur shouted. "He is a despicable, unreliable, egotistical, amoral piece of shit who never does anything for anyone's sake but his own."

"But he got your body out of Odinmont." My voice trailed off as Arthur's seething green eyes looked straight into mine.

"What's he saying?" Elias tried again.

"Um."

"You can tell him what I said!" Arthur put his hands on his hips.

"Later." I cleared my throat. "Listen." I updated my father's ghost on the theory of Loki's alliance with Ragnara and the gods' blood in Helheim. "If we can get ahold of the gods' blood, then Ragnara will become mortal. And then we can . . ." I left that statement incomplete.

Arthur nodded in comprehension. "Is there a way we can find out if that theory holds up?"

Now Elias interjected, and as usual, he replied as if he had actually heard Arthur's question. "We can look for the blood in Helheim."

"We . . ." Arthur's green eyes flickered.

"*You*, specifically," I said.

Arthur thought a little, but then it seemed he had made his decision. "I'll go."

I looked at him. "If it's dangerous, then you shouldn't."

He winked. "I'm already dead. Nothing can kill me."

He lied. Gods, how he lied.

Elias drove me home.

"I knew it was too good to be true," he said with his eyes aimed at the road. When the car's headlights hit the reflectors along the side of the road, they flared.

I was deep in thought, so I didn't respond.

"Should I just forget about it? I can just file it away as a beautiful but highly improbable dream." His voice was both teasing and disappointed.

I raised one corner of my mouth. "It was stupid. I thought I could suppress thoughts of Varnar and Rorik." I cursed quietly. "Sverre. I can't get used to calling him that. But I'm sorry I used you."

Elias chuckled. "You can use me for your suppression needs any time." In the light from the dashboard, I saw his face grow serious again. "Sverre. You got close to the prince."

"A little too close."

Elias was polite enough not to comment. "Which side is he on now?"

"I have no idea, and I don't care, either."

"Yes, you do. You're hurt, but you've gotten close to both the commander of the resistance movement and the prince of the regime. Do you realize what position that puts you in?"

"Eww!" I gave him an angry look.

Elias tapped his palms on the steering wheel. "I'm just pointing out the obvious."

"Well, not everyone thinks so cynically. And why am I even discussing my love life with you?"

Elias's face was hidden by curls and darkness. "Because I'm more cynical than most."

I sighed and leaned my head back against the soft upholstery. Everyday things like seats, beds, duvets, and pillows still seemed like the height of luxury.

"Are you coming this year?"

Elias's question jerked me back to the here and now. "Where?"

"To the equinox ball. It's next weekend."

"I had forgotten all about that. Am I even invited?"

"The invitation was sent to your address at Frank's."

"This year I'm not required to participate, so I'll pass."

"It could be advantageous."

I sat up a little straighter in my seat. "Why?"

"If Arthur goes to Helheim that night, when everyone else is at the party, then they'll be busy celebrating the equinox, and we can be there when he comes back."

"There? Where is *there*?"

Elias sighed. "Just when I think you're in on all the secrets."

"Just tell me."

Frank's, which at this time of night was closed down, came into view at the end of Bredgade. There was a light on in the apartment above.

"The entrance to Helheim is in Od's office, along with the other portals to the various worlds. The one leading to Helheim is in a hatch in the floor, under the big cowhide."

"Does it have to happen at The Boatman? Can't Arthur just go there?"

We were quiet now, and I saw a silhouette in the illuminated window. Frank was looking down at us.

Elias also looked up, but then focused on me again. "He can, but he has to come back through a portal if he's going to bring a physical object with him. And gods' blood is physical."

"And The Boatman is the only place with a portal?"

"As far as I know."

538

"Luna?" My voice was light and gentle.

We sat on the red sofa in The Island during the break between Danish and history.

Luna turned her head. She didn't even realize I was trying to convince her of something.

"What is it?"

On Luna's other side, Mathias leaned forward slightly and cocked his golden head. "What are you buttering us up for?"

"Drop it, Mathias," I snapped.

"You're gonna ask us to do something, aren't you?" Mathias asked with mock seriousness.

I looked away from their interlaced fingers. "Are you going to the equinox ball?"

Mathias's eyebrows flew up. "Of course. Are you? You don't usually like that kind of thing."

"Sure I do," I lied. "I totally want to go."

"Seriously?" Luna's forehead wrinkled.

"Yes, seriously. But I don't have anything to wear. The dresses you sew for me have a way of getting ruined. The only one that's somewhat intact is the one you made for my birthday last year, and I don't feel great about wearing it. It reminds me of . . . what happened. Frank's attempted murder."

"What happened to the green silk one I made you for New Year's Eve?"

I busied myself by looking out the large panoramic window. Outside, it was gray and misty. Large raindrops clung to the foggy glass.

"I gave it away." I composed myself as the image of Faida hanging from the tree in the green dress faded. Sometimes it wasn't that great to be so connected to the past. "You don't have to make a whole new one for me. Don't you have one I can just borrow? And Mathias, could you do my makeup?"

Luna beamed. "I just made a lavender jumpsuit."

I looked desperately at Mathias.

He was completely serious. "I can paint your nails to match. Your eyeshadow should be light purple, too."

As I searched for a diplomatic way to say I would rather die than wear a purple outfit, they burst out laughing.

"I'm just kidding." Luna wiped her eyes. "I'll sew you a new dress."

"And I'll make sure you're made up like the queen of the night," Mathias added.

"Who are you taking?" Luna asked as we headed toward the history classroom down Brown Hall.

"Taking?"

"As your plus one. Or are you going with Od again?"

I shuddered. "No. Do I have to bring a date?"

Mathias leaned forward. "It doesn't need to be romantic. Just a friend." He hurried to pull Luna close. "Not one of us. We're going together."

"Hmm. Actually, I have an idea of who I can ask."

"They'll kill me."

"No one is going to kill you, Frank." I folded a dish towel and tossed it in the basket on the coffee table.

"Od Dinesen and Niels Villadsen wanted to hand me over to Ragnara, last I saw them."

"That's why it sends a message if you go with me. I'm starting to understand the political game, and I'm trying to play it. I've been someone else's pawn for too long."

Frank crossed his arms, and the anchor on his biceps peeked out beneath his T-shirt's sleeve. "What game are you talking about?"

"Last year, I went with Od. In doing so, he showed that he would protect me. If I bring you, I'll be doing the same." I picked up another towel and folded it. It was still warm from the dryer, and the static electricity crackled in my hands.

Frank looked at me. "You don't think they'll throw themselves at me and kill me and arrest me?"

I raised an eyebrow. "In that order?"

"I have Halfdan to think about. If something happens to me, he'll have no one. The only reason I can walk free here is that the bar is enchanted. I'm in bad standing with Ragnara now that I've acted directly against the regime, and here at home, I've committed murder." His voice broke on the last word.

This made me grow serious. "They won't do anything to you. If they mess with you, they mess with me. Niels won't hurt anyone under my protection."

Frank smoothed a calloused hand over his silver-gray hair with a twinkle in his eye. "Under your protection."

I tossed down a rag. "Are you coming or not?"

He laughed. "Of course I'm coming. I've always wanted to go to that ball."

It felt like an unfortunate rerun as I sat on a chair with wet nails and the ecstatic Luna and Mathias talking and laughing over me.

Mathias was working on my hair, and Luna smoothed my dress, which she had sewn with impressive speed. It was blue, a shade so deep it was almost black, with red beads that matched my hair color exactly.

I let out an *ow* when Mathias tightened my ponytail, which practically gave me a facelift. He pulled more, and my head wobbled from side to side. Then he started to tease it.

My palm brushed against Hakim's khamsa.

"It goes with your nails," Mathias said.

"What?"

". . . and the bag."

I looked down at my shining metallic fingertips. My hand rested on a little bag of the same color.

Luna took a step back. "What a hairdo."

"What?" I said, frightened, but I couldn't touch it for fear of getting nail polish in my hair.

"I can't help it." Mathias released me and came around to the other side. "Anna's hair is so nice. And it's getting really long. A wide braid goes well with the rest of the outfit."

He wore a suit and, of course, looked like he'd just stepped off the runway. Luna's dress was copper-colored, and her hair was back to its natural brown color.

"Mathias, can you boost me?" I asked. "There are going to be a ton of people there tonight, and I can't shield against all of them."

I didn't dare take klinte, in case I needed to use my powers. How strange, to see my clairvoyance as a plus.

"Of course." Mathias wrapped his arms around me and pulled me close, as his divinity seeped into me. It felt different from Od's—fresher, and it smelled a little like grass, but afterward I was just as strong as when Od had filled me up.

I carefully ran my fingertip over a nail and determined that the polish was dry.

"Are we ready?" I asked. The party hadn't even started yet, and I was already exhausted.

There was a knock at the door of my apartment, and when it swung open, Frank stood outside. He was also wearing a suit, with a long coat over it, and he looked like a movie star from the fifties.

"Are you ready?" Though Frank tried to hide it, I saw that he had a worried shadow over his face.

"Did you say goodbye to Halfdan?" I asked, grabbing my silver bag.

"Three times." Frank smiled. "He's having fun with Mina."

I nodded resolutely. "Then let's do this."

We drove up there in Frank's pickup truck. Luna and Mathias sat in the back in a tangled heap, and I sat next to Frank, who maneuvered the truck down the dark country road. We were driving right behind a car bearing the royal family's crest, but that was the

542

only reminder that we were heading to a fancy ball. Everything else was trees, naked fields, windmills, and the whisper of the wind.

In the parking lot in front of The Boatman, I was struck by how the bar called to mind Hrafnheimish architecture. It wasn't old-fashioned—quite the opposite—but it radiated history. Od must have hired people from the parallel world as consultants.

Unlike last year, when I was brought in through the back entrance with no idea of what I was walking into, we walked in the front door. Frank opened the door with a forceful grip on the doorknob, which was shaped like the head of a wild boar. Veronika— the small, black-haired, elfin bartender—met us and, with a brusque exclamation, held out a flat hand.

I started fumbling for my wallet, thinking she wanted money, but Luna gave her her invitation. Awkwardly, I pulled mine out and pointed at Frank.

"He's with me."

Veronika gave him a surly glare.

"Murderer." Her voice sounded like that of a man who had been on a week-long bender.

We looked at her with alarm until we realized this was a formal greeting. Not an accusation.

I leaned toward her. "And thank you, by the way. Od told me what you did."

She pushed me so hard it left a bruise on my shoulder.

"You're welcome!" she hissed, and I stumbled into The Boatman.

There were sheaves of grain hanging from the ceiling, alongside apples with ribbons tied around them and round loaves of bread in glistening fishnets. The walls were draped with tapestries, with patterns I recognized from Sént. The tables were piled with food, and the glasses of mead were matte and decorated with reddish-brown wires. I had seen glasses exactly like them in the elf mound. Shaking my head, I smiled. The other worlds were so present at the equinox ball, it was a wonder I hadn't noticed it last year.

This year, the staff were buff men whose uniforms didn't conceal much of their muscular, fake-tanned bodies.

"They're here in your honor."

I didn't have to turn around to know it was Elias standing behind me. "Who's here in my honor?"

He breathed in my ear, and I turned around. Then he gestured toward a particularly fit guy with stick-straight, plucked eyebrows and an almost orange complexion. "You do enjoy a wide range of male company."

He looked toward Hakim, who had just walked in with Niels Villadsen. Hakim immediately looked at me, and I gave a small nod in response.

I tilted my head back toward Elias. "Do you feel overlooked?"

A cheeky smile crossed his lips. "Quite the opposite."

He winked at a girl standing at the bar. She blushed and smiled back.

I rolled my eyes. "So it's fine for *you* to have a harem, but if *I* . . ."

Luna and Mathias came over to us.

I swallowed my final words as Elias bowed formally at them.

Neither of them returned his greeting. They just stared at him.

I had told them that Elias saved me from being assaulted at Sverresborg, but they insisted I couldn't trust him.

I had to agree with them.

Frank appeared behind me, and Elias's eyes shone. "The evening's pièce de résistance. Interesting choice of date, Anna."

"It's a statement," I said, my lips tight.

"And a strong one. But right now, I need to speak with you in Od's office."

We took a few steps. Luna, Mathias, and Frank followed us.

Elias stopped and looked over his shoulder with an expression of astonishment. Then he sighed and scratched his forehead. "Fine, come on, everyone."

As discreetly as possible, we slipped into Od's office, which luckily was empty and free of any cages. Frank looked to the corner where he had been detained.

I laid a hand on his arm. "They won't imprison you again."

"I deserved it. It's just Halfdan—"

"I'll make sure it doesn't happen." I don't know where my confidence came from.

Elias clapped to get our attention. "Anna. You're going to call Arthur and send him to Helheim."

"I knew it," Luna sputtered. "You had no interest in coming to the party."

I made a face. "No. I lied."

"Why do you always do that?" she complained. "You know you can tell us things."

I didn't respond.

"If the blood is in Hel's hall, then by my calculations, Arthur should get back while Od is giving his speech. We can wait for him in here. At that time, everyone will be pretty . . ." He smiled deviously. "Distracted."

"You mean hypnotized?" My voice was dry.

"Yes," Elias said without so much as a smile.

Luna's mouth hung open. "That's what he did last year. I felt totally high afterward."

"Why do you think we even throw these parties?" Elias turned his head. "But that's irrelevant now. Anna, Are you ready?"

I stepped away from the others.

"Arthur," I said. "Dad," I whispered afterward.

Arthur immediately came through the wall. He simply materialized out of nothing. He grabbed my shoulders and held me away from him to get a look at me.

"That dress. That hair." There was light reflected in his green eyes. "You're a grown woman. So strong." He wanted to say more but stopped himself.

"Are you sure you want to do this?"

His red brows came together. "Of course." He shifted his gaze to Mathias, who greeted him with a wave. Everyone else saw only empty space.

"Okay. Go on. I'll be here when you get back." I pointed at the large cowhide on the floor. "It shouldn't take more than an hour. I don't understand how you can find the gods' blood in such a short time."

"Time works differently down there," Elias said behind me. "Arthur will experience it as a day or longer. You of all people should know that time passes differently depending on the world you're in."

Panic rushed through me. "Should we drop this whole idea? There must be another way."

Arthur pulled me close. "There isn't. I'm doing this for you, your sister, and your mother."

His body felt alive and real against mine. My breathing was unsteady. "And for everyone else in Midgard and Hrafnheim."

"To be honest, you're the only ones who mean anything to me."

And then he was gone, and I was holding empty air. Slowly, I let my arms fall to my sides.

"Now all we can do is wait."

At the party, we all tried to act like nothing was up, which was not at all successful.

I kept checking my phone to keep an eye on the time, Mathias kept looking down the mirrored hall to Od's office, and Luna jumped every time there was a loud noise, which was often. Frank stood up straight when people looked at him, unsure which attendees were aware of his murderer status. At one point, Niels Villadsen brushed past him and whispered something in his ear that caused him to stiffen.

Od suddenly stood right in front of us. He smiled mildly, and I didn't have the chance to put my defenses up. I could therefore do nothing but stare at him. The others seemed to be in the same boat, aside from Mathias, who could resist him with his own divinity. He reached his hand out to Od.

Od took it, then turned his head slightly toward me. "Anna. Let me tell you again how unbelievably glad I am to see you back home."

"Oh, right," I said. "Did I ever remember to thank you for your help with the elf mound?"

Od looked quickly at the others, but they only looked back dazedly.

"That didn't happen," he told them, and his eyes gave a silvery little wink.

Only Mathias noticed it, but he didn't say anything.

He turned back to me. "You left pretty abruptly on New Year's Eve."

The room spun. "I'm sorry I took advantage of your hospitality that night."

Od's head tilted a bit more. "And that you let my prisoner go." He looked at Frank.

This shook me out of the mindless stupor, and I stepped in front of Frank. "You dare to . . ."

For a millisecond, surprise flew across Od's face. Then he bowed his head.

Without noticing it, my arms had spread out between Frank and Od.

Od's strong hands grasped my arms and pulled them forward, so I once again stood normally. "I support your choice." He looked to Niels Villadsen, who stood nearby with the Earl and Hakim. "So does the DSMA." He bowed at them almost imperceptibly. "Please forgive me."

He vanished into the crowd, and someone called out to him.

I exhaled tentatively as Frank's tense aura pounded on my back.

"I simply don't understand why you go against demigods, government agencies, and despots for my sake. I killed innocent people."

I breathed raggedly, and a bead of sweat rolled down my spine under the dark blue silk of the dress. "I think a lot of the attendees have, actually."

I was no exception. There was no guarantee that the soldiers in Hrafnheim had even asked to join the army.

Elias's eyes met mine from across the room, but I looked away.

"You're here again this year." The voice was right by my ear.

I turned around.

Bubbly laughter flowed over me. The first lady and internationally famous actress slash mind-reading witch laid a hand with red painted nails on my shoulder. I had met her and her husband at last year's ball.

"It's nice to see you so . . . alive. Your trip was extremely dangerous."

"Stay out of my head!"

The laughter rang out again. "Can you stop seeing your visions?"

"You shouldn't read my thoughts."

She shrugged in her wildly expensive designer dress.

"I'll try to stay out," she said. "There's just so much exciting stuff that goes on in there, with your father in the realm of the dead and your secret trip to Hrafnheim and all that." Her fingernails brushed my temple as she said the forbidden name.

My fists clenched. She pulled her hand back and ran the back of it along her jaw in a diva-like motion.

"I'll keep your secrets. That's a promise." When she said *promise*, her aura bubbled.

"Is your husband here this year?"

She raised a glass and handed me one, too. She clinked them against each other. "He's busy leading the country. You know, elections and wealth distribution policies, international crises, a whole bunch of other boring things."

"Is he aware of the doomsday threat and a parallel world on the brink of civil war?"

Her lipstick-painted lips closed around the edge of her glass, and she took a little sip of the bubbly, golden liquid. She looked at the imprint her lips had left on the crystal. "Yes, of course. Being prime minister is a busy job."

I inhaled. "And you came without him."

"He has always been my companion. And before that, hundreds of years ago, others were my companions. Look out for yourself, seer. There are many who wish you ill." And then she was gone.

"You look beautiful tonight."

I jumped, startled. It was Hakim, standing next to me. It was strange to see him in a suit, but I had to admit, it looked good on him. For once, he had managed to tame his dark hair somewhat.

"You, too," I blurted, and my cheeks prickled with heat. "I mean . . . you look . . ."

I quickly took a gulp of my bubbles.

He looked at me. "What are you plotting?"

"What makes you think I'm plotting something?"

He gave a low chuckle. "They're freaking out about your trip over at the DSMA. They've spent years trying not to disturb the peace between Midgard and Freiheim, and then you come along and wreak havoc."

"Why are you telling me this? Aren't you high up at the DSMA?"

His dark green eyes met mine. "I know where my loyalty lies."

"With the Danish government?" I made a face, but I don't know why.

"Anna . . ."

"I feel like I'm talking to a spy," I said. "Are you feeding me information?"

Hakim looked toward the stage, where a band played. His head bobbed almost imperceptibly in time with the music.

"I think I'm warning you, but I'm not completely sure of what. Maybe someone in the DSMA is helping Ragnara. Someone who will go to great lengths to preserve the peace. You're . . ." He searched for the words, ". . . an obstacle, in that regard."

I nearly threw up my arms. "Are you saying the DSMA is after me, too?"

"No!" His reply was immediate. "The DSMA is not after you. But I've heard chatter in the halls that you're destroying the peace. I can't convince them that you're actually trying to protect it."

"Protect the peace." I saw a glimpse of Faida being impaled, and Tíw, whose stump protruded from the torn sleeve of his shirt. "There is no peace to protect, Hakim. None whatsoever. And I'm afraid that the unrest will come here, too. My sister has seen it: Ragnara is coming."

He breathed heavily, and, as always, I could read him clearly; I caught a vision. It was an asphalt road, speckled with gasoline or water. I heard sharp sounds—*plock, plock, plock*—in the distance, and someone was running, breathing heavily. I sensed it was Hakim. Yes, Hakim knew all about unrest.

"Just be careful," he said. "Not everyone likes your way of solving problems."

"Do *you* like it?" I don't know why I was so direct.

This gave him a little jolt, and almost as though he weren't thinking, his hand touched the silver pendant hanging from my neck. The metal pressed into the hollow above my artery, and my pulse pounded in my ears.

"Don't you know that?" he whispered.

I took a small step backward.

Hakim pulled his hand away, turned around, and hurried off.

My eyes followed his back and broad shoulders as he crossed the room. Breathless, I tore my eyes away and looked around.

We had finally reached the moment when Od stepped onstage. The male singer made space for him. My eyes caught Elias's, and he tapped Luna on the shoulder. She pulled Frank and Mathias with her.

We hurried to reach the office before we were swallowed up by Od's mass hypnosis.

I looked over my shoulder.

People were already lost to the world, and they stared, enchanted, at the handsome demigod. I quickly walked away from the stage, singing *la-la-la-la* in my head. It was so quiet, you could have heard a pin drop. But you could have also thrown a bomb without anyone noticing.

"Thank you all for coming," came Od's voice behind us. It carried through the room, even though he didn't have a microphone. "Tonight, we celebrate our ability to meet the coming winter . . ."

Elias carefully shut the door with a *click*.

I paced back and forth, which made my dress rustle. Luna and Frank sat on the leather sofa with their hands balled up in front of them. Mathias kept his blue eyes, which were shining like blowtorches, directed at the floor. Elias knelt and cast the cowhide aside, revealing a hatch in the floor. He undid the latch and took a step back. For a while, nothing happened, but then the ring on the hatch began to shake a little. Then it shook more and more, until finally the floor was vibrating.

Frank spread his hands and clutched the edge of the sofa. Mathias went to Luna and held her. Something started banging on the underside of the hatch. Fists or kicks.

"Arthur?" I called, getting to my knees. "Dad!"

I pulled on the latch, but something held it closed. There was suction or something sticky down there, but I pulled with my full body weight and clawed at the edges, and there was a high-pitched sound like a boiling kettle.

Finally, the hatch flew open with a loud *pop*, and a greenish gel splattered on me, along with a chlorine-like vapor. There was a sound like giant grasshoppers running amok, as well as plaintive voices. I stuck my head into the hole and shouted as loud as I could, but Frank yanked me back.

An eggy, sulfuric smell that I recognized from the Midgard Serpent rose toward me, and a weak *Anna* echoed.

"Dad!" I screamed. "Arthur!"

The air crackled with electricity, and Luna's curls stood up.

"Dad," I called again, hoping the many guests at The Boatman really couldn't hear anything.

Arthur's head rose up slowly, as though he were climbing up the side of a tall mountain. The sight of him made me lose my breath. Sallow, with dark blue blood vessels protruding along his jaw. His eyes were colorless, and his hair was straggly.

I screamed, and Mathias shouted in fear.

Then I pulled myself together and grabbed Arthur's gnarled, white hands to pull him up. Mathias helped me and tugged on Arthur's wrists, while Luna, who of course couldn't see my father— lucky for her—tried to grab him, but only swung her hands through the air. Frank held on to my waist and tried to keep me from falling into Helheim.

Arthur let out a sound, and I realized the insect-like clicks were coming from him.

"Cure," he forced out between clicks. He pulled at us, and I got the feeling he was trying to pull Mathias and me to him, rather than pull himself up. "Blood. Cure."

"What? Cure what?" I didn't understand anything he was saying.

He pulled harder on me.

Now Elias jumped in between us, and even though he couldn't see Arthur, he pried our hands apart.

"Living people can't go that way," he shouted. "You'll be in limbo forever." Elias shoved the invisible Arthur, and he fell back into the hole with a *svoop*. Then Elias slammed the hatch shut with a bang.

Mathias, Frank, and I flew backward and landed in a pile,

smeared with the sulfuric slime. Luna's brown curls stuck out in all directions. I was bleeding from a scratch on my arm, and the red liquid mixed with the filth from below.

"What just happened?" I squeaked as I crawled over and ran my hands over the hatch, as though it could bring my father back.

"He didn't make it," Elias panted. "And now he must stay in Helheim."

I was about to say something, but just then, the door to the office swung open.

Od appeared in the doorway. He studied us, slime-covered and battered on the floor. His beautiful eyes were wide, silvery beams radiated from him, and his breath came out as steam.

"What have you done?" he bellowed. "I just spoke to my wife, and she's furious."

CHAPTER 44

We sat in a row on the sofa with Frank standing behind us. Od stood in front, and I stared down at my feet. My hands were clenched in my lap, and every once in a while, slime dripped from my hair with a big, greasy *splat*.

Od spoke angrily and continuously.

"I didn't know," I interrupted Od's monologue.

Everyone looked at me, and Od was quiet.

"I didn't know he risked getting captured down there."

"Risked." Od's voice was low. Ominously low. "He didn't take a risk. The outcome was certain." When I just stared at him, un-comprehending, he added, "He knew exactly what he was doing."

I was unable to speak.

"When a dead person goes to Hel, he gives himself willingly to her," Od said. "And she doesn't let go easily."

I inhaled. "He sacrificed himself. He thought he would man-age to find the blood and give it to me, but he knew he would be forced to stay down there."

"Do you understand how angry Freyja is?" A silver beam shone from Od's eyes. "She's relinquished her claim to him."

I looked up.

"What does Freyja have to do with any of this?" Even though my lips were moving, it didn't feel like the words were coming from me.

Od's already broad shoulders grew, and he glowed white with agitation. "She had laid claim to his soul, and now it's been sto-len from her."

"Arthur's soul isn't an object you can just own."

"Yes, it is."

"But he has free will."

A cold laugh escaped through Od's teeth, and at that moment, he was truly frightening. "None of us have free will."

"How do we get him back?" Luna's voice was thin. Her curls had calmed down a little, but her dress was ripped, and there were streaks of green slime on her cheeks.

"We can't get him back." Od's voice was so piercing, we all jumped.

The room went completely silent.

Mathias and Luna clutched each other's hands. Frank moved his feet, and Elias stared straight ahead with his teeth bared. I had unconsciously started to stand up, ready to flee.

Hey, wait a second.

I turned my face toward Elias. "You knew."

He closed his eyes as though he feared what came next.

"Of course he did," Od barked. "Whatever you sent Arthur to Helheim for, Elias knew what the consequence would be."

A feeling like cold pinpricks spread through my arms, and I was momentarily stunned. The pricks turned into flames, and, without thinking, I threw myself at Elias and hit him with closed fists. He raised his arms but let me pound on him.

Mathias grabbed me and pulled me back.

"Arthur knew it, too," Elias attempted, but this only made me throw myself on him again.

"You're willing to do whatever it takes to get that blood. You were willing to sacrifice my dad. How many times will you betray Arthur?" I shouted, writhing in Mathias's grasp.

Elias, who now—in addition to green slime and torn clothes—also bore cuts and bruises from my nails and fists, looked calmly at me. "I plan to betray him as many times as necessary."

I panted in Mathias's arms.

"I'll kill you," I said slowly. "For your own sake: get away from me, and stay away."

Elias's expression was impossible to interpret. His blue-gray eyes stared at me. Then he bowed and left through one of the many doors in Od's office.

The corners of my mouth twisted downward, and I couldn't hold back the sobs. Luna embraced me, and Mathias embraced us both.

I sniffled into Luna's shoulder. "I convinced Arthur to go down there, and now he's gone."

"He knew what it meant," Luna said. "It's not your fault."

"But he would do anything to help me," I said. I had gotten control of my breathing, but the realization made me cry again. "Everything's going wrong."

My friends hugged me, but the doubt wouldn't go away. It hammered at my conscience, and every time I thought of another failure, I collapsed a little more. Eventually, I slipped out of Luna and Mathias's embrace and slid to the floor. I didn't register anything, only looked blankly into space. I realized that my gaze had fallen directly on the blue door that was the portal to Hrafnheim.

My friends tried to pull me up, but my body was limp, and before they could get me to my feet, Od laid a hand on Mathias's shoulder.

"Go home," he said gently. "Anna will stay here."

"But . . ." Luna tried again to pull me up.

A whisper from Mathias made Luna let go. Frank mumbled something, and the three of them disappeared through the door. I was alone with Od.

He squatted down in front of me. "Come."

I didn't even have the strength to lift my head. "Where?"

"You're going to see something very few people have seen."

"Yay," I said. I meant it sarcastically, but it came out sounding hollow.

A warm finger was placed under my chin, and Od turned my face up. He stared into my eyes and unleashed his persuasion magic.

I blinked drowsily and stood up. It felt like I was levitating. Without sensing much, I followed him through one of the many doors. It closed behind me, and I studied the room, which seemed to be in a small apartment.

The room wasn't very big, and the walls were full of bookshelves, framed paintings, photographs, and colorful tapestries. One entire wall was a large pane of glass, like in Elias's observatory. But where Elias's window faced the sky, this one looked out over the dark North Sea and the wide sandy beach. Right now, it was almost pitch black out there, and the only thing I could see was the light from the party hitting the sand and small, shining spots floating far out at sea. The waves crashed, and it seemed the glass was embedded in the dune beneath The Boatman.

"Through there," Od pointed to one of the room's other doors, "is a bathroom. There are fresh clothes. Clean yourself up while I go end the ball."

I stared apathetically at his back as he left. Then I stepped carefully into the tiled room.

It looked like something from Sént, with its blue and white tiles decorated with everything from Arabic calligraphy to serpent knots, runes, and griffins. Hot water was already flowing into a large tub, the edge of which was level with the floor. It smelled of sandalwood and lavender.

I slipped out of the dark blue dress, which was ripped and bloody. My hair was a sticky mess, so I pulled out the many bobby pins and ribbons, spoiling what remained of Mathias's work. With a sigh, I glided down into the water and studied the green blotches that came off my skin. On the edge of the tub sat something I hoped was soap, and I lathered it in my hair and tipped my head back.

When I was as clean as I could be, I got out of the water and dried myself with one of the big fluffy towels that sat folded on

557

a wooden table. Just as Od had promised, there were some simple clothes there as well, in beige and dark brown. I threw them on and already felt more like myself, even though I flinched every time I recalled the desperate expression on Arthur's face as he was pulled down to Helheim.

Back in the room, I walked soundlessly across the thick carpet to the shelves and let my fingertips glide over the spines of the books. Some were ancient and frayed, others new and glossy. There were poetry, religious texts, and history. Then I looked at the pictures.

I recognized a painting of Elias's mother, whom I had seen in Od's past nearly a year ago. There were also photographs. One of Arthur, and one of a woman who looked unmistakably like Mina. It must have been her mother, who was also killed by Ragnara in the Windmill Murders many years ago. In fact, there were only pictures of dead people.

Someone stood behind me.

"Will my picture hang here, too, some day?" I asked.

Od didn't respond, and I turned to face him.

His eyes glided over the many faces. "Maybe I'm the one who'll go on your wall."

"What do you mean?"

His gaze shifted to my face, and he smiled kindly.

"Ragnarök is coming soon." His mild facial expression didn't match his words.

"I'm trying to prevent it. But it keeps going wrong." My voice was thin.

His warm hand cupped my cheek. "Maybe it isn't meant to be stopped."

I brushed him away. "I don't think anything is *meant* to happen."

His hoarse laughter flowed around me.

I furrowed my brows. "What are you laughing at?"

"You take everything so seriously."

I glanced at the smiling photo of Arthur on the wall.

"I think this is all pretty serious. For example, I just lost my father." I wanted to say this in a measured, controlled way, but as soon as the words left my lips, they quivered, and it took me a little while to regain my composure.

Od tilted his head. "I understand your pain."

With great effort, I forced the tears to stop. "Then tell me how to get Arthur back."

Od was clearly searching for merciful words, but I held up my palm. "You can't tell me I can't get him back. That's the one thing you're not allowed to say."

Od was silent for a while.

"It's gotten more complicated," he said finally.

I lowered my hand. "How can this have gotten any more complicated?"

"Before, only my wife had a claim on him. Now there are two goddesses, and one of them already has him."

"So Freyja is prepared to go against Hel?" Hope made me stand a little straighter.

"You shouldn't get between those two."

I threw up my arms. "How do you feel about your wife running after dead men?"

Od looked out the large window at the dark North Sea. If it weren't for the pleasant warmth of the small room, I would have felt like I was standing directly on the beach.

"The gods don't look at it that way. Dead or alive. They don't distinguish them."

"That's not what I meant. Don't you get jealous?"

Od's finger traced the end of the shelf, which was carved with a wild boar's head.

"No," he said. "I also love people other than her." He pressed his lips together, as if to say, *and that's all I have to say about that.*

I didn't let him off that easily. "You have a very modern relationship, considering you're over a thousand years old."

His eyes sparkled. "Everything comes around."

I put my hands over my nose and let my fingertips massage the spot between my eyes.

"The only thing I want to know," I said, feigning patience, "is how my father can come back."

Od lowered himself into a soft chair and pointed to another one next to it. I sat down and folded my legs as he poured something golden into two glasses and handed me one. The taste was sweet and warm, and I recognized the drink as the mead of poetry. Intoxication rolled through me after the first mouthful, and I ran my tongue over the edge of the glass.

Od spoke slowly. "You don't come back from Helheim." I wanted to speak, but he held up a finger. "Unless there's someone else lined up."

I turned my head, uncomprehending. "Someone else?"

"If, theoretically"—he raised an eyebrow as he said *theoretically*, as if to say it was completely impossible—"one manages to get out of Helheim, someone from another of the realms of the dead has to claim their soul."

"What other realms of the dead are there?" I leaned forward slightly.

"Fólkvangr and Valhalla," Od said and took a sip from his glass. He exhaled slowly as his shoulders dropped.

"Freyja and Odin."

He sighed. "If you can get one of them to take Arthur for themselves, then Hel can't keep him."

"Odin hates him, and Freyja renounced her claim."

"Maybe one of them can still be convinced."

"Even if it succeeds, wouldn't it just be status quo?" I asked and took a large gulp. The liquid burned all the way down, and I coughed discreetly. "Then he'll just have to go to their realm instead."

Od shrugged. "If you acknowledge the gods, you'll end up in one of those places regardless."

I drank again. "What if you don't acknowledge the Norse gods?"

"Those who belong to another faith are, in death, forever cut off from the followers of this faith."

"And what if you don't acknowledge any gods at all?"

"Then you disappear when you die."

I wagged a finger. "Says you, because you believe in the Norse gods."

Od smiled almost imperceptibly. "Of course. In reality, no one knows."

Another mouthful emptied the glass, and the liquid warmed my throat in a pleasant way.

Od poured us more. I drank greedily.

"Tell me about the goddess Hel." I leaned my head back in the soft chair as the room's contours became a little fuzzy. In fact, I had the feeling that space and time were sloshing around me.

Od shifted in his chair, and it creaked faintly.

"Hel is Loki's daughter, and she rules over Helheim." His voice was calming and sounded almost like a lullaby. "To get there, you must pass the maiden Modgud, who guards the entrance. She requires payment in blood."

I emptied my glass with one last sip.

"Hel's hall is called Eljudnir. It means *wet with rain*. Her dish is called Hunger, and her bed is called Kör."

"Ohhh . . . Kör. That's what Arthur said before he fell back down to Helheim. I didn't understand what I was supposed to cure."

Od's warm laughter surrounded me. "Kör means *sickbed*."

I could no longer keep my eyes open, and the empty glass rolled out of my hand and landed on the soft carpet.

Now Od's voice was everywhere. I felt myself being picked up and laid on a soft surface. "Hel is beautiful on her right side, but ugly on the left."

"Have you met her?" I whispered.

Od lay down next to me, and I nestled close to him. His arms

561

folded around me, and the current of divinity flowed from him into me.

"Of course I've met her. I went down there to get someone. But I didn't succeed. I couldn't even get in because I'm a demigod. My human half kept me out."

My fingers found his shirt and clutched it.

Tentatively, he stroked my hair. "Sleep." His hoarse voice and the crash of the waves were the last things I heard before I drifted into my dreams.

I woke alone in the bedroom, where a giant window also displayed a view of the beach. It was gray and foggy, but it was light enough that I judged it to be early morning. Down by the water, someone walked a dog on a leash, and the waves lapped against the sand. An orange barrel had washed ashore, and lyme grass swayed intermittently near the window, though inside there was neither a draft nor wind.

In the kitchen, Od stood over a stove, and a table was set with fresh fruit, plates, and cups. It seemed strangely banal to see the demigod puttering with the food. That is, until he turned and smiled at me in a way that nearly knocked me to the floor.

Nope. Nothing banal about this at all.

I looked out yet another large panoramic window. "Is this where you live?"

Od stopped mid-motion over the pan, but then continued. "Not many people have been here."

"You're like bears, all of you. You hide away in caves, and then people are supposed to feel really special if you let them in, even if their lives are at stake."

Od didn't reply, but he cocked his head slightly.

I racked my brain for an apology.

"I didn't mean it like that," was all I came up with. I sat and looked down at the beach again. "Thanks for letting me sleep

562

here," I mumbled and dug into the food. "And for this." I turned a gleaming lock of hair between my fingers. The night with Od had clearly boosted me.

Od kept his face directed at the table. "You'll need it."

"I'd better get going soon," I said between two bites. "Looks like there's a bus stop down the road. I just need to look up the schedule for the 71."

A laugh escaped Od's mouth.

"What?"

"Anna, you always surprise me." When I looked at him, confused, he continued. "I'll take you home."

"Do you have a car?"

"Nah," his eyes glinted. "I thought we would travel like demigods."

Faint nausea simmered in my stomach, along with pure adrenaline. Sitting on Od's back as he sprinted made the tips of my fingers and toes quiver. I had tried it before with Mathias, but Od ran much faster. He plopped me down in the yard in front of Rebecca and Ben's house. Quick as a flash, he was gone again.

Luna came running.

"Anna." She laid a hand on my back.

A contraction of my upset stomach told me it was time to run to the bathroom. Luna followed me in and held my hair back as I threw up.

"What are these clothes?" Luna asked and helped me to my feet.

I leaned over the sink and turned on the water. "I borrowed them from Od."

Luna narrowed her eyes.

"Is something going on? Your teeth are super white." She bared her own teeth, which also gleamed, but then again, she was with Mathias all the time.

I looked at her as the water I had just splashed on my face ran down my cheeks. "No. Nothing's going on. He just got me drunk and I passed out cold. Then he took me to bed."

Luna's lips formed an *oh*.

"Can I borrow a T-shirt? This one got wet."

"Of course. But I don't have any black ones."

"That's fine."

"Or brown or gray."

I groaned. "What about dark blue?"

She shook her head, her curls bouncing. "Everything's in the wash. All I have is a yellow one."

"You're lying."

She bit her lip, laughing. "Yes. You've taught me how to lie, and if that's what it takes to make you wear colors, I'll do it."

Even with the spells, people noticed me that day at school. In a neon-yellow shirt, Od's beige pants, and my mom's high-heeled boots that I had been wearing the day before, I felt like a walking color wheel.

"Wow," Mathias said when we met him in Blue Hall.

I gave him a tired look. "I know I look like shit."

He glanced at Luna. "Isn't it a little much with the red hair? Speaking of which, is it shinier than usual?"

I touched my hair. "Oh no. I had forgotten all about that."

Lunas put her hands on her hips, her green nails pressing against her purple dress. "Is there something wrong with wearing different colors? I think they're protecting her."

"No, no." Mathias tugged on her orange necklace to bring her close to him. He planted a kiss on her nose, then one on her mouth. "I love it on you. It's just because Anna—" He stopped when I growled.

"Enough about my appearance. Can we have five minutes where we don't talk about clothes and hair?"

They walked with me to the plush red sofa, which only added to the explosion of colors. I gave them a brief rundown.

"Od said Arthur needs another god of death to claim him so he can get out of Helheim."

Luna's forehead creased. "Didn't Freyja already claim him?"

I nodded. "But she's renounced her claim because she's pissed that he willingly went to Hel. Also, someone has to go get him and the gods' blood from down there."

"And how will that person get back?" Mathias asked, squinting. Maybe the combination of mine and Luna's outfits, and the red sofa on top of that, made it hard for him to concentrate.

I threw up my arms. "Humans can only go to Helheim by dying, so if anyone's dumb enough to volunteer, that person would also need a god to claim them."

We pondered silently.

"Can I go there?" Mathias's voice indicated that he most certainly didn't want to.

"Demigods can't. Od said he had been down there himself, but that he couldn't get in." I sighed and looked at my phone. "Class is starting soon." I stood up.

The others got up as well. "Isn't Helheim big?" Luna asked as we started walking toward the French classroom. "How—even if we got someone to go down there—how would they find the gods' blood?"

"I have an idea of where it is," I said. "Hel lives in Helheim. And in her hall, there's a bed. Arthur said the bed's name, Kör, when he tried to come up. I think he found the blood, but he wasn't able to steal it."

"Great," Mathias said. "So we just need to convince someone to die and go to Helheim and steal gods' blood that Loki has hidden in the bed of the goddess of death. That shouldn't be a problem."

"What do you want?" I focused on Mina when I finally noticed she was sitting in front of me.

I stood behind the bar at Frank's, deep in self-pitying thoughts. I was alone at the bar, as Frank had run up to the apartment to see Halfdan, who was crying inconsolably.

Mina played with her shiny, brown ponytail and said with a suppressed smile, "You should really work on how you talk to customers. You do have a service job now."

I tossed the dish towel I was squeezing in my hands behind the bar. "Okay. Let's try that again," I said with a grimace. "How can I help you, honorable paying customer?"

"Super. If you lose the sarcasm, it's even better."

I cocked my head.

"A cola," she said.

"Coming up." I grabbed one and set it in front of her. "Did Frank let you off?"

"Yeah." She nodded. "He didn't want to leave Halfdan when he was upset. I think his soft grandpa feelings took over."

"Aww," I said, as I had learned was the correct response when people talked about kids and feelings.

"I need to talk to you about something," she said between sips.

I grabbed the dishcloth again and wiped the counter, mostly to keep my hands busy. "Mhmm."

"I have something you should see. I found it yesterday." Mina rummaged in her bag. "My dad will kill me if he finds out I took it."

She laid a piece of parchment on the counter. It was yellowed, written in a neat hand, and had a red wax seal.

I turned the paper around on the shiny steel counter and gasped. "It's the deed to Odinmont. My caseworker got it from Ben because I wasn't of age, but she sold it. Why does your dad have it?"

"I was gonna ask you the same thing."

I held up the paper and studied it longingly. "No idea. The deed was gone when Greta sold the house."

"There's something strange about that paper," Mina said. "I've been over by Odinmont, after you moved out, and I simply couldn't get up the hill."

I said nothing, but this matched my own experience of Odinmont being magically sealed after it was sold.

"But as soon as I had the deed, there was no problem. I could stroll right up the hill and into the house."

With a gasp, I almost shouted: "You've been inside?"

She nodded.

"Will you take me there?" I leaned all the way over the counter toward her. "Please?"

Begging wasn't really my thing, but I was ready to get on my knees and plead.

"Of course."

"What do you want in return?" I asked, suspicious.

She furrowed her brows. "Nothing."

I nearly cried when I stepped through the blue front door. Okay, I actually did sniffle a few times, but I kept it hidden from Mina. I let my fingertips run over the kitchen table and walls, and along the long crack in the dining table.

Mina stopped in front of the long spear, Gungnir, that Svidur had hung on the wall many years ago. She reached out.

"Don't touch it!" I shouted, afraid that Mina would explode on the spot if her skin came into contact with the rusty iron.

She lowered her hand slowly. "Is it fragile?"

"Very," I lied. "I'm going upstairs."

In my bedroom, I sat on the bed and lay down on my side. My cheek hit the pillow, which inexplicably still smelled like Varnar. Unaware of much else, I held it against myself.

"Are you tired?" Mina stood in the doorway.

I couldn't get up when she sat at the foot of the bed.

"This house is the only home I've ever known," I said.

Something crackled.

I looked up at Mina, who held the deed out toward me. Intense longing shot through my arms and out my fingertips when I reached for it. The paper landed in my palm.

"It's yours," Mina whispered. "It's always been yours."

I clutched the deed, unable to let go of it.

"Now, I'm no lawyer, but even if you give me the deed, I don't think it's completely legal to just take a house." I almost added *back*.

Mina stood and looked out the angled window, and I realized it was Ostergaard she was looking at.

"That paper isn't a normal deed. And something tells me my dad won't notice. He seems cool, but ever since my mom died . . ." She stopped.

I furrowed my brows, the Varnar-scented pillow still pressed to my chest. "Are you sure?"

She stared inscrutably at me. "I'm not sure of anything at all."

CHAPTER 45

I sat up in bed, breathless.

Images of the broken birch tree in Kraghede Forest, next to my lifeless hand, lingered from the dream, even though my eyes were open. Frank's footsteps disappeared across the field toward Odinmont. Serén's words echoed in my head.

"She's coming, Anna."

My death was going to happen. It must be in the near future, as Serén kept seeing the vision, and she sent it to me. She didn't show herself to me, but I felt the chill crawl under my skin and spread through me as I watched myself die. It all ended with Frank snapping the birch tree.

Crap! Was someone threatening Halfdan? Was Frank about to turn on me again?

I moaned.

Maybe . . .

I pondered as the sleep drained out of me.

Maybe I can change it. Maybe I can stop Frank.

Even though I didn't want to, I threw off the covers and padded over to my dresser.

Beneath scarves and gloves, I found Auka, which I hadn't used since Hrafnheim. Holding the axe's handle felt a bit like being reunited with an old friend. The metal head pulled forward slightly, but after a couple of swings through the air, I lowered my arms with a sigh. It wasn't going to cut it. It was too small for what I had in mind. I put it back and pulled on a pair of boots and a sweater.

I closed my door with a click and took the few steps across the hall to Frank's apartment. The entire building was protected with spells from the outside, but nothing hindered me from moving around within its walls. With a little creak, I opened the door into Frank's bedroom.

His breathing was slow and heavy, and behind it, I could hear Halfdan's, light and quick. I held my breath as I snuck in and reached out for the heavy axe that hung on the wall. It was much heavier than Auka, and I had to be careful not to let it hit the floor, but I succeeded in getting it down soundlessly.

Halfdan had kicked his blanket off and lay on his back with his little arms and legs out to the sides like an X. His stuffed animal had rolled to the side, and, holding the axe in one hand, I went over to him. His shirt had slipped down, so I could see the round scar on his chest. It looked like a bullet wound, but I knew it was where Sverre had healed him. I also knew that Frank would do whatever it took to keep him safe. I draped the blanket over Halfdan. Encumbered by the heavy, sharp weapon, I grabbed the stuffed animal and tucked it in next to him.

Then I looked at the sleeping Frank, who looked defenseless with his loose gray hair, his white T-shirt, and his arms stretched out, relaxed and with the palms of his hands facing up.

I raised the axe.

I felt a jolt when I saw Kraghede Forest, illuminated by the moon and covered in small frost crystals. It looked exactly like it did in my dream. Like in Serén's vision.

The journey down there had been cumbersome with the heavy axe in tow, lurching down the road on my bike. Now I stood nailed to the ground, unable to move for fear.

The wind tugged at the crowns of the tall trees, and I jumped to the side, startled, when a bird high above me screeched in protest. A breeze reached through the spruce trees, and the sound of the birch leaves rustling was laughably weak in comparison to the deep creaking of the old, sturdy trees.

I stood before the birch tree. It swayed slightly, and I got the feeling it would flee if it weren't bound to the earth by its roots. I raised the axe and took a swing.

The metal struck the fragile trunk, and both the tree and I shook from the blow. Frank's axe embedded itself in the tree, and I had to ease it out. Birch sap ran from the cut, the oily liquid glinting in the moonlight.

I raised the axe and chopped again, this time letting out a little cry to give the blow more force. The tree was stronger than I had expected, and my fingers trembled from the impact.

It didn't make sense that Frank could snap it with his body-weight alone if it was so tough. Again, I swung the sharp axe back and raised it, aiming to take the tree down.

"What are you doing?"

I spun around, the axe still raised.

Frank stood in the moonlight in a pale-colored jacket with the hood pulled up.

I pulled the axe back to indicate I wasn't afraid to use it against him.

He held up his arms with a look of confusion. "I'm not going to hurt you, Anna."

"Then why did you follow me here?" My heart was pounding, and with a shiver, I realized that the moon looked exactly as it did in my vision, that the fields were covered in snow, and that Frank was wearing the same clothes.

"I thought someone had given you stjórna." He stood completely still.

I breathed rapidly. "Why are you wearing that jacket?"

Frank looked down at himself.

"This?" He rubbed his hands on the fabric. "Because it's cold out." When I only stared at him, he took a small step toward me.

"Did you really think I wouldn't notice that you snuck into my bedroom and stole my axe?"

My arms were starting to tremble from the effort of holding the heavy weapon over my head. "Yes, I really did think that."

The smile lines around his eyes deepened.

"I promise you . . ." He stopped. "No, I swear on Halfdan's life that I won't hurt you. Ever again."

The axe lowered slightly.

"I don't know who to trust anymore." Finally, the metal head landed with a *thunk* in the dry leaves in front of my toes.

Frank walked up to me. "Why are you trying to cut down that tree?"

I looked down at the ground and kicked a twig. "I keep seeing it."

A warm hand landed on my shoulder but didn't squeeze. "What do you see?"

"I see you killing me. Here." I pointed around the forest. "And then you crack the tree with your weight. I thought that if I cut down the tree, I could change the vision." I exhaled, defeated. "It was stupid."

Frank's hand went away. "You see me killing you?"

I nodded.

"Here?"

"Yeah."

"Are you sure it's not . . ." His voice faded before he spoke again. "The thing that happened last year?"

"Last year you didn't succeed." I shook my head. "In this vision, you do."

He was silent for a while. Finally, he spoke. "Are you sure it's me?"

I raised my head. "Yes. It has to . . . Well, no, I guess not. I see you from behind. I just assumed it was you, but I don't actually know."

Frank put an arm around me and led me out of the forest.

"So it could be someone else entirely." He let go of me quickly, as if to signal that I had no reason to fear him.

"Great! You just added yet another mystery murderer to the list."

Frank gave my back a little shove in the direction of his pickup truck, which was parked by the side of the road. "I'm just glad you've realized it isn't me. Here, let me take the axe. It's heavy."

I handed him the deadly weapon. "Oh, I haven't realized anything. Don't expect me to trust you. Or anyone else, apart from a select few."

Behind me, Frank whispered: "That is quite sensible."

"You did what?" Mathias sputtered.

I blinked my eyes tiredly on the red sofa in The Island the next day. "It was stupid, but I wanted to change the future."

"A felled tree doesn't change anything." Mathias studied me critically.

"Maybe it's a little thing, but if I can change it, then there's hope." I shook my head. "It didn't work, anyway. The tree was really strong. I don't understand how anyone could break it with their weight alone."

"Maybe they can now that you've hacked at it," Luna said, who was busy braiding a lock of my hair.

I put my hands on my forehead and let out an *ughhh*. "I'm such an idiot. Instead of preventing my own murder, I've just made it easier for whoever-it-is."

My hair slipped out of Luna's grasp.

Just then, Mads came over and plopped down on the sofa between us. "What's wrong, Anna?"

"She just made a little mistake," Luna said, taking my hair again.

"Little?" I leaned back. "I've made a fatal mistake."

Mads's face went pale, and he nodded. "What did you do?"

"I made it easier for someone to kill me." I let out another frustrated groan and hit my forehead with clenched fists.

573

Mathias removed my hands. "Stop that. Hurting yourself doesn't help anything."

"Maybe," Mads said, "it's a blessing in disguise. Maybe this'll turn out to be a good thing." He patted both Luna and me on the thigh. "Come on, we'll be late for Danish class."

The others gathered their things and stood up, while I sat frozen and stared into space.

The solution.

"You coming, Anna?" Luna took a couple of steps, then looked back over her shoulder.

I raised my head toward her. "You go ahead. I'll be there later."

"Svidur." I exhaled cautiously. "All-Father."

It felt strangely irreverent to be summoning a deity while standing in the middle of my small kitchenette, but he probably wouldn't care if I was in a temple or a kitchen once he heard what I had to say.

"Svidur. Come on." I wrinkled my nose. Okay, he probably wouldn't show up if I asked him like that. I made an effort. "I know we parted on bad terms, but I'm certain you're going to want to hear this."

No response. I could sense only resentment in some unspecifiable place in the air around me.

"I think I've found a way to make Ragnara mortal and get rid of her. But I need help from a god of death, and you are, you know . . ." I looked around, ". . . one of those."

A sound behind me made me bow my head with relief.

"Thank you, Svidur. I've realized something. I've . . ." I turned around, and my voice faded into a breath. "Holy shit." My mouth hung open.

The woman in front of me came close and bowed her head. She was noticeably taller than me, so she had to lean over to reach me.

I thought the goddess might be a little pissed at me, since I had slept with her husband and deprived her of my father's soul, but she locked her amber-colored, almond-shaped eyes on me. There was a smile on her lips, and an intoxicating fragrance flowed from her body. I simply stared at her like an idiot. Her hair, which was the same color as ripe wheat, cascaded over her shoulders in waves, and she wore a golden, floor-length dress, which was just transparent enough for me to make out her exquisite naked body beneath it. Bare feet stuck out from the bottom, and although it sounds dumb, they were so beautiful, I had to tense my back to keep myself from kneeling and worshipping them.

She placed her mouth against mine and kissed me. And it wasn't just a peck. *No, no.* It was a real, deep, passionate kiss, and I was left standing there, breathless, when she pulled away.

A honey-colored halo radiated around her whole body. Then she sniffed my neck, and the warmth of her breath sent pleasant tingles up and down my spine.

I swayed.

"You called for a god of death?" she asked, as though she had just been in the other room.

"Svi . . . Svidur?" I could barely say the name.

She tilted her head. "He's pouting. Something about a hanga-drott in Hrafnheim. Do you know anything about that?"

I shook my head, trying to clear it, or to at least be able to speak clearly. "Freyja?"

"Mhmm." She studied her nails, as though I were boring her already.

"Arthur is in Helheim," I stammered.

She looked at me.

"Hel. My archnemesis and mirror image." She pursed her lips. "I don't like that she has Arthur."

"Yeah, I've heard."

She leaned her head back. "What are you going to do about it?"

575

I pulled myself together. "I'm going to get him back. But I'll need help."

Her slim hand touched my chin. "You resemble Arthur so much."

I jerked my head away, wanting to get back on track.

"Help?" I had once again lost the ability to form a complete sentence.

Her feline eyes grew cold. "Help you?"

"Would you?" I jutted my jaw forward. With effort, I stopped myself from casting my eyes down.

She released me by looking away, and it felt like the floor opened beneath me and I fell several feet down.

"I'll help." Her voice was nonchalant, but I got the sense it was an act. "I want to have Arthur in my realm, and you amuse me with all your antics. I'll even let your father stay in Midgard for a while if we succeed. I'll get him in the end, anyway."

I relaxed a little. "It's strange that you rule over a realm of the dead, when you represent love and beauty."

Suddenly, her amber-colored eyes flashed, and she grew quite a bit taller. The air around her sparked.

I stepped back, stunned.

"Love and beauty." She sneered. "I'm a goddess of war. I'm a goddess of death. I'm a goddess of creation. I'm a witch. I'm a healer. I am love." She flung out her arms, which were now each as long as a whole person. "There's one single stanza about my beauty in the old poems. One." She extended a long finger. "The male gods are also warriors, protectors, conquerors, and masters, and *that* gets remembered. But I'm always just referred to as that beautiful goddess of love."

"It's just . . ." I whispered. "You *are* really beautiful."

"All gods are beautiful." Freyja's large face moved right in front of mine, heat radiating from it. "All gods!" she yelled, and the sound made the windowpanes rattle.

576

An alarm went off on the street, but otherwise, no one seemed to notice the noise from my apartment.

"Sorry," I stammered.

Freyja shrank back to normal human size, then installed herself on one of my plastic chairs. The sight of the goddess in her transparent dress sitting on a cheap chair in my kitchen was more than a little strange.

With an expression of only mild curiosity, she looked at me. "What's your plan?"

"I'll tell you, but before I say more, please convince Svidur to come." My breathing was still heavy. "We need to talk business."

Freyja craned her head back and opened her mouth.

I expected a howl loud enough to rip my face off, but all that came out was a barely audible whisper. It continued for a while, as though she were arguing with someone.

Finally, a sound on my other side let me know that Svidur had arrived.

"Little seer." His voice was surly, and I turned toward him.

He was shorter and quite a bit thinner than the last time I'd seen him. His hair was completely white, and deep furrows lined his face.

"Is something wrong?" I asked.

His one eye glinted in its deep socket. "I'm losing my strength. There aren't enough people who believe in me."

I glanced at Freyja, who had wandered over to the apartment's only mirror. She looked at herself and turned her face from side to side.

"She looks good, though."

Freyja shook her head, her golden mane swishing behind her.

"I can feel it, too," she said. "Look," she held up a strand of hair. "I got a gray hair."

Svidur took an unsteady step.

"Would you like to sit?" I gestured at the plastic chairs around my small table.

He prepared to protest.

I held up my hand. "Just stand. I have a suggestion. An offer." I nodded to Freyja. "For both of you."

I stood in Elias's driveway in front of Stjerneborg.

The yard was empty and dark. The cold bit my cheeks, but I knew this was a negligible pain in relation to what was coming. I looked at the sky, which was shifting from deep blue to pitch black. The moon was the exact same shape as it was in the vision, and small snowflakes drifted down toward me. Footsteps approached in the gravel behind me.

"Am I back in your good graces?" His voice was cold, and I wasn't sure if Elias wanted to be in my good graces, even if he had the chance.

I turned. "We need to talk."

He stood completely still. "How can I help you? You only come to me when you need something."

"Maybe you shouldn't throw stones."

"Maybe you should just say what you want." His fists clenched.

"I need you to . . ." I had a hard time saying it.

"What?" A muscle tensed in his jaw.

I exhaled. "I've realized that the two of us have a joint task. Something I never expected to ask you for."

"I've never doubted the day would come when you acknowledged we belong together." The corner of his mouth turned up, but there was an ironic distance. "The question is whether I still want to."

"I need you to do something for me. Something I can't get anyone else to do."

His tongue ran across his parted lips.

"I can't imagine no one else wants to." He stopped and looked at my clothes for the first time. His eyes ran across the delicate, slightly transparent blue-and-white fabric. "That's the dress Luna made for your birthday last year, isn't it? Why are you wearing that?" He let a tentative hand sweep across the fabric.

I removed Elias's hand and squeezed it in mine for a moment, unable to say anything.

Elias's eyes narrowed, uncomprehending.

"Why are you wearing it?" he asked again.

I took a moment to work up my nerve before I could respond. "Because I need you to kill me."

CHAPTER 46

"This had better be a joke."

I shook my head.

"Completely out of the question." Each syllable was pronounced with extra emphasis.

"It's the only way."

"To do what?"

"It's the only way I can get down there. To Helheim. To get the blood and Arthur."

Elias looked at the stars as he forced the words out. "Your father would rather stay down there than have you sacrifice yourself for him."

"It's not a sacrifice. I'm betting that I'll get to come back."

Elias tore his gaze from the blinking pinpricks above us and looked at me again. "How?"

"You can reanimate me if you have the gods' blood. You and Luna together. She and Mathias know to meet you at Odinmont after . . ." I fiddled with a silk ribbon, ". . . after you've done it. That gives you an hour to get yourselves, Arthur's body, and my body to The Boatman. That's where you'll get the gods' blood. Luna's magic energy, together with the blood, should be able to reanimate us both. Divinity, magic, and science can work together. You've always said that. The solution has been right under our noses the whole time."

Elias looked more and more horrified with each sentence.

"You are absolutely the most reckless person I've ever met, and I've met a *lot* of people." He moaned desperately. "How did you get

Luna and Mathias on board with this plan? I would have expected them to have you committed if you aired these kinds of insane thoughts in front of them."

"They don't know about it yet." I cleared my throat. "You'll have to explain."

He was silent for a moment. "They'll kill me."

"Not when you show them my body. They'll be forced to listen to you."

"Even so." It was clear how unlikely he thought this was. "Even then, you and Arthur can't come back. Your souls aren't bound to anything."

"Svidur will claim my soul, and Freyja will claim my father's."

Elias blinked a couple of times. Finally, he composed himself. "How in the worlds did you convince them of that?"

I jutted my lower jaw forward. "I promised them something." I waved my hand. "It doesn't matter what."

"Have you no fear?"

"Fear is what's making me do this. Ragnara is on her way here to kill me, and that will start Ragnarök. My sister keeps seeing it. I've turned it over in my head. This is the only way." I held Elias's face. My palms rested on his smooth cheeks. "You're the only one who can do it."

He twisted his head free. "The only one who can make himself kill you? I would think you'd have a whole line of people who would gladly do the honor."

My hands remained in the air next to him, but I didn't try to grab him again. "I meant you're the only one who can bring me back to life."

"I don't want to do that, either."

"Don't you want Arthur back?"

"Yes," he whispered.

"So do it."

He spun around and took a few strides away from me.

I followed and stepped in front of him.

"Do you remember," I asked, "the time we visited Justine in Sømosen?"

He didn't respond.

"She said that our fates are bound by love or death. Or both." I stepped closer. "This must be what she meant."

He raised the corner of his mouth in a bitter smile. "She meant your death and my love."

We sat at the little wooden table in Elias's living room while Elias drank a large glass of mead.

I played with the ribbon on my dress again.

Finally, Elias drained his glass. "How is it supposed to happen?"

I straightened. "In Kraghede Forest. If we do it anywhere else, Serén will see it and figure out that it's a different murder. She'll try to prevent it by sending past-me the vision. I won't understand that it's necessary for me to be killed to prevent Ragnarök, so I'll stay away from you. You'll need to hide your face, and we have to reenact the vision as closely as possible."

"I don't understand."

I made my voice slow and pedagogical. "We need to trick my sister and myself. In the past."

Elias poured himself another glass, and I threw up my hands in frustration. A large sip kept Elias from speaking, but I got the feeling that he was struggling to keep up.

I continued quickly. "Time is in constant flux. I can see it when I'm with other seers. It sounds strange, but this might not even be the present. It's both past and future."

Again, Elias drank without responding.

"That's why we clairvoyants can see forward and backward. I'm only just now figuring it out. But I think that's how it works." He wanted to say something, but I cut him off. "Serén has already seen that it happens, but she can't make sense of it. If she starts to suspect what I'm planning, she'll try to stop me. But it's necessary. It's the only way! I've spent so long working against fate. Instead, I should work with it, use it to my advantage."

The eyes in front of me followed my lips, but I wasn't sure if he completely understood me.

"It must have been predestined since my birthday. Maybe before. Maybe it was never Frank we saw." I stared out into space as the realization set in. "Maybe it has always been you."

Finally, Elias found his voice. "So, to trick you and your sister, how do we need to do . . ." his voice cracked ". . . it?"

"You. I'm not doing anything."

He inhaled sharply. "What do I need to do?"

"You need to recreate the night Frank almost killed me. You have to strangle me with a leather cord and carve the rune ansuz into my back. Finally, you have to snap the little birch tree with your weight."

CHAPTER 47

It's happening.

I breathed shakily as the winter chill crept up my legs. My heart pounded, and the trees creaked above me.

I moved forward as though sleepwalking. In a corner of my consciousness, I knew that both my sister and I were watching, so we had to make it resemble the vision as closely as possible. I walked past the place I knew I was seeing the vision from, and quickly lowered my head so that my face was hidden by my long, matted hair.

I heard footsteps behind me as Elias crunched noisily through the dry leaves and twigs. I didn't dare turn around to see if he had followed my instructions to pull the hood up and keep his head turned away from the spot where Serén and I were watching the whole thing.

My heartbeats drowned everything else out. My pulse thundered inside my head, and I had to force myself not to run in the opposite direction. With a couple of deep breaths, my heart calmed down a little, but it started racing again as soon as I thought about what was going to happen.

Calm down. You're just going to die. It'll be fine. It'll only be worse if you resist.

Okay, now my heart was pounding even faster.

Elias caught up to me, and I sensed him raising the leather cord over my head. He laid it against my neck as softly as one of the caresses I was beginning to long for.

"This is wrong," Elias said, breathlessly, from behind me. His mouth was right next to my ear. "I don't want this."

With great effort, I sent all the willpower I had out into my limbs so I could let Elias do what he needed to do.

He pulled the cord back, hard. "I give life. I don't take it."

I wanted to snap, saying he'd never held himself back before, but I was unable to let out so much as a tiny squeak.

A voice, perhaps inside my own head, shouted: *Run, kick, hit. Do something. Anything.*

The leather cord was ice cold. It felt like frozen wire, but I forced myself not to fight, even when my body bent backward. Even when my throat squeezed shut, and panic spread through every fiber of my being.

My heart beat slower . . . and slower . . . and slower. Consciousness—and, along with it, life—seeped out of me.

With one eye cracked open, I saw the ground rise to meet me. I didn't even feel the impact when I landed on the forest floor. Above me, Elias continued his work.

"The things you convince me to do," he muttered.

There were now several seconds between each heartbeat. Either that or I was in a place where time was suspended. Far away, Elias screamed, but it seemed irrelevant. Trivial.

Thump, my heart said. Then there was a long pause. *Thump*, it said again, but it had realized what was going to happen. *Thump*, it said one last time. And then it was still.

I sank down below myself and lay encased in a thin layer of ice. Above me, just on the other side of the ice membrane, Elias ripped my dress open and moved his arm jerkily, carving ansuz into my back.

It should have hurt. It should have stung. But I felt nothing.

The ice surrounded me now, and I couldn't figure out what was up and what was down. I couldn't even blink, as my eyes were frozen, too.

There's a small chance that this maybe wasn't such a good idea.

Elias stood over me and snapped the birch tree before running toward the edge of the forest.

On the other side of the ice, sharp light shone, winds blew, and water flowed, but inside my tiny, frozen room, it was still.

What now? I thought, just before a cracking sound began to spread. It started as faint background noise but grew louder and louder. The ice around me crackled, and I tried desperately to cling to some of the shards, but they crumbled in my hands. Then I burst through it and tumbled down.

I won't say I simply fell, because that could mean a graceful, twirling descent, like that of a snowflake or feather. No, I soared toward the bottom, or wherever I was going. Far above me, I saw the outline of my own silhouette, lying completely still.

Around me there were both total darkness and angry, chalk-white light. Voices blared. Both loud laughter and manic screams. Behind it all was the hoarse laughter of ravens. Gusts of wind tore at me as I tumbled downward. The space around me filled first with gravel, then larger and larger stones. Finally, I hit large boulders and bounced around like a stray ball.

My body made a final sharp *boing*, and I cursed as it sent me down a gravel road. I skidded along, finally stopping on my stomach, my mouth full of dirt. I couldn't see out of my eyes, which were caked with dust.

Feverishly, I spat out the dirt and got to my feet. I brushed myself off and looked around, squinting through a thick bank of fog that lay over the landscape.

I was underground, in a way. High above me was a stone ceiling, and I involuntarily remembered all the caves Rorik—*ugh! Sverre*—and I had spent the night in on our travels through Hrafnheim. Even though I was far below ground, there was a light source somewhere.

Something rattled and roared, and I walked in the direction of the sound. Multiple times, I tripped over branches. I couldn't see the ground through the thick fog, but it was bumpy and uneven, and sticky in several places, like walking over large gobs of chewing gum. At one point, one of the branches grabbed my ankle and held tight, causing me to trip and fall to my knees in the dim veil of fog. Without looking for what I had tripped over, I got up and continued.

Finally, I fought my way over to the frothy sound. It was a river, and I had to walk right up to it to look down into the water.

Which wasn't water at all.

When I got close enough, I saw they were weapons, flowing like a dark, thick liquid. Swords, axes, bludgeons, and knives clinked against each other and flashed in the unidentifiable light.

"That's Gjöll," a voice said behind me.

I shrieked and jumped.

A woman stood there, her skin chalk white.

"It's what?" I panted.

"The river." She pointed. "It's called Gjöll. It means *noise*."

I looked down into the current. "That's a very fitting name."

Many of the weapons had runes etched into them.

"What are they doing there?"

She smiled inscrutably. "They're offerings. They were all offered to the gods over the years."

I studied the woman, who wore a brown shift dress. Looking down at myself, I realized I still had my nice dress on. I might have been a little overdressed for death.

"Who are you?" I asked.

She wrinkled her forehead, her mouth open. Her eyes stared far off into the mist.

"I don't know," she said.

My brain was foggy, too, as though all my memories were wet pieces of soap that kept slipping away from me. I squinted. "Can you not even remember your name?"

She turned her head. "I'm supposed to take you across the river. That's what I'm supposed to do. Take the people who come here across."

With a decisive wave, she gestured across the wild maelstrom of sharp blades and started walking.

"Hey, wait a second. You can't just go around without a name."

"It's totally empty in there." She tapped a finger on the back of her head.

"Even so, I can still call you something."

Her face turned up toward me. "Yes. Give me a name."

I rummaged around in my own brain, but it wasn't working, either.

"Your name is," I stared intensely at her, "uh . . ." Okay, there was no activity in there, just useless mush. "Your name is . . ." I shook my head forcefully. Something was coming to the surface.

The woman came closer. "What's my name?"

"Your name is," I pulled myself together, "Modgud," I blurted, surprising even myself when the name Od had said when he told me about Helheim appeared from my blurred memory.

"Modgud? That's a strange name," she said.

I flung out my arms. "It's a nice name."

"Okay, then. Modgud." She shivered but got a little more color in her cheeks. "What are you doing here?"

"I think I'm supposed to do something," I replied slowly. "But I can't remember what."

Modgud put her hands on her hips. "I mean, how did you die? I have to make sure you're in the right place."

"Isn't there something about how you're not supposed to ask dead people about that?"

Modgud looked up at the cave's ceiling and explained patiently. "That only applies to dead people who are spirits in the world of the living."

"Oh, okay. Someone named Elias killed me."

"Elias . . ." Modgud seemed to taste the name and almost recognize it. Then she looked sternly at me. "Were you in battle?"

"No. Not at all."

She looked intently at me without blinking. "Did you die while protecting your family?"

"No, not exactly."

She counted silently, as if performing a complex calculation in her head. She came to a result and said: "Fine. Murder. That's accepted."

I raised a hand, which was strikingly white. "What now?"

"We go over the bridge." She pointed.

"What bridge?" I didn't see any . . . *whoa*. Where had that come from?

In front of us, stretching all the way across Gjöll, was a gleaming, golden footbridge. That must have been what gave off the gentle light.

"Gjallarbrú leads to Helheim."

I exhaled hard. "Perfect. That's where I'm going."

"Come on, then. There's nothing worse than being late to your own death."

I cleared my throat. "Actually, I'm planning to get out of here. I just don't remember how."

"No one gets out of here."

"I will."

Modgud gave me a doubtful look. "I've been here for an eternity, and no one has ever gotten out."

"Whatever. I'll see you. Or . . . actually, I hope I don't."

Together, we pushed on the large gate that hadn't been there moments before. I took a couple of steps through the opening, but Modgud stopped me. "What's that on your back?"

My hand felt around behind me and came back bloody. I stared at my red fingertips.

"It's a symbol. I have it because . . ." I struggled to think. "Something about blood. It symbolizes something." My mission was right on the tip of my tongue, but I couldn't formulate it.

"It looks like the symbol for *god*," Modgud said behind me and brushed her hand across my back. She waved her bloody palm. "I needed some of this anyway. Now I don't have to cut you."

God, ansuz, blood.

"Oh, right . . ." I sighed, panicked that I had nearly forgotten the whole reason I was there. "Thanks. Thank you so much!"

I walked in and looked back once to see Modgud staring at her red hand.

I came up with a simple mission statement.

"Find gods' blood in death's bed and Arthur. Find gods' blood in death's bed and Arthuuur . . ." It turned into a little song that I hummed again and again, terrified of forgetting my objective, which was apparently a real danger in the underworld.

I continued into the misty, gloomy land, all the while singing my song.

"Find gods' blood in death's bed and Arthuuuurr," I whispered. Then the shock set in. What was my name? I fumbled around in my memory for a few seconds before it appeared. "My name is Anna," I added breathlessly to my song. "Find gods' blood in death's bed and Arthur. My name is Anna."

It was cold and damp, and I was continually struck by gusts of humid wind that cut through to my bones and marrow. Along the road were figures, their feet buried in the mud. They wore all different kinds of clothes, and their faces were expressionless. Some of them jiggled, but they couldn't get free.

"Find gods' blood in death's bed and Arthuuurrr," I wailed as I jogged along. Finally, I swung my arms around because I kept getting a tingling feeling in my fingertips, like they were falling asleep. I focused on a person who stood in the foggy ditch.

He looked straight ahead with milk-white eyes, yellowish skin, and messy hair. An insect crawled across his face and into his mouth, but he didn't notice, and though his eyes were directed toward me, they stared out into space.

"Find gods' blood in death's bed and Arthuuuuuuurrr," I shouted to myself and ran past him, my arms flailing. "My name is Anna."

Even though the road sloped down, there was pressure on my body as though I were running up a steep hill. At the same time, I was weighed down by invisible boulders. I heard the distorted sound of waves crashing, and when the road changed direction and curved around some iron-colored, leafless trees, which I suspected were the same as the ones in the Iron Forest, I saw that I had reached a sea.

The beach was as wide as the west coast of Jutland, but the sand was gray, and the waves lapping over it were bright green. Scattered on the beach were corpses in varying states of decay. Figures crawled around, biting into the motionless bodies. Black birds sat on cadavers' heads, pecking at them.

"Find gods' blood in death's bed and Arthu—"

I stopped mid-leap, gasping, and stared. Mist sprayed me from the green sea, and everywhere the drops touched my bluish skin, it sizzled. Smoke rose with the stench of burnt hair. I couldn't feel anything, but I brushed my palms over my arms to remove the corrosive, oily liquid. Something nibbled on my leg, and I kicked before looking down.

A repulsive creature looked up at me with pointed teeth and red eyes.

"Stop. I'm not dead . . . Well, I am, but you can't eat me."

The creature turned its head 180 degrees and studied me.

"Corpse-swallower," it clicked.

I backed away. "Yes, I see that. But you can't swallow me."

It crawled. Its hind legs were twice as long as the front, and had no joints, so its rear end stuck up behind its head.

"Where am I?" The words got stuck in my mouth from sheer

591

terror, but the corpse-swallower fortunately seemed not to want to bite me anymore.

"Nastrond. The beach of corpses."

I looked around, my lips quivering.

"How apt." I pulled myself together. "I need to find Hel's hall."

A hall she saw, far from the sun
On Nastrond it stands, and the doors face north;
Venom drops through the smoke-vent down,
For around the walls do serpents wind.

The corpse-swallower's voice buzzed like a fly, but the words were familiar. I turned around and shook more of the toxic droplets off my arms. Hejd had said the same thing to me in a vision.

I let the words roll around in my head. Hejd had given me a clue.

The doors face north.

I forced my brain to work, even though it felt like oatmeal.

"Does the sea face north?" I asked the frightening creature.

The corpse-swallower's head rotated in a way that looked totally unnatural, but which must have been a sign of confirmation.

I looked down at my hands, which were covered in the green filth that drifted from the waves. Something was swimming out there. It looked like the ripples the Midgard Serpent's large body had made in the sea outside of Sverresborg—but these ripples were smaller, and there were more of them.

Okay—here goes.

I walked to the water's edge with my head up. Out of the corner of my eye, I saw a figure whose feet were being eaten, and I swerved around it. I hesitated for a moment in front of the neon-green water, but then I forced myself into the waves.

It stank of sulfur and rot. It smelled like the Midgard Serpent, but that made sense, as I was heading toward its sister. I waded but struggled to get very far; the water was a thick soup. When it was up to my waist, I felt something moving below. Like I was surrounded by eels. Long, smooth streaks appeared at the surface of the jelly when it reached my chest.

Serpents wind.

I continued, even though my breathing was raspy and terrified.

I really, really hope I'm right, I thought before ducking my head into the green slop.

For a while, I was surrounded by green light. There were loud *blup* sounds, and the snakes—the living serpent knot—wrapped around my body and nearly squeezed the life out of me.

Oh, right. There was no life to squeeze.

But they fastened themselves to my wrists and ankles. Eventually, they pulled me down, and I tried my best to relax and not fight my way back to the surface.

Farther and farther down the snakes pulled me, and finally, my feet hit a surface, which I leaned over and fumbled with. Only a small amount of light reached down through the cloudy green water, but finally I found a handle, which I turned with all my strength.

After a struggle, it gave, and I splashed through a short hallway that I just barely fit through. At the end, I had to dig and plow my way through, until my head finally popped out through a membrane, and I landed in a puddle of green, foul-smelling water on a stone floor. I crawled to my knees, regurgitating mouthfuls of green liquid.

Death is hard work. I hoisted myself up and turned around in the large hall. This must be Eljudnir—Hel's hall, which Od had told me about.

The stone walls were so tall, I couldn't see the ceiling, and the benches and tables were so large, I felt like a Lilliputian. Although I was indoors, drizzle trickled down in a steady stream. There were people on the benches, but they could barely see the tabletops, so they stood on their toes to reach. On a hunch, I climbed up and peered over the edge.

There was a platter, the middle of which was a bottomless pit. A force pulled at me from the black hole, and though an enticing smell of food rose from it, the platter was empty.

The pale, thin people reached out for the invisible food, but they were empty-handed. Occasionally, someone got too close to the giant platter and was simply sucked into it.

I let my gaze glide over the sunken cheeks; deep-set, dark eyes; and bloodless lips. My eyes lingered on a particular man. He snatched at the fragrant, yet empty, platter, and a look of frustration flickered across his face, which had noticeable blue veins.

"Arthur!" I exclaimed.

He looked around but quickly turned his attention back to the empty platter. He had to stand on his tiptoes to reach it.

I balanced on the outer edge of the bench, which was wide enough that my feet had just enough room to stand behind the bony people.

"Dad," I called again, but he didn't react.

When I reached him, I grabbed his shoulder and felt the bones through the worn fabric of his shirt. He slowly turned his head toward me with no sign of recognition.

"Hey, I found you!" I said. "Where's the blood? We need to get it so we can go back. The others are waiting with our bodies."

With a disinterested expression, Arthur turned back to the platter and reached his hand toward it. He got so close that it pulled at him, and his feet lifted from the bench like a piece of iron to a magnet.

With a frightened shout, I pulled him back. "Wake up."

"Who are you?" Arthur's voice had the same clicking sound that it had that night at The Boatman.

For a terrifying moment, I had forgotten it, but then the name came back.

"Anna," I said.

"Anna?" He swayed and leaned toward the platter again.

"I'm your daughter!" I screamed and yanked him back. My thin, pale fingers clutched his face.

This gave him pause. "Daughter?"

"You're here because of me. Your name is Arthur, and you're my father."

His eyes took on a vague hint of green.

"Arthur," he repeated. "Father. Daughter." With each word, a little more color returned to him.

"Yes," I whispered, ready to cry with relief.

His eyes wandered, as though he was searching for something in his memory.

"Anna," he said finally, sighing. Then he embraced me. "You came."

He was silent for a moment as he held me. I could feel his sharp bones through his shirt.

"You came."

Another pause.

"You came here." His voice had returned to normal. He held me at arm's length.

The eyes in front of me flashed—now, fortunately, as green as ever.

He shouted. "What on earth are you doing in Helheim?"

"I came to get the gods' blood and you."

He raised his arms. "That can only mean one thing. You're dead."

"Yeah, but—"

"That was the one thing I wanted to avoid." He raised his voice further, but none of the skeletal figures around us noticed. "My one objective was to keep you, your sister, and your mother alive." He clenched his fists. "Who killed you? Who? I'll avenge your death. I swear it."

"It was Elias, but—"

He interrupted me with another shout. "Elias. I knew it. He's a—"

"I made him do it."

Arthur stopped. On the plus side, he now looked like his normal self. Anger apparently worked wonders for the dead.

"You. Did. What?!" The final word was even louder than the rest.

"It was the only way for me to get down here."

Arthur's lower jaw went first to one side, then the other, and for the first time in my life, I feared my father would slap me.

I stepped toward him and placed my palms on his chest. "Can we do this later? I have a plan."

An imperfect, uncertain, and completely insane plan—but still.

He stared at me, unmoving.

"We have a lot to do," I added.

Arthur massaged his temples. "You and I are going to have a serious talk if we make it out of this."

"You can ground me later. Right now, you need to come with me."

He hopped off the bench and held out his hand so I could climb down.

"The blood is in the bed," he said.

"Where?"

He pointed to an enormous alcove that took up most of one wall.

It took several minutes to cross the large room, and I felt like a little mouse in a giant house. At the foot of the alcove, I looked up. The entrance was several yards above us. The wood was rough and worn, and we used the holes as steps. We climbed up the steep wooden surface.

A couple of times, my hands slipped. They were still greasy from the sea, but I managed to hold on. Next to me, Arthur climbed while keeping a constant eye on me, ready to reach out his hand and grab me if I fell.

We reached the top and tumbled onto the mattress. It sagged under the thick cloth.

"Don't touch the veil," Arthur said.

When I looked more closely at the transparent net that hung along the edges of the bed, I saw that it was full of sticky bodies, like flies on flypaper.

I backed away from it.

"I found the gods' blood over there." He pointed to a pillow, and we waded through an animal pelt with fur as long as my entire body.

When we were almost there, we heard a shrill whinny. Arthur cursed and pulled me through the bristles so we could hide in the gray fur. An enormous, yellow horse trotted into the hall. It had only three legs, but that didn't seem to slow it down.

"The Hellhorse," Arthur whispered.

On the Hellhorse's back sat a figure.

The figure, who was as tall as a house, came toward us, and only her silhouette could be made out through the deadly veil. She pulled it aside and brushed a couple of bodies away, which landed with a deep *plunk* on the stone floor far below us.

Then she lay down with a sigh. She placed her head on the pillow, and a feminine *mmmmm* was followed by a yawn. It didn't take long before her breathing slowed.

Arthur started crawling and signaled for me to follow him. We crept through the gray tunnel of fur toward the large woman's face.

Hel lay on her side, her right side facing up and the left planted in the pillow. She was beautiful to look at. Not intoxicating and sweet like Freyja, but wild and dark, with sharp black eyebrows and shiny hair. What I could see of her mouth was formed of soft arcs, and her cheekbones were very high, golden skin stretched across them. I stared, hypnotized, at the beautiful goddess of death, who slept peacefully.

"It's under here," Arthur whispered and slipped his hand under the pillow.

At his movement, Hel stirred slightly and rolled onto her back.

I gasped loudly when her left side became visible. It was half rotten, blue-black, and maggots crawled in and out of large holes in her cheek, through which I could also see her teeth. Each tooth was the size of my body.

I muffled a scream, and Arthur, whose hand was now lodged under the pillow, looked at me with a furious *shhh*.

"Sorry," I whispered. "She's just so . . ."

Even though it was freezing and damp, a thin layer of sweat broke out across my forehead.

"Help me," Arthur hissed. He tried to pull his arm back. "I have it, but I can't get it out."

I leaned into him and pulled his arm, which was as heavy as lead. Whatever he had a hold of, it weighed a ton.

"How much blood is there?" I hissed. "A whole swimming pool?" I pulled and tugged.

Finally, Arthur's hand loosened, and we toppled backward.

In Arthur's palm, which was weighed down against the mattress, was a small bottle. In it, a rust-red liquid glowed. It was only half the size of Elias's ampoules, but he could barely lift it.

I held the bottle, too, which we dragged along the mattress through our combined efforts.

"The passageway is over there." With a groan, Arthur nodded toward the wall behind Hel's half-rotten head.

I saw a small hatch that was strikingly like the one on the floor in Od's office. I pulled as hard as I could on Arthur's hand with the bottle, and slowly but steadily, we made our way over to it.

Sweat was dripping off me, and Arthur was panting from exertion. Arthur cautiously knocked on the door with a clenched fist. Behind us, Hel smacked her lips in her sleep. I turned and looked at her.

Noooo.

She wasn't asleep. The goddess had opened her eyes—one iron gray and one milk white. She studied us with her head cocked. Mild amusement crossed her face, and she blew on us with a breath that smelled of chlorine.

I kicked at the hatch, and it swung open. A dark blue claw reached after us as we squeezed ourselves through the small door. We crawled through a narrow corridor, dragging the blood behind us.

Slowly, almost as if to torment us, the hand crawled after us. The fingers, which were as long as Mads was tall, crept along the floor. They looked like giant legs.

I saw the hand in the red glow of the blood.

I heard Mathias's voice far away at the other end of the tunnel. "Anna."

"Mathias," I screamed. "Luna."

"I can hear you," Mathias shouted.

"I can't hear anything." Luna's voice grew clearer. "But damn, it smells down there."

"Get away from the passageway, Luna. You'll fall in."

"We're coming," Arthur shouted as Hel's hand fumbled after us. At one point, it grabbed my dress, but I kicked the fingers away.

There was an angry shriek at the other end of the passage, and the hand was no longer teasing and playful. It clawed at us and sent a clenched fist in our direction.

Finally, Mathias became visible in the distance. I couldn't tell if it was up or down. A hand reached out, and I shoved the blood into it. He must have extended his arm by several yards.

The hand disappeared, and he cursed.

"Not the blood." There was a crash as something was tossed aside. "Give me your hands."

His neon-green hand appeared again, and Arthur and I each grabbed a finger, which were as large and solid as ropes.

599

With Hel's angry hand flailing behind us, Mathias hoisted us the rest of the way, and Od's office came into view. I clung to the finger, and in a cloud of mist and water, I was flung into the room, where Luna looked around as if to locate something, and Elias struggled to lift the minuscule but very heavy bottle of gods' blood from the floor. Behind me, Hel took one last swing, but her claw vanished as Mathias slammed the hatch shut.

A strange apparatus was connected to cables and IVs, which were inserted into two dead bodies that lay on the desk.

Our dead bodies.

CHAPTER 48

Elias concentrated on pouring the blood into a flask attached to one side of the apparatus, while water simmered in the other one. Luna had closed her eyes and was mumbling spells, while Mathias alone stared at me.

I couldn't move, but I looked up at an angle. Behind Elias, I saw Od's desk with the two lifeless bodies.

"Anna," Mathias sounded terrified. "You're all . . ." He couldn't get the words out.

I couldn't answer. I looked at my hand, which was yellow. The skin hung loosely, as though the bones beneath were about to burst through.

"Can you see them, Mathias?" Luna asked. "All I can see is that green splat."

"There, on the carpet." He looked desperately at Elias. "Is it too late?"

Elias had rolled up his sleeves and was working intently at the machine, which now shook and bubbled. "Is she moving?"

I wanted to speak, but I simply couldn't.

She? Why not they? Where is Arthur?

Mathias's hand hovered over my shoulder, but it fell right through me.

"Is she moving?" Elias's voice resounded through the office again.

I shivered as Mathias's hand penetrated my torso. It rummaged around inside me, giving me a tiny bit of his divine strength.

"Her spirit is moving," Mathias announced. "A little bit." His voice was shrill and didn't sound like him. "But she's all dried up. And Arthur looks like one of those bodies they find in bogs."

I turned my head minimally and saw that my father's face was brown, his skin thin as parchment.

"They're in limbo. None of the gods of death have claimed them." Elias didn't even raise his head. "Their souls are about to expire. Luna, now!" he commanded and held out two wires. Each of them ended in a needle, which had been inserted into our hearts and held in place with white bandages. IVs were attached to our wrists.

"Svidur and Freyja. You promised," I rasped.

Like a faint echo, I heard Svidur's gleeful laughter. "The last time we made an agreement, you were the one who backed out at the last second."

"Promise," I panted.

"You might end up regretting our deal. Are you sure, little seer?"

"Sure?" I whispered, unable to muster the strength to sound angry. "Of course I'm sure!"

"What do I do?" Luna asked. Beads of sweat broke out on her forehead.

"Send magical energy into the wires."

Luna inhaled through her nose and clenched her fists resolutely around the cables.

"If you use too much force, they'll explode. Too little, and it won't be enough to jump-start them."

"How many tries do I get?"

"You get *one* try. On three." She wanted to object, but Elias started to count. "One . . ."

"Svidur," I whispered. "Help us." My bones creaked, and a faint taste of dust spread through my throat. "I stand by my word, All-Father."

Again, I heard a hoarse voice right next to my ear. "I can see time, and I'm telling you, this will cost you dearly."

He laughed, as though the thought exhilarated him.

"This is no laughing matter. Get Freyja, too."

"Two . . ." Elias said.

My teeth were loose in my mouth, and a glance at Arthur revealed that the bridge of his nose had vanished entirely.

"I'll keep my promise!" I said, without moving my jaw, as I could feel my teeth starting to fall out of my gums.

There was a sigh so deep that my now completely white hair swirled around my head. "So, you'll worship me from now on. You renounce all other gods. You are mine."

"I swear it."

"Then we'll claim your souls," came Svidur's rough voice. Freyja's sensual laughter sent shivers down my disintegrating body.

"Three . . ." Elias said, and Luna let out a concentrated scream as sputtering electricity danced around her fists. At the same time, Elias turned a handle, and steam poured from the machine.

The gods' blood ran through a glass spiral tube and met the boiling water in the middle.

Svidur's voice still rang in my head.

Luna's magic reached my heart, and I recognized the feeling from when Védis tried to remove my spells. A current—one that was hundreds of times stronger than the divinity Od and Mathias could emit—flowed into my veins through my wrists and dispersed throughout my body. Elias's machine produced a loud bang, ending with a large cloud of smoke.

Suddenly, I was lying on the desk, not on the floor. I gasped, and next to me, Arthur did, too. My body protested as life gushed back into it, and I went from not being able to feel anything to being torn apart by overwhelming pain.

The needle in my heart scratched with each thunderous heartbeat and the IV pinched my wrist. My throat, which Elias had throttled with the leather cord, burned; and my back, where he had carved the rune, stung like hell.

But I wasn't in hell—not anymore. I was in Midgard again, and I was alive.

I looked at Arthur, who lay right next to me. His eyes, which had been clear and dead on the stone platform in Odinmont, were now green and full of life, and he was staring back at me. And for the first time, we embraced.

Od's office looked like a war zone. The floor was coated in a layer of green slime, there was a singed spot around Elias's apparatus, blood—primarily from my back—was smeared across the desk, and the chairs and papers in the room had been toppled and blown around.

Arthur and I sat on the sofa, leaning against each other. Elias had wrapped us in blankets, but the cold wouldn't let go of our bones and flesh.

My body felt like it weighed a ton, and I didn't even want to think of how my dad felt after having been dead for over eighteen years.

"I died here," he whispered. "Right on this sofa. My last memory is lying here with my head on Benedict's lap."

"How fitting that you were brought back to life here, too." My lips were ice cold, and my fingers wouldn't stop quaking.

Elias handed us each a glass of mead. He said nothing, but his eyes lingered on Arthur.

Arthur looked at him as he accepted the drink. "You killed my daughter."

The words hung in the air, and for a moment, they both held on to the glass.

"But I asked him to," I protested.

A muscle tensed in Elias's jaw, and his eyes moved over Arthur's face. Quickly, Arthur took the glass and looked down into it. "You also saved her life. You've done so several times."

Elias didn't respond.

"He also brought you back," I said. "No matter how mad at him you are, he did bring you back to life."

"Yes," Arthur said quietly. "He did."

The door swung open, and I feared it was Od coming in with all his divine fury, but it was Ben and Rebecca, and within two seconds, we were surrounded by embraces and voices.

Rebecca mumbled spells that blew heat under the blankets and into us both, and amid the commotion, I saw Elias turn around and walk out the door. His eyes locked on mine briefly before he disappeared.

"Praise the gods," Rebecca sobbed as she hugged Arthur.

Luna and Mathias stood arm in arm before us.

"You're crazy, both of you." Even Ben's self-confidence was gone, and his brown eyes shone. "You're . . ." His voice cracked, and he held Arthur close. "I never thought I would see you alive again."

Arthur's red hair stood out between Rebecca's white mane and Ben's brown dreadlocks.

"All we're missing is Thora." Rebecca sniffed. "Then we'll be together again."

In bed in my old room at Odinmont, I lay under stacks of blankets, shaking with cold. My dreams were plagued with images of Helheim, and every time I thought I was back in the underworld for real, I woke up and had to process all over again that Elias had succeeded in bringing me back. Me and my dad. Maybe . . . maybe everything would be okay after all. This was the first time in a long time that I allowed myself to have that thought.

Then I sank back into my dreams, and it all started anew.

Arthur slept in the crypt. He simply couldn't fall asleep if he wasn't in his old resting place, so he had climbed up onto the large stone platform.

I had at least gotten him to take a pillow and blanket down with him.

Something made me wake up fully, and my eyes flew open.

I lay there for a second with my heart pounding before I got out of bed. I kept a blanket around my shoulders, as I still couldn't get warm. As quietly as possible, I tiptoed downstairs. I looked at my phone. It was just past three in the morning.

In the kitchen, I drank a glass of water. The cold liquid felt like ice going down my throat, and I felt it spreading through my body. After having been dead, I noticed these kinds of details.

Halfway up the stairs, I heard a noise from outside. It was a little tap on the door, and I jumped, frightened.

I walked barefoot down to the door and stood behind it, motionless.

"Anna?" called a muffled voice. "Anna."

"Hakim." I opened the door.

It was dark outside, and I heard the wind whistling through the trees. Cold hit me, and I wrapped the blanket more tightly around my shoulders. I curled my toes under as a frosty breeze swept across them.

Hakim stood in the doorway, illuminated by the little lamp I had turned on in the hall. At first, he squinted his green eyes, but when he saw me, he smiled, as though breathing a sigh of relief. "You were so hard to find."

I was surprised. "Were you looking for me at Frank's? I'm going to live out here again from now on."

His eyes were still trained on me, as though he didn't quite believe I was really there. "It's a good thing you heard me."

"I can't sleep. It's like death won't let go." I shuddered involuntarily.

"But you made it. You survived." Hakim smiled again.

Damn, there was a reason why girls were always staring at him. I was lucky to be on the receiving end of that smile, and I returned it instinctively.

"Oh, Anna . . ." Hakim raised his hand and nudged the blanket wrapped around my shoulders a little to the side. Tentatively, he touched the khamsa that always hung around my neck. His finger followed the silver chain, and I got another chill, but this time it wasn't death's fault.

"What are you doing here?" I could hear that my voice sounded strained.

"I wanted to see you." He swallowed. His eyebrows drew together. "I wanted to be sure it was true that you survived."

"I'm alive. You can relax."

He kept his finger on my neck. Then he searched for the words that seemed difficult for him to get out. "There's someone you can't trust."

"Who?"

He shook his head in frustration. "I don't know who it is, but there is a traitor among us."

"Is this something you know from the DSMA?"

He was still staring at me.

"I can see everything clearly now." He composed himself, as if to keep on track. "I'm here to warn you."

When I spoke, my breath came out as steam that wrapped around Hakim's face. "Warn me of what?"

He closed his eyes. "Ragnara is on her way."

I stiffened. "What do you mean, she's on her way? As in right now?"

I raised my hand to his. It was cold, but the wind was also rustling through the trees, and small snowflakes fell from the sky.

"Right now," Hakim said.

I opened my mouth to speak, but suddenly Hakim's arms were around me. He was still cold, but the lips that met mine were soft. Unexpectedly soft. The kiss grew deeper and more fervent.

I was so caught off guard, I let him kiss me. In fact, I reciprocated, but I wasn't sure if that was because he surprised me or if I had always wanted to. When he finally released me, I whispered,

"Hakim," shocked that he was being so forward. He was never like that. "What are you doing?"

"Sometimes you realize how close you are to losing everything. How close you are to not even trying to reach happiness, even if it only lasts an instant."

I was a little out of breath and dazed, on top of the kiss. "I'm very much alive, Hakim. I made it."

"You've been so clear to me," he said. "Ever since I first met you."

His hand was still resting on the silver pendant.

"You're the only one who has seen past my spells on your own," I said quietly. "Everyone else needed magical immunity, but you did it out of sheer will."

"I saw something beyond the spells."

"What?"

"You. There is so much of you in my heart." He took his hand away and started walking backward. "Ragnara will be here soon. I'm getting help."

"You're leaving?" I followed him, but he disappeared into the shadows. "You can't just come here and say Ragnara's on her way, kiss me, then leave."

"If it's real, it will never be over," were his last words.

I stood in the driveway alone in the cold western wind. My palm rested on the pendant that Hakim had just been holding.

"Anna," called a voice from the doorway. Arthur stood there, half-awake, his hair sticking out in all directions. "What are you doing out here?"

"Hakim was here." My bare toes were starting to cramp from the cold, and I walked back into the hall.

"What did he want?" Arthur wrapped the blanket tightly around me and rubbed my arms. For the first time, I felt how strong he really was.

"He said Ragnara is on her way." My hand was already reaching for my phone. "We have to get ahold of the others. Could you teleport . . . oh, right. Run down and get the witches, and I'll call Mathias."

My pulse pounded in my mouth and temples.

I didn't manage to make a call before my phone buzzed in my hand.

"It's Niels Villadsen," I said. "I'll take it, just run." When Arthur hesitated, I repeated. "Run."

He gave me one last squeeze before speeding off across the field toward Ben and Rebecca's house.

"Hello," I said into the cool glass screen.

"Anna." Niels sounded out of breath.

"I'm glad you called," I began. "Ragnara is on her way here. We need help."

It was quiet on the other end.

"Maybe you knew that already?" I asked. "Did Hakim tell you?"

"Hakim?" Niels repeated. He sounded confused.

"Yeah. He just stopped by to tell me Ragnara will be here soon." I didn't mention the kiss that still hummed in my mouth. Despite the danger that was to come, I couldn't help but smile to myself and run my little finger across my lower lip.

The normally composed Niels made a strangled noise.

"Anna. I'm sorry to have to tell you that my people just found Hakim's body in Kraghede Forest. He went there looking for you, but someone killed him. It must have been someone he trusted, as there was no sign of a struggle."

"What . . ." Everything spun around me, and the cold that had previously gnawed at me was dissolved by a wave of scalding heat. "But I just talked to him."

"He's been dead for several hours."

CHAPTER 49

I stood in the hall with the phone to my ear. Niels may have been talking on the other end, but I didn't register it.

Someone grabbed my shoulder, and I jerked. The phone hit the tile floor with a hollow *clunk* followed by a sharp crack as the glass screen shattered.

Mathias and Mads stood there, both in their pajamas. Mathias glowed green. It was his hand that rested on my shoulder, but I only looked at him, uncomprehending.

"Hakim's spirit came to me, and I got ahold of Mads," he said. "Od will be here soon."

"Hakim . . ."

"I know," Mathias whispered. "I'm so sorry."

Something flickered down at Ostergaard. It was a cold light, perhaps from a giant crystal.

There was a faint *baaah* sound from down there.

I was still looking at Mathias, paralyzed. "He was just here. We kissed. He felt so real."

"Anna!" Mathias shook me lightly as if to wake me up. "You can think about that later." He looked in the direction of the flickering light, which was approaching us from across the field.

Leather wings fluttered, and I saw the silhouettes of fingalks.

"Go inside."

"What did Hakim say?" I insisted.

Mathias gave me a long look with his burning blue eyes. "He said goodbye."

I opened my mouth but could do nothing but exhale a whistling moan.

"Go. Inside!" Mathias shoved me inside with his superhuman strength. The door slammed shut, and though I pounded on it, Mathias held fast to his side.

I had the sense that some of Ragnara's fingalks had reached my yard, and at that moment, one of them shrieked, and I heard Mads let out a half-strangled cry.

The fingalk brayed with pain, after which a stench spread. I could smell it all the way from inside Odinmont. It then sounded like another one attacked but suffered the same fate.

"Hakim," I called. "Hakim." If he was dead . . . I clutched my stomach as a sharp pain tore through it. "If you're a ghost, then I can talk to you," I shouted. "You must have a really strong spirit if you can already upgrade yourself to poltergeist."

There was no reply.

"Hakim." My voice ended in a sob, and I slid down along the cool wood of the door.

"You can only talk to spirits in this world, and he's moved on," a voice said inside my head.

"Then I'll follow him." I looked around, but I was alone.

"He belonged to a different religion, and you worship the All-Father now. That separates you."

"Svidur?" I asked. "Is that you?"

Outside of Odinmont, there were screams and the flapping of wings. Mads and Mathias had to fight off the fingalks with their bare fists.

"Where is my blood?" Ragnara's childlike voice called from the field below. "You stole my gods' blood."

I couldn't see her, but the violent aura struck me through the door. It was as though a dark hand were trying to strangle me, and I grabbed my neck. My fingers hit the silver hand.

"Didn't that blood originally belong to someone else?" Mathias retorted. His voice sounded metallic, as it always did when he went into god mode.

"Originally . . . Pfff . . . Nothing is original. Power is always changing hands."

"It seems the power is about to slip away from you." Mads's deep voice rang out in the night.

Ben, Rebecca, and Luna's voices joined the fray. They shot out balls of energy, but something zapped back at them. Ragnara had her own sorcerers with her.

"All-Father. I summon you!" I yelled, and suddenly Svidur was sitting on the stairs, relaxed. One moment he wasn't there, and the next, he was. His hair was pitch black, his skin smooth, and his eye glinted brightly.

"Look at me," he said. "Your belief in me has worked wonders."

"Let me speak to Hakim," I demanded.

"I said it would cost you dearly to bind yourself to me, little seer."

The oxygen was sucked out of me.

"Svidur," I begged. "Not Hakim."

I had fought so hard to keep everyone alive, but I had failed. Now I couldn't even hold on to Hakim's spirit.

"You think you can have everything?" Svidur tilted his face. "If you make *one* choice, you exclude something else."

He leaned back and looked even more relaxed as he draped himself across the stairs.

"Just not Hakim."

Svidur raised his thick, black brows. There wasn't so much as a single wrinkle on his forehead. "Would you rather lose your witch friend? The giant wolf, or the demigod who's fighting so bravely out there? Or your father?"

"I don't want to lose anyone."

There was crunching in the gravel outside.

"You are the son of my rival," came Ragnara's high voice.

"Where is Baldr's blood?" Her voice snapped like a whip. Her thirst for power struck me with a pang.

It was Od who answered her. "There is no more."

"I want it!"

Eskild's voice barked as he commanded his troops. "Berserkers, take the north side. Fingalks, attack from above. Herders and sorcerers, stand in a circle."

Arthur exclaimed with an *arrrgh* as he collided with someone. I didn't dare imagine who, but I suspected it was a berserker on demiblood. Luna shouted, too, and Od sounded completely different from how I had ever heard him before. He let out a war cry as he crashed into someone.

I tried the door again, but it was impossible to open.

"Ragnara has taken demigod blood," Svidur said. He leaned up against the railing, and I thought he looked like a large, cuddly cat. "Combined with the rest of the gods' blood she has in her body, she's even stronger than the two children of gods out there."

I pulled the door handle with all my strength.

"You can't go out there, little seer. You'll only get yourself killed." It was clearly Svidur doing some kind of hocus pocus with the lock.

"Can't you help them?"

Svidur shrugged, and the corners of his mouth turned down. "I've already won. The gods' blood is fleeting, so I just have to wait until she's a human again."

He said *human* as though it were a dirty word.

"Those are your followers." I inhaled. "That's your son out there."

He yawned.

"I'm only interested in my ravens." He gave me a cheeky look. "You and your sister."

"They'll all be killed!"

His eye blazed with excitement. "Yes. And they'll die in battle, so they'll come directly to me, aside from your father, who is

613

trying to protect you. If you die protecting your family, you go to Fólkvangr, and Freyja longs for him so."

I screamed. It was a panicked, animalistic sound that came from my throat. Everyone I loved was going to die. Hakim was already gone, and now the others would follow.

Outside, I could hear fighting, but Ragnara's people outnumbered us, and even with two demigods on our side, my friends were at a significant disadvantage.

I walked up to Svidur. Something rushed inside me. A force. I wasn't quite sure where it came from. It started in my bare feet, rolled up through my legs, groin, and stomach, and ended in my chest. It was a snake uncoiling itself.

"I won something, too, when I bound myself to you," I said, even though I didn't understand what it was I had won.

Svidur stood up from the stairs and pulled his chin back toward his neck to stare intensely at me. "What did you win, little seer?"

"I'm a völva now," I said. My voice was an octave deeper than usual. It was like a myriad of völvas were pushing it out of my mouth. Behind them all stood Hejd.

One corner of Svidur's mouth pulled back in an approving smile. "And have you understood what it means to be a völva?"

> *The wide-seeing völva*
> *Wolves she tamed*
> *Went where she could* ·
> *Went with madness*
> *Awaited with joy*
> *Commanded the All-Father*
> *Defeated the evil woman*

The words came from all the völvas, but they resounded from my mouth. The past pulled at me, but I held on to it as though it were the reigns to a team of wild horses.

Svidur came closer. I had caught his attention.

"What do you command me to do, völva?"

I know all, Odin!
Your eye is hidden
Deep in the wide-famed well of Mimir
Necklaces and rings had I
Wise was my speech and my magic wisdom
So I see more widely
Over all the worlds

Svidur breathed heavily.

"Raven." His large hands cupped my cheeks. "Soothsayer. Völva."

I placed my hands on top of his and held fast as I stared into his burning eye.

The war I remember
The first in the world
When with spears
Guldveig was smitten,
And in the High One's hall she burned
Three times burned and three times born

I pointed into the living room, where Gungnir hung on the wall. Odin's spear, which had nearly taken my life. It sang in my head. *I was forged by the Sons of Ivaldi using rune magic. Kill.*

"Take the spear," I commanded Svidur.

"I am Gungnir," the spear whispered, and I let the words come out of my mouth.

Svidur grew taller with every word I said, until he had to duck his head beneath the ceiling. His face became more and more youthful, and his biceps swelled. Then he reached out, and his arm reached all the way from the hall into the living room and up the wall. His large fingers closed around Gungnir and pulled it down from the wall.

"Kill," I ordered the god, and he moaned. His chest was now broader than a car.

"My raven. *There* you are," he said, and the breath that hit me was warm and pleasant. Then he let go of me, flung the door open, and went out into the yard.

I followed him with long strides, and I felt the strength of the many völvas behind me. I stood tall on the threshold and looked out over the battlefield that Odinmont's yard had become.

All my friends were alive, but there were dismembered fingalks everywhere, Rebecca's hair was in flames, Ben's clothes were smoldering and blackened, and Mathias was bleeding fresh demiblood from a gash in his neck, while one of Mads's arms hung limply at his side.

My father lay on the ground, but he was alive.

Oddly enough, I felt totally calm, even as I looked at my battered friends. I knew they would survive this.

"Kill the usurper," I ordered Svidur. "Use Gungnir."

Everyone stopped and looked at me.

My voice unfurled over them, forceful yet controlled. I could feel the völvas looking out through my eyes.

Even Mathias and Od looked at me with reverence.

Giant-sized Svidur stomped out.

Ragnara, who had been about to swing her green knife at Arthur, stopped mid-motion. She stared at Svidur with a blend of fear and fury. Then her gaze shifted to me.

"Thora's blood will lead to your death," I said with my head held high.

Svidur walked slowly forward. Gungnir had grown along with him, now the length of a flagpole. With a single stroke, he took down the berserkers. The fingalks fluttered to the ground, and the herders collapsed.

"All-Father," Ragnara whispered. "You have never appeared to me before. Do you want me now?" There was a hint of supplication in her voice.

He lowered his head and stood right in front of her. "Want you . . . Want you . . ." He laughed, and the sound made the earth shake. She fell to her knees in front of him. "Yes, I want you. The völvas want you. To die."

Ragnara's eyes flickered. "Help!" she screamed. "Help me, Loki."

She looked out across the field, which was dark and silent.

No response.

"Help me," she called again. "We had a deal."

She was answered with silence.

Svidur raised Gungnir and looked at me.

I nodded. I could feel the völvas' eyes blazing coldly through mine.

Svidur smiled when he saw my motion. Then he thrust Gungnir forward and pierced her again and again.

"One. Two. Three," he counted.

She fell to the ground, and her desperate need for power, which I could almost taste, vanished. Her spirit rose from her body, which Eskild had thrown himself over.

The spirit looked around, and her expression was different from before. It was shocked, indignant, and, honestly, not unlike my own when I looked in the mirror.

She looked at me, and I returned her gaze. All the völvas watched through my eyes.

With dignity, she bowed her head.

"Thorasdatter, you have won," the spirit said.

"I understand you," I said. "I understand your resentment that everyone always made decisions for you when you were a slave. I can understand why you fought against it. At all costs."

"Slave." The spirit tasted the word. "Fehu." She pointed at my forearm, where the rune was tattooed. Then she came closer, and her transparent hand reached through me. I shivered as the chill of death once again spread through my body, but I remained standing. For a second, I thought the spirit would squeeze my heart, but her palm brushed the inside of my back, where Elias had carved the ansuz. "You, too, are both slave and god. Like me."

"Actually, I think we're just human."

"Human." Ragnara said the word as though she didn't quite understand it.

"You have to rest now." The words were hard, but my voice was soft. Ragnara's ghost was right in front of me, her hand still buried in my body. I looked at her face. The brown eyes, which looked so much like Rorik's, were the most solid part of her. "It's over now," I whispered.

She leaned close to me. "If you think it's over with me, you're mistaken."

Then she disappeared, and Eskild let out a howl of anger and pain.

Svidur raised Gungnir again, but I shouted: "No. No more."

He lowered the spear and bowed his head. "You command me, raven. You command me, völva."

EPILOGUE

I walked out through Odinmont's blue front door—there was no reason to lock it behind me, since no one could get into the house without the deed that was tucked into my pocket.

For a moment, I stood there at the top of the hill and looked out over the flat North Jutland landscape.

The sun was setting, though it was only half past three, but that's how it is in Scandinavia on the day of the winter solstice.

My birthday.

I had—against all odds—survived another year.

Miraculously, there was no wind. Normally it mercilessly flattened the trees and bushes on their west-facing sides, but today there was only a light breeze. Above this calm scene, the sun's rays flowed blazing orange. The giant ball of fire rested on the horizon, waiting patiently.

I sighed. No way around it.

I took in one last panoramic view, and maybe my eyes were playing tricks on me, but I thought I saw figures in Kraghede Forest. Right at the edge, in front of the now-broken birch tree. The red sunbeams flashed on the bare tree trunks.

I shook my head. Maybe I should stop being so vigilant. The corners of my mouth turned up involuntarily as I turned around and accepted the peace that my home always instilled in me. There was a little twinge in my back when I turned my head.

The wound on my back had only just healed, and it was still a little tender whenever the skin was pulled. I would have a large scar shaped like the rune ansuz forever.

My smile froze when I thought of Hakim. I fingered the silver hand at my neck. Though the metal was cool, warmth flowed into my fingers.

I turned around so my face pointed at Ben and Rebecca's house, and I saw something I couldn't quite make out at the side of the whitewashed wall. Were they cutting down one of the large trees in their garden?

I pulled my mother's coat tight around me and started walking down the hill.

In the yard, I met the quirky family, Mathias, and my dad. The sight of Arthur's red, spiky hair made my stomach do a somersault.

Strange to have such opposing feelings of pure joy and raw sorrow at the same time.

When he turned around and looked at me with a love so deep I almost couldn't fathom it, it was impossible to stop the grin spreading from ear to ear. He reached out to me.

"I came down early," Arthur said, giving my hand a squeeze. "Is that okay?"

"Of course," I replied. "I just have to get used to not panicking when you disappear."

I panicked a little anytime anyone disappeared.

The winter sun bathed the ground, the trees, and the house, and its rays had taken on a pink tone that made the scattered clouds look like cotton candy.

Rebecca had her large basket in her arms. It was full to the brim with bones, fresh pieces of meat, and a bowl of steaming dark-red liquid. Despite the below-freezing temperature and the fine dusting of snow that covered the ground, her bare feet stuck out from under her long dress. She raised her head toward me with a soft expression that did not match the bloody items she carried.

"Happy birthday, dearest Anna Stella. We're about to begin our jólablót."

I took a bird carcass, dripping blood, from Rebecca. "I'm ready."

"Yay! You're Norse pagan now." Luna did a little victory dance.

I grunted. The price of my newfound religion had been incredibly high.

Mathias looked at me. "We're going to Frank's afterward to celebrate your birthday."

I gaped. "I said I didn't want a party."

Mathias patted me on the shoulder. "There are a lot of people who are happy to see you alive on your nineteenth birthday, so let them have this time with you."

"Who?"

"Mads, Frank, Elias, and Mina are waiting there." Mathias's warm hand gave my arm a squeeze. "Let's do this."

He took a clump of meat.

The others took animal parts and bloody bones, and we walked in a solemn line with Rebecca in front to the other side of the house.

"We upgraded this year," Luna whispered and lifted a brown bird's wing, a white bone sticking out the end. "All else being equal, Odin saved our lives as soon as he had the strength to do so." She looked at me out of the corner of her eye. "How did he get so much strength?"

"Upgraded? How?" I asked to avoid commenting on her question, but she didn't get the chance to answer.

On the side of the house that faced Odinmont, I saw what she meant. The form I hadn't been able to make out in the dusk was now clearly visible. It was a tall pillar that looked like a totem pole.

Ben and Rebecca had evidently peeled a living oak tree. It was carved and painted, but the roots were still anchored deeply in the ground. Green branches protruded from the trunk, but most notable were the painted heads stacked on top of one another.

I saw a woman's face with golden hair and a teasing expression, a stern man's head with a mane of red hair, and a white face with burning blue eyes the exact same shade as Mathias's. At the top of the tree was a face with a pointy hat and an empty eye socket. A ladder was leaned up against the carved trunk.

In front of the pole stood a tall man, who studied it with his hands at

621

his back. When we reached him, Od turned around and looked at me in that way that threatens my willpower. His eyes met mine without saying a word.

Rebecca, Arthur, and Ben bowed to him.

I wanted to snap at them to stop ingratiating themselves to the demigod, but my dad sent me a warning look. I made myself curtsy vaguely at Od, which made him smile in amusement.

Rebecca guided us into a circle and splattered blood on the pole with a bundle of twigs.

"Gods," she chanted. "We acknowledge you."

There was a slight vibration under my feet.

"We worship you."

The ground rippled again.

"We make offerings for you."

The sun had nearly set, so it was getting pretty dark, but a little glimmer flashed in the sky.

I saw the silhouettes of two shapes appear from above. They encircled the conical hat at the top of the pole.

"Roooark." One of them laughed. The other joined in with a corresponding shriek. The birds turned their heads and looked at us with beady eyes. Their black feathers gleamed.

Mathias shifted uneasily but stayed where he was, with the piece of meat in his hand.

First, Ben climbed up the ladder. He whispered something to the red-haired head and placed his bone in its open mouth. Luna followed him and hung her bird's wing on a branch that protruded from the white god's ear. She said something inaudible before climbing backward down the ladder again. Mathias simply reached up; his arm was suddenly much longer, and he threaded his piece of meat onto the same branch at Heimdall's temple. Arthur went reluctantly to the golden goddess. She was at eye level, so he didn't need the ladder. He dipped his hand in Rebecca's bowl and brushed it across the wooden figure's cheek.

I thought I heard a feminine sigh from the tree, but I might have been mistaken.

"Thank you for letting me stay with my daughter," Arthur mumbled.

Od reached up and wrapped a golden thread around the highest god's neck.

When it was my turn, I climbed up the ladder. I didn't really know what to do, as there were no empty branches or flat surfaces left, so I stood for a while at the top, thinking.

The ravens studied me from above, circling.

Resolutely, I impaled the bird carcass on the pointy hat.

"Here, Svidur," I whispered. "I recognize you as a god. I guess I'll worship you, but I don't know which of us it'll be worse for."

The birds dove down, screeching, and I nearly fell off the ladder in fear. They perched on the cadaver, where they picked flesh off the bones, their glittering, black, beady eyes still scrutinizing me.

"I suppose that's a good sign, Svidur," I said quietly.

There was a little flash of light in the sky, and someone laughed from high up.

"Call me by my proper name," he breathed inside my head.

"Okay, Odin," I whispered. "I'm against the concept of gods. Strongly against it, but you win this round."

He laughed. "I always win, little seer. Always."

In Kraghede Forest, not far from us, Elias watched our small silhouettes on the other side of Odinmont. We were barely visible in the twilight. He, too, saw the flash of light in the sky.

He laid his hand on the almost broken birch tree.

"I did it," he said. "I held up my end of the deal."

A dark figure stepped closer to him.

"Did she die?" The figure was wrapped in a gray cloak, and its voice was deep and sharp.

"She thinks it was her idea, but Anna died by my hand. She was dead for a while, anyway."

"And you worked for Ragnara when she was alive." The name came out sounding hard, like it had sharp edges.

Elias didn't respond.

"The raven is back on the hill. Good," the person said to themselves. "Everything's going according to plan. And I can move in their midst without anyone growing suspicious."

"What about my payment?" Though anxiety made Elias's voice tremble, he forced the question out. "I did everything I promised."

The hood was pushed back, and Elias opened his mouth with a gasp.

The person standing before him was a woman with freckles, a mild expression, and a thick, wheat-colored braid on the top of her head. Her eyes were blue-gray. She laid a warm hand on Elias's cheek and smiled.

His eyes grew shiny. "Mother?"

"Elias." The sharp voice had changed into a woman's gentle voice. "My child." She tilted her head.

"Stop it," Elias whispered. "Can you please stop it?"

A playful laugh came from the woman's mouth, and her eyes glinted mischievously. "Isn't this what you want?" the woman asked. First her face flickered, then her whole body, and finally, the person transformed. Bright red hair flowed down over the shoulders; the dark eyebrows gathered defiantly—one with a scar through it. "Do you want her?" The voice was deeper now, but still feminine. She drew closer to Elias. The hand that was still on his cheek moved down along his neck. Her nails scraped across his skin, sending a shiver through his body. "Do you want me?" she whispered. "Do you want me, Elias?" The name was dragged out, and the s continued until she got right up close to Elias's face and cheek.

With a brutal motion, Elias shoved her away.

"Stop it, Loki," he said.

The head shook, and gray hair fell in thick locks around the face. The eyes were the color of polished iron. The mouth twisted upward in a sardonic smile. He grew taller than Elias, his shoulders became wider, his

chest more powerful, and the hand around Elias's neck doubled in size.
His thumb rested on his jugular, which pulsed beneath it.

"Would you rather have me as I am?"

"You know what I want."

"You'll get what's coming to you." Loki's gray eyes glinted.

In Hrafnheim, the rays of the setting winter sun flowed over the realm.
Over Særkland's brown fields, the herds of animals in Frón, the salt
mines in Danheim, and the broad rivers of Gardarike.

The black dunes of Hibernia glinted in the orange beams, and the
carvings on Gytha's house were dry and cracked.

A single snowflake floated down and landed on the wooden surface, but it melted immediately. Another flake followed, and then another and yet another. Soon, the air was thick with falling crystals. A
layer of ice spread over the wooden carvings, and the glassy coating
crackled.

On the main street of Dyflin, people raised their heads to the snow
that was settling over them. The lindworm bones of the buildings glowed
green, but they, too, were soon covered in frost.

"So cold," they mumbled, blowing on their clenched fingers.

The dream catchers hummed, then went silent as they were encap-
sulated in ice.

A ship floated lazily down a river, but it stopped with a creaking noise
as the water around it first became a thick, milky white, then froze solid.
It happened so quickly, even the small waves grew stiff mid-movement.
The men and women on deck shouted at one another in surprise, the
breath steaming from their mouths. The frost was so strong, it ran up
the mast and, finally, pulverized the wood with a bang. The sail toppled
down, and the people jumped for their lives.

The cold spread like fire across the flat plain, heading toward Ísafold.
Birna, who stood on the heath, raised her head in the direction of the
sputtering noise. Styrr placed an arm around her shoulders, squinted,
and looked toward the horizon as the rime rapidly came closer.

The frost reached the grove of Barre, and the rustling of the trees went silent as the river Iving splashed angrily.

Birna and Styrr turned and ran, but the ice caught up to them and covered the legs of their pants with small crystals.

Tíw shouted to them from his open door. The sleeve of his shirt hung limply on the right side, but he used his remaining arm to hold the door open. Birna and Styrr reached it with frozen boots and blue lips. Tíw slammed the door once they were inside, and the ice sealed it shut.

Fimbulwinter had begun.

CHARACTERS

AELLA [EYE-ELLA]	Varnar's friend and Serén's girlfriend
ARTHUR	Anna's father
BENEDICT SEKIBO [SE-KEE-BO]	Luna's father
BIRNA [BEER-NA]	a girl from Ísafold
BODA	a giant wolf, the wife of Monster/Etunaz
BORK	foster father to Serén and former adviser to Ragnara
CHRISTIAN MIKKELSEN	Peter's friend, who Anna calls the psychopath
ELIAS [EH-LEE-AHS] ERIKSEN	potion maker and Od's assistant, also known as the Brewmaster
ESKILD BLACK-EYE	Ragnara's adviser and commander of her army
FAIDA	girl from Ísafold
FINN	a fingalk
FRANK	Anna's friend and would-be killer, owner of Frank's Bar and Diner
FREYJA [FREY-A]	the goddess of love
GEIRI	one of Ragnara's men
GRETA	Anna's social worker
GUSTAF	one of Ragnara's soldiers, a man with no aura and yellow eyes
GYTHA	a woman who sells clothes near Dyflin
HAKIM [HA-KEEM] MURR	a young police officer
HALFDAN	Frank's grandson
HEL	the goddess of death
HUGINN AND MUNINN	Odin's ravens
INGEBORG	Prince Sverre's fiancée
JUSTINE	a clairvoyant friend of Elias's

KNUT	one of Ragnara's soldiers, part of the raid on the giant wolves
LOKI	a jötunn/giant
LUNA SEKIBO [SE-KEE-BO]	Anna's friend, a witch
MADS	Anna's friend, a half giant
MATHIAS HEDSKOV [MA-TEE-AHS HEDH-SKOH]	Anna's friend, a demigod
MERIT	a girl afflicted with splittr who helped Anna and Rorik in Kyngja
MINA OSTERGAARD	Anna's neighbor and classmate
MODGUD	guards the entrance to Helheim
MONSTER	Anna's friend, a giant wolf
MR. NIELSEN	Anna's Danish teacher
NAUT KAFNAR	a murderer; Anna calls him the Savage
NIELS VILLADSEN	Anna's contact at the DSMA
OD DINESEN [DEE-NE-SEN]	owner of The Boatman, a demigod
ODIN	the All-Father, the primary god of the Norse pantheon
PETER NYBO [NEE-BO]	Anna's nemesis at school
PRINCE ETUNAZ	Monster's real name and title
PRINCE SVERRE [SVEHR-A]	Ragnara's son, the crown prince of Freiheim
RAGNARA	the ruler of Freiheim
REBECCA SEKIBO [SE-KEE-BO]	Luna's mother
ROKKIN	Monster's daughter, a giant wolf with black fur
RORIK	a deserter from Ragnara's army who travels with Anna
SERÉN [SE-REN]	Anna's twin sister
STYRR	a man from Ísafold
SVIDUR [SVEE-DUR]	Odin's alter ego
TALIAH	a clairvoyant girl from Miklagard
THORA BANEBLOOD	Anna's mother and Ragnara's enemy
TÍW	a man from Ísafold

TRYGGVI	a skald Anna meets in Ván
VALE [VA-LEH]	a giant wolf with white fur
VARNAR	a resistance fighter Anna has developed feelings for
VÉDIS	a witch
VERONIKA	a bartender at The Boatman
VÖLVA HEJD [VOHL-VA HAIT]	the mother of all seers

PLACES

BARRE [BAR-A]	a grove in Frón
THE BOATMAN	Od's bar in Jagd
THE BRONZE FOREST	home of the Forest Folk
DANHEIM	a kingdom
THE DARK FOREST	where the berserkers live
DYFLIN	a town in Hibernia
FÓLKVANGR	Freyja's domain, where she takes her share of those who die in battle
FREIHEIM	the official name for Hrafnheim
FRÓN	a small, flat kingdom
GARDARIKE [GAR-DA-REE-KA]	a kingdom
HARALDSBORG	the rebels' castle
HELHEIM	Hel's domain
HIBERNIA	a kingdom
THE HIDDEN WORLD	the world of the gods and other supernatural beings

HRAFNHEIM	a world created for believers in the old faith
THE IRON FOREST	home of the Wolf Folk
ÍSAFOLD [EE-SA-FOLD]	a small town in Frón
THE ISLAND	the student café at Anna's school
IVING	a river between Frón and the Iron Forest
JAGD [YAGD]	a coastal town in northern Denmark
JORVIK [YOR-VEEK]	a town in Hibernia
KONUNGSBORG	Ragnara's castle in Sént
KRAGHEDE [KRAG-HEY-THE] FOREST	a forest bordering Ravensted
KYNGJA	a deadly swamp
MIDGARD	the human world
MIKLAGARD	a kingdom
NASTROND	the beach of corpses
NORVÍK [NOR-VEEK]	a kingdom
ODINMONT	Anna's home
OSTERGAARD	the property next to Odinmont
RAVENSTED	a town in northern Denmark
RIPA [REE-PA]	a city in Ván
SÉNT	the capital of Hrafnheim/Freiheim
SØMOSEN	a swamp in northern Denmark
STJERNEBORG	Elias's observatory
SVEARIKE [SVAY-A-REE-KA]	a kingdom
SVERRESBORG	a prison in Svearike belonging to Prince Sverre
SÆRKLAND	a kingdom; supplies crops to the rest of Freiheim
VALHALLA	Odin's domain, where he takes his share of those who die in battle
VÁN	the kingdom where Sént is located
VIGRID	the red plain surrounding Sént
VINDR FEN	a desolate stretch of land in Hibernia

CONCEPTS / OBJECTS

ANFARWOL	a word meaning immortality, commonly used as a greeting in Freiheim
AUKA [OW-KA]	Anna's axe
BERSERKERS	a group of warriors
BLÓT [BLOHT]	a ceremony
CLAIRVOYANT	someone who can see the past and/or future
CLINGY SPIRIT	a type of ghost
DEMIBLOOD	the blood of a demigod
DEMIGOD	someone who is half human, half god
FEHU	a rune designating property, adopted as a symbol by Ragnara
FIMBULWINTER	a three-year-long winter that signals the coming of Ragnarök
FINGALK	a frightening winged creature, described as part bird, part ape
GIANT CRYSTAL	a crystal made by a giant; it keeps its user hidden from their enemies but glows red when their loved ones are nearby
GUNGNIR	a magical spear
HÁLFA	a holiday celebrated in Ísafold to mark the halfway point of winter
HANGADROTT	the sacrifice of a royal
HERDERS	priests who work for Ragnara
HNETAFL	a game of strategy
JÖTUNN [YUH-TUN]	another name for giant
KLINTE [KLINT-A]	a potion that dulls the senses
LAEKNA [LEK-NA]	a healing potion
LINDWORM	a type of large serpent with glow-in-the-dark bones

MEDIUM	someone who can communicate with the dead
THE MIDGARD SERPENT	a giant lindworm, also known as Jörmungandr, that wraps around the whole world, holding its tail in its mouth
RAGNARÖK	doomsday
SEID [SAIT]	a magic ritual
SKALD	a traveling performer who recites news and poetry
SPLITTR	leprosy
STJÓRNA [STYUR-NA]	a sedative potion
TILARIDS	Rorik's sword
ULFBERHT SWORD	a sword into which the blacksmith puts part of their soul
THE VARANGIAN GUARD	Ragnara's army
VÖLUSPÁ [VO-LU-SPA]	a tenth-century poem containing the völva Hejd's prophecies
VÖLVA [VOHL-VA]	a female clairvoyant, also called a seer
YGGDRASIL [IG-DRA-SIL]	the World Tree of Norse mythology, where Odin was hanged

© Sara Galbiati, Gyldendal Medie

AUTHOR

MALENE SØLVSTEN made her debut in Denmark in 2016 with the first volume of the fantasy trilogy Whisper of the Ravens and was nominated for the Readers' Book Prize in the same year. The series quickly became a bestseller in Denmark, for which the author received the 2018 Edvard Prisen, awarded annually by the Danish Library Association. An economist by training, she lives with her family in Copenhagen, where she now works as a full-time author.

TRANSLATOR

ADRIENNE ALAIR is a literary translator working from Danish, Norwegian, and Swedish into English. She studied Scandinavian Studies at the University of Edinburgh and has lived in Sweden and Denmark. She is now based in Charlotte, North Carolina.

The thrilling fantasy adventure continues . . .

Malene Sølvsten
Mannaz
(Whisper of the Ravens Book 3)
On sale Fall 2025
ISBN 978-1-64690-028-2

Eternal winter is ravaging the world, and disease and hunger are spreading. Nothing seems to be able to prevent the prophecy of the end of the world from coming true. But perhaps Anna misinterpreted the signs?

To understand the fate that threatens them all, Anna must tame her powers, and she must learn to tell the difference between friend and foe. The closer she gets to the truth about Ragnarök, the more it becomes clear that someone close to her is working against her. Will she manage to uncover the traitor before time runs out?

If Ragnarök can be averted, Anna is prepared to pay , even with her life. But the price is higher than she knows. . . .

Discover the exciting Rosenholm fantasy trilogy!

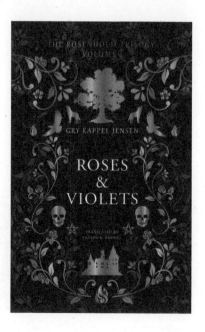

Gry Kappel Jensen
Roses & Violets
(The Rosenholm Trilogy Volume 1)
On sale now!
ISBN 978-1-64690-012-1

Four girls from four different parts of Denmark have been invited to apply to Rosenholm Academy for an unknown reason. During the unorthodox application tests, it becomes apparent this is no ordinary school. In fact, it's a magical boarding school and all the students have powers.

Once the school year begins, they learn that Rosenholm carries a dark secret—a young girl was murdered under mysterious circumstances in the 1980s and the killer was never found. Her spirit is still haunting the school, and she is now urging the four girls to bring justice and find the killer. But helping the spirit puts all of the girls in grave danger . . .

Read Siri Pettersen's first trilogy
—The Raven Rings—out now!

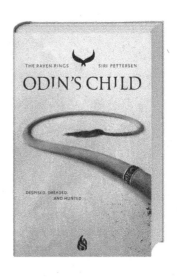

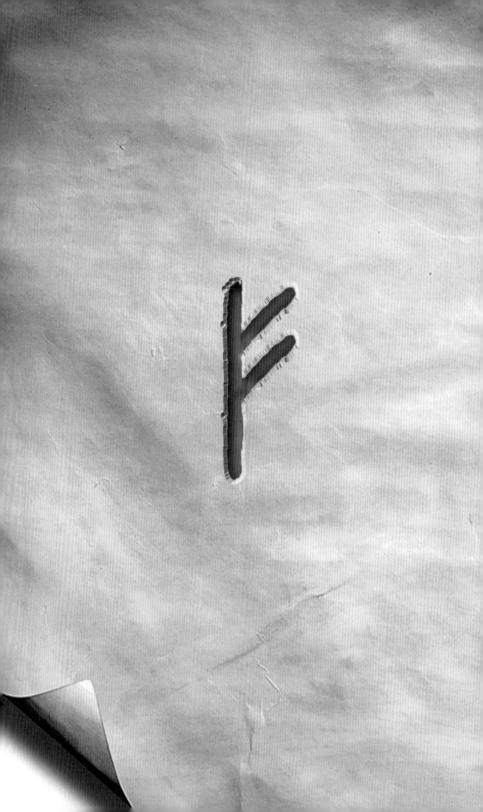